Collected Poems of ELINOR WYLIE

". . . Here was a poet indeed, one whose early promise and later fulfillment have withstood the stern measure of the years. Her poems now seem even better and nobler, read finally in one embracing volume. They bear the imprint of a sensitive spirit; they are drenched with beauty; they have fire and fury, mixed with passionate restraint; and underneath there is a profound philosophy of life and death and love which is sane and steady, and at once august and simple."

— CHARLES HANSON TOWNE

A BORZOI BOOK *published by* ALFRED A. KNOPF

Collected Prose

OF

ELINOR WYLIE

Collected Prose

OF

ELINOR WYLIE

1933

ALFRED A. KNOPF
NEW YORK

Contents of the Volume

JENNIFER LORN

A Sedate Extravaganza

Currite ducentes sub tegmina, currite fusi.

CATULL.

ILLUMINATING EPISODES IN
THE LIVES OF THE
HON. GERALD POYNYARD
AND HIS BRIDE

Complete herein in *Three Books*

WITH A SPECIAL PREFACE BY
CARL VAN VECHTEN

TO

MY MOTHER

Jennifer Lorn

PREFACE

A certain difficulty arises in writing about a book to which one awards an unreserved enthusiasm, an agreeable difficulty, no doubt, but none the less a difficulty. This unnatural situation was the cause of a great deal of perplexity on my part after my earliest reading of Jennifer Lorn in 1923. Determining, therefore, to discover some slight flaw, some rift in artistry, some hesitation in the creator's precision, I went straight through the book again — in vain, I may add, in so far as the purposes of my pursuit were concerned. A third and more recent reading banished all uncertainty. My enthusiasm has mounted in ten years rather than ebbed. I am confirmed in my belief that Jennifer Lorn is the only successfully sustained satire in English with which I am acquainted.

A satire of what? the reader may reasonably demand at this point and the rather vague reply I must give to the question is another proof to my mind of the authentic quality of this " sedate extravaganza," for, unlike

3

There is, it may as well be proclaimed, a kind of perfection about Jennifer Lorn, the perfection of an artist who has completely realized her intention, the only perfection, perhaps, with which the critic should concern himself, although there is another approximate perfection which causes a book to arouse feelings in the reader of which the author was never aware. Certainly the perfection of this book is miniature, like the perfection of the red jasper bowl which Gerald loved so much he could not bring himself to bestow it on Jennifer, but this condition should be obvious, that perfect works of art are always conceived on a small scale. Moby Dick and Hamlet have their greatnesses; they also have their faults.

For its life, which I believe to be, if not immortal, at any rate as nearly immortal as any other work of art of its period which can be named, the story depends to a remarkable degree on the character of Gerald, that " fine flower of English gentlemen," of whom Jennifer, thinking him dead, remarked:

" My dear husband was a superb horseman; his knowledge of history was amazing, and his fund of anecdote inexhaustible. As a travelling companion, and indeed in every other relation of life " — she explained with a loyal little sob — " he was the most superior person whom it has ever been my privilege to know."

Gerald, in fact, is incomparable, with his air of passive and polite contempt, his amiable and cold composure, thieving in India, the seat of his enormous for-

tune; Gerald, reading Candide and drinking brandy to relieve the tedium of an ocean voyage; Gerald, entertaining his wife during the honeymoon with long anecdotes which for the most part concerned her own family history with which she was entirely familiar; Gerald crushing the white roses, dispatched to Jennifer by her youthful admirer, under his heel in the courtyard of the Paris hotel; Gerald astride an elephant on the road to Delhi, " straight as a lance and stiff as a poker, accommodating himself in some uncanny fashion to the swinging pace of the monstrous animal; his face as immobile as a carven Buddha beneath the green umbrella which he habitually carried," an umbrella which he transformed by his grasp into an object " as awful as a sceptre and as ornamental as a lotus-flower "; Gerald beset by bandits, firing coolly until his ammunition is exhausted, hurling then his pistols at the heads of his assailants and, finally, fencing with his cane; Gerald, overpowered by numbers, ostensibly staked through the heart and buried under stones, saved by his slenderness (the stake had penetrated his cloak alone); above all, Gerald, the magnificent, appearing to Jennifer and her Prince before the ruins of Persepolis, bearing himself " with such an air of elegance and pride that the very column lowering over his mortality seemed somewhat dwarfed by the perfection of his poise," quoting Marlowe with a slightly satirical smile: Gerald, indeed, is the epitome of maleness with all its vanity and self-importance transfigured by the smiling art of the writer, who succeeded in sympathetically identifying herself with him, into a comparatively irresistible decorative figure. So puissant is Gerald that any author who had created him might safely permit her future reputation to rest on that accomplishment alone. In this instance, moreover, the character is happily set in what can scarcely fail to continue to be regarded as a permanent masterpiece.

It has long been my contention that the relation of the acts and deeds that make up the externals of a person's life, the incidents, indeed, from which most biographies are pieced together, give a most faulty impression of their model. This would, I think, be especially true of Elinor Wylie. The facts of her life as they have been related to me were completely at variance with her character as I was acquainted with it. This character apparently contradicted at every turn the evidence of her semi-public actions. For myself then, if I wish to quicken my mind with a memory of my dead friend, no account of her birth, childhood, marriages, and child-bearings has any value. I turn rather to her work, in the best of which is to be rediscovered the beautiful essence of her nature. Elinor lives again for me in a rereading of Jennifer Lorn and breathes as warmly as if the breath of her very lively conversation again brushed my cheek.

CARL VAN VECHTEN

JUNE 4, 1933
NEW YORK

Jennifer Lorn

CONTENTS

Jennifer Lorn

BOOK I: *GERALD*

1

A GROSS OF BRASS KNOCKERS

WHEN WARREN HASTINGS became Governor-General of India in the year 1773, he had among his associates a young man whose abilities, if somewhat less than those of his chief, were so peculiarly marked that Hastings soon found it necessary to decide whether this person was to be broken as an enemy or raised to the illustrious eminence of a friend. Having fixed upon the latter course, the great man never regretted his choice, and the able associate was content to remain just that and nothing more, knowing very well that though under other circumstances he might himself have joined the perilous and thinning ranks of great men, his own position was far safer and only a little less lucrative in the long run.

The Honourable Gerald Poynyard was the heir to a barony whose extreme antiquity was the only satisfactory thing about it, and at an early age he made up his mind finally and firmly that the other satisfactory things of life were so essential to his happiness that he could even bring himself to work, and to work hard, in order to obtain them. In his day and generation, this was an idea so original and surprising that Gerald, at one time, came very near to being regarded as the black sheep of an otherwise respectable family, but his almost immediate acquisition of vast sums of money did much to remove this prejudice from the minds of his more critical aunts and cousins.

The natural question raised by these gentry was, " Why doesn't Gerald make a good match? " but to this he had always the same answer: " Because I happen to want a beautiful wife." Suggestions that beauty and money might sometimes be found in exquisitely balanced portions he pooh-poohed, reminding his relatives that the smallness of his estates and the largeness of his nose forbade any such plan unless he was willing to make a victim of some romantic ward in Chancery, or discover a banker's daughter who weighed in at less than thirteen stone. His father, having no choice whatever in the matter, gave in with a good grace, and let the boy have his own way, remarking only that since decent class distinctions seemed to count for nothing in Gerald's estimation, it was a pity that he was tossing aside a splendid career in the diplomatic service to become a clerk in the East India Company.

Gerald considered his three years at Cambridge sadly wasted; he took a deep interest in Greek History and nourished a secret passion for mathematics, but on the whole his university career was a mere marking of time, chiefly memorable for the extreme pleasure he took in the Newmarket Races and for several visits to the continent during the Long Vacation. During these visits he perfected his knowledge of French; it was customary among his friends to say that Gerald's accent was the best possible earnest of the stainless aristocracy of his acquaintance in that delightful country. As early as 1765 he was a familiar figure at the more exclusive coffee-houses in London; he possessed a sort of cold and deadly skill at gaming, seldom exercised, but almost never without success.

In this same year, when he was barely twenty, he first appeared at Versailles, where his odd but distinguished type won him a decided measure of appreciation from the various societies into which the good offices of his connections easily introduced him. Perhaps these connections still hoped that he would have the wisdom to select a wife from among Parisian banking circles rather than to haunt the court in a determined pursuit of knowledge of the morals and manners of the *haute noblesse* of France;

if so they were disappointed. He was polite to the bankers and tax farmers; they found him charming, and honoured his small draughts with real pleasure, but he never looked at their daughters' faces however gallantly he bowed over their hands. At the court he deliberately attached himself to certain ladies of great but diminishing beauty; as they were all at least twenty years older than he they possibly knew more about the ways of the world than he did at the beginning of their association; it is certain that at the end what little he did not understand about life at the French court could have been written upon the proverbial sixpence.

At Versailles he was accepted without question as a young and clever Englishman of good family; his great height, the prominence of his pale blue eyes, and his thin bony nose satisfied the recognised conception of an Englishman, and with the help of a fair skin, and thick hair shining flaxen under the powder, he passed for handsome. Agreeable he undoubtedly was; highly agreeable, with perfect manners, not too strikingly in evidence, and a wit just subtle and serene enough to please those most captious critics. He had a fine figure, and when he had money he was generous with it. Altogether, he was rather more than liked. There is a spirited portrait of him in one of Voltaire's most famous letters, written at this time. He is introduced as " a young Englishman, truly intelligent." This, from Voltaire, is much, but no more than the truth.

Upon attaining his majority, Gerald immediately applied for and received the position of clerk in the East India Company. The consternation of his family has already been dwelt upon; it is only necessary to add that his creditable record at the University, and his really brilliant successes at Versailles made the blow all the more crushing. When he left Cambridge, the preceding year, his most influential cousin had informed him that the Diplomatic Service might have been founded for no other purpose than to give scope to his indisputable talents; even going so far as to state, in a stage whisper, that he was practically authorised to offer him a small but honourable post at the court of Saxony. Gerald asked what stipend he might expect, and on being enlightened as to what his cousin assured him was an unimportant point, sniffed loudly and disdainfully. A year later he was in Calcutta.

Gerald, who loved all courts except the smaller German ones, was now in a counting-house, but he had reached the counting-house by way of many courts, amusing and various as the jewelled stars and ribbons which they had bestowed upon this young and ingratiating foreigner. Following a week of amazing luck at White's, the results of which were augmented by a modest, but timely, bequest from an adoring old nurse, he discovered that he was in possession of sufficient funds to travel at least part of the way to India in the proper style for the Grand Tour; while he traversed Europe by the lengthy and circuitous route of his own choosing he was in all respects the young nobleman setting forth to see the world. This curious circumstance, taken in conjunction with the fact that the same sum of money invested in the business of a merchant in Spanish wines or a new and progressive banking house in the City would have given Gerald a tiny but assured income for the rest of his life, might lead the ignorant to suspect him of profligacy and extravagance. This was not the case; he was simply investing the money in himself, with a nice appreciation of his own powers. By the time Gerald took ship at Marseilles, his brocades and velvets were wearing threadbare and his purse was exceedingly depleted, but he had polished his French *ad unguem,* and given the last perfect twist to his swordsmanship; improved the soundness of his chess in Germany and heightened its brilliance in Italy; shot bears in the Pyrenees with Spanish peasants and sharpened his steely wits against the best brains in Europe. After buying a complete outfit at the proper shops in Marseilles, an outfit including such delicate linens and nankeens that he shuddered to contemplate them in the aguish grip of the *mistral* under a sky which set his teeth on edge, he spent his every penny on chincona bark, six dozen bottles of the finest brandy, and the works of Voltaire bound in dark rose-coloured morocco and having his own arms blind-tooled on the covers at an extra cost of twelve louis. Then he boarded an East Indiaman, and, passing Gibraltar under a tiger-striped December sunset, looked his last on British soil until he landed on a mud bank in the Hoogli.

He had made all the necessary arrangements with the East
India Company; aboard the ship his passage had been taken for
him, and the voyage passed pleasantly enough. His fellow pas-
sengers were dull in the extreme; a sandy-haired Scotchman,
going out to the same counting-house in Calcutta, was soon
driven to saturnine and scornful silence by Gerald's godless conversation; two ingenuous youths, destined for military service in
the Sepoy army of the Company, began by assuming airs of superiority and ended in a state of abject fear which threw them into
paroxysms of laughter at the subtlest and most abstruse of his
jokes, which they invariably failed to comprehend and which
were invariably directed against themselves. The Scotchman often
wanted to laugh, but his conscience forbade. Gerald would have
been wretched without the brandy and *Candide;* with the help
of these the long blue days and black silver nights melted away
like a dream.

When he woke in the counting-house, he was very wide
awake indeed; he was greedy for work, tireless, watchful, terrible with a sort of guarded and restrained passion. He was
quickly promoted. As he rose his associates came to fear him.
The Scotchman, Macallister, maintained he was the devil, and
Macallister feared him less than the others did. Oddly enough,
the natives adored him; in dealing with them he always drew
the velvet glove over the exceeding hardness of his hand, but the
same hand was there, the same texture and weight of iron. Going
out in 1766, at the age of twenty-one, he was from the first a
marked man; his aristocratic connections and his striking appearance probably contributed to his success, but in the main it
was the result of sheer ability and the cold and enduring determination to encompass certain ends. His health was astonishing;
during his seven years as an employé of the East India Company
he lost every scrap of fat with which European cooking had
padded his bones; his freckled face grew as yellow as his hair;
his predatory hands were claws, and yet he was never ill, never
even tired; he combined the work of a navvy and a prime minister, and throve upon it. Soon he was the recognised ambassador to the more peevish of the native princes, his perfect
firmness and impeccable suavity made him invaluable to the

Company and acceptable to the most pampered of rajahs. Here was a man who had every grace, every accomplishment; a man whose chess was as magnificent as his marksmanship; a man who could manage a horse or a political intrigue with light and masterly touch; a man who had no fear and who was beginning to have a great deal of money.

In 1772, the year before Warren Hastings became Governor-General, Gerald was considerably more than beginning; he already had a great deal of money, and he was a distinct power in India. The Company recognised this fact, and profited by it; Gerald was well satisfied to be made use of by the Company, so long as he was permitted to make use of India. He was now twenty-seven years old, and in one way or another he had managed to save fifty thousand pounds. Into some of the other ways it is perhaps best not to inquire, but his worst enemies never accused him of lack of industry, ingenuity, or intelligence. Taking it all in all, it may be said that Gerald earned his money.

He was now determined to use his fortune to the best advantage; before investing it he wished to make certain acquisitions and to fulfil certain ambitions. They were singularly definite; they included the purchase of four cream-coloured horses from one rajah, and a string of pearls from a second; these he obtained, together with one magnificent diamond and a small palace of marble, gilded under the sun and frosted silver by moonlight, the forfeited property of the richest native merchant whom the Company had succeeded in ruining that year. It stood on the outskirts of Calcutta, where the houses were all of dressed stone, drab and low, and as it was new and shining and white it looked very cool and beautiful above the yellow Hoogli.

Having deserved well of the Company, Gerald had no difficulty in arranging for a year's leave of absence and his passage home. It was generally understood that he was going back to England to be married; when offered congratulations he accepted them simply and affably, without troubling to explain that as yet he had not selected his future wife. Indeed, he was hardly himself aware of this fact, so very real and clearly defined was his own idea of the lady he was about to wed. After making a few more purchases, which included hangings of indigo and silver for the more important rooms of the palace, and an uncut sapphire of great size and beauty, he again took ship, sailing this time straight for England. On board the East Indiaman he was the object of much adulation; this annoyed him greatly until, remembering his former experience, he decided to re-read *Candide* and drink brandy; the weather was like his own sapphire taken out of its ivory box and dissolved in sunlight; he sat on deck, upon cushions of scarlet silk with a snow-white awning like a great cloud between him and the sky, and though the quality of the brandy left something to be desired, he had never enjoyed *Candide* half so much.

Gerald was an excellent sailor; the Bay of Biscay upset him only because his servants were all seasick. Upon arriving at Bordeaux his equanimity was completely restored by a delightful addition to the ship's company, a young Frenchman of good family and a refined taste in literature and wine. The last quart of brandy had been requisitioned in the middle of a violent storm to save the life of a female passenger; only the heavier tragedies of Voltaire, which he had never cared for, remained to be read. The appearance of a youthful Parisian, mad with joy at escaping from the offices of the Bordeaux wine-merchant whom he had the ill fortune to own as an uncle, and to whom his mother had sent him in a moment of insensate sisterly affection; a youthful Parisian transported with happiness at the prospect of meeting his fiancée in London, and carrying with him to beguile the tedium of the voyage four cases of superb claret and the first published writings of Mirabeau; this was indeed a welcome distraction. Gerald was almost sorry when the grey shape of the Lizard raised its lighthouse and threw a shattered beam of gold into his searching eyes.

Hiring a chaise at Gravesend, he drove straight to the London house of his most influential cousin, who in the course of seven years had shrunk and stiffened in an alarming manner. Nevertheless, he appeared overjoyed at the sight of Gerald, in whom his perspicuity recognised a potential influence even greater than his own. This lean and yellow young man, shivering on the doorstep with his new bottle-green greatcoat huddled around him, was magnificent in the chrysalis, cold as yet, and torpid, but with the germ of glory concealed somewhere among the folds of stiff cloth, like the golden guineas hidden in the obscure cavern of his pocket. Lady Dicker, who had herself shrunk and softened almost out of knowledge, hurried downstairs with her hair unpowdered and a puce-coloured satin dressing-gown hastily thrown about her shoulders; she begged her dear cousin to regard their home as his during his sojourn in England. "At least you'll stay the night?" she besought.

But Gerald would trespass on their generous hospitality no further than to partake of a glass of sherry and to warm his toes in front of the study fire while his cousin informed him as to the schedule of stages on the Exeter Road. Gerald was going down to Basingstoke immediately to see his poor old father. He had not remembered that the month of April was so chilly in England. Yes, he was glad to be home, but it was cold; devilish cold. And he threw another log on the study fire and swallowed another glass of sherry. In the panelled hall his two turbaned servants shuddered with chattering teeth, their feet drawn up from the black and white marble floor.

After a wretched journey by stage to Basingstoke, and a delicious drive in the best hired gig that town afforded, through a spring landscape laced with bloom, Gerald arrived at the quaint hamlet of Camphileden, and stood once more upon his father's doorstep. An east wind blew a shower of frail petals about him; the servants, whom the carter was bringing, along with the seventeen portmanteaux and two sole-leather trunks, shivered so violently that they were unable to admire the blackthorn hedges; but Gerald was enchanted with everything. A blossoming cherry tree in a sheltered southern corner of the garden sent him into the house with an ecstatic smile upon his wooden countenance; the white hyacinths almost moved him to song. Lord Camphile met his son with an aggrieved air; he had a bad cold in his head, but his gout was somewhat improved. Otherwise he had altered very little; Gerald found him looking rather younger than the most sanguine of filial hopes had seemed to warrant.

Gerald was properly pleased to see his poor old father looking so well; he was now far too important a personage in his own right to have any lurking regrets about that. In India he was

Poynyard; he thought of himself as Poynyard and, when he considered the subject at all, felt distinctly annoyed at the idea of suddenly becoming Camphile. It was a real satisfaction to see his father in such excellent health, and to know that the poor old man was no more than fifty-six years of age and might reasonably be expected to live for some time. He wrung his father's hand with unaffected warmth, and observing that the paternal dressing-gown was slightly frayed, decided to replace it as soon as possible by a much finer one of dark blue brocade with a wine-coloured cord and tassels.

In the morning Gerald rode into Basingstoke on the only decent mount his father's vast stables contained; the pretty little mare had originally belonged to a sporting farmer who, unable to pay his entire rent of fifty pounds for one farm and three pepper-corns for another, had left Dolly and the pepper-corns at Camphileden and driven away cursing behind his flea-bitten grey. Lord Camphile was thoroughly disgusted, but the solitary stable-boy was the happiest man in Hampshire; no lapidary ever polished a gem with a more meticulous care than the delighted Hodge henceforward bestowed upon the smoothing and sleeking of Dolly's silken coat. Gerald, riding into town through flowery fields, himself attired like the lilies in dazzling brown boots, cream-coloured breeches, and a pale grey coat with gilt buttons, had no reason to feel ashamed of Dolly; she shone brighter than his boots.

Gerald went immediately to his father's agent, who since the decline of the Camphile fortunes had been forced to eke out his meagre income with the help of a solicitor's business in Basingstoke. Mr. Jackson received the young heir obsequiously; at the end of half an hour's close conference he was in a state of trembling rapture. " A thousand pounds will do wonders . . . wonders! " he kept repeating, and wished he might add, " your Lordship," for he had no love for Gerald's father, nor indeed for any impoverished person other than himself. Gerald broke away from his eager conjectures about the relative merits of whitewash applied to the outside of cottages and oaken joists applied within; the young man now visited a wine-merchant's, the best in Basingstoke, but in so humble a way of business that his webbed and furry bottles failed to satisfy the exigencies of his customer's taste. However, he was permitted to dispatch a case of port to Camphileden, together with a small quantity of really good brandy which the worthy fellow had secured at an executors' sale. His claret was impossible; Gerald, who drank no other wine, lost no time in sending a large order by post to one of the leading London houses. That night, at dinner, his father begged him to help him finish the second bottle of Basingstoke port; he refused with the utmost politeness and hauteur, though he knew it to be a very good wine indeed. He sniffed thankfully at the brandy in his own glass before swallowing it.

Lord Camphile indulged in one curious affectation; he persisted in treating his son as a failure. Gerald would have been keenly annoyed by this absurdity had it not happened to appeal to his rather sardonic sense of humour. To hear his father's constant references to the disgraceful depth of commercial careers and the ridiculous height of counting-house stools was merely amusing to him, who had sat on cloth of gold among swansdown cushions and diplomatically allowed a prince to beat him at chess; even his father's seat in the House of Lords was lowly compared to a swaying howdah perched on the back of some crimson-caparisoned royal elephant, and he had placed many more bullets behind tigers' ears than pens behind his own. Therefore he could afford to laugh at his father, and he did. But on the whole the two managed to agree fairly well, and the next month passed very pleasantly.

The weather was all that could be expected of April, and the workmen made good headway with their whitewashing of cob walls and thatching of roofs; the village became so tidy that the high street looked like a Dutch toy. Gallons of green paint were splashed upon front doors, and it was said that Gerald had ordered a gross of brass knockers from London. This was the famous year in which a local wit recalled the ancient form of the hamlet's name; Camphile Eden; saying that in spite of a serpent he might mention being the cause of it all, they had damn near gone back to Bible days what with rose-bushes and clean curtains. To every one's surprise Gerald took the matter up eagerly, not with a cane, as some people had expected, but with energy and enthusiasm and the help of that submerged antiquarian, the Vicar of Saint Cuthbert's. Soon the village found itself with a name which seemed as new and disturbing as the brass knockers; a name split into two parts and therefore just twice as hard to write, as the schoolmaster told various indignant inquirers. Nevertheless, the name, being Gerald's choice, stood, and probably stands till this day, and if you look close enough at a map of Hampshire you may perhaps find it so written: Camphile Eden.

The Hall itself, so-called, although it was in reality no more than a little grey dower-house, of crude and unfashionable Tudor construction, was given a charming new face of blushing rose-coloured brick; an improvement so manifest, at least from the south lawn, that Gerald almost ceased to regret the enormous Elizabethan pile which had been destroyed during the Great Rebellion much to the annoyance of his grandfather's grandfather. That gentleman, known severally to his friends and foes as Handsome Phil Camphile and the Devil's Twin, was said to have greeted the disagreeable tidings of the burning and sacking of his country-seat with the sprightly comment that he could bear the loss of the Towers; the cellars were all he really cared about. Gerald, examining the gigantic blocks of calcined stone, the heaps of blackened bricks, decided that the house must have been an example of the worst possible taste, barbarous and shocking in the extreme; he had made up his mind then and there to have some competent architect build him a suitable mansion, on this same site, as soon as he had saved a little more money. And he reflected comfortably that owing to the unusual nature of his Indian investments, into which it might be instructive but alarming to inquire, his fifty thousand pounds was still fifty thousand pounds and perhaps a trifle over, in spite of the fact that he had spent rather lavishly of late. The Adam brothers, of whom he had heard great things, would be the very men if he could afford them; they would understand to perfection the chaste and stately simplicity which this landscape required to crown it. At the same time he remembered with pleasure his pretty little marble palace above the Hoogli. In the carven richness of the stones about him he could see no beauty; on the contrary, they filled him with disgust, and he kicked a rampant lion so hard that he stubbed his toe severely in addition to ruining a particularly elegant varnished boot.

The Gardens at the Hall were already well established; Gerald's mother had found her chief solace in them after her husband ceased to interest her and she ceased to interest her son. She was a gentlewoman of fair intelligence and no little beauty, but her husband was too stupid and her son too clever to understand her, and she was forced to seek companionship among standard roses and espaliered fruit trees. The winters were her worst times; in spite of a small conservatory she died of loneliness in February, 1757. However, the roses and fruit trees survived, thanks to the devoted care of an old gardener, who had conceived a romantic love for her when she first came to Camphile Hall fifteen years before, and who watched her yellow hair turn silver-streaky with a sort of dumb and helpless agony; if she had been a rose he could have blown strong smoke from his pipe and killed the trouble; for a dying lady he could do nothing. But in 1772, when the old man was nearly ninety, her gardens were a living marvel.

Gerald had the interior of the Hall redecorated in the fresh and delicate style of the period; he employed labour from Basingstoke, and a local architect, who had the sense to recognise his client's faultless taste and to profit by it. The expense was not great, but the effect was charming. The green morning-room was especially successful, though the white parlour on a sunny afternoon elicited more praise from the general run of calling ladies. The library was left untouched, partly out of respect for Lord Camphile, but mainly because Gerald realised that the chairs, if done at all, should be done in morocco; a needless waste of money which could be used to better advantage elsewhere. On his next trip to London he acquired some exquisite peach-blow porcelain and the *Fermiers Generaux* edition of La Fontaine.

The entire county called, first out of curiosity and then again out of sheer amazement; presently Gerald was very much in demand. Reports of his vast wealth were circulated on all sides; at Lady Andover's *fête champêtre* he was mobbed. During the

months of May and June he did not dine at home more than half
a dozen times, and then with a distinguished company about him.
His clothes were impeccable, his manners consummate, his poise
beyond praise. Many daughters of good houses shook with fearful
delight in his presence; he seemed a fairy prince, with just
enough of the ogre about him to make him totally irresistible.
But there was never anything to resist; Gerald remained unmoved.

Meanwhile, it must not be supposed that London offered no
attractions to the returned wanderer; the influential cousin saw
to it that London should. Sir Richard Dicker, or Cousin Dick,
as with a double inevitability he was known to half the peerage,
baronetage, and landed gentry of Great Britain, saw no reason
whatever why Camphile's boy should vegetate in a deserted
village. Without wishing to dwell too lovingly on the riches of
his young kinsman, lest Parliament's already somewhat nervous
interest in the East India Company be aroused to a pitch commensurate with that which caused the Governor-General of India
much inconvenience at a later date, he nevertheless allowed it to
be understood that Gerald was able to support a well-born wife in
a style far beyond that to which she had been accustomed. No
unnecessary questions were answered, or indeed asked, for to
most people's minds it was much more suitable that Baron Camphile's son and heir should possess a hundred thousand pounds
than that he should not. A hundred thousand was the figure at
which Gerald's fortune was commonly reported, and by a curious and pleasing coincidence that was the figure at which it
actually stood in August, 1772, thanks to the quite unprecedented luck attending certain obscure Indian investments. Warren Hastings, getting wind of these negotiations, considered
very seriously the advisability of having a warrant sworn out for
Gerald's arrest immediately upon the latter's return to India, but
thinking better of it, decided instead to accept the young man as
a trusted associate; a decision which, as has been said before, the
great man never had cause to regret. But in 1772 there was as
yet no Governor-General in India, and Hastings was still sweating in Calcutta while Gerald was making his bow at St. James's.

His experiences of court life were very different from the

brief and glittering dreams which had engaged his youthful fancy at Versailles; his sovereign's quiet domestic life, though varied by intervals of insanity, was too essentially German to interest Gerald; he did far better during the days of the Regency, which really suited him and permitted his magnificence to shine forth unobscured by the stupidities of bad manners and good morals. At present he found much to amuse him, but little to charm; he began to think that English life was not for him, and spoke seriously of removing to Paris and marrying the daughter of one of his old French friends.

"There was a little Solange," he used to say, "who was utterly charming at eleven years of age; she would now be just eighteen. Her mother was the wittiest and possibly the most beautiful woman I ever knew; her father . . . well, he had not too much to bequeath in the way of brains, perhaps, though I come near to committing *lese majesté* in suggesting it . . . but if the best blood in France can be said to count, the little Solange should be all that there is of the most exquisite." And he would sigh gently, smoothing an invisible wrinkle out of his silk stocking. In the main, he found the English ladies handsome and extremely dull; at the great Whig houses where his cousin introduced him he had every opportunity of judging, and as in Hampshire he was *persona grata* among the leading county families, it may fairly be said that Gerald deserved the criticism which was undoubtedly made. He was, indeed, absurdly hard to please.

"My dear sir, what I require is something very different from any of these excellent females," he remarked to his father one evening in late July, as the two sat sipping their wine in the panelled dining-room, fresh-painted a clear yellowish white which showed up the new Chinese Chippendale chairs to much advantage. The western windows were open, and Gerald was not so deeply preoccupied with his *Château Margaux* as to render him incapable of appreciating the shining lemon-coloured sky or the scent of a charming shell-pink climbing rose which he had saved from the builders' vandalism at the slight cost of horse-whipping a day-labourer and threatening a carpenter's apprentice with a pocket-pistol. "The country ladies are all too red, the London ladies too pasty, when they are not rouged out of all resemblance to humanity. Nevertheless, I prefer these last to the Blowsibellas of our own sweet countryside. I suppose when I venture into Cornwall next week I shall be suffocated in an atmosphere of clotted cream and over-ripe apple cheeks. God damn Dicker and all his cousins! "

He had upon his Chinese Bristol plate a superb bunch of white currants; when he held them up to the light they were like a little cluster of grapes, translucent, veined with green and amber, delicate as fruit blown in Venetian glass. He tasted a currant with pursed lips, and continued the conversation; his father was silent.

"I most certainly have no hope of bringing home a bride from Saint Mary's; I may possibly acquire one of Dick's Hereford bulls to improve our wretched breed; beyond that I have no plan, other than my invincible determination to limit my visit to a week's time. The fact that my mother used occasionally to spend the Christmas holidays at the Old Rectory does not appeal to me as a reason why I should be boiled to death; boiled in oil I may say, in discreet reference to our worthy cousin's gift for flattery. Thank Heaven that my engagements for August are so numerous that they will require my absence in Scotland during the whole of that month; the devil take the probability that Dick's are precisely the same. If I find myself in his company on some lonely grouse-moor, I warn you, sir, in all gravity, that there will be considerable danger of a fatal shooting mishap."

He ate another currant and laughed. "I feel no alarm," said Lord Camphile, after which ambiguous comment he fell asleep. Gerald rang for the butler. "Brinton," he commanded, "I desire you to inform Mrs. Barnes that the remainder of that excellent saddle of mutton is under no consideration to suffer metamorphosis into a shepherd's pie; in that eventuality I should be forced to take steps which would be painful both to myself and to Mrs. Barnes; Mohammed will curry the mutton."

"Yes, sir; very good, sir," said Brinton. "Gerald," said Lord Camphile, waking up, "I should like a little, minced on toast." "My dear father," said Gerald, "it is ever my pleasurable duty to yield to your slightest wish; Brinton, you hear what your master says." With which he rose smiling from the table, and spent the evening pacing softly up and down the east terrace, inhaling snuff and watching the full moon as she languidly detached herself from a tangle of beech trees in Camphile Eden Bower.

2

THE EARL'S ELZEVIR

SIR RICHARD DICKER was the son of a clergyman; his father had been the Reverend Sir Ambrose Dicker, Rector of Saint Mary Pengwynne's in Cornwall. A deserving cousin now held the living, but the Old Rectory, a commodious dwelling of the Jacobean period, had been purchased by Dick as a country retreat, endeared to him by childish memories; he needed some such haven of rest in the intervals of his London activities, and thoroughly enjoyed the small farm which was attached to the place and managed for him by a reliable resident agent. The New Rectory was much better suited to the present incumbent's requirements; a well-built modern house with a good kitchengarden and neat lawns, in the shadow of Saint Mary's tower, it enabled him to keep up the proper appearances without making unnecessary inroads upon his slender resources; unlike his predecessor, he was entirely dependent upon the living. The Dickers showed him every possible kindness, and he dined with them at least four times a year; he was a widower with several young children, and an agreeable person in all respects save the very poor quality of his play at whist.

The village of Saint Mary Pengwynne was so close to the borders of Devon that the surrounding landscape possessed rather the green and luxuriant quality associated with the latter county than Cornwall's own air of wild and rugged grandeur. The Old Rectory was situated among scenes of surpassing beauty; Gerald was pleased in spite of himself, and when he was pleased his manner was enchanting. The local gentry were impressed, those who dined at the Old Rectory the first evening of his stay pronounced him delightful; the second evening he was called distinguished; it was not until the third that the disappointed mother of three lovely girls labelled him morose.

The next morning at breakfast his brow was dark and corrugated; he hardly touched the kedgeree which his own servant had prepared for him. Dick talked of Hereford bulls with patient cheerfulness; his wife remained discreetly silent as she poured the tea. After Gerald had drunk five cups he commented upon the pretty Chelsea porcelain; his hosts breathed again, and Mohammed went out into the Italian garden and wept for joy.

" Dear boy," said Dick courageously, " you have heard me speak of my Devonshire cousins."

" Often," said Gerald.

" The Nevilles and the Cleverlys," said Dick.

" Just so," said Gerald. But he consented to ride over to Cleverly-Neville that afternoon.

" You'll like Tam-Linn; he has the finest library in the United Kingdom." Dick was growing venturesome.

" Oh, yes," said Gerald, " I know the man well. He tricked me out of an Elzevir Cicero; an intelligent fellow. I'm engaged to help slaughter his game in August. But what the devil is a Scotch Earl doing in Devon? "

" His wife was a Cleverly," Dick informed him proudly; Gerald nodded with perfect politeness.

" And his daughter is the most beautiful girl in Devonshire." This time Dick had gone too far; Gerald rose without a word and stalked from the room.

Dick was intimidated; that afternoon at Cleverly-Neville he drove his female cousins away from Gerald as though they had been a parcel of hens striving to reach some rich and indigestible food; he felt sincerely that in the event of one of the more talkative of these ladies managing to corner Gerald, the consequences might be really dangerous. The Earl of Tam-Linn did the honours of his wife's house with true Scotch hospitality; he and Gerald had taken to each other from the moment of their first meeting, and the hours passed smoothly in the congenial discussion of the relative merits of English and French binders. Six o'clock came, with lengthening stripes of darker green across the shaven turf; the tree-tops rustled in the sweet airs of evening, the sky was silver and gold. Within the library the cloudy amber sunlight gave lustre to glazed leather and gilt lettering; the Chinese brocade which covered the chairs flashed into spider-web patterns of tinsel thread traced upon orange and dull blue. "Perfection; complete perfection," murmured Gerald as Lord Tam-Linn placed a marvellously-preserved palimpsest of Vergil in his long thin hands. The Earl was much gratified by his young guest's unaffected admiration for this treasure, but Gerald was not referring to the book alone; the room with its oak panels, faintly gilt along the mouldings, its Chinese brocades, its *Famille Jaune* vases on the carven chimney-piece under the portrait of a lady by Sir Peter Lely, all these things appealed to his passion for perfection; the smell of Russia leather and of pot-pourri perfumed the fresh breeze fluttering the curtains, the sound of a spinet tinkled from above; the only jarring note was Lord Tam-Linn's loud voice roughening the "r" in Vergil. Presently this was removed; its owner had gone to look for the Elzevir Cicero. Gerald drew a long breath of relief.

"Our good friend hardly deserves this exquisite house; his own top-heavy granite castle of Carterhaugh suits him far better. After all, there is nothing to touch these little Queen Anne manors for the nice combination of beauty and comfort." He turned his head upon the high cushioned back of his chair and closed his eyes for one luxurious instant; when he opened them again he was looking straight out of the window at a young girl who leaned upon the sundial; the cloudy sunlight fell faint and diluted upon her burnished head.

Her hair was red-gold, looped and curled in innumerable ringlets; unpowdered and unbound, its brightness was amazing. She wore a dress of cream-coloured muslin; against her pale blue sash certain petals of a large cream-coloured rose drooped defined, the rest melted into the tinted fabric of her bodice. Her eyes were dark, dark grey or hazel contrasting strangely with a skin of singular fairness; her features were formed in lines of the most wistful and appealing beauty, delicate and clear.

"In the name of God, who is that girl!" cried Gerald in a strained and choking voice. "That," said Dick coolly, "is my little cousin, Jennifer Lorn."

Jennifer Lorn was the most beautiful girl in Devonshire; indeed, with the possible exception of a few Genoese and Sicilian peasants and a shawled colleen or two in Galway, she was the most beautiful girl in the world. At this time she was exactly seventeen years old; as her father preferred to spend his money upon first editions there is no contemporary portrait of her in existence; the vision of her early loveliness faded from reality like dew licked up by the sun. The miniature which Gerald ordered in Paris a year later was destroyed during the Revolution; its owner had not the heart to claim it on his return from the East in 1773, and it remained in the artist's hands for twenty years before Fouquier-Tinville chanced to see it lying in the blood and mud of the streets; because it smiled so innocently at him he ground it under his boot. As the old miniature painter's head had just fallen into the basket, the incident appeared unimportant at the time, but now it seems a pity that the little ivory oval did not survive the Reign of Terror, as by all accounts it must have been not only an excellent likeness but a delicate and distinguished work of art.

The daughter of the Earl of Tam-Linn and the Honourable Clarinda Cleverly-Neville, Jennifer was almost bound to be a beauty, but no one could have foreseen the remarkable success with which she contrived to fuse and combine the good looks of both families into an exquisite concord quite her own. Tam-Linn was now nearing seventy; he was still an extremely handsome man; a lean Scot, tall and proud and very fierce, with bright eyes and bright red hair as yet hardly dimmed by grey. Jennifer had taken his eyes and hair and made them more amazing; she had taken as much of his height as she needed, and the scornful lift of his forehead, and his long throat, and his slenderness. But she had rejected his harsh burring voice; she had rejected his nervous energy and a good half of his brains. From her mother she had chosen a charming languor, a complexion of rose and cream, little bones, and soft flesh to lie sparingly over them; her hands and feet were her mother's, and so were her laziness and her good nature. She had her mother's minute teeth and extravagant eyelashes; if she had ever grown plump she would have had her mother's dimples too, but the

Lorn blood running wild and chilly in her veins kept her thin and clear as green leaves in April.

Besides her beauty, she had all manner of engaging tricks and traits; people smiled when she spoke, and the more susceptible, seeing her praying in church on Sunday, were not infrequently moved to tears. But she was neither very strong nor very clever; the suave warm air of Devon tended to increase her natural lassitude, and none of her governesses had taught her more than the use of the globes, a little music, and the ability to converse unintelligently in French and German. However, her accent in each language was beyond reproach; her singing voice, a strange little muffled contralto, had been so far neglected that it remained quite adorable, and her touch upon the spinet was too light and casual to be really distressing. She was excessively fond of sitting upon a garden seat and reading Bishop Percy's Reliques; she would have preferred to lie down in the grass under the shade of the copper beeches, but this was forbidden owing to the supposed delicacy of Cleverly-Neville chests, long her mother's excuse for protracted absences from Carterhaugh. This lady shared her daughter's taste for poetry, but she was perfectly satisfied with garden seats and the works of Mr. Gray and Mr. Goldsmith; she was much more intellectual than Jennifer, and a valued friend of Mr. Horace Walpole's. In her youth she had been romantic; to marry Tam-Linn was a more adventurous manner of indulging a passion for Scotch history than a mere reading of Bishop Percy's ballads. In her early married life she had found Caxton's Malory among her husband's books and forthwith insisted that her infant daughter should be christened Guinevere in the Parish church of Cleverly-Neville; Tam-Linn insisted that the child should be baptised by the minister at Carterhaugh, and given the name of Janet; they compromised upon Jennifer, an old Neville name. A journey to Scotland during a particularly wet April proved impossible under the circumstances, but Tam-Linn was allowed to call his daughter Jenny.

The more robust of her Carterhaugh cousins called her Jenny Forlorn; her mother was accustomed to dress her in white muslin all the year round, and this habit, though highly satis-

factory from an æsthetic point of view, produced during the
Scotch winters a type of sore throat which did not tend to raise
the spirits. Lady Tam-Linn saw her chance and took it; Jennifer's health could not possibly support so severe a climate except for the month of August. Lady Tam-Linn was happier in
Devon; Jennifer was happier in Devon; Tam-Linn himself was
happier in Devon after his wife had the most valuable portion
of his library, including all his classical manuscripts and every
Elzevir he possessed, removed to Cleverly-Neville. He stayed at
Carterhaugh from the beginning of August until he joined his
family at Christmas; his sons sometimes stayed with him, and his
daughter sometimes wished she could. Had she done so, and
joined the other Lorn and Carterhaugh girls in their racing and
chasing over the moor, it is probable that her vitality would
have been higher; it is a pity that she was not permitted to kilt
her green kirtle as bravely as the original Lady Janet for whom
the minister did not, after all, baptise her. Her muscles and her
brains were perfectly capable of development; she should have
lived in Scotland until she was sixteen and then been packed
off to Oxford with her brothers, Jock and Jem; perhaps she
might have struck the authorities as looking rather like a pretty
girl in boy's clothes, but that, being precisely the way in which
her brothers struck them, would not have mattered very much.
In spite of their names, Jock and Jem were thoroughly Cleverly-
Nevilles. Their mother adored them, and their father teased them
and felt like a brute when their blue eyes blinked at him in polite
protest. Jennifer was his favourite; he liked to see his own falcon
eyes burning in her small pink and white face, and he knew instinctively that she was neither a fool nor a coward, only egre-
giously lazy.

"God damn my soul, the girl's even lazier than her mother!"
he would say, and then he would laugh and laugh and laugh.
The boys would jump in their chairs and shrink back in alarm,
but neither little Jennifer nor her mother jumped or shrank at
all; they laughed too, and they were laughing at Tam-Linn. The
next day, very likely, the whole family would leave for Devonshire, a full fortnight earlier than the Earl had expected. He loved
the dripping rocks and spongy heather of Carterhaugh with a

fierce intensity, and yet when he reached Cleverly-Neville on Christmas Eve, and kissed his wife and daughter again, he was so wild with joy at the sight of them that he could very nearly, as he himself put it, have eaten them both up like a nice little pat of butter and a nice little pot of cream.

Thus Jennifer Lorn was brought up within sight of a warm pearl-coloured sea, in a garden where the roses bloomed all winter if they had a bit of south wall to hold the sun behind them, and where the lilacs and laburnum came out so ridiculously early that your mind was never quite made up to look for them, and they carried a slight air of miracles about them every spring. She was brought up to eat bread and butter, and milk and honey, and rice pudding, and strawberry jam for a treat. She was brought up to wear frocks of fine India muslin and to tie blue ribbons about her waist; to go to church and sing hymns out of a velvet hymnal with a gilt cross on it; to sit on a green silk chair while her maid brushed her curls to splendour; to sit on a white bench and read Percy's Reliques; to lean over a sundial on a summer's day and wonder drowsily why she loved cream-coloured roses better than yellow ones, and why she had ever been born. This is the way in which she had been brought up, and this is the way she looked; it is easy to understand why Gerald uttered a choking cry and sprang violently to his feet when he first saw her in July, 1772, falling asleep at six o'clock on a golden-cloudy afternoon, with her red ringlets heaped like a little fire above the circle of stone.

She was precisely what he had been searching for ever since his return to England; she had been in his mind's eye all the time, correct in every detail with the possible exception of the red hair; he had imagined that her hair would be ash-blonde or pale chestnut. But that was natural enough; such a complexion had never been seen before save in combination with the fairest of flaxen tresses. He had not made the mistake of supposing that she would have blue eyes; these eyes, the colour of a thunder-storm streaked with yellow lightning, had blazed for an instant into his before the lazy eyelids covered them up, and he had known them for the most beautiful eyes in the world; he had always intended that his wife should have such eyes. He fell back rather limply against the Chinese brocade; the girl was almost too perfect.

" Pretty little thing, isn't she? " Dick asked complacently. Gerald stared at him in silent disdain.

When Tam-Linn came back with the Elzevir Cicero, Gerald drew him aside. "Lord Tam-Linn," he said in a quiet, admirably controlled voice, " I should like to ask for your permission to marry your daughter." Tam-Linn, who had thought that Gerald was going to attempt to buy the Cicero from him, was very much relieved. He had been surprised and embarrassed by the prospect of having to refuse his young friend's request; this was another matter. It never occurred to him for an instant that Gerald had seen Jennifer for the first time just five minutes ago; he took it for granted that the acquaintance was of reasonable standing, and he knew that Gerald's own standing was rather more than that.

To tell the truth, Tam-Linn did not entirely realise his daughter's astonishing beauty; he admired plump dark-haired women, of the type of his own Clarinda. Privately he thought his child had a slightly starved and eccentric air; he gave her a great many buttered scones and girdle-cakes whenever he had the opportunity, and loved the poor girl none the less for her pathetic appearance, but of course it made a difference to him in his estimate of her matrimonial chances. As for her hair, the Black Tam-Linns had always been the handsome ones; they had square impassive faces bearing the unmistakable stamp of the blood of those southerners who once built a wall across Scotland; their cleft chins and calm brown eyes were still classic. The Earl knew what it was to be called Red by cousins who looked like Roman consuls. It always gave him a shock to see Jennifer standing knee-deep in purple-red heather with her copper-red hair streaming out against a hot blue August haze; when the high wind lifted the tangled locks and bent the heather, whistling all the while like a mad thing, he thought of witches. It comforted him to remember that the lassie would soon be old enough to wear a decent snood and a sprinkling of powder.

Therefore, it is only natural that when Gerald asked Tam-Linn for his daughter's hand, the Earl made no objection, merely remarking that he would have to ask his wife, but that for his own part he would be thoroughly pleased to see his girl the daughter-in-law of his old friend Camphile.

As a matter of fact, Lord Camphile and he had never liked each other; still, it seemed the simplest thing to say under the circumstances, and in a rush of relief about the Elzevir, he said it with much geniality, reflecting meanwhile that he thanked his God that the real decision lay in Clarinda's province.

" Then may I have the privilege of a word with Lady Tam-Linn ? " asked Gerald urbanely, but with a slight emphasis on the " Lady " which would have annoyed the Earl very much had he not been far too absent-minded to notice it, and which caused Dick to quiver with mingled joy and fear. Dick's head was swimming, but on the whole he felt great pride in his youthful kinsman; in addition to this he was conscious of a pleasing sense of triumph; he had not forgotten how haughtily Gerald had stalked from the breakfast-room that morning at the mention of Jennifer's name, and he debated within himself as to the advisability of rallying the dear boy upon the subject. Just as he had reached the conclusion that after dinner was always the best time, Lady Tam-Linn appeared in the doorway.

She was a very pretty little woman, much younger than her husband; her dark hair, silvered only by its sprinkling of powder, grew into a peak on her forehead; the mingled rose and dove-colour of her dress set off her fine complexion to advantage; her small feet were almost concealed by the shining buckles on her shoes. Only her lively and satirical blue eyes made her other than the charming wax doll whom Tam-Linn had longed to set above the incongruous savagery of Carterhaugh. He had fondly believed that because a woman had pink cheeks and plump white hands she must of necessity be pliant and docile; Clarinda was neither of these things. Under her lazy amiability she was both wilful and obstinate, but as her strongest desire in life was to make her husband and children happy, no great harm was done; she always encompassed her desire in her own way, and they soon learned to be satisfied with the sort of happiness she considered good for them, knowing very well that any other sort was simply out of the question. They were an exceptionally united family.

" My love," said Tam-Linn, " Mr. Poynyard wants to marry Jennifer."

His wife inspected Gerald closely before replying; she was

still far too romantic to tolerate the thought of a mere marriage of convenience for her daughter. Lady Tam-Linn liked tall fair-haired men; she found Gerald's appearance most satisfactory, and considered his nose a mark of race, which indeed it was. His commanding presence and air of impassive and polite contempt impressed her; in a word, she thought him magnificent. She was not sufficiently vulgar-minded to allow the idea of his wealth to obtrude into her upper consciousness, but an aureate background swam behind him, throwing into cold and clear-edged relief the sharp lines of his figure, clad in metallic grey, with shimmering buttons on a coat the colour of steel.

His chill eyes compelled her; she was won in a moment. Gerald realised his conquest as he followed her into the Blue Parlour, but his taste was too perfect to permit of strutting; he went gravely and decorously behind her without so much as a glance in Dick's direction; his slight bow to Tam-Linn was a masterpiece of dignity and reserve.

BOOK II: *JENNIFER*

1

PHŒNIXES AND POMANDER BOXES

WHETHER GERALD now fell under the disturbing influence of a true passion for Jennifer's fine-spun flesh, or whether he merely wished to possess her as he might have possessed a Chelsea figurine or a delicate piece of Meissen, is a question which, at this late date, may not improbably remain forever shrouded in mystery. He was, with all his faults, a person slightly superhuman; Jennifer, on the contrary, little more than half animate. Her vitality would have been amply sufficient for a sleepy water-sprite or a pink marble nymph waking at night among cypresses; before the prospect of a London wedding it swooned into a daze of terror, whence it was slowly revived by her father's caresses and Gerald's gift of a swansdown hood. Lady Tam-Linn was not averse to avoiding the necessity of an Amazonian bevy of Lorn bridesmaids; she silenced her aunts by the discreet use of sentiment, and the reminder that poor little Nelly Cleverly and dear little Kitty Neville would now have a chance to shine unobscured save by Jennifer's own shrinking presence, veiled and drooping as it must inevitably appear. Among sniffs and one-sided smiles, a small and simple wedding in the parish church was confessed to be suitable; there the elfin creature had been christened, as her mother's breaking voice remembered; there she would in all probability be laid to rest, as Aunt Susanna's croak sarcastically reminded.

"Gerald will himself attain the Abbey," said Aunt Jane, who had in her youth been promised to a Post Captain in the Royal Navy, a tall fair man. This gentleman having unfortunately perished of an intermittent fever during a cruise of the West Indies, his betrothed ever afterwards wore a becoming sense of bereavement and a strand of yellow hair encased in a locket of Whitby jet. The colour of Gerald's hair approximated closely to that of the plaited circlet upon Aunt Jane's breast; it needed only the length of his legs to make her his fluttering champion upon all occasions.

Had the honeymoon extended no further than Bath, Jennifer could have danced in glass slippers indefinitely, without fear of splintering them upon anything rougher than the polished floor of the Pump Room. The languorous measures of a gavotte invited her indolence; her extreme beauty dazzled all eyes and tripped all tongues to stuttering. Even her half-humanity could not receive with complete indifference the love of the entire population of a fashionable watering-place. During the fortnight which the newly-wedded pair spent within its purlieus, a sort of midsummer madness descended upon the simmering town. Gerald had insisted that all of his lady's gowns should be either black or white in hue; if he found a stray garment of sea-green or azure he incontinently consigned it to oblivion, careless of her ineffectual tears. A long apprenticeship to white book-muslin had bred in Jennifer a strong distaste for the blanched pearliness of satin or the frosty bloom of velvet without colour; she therefore dressed exclusively in black, to her husband's vast amusement and her mother's rumoured distress.

With what delight she now obscured her flaming curls in clouds of powder and her little limbs in stiffened furbelows of black brocade can only be conjectured; at the least she felt her slippers to be veritable glass and conceived of Gerald as a very passable prince. Her sable magnificence soon won for her the pretty title of the Mourning Bride; a vague aura of sadness haloed and surrounded her, and twenty romantic stories were born during three silver nights of the full harvest moon. A lover murdered upon the banks of the Euphrates and another killed in action upon the coast of Coromandel were among the tamest of these inventions; dawn frequently discovered various young blades of Bath shedding tears among the claret cups for the gallant death of Captain Corydon at the hands of Hyder Ali.

Jennifer accepted the tales of these visionary lovers with a certain pleased composure; such legends carried with them none of the inconveniences of mortality. Gerald entertained himself hugely at her expense, without in the least disturbing her grave self-esteem. She owned to a distinct preference for Colonel Clitander.

"My dear, you do well to cherish the memory of this brave officer. Modest and unassuming in demeanour, his hardihood was well-nigh proverbial in India, and his riches so great that he was enabled to retire from the service after four years spent in Bengal. As you know to your lasting regret, he attempted to make the homeward journey overland attended only by servants, in whose integrity, alas, his noble nature trusted. These he unfortunately permitted to have sight of some valuable diamonds and other gems which he habitually carried in his writing-desk, and which were doubtless intended as gifts for his lovely girl. In consequence of his imprudence, the abandoned wretches were unkind enough to slay him and cast his lifeless body into that historic stream, from which it was never recovered, nor does any man know the fate of the murderers."

At this point Jennifer invariably saw the dark and terrible night studded with outrageous stars, and heard the sinister lapping of the river; the face of the hapless Colonel Clitander shone pale with sleep in the midst of gathering dangers, while the bodies of the servants crept nearer and nearer, like black and glistening snakes, to the couch of their victim.

"As for Captain Corydon," Gerald would continue with the utmost urbanity, placing the tips of his long fingers together and gazing dreamily into the distance with his large and somewhat glassy eyes, "his end was admittedly a sad one, yet I hardly think, my love, that you would have favoured his suit in the event of his return to Devonshire, for as you doubtless remember, that beautiful county was his home, making him your neighbour and your childhood's playmate. The only son of Squire Corydon of Market-Arcady, Tom Corydon was blessed with a sunny disposition and the finest head of auburn hair which I ever beheld, naturally waving, egad, and of a thickness quite hyacinthine. He had an uncommonly good figure, too, a poetic mind, and accomplished manners. However, by a most unfortunate accident which befell him while still a mere lad attending Eton College, he had during some bout of fisticuffs or other boyish sport broken his nose, thus totally destroying the natural symmetry of his features and disfiguring himself for life. This circumstance rendered him less pleasing to the eye; it could not dim his genius or corrupt his virtues. It seems a thousand pities that owing to the unreasonable and hypercritical nature of womankind in general and of you, my darling, in particular, he should have lived the brief remainder of his days a lonely and disappointed man. My personal good fortune cannot stifle my sympathy for his distressing lot; I feel that the swords of Hyder Ali's assassins clove a broken heart as well as a broken nose."

With this he would smile blandly upon his bewildered wife, at the same time delicately tapping the elevated bridge of his own nose before curling his nostrils for the fastidious reception of a pinch of snuff. Jennifer conceived a violent antipathy for the brave Captain Corydon; she had a clear and rather horrible picture of a slim young man on a dappled grey mare riding down the lime avenue at Cleverly-Neville; as he approached the terrace she could see first his straight shoulders and the bronze abundance of that hyacinthine hair, then the flat and ape-like ugliness of his face smote upon her shrinking vision, and she closed her eyes against the neat foil-lace of Gerald's left lapel. His words were always real to her; they carried a sibylline quality of revelation, and lived in her consciousness more vividly than the waistcoat buttons cold below her chin or the light touch disarranging her ringlets.

Gerald refused to remain at Bath for more than the fortnight of their original intention; he found the climate enervating and the company provincial, nor would he take the place seriously as a resort of the first fashion of the day. He was excruciatingly bored by Balloni, and thought the stakes at all games of hazard so low as to be negligible as a means to excitement. The capital band of French horns and clarinets then performing in the Pump Rooms he pronounced overestimated; Jennifer's dancing partners excited his rare and secretive mirth.

"Phœnixes and Pomander Boxes!" he whispered with cryptic sibilance in Jennifer's ear as he brought her a small glass of negus at supper time, gently removing from her unresisting hand the bumper of champagne which the aged Earl of Wessex had just placed there. "Phœnixes and Pomander Boxes!" His nearly soundless laughter, thin as a bat's cry, lost itself among the crystal lustres of the enormous chandeliers.

If the deceased lovers of the Mourning Bride were legendary, she herself was fabulous within a week, nor did it require either time or absence to endow her with all the attributes of a mythological paragon upon Olympus. After a swift post-chaise had indeed removed her from their view, leaving sorrow to add poignancy to her imagery presentment graven in their hearts, her admirers were seldom able to command their voices in enunciating her name. She departed upon a fine sunny morning of mid-September; Gerald had ordered the horses for the fresh and virginal hour of six in order, as he said, to avoid the heat of the day and the impetuosity of crowds. Marching downstairs in all the majestic austerity of a long grey cloak and a black hat severely laced with silver, he had somewhat the air of an aristocratic highwayman. His scornfully detached gaze swept the Crescent without seeming to perceive the score of young gentlemen who surrounded the post-chaise, nor did the excessive absurdity of their appearance bring the slightest smile to his pallid and compressed lips. It may be that the long yellow hands, half-concealed by the fall of spider-web Mechlin, tightened significantly upon the Malacca cane; so Jennifer's timidity certainly fancied. With the highest degree of apprehension she realised that her attendant squires were dressed to a man in sombre habits, that their arms bore bands of crêpe, and that innumerable festoons of white flowers, of a most deathly and oppressive sweetness, dangled from their grasp. As the foremost stepped forward, proffering her what appeared to be an engrossed parchment of some solemn description, she turned the empty splendours of her eyes upon him; her small mouth formed itself into an expression of helpless entreaty. She was beyond words and felt that she should faint in another instant, the instant, probably, in which her young friend Mr. Shepherd put his ebony flute to his lips.

"Ignore this mummery!" cried Gerald in a voice like cracking glaciers; the grey cloak enveloped her in a cold whirlwind of speed, and she fell back upon the purple cushions of the post-chaise, her drowning senses aware of a prodigious noise of wheels and whips and thundering hooves, through which the diminutive sound of the flute trickled in mournful farewell. The autumnal breeze soon revived her; she saw that a white tuberose, flung by some brave spirit, had fallen into her lap. Her husband's immobility was so alarming that she dared not remove this object, lest it should attract his terrifying attention; it lay wilting in the hot parallels of sunlight that shifted over her knees; its lugubrious incense sickened her. When they stopped to change horses at "The Bear" in Devizes, she let it drop into the deep golden dust of the road; Gerald set his heel upon it with careful and exquisite precision.

London in 1772 was a scene of wild profligacy which Gerald viewed with a calm amusement having no little of the sinister in its smile. Possibly he enjoyed the sense of superiority which his own wire-drawn moderation produced; possibly he agreed with Mr. Hume, who, writing from Edinburgh in that year, employed the following curious words, which must be taken with a salty grain of reminder that Mr. Hume was a Scotchman and an historian: "I am delighted to see the daily and hourly progress of madness and folly and wickedness in England. The consummation of these qualities are the true ingredients for making a fine narrative in history."

It is not improbable that Gerald saw these sentiments soon after they were penned; if so he certainly read them with sympathy and pleasure. Possessing a wit of the most cynical and subtle description, exactly suited to the fashion of the day, he might well have rivalled Selwyn in this particular had not his indolence and reserve prevented. He drawled his graceless comment upon life quite irrespective of his company; he would not wait for a duke or a prime-minister to be present when he made a joke, and a passing butcher-boy or milliner's apprentice might extract what benefit they could from a muttered remark which should have convulsed Bellamy's. He teased his wife into white-faced apathy and her lady's-maid into hysterics, but he would not take the trouble to talk at Brookes' or the Chocolate House; he preferred to sit idly fingering his coffee-spoon and emitting an occasional and acid laugh at the expense of another's reputed brilliance. By every human law he should have been hated; instead he was triumphantly popular without the slightest effort on his own part.

Chances were the vogue; gaming now constituted Gerald's only vice, and as he was invariably lucky in the long run, he was enabled to be at once fashionable and provident. Mohawk and anti-Mohawk, Medmenham Abbey and the Houses of Parliament were equally dull and distasteful to his curious mind. Dick urged his entrance into politics; he replied with perfect candour that he would rather persuade Horace Walpole to sell him the little silver-gilt clock given by Henry the Eighth to Anne Boleyn than have the entire Cabinet in his pocket.

It had long been Gerald's declared design to take a London house for the ensuing year; Mrs. Forrest's magnificent mansion in James Street, with one front facing on the Bird Cage Walk in Saint James's Park seemed a suitable choice, and negotiations were already in progress when his wife's unaccountable horror of the town forced him to make other plans; his kindness to her in such matters was always beyond reproach. He had, indeed, looked forward with considerable amusement to this opportunity of studying the follies and dissipations of London life; the circumstance, however, of Jennifer's falling into a violent fit of hysterics in a Hackney coach on the way home from Ranelagh decided him in the intention of removing to Paris at once.

Jennifer's own idea of a small house in Devon was of course out of the question; he could only assure her that the gloomy and marmoreal atmosphere which so oppressed her spirit would be entirely lacking in the French capital; the sprightly elegance of that country must infallibly prove a more potent tonic than all the thatched roofs and clambering roses which her romantic

fancy had been busily painting in the style of the best contemporary water-colours. She lay upon the looped and tasselled four-
poster in Dick's suite of guest-rooms; below her Saint Albans
Street was spread with straw in compliment to the accouche-
ment of a next-door neighbour, but the mat of brittle gold-brown
strands muffling the clatter of iron and the click of leathern
shoes, served only to increase her distress. From its beaten thickness there rose a smell of farmyards and fields which mingled
with the scent of tobacco and patchouli to form a perfume grotesque and tragic to her imagination. The Honiton handkerchiefs of her trousseau were wetted with tears and lavender-
water in equal proportions; Gerald grew politely weary of her
delicate features drowned and her large eyes darkened in woe.
Consultation with several eminent medical men resulted only in
the pronouncement that Lady Jennifer Poynyard was suffering
from severe nostalgia; chivalry demanded that her husband sacrifice his personal inclination in the interest of her health, and in
gently refusing to spend the Christmas season at Cleverly-Neville
he contrived to make the delights of the French court so invigorating a prospect that Jennifer at once demanded her mirror,
her maid, and her Spanish lace scarf.

That evening, seated with his bride in one of the most retired
upper boxes of Covent Garden Theatre, Gerald laughed so heartily at the tragedy then occupying the boards that Jennifer herself
was moved to mirth; his comments upon the audience were
charmingly satirical, and only the knowledge that no one in the
house could observe her new frock cast the slightest cloud over
her quiet enjoyment. She was attired in a dress of white satin, embroidered in rose-buds, convolvulus, and vine-leaves shaded after
nature; her hair was dressed in the latest fashion sponsored by
the young niece of the Duc de Nivernois, the French Ambassador, and Gerald had permitted her to dust the faintest imaginable bloom of rouge upon the porcelain pallor of her cheek, so
that it seemed merely to reflect the pink petals of her bodice. On
leaving the theatre she attracted such favourable attention that
Gerald was considerably annoyed and she experienced the strange
sensation of swimming to her coach through a sea of languishing
masculine glances, bright blue and amber and inky black. She

felt rather frightened, and shrank so swooningly within the protecting curve of her husband's arm that he was able to think of
her with pity no less than pride; this put him into a high good
humour, and, after supping upon hot jellies, he kissed her affectionately and retired to rest.

Jennifer lay awake for many hours; her thoughts, as ever,
were vague and evasive, concerning themselves chiefly with Parisian vistas diminishing into dreams of the Parthemont Convent
where she had spent her fifteenth year, to the vast improvement
of her French and the temporary disablement of most of her reasoning faculties. She had for a time desired passionately to join
the Roman Catholic Church, but the amused opposition of both
parents soon put an end to what appeared to them the merest
febrile and fantastic strivings after novelty. It had been the frequently expressed wish of her early adolescence that she should
take the veil; had she proposed entering the harem of the Sultan
of Turkey or going as a missionary into the interior of Mon-
golia the plan could not have seemed more ridiculous to her
mother's decorously ordered mind. "Pray do not mention this
absurd idea to your father; he would be seriously displeased, my
love," said Clarinda, suppressing her smiles under a tender gravity. Jennifer went immediately to the library and informed Tam-
Linn of her intention; the storm of chuckles with which he met
her was far more discouraging than anger. The result of these
conversations was that Jennifer did not return to the convent, and
was therefore always somewhat doubtful about the conjugation
of certain irregular verbs in her use of the French tongue, though
she retained an admirable knowledge of the Letters of Fénelon,
the *Telemachus* of the same author, and the *Athalie* of Racine.

"Dear Gerald assures me that Paris will restore my spirits,"
she thought, as she lay watching the bluish flame of her night-
light diffused in a dim radiance beside her bed, spreading thinly,
like milk in a muddy pool, through a darkness rendered more
brown than black by filtrations of fog from without; beyond
the window-panes an evil yellow gloom mirrored and magnified
the ring of brightness. "He is extraordinarily kind to me; I ought
not to allow myself to fall into these moods of melancholy. I
think the climate of London must be ill-suited to my constitu-

tion; I remember that the east wind in Paris is said to be decidedly bracing; I must ask Gerald about a new fur pelisse tomorrow, without fail. ' So shines a good deed in a naughty world.' —Shakespeare. The French consider him barbarous. It is a pity that Mr. Gray should have died after all, in spite of the Duke's kindness. I had so wished to meet him; I prefer his ' Country Churchyard' to Mr. Goldsmith's ' Deserted Village'; I believe Mr. Goldsmith to be a little lacking in elegance. ' Out, out, brief candle.' Shakespeare again. Papa admires Shakespeare. How dreadful it would be if the light were actually to be extinguished; this room is very draughty. ' 'Tis but a night, a long and moonless night. . . .' Blair's Grave . . . my Aunt Susanna's favourite poem. ' To paint the gloomy horror of the tomb. . . .' I wish I did not remember it so well; my aunt continually read it aloud to me when I was a child. Paris . . . Paris . . . how delightful to see it once more! I trust the good sisters have none of them died; impossible to conceive of Paris without them. La Rêve . . . Racine . . . Corneille. ' Ne verse point de pleurs sur cette sepulture passant: ce lit funèbre est un lit precieux.' Death; poets are forever writing about death. These purple curtains always turn black at night; they are too sombre a shade. ' My love is dead, gone to his death-bed. . . .' Ah, that unfortunate youth Chatterton . . . dead by his own hand! Dead . . . dead . . . I am becoming excessively morbid; let me resolutely think of something else . . . the beauties of nature . . . Devon. . . . Ah, no, not that! Pictures; I have seen many beautiful pictures in London. . . . I wish Sir Joshua had given the Academy's gold medal to young Mr. Flaxman. . . . Gerald says he is a most deserving person. I am to have my miniature taken in Paris . . . à Paris . . . Paradis . . ."

Jennifer fell asleep at that moment when the shadows dropped a monstrous lid over the night-light's little azure eye; swiftly the room dissolved into pure darkness.

Preparations for their departure were soon under way; Gerald, while himself preserving a princely calm, looked indulgently upon Jennifer's fits of childish mirth. The miasma of her homesickness was quickly dissipated in a high wind of excitement; no bonnet nor mantle was laid in her boxes but found a more dazzling counterpart in her imagination; Paris was to materialise these visions in actual straw and silken weaves. Under her husband's encouragement a good half of her wedding garments were given away to her prettier cousins; he would not permit the really plain girls to receive anything but the products of the Cleverly-Neville sempstress. But the most flaxen-and-cream of the Devonshire lot was rendered ecstatically happy by the gift of an apple-green gauze, while a certain black-haired Eleanor Lorn looked statuesque for three Edinburgh seasons in a sapphire velvet of the richest quality.

Jennifer was beginning to understand that her earlier incarnation as a beauty of Bath was to be no more than a farthing dip in comparison with the approaching dawn of her glory; she was to rise from the foam of the English Channel like a copy of Venus Anadyomene in gold and ivory, presently to be clothed in suitable raiment by the inspired mantua-makers of Paris.

2

THE ITALIAN VINAIGRETTE

ONE disagreeable incident marred this happy period in the life of the newly-wedded pair; the Directors of the East India Company were sufficiently ill-advised as to ask Gerald to join their Board. Probably Sir George Colebrooke was largely responsible for this step; its result was a two-days' rage on the part of Gerald, natural enough under the circumstances to one of his haughty and uncompromising habit of mind. He shut himself up in his apartments and refused to speak to any member of the household for forty-eight hours; Mohammed had strict injunctions to set his meals, neatly arranged on a tray, outside the door of his study at stated intervals and with the least possible noise. Dick was genuinely distressed; his kind heart could not share in his wife's more critical estimate of Gerald's conduct.

" My dear," he said hesitatingly, " is it not after all the Directors who are at fault? Our cousin is slow to wrath, but this extraordinary suggestion could not fail to disturb even an equanimity so admirable as his. Think of what this would mean; a complete cessation of his more important Indian activities; an enforced residence in London; association with dotards. The thing is unthinkable. The boy is brilliant and is, very wisely, aware of the fact; this preposterous plan would fetter him, deprive him of his freedom of action; in a word, clip his wings. I hope my estimate of human nature is not too cynical if I suspect an undercurrent of jealousy in the minds of these gentlemen; they are well informed as to Gerald's status in Bengal; it is, indeed, an enviable one. . . . The rest is only too clear. I have the greatest sympathy with his agitation of soul; the difficulty of resenting this sort of sly and subtle insult sticks in the throat of a proud man. I honour him for his keen sense of personal dignity; I took pains to give him the liver-wing of the goose and to see that his claret was at the proper temperature to-night."

"Cook grumbles at trays, and the maids are all afraid of that Ethiopian when he comes into the kitchen," his wife replied with considerable asperity. "In my opinion Gerald is extremely selfish; Cook would be very hard to replace, and you know how dependent I am upon Miles for my comfort. However, I say nothing; remonstrances are quite useless where your distinguished relative is concerned. Thank heaven he is no kin of mine; my heart bleeds for his poor young wife." She was silent, to Dick's relief; her averted eyes spoke for her.

"The Moslem population of India has little admixture of Ethiopian blood," he said with great mildness. His wife walked out of the room; he heard her speaking gently and placatingly to Miles in the corridor.

"I assure you, my excellent creature, that there is not the slightest danger of rape; pray set the kitchen-maid's mind at rest upon this point," she whispered. He picked up a still-folded copy of that new and fashionable journal, the *Morning Post,* from his wife's work-table and, laying it down almost reverently outside Gerald's door, tiptoed softly away.

Jennifer was awed into silence; she felt, nevertheless, that the dispensation of Providence which temporarily deprived her of her husband's society was merciful rather than otherwise. His face, as he strode away from her simple-minded inquiries, had not been reassuring.

" This is the work of Laurence Sullivan; you may depend upon it that Sullivan has had a hand in this," he informed her accusingly. " He knows I am of Clive's party, and that I understand the true state of Indian Stock. Verney will drop a couple of hundred thousand in this affair; I told him so only last week. Observe that this offer is very nearly coincident with our conversation. I wish my quilted dressing-gown at once."

Jennifer leaped to her feet in a shower of coloured spools from her sewing-case; she brought him the dressing-gown herself, her small shaking hands thrusting it through a door so grudgingly opened that it afforded but a fleeting glimpse of a countenance composed to the inhuman colour and impassivity of stone.

On the second night she woke startled; her eyes flew open at the click of a key in the lock, her glance strove wildly to penetrate the uniform obscurity of the room. She was aware of the immeasurably slow creaking turn of the door-knob, wherein oil and rust alternatively soothed and retarded the scrape of metal upon metal. A thin slit of flame-colour spread to a band dappled and pied with shades; then against a background of fire-light, paling as it broadened behind him, the silhouette of her husband stood revealed. His crest of sandy hair and the extreme edges of his crimson dressing-gown were tinged with a reddish glimmer; for the rest he was a figure carved from darkness. As he stepped noiselessly towards the bed he might have been cloaked and masked in black velvet; even his eye-balls held no lustre. The acidulated softness of his voice steadied her nerves by pulling them tighter; it slid along them like a slender bow drawn athwart the strings of a violin. He towered above her, prodigiously tall, elongated into the semblance of his own shadow.

" Come," he said, " I wish to talk with you." She was unable to answer; without another word he swooped downwards, lifting her from the pillows as if she had been a doll. Like a doll she dangled in his arms; under the fine lawn of her nightgown her flesh was cold as wax. He dragged the great purple counterpane from the bed and enveloped her in its heavy and voluminous folds; she was swathed in thick brocade like a little mummy in imperial cerements. He threw her back over his bony shoulder with a movement so adroit that it succeeded in being gentle; her head drooped low, the confusion of her hair swung against his shoulder-blades like tawny clusters of grapes; she appeared lifeless. Inwardly she was calm; she felt exhausted by the shock of her surprise, but nevertheless a vague sense of satisfaction possessed her mind; she was conscious that Gerald was paying her a compliment. If his flattery was amazing it was none the less unmistakable; he was about to consult with his loving wife the matters of importance which had engaged his solitary reflections for two days.

In the study a large fire had fallen to a heap of rose-red embers, stirred here and there by airy wings of flame. Two extravagantly rococo armchairs faced the fender; their golden scrollwork and Tyrian upholstery turned them into thrones; the tiger-skin rug beneath them lent a touch of barbaric splendour to the scene. Jennifer knew in a flash that Gerald had shot the tiger in the most perilous wilds of Bengal; the stock of his gun had rested upon the spot where her heart now beat. She realised with respect that neither her own proximity nor that of the tiger could ever accelerate the measured pulses of her husband's blood; he was above fear, and though love might move him to tenderness it could never submerge him in folly. A small painted table held the remains of a partridge and a cut glass decanter; the bones of the former were picked to a pale filagree ghost; the latter's sole reminder of the generous wine which it had undoubtedly contained was a faintly roseate tinting of its pattern. The floor around one of the chairs was littered with portentous folios and documents; a great sheet of vellum decorated with a scarlet seal lay in the midst of a heap of letters. Gerald deposited her in the other chair; so seated, she was at his right hand; at his left a solitary candle burned above the supper tray's silver dishes.

She sat half reclining in the vastness of the chair, a delicate and fantastic creature overwhelmed by uncongenial grandeur; her little face seemed suspended upon its sumptuous background, as if she were the youngest and most beautiful of Bluebeard's wives, decapitated in her sleep, and still smiling.

Gerald drew a book from the table; she noticed that it was bound in morocco, and that its pages were propped open with a richly chased nut-cracker.

" My child," he began, in a serious but affectionate tone, " you have probably felt the loneliness of the last few days weigh heavily upon the natural cheerfulness of your disposition; you are in need of a little mental relaxation. I do not propose to weary you with the recital of my own affairs, which would certainly fatigue and probably perplex your understanding. Instead, I intend reading aloud to you extracts from a delightful work which my Paris bookseller has but just sent me; he has orders to transmit to me immediately upon their publication all the best novels, plays and books of travel that are produced in France, first having them suitably bound in order that I may later include them in my library. This volume is by Bernardin de Saint Pierre; its title is ' *Voyage à l'Ile de France.'* You may possibly know this island better under its other name of Mauritius; the author's long residence there has rendered him peculiarly fitted to write upon this subject; his style is charming. I desired to share my pleasure in it with you, my dearest girl. Forgive my apparent neglect; let us be happy together. In view of our imminent journey to the East this work will be of especial interest to you; the events of the past few days have warned me that I must not prolong our stay in Paris beyond six weeks at the latest. You are looking very lovely to-night; allow me to kiss your hand."

He stooped and brushed her small and chilly fingers with his lips, which did not lose the slightest part of their habitual compression in the act of gallantry. His eyes, however, pale, prominent, and now very lustrous in the firelight, devoured her with a curious intensity of gaze which seemed, mild and deliberate as a cat's tongue, to lick up the cream of her beauty and swallow it with quiet satisfaction.

He sat, a supremely elegant figure, lounging in the enormous chair, his slim ankles crossed and thrust towards the heat of the embers, his narrow hands supporting the heavy book in midair without apparent effort. His low and somewhat sibilant voice caressed the French words with soft precision; his large white eyelids concealed the curious look which, gradually fading from his wife's mind, left it vacant of everything except the images of dreams. Under successive waves of sleep she grew unconscious of the dulness of the book, the gentleness of Gerald's voice, and the comfortable warmth of the fire, all these causes combining none the less to smother her beneath a drowsiness so deep and pleasant that she believed herself to be lying on the sunny side of a haycock in the south meadow at Cleverly-Neville.

She woke to a room thinly silver-gilt with winter dawn; Gerald was still reading, in a low, perfectly modulated voice.

Gerald breakfasted on China tea and a couple of well-peppered mutton chops; facing him Jennifer drooped somewhat pallidly over the *Critical Review*. Afterwards he permitted her to assist him in dealing with his varied correspondence, grown more voluminous than ever since the news of his impending departure had spread through London. Several gentlemen of reputed importance were the recipients of short and savage notes which, composed by him in a mood of tranquil enjoyment, were transcribed in the delicate and spidery scroll-work of his wife's handwriting; the barbed and poisoned arrows of his wit struck home all the more shrewdly from behind the cover of the amber-scented sheets of paper which she turned so meticulously into the likenesses of little cocked hats.

Gerald's good humour continued throughout the day; that afternoon at dinner his merry laughter at the expense of most of their acquaintances proved so infectious that Lady Dicker told the story of her sister Selina's affair with the Cornish curate, and Dick, on joining the ladies in the drawing-room, obliged them very much by singing that popular song, " Cease, Rude Boreas . . ." He then proposed an adjournment to Covent Garden Theatre, where a new ballet had just been put on.

" A charming idea, Dick," said Gerald calmly, " but impractical under the circumstances; the necessity of our being up betimes would render such a course extremely fatiguing to Jennifer." On Dick's protesting his ignorance of any such necessity, Gerald informed the others that he and his wife were leaving for Dover the next day, he having previously written to hire a vessel to convey them across the Channel. Reasoning was without avail; remonstrances were so much wasted breath; his decision was irrevocable.

Jennifer discovered to her amazement, on going upstairs to warn her maid Sallie of their immediate journey, that Gerald had already caused that young woman to pack her mistress's boxes to the last ribbon, and had himself escorted Mohammed into the room to strap and cord them. One portmanteau alone gaped half-empty upon the carpet, waiting to swallow up her little slippers and the flimsy elegancies of her peignoir and her fringed shawl. On the dressing-table a sparse selection of perfume bottles and ivory-backed brushes remained to tell of her husband's attention to every detail of their arrangements. Sallie, her face blubbered with tears, moved distractedly about the dismantled room; when Jennifer entered the girl jumped as if a pistol had been discharged at her ear.

It had been tacitly arranged that Tam-Linn and Clarinda were to come up to town before their daughter left for France; Jennifer knew beyond a doubt how deeply her father and mother would resent her apparent indifference to the claims of filial affection. The reflection troubled her, but she felt too dazed and weary to think with any degree of continuity of the unfortunate results of this strangely hurried farewell to England. That it was indeed farewell she realised quite clearly; Gerald often spoke of embarking for India from some Spanish port; even if he finally decided to take ship at Gravesend their stay in London would probably be a matter of a few hours at the most. Her brain whirled like a shuttle-cock thrown violently across enormous distances; she felt positively light-headed in the endeavour to concentrate her thoughts. Sitting down at the writing-desk, she picked up a long green quill pen; she observed that it had recently been mended with the most consummate skill, and recognised the work of her husband's penknife.

She drew a sheet of paper towards her; she had every intention of writing to her parents in a manner which would leave no room for dubious question as to her sorrow in parting from them. Then the vast black curtain of the future seemed to sway before her swimming eyes; it was all at once a portent, a thundercloud, a pillar of thick smoke; it grew like a tree, its broad trunk blotting out imagination, its branches obscuring time and space. She laid her forehead against the cool smooth satin-wood of the table, which danced a little upon its spindle legs in rhythmic accompaniment to her sobbing. She regained her composure almost at once; a desperate languor descended heavily upon her, and she slept with her brow bowed down upon the desk, the green quill pen still clutched between her fingers.

She slept, and sleeping saw the events of the day pass before her vision, little altered from their original course, but grown more vivid and at the same time more menacing. One incident in particular, trivial as it had seemed at the time, was revived into a mysterious and elusive significance. She was walking home from a shopping tour; Lady Dicker walked beside her, with short steps and inconsequent chatter of stay-laces. The lady's presence had jarred but slightly on Jennifer's waking self; now the dream made her a gadfly, a miniature fury not to be shaken off even by winged heels and streaming banners of hair. They went faster and faster; the grey streets flew by in a lateral frieze of faces; behind were voices and clattering shoes, before, some unknown peril quaked or yawned in quagmires and precipices. Then at a noisy corner, where horses, suddenly pulled up, snorted with steaming red nostrils and the muddy brooms of crossing-sweepers drew crescents in the mire, Jennifer beheld a tall figure approaching, threading its way adroitly and delicately through the dingy rout of pedestrians.

The figure resolved itself into a youth of pleasing appearance, of slight build and military carriage; his head was bowed as if in dejection or profound thought. He was attired in full regimentals; certain modifications of his dress made it clear that he was in the deepest mourning. The result was at once affecting and elegant; the scarlet coat was lined with black silk, and worn with black waistcoat, breeches, and stockings. A black sword, adorned with a sword love-knot of the same sable hue, completed the costume; the countenance of the young gentleman matched it to a nicety in combining extreme good looks with an expression of heart-rending melancholy. He could not long have passed his twentieth year; Jennifer was grieved to observe the evident marks of sorrow upon the features of one so pre-eminently fitted for a life of happy adventure. He was pale; his dark hair curled above a candid brow too early traced with lines of suffering. Between his large eyes and his pointed chin the contours of his face still held a childish purity of outline; the little hollows under his cheek-bones and the firmness of his small lips were touchingly incongruous. His air of fashion merely succeeded in making him more pathetic.

He carried his hat in his hand; during their brief meeting in the morning's reality he had only gazed at her sadly and passed on in silence. In the dream his gaze was the same; his brown eyes were full of a hurt and startled recognition; he seemed to wait for some sign on her part, the lack of which bewildered him. Then he stopped and spoke; his voice was strange, it seemed to traverse wild spaces before it reached her ears, and yet it fell like comfort on her heart.

"Madam," he said, with a grave little bow, "do you wish me to save you? You have but to command me; I am yours." Her own voice also sounded strange; it might have travelled from the moon before it answered him.

"Save me, sir? From what do I require to be saved?"

He shook his head with a sort of vague and absent-minded despair; his eyes searched hers hopelessly; he was gone. The crowd surged around her, ugly and evil-smelling; a grotesque painted face spat an unknown word in the direction of her questioning glance; another, between a fuzz of silvery hair and a clerical collar, leered ambiguously. She woke screaming; long after she had dragged herself across the room to sink shuddering into the softness of the bed she continued to feel a sharp and peculiar anguish of sorrow and fear. . . . At last she fell into a deep slumber in which no memory remained of the day's events or the night's dreams; the image of the pale-faced youth was expunged from her mind. She never thought of him again.

The sailing vessel which Gerald had engaged for their conveyance across the Channel was new and commodious; every preparation had been made for their comfort, and Jennifer was delighted with the little cabin with its look of a nautical doll's-house; only an unfortunate change in the weather prevented her from appreciating the interest and novelty of the voyage. A severe storm rose during the night; the danger was real and imminent, but Jennifer was completely indifferent to the outcome of the situation. She wondered feebly how Sallie could evince such a liveliness of terror when Gerald, drenched to the skin but calm and suavely stoical, came into the cabin in search of a heavier cloak and a larger flask of Cognac.

"A stiffish breeze, my love," he told her reassuringly; his amiable composure was unshaken when she peevishly declined the sip of brandy which he offered her with such courteous solicitude. When she turned her face to the white-panelled wall and then turned it back again with a groan because the wall smelled so strongly of fresh paint and turpentine, he smoothed her forehead with a cold salty hand; when she pushed his hand away he only smiled indulgently and ordered Sallie to find her mistress's vinaigrette at once. The girl obeyed with blanched cheeks and tottering footsteps; she was an admirable sailor and felt not the slightest inconvenience from the fury of the waves, having passed most of her early childhood in her father's fishing-boat off the coast of Devon; the certainty of drowning in this foreign sea was less disturbing to her nerves than Gerald's touch upon her shoulder and his simple incisive word in her ear.

The vinaigrette, a delicate trifle of Italian workmanship, immediately slid from Jennifer's listless fingers and rolled under the bunk, where it lay until the Captain found it the next day; he presented it to his wife on their silver wedding anniversary, which happened to fall on Wednesday of the following week. She liked it none the less for being golden as a guinea; the consensus of opinion among her friends inclined to silver-gilt as its probable material, which, if it rendered it not quite so valuable, made it infinitely more appropriate to the occasion.

Gerald remained upon deck during the entire night; the storm merely served to exhilarate his spirits and occupy his mind. When he thought of the Dickers reduced to backgammon instead of four-handed whist he laughed above the booming of the gale; his blood was up, and as he sprang out of the lighted cabin into the ink-black pandemonium of the elements he thought of a warm fireside as the most detestable prison that a degenerate race had ever constructed.

"Sodden and torpid . . . sodden and torpid!" he shouted defiantly into the teeth of the wind. It was one of his rare moments of enthusiasm; the knowledge that he was the only human being on board who remained totally devoid of fear sent a fire through his veins which no distillation of grapes grown under the hottest suns of the Midi had ever kindled there. The little crew was divided between admiration and loathing; the men felt that as self-respecting seamen they should not permit any one but the Captain to swear at them so savagely, yet when they saw this tall devil leap well-nigh half-way up the mast in a single movement of incredible agility, when they perceived the palms of his white hands flayed raw and bloody by the ropes upon which he hauled with such strength and skill, they allowed the admiration to triumph; not one of them but had a swig from his flask before the night was out.

When the milk-white dawn lay reflected in the darkness of Calais sands, Gerald sluiced a bucket of cold green sea-water over his scarred fingers; his face was crusted with dried spray, and he scrubbed it unmercifully with a bit of oily oakum, at the same time reflecting pleasantly that Paris afforded a larger selection of soaps, medicated lotions and perfumed unguents than any other spot on earth. He reached deep into his pockets only to discover that his roll of bank-notes was soaking wet; the yellow sovereigns which he distributed among the crew turned their awed regard into a more jovial expression of their sentiments concerning him, and Jennifer was wakened to a splitting headache and a blaze of early sunshine by the loud three-times-three which re-echoed from the deck above her cabin.

3

EXCESSES IN VENEER

THE *voiture* which he had bespoken in advance was already waiting them at the Lion d'Argent, but Gerald would not hear of Jennifer's continuing the journey until she had rested upon one of the best feather-beds in that celebrated hostelry, while he himself hovered over her with every possible attention to her comfort, including lavender-water, sal volatile, and strong tea brewed by Sallie in the kitchen of the inn, to the great anger of the cook and Mme. Dessein herself, who were engaged in preparing a parsley omelette and a filet of sole for *Milord*. With this and some passable coffee he made a very fair breakfast; later he sought to rouse Jennifer's spirits by an amusing account of his first visit to Dessein's in the year 1765, when as a mere lad he had enjoyed the good fortune of dining at the same table with Sterne, then engaged in collecting material for his agreeable work, later published under the title of " A Sentimental Journey."

"In those days I was more easily entertained," he said smiling. "I should not have relished Mr. Sterne at breakfast this morning."

Gerald had arranged to go by post from Calais to Paris, with four horses, two postillions, and his own servant on horseback. Mohammed had protested in vain; his swarthy face looked darker and more dazed than ever above the ordinary livery of an English lackey, which Gerald considered more appropriate for the journey than the man's usual white robes and turban. Sallie was to share the coachman's seat, being quite content to do so after she had been informed by her young mistress of the exorbitant sum which this privilege was to cost them. Altogether, taking the whole procedure as easily and comfortably as possible, they could hardly hope to get to Paris under twenty pounds, ten or twelve of which would go for the expenses of posting in the grand style; Gerald was sure to insist upon patronising the best inns, nor would he condescend to concern himself about the double charges for the so-called royal posts.

His French acquaintances had always spoken of him as *un homme prodigue,* which appellation he received as a compliment in spite of the fact that he knew it was intended as a somewhat severe criticism. But now his money-belt was so corpulent that he was forced to lock it in his portmanteau lest it interfere with the refined slimness of his figure, and he had draughts upon Messieurs Panchaud and Foley, the well-known bankers of the rue Saint Sauveur for such truly magnificent sums that Jennifer need not have felt any uneasiness, as she undoubtedly did when they were charged forty sous apiece for a very poor dinner at the inn at Abbéville.

Jennifer's fatigue and his own desire to view the curious structures of this quaint old town strengthened Gerald in his determination to spend the night in Abbéville instead of pushing on to Amiens, which their excellent horses could quite well have accomplished. The churches were somewhat disappointing; the best inn which the place afforded was both small and dirty; the pleasant crimson-curtained parlour of its Devonshire equivalent was entirely lacking. While dinner was preparing, Jennifer lay miserably on the high uneven bed; the lavender-scented sheets and silken coverlid with which Sallie had sought to mitigate the dinginess of this equivocal couch giving little peace to her mind however much they might soothe the exhaustion of her body. When Gerald proposed a stroll through the streets " in order to prevent our chicken from being under-done and to allow them sufficient time to wash the salad properly," she accepted the suggestion with docility and sweetness. Below in the courtyard the inn-servants were quarrelling violently among themselves; with a shudder of relief she took Gerald's proffered arm and turned into the principal thoroughfare of the town.

The clear pale saffron of the sky hung tenderly above the ancient houses; the yellow stone-crop on the roofs, the coppery rust streaking the iron-barred doors, were painted in colours of flame. Jennifer, in her swans'-down hood and black-velvet pelisse, picked her way cautiously over the huge cobblestones; Gerald conducted her down a roughly paved street, immensely broad, and at this hour almost totally deserted. Behind the reticence of the house-fronts, bolted and grim as fortresses, secret as graves, she imagined horrors of imprisonment long drawn out and of murder quickly consummated; once a stifled scream turned her blood cold as winter rain.

Finally their ramble led them to the brink of a small stream or canal; its margins were trimmed with emerald water-weed; in the midst of the dun and purple tints of the surrounding landscape it wore an air of country gaiety and grace. It was crossed by a little rustic bridge; a flock of geese made lively its farther side, while numerous ducks in variegated plumage swam upon its looking-glass surface. The whole scene was happy and pastoral, in perfect harmony with the hushed tranquillity of the evening sky. Some women in grotesque foreign caps and aprons came to lean upon the railing of the bridge and gossip volubly; if they had been clothed aright in pretty prints and calicoes, if their voices had been softer and their countenances more prepossessing, and above all if they had not been speaking French, poor Jennifer might almost have imagined herself to be safe in Cleverly-Neville. Even as it was, she returned to the inn considerably refreshed in mind and body, to dine on a sliver of chicken breast and a thimbleful of white wine; the salad unfortunately tasted of garlic.

Afterwards she took out her new writing desk, and penned an affectionate letter to her parents, containing a full account of their stormy passage across the Channel, the scenery of that portion of France which lies directly east of Calais, and concluding with a poetic account of sunset gilding the spires of Abbéville, during the course of which, out of respect to her father's and mother's several tastes in literature, she quoted once from the Tempest and three times from the Deserted Village. Her mother forwarded this epistle to Horace Walpole, who seems never to have acknowledged its receipt; there is not the slightest reason to suppose that he read it.

The following night the travellers spent at Amiens; Gerald found it difficult to accord an unreserved admiration to the celebrated Cathedral, which he nevertheless allowed to be impressive and in a measure sublime. Since Gothic was the fashion he magnanimously felt that it should be given every opportunity of pleasing a man of taste; when it failed to do so, however, he had no hesitation in blaming the Cathedral rather than himself. " It has a rude magnificence, a romantic charm . . . but there is a lack of restraint . . . almost, one is tempted to say, a touch of vulgarity. The fad will pass . . . we should not concern ourselves too deeply with these gigantic monuments to superstition. Only the classic can endure the tooth of time; I shall take you to see the *Maison Carrée* at Nîmes, a very perfect example of Roman architecture of the best period; it dates from the year one. It has infinite lightness and grace; I much prefer it to the amphitheatre in the same town or the still finer one at Arles."

On the third day the easy stages of their journey brought them to the famous town of Chantilly; Gerald found himself both hungry and thirsty, so though it was no more than mid-day, and they could have pushed on to Paris that same night, he decided that it was his bounden duty to exhibit to Jennifer the palace, long the seat of the princes of Condé, and the extensive forest so vastly improved by M. le Notre during the previous century; its birds, fountains, cascades, canals and other more or less natural beauties filled her with delight after the dusty road, and, notwithstanding the fact that it was already November, its sylvan glades and picturesque water-courses were still dressed in tints of gold and blue under the silver sun of noon. At dinner he further regaled her with the story of the suicide of Vatel, cook to the great Condé, subsequent upon the non-arrival of a fine salmon from Paris which should have preceded by several hours the advent of Louis the Fourteenth as the guest of his renowned master.

" Over-conscientiousness, my dear, has wrecked many a promising career; I honour scruples, but they, like everything else under heaven, have their place and should be kept there; in this case they should have remained in the kitchen." He leaned back in his chair, which was fairly comfortable, and sipped his wine, which, if it left something to be desired, was at least the best to be procured in Chantilly. Jennifer regarded him with servile wonder and admiration; she was no more awed by his intimate knowledge of such amusing historical incidents than by his ability to carve a roast duck or eat a French artichoke with neatness and grace.

" How very distressing," she murmured sadly, struggling with the spiny leaves upon her own plate. Gerald possessed himself of it with quiet dexterity; in an instant he had bisected the whole recalcitrant vegetable, transferring its delicate inner portions to a clean saucer and adding thereto a large allowance of Holland Sauce and the half of a carefully buttered roll. Later, while he peeled and quartered a small apple for her dessert, he related several stories of the gorgeous past, when the great Condé had enjoyed the society of Racine and Molière amid these sympathetic surroundings.

They left Chantilly early the next morning; a white mist enveloped the earth; the sunrise at its heart turned it into a fire-opal. They moved remote and lost through the colourless silence, which seemed to make their progress slow and solemnly portentous. Gerald discoursed lightly of the subjects which had occupied his mind during the preceding night; he was urbanity itself beside the languor of Jennifer, the impatience of Sallie, and the dignified bitterness of Mohammed. He alone spoke before eleven o'clock; the servants may have been silent out of respect, but no such excuse can be offered for his wife's conduct. She undoubtedly slept during a large part of the journey, owing to the circumstance of her nights being disturbed by dolorous cogitations and waking dreams. The suicide of Vatel had engaged her fancy during the previous evening after she had retired to the questionable peace of her chamber; the ministrations of Sallie, though well-intentioned, were not particularly effective in calming her agitated nerves.

"Cut his throat with the bread-knife, I'll be bound, ma'am," was that young person's contribution to a subject unwisely opened by Jennifer in the hope of receiving comfortable assurances that at the worst the poor wretch had experienced no difficulty in obtaining an opiate poison from the stores of the Prince's apothecary. "If it had been a murder, now, he might have used the meat chopper, but a suicide's different; depend it, ma'am, that it was either the bread-knife or one of those little sharp affairs as cooks set such store by for vegetables."

During the day Jennifer revived considerably; she was able to take an intelligent interest in the great Abbey of Saint-Denis, though the close proximity of the illustrious dead now occupying such superb tombs within the sacred precincts afflicted her weak spirit with a noticeable melancholy towards the approach of evening.

"They sleep well," said Gerald kindly; she had no idea that the words were not original, and agreed hopefully, at the same time making a slight mental reservation to the effect that the sculpture looked monstrously heavy to form a coverlid for the daintily articulated skeleton of a queen.

With her mind more and more preoccupied with fantastic imaginings, she began to plan a dream-progress through the golden castles and green forests of the past; a Una all snow and innocent fire, she would wander forever companioned by a chivalrous and courageous lion, her thin white hands warmed in his tawny mane, her shining head pillowed upon his broad bosom at night. It would be far more romantic than a chaise, and also more comfortable; when the way led over velvet mosses and soft violets, she could walk barefoot in the dew; when she encountered stones or thorns or shifting sands, she could mount upon the thick-furred saddle of her champion's back, and ride unscathed into the next valley of enamelled lawns. She saw this noble animal quite plainly in her mind's eye; he looked very much like Tam-Linn attired in the hide of the Scots sheep-dog which her father had given her on her seventh birthday; the strange creature inspired her with the utmost confidence. She could have wept for the grotesque consolation of its presence.

Roused from her reflections by their proximity to the great city, which soon made itself evident in a closer grouping of buildings and a denser crowding of vehicles of every description, from rude wooden carts harnessed with ropes and adorned with sheep-skins to richly painted chariots, Jennifer soared into a state of exhilaration very unusual in one of her pensive disposition. The Calvinistic principles which her father's family had sought to implant in her youthful understanding had not unnaturally produced a contrary effect, including a pronounced leaning towards the Jacobite cause and the Roman Catholic faith. She now begged that their excursions might shortly include a pilgrimage to Saint-Germain-en-Laye, where she might follow in fancy the slow pacing of exiled princes along its melancholy and autumnal alleys of deflowered lime-trees. She evinced no interest in Henry of Navarre, merely remarking, to her husband's vast delight, that she had always understood he was a dissenter.

Night fell; in front of them a smoky radiance hovered suffused and vague in the dusty atmosphere. "Paris at last," cried Gerald with suppressed emotion; Jennifer very nearly fainted from fatigue and excitement; Sallie laughed hysterically, the postillions swore at the sweating horses, Mohammed prayed audibly, his lips set and sombre within his curling beard. In another ten minutes' hurry they drove swaying and clattering up to the Porte Saint-Denis.

They lodged at the Hotel de l'Impératrice in the rue Jacob, where they had an elegant apartment on the first floor; the situation was good, and the furniture, in Jennifer's estimation, magnificent, but Gerald found fault with it from the beginning.

"I detest stamped velvet," he said with acerbity; "Beauvais tapestry is, of course, infinitely worse; the violently rococo forms in furniture have always repelled me. As for this fellow's claim, my dear, that the contents of our apartment was formerly the property of some grand seigneur, I am but too well acquainted with the type of person to whom the acquisition of such lamentable objects is as a second nature, effortless as breathing, inevitable as death. Such chairs and settees were obviously purchased by a man of middling family and questionable breeding, to whom the concurrent possession of great wealth and execrable taste gave power to mark down and make his own these spoils of barbarism. I imagine that the wretch lost his money in no such gentlemanlike way as the gaming-tables provide; he was the victim of various shady speculations and ill-bred enterprises, into which no man of true quality could ever have been drawn. His fate was richly deserved; my one regret is that after having fallen beneath the avenging hammer of the public auctioneer, these distressing excesses in veneer and debaucheries in gold-leaf should have found shelter under the same roof with people of acute judgment and refined sensibilities. I fear their effect upon your appetite, my beloved girl; your déjeuner this morning would not have supported the vitality of an invalid humming-bird. It is only the tonic influence of this excellent burgundy which saves me from a like sad state of health. Supping in a chamber of horrors must necessarily be followed by results extremely deleterious to the strongest constitution; can I not persuade you to eat a small piece of this omelette, to which the addition of peaches preserved in brandy lends much simple charm?"

Jennifer accepted a moderate portion of omelette and consumed it with a measure of appreciation; the French cuisine pleased her, and she preferred a little meal of Strassburg pâté, with three young lettuce leaves, crisped and blanched, and a glass of bright champagne, to all the roast mutton and rice pudding of former years. It is possible that a really protracted residence in Paris might have encouraged in her a delicate imitation of Clarinda's plumpness; her brief stay in that paradise of gourmets could do no more than endow her with a mild taste for apricot tarts, doomed to complete frustration amid the vicissitudes of her subsequent career.

She reclined upon the smaller settee in that attitude later popularised by Madame Récamier; Gerald would never have admitted how well the discoloured gilding and pinkish-purple upholstery of the couch set off her powdered head curled like a Bellini cherub and her gown of white gauze sprinkled with diamond points and stars. He had engaged the leading hairdresser of the day to arrange her hair every evening; its ardent hue and extravagant quantity made it amenable only to the highest skill; now she was crimped like a lamb and winged like a dove and crested like a breaking wave according to the artist's fancy, and all for the trivial price of twelve *livres* a month. She looked like nothing under the drab heaven of that hemisphere; such creatures infest the silver linings of thunder-clouds and the farther side of the moon. Gerald himself had not fallen in with the usual superstition which rendered an immediate visit to a tailor and barber absolutely requisite for the Englishman arrived in Paris overnight. He wore his flaxen hair powdered and dressed plainly and elegantly according to the accepted standards of a man of fashion in London; his black velvet suit, with very rich gold waistcoat and ruffles of the finest needlepoint Alençon, had nevertheless an air of sober dignity and restraint, befitting an Ambassador or a Prince of the blood.

"Would you have me blossom forth in the character of *petit maître*," he inquired loftily, when Jennifer ventured to admire a superb length of sky blue brocade which the tailor had submitted to her husband that very morning, "or execute a graceful and spirited harlequinade upon the stage of the Opéra Comique?

I have no doubt that our dear good Grètry would be transported with joy at the prospect of composing the music incidental to such an exhibition on my part. We shall judge to-night whether indeed the fellow's skill be worthy the essay."

He laughed and sighed in the same breath; Paris had altered much since the halcyon days of his resplendent youth. " I remember his first success made a great stir in Paris; it met everywhere with unparalleled praise; *Le Huron,* I believe it was entitled. I did not witness it, being in India at the time; many of my French correspondents, writing to me of the season's musical and dramatic events, confused the inhabitants of that country with the North American Indian, among whom the Hurons are a horde or tribe. It was a diverting error on the part of a highly cultivated class of people. The piece which we are to attend this evening is called *Zémire et Azer;* I judge by the name that the story is Oriental in origin; I trust you will find it both edifying and delightful. But music in France has suffered a sad decline; it was very different during my early Parisian visits; I recall vividly the fact that during my sojourn in this city in '64, Rameau was given a patent of nobility and the order of Saint Michael; *eheu, fugaces* . . . ! Things are in a very bad way; Lulli has found no successor, and he, as you know, was an Italian. France is only less degenerate than our own unhappy nation; we must search further for signs of the ancient grandeur of art. The tragic drama in these days awakens sentiments of pity and terror of a nature very dissimilar to those aroused by the masterpieces of the Greeks; hysteric laughter chokes the tear ere it has fallen."

He desisted and, leaning his handsome head upon his beautifully moulded hand, appeared sunk in the most profound dejection. Jennifer had never seen him so deeply moved; she feared to address him, and was vastly relieved when the charming painted chariot drawn by a smart pair of horses, which attended them every day from seven in the morning until midnight, was announced by Mohammed; they drove at once to the opera. Gerald's darker fears were not realised; the performance was excellent, the audience brilliant and vivacious in the extreme; the number of distinguished members of the *haut ton* who stared at

Jennifer and bowed to Gerald made the evening one of almost undiluted pleasure to both.

At breakfast the next morning Gerald was in admirable humour; he reverted to his conversation of the night before, and dilated upon the same subject with an easy mastery of his theme and all the enthusiasm of hope. " I should not have said that Lulli has found no successor; such an one has been discovered in Vienna, by my old friend Le Blanc du Roullet, a musical amateur of faultless taste and exquisite discrimination. . . ." While dissecting his partridge with meticulous care he continued to address his wife upon the kindred arts of music, painting and letters; the drama he naturally placed under the latter classification. Jennifer could form no clearer idea of the meaning of his words than if he had been declaiming, as he frequently did, from the Greek of Æschylus, or debating with himself in one of the lesser-known Bengalese dialects.

" Beaumarchais is out of luck this winter; he has poisoned his wife and cannot get his play produced; there's a *Comédie Larmoyante* for you, more amusing than Diderot's. I have just received the last volume of that fellow's immortal work, the one containing the plates; the subscribers have been very patient."

" What is M. Diderot's great work, Gerald? " inquired Jennifer eagerly.

" Why that question? You are not generally so inquisitive? " He was laughing at her, but she persisted.

" Because a lady asked me last night whether or not I was happy in a marriage with M. Diderot's great work; I could not comprehend her meaning in the least."

Gerald laughed again.

" She meant that your husband was well-informed, my dear; I cannot take such a remark amiss."

" She also wished to know whether you were going to Russia with the rest of his library."

This time Gerald's face paled slightly with annoyance; he recovered his poise instantly; his third laugh was a little acid.

" They cannot forgive me for being cleverer than themselves; their Simian wits are exercised over my evident superiority. My eyes have been purged with euphrasy and rue; I see the mud in the kennels now, and the cracked lanterns, and the garbage on the Seine thicker than the lily-pads on the ponds of Versailles. They say of me, as Candide said of the noble Venetian, " *Rien ne peut lui plaire.*" I think in their hearts they are inclined to say also, in the words of the same simple fellow, " *Quel grand génie!* " Do not submit to their impertinence, my love; I shall be glad to provide you with a set of answers for all occasions."

Jennifer nodded meekly, shaking the powder from her loosely arranged hair until it shone red as copper leaves and festoons on the worn silver surface of well-polished Sheffield. She had a vague distrustful notion that he had been teasing her; she always experienced a like sensation when her father attempted to teach her Scotch history.

"It is an honour no less than a joy to instruct you, dear child," he went on affably. " You are as well born as any of these aristocrats, if we but accord belief to the widely credited story which assigns to the Earl of Tam-Linn the honour of being descended from Tamburlaine the Great; a not inconsiderable claim to royalty. I think your enormous eyes have a slight tendency to tip upwards at their outer corners; the length of your lashes is confusing to an inquiring gaze, but I believe this to be true. You are a Tartar princess, and I no more than an Asian Jade in an undignified but admiring attitude."

" It isn't necessary to go back so very far as that, Gerald, in order to know that the Lorns have kingly blood in their veins," replied Jennifer with all the haughtiness of which her languor was capable. Gerald appeared distressed; he held up his hand reprovingly and the fine lace fell back to exhibit the blue veins in his own elegantly turned wrist.

" My darling," he implored, in a pained voice, " I beg of you, let us have no scandal. I should be heart-broken to believe that Paris was in any degree corrupting your exquisite mind; I have heard *that* story from your father; may its tragic nature excuse it somewhat from the charge of immorality."

" I confess I fail to understand you," cried Jennifer, almost reduced to tears. " I know very well, however, that the Tamburlaine tale is strictly true; my father has proven its veracity from ancient documents and ancestral jewels."

"I admit," said Gerald magnanimously, "that this legend is entirely proper, whether or not it be true."

4

THE SHAGREEN SLIPPERS

WHEN ZENO, Barbaro, and Contarini came from Venice in 1474, as envoys to the court of Uzun Hasan, leader of the celebrated White Sheep Turcomans, they brought with them from the great republic a Scottish lady of surpassing beauty and unblemished character, one Lady Helena Lorn, of the famous house of Lorn and Carterhaugh. The fact that her sister had married Contarini probably accounted for her inclusion in the little party which arrived at the court of Uzun Hasan, in his magnificent city of Isfahan. This monarch's queen was a Christian princess, daughter of the Emperor of Trebizond, Calo Johannes, of the family of the Comneni; her name was Despina. Imagine the delight of the well-born Scottish sisters at being received by a lady who was at once a queen and a Christian; in those days there were no Calvinists. Alas, their happiness was but short-lived; the treacherous Barbaro conceived the dastardly plan of disposing of Helena Lorn by barter to a wealthy merchant of Isfahan; during the absence of her brother-in-law the horror was nearly consummated; the king was suffering from a passing indisposition, caused by the incautious consumption of a cup of sherbet prepared by his cousin's cook; the queen could not be summoned from her husband's bedside; the excellent Zeno was absent on a pleasure tour of the provinces. No course remained but flight, instant and swift; Helena bade her sister an anguished farewell and went forth alone into the night, disguised as a Kurdish shepherd boy in one of the woollen cloaks of immense and shaggy thickness much affected by these savage tribesmen, who employ them indiscriminately as great-coat and bedding; her little feet were shod in shoes of a bright emerald dye, fashioned from that shagreen leather which is still common in Isfahan. Her disguise was not penetrated; she had the good fortune to be a brunette, and though she was forced to sacrifice the rich abundance of her hair, there is small doubt that she appeared a youth of singular grace and symmetry of form and feature."

"Pray go on," exclaimed Jennifer, enraptured by this recital. "You lend the old story a fresh distinction by your manner of relating it; Gerald, I entreat you to continue." With a courtly bow, he complied with her request, which seemed to flatter him prodigiously.

"She wandered far, and passed through many astonishing and frightful adventures, in the midst of which her virtue and beauty were miraculously preserved. The belief persisted, however, in all who beheld her, that she was no more than a comely shepherd boy, and as such she was conveyed to the royal observatory at Samarkand, where a lad was required to polish the lenses of the great telescopes and assist the astronomers in the simpler mathematical computations; since the wild tribes of the desert first traced the circles of heaven upon the ruddy sands, Kurdish shepherds had always enjoyed an enviable reputation as astronomical assistants. This renowned observatory had been built by Ulagh Bey, grandson of the great Tamburlaine himself; his father, Shah Rukh, had removed his capital to Herut, but the university at Samarkand continued to be a haunt for scholars, scientists and poets, where they found opportunities for study and meditation not afforded them by the more brilliant society of the court at Herut. Ulagh Bey was himself a poet and a patron of literature; his son had the bad taste to murder him, and was very properly put to death by his own troops some six months later. You are to understand that Persia is an extensive country; in this era it had a large variety of rulers, who saw fit to disagree among themselves at the cost of much bloodshed and insane violence. I cannot inform you with any degree of exactitude what particular descendant of the illustrious Tartar occupied the throne of his ancestors at Herut or Samarkand while Uzun Hasan reigned gloriously at Tabriz or Isfahan. This much is certain; the seventh son of the ruling monarch, in whose body flowed a divine elixir derived from Tamburlaine the Great, was at the time of Helena's desperate flight in charge of the royal observatory at Samarkand, whither he had been sent in order to complete his education under the kindly supervision of the historians Mirkhond and Khwadamir and the poets Jami and Hatifi.

"He was a young prince of pleasing address and engaging manners; his good looks were proverbial among the court beauties of Herut, several of whom had most immodestly followed him from home. He became interested in the pretty boy who showed such skill in polishing his favourite lenses; upon discovering the sex of this charming creature he at once proposed honourable marriage, which was subsequently performed according to the ceremonies of both great branches of the Mohammedan faith and also those of the more ancient religion of Zoroaster; the young man was a convinced Sufi, but he desired to do all that lay in his power to protect the good name of his lovely bride; your father assures me that they were later united by the rites of the Roman Catholic Church by the Chaplain of King James the Second of Scotland in the royal chapel at Holyrood. . . . So much for any shadow of disrepute attaching to the name of Lady Helena Tamburlaine, or Tam-Linn, as the rude dialect of your peasants persisted in pronouncing it. The wedded lovers lost no time in repairing to Edinburgh by way of Constantinople and Venice; they made quite a stir in Scottish society of the period, and are even said to have visited persons of distinction in London, where they had the honour of being presented to his Majesty King Edward the Fourth of England."

"But my dear Gerald," exclaimed Jennifer with sparkling eyes and flushed cheeks, "the wealth of detail which you have lavished upon this truly fascinating story delights me beyond words; my father never made it half so entertaining. You have a wonderful gift for narrative; this is far better than the Castle of Otranto."

"Assuredly, my love," replied her husband with complacency. "Would you like to hear a little more, which I have discovered from the same sources?"

"By all means; I need not be at my dressmaker's for another hour, and then it is only to be fitted for a riding-habit which I shall never use, although it is a most becoming shade of green."

"There remains only to tell of the exceptional happiness of this strange union, then," said Gerald, "and to explain the fact that by means of various regrettable mishaps the male heirs to the Earldom, then of Carterhaugh, were one by one snatched away to the grave; finally only Helena and Signora Contarini were left; the sisters were twins, and the decease of a nurse had made the two noble orphans extremely doubtful as to which was the elder. If they had been boys it is probable that their sentiments would have been different; the curious tradition is that neither was willing to admit her seniority, and only the absence of the Signora at the Doge's scintillating court forced Helena to accept the title, which she naturally held in her own right, as Countess of Tamburlaine and Carterhaugh. She had some difficulty in persuading the king to allow her to incorporate the name of the conqueror of Asia in the good old Scottish appellation; the intervention of the Earl of Mar, a close family friend, decided the matter to the lady's satisfaction. The imprisonment and subsequent execution of that great noble was an unfortunate result of this act of kindness on his part; he was arrested on a charge of magic, and there is little doubt that his absorption in Persian poetry and the doctrines of Sufism were the original cause of the rumours which ended only with his death. A pity . . . there is nothing sadder than the sight of despotism discouraging literature and the mental graces.

" On the other hand, Mirza Tam-Linn, as he soon came to be called, took a vast interest in what must now be regarded as his ancestral estates; he became a devout Catholic and a model landlord, and eschewing forever the secular poems of Jami and Hatifi, became deeply immersed in the works of the mediæval scholiasts; he was the real founder of your father's fine library; to him your family owes the large collection of manuscripts, including rare controversial writings by John Duns Scotus; your forebear ranged himself on the side of this cleric, as opposed to Saint Thomas Aquinas, on the subject of the Immaculate Conception. The early sacred carols of Scotland also engaged his attention; he wrote a number of ballads which are sung about the countryside to this day. He was one of Caxton's first patrons; during his visit to London he met this ingenious fellow at the house of Lord Rivers, the king's brother-in-law, whose ' Sayings of the Philosophers,' Caxton was then occupied in printing. Mirza acquired this valuable book, together with the *Morte d'Arthur;* your parent has not infrequently given thanks in my hearing for his ancestor's foresight and excellent taste.

"Always a poet to his finger-tips, he had no regrets for the astrolabes and mural quadrants of Samarkand; his time was passed in writing religious verse and riding over his vast but somewhat barren estates in company with his adored wife. He had the misfortune to lose this beautiful and intellectual woman at the birth of their sixteenth child; the remainder of his days was passed in study and literary composition. His favourite book was Caxton's edition of the 'Golden Legend, or Lives of the Saints,' based upon the 13th century 'Legenda Aurea' of Jacobus de Voragine; of his own writings, which were unfortunately never published until Bishop Percy included some of them in his recent collection, he was inclined to give first place to his re-freshingly romantic Ballad of Tam-Linn, though he composed various dirges and elegies which were more in keeping with his own incurably serious habit of mind. His mastery of the Scots tongue was amazing; he knew Gaelic in all its branches, and was an accomplished performer upon the bag-pipes."

Gerald paused for breath, and drained his glass; his face was intent and almost melancholy in its expression.

"I cannot really like that part so well as the beginning," sighed Jennifer, "though, of course, it is highly interesting in its way; he must have been a very remarkable man."

"He was," said Gerald.

"One small point may still be worth mentioning," Gerald continued. "As it partly concerns you, my dearest, you may not find it entirely dull, though there are some fairly long words in it. I have said before that Helena was a pronounced brunette; one of the Black Lorns, you observe. On the contrary, Signora Contarini was radiantly red like yourself; in Venice this colouring is immensely admired, and she was by all accounts considered the most beautiful woman at the Doge's court. She had a daughter, even lovelier than she, by name Grizel Lucretia Cecelia Contarini; tradition has it that this incomparable creature was the original of many of Titian's most resplendent ladies; her exalted social position precludes the possibility of her having sat for some of these masterpieces, but it is certainly true that the painter used to follow her about the watery highways of Venice, his little gondola, equipped with a small telescope and a portable easel, gliding in the wake of her gorgeous barge through long azure afternoons and yellow sunsets, in the course of which he produced a large variety of sketches immortalising her superhuman beauty forever.

"On a visit to her uncle and aunt at Carterhaugh during her nineteenth year she conceived a violent attachment for her cousin Malcolm, eldest son of the Tam-Linns; the young man warmly reciprocated her affection. Some objections were raised by Helena on the score of consanguinity; these were ably seconded by Signora Contarini, who had every hope of uniting her daughter to the heir of one of the great Roman or Florentine houses. She, as a well-born woman, had always regretted the fact that Venice was a republic, and as such not fit to rank with ancient empires and dukedoms; the idea of losing her little girl in the black frosts of a Scotch winter was too much for her patriotism, however; she wrote to Grizel bidding her return at once to Venice.

"The course of true love was in this case not to be so easily interrupted; Malcolm's evident misery softened his mother's proud heart, while news of Grizel's imminent decline caused the more emotional Signora Contarini to dispatch her consent instantly, together with a number of costly jewels and several hundred yards of the richest products of the looms of Venice; a small copy of Titian's Sacred and Profane Love was included as a wedding gift to Malcolm. This could not fail to please him owing to the fact that of the two figures occupying the canvas one was said to be an excellent portrait of his bride."

5

THE BASKET OF WHITE ROSES

GERALD desisted, and helped himself to a small bunch of white grapes. Jennifer was pleased with that part of the story dealing with the red-haired Contarini; she besought him to continue, but he was firm.

"You are already long overdue at your dressmaker's; go at once, my dear, and while you are there, kindly order a white velvet riding-habit and a hat to match, with the longest plume it is possible to find in Paris; the hat itself should be fairly large, but sharply turned up on the right side. I wish you to wear it with your hair unpowdered; here the effect would be too startling, but in India I think we may allow ourselves a little *bizarrerie* to brighten the monotony of our days. You will ride only in the evening; the effect under a tropic moon should be picturesque in the extreme. If you fear the weight of velvet — though the best velvet of Lyons is remarkably soft and light — I should suggest a heavy corded silk. But follow your own inclination, by all means, my dear; you understand my idea about the hat, I am sure."

He kissed her good-bye with unusual tenderness, and reflecting that he had been perhaps a thought trying in his educational methods of late, went out determined to discover some charming trifle as an appropriate gift for the poor child. He intended originally to buy her some lace, of which she was inordinately fond, but while he was engaged in examining a scarf of French needlepoint with ground of *réseau rosacé* almost entirely covered by a design of great intricacy and beauty, he remembered that only the preceding week he had been told of an exquisite red jasper bowl, or *brûle-parfum,* mounted in gilt bronze by Gouthière and now going at the ridiculous price of one thousand *livres* thanks to its owner's sudden financial embarrassment; d'Aumont would already have possessed himself of the treasure but for the fact that he had recently purchased a duplicate; it was great luck, thought Gerald, that the duke had not availed himself of this opportunity of having the pair. Such a chance could not be idly thrown away; Gerald hurried to the house of the unfortunate banker whose double personality had attempted to combine the pursuit of high finance and the collection of various airy or sumptuous works of art.

Bailiffs were already upon the scene; the auctioneer, a small sagacious individual in black merino, was directing his two blue-jowled assistants in the business of displaying to their best advantage the remaining pieces of furniture and bits of porcelain and ormolu; an immense Aubusson carpet, of tender colouring and chaste design, was flung to one side of the long drawing-room; pushed back against the panelling were many precious lacquer cabinets, consoles and tables in marquetry, columns and vases in porphyry, jasper, and choice marbles and transparent clays of China and Japan. Gerald was sincerely touched; the sight of the library beyond, its walls a rich and sombre mosaic of gilded leather, faintly scented with the exotic perfumes of Morocco, Russia, and Spain, affected him painfully; the glimpse he caught of a lean figure bending over a disordered writing-desk forced him to have recourse to his pocket-handkerchief and a cleverly simulated cough.

The tragedy would have been more intolerable if its protagonist had been able to boast of aristocratic connections; nevertheless he was deserving of the heartiest sympathy. Gerald debated within himself whether or no he should venture into the library to offer a word of well-bred condolence on the loss of those cherished volumes whose absence was already blackening the walls with unsightly patches of sheer emptiness; only the immediate necessity of bidding for the jasper bowl prevented him from translating this humane thought into suitable action. . . . He obtained the ravishing object for nine hundred *livres;* it was a decided bargain at the price.

Gerald carried it home in his own hands; in spite of its great weight he was able, with the help of a hired cabriolet and his remarkable muscular strength, to convey it direct to their hotel, where he spent the entire evening regarding it with a passionate admiration, refusing to attend a small and select gathering in a certain celebrated salon at the Convent of Saint Joseph, though he had since his earliest visit to Paris been *persona grata* in that particular quarter. Jennifer was relieved; she enjoyed examining the minutiæ of detail which Gerald pointed out to her so eagerly, and she was glad enough to escape the terrifying formality which froze her chilly young blood in most of the great drawing-rooms of Paris. The jasper bowl was too lovely to part from, even for a matter of hours; Gerald knew in his heart that he would never give it to his wife so long as he lived; at the moment he could almost have sworn that if it had come to a choice between them, he would have selected his newer acquisition to have and to hold forever. This is not so strange as might appear at first when it is taken into consideration that the bowl was cut from a superb piece of jasper, mounted in gilt bronze, with satyrs' heads bearing dependent festoons of vine-leaves; within the feet a serpent was coiled to spring. It stood upon his writing-table until the day of his death.

The following day he purchased for his wife, for the sum of exactly one hundred *livres,* a scarf similar in design and only a little inferior in quality to the one he had first considered. She was enchanted, and wore it that very same night to an important reception at the British Ambassador's; Gerald, viewing the charming effect of the frail web of lace encircling her white shoulders between the ivory satin of her gown and the string of Indian pearls which he had picked up under such strange circumstances at the court of the Nawab of Murshidabad, decided that his gift was far prettier and more appropriate for a lady than even the most exquisite of *objets d'art;* women always preferred something to wear, and by no stretch of the imagination could he conceive of Jennifer's fragility striving to support the heavy burden of the jasper bowl; she would have to be transformed into marble first.

For a moment his fancy saw her thus, with flying draperies by the royal goldsmith, set in a blue vista at Versailles; then he realised that under those circumstances she would undoubtedly be the property of the king; he dispelled the vision from his eyes with one sweep of his long fingers, and went on with his game of vingt-et-un as soberly as if he cared for nothing on earth but the cards and the supper, being enabled to practice this dissimulation the more readily through caring quite sincerely for both of these mitigating and blameless pleasures amid the vast melancholy of the universe.

Meanwhile Jennifer was engaged in an adventurous exploration of the conservatory; the fact of finding herself in an English house had encouraged her greatly, and she was now valiantly setting forth alone in search of a white camellia and a spray of maiden's-hair fern, which floral ornament she rightly considered would lend the completing touch of modishness to her costume; the roses, jasmine, carnations, exotic lilies, and streaked and spotted orchises upon the laced and jewelled bosoms of the other ladies strengthening her in the supposition that this final grace was as necessary to the woman of fashion as a painted fan with mother-of-pearl sticks or a pair of gloves of glazed and supple kidskin.

The long conservatory was dimly lit; after the scintillant atmosphere of the ball-room, where brilliance was shattered into prismatic confusion by countless tinkling icicles of glass in sconce and chandelier, it was a lane of blue dusk, a tropic night striped with stupendous fronds; it was vaulted with palms and hung with ropes of fragrance. High overhead three incredible moons floated in space; the yellow Chinese tissue of which they were fashioned bore a thin tracery of wave and cloud upon its distended surface, where golden dragons wallowed and swarmed in battle. Jennifer drew a shivering breath of amazement; the scene enchanted her to the point of tears, disquieting her slightly at the same time; she leaned against a great black lacquer cabinet in an attitude of unstudied innocence tinctured with timidity; her head was turned over her shoulder, her little hand was laid upon her breast.

In another instant she might have become a crystal fountain or a tree of white flowers, to be immemorially lost in the British Ambassador's conservatory; some such catastrophe was perhaps averted by the sudden appearance of a young man, who burst through the elaborate trellises and festoons of foliage evincing the same charming impetuosity with which the nimble prince clove his way through the prickly half-acre hedge around the Sleeping Castle. The nymph, who had feared the advent of Apollo in the character of an elderly Academician or a verse-making Marquis with a lisp, relaxed again into mortal flesh; a glance at the stranger's frank and open countenance sufficed to show that the danger was at most pleasantly negligible; the conservatory was the poorer by one silver cascade or scented rose-bush, and Jennifer was weeping distractedly in the arms of the unknown.

"At last I have found you!" cried the young man in accents vibrant with joy; "I have even had the supreme good fortune to find you when you were evidently in want of assistance; to speak of beauty in distress were impertinence; to liken you to Ariadne were immediately to suggest the absurd comparison of myself with Perseus; may I venture to recall to your mind the homely proverb that a friend in need is a friend indeed? " With which gallant and respectful speech he produced a pocket-handkerchief of fine cambric and applied its softness to her streaming eyes, at the same time patting her gently but firmly upon the shoulder. Jennifer derived great comfort from his reassuring actions; the lively terror which she had experienced in the expectation of beholding a foreigner was entirely dissipated by the youth's appearance.

"Oh, my dear sir," she cried somewhat hysterically, " what felicity to know that you are English, or at the very worst, Scotch! I do most deeply appreciate your kindness, coming as it does from one with whom I am as yet unacquainted! "

The young man wrinkled his pale-brown eyebrows in bewilderment, simultaneously implanting upon the highest curl of Jennifer's *coiffure* a kiss so light and fleeting that its pressure failed to disturb even so much as a grain of powder from that airy convolution, which resembled nothing half so much as a butterfly poised for flight.

"But why — why — my adored angel — if I may be permitted so to address in all reverence one whom I have long dared to worship from afar — why should I be, of all things under heaven, Scotch? I was born in Kent, near Sevenoaks, where my ancestral mansion is prettily situated. My mother's family are natives of Berkshire; their home is the most northerly point I have as yet attained in my travels through Great Britain. It is true that my tutor, though a Welshman, is a friend of Mr. Hume's; possibly I may have picked up an accent from the worthy man, but it seems more probable that what you mistake for a Caledonian twang is in reality a trace of the Italian language lingering upon my tongue; I have but lately arrived in Paris after an extended stay in Rome and a tour of the more important Italian towns. I hope you do not find my manner of speaking distasteful to you; if so I will hasten to alter it to the best of my ability; I will intone to you the sonorous chants of the priests of Baal or the songs of the ancient Chaldean shepherds if it will but please you a little; if you will smile I might even be valiant enough to speak French."

"Oh, no, no," entreated Jennifer pitifully, "I never wish to hear that detestable jargon again. . . . It is a veritable *mélange* of truly shocking improprieties, so far as I can judge. How different was the vocabulary of the good nuns of the Parthemont; I am quite sure they were totally ignorant of most of the expressions commonly used in the most exalted society in France. There was *Athalie,* to be sure . . . but that was poetry. Now I hear nothing but such words as *amour — admiration — désespoir — adoration — ange pur — cœur dur — cœur insensible — beauté terrible — cruelle — tellement belle — o ciel!*"

Jennifer was rapidly losing her self-control; dreadful memories of even more passionate phrases, murmured in low voices and looked as speakingly from imploring eyes, caused her to shudder violently and cling closer to the young man's protecting arm.

"But that is poetry too, in a way — though I doubt whether a severe stylist would admit that last rhyme. Those are not wicked words; in fact I am at this very instant planning to translate them into English and repeat them to you, with such connecting verbs, articles, and prepositions as will presently make clear their very humble meaning. Only tell me this; why did you think that, at the worst, I might be Scotch?"

"Because your voice reminded me of my brothers, but they, to be sure, went to Oxford, and all the Lorns laugh at them."

"Ah, that accounts for it, then," the sprightly youth continued, "I also attended that University; I have little hope that I should escape the Lorns' laughter, which I am sure is disconcertingly hearty."

"Oh, it is indeed," agreed Jennifer fervently. "You know they are so unfeeling as to call me Jenny Forlorn, and to make great game of my wrists and ankles."

"Your wrists and ankles are the most delicate experiments in turned ivory that I have so far had the privilege of observing," he returned. "The Pope's smallest comfit-box is clumsy in comparison. I have no objection to your being Jenny, but Forlorn you shall never more be, now that I have found you."

This time Jennifer felt the kiss upon her hair; the fact that the boy's light voice was so singularly like her brothers' seemed to make the caress a mere matter of course.

" Let us sit down," said the young man, " I have much to say to you."

They sat side by side upon a small couch of vermilion lacquer; they made a remarkably pretty pair, and numbered a possible thirty-six years between them. If the boy was nineteen, as he subsequently stated, his appearance was juvenile even for that inconsiderable degree of age; Jennifer had not seemed so ridiculously young since she had picked cream-coloured roses in Devonshire, during the preceding summer. Next to her shimmering white gown, the blue of his suit was black in the half-darkness; she stared intently into his face, and saw that he had a fair complexion and very brilliant hazel eyes, wide-open and rather round, a short nose, and the mouth of an irresponsible angel; his powdered hair she judged to be of the same pale brown as his straight furry eyebrows. He looked charmingly and obscurely mischievous; his mouth was grave, but his eyes were full of a wild hilarity and a wilder triumph.

Without the door a capital band of stringed instruments was rendering a selection of Italian airs; supper was in progress, the dancing had for the moment ceased, and none drew near to disturb them. A tenuously stately toccata seemed to allay the moving atmosphere of light and perfume and far-off laughter; Jennifer listened in a quiet enchantment, her hands clasped loosely around her slender knees. The boy was silent also for a moment, but she could feel the tense excitement and exultant restlessness in his thin body; his pointed fingers beat irregular time to the music; within his throat a little sound of humming began and ended and began again; once he sang a line or two in the lively ghost of a tenor, pronouncing the words clearly in an unpretentiously impeccable accent, and glancing sideways at Jennifer with his bright faun's eyes to see whether she was admiring him. He was completely at his ease; he seemed to be savouring a secret happiness which filled him with hardly restrained mirth. Jennifer liked him enormously; she felt as if she must have known him for years; as if he must have come to her Christmas parties long ago in a pale blue suit and a white ruffle and a close fitting cap of golden curls. She waited patiently for him to speak; she knew he was about to say something interesting.

"At last I have found you!" he repeated, in accents rendered thrilling by the little vibration in his voice, compounded equally of laughter and emotion. "I saw you first in a Hackney coach in London, last October . . . I do not recall what you were wearing at the time, but I know that you appeared to me a seraph robed in snow—"

"That must have been my ermine mantle—"

"And again in the gardens of the Tuileries; night was falling; you seemed a star in darkness—"

"And that was my black velvet *pelisse,* without doubt," cried Jennifer with warm interest. "Was I not wearing at the same time a white veil?"

"Veil?" exclaimed the youth. "O lovely sound—sweet augury, ecstatic hope—what visions are conjured up by that one word! And there above our innocent heads hang clustered oranges, by all that is holy I declare they do, wreathed in their own blossoms; how different from that insidious fruit of Eden whose coarser grain should never be permitted to intrude into the diet of pure romance! I refer to the apple, whose part in the story I always thought the more contemptible because of its wicked passivity throughout; a veritable copper's nark of apples, in my opinion, and far worse than the snake. But this is no fit conversation for your remarkably small and symmetrical ears; the question I desired to ask you was quite simple, yet full of homely morality; it is this; will you be so good as to marry me at once?"

For an absurdly happy second Jennifer's whirling thoughts flew like a released swallow towards a minute and sunny opening at the end of a dark tunnel; then they folded their wings again in resignation; in spite of the fact that it was impossible to avail herself of the young man's offer, it gave her a sense of security.

"My dear sir," she faltered, "I cannot accept your highly flattering proposal; unfortunately I am already married."

"Ah," said the youth, rather wanly, and again with a slight sigh. "Ah, that is indeed a pity."

Then his face brightened once more, and he recovered his spirits with something like a mental pirouette.

"But perhaps your husband is very old, or perhaps, though still in the prime of life, he will perish shortly of one of those malignant fevers which so often follow an indulgence in Seine water as a beverage; I trust he is an abstainer from wines and liquors, unless of course he is an habitual drunkard, which would, unless his constitution be of iron, answer quite as well the exigencies of our case. For your own part, I entreat you to drink only the *Eau du Roi* of Chantilly, a pure spring water imported into Paris at some expense; you must give me your word of honour that you will on no account touch any other drink, at the same time religiously concealing from your husband the existence of such an article; I shall send you some to-morrow concealed in a gigantic basket of white roses; if your husband has the bad taste to look into the basket, the crystal element will be at once metamorphosed, rather in the manner of Ovid than of Saint Elizabeth, into creamy petals impearled with dew; there will be no card in the basket, but your heart will tell you whence it came. Drink the water, eat the roses — you perceive of course that I have been studying, under the guidance of my tutor, the Latin of Apuleius — and all may yet be well. Meanwhile there is surely no marital duty so severe and pressing as to render you unable to join a small picnic, jaunt, or excursion which my aunt is making to-morrow into the wilds of Fontainebleau. My aunt is the first cousin of our Ambassador; I am her favourite nephew; need I say more? "

Jennifer looked at him carefully; she thought she had never seen so engaging a countenance, having naturally long ago forgotten the young man of the black loveknot.

" I cannot tell you," she cried in a voice which for her was remarkably enthusiastic, " with what gratitude and pleasure I have listened to your words; surely the superiority of the English is well demonstrated by the fact that whereas the majority of the French gentlemen whom I meet insult me with proposals of the most heinous nature, you have at once made me an offer of marriage and, finding that I was quite powerless to accept this, have courteously followed it with a plan for formally introducing me to your aunt and conveying me to Fontainebleau under the protection of this lady. It has also been a great relief to talk to you of my troubles; I can hardly express to you the agony of mind which I have endured recently, and which I have feared to impart to my husband lest it result in the death of various persons of rank and fashion, none of whom are to be sure particularly worthy of esteem, but who possess in nearly every instance either an aged mother or an affectionate wife and family to whom their loss could hardly fail to be disturbing."

" May I inquire your husband's name, Madam," the boy asked with gravity; when Jennifer whispered low the one word " Poynyard," pronouncing it with a measure of awe, he nodded sagely.

" Ah, yes, to be sure — I might have known. But let me hasten to set at least a portion of your fears at rest; I am acquainted with your husband; he would never kill, only cane with extreme severity. I know precisely the sort of cane which he would employ; a thin and sinister wand, of pale straw colour, with spots of a most peculiar and malignant brown; a truly serpentine cane, which might be one of Medusa's locks fallen down over her eyes and forthwith magicked into supple stone for the flaying alive of poor lovers. I should dislike extremely to feel its fang in my own meagre shoulder-blades, I assure you; none the less I am determining upon venturing so far as Fontainebleau. Let us, for one day, be babes in the wood sheltering from a more than avuncular wrath behind the petticoats of my excellent aunt, a rare and lovely creature, a good twenty years my deceased uncle's junior; she is a woman of brave spirit tempered with discretion; would that my dear mother were like her in certain qualities which it would be unfilial to formulate into words! We are singularly lucky in being able to count upon her assistance in the matter of the picnic."

He leaned back with a lazy smile upon his countenance, after allowing an apparently wholly unconscious kiss to smooth away the bewilderment from Jennifer's innocent brow.

" But, my dear sir," she began, " how is it possible for you to escape asking my husband to join your proposed excursion, and if my husband comes . . ." Her pause was eloquent, but less so than the tongue of the persuasive young man.

" Of course, my dearest love — or rather I should say, as more *convenable* as yet, my dear Madam — of course if he comes our day will be completely ruined. Are we not to hire a pair of dashing steeds and gallop madly through the forest glades, avoiding by the veriest hair's-breadth the vast and polished trunks of beeches, painted a strange subaqueous green by the light that

filters through their leaves — but no, it is now November — let
us avoid instead the stately boles of great oak trees — shall we not
avoid those russet monarchs of the wood by the unlikeliest fraction of an infant's hair, while my pretty aunt is plucking lavender
and reviving memories of Sevenoaks in the English Garden?
Shall we not moreover wander along the more exiguous paths
and alleys, treading warily lest we step upon the adders which
infest these sylvan haunts; shall we not explore the celebrated
Gorge aux Loups, plumbing its caverns in the fearful hope of
arousing one of the lean grey shapes which roam it still by moonlight? Do you not, in short, adore danger of the most deadly description, and would not the presence of your husband dust a
bright romantic bloom from the appalling adventures which we
are about to undertake?"

Jennifer considered his words with demure composure; she
harboured not the slightest doubt of the high seriousness of this
surprising speech, but the idea of peril, usually so repellent to her
mind, was by some curious alchemy made alluring by the spell
of the young man's conversation; the adders even lost their terrors
in her prophetic conviction that he would prove competent to
deal with snakes, wolves, and spirited horses with equal facility,
and that without the necessity of drawing his sword or raising
his voice.

"I should certainly enjoy myself more if dear Gerald did not
accompany us," she admitted. "But how can you possibly contrive
to prevent his coming, since in common courtesy he must be
invited?"

"The simplest thing in the world," the youth explained with a
wave of his hand. "My aunt shall invite him; she is unfortunately
quite beautiful, but I will instruct her to wear an unbecoming
costume; I have in mind a snuff-coloured cloth mantle the purchase of which I strongly deprecated at the time; a use has now
been found for it, which is very gratifying, as it is both costly and
durable, and I had forbidden her to wear it in my presence. She
shall speak encouragingly of certain ladies languishing to meet
Mr. Poynyard; they shall be the most egregious bores to be found
in Paris; my aunt knows an astonishing number of bores, as my
late uncle insisted upon her making his friends her own. Your

husband is certain to refuse; he does not suffer fools gladly. For your part, you have but to exhibit a mild reluctance, and the day is won; we shall be eating white grapes at Fontainebleau before the week is out."

He clasped her to him in an ingenuous embrace, at the same time kicking his smart scarlet heels in the air and clashing his silver shoe-buckles together in a somewhat frivolous elation of soul. Jennifer gave a long despairing sigh; his final words had killed the last little fluttering hope in her breast.

"Alas," she moaned. "I might have foreseen this; all is lost, my friend." And she subsided into bitter sobs once more, to the vast derangement of his Italian point ruffle, which in her confusion she used to staunch her tears under the impression that it was the fine cambric pocket-handkerchief of her first consolation at his hands. "The white grapes of Fontainebleau; how could I have forgotten the ominous sound of those words, which I hear pronounced above the breakfast table every morning of my life? My only excuse is that I am customarily very sleepy, but this does not explain my extraordinary stupidity. Oh, if that is the spot where they grow exquisite white grapes under glass I fear we must abandon hope at once; if it is also the spot where some one signed the revocation of the Edict of Nantes and some one else murdered her secretary, there is no conceivable chance remaining to us. There is an end forever and ever to our poor picnic; I do most heartily wish I had never been born."

The young man held her closer; there were tears in his own eyes, and having found the handkerchief, he dabbed at them quite openly.

"How very unlucky — but how amazingly unlucky — " he kept repeating. "And are you sure the place has such an attraction for him — might not the adders counteract the Edict of Nantes? "

"Do not waste your time in vain imaginings, my dear friend, my dear . . ." said Jennifer sadly. "I knew in the bottom of my heart that such happiness could not be for me." And she fell into quiet weeping, while endeavouring to draw her string of pearls far enough in advance of her pointed chin to observe their lustre and extract a minute but present comfort from their pierced and luminous globes. "But, oh, if only I might have worn my new

green riding-habit; if only we might have discovered the wolves'
cavern; if only we might have picked lavender with your aunt
in the English garden! "

He gazed at her with childish and companionable pity; he had
no more gay words wherewith to console her.

With clasped hands and questioning eyes, they looked long
at each other; he noted the length of her drenched eyelashes and
she the engaging golden freckles upon the straight bridge of his
nose. At last they drew slowly apart; an unreasonable but utter
hopelessness blurred their steady gaze. Jennifer had in some mysterious fashion infected the mercurial youth with her own quiet
lassitude; it seemed useless and wearisome to struggle against
odds which now assumed the aspect of a monstrous growth in
shapes of fear and shadows of disaster.

The boy saw this lovely child immured in solitude and deprived of sustenance; he saw a room without a fireplace whose
one long dusty window afforded a grey prospect of chimney-pots;
the place was draughty and rats scampered behind the crumbling
plaster of the walls. Jennifer imagined the flick of the cruel cane
across that white and ingenuous brow, and the red mark drawn
there seemed to draw blood from her heart; she saw a youthful
hero, lacking weapons, in a suicidal leap at a giant's throat; her
hands went over her eyes and she shuddered. Both shuddered;
both despaired; they were silent as a pair of exquisite wax dolls
under the enormous canopy of flowers.

In the mind of each the pitiless play continued; the door of
the narrow room opened with a mercifully blinding burst of
light; the little figure by the window screamed and swooned away
in the renewed darkness, now stirred into sinister motion by an
unknown presence; at this dreadful presentiment the boy leaned
limply against Jennifer's shoulder, while she swayed dizzily in
contemplating the cane extended into a huge snake, mottled yellow and brown upon the pulsations of its scales, and now slowly
encircling the slight body of her young friend; she heard the
small bones snap under the relentless pressure.

Perhaps the cloudy and suffocating fragrance of the tropical
plants may have contained some taint of a narcotic poison; the
boy found it necessary to bring the flint and steel of his wit and

courage very sharply together to waken a flash of his former gaiety; he prattled for a doomed instant of the gardens of Luxembourg, Condé, and Soubise as possible meeting-places; he spoke of the promenade along the fortifications and the *parterres* of the Archbishop near Notre Dame, but in his soul he knew that their pretty dream was ended; each was a coward for the other's sake. In all the strange and varied trials and adventures of his later years, the memory of that night remained intact and perfect, like a pastoral scene upon a prince's coach-panel or a classic instance modelled skillfully in tinted clay.

They kissed, gently and sorrowfully; their fingers clung and fell apart; in another moment a tall Hungarian officer in the green furred jacket and pale grey breeches of the Nadasdy Hussars was bowing over Jennifer's cold hand to claim the dance for which the Italian musicians were already tuning their delicate instruments; she went without a word or a backward glance, a young Eurydice never to be reclaimed by the blithe Orpheus of Fontainebleau Forest.

The boy sat whistling softly for perhaps half an hour; he was very tired. At the end of that time he rose and entered the supper room; after three glasses of champagne and a *meringue glacé* he felt much better; he then most sensibly proceeded to go home, where he had an excellent night's sleep, quite untroubled by dreams of love or indigestion.

For a whole week Jennifer was inconsolable; she wept continually, and grew so thin that Gerald spent many hours seated by her side, with a silver spoon in one hand and a glazed pot of Chantilly cream in the other; every time she opened her little mouth he put a spoonful of cream into it, and as she was not in the least hungry she found it simpler to preserve an absolute silence which assisted her greatly in concealing the reason for her extreme sadness. Gerald took it for granted that another access of nostalgia had descended upon the poor child; as he could not consider even the briefest stay in Devonshire he talked for some time of a restful month at Montpellier; only the atrocious hotel which he remembered as the best afforded by that notoriously salubrious town prevented him from putting this kindly plan into execution.

The proposal, brought forward by Gerald, that his wife should have her miniature painted succeeded in restoring her to her natural health and spirits, never very strong or vivid at the best. Her husband had entertained strong hopes of Greuze; a canvas by that incomparable hand would be the very net for trapping all the wings and petals and diaphanous airs of Jennifer's beauty. The thing was not to be; the artist was still sulking and remote; he had refused to exhibit since the unfortunate incident of *Sevère et Caracalla* in '69. Gerald could remember the storm of ridicule brought down upon the painter's head when this amazing historical work was suspended side by side with the delicious *Petite Fille au Chien Noir;* it was one of those dreadful attempts at the grand manner which upon the stage turns Mercutio into Timon and upon the printed leaf spoils an excellent rondeau to produce a vile imitation of Racine. Gerald had been deeply distressed at the time; his clear recollection of the *annus mirabilis* of '65 sharpened his regret at the fiasco; when he thought of those thirteen small casements opening upon Arcadia he could have wept as bitterly as the young girl who wept for her dead bird in that pure atmosphere.

He had himself condescended to wait upon M. Greuze, immediately following his arrival in Paris; a half-promise was made but never redeemed; the painter forfeited the privilege of beholding that lady whose loveliness he failed to embalm forever behind a few layers of pale and rosy paint and a thin lacquer of tawny varnish. If he conceived of her as the typical Englishwoman of the Frenchman's fancy, he might easily have drowned himself in the Seine upon realising the chance he had missed; there lived no dove in any golden age whose death produced a grief so exquisite as that which overflowed the eyes of Jennifer Lorn, as she lay along the faded crimson couch in a translucent garment of black gauze, while tears of an incredible brightness blinded her with their prisms.

A fashionable miniature-painter begged for the favour of transferring some small portion of her charm to ivory; Gerald consented, and the thing was done. It served the purpose of rousing Jennifer to life; her vanity prevailed upon her to smile, and her sense of duty forced her to give faithfully a sufficient number of sittings to permit the little work of art to be finished in time for Gerald's birthday. Only the fact that at the last minute it was discovered that the pearls were not included among the accessories of the painted costume caused a delay which eventually resulted in Gerald's forced departure without the delightful object; Jennifer bought a snuff-box as a substitute, but being upon the high seas at the time, totally forgot to present it to him. Later she found it extremely useful as a receptacle for pins.

The poor girl's exceeding sorrow lasted a full week; she could not, during all that period, free herself from affectionate memories of the young man of the conservatory. At the end of the seventh day, she was forced to interview the miniature-painter in order to arrange a sitting for the morrow; his intelligent suggestions as to her dress, which was to approximate as nearly as possible to that of an ideal Diana, and his very interesting anecdotes of his youngest and favourite daughter distracted Jennifer's mind, gave her a slight appetite for supper, and sent her to sleep dreaming of the precocious comments of Mathilde upon the occasion of her first communion.

The sittings were uniformly pleasant; the artist's timidity would have precluded the possibility of presumptuous compliments had his virtue not rendered such liberties naturally repellent to his mind; Jennifer always recalled him with satisfaction as the only Frenchman who had neglected to make love to her; she never forgot the names of his children or the different species of roses which he proposed to cultivate on retiring to a peaceful old age in his native town of Tours. She would have regretted profoundly his death at the hands of the public executioner at a considerably later date, had there existed the remotest chance of the sad story being brought to her attention after the passage of so many unimaginable years.

She was sitting, in her character of Queen and Huntress, as close to the fire as her voluminous draperies permitted; a gilded bow slung across her shoulders adding but little to the warmth of a costume better suited to Mount Olympus than to a Parisian *salon* whose six long windows were even now bombarded by a wind from the Steppes of Russia; a peppering of sleet teased the window panes and hissed upon the fire. She shivered like a silver aspen, and then, less romantically, sneezed in a pathetic manner; the artist's heart was torn, because the necessity of doing full justice to the pearls made it unadvisable to allow her to transfer her ermine scarf from the chair-back to her own throat. He bent above his table, balancing the magnifying-glass carefully in his left hand while his right stippled a transparent shadow of carmine upon the minute presentment of her mouth smiling from the ivory; it was simple, since the child was tired, to add a touch of rose-colour to the counterfeited cheek, instead of demanding a rouge box and a hare's foot to improve the pallor of the true one.

"Oh, yes," he said with gentle satisfaction, "Armand and Pierre rarely quarrel now; the incident was very amusing, but their mother would have been alarmed at its repetition; I was obliged to speak quite seriously to them, and I am happy to say that they are now another David and Jonathan among brothers."

"How charming," cried Jennifer with sympathetic pleasure. "And do not forget to relate the story you promised me of Suzanne's adventure with the currant-jam!"

At this moment Gerald entered the room; his air was cheerful, but a look of strong determination narrowed his lips and eyes in a way which to his wife's quick apprehension portended words or deeds of a strenuous and fatiguing sort.

"I have heard direct from Calcutta," he exclaimed with emphasis; "Sullivan works against me in London; there is no time to be lost; I must have the friendship of Hastings himself, or go down like a nine-pin. We sail from Gravesend in three days; if the winds are favourable we may perhaps achieve a single night in Saint Albans Street, if you think it worth the trouble. I regret that we shall have no time in which to acquaint your parents with our plans; I myself shall be infinitely put out at the impossibility of bidding my poor old father farewell; I can scarcely hope to find him alive on my next visit to England. I trust you will endeavour to subdue your filial sentiments of sorrow in so far as to assist me in every way in making the journey as expeditious as may be; wifely affection should give you courage for this small sacrifice; it is rarely I make any demand upon you whatever."

Jennifer rose hastily, gathering the folds of her tunic and

mantle over her arm; as she fled from the room the parquet flooring struck cold as the black ice of mid-winter through her flimsy gilt sandals. The painter flung the heavy ermine scarf around her shoulders as she passed, earning thereby a dark look from Gerald and a word of agitated gratitude and farewell from the lady.

"It is a pity," he told his wife that evening, "that one could not have adopted this unlucky child; I fear she is destined for great unhappinesss."

His wife looked up from her embroidery frame; because he was a fashionable miniature painter she no longer knitted. The excellent soup for which they were even now waiting, the like of which had nourished the artist's soul for twenty years, was in these days of affluence prepared by the cook; it was not quite so good as formerly, but Madame took infinite satisfaction in the recovered whiteness of her tapering fingers. She examined him kindly with her quizzical brown eyes before replying.

"How old is she?" she questioned.

"Not yet eighteen; a child, only a child, beautiful and unfortunate. She would have been exactly the proper age for Pierre." A different quality crept into his wife's voice; she gazed at his bent head with an expression which she would have thought it pure folly to permit him to observe.

"You are very romantic, my friend, and not very practical. Do you think the possessor of those pearls" — she tapped the ivory sharply with her pointed finger-nail — "could ever have been content to wed a mere civil-servant — brilliant, it is true, but — ?" Her shrug was eloquent of many things, incredulity, amusement, and a slight contempt for Jennifer, a restrained but fiery pride in Pierre, an exasperated adoration for her husband. His lowered eyes missed the pantomime of gesture and glance; he was intent upon the picture.

"Undoubtedly, if they could have known each other," he said calmly; he was too wise to add, "Her tastes are very simple." She leaned towards him; her clever eyes surveyed the small seraphic face lying so helplessly in the palm of his hand.

"You are right, my friend," she said. "The girl is unhappy; she has need of peace. Perhaps Armand, and the little farm at

Tours, would have been best." They looked at each other and smiled; then, somewhat to his surprise, she kissed him. This gratuitous mark of affection inspired him to tease her.

"You are not willing to relinquish Pierre," he said.

"Nor you the little farm at Tours." She had him there; he sighed and polished his spectacles before resuming work.

The subject had all at once grown depressing; it was never re-opened between them. He completed the miniature according to Gerald's instructions, taking great care to reproduce the pearls to perfection and to alter slightly the expression of the eyes, as his patron had commanded. The generous sum which he had received for the work was put aside as a marriage portion for his eldest daughter; the picture itself he habitually carried in his breast pocket, to be the more easily forthcoming, as he told himself, upon the Englishman's arrival to claim it. It passed out of existence at the moment of his own death, in the singular manner before related; it was without doubt his masterpiece.

The next morning, as Jennifer passed through the courtyard of the hotel on her way to the luxurious chaise which awaited them in the street, she was aware of a neatly-dressed man-servant bearing a large hamper from which ascended in the chill November air a miraculous scent of roses; she assured herself that the hamper could contain nothing more enthralling to the imagination than the fine linen of a dandy laundered with perfumed soap, yet when Gerald strode to the basket and raised its lid with a supercilious sniff, her heart beat against her ribs like a wild-cat kitten in a cage of silk.

"White roses — at this time of year!" he cried with polite fury. "I congratulate you, my love, on having made a conquest; your admirer must be either a millionaire or a gardener; he must have posted straight from Naples or robbed the conservatory of our own ambassador, which I noticed as being well-furnished with like blooms; in either case he must be a man of courage and determination; I should like to meet him."

His laugh was frigid; he plunged his long hands into the tangle of pearl-coloured flowers and fresh green leaves; Jennifer's heart stood still. She expected every instant to see a great crystal flacon of *Eau du Roi* flourished against the sun; the vision ap-

peared to her mind as alarming as the appearance of a phial of
arsenic would have been, and when the basket finally gaped
empty upon the frosted cobble-stones of the courtyard, with the
flowers scattered like a snow-drift beside it, she felt indeed that
a miracle had been performed, an Ovidian metamorphosis
achieved; she came very near to believing that the bright-eyed
youth himself had assumed the finer substance of a heap of rose-
leaves.

When her husband stepped with great deliberation up to this
heap, and with the utmost composure proceeded to stamp it into
shreds, she screamed three times and fainted. Sallie revived this
swoon to semi-consciousness by the simple expedient of shaking
the moisture from such flowers as had escaped her master's boot-
heels into the face of her mistress; Jennifer was carried to the
chaise almost completely covered with white petals and drops of
dew. Gerald asked her no question; he seemed to consider the
incident closed, as indeed it was in reality.

The youth, finding his nymph had departed, remembered her
with despairing rage for fully six months, at the end of which
time he married at the earnest wish of his mother and lived happily ever after; Jennifer never entirely forgot him, though her
curious experience with M. Saint Amond in Calcutta relegated
the English boy to the limbo of half-remembered and wholly unintelligible dreams.

6

THE RAJAH'S RUBY

GERALD and his wife spent a night in London after all; Dick was
overjoyed to see them, and took them to the *Ombres Chinois,*
undoubtedly the most elegant performance then to be witnessed
in town. Lady Dicker would have preferred a table of four-handed
whist, but Gerald pointed out with the most perfect courtesy and
firmness that Jennifer was in no fit state to play an intelligent
game of cards after the acute misery which she had experienced
in crossing the Channel. His cousin's kind heart was touched;

she gave in with an excellent grace, and enjoyed the evening without a single regret for her favourite amusement; she allowed Jennifer's nodding head to rest against her dumpy little shoulder more than once in the course of the entertainment.

Gerald eyed his wife solicitously several times, but he was convinced that a sea voyage was precisely the tonic which her evident fatigue required. Their box was somewhat withdrawn from prying glances; its velvet curtains afforded a consoling shade in the midst of swaying lights and clamorous gongs; Jennifer was fortunate to be able to sleep during the greater part of the bizarre and brilliant spectacle which was so obviously delighting the remainder of the audience.

After posting through a snow-storm to Gravesend the next day, Gerald and his wife dined at the Falcon Inn and went immediately aboard the Phœnix East Indiaman. Jennifer was delighted with her cabin, which was neatness itself, and most elegantly fitted up, being painted a light sky blue with gold beadings; the bed and curtains were of the richest Madras chintz, and a capital mahogany dressing-table and bureau completed the furnishings. Her inspection of the entire ship was less reassuring, though productive among the ship's crew of an instant and surprising predilection for her which would have caused any one of them to relinquish without a murmur his share of rum and plum-duff had she ever felt inclined to demand this sacrifice.

She could hardly, however, have realised her extraordinary popularity among the seamen; and certainly any such manifestation on their part would have distressed her beyond words; during the two weeks in which she lay supine under the swinging curtains of her berth she was frequently inconvenienced by the strong scent of tobacco which the fresh breeze conveyed through the porthole of the cabin. She could not know that this was the result of a devotion which forced many a sleepy sailor to forgo his well-earned hours of rest in order to keep romantic watch near the couch of his divinity; the fact that such a proceeding was ill judged cannot detract from its simple nobility.

Nothing could rouse her; the prodigious seas of the Bay of Biscay merely toyed with her inanimate form as if she had been a very small mouse in the power of a playful but gargantuan cat.

Fortunately the wind, though tempestuous, was uniformly fair; the ship's progress was consequently extremely rapid; within twelve days they were approaching the Canaries. One bright evening Gerald entered her cabin door; he was feeling particularly fit after a dinner of boiled fowl and claret and a few games of pagoda whist with a group of gentlemen returning to India to resume their duties in the armies of Madras or Bengal or the no less arduous Civil Service.

"My love," he said firmly, "I am going to carry you up onto the deck; the air will do what medical attention has failed to accomplish, and you will have the pleasure of beholding the truly glorious spectacle of sunset upon the peak of Teneriffe."

The prescription, though Spartan, was efficacious; the snowy eminence scarce stood more quietly among the clouds than its reflection lay upon the waters. The natural beauties of the island, combined with a spoonful of port wine jelly, went far towards reviving Jennifer to a faint interest in the affairs of the world, and as day by day her loveliness was augmented by a sea-shell colour in her cheeks and a long succession of becoming bonnets, the sailors' admiration grew apace, and they strove constantly to excel each other in feats of strength and skill, which, if they did not at all attract her notice, at least caused a noticeable improvement in their manner of hauling upon ropes and holystoning decks.

On approaching the Cape of Good Hope, where the captain had given them all lively expectations of stopping, they were attended by so fair and favourable a breeze that this worthy man immediately informed them of the advisability of rounding the giant promontory as speedily as might be, very sensibly observing that a month gained in the passage to India was of far more importance than eating grapes at the Cape town. Putting into Johanna for a fresh supply of water and provisions, he was soon able to mitigate their disappointment by permitting them to enjoy a considerable purchase of the excellent pineapples, oranges and guavas of that luxuriant island.

Poultry and fish appeared again upon the table, transformed by Mohammed into the most savoury curries and kedgerees; a personal friend of Lord Clive's was the lucky possessor of a Caffree servant who had been taught to dress turtle in the West Indies, and who had cost his master upwards of fifty guineas in Jamaica; Gerald's cases of foreign wines and liqueurs, obtained at an Italian warehouse in the Haymarket during his last hurried hours in London, contributed much towards the general good-fellowship, and it needed only the very high stakes at hazard prevailing among the gentlemen to make Jennifer comfortably aware that her husband was well pleased with the conditions of the voyage. She was the only lady on board, and as such was the recipient of a prodigious quantity of oranges and guavas and an even more generous supply of compliments, carefully kept in check by Gerald, who spent almost every afternoon at her side reading aloud from the French philosophers, and insisted upon her retiring every evening at an early hour in order to preserve her health; a Supreme Councillor returning to Bengal once had the audacity to send a glass of champagne and a magnificent pineapple to her cabin, with his respectful queries as to her welfare; only this personage's obvious senility prevented Gerald from giving him a glance over the card-table which would have curdled his blood forever against the most torrid suns of India.

Upon another occasion a comely youth, going out to his initial service in the Madras army, happened to observe, through the open door of Mr. Poynyard's cabin, a tableau consisting of that gentleman, a beautiful fusee, and a pair of pistols of exquisite workmanship, which their owner was engaged in cleaning with the most meticulous attention; the youth had spent the greater part of the preceding night in pacing the deck and composing a poem, after the manner of a Greek ode, to celebrate the glad New Year and the remarkable beauty of Lady Jennifer Poynyard. It may have been merely the vivid imagination of one whose mind was already infused with poetic fancies, but the Cadet could have sworn that a sudden and terrifying look, swifter and more deadly than a basilisk's, darted from Gerald's steely eyes into the innocent blue of his own; he at once bethought him of his fond parents' farewell admonitions and the sage advice of his kind old friend the vicar, and reached the decision, after regaining the privacy of his favourite corner of the deck, that the poem was rather too impassioned in tone to render it a suitable offering to a married woman.

He ended by presenting Jennifer with the sewing-case which had been his mother's parting gift, and locking the ode away in the respectable privacy of his writing-desk, thus solving the whole matter in an eminently satisfactory way; the sewing-case had long been the subject of many unfilial maledictions, owing to the presence within its inoffensive cover of a number of painfully sharp pins and needles; the ode he often found invaluable during the course of his subsequent prolonged career as the handsomest subaltern in the Company's two armies.

If Gerald read *Candide* upon this particular voyage, he did not share his enjoyment of it with Jennifer; perhaps he thought that the pessimistic conclusions of that romance might produce a disheartening effect upon his wife's tender and malleable understanding. Nevertheless, it must not for an instant be supposed that Jennifer was excluded from her husband's intellectual interests; the Encyclopædists, if sometimes irrelevant to his personal tastes, could not fail to engage his active mind, which anything of a controversial nature invariably intrigued.

His wife always preferred Diderot to Voltaire, owing to the fact that the last volume of his great work, the one containing the plates and comprising a marvellous selection of steel-engravings of all the wonders of the universe, had but just reached them during their stay in Paris; this edifying and instructive book was her comfort and stay on many a long azure afternoon when Gerald denied her the relaxations of Mrs. Elizabeth Griffith and Mrs. Frances Brooke, whose novels he did not consider worthy of her attention even on a sea-voyage. The *Pensées Philosophiques* she could never sincerely enjoy; it seemed curious that it should require so much time for reading; Gerald himself had informed her that M. Diderot wrote it between the morning of Good Friday and the evening of Easter Monday, which appeared a short period for the putting together of so many words, if a somewhat rigorous and Lenten manner in which to pass the happy festival of Easter; the penance should have stopped by Saturday. The volume of plates, in her estimation, never ceased to be Diderot's supreme achievement.

They reached the mouth of the Bay of Bengal early in January; it being then too late in the season for them to venture upon the coast of Coromandel, having an admirable good run for seven days, and then making the land; the captain entered this in the log-book as the Island of Cheduba, but Gerald stated, with the most complete assurance, that it was more probably the mainland of Aracan. They cleared the coast, and stood to the westward for the purpose of making Point Palmiras. Gerald was proved to be, as usual, correct in his supposition; the captain's remark that it was a pity Mr. P. hadn't the job of navigating the vessel himself loses the force of sarcasm when it is taken into consideration that Gerald could almost undoubtedly have acquitted himself in a manner to make the assertion no more than simple truth.

At the end of another week a light breeze from the southwest carried them into Balasore Roads; they anchored off the Island of Sangor on the nineteenth of January, 1773. In London upon this very same day Junius was writing his farewell letter to Woodfall; in less than a year from that time Philip Francis was on his way to Bengal. At the identical moment of Gerald's arrival in that province the Governor of Bengal was in the act of dining, noon being the customary dinner hour in that part of the world; his good digestion and peace of mind were no more disturbed by the projected journey of Junius than by the proximity of his young friend Gerald.

The knowledge that he was upon the eve of becoming the first titular Governor-General of India, on the retirement of Mr. Cartier, was his first absorption at that instant; next in interest the plans for his country house at Alipur; lastly he was seriously considering the advisability of sending his secretary in search of his body servant and bidding the latter tell the cook to overcome the habit of mixing so large a quantity of turmeric, chilies, ginger, coriander, aniseed, black cummin and cardemon in the simple sauces he had expressly ordered for his curries; he was a man of plain taste and spare diet, and could never quite understand Gerald's minute attention to gastronomic affairs. He was no more gratified by the thought of friends than vexed by the suspicion of foes; such are the curiosities of history, of which this tale is too trivial in essence to render much account.

Gerald immediately engaged a paunceway, or Bengalese boat, to convey his small party to Calcutta; the novelty of this mode of travelling went far towards reconciling his young wife to the extreme discomfort of the trip; the motion was inconsiderable. On the evening of the second day the voyagers came within sight of that magnificent suburb known as Garden Reach; here numbers of gentlemen of the highest rank in the Company's service had erected luxurious villas for occupancy during the hot weather; a few of these houses were utilised by their owners the year round as a means of escaping the unhealthful airs of the city. Gerald could not forbear remarking somewhat censoriously upon the spread of pomp and splendour in the vicinity of Calcutta; his own palace, which enjoyed a noble prospect of Garden Reach in one direction, and of the recently-completed Fort William in the other, with the great town as a fitting background for the fortifications, was now slightly dwarfed by one or two of the newer residences of Justices and Councillors. He had, however, the satisfaction of knowing that in point of elegance and beauty his own excelled all the other mansions, in addition to commanding incomparably the most extended view of wide waters and verdurous landscape, so refreshing to the eye amid the burning climate of Bengal.

This miniature palace was originally, as has been stated, the property of a native merchant, a man of opulence and a friend of the celebrated Gocal Gosaul; Gerald was always inclined to give credence to the rumour that the plans for its construction had been supervised by a pupil of the mysterious M. Austin de Bordeaux of Agra; the story alone seemed to account for an extreme delicacy of design, contrasting strongly with the solid brick and masonry of the neighbouring buildings, which wore the tawdry detail of their stucco ornaments with an air of ostentation which could not blind the discerning glance to their innate vulgarity.

Jennifer was charmed by the exotic richness and exquisite purity of style and workmanship prevailing throughout her new home; the mosaics of *pietra dura,* the pierced complexities of snowy marble, filled her with childish appreciation and delight; she kissed Gerald at least twenty times before exhausting herself and her vocabulary in ecstatic survey of the fairy castle. The indigo hangings and silver arabesques of the principal drawing-

rooms especially pleased her; their subtle fragrance of sandal-
wood, aloes, musk, cassia, and sweet calamus, persisting among
the rich folds long after the brazen perfume-jars and incense
burners of their vanished mistress had been broken and cast into
the dust-bin, intoxicated her to a pitch of laughter almost impossible to one of her temperament; she fell asleep at last singing
Scottish melodies of an inconceivable sadness in a little voice by
no means devoid of merriment, to the vast disappointment of
Sallie, who was accustomed to brushing Jennifer's bright locks
every night while her kind lady read aloud, for the benefit of
both, from the fascinating pages of Samuel Richardson.

The girl found the romance of Clarissa so enthralling that
she not infrequently bedewed her mistress's glittering red-gold
curls with showers of tears of sincerest sympathy for the sorrows
of that lovely and unfortunate heroine. Upon this occasion, she
was forced instead to listen to a recital of Border Ballads, winding up with a very spirited version of Kinmont Willie and a
somewhat frivolous rendering of the Bonnie Earl of Moray; as a
native of Devonshire she declared before God that the words
were so much Dutch to her, while the un-Christian dolefulness
of the tunes reminded her of the Methodists. She drew the gauzy
azure curtains of Jennifer's gilded bed to the accompaniment of
a queer minor caroling.

"Werena my heart licht I wad dee!" sang Jennifer; Sallie
minced out of the room sniffing an atmosphere of heathen perfume and unholy music which set her refined Church of England teeth on edge.

"There was always a touch of Chapel about the Earl," she
reflected sagely, remembering the minister at Carterhaugh and
the porridge of a cold October morning. Lady Tam-Linn had
ever been her ideal of fine ladyhood; she was devotedly attached
to Jennifer, but she often pitied the strange little soul because she
wasn't pure Cleverly-Neville undiluted by that wild and lonely
blood of the Lorns.

Meanwhile Gerald, after surrounding himself with a sufficient
number of writing-desks, newly-mended pens, silver candlesticks,
bronze and crystal paper-weights, enamelled snuff-boxes, travel-

ling-clocks of tooled Italian leather and Swiss workmanship, and ancient and modern books in vellum and morocco, to cause him to feel comfortably at home in his sumptuous library, was engaged in composing a letter to the Governor of Bengal; it was a model of respectful modesty and masterly tact.

"I have selected him for success," he said inwardly, smiling a trifle at the perfect phrasing of his literary effort, in which he had contrived to combine the demure and graceful wit of the period with an ageless force of expression all his own. "He will climb far enough for me to take a flying spring from his shoulders which shall assure me of landing as high as a wise man should ever care to be above his fellows. I had rather, any day, take the chance of utilising a top-heavy genius for a ladder than seek a safe footing on the flaccid lumps of humanity who have lacked strength even to stand erect; my ladder may fall, but I shall feel it swaying, and, thanks to the athletic lightness of my frame and the activity of my senses, I shall save myself in time. Meanwhile, it is more profitable to the mind and soul of a gentleman to owe promotion to a genius than to accept favours from swine."

Having neatly folded this important letter, he sealed it with peculiar care, employing the best quality of sealing-wax and an amethyst signet-ring; he seldom had recourse to the common wafer, and his letters were always delivered by hand unless they must traverse great distances; in the latter case they were invariably franked by men of rank and great political and social distinction. Waking Mohammed, who was slumbering outside the door in the happy dream of a returned exile for whom the bazaars would be open on the morrow, Gerald gave him clear and concise instructions for the note's forwarding during the next forenoon, and after swallowing a mild chincono febrifuge as a precautionary measure, retired to a well-earned and invigorating rest.

"There at least is something accomplished," he told himself, as he snuffed the last candle. "It may be no more than a first step, but I feel infinitely relieved to know that it has been taken." It is quite possible that the sound of Jennifer's voice had penetrated to the library and made some unconscious impression on a mind occupied with affairs of state to the exclusion of all other interests; it is certain, at least, that he climbed into bed softly humming a minuet of Lulli's; his whole being was pervaded by a sense of quiet but enormous satisfaction.

A succession of large and formal dinners followed the arrival of the married pair among the scenes of Gerald's early triumphs; every one spoke of him as a coming man, and his allegiance to Hastings seemed never sufficiently well-defined to make the Governor's secret enemies feel safe in alienating him, he might prove useful after all, at a pinch; he had brains of a very uncommon sort, and in spite of his breeding it might not be wise to bank too confidently on his incorruptible character. His wife's beauty and his own distinction caused them to be much in demand as guests; his whole establishment was conducted upon a scale of a well-nigh fabulous splendour; his entertainments were extravagantly brilliant; dazzling lights, exquisite harmonies of flute and clarinet, choice viands and a variety of rarest wines turned a mere dinner-table into a vision of Paradise. He kept three handsome phaëtons and three pairs of beautiful carriage horses; his saddle-horses were of the noblest Arabian breed; the little equipage of fine wicker which he caused to be fashioned expressly for the purpose of affording the cream-coloured ponies a chance to draw Jennifer behind them in proper style was soon one of the sights of the evening's drive to the race-course; the fact that she was romantic enough to prefer a palanquin gave Calcutta less opportunity than it would have liked to observe her in her Parisian clothes with the blue silk reins between her little fingers; the scarlet whip she never saw the necessity of using, since the ponies were now quite old and completely reliable.

The fancy for the palanquin was of course utterly unreasonable, but Gerald with his customary generosity gave way to it; it was richly fitted out in every particular, and only the bearers' distressing habit of uttering groans of a profound and awful character caused Jennifer anything but the utmost pleasure in its use. Owing to her extreme fragility and slenderness she was totally at a loss to account for this practice until her husband informed her that such was the invariable way of palanquin bearers from time immemorial, and that had the conveyance been entirely empty they would have conducted themselves in precisely the same manner.

Among the Burra Sahibs of Calcutta Gerald was now incomparably the most magnificent in his mode of living; the reflection that as yet he held no other official position than his original one of Writer to the Company would now have appeared ludicrous had it been present in any mind but his own. For his part, he was well content to wait, winning the approbation of his chosen chief by a series of secret intrigues and manœuvres truly astonishing in their subtlety, and enjoying meanwhile the possession of the wife of his express selection and the manner of living which he was still young enough to consider amusing in spite of a clear realisation that it could not fail to weary him after the lapse of years.

In contrast to his sumptuous surroundings, and to the very delicate and fantastic beauty of his wife's apparel, Gerald now affected a dress of elegant severity; he wore his hair unpowdered, and his clothes were of so quiet a colour and so austere a cut that even Mohammed, remembering the Prophet's injunction, could hardly fail to approve. The valet was submerged in the Mussulman, and he took considerable pleasure in quoting to Sallie such proverbs as "It is lawful for woman to clothe herself in silken garments, but it is forbidden to man; any man who shall wear silk in this world shall not wear it in the next."

On another occasion, when his master insisted upon donning, for the sake of coolness, a pair of skillfully woven Lisle hose with embroidered clocks which he had purchased along with many other articles of the finest cotton and linen materials and the best grades of Nankeen in Blunt's Warehouse in the Haymarket, Mohammed had the satisfaction of silencing Sallie with the well-known saying, "God will not be merciful to him who through vanity wears silk stockings." A French valet would probably have sulked; among the faithful a deeper wisdom prevails, and to the good servant Mohammed Gerald never appeared to greater advantage than in the cold simplicity of his flaxen queue and the grey or fawnish cloth of his superbly-fitting coats and breeches, in decorous contrast to the prevailing tendency among the youthful members of society to cover themselves like marionettes or monkeys with a profusion of lace, spangles, and foil.

His refusal to smoke a hookah was another proof of his independence of mind among a group of rattling and flighty gentlemen to whom this habit, begun as a fashionable diversion, had soon assumed the importance of an indispensable necessity of existence. He seldom condescended to attend gatherings at the Harmonic Tavern and similar places of entertainment; his tastes in wine and music were almost captious in their perfection; his domestic life was always beyond reproach.

Jennifer also was bidden to remove the powder from her flame-coloured tresses; their revelation created a sensation in Calcutta and gave her a new interest in the innumerable frocks of white material, ranging in hue from pearl to thickest cream, with which Paris had provided her; she knew at once that the effect was far more striking with gold instead of silver locks; divergence rather than concord between costume and coiffure struck the high note which her simple vanity approved and her proud husband demanded.

Gerald was invariably correct in these little ideas, and had a well-nigh uncanny gift of discerning the latest mode before it was fully hatched; in this as in other and more important matters the thin egg-shell of the future was transparent to his pale and rapacious eye. Though it was utterly impossible that he could have informed himself as to the question until many months later, this was the precise date at which the united peruke makers of London were petitioning His Majesty the King to pass a statute whereby it should be unlawful for a man to wear his own hair; the trend of fashion was turning slowly but inevitably away from powder, pomatum and the six-tiered wig of the macaroni; it would soon be extremely *démodé* to be bald, and young ladies with an abundance of chestnut curls could presently have the joy of exhibiting these natural adornments almost anywhere except at Court.

Jennifer lived more than ever in a dream of lights and perfumes and unreal sounds; the routs and concerts of the evening were hardly more exotic and singular to her senses than the ordinary glare and noise and clatter of the Indian every-day running beside her palanquin as she passed. The air smelt like the chapel at Parthemont set in the walled garden at home upon the hottest day of summer; it stifled her shallow lungs, and she was rejoiced when the rough northwesters of March and April beat the flimsy verdure of Garden Reach into a tangle that matted the ground with green and fell in torn ribbons along her window sills.

The hot season she could never for an instant have supported; regarding all extremities of heat and cold with an equal repugnance, she had never scrupled to faint in church upon a sultry Sunday in August if the family's departure for Carterhaugh was postponed by any mischance; her habit of contracting a severe sore throat when the Scotch autumn stiffened into winter was too generally recognised among her relations to render it a measure to which she was often compelled to resort. It must not for a moment be supposed that she practised the slightest degree of dissimulation at these times; she simply utilised to its fullest extent the natural delicacy of her constitution and the affection which her appearance immediately wakened in all beholders to obtain certain attentions and privileges which she had neither the strength nor the courage to gain by bolder methods; her ethical right to these pathetic stratagems seems fairly well established.

Upon the advice of the celebrated Laird brothers, the foremost physicians in Calcutta, Gerald determined about the middle of April to allow his wife to accompany him upon one or two of the secret missions and amazing enterprises with the execution of which his leader continued to honour him. He was entirely whole-hearted in his devotion to the cause of Hastings; that great man, on the other hand, had the good sense to trust his associate and the good nature to give him a very free rein in certain matters more important to Gerald himself than to the Governor-General of India. No one knew better than the astute Mr. Poynyard that his chief's position was precarious; he knew to a day when the new Council proposed sailing, and he weighed the enmity of Francis against the allegiance of Barwell with his usual cool and cynical clarity of vision. When all was said and done, he felt convinced that, in the words of the Eastern poet, the enemies of the Governor-General might chance to find a tiger while beating the jungle for a deer. Nevertheless, he saw no reason to parade his considered and decided loyalty, such an exhibition were at once injudicious and in the highest degree vulgar; its omission left Hastings no less obliged and his adversaries the more hopelessly baffled.

He declined all promotion for the present; upon the Company's books he still figured as a mere Commercial Resident, but few Members of Council would have grumbled at changing places with him. Only the appalling number and dangerous nature of the diplomatic missions upon which he was sent prevented their admiring envy from becoming rancorous and unkind; he might be saving money for himself, but he was indisputably saving the skins of a number of worthy Anglo-Indians at the same time. These seasoned men of affairs were far too skilled in worldly matters to be unaware of this circumstance; the quality of his entertainments and the beauty of his wife completed the conquest of their better natures.

Whether Gerald had any hand in the transaction whereby the Nawab Wazir of Oudh became sole proprietor of that province at the small cost of contributing half a million sterling towards the expenses of that war which resulted in the massacre of Patna and Major Munro's efficient discouragement of the first Sepoy Mutiny is a matter for conjecture. These sanguinary events occurred before his earliest appearance in India; the dealings with the Wazir marked not only Gerald's own arrival in Calcutta, but also the beginning of Baron Clive of Plassey's second administration as Governor of Bengal.

Lord Clive has certainly received at the hands of History a larger share of praise and blame for the affair than was ever accorded Gerald, but it is impossible to tell into what royal peacock pies of diplomacy the latter's long forefinger was not gently introduced. It is probable that his extended and cordial friendship with the Wazir himself, certainly dating from '65, had its origin in some such kindly act on the part of Gerald; it was now a sincere pleasure to him to renew this friendship.

Scarcely less delightful was his frequently postponed visit to the court at Murshidad, where years before he had obtained the remarkable pearls now adorning Jennifer's gracile throat. Having persuaded the higher powers of the real necessity for this mission, he undoubtedly succeeded in changing the sentiments of the rajah from vexed and helpless discontent to lively gratitude and appreciation; he gave the monarch a much clearer notion, not only of the generosity of the British in allowing him a handsome sum in annual exchange for his power, but also of their genius as a military nation, and of the important advantages to be derived from cordial relations between native princes and English gentlemen. The unyielding yet tactful force of his arguments left the rajah pluming himself upon his wealth and his desirable allies instead of toying pettishly with dancing girls and dreams of revolt; Gerald went home with a magnificent ruby in his pocket.

Oddly enough, he felt its presence there rather an embarrassment than otherwise; he could not by any stretch of the imagination picture it adorning his own person; for Jennifer the colour was inconceivable and the size unsuited in the extreme. Conjured from æther and diaphanous fire as she so miraculously appeared, her flesh was too light a framework for the thick splendours of the majority of jewels; their tints of life and living things seemed carnal in direct comparison with the angelic amalgams of her body. Gerald understood this; the star sapphire which was to have been his wedding gift to her shone like a planetary sphere in its ivory box; invisibly suspended from her little neck its solidarity was like a bruise marring the superfine tissue of her skin. He accepted the disappointment with a philosophy that matched her own indifference; he turned the tiny key in the carven lock, and because it was a charming plaything in its own right, wore it on his watch chain for seven years, at the end of which time he found a use for the star-sapphire with which our narrative has no concern.

If a blue jewel was a bruise against Jennifer's flesh, an emerald was an asp, and a ruby a veritable death-blow. When Gerald adjured her to wear nothing less ethereal than air-clear diamond or inward-lighted pearl, she did not consider this command a severe deprivation; her twenty trinket-boxes were already overflowing with an abundance of such treasures, augmented daily by her husband's thoughtfulness and the admiring regard of almost every crowned head in India; it was said that the chief of the Rohillas himself sent a fair-skinned Caucasian free-booter into the streets of Garden Reach, with a flag of truce, a letter for Gerald written in a Hindustani cipher which he alone of living Englishmen could read, and for Jennifer a necklace of yellow diamonds fashioned in those golden days when Afghan princes ruled in the valleys of Rohilcund.

Though this strange embassy could not avert the subsequent slaughter of the brave Rohillas by Colonel Champion's brigade, it is certain that Gerald tried his best, when the question arose, to prevent this most unfortunate occurrence. He always encouraged Jennifer to wear the necklace; the curious colour of the diamonds matched the lightning flashes in her eyes.

As for the rajah's ruby, Gerald never found the woman to whom he could offer this noble gem; his æsthetic sense always held him back at the last minute because he felt sure that the result would be incongruous. At one time he cherished a vague notion of presenting it to Pauline Bonaparte; the shocking effects of the West Indian climate upon her health and the clarity of her smooth olive complexion made his non-pursuance of this plan a lifelong source of mental satisfaction.

At last, in his old age, he beheld the indubitable face gliding like a pensive Muse through the distressing confusion of the carnival at Venice; the brows, the smoothly-banded, burnished darkness of the hair, the very laurel wreath, proclaimed the exact Melpomene, drawn down to human sadness by a shabby black domino. The girl was obviously poor; the gift of the ruby would have assured her a permanent affluence, but Gerald realised that he would cheerfully support a husband and several young children or a brace of lovers rather than forego the pleasure of seeing the great stone hanging like a mortal drop of blood upon her breast. He followed her with the long dignified stride from which the years had ·purloined nothing but speed; in her quick step the goddess was revealed, and she left him far behind.

Had he been able to subdue his natural sense of importance to the level of a little hurry this pretty idyll might have had another ending; its true consummation was no more than an old man preserving a lovely girl's virtue and his own majestic vanity at one and the same moment. He went home, looking, among that noisy crew, like a captive Roman emperor in the hands of the barbarians; he felt curiously thwarted and weary. The happy ignorance in which the fair Venetian returned to her father's shop was never disturbed by the remotest suspicion of this equivocal aversion of Fortune's countenance from her humble and contented lot.

7

THE GRADUAL DUSKY VEIL

GERALD returned to Calcutta after the last of these interesting diplomatic enterprises so stimulated and amused by his adventures that he felt more than ever convinced of the benefit to his wife's health to be derived from a like pleasure trip in his company. Her medical men at first protested against the fatigue of such an undertaking, but Gerald honestly persuaded them, during the course of a simple dinner, of the advisability of his plan; his triumph must be attributed almost entirely to his eloquence and urbanity, for neither of the Lairds allowed himself more than the very moderate portion of whiskey necessary to render the drinking-water wholesome and agreeable.

" She shall have every luxury," Gerald assured them, " and what is harder come by in this infernal country, every comfort to boot. She shall have a dozen or more palanquin and a regiment of bearers; she shall have cool wines and dainty food and skillfully concocted febrifuges, wherein the taste of the chincona bark is concealed among a multiplicity of flavorous spices, and the saps of trees join with delicious fruit juices to relieve the thirst of mid-day. She shall have a tent to sleep in damasked with more fairy nightmares than filled the head of Scheherazade, and she shall ride one day on a great granite tower of elephant flesh and the next on a milk-white doe, according to her fancy and the exigencies of the weather."

James Laird cocked his eyebrows at this; he cut a careful slice of pineapple and looked interrogatively at John. John's nod was at once an affirmative reply to his brother's question and a complete agreement with Gerald's ideas.

"She will have, in addition to all these things, a devoted and attentive husband," he said with a low bow which suggested the courtier and seemed at variance with his grim Scots voice.

At this time, in spite of the somewhat apocryphal legends which in Europe clustered about Cagliosto's name, little or nothing was known of the mesmeric art; an intelligent observer might have deduced many valuable facts as to the useful and practical nature of this science from the words and actions of the two distinguished brothers during the remainder of the afternoon and evening; Gerald's fee was generosity itself, but they both felt that their host's warm heart and delightful manners were better than many golden guineas.

The next morning Gerald himself drew the blue curtains of his wife's couch with one hand, while with the other he carefully deposited her breakfast-tray upon the little knees drawn up under the thin linen sheets for its reception.

"Do me the favour to eat your *chota hazri* for once, my dear child; as it includes nothing but a cup of tea and a mangosteen the task should not be too cruel; even a sprite should subsist with pleasure upon infusions of flowers and rosy-ripe apples of Eden. . . . And now, I have some excellent good news for you; we are to leave this dull and malarial spot to-morrow for the express purpose of visiting your relatives at Delhi."

Jennifer was totally at a loss to understand him; she blinked sleepily at the close-shaven lines about his lips and saw that he was smiling amiably down upon her from his commanding height; he appeared very proud and handsome in his pale-grey coat.

She felt a sudden access of anxiety, accompanied by a vivid but incorrect premonition that a fleet of East Indiamen had arrived at the entirely problematical Port of Delhi with scores of her most unsympathetic aunts and cousins turning the decks into *parterres* of parasols and Sunday bonnets, set in a formal pattern. The thought troubled her; she was convinced that Gerald could not possibly tolerate her kinsfolk; many of the Lorns were opinionated without being witty, while all the Cleverlys were silly without being silent.

She stared at her husband in alarm; her golden-hazel eyes were black with apprehension; she seemed a newly-wakened Naiad with the deep-sea light of her darkened room falling about her from the bluish green jalousies at the windows and the indigo curtains above her head.

"Explain, Gerald, please explain; I am afraid you are teasing me," she murmured feebly, sipping her tea with a shivery sense of comfort in its heat and fragrance. Gerald noticed the minute convulsion of her shoulders under the lace and lawn of her night-gown; in a moment he was all gallant anxiety and solicitude.

"Ah, I was determined upon a change of air for you; I knew that you could not long survive this climate even under the most favourable conditions; thank God we have acted in time; you are upon the point of contracting a fever, you are at this very instant the victim of a slight chill. A morsel of this preparation of chincona will cure you at once; a spoonful of ginger conserve will immediately remove the taste of the medicine. Nevertheless, such simple remedies cannot long hope to preserve life in one of your transcendentalised substance; you must not be subjected to the pestilential miasmas of Calcutta during the coming season. We leave at dawn to-morrow; I am engaged to dine with three Members of Council; I have invited a few of our close friends to assemble here for tea and coffee and more convivial farewells at seven this evening; I affectionately direct you to wear your pearls and your silver tamboured gauze and to look your loveliest for me; the music and dancing will not commence before eleven, so no fatigue beyond quietly agreeable conversation is incumbent upon you; the requisite beauty you achieve without effort. Take only chicken broth for dinner, with a little rice; I deeply regret the necessity of your dining alone, but the rest will do you good; be sure to drink a glass of champagne and to follow it *instantly* with another of these pellets."

He stooped swiftly and kissed her; the next minute his grey coat-tails had whisked into the hot sunlight of the small ante-room where Sallie sat mending one of her mistress's silk mantles;

his few words were sufficient to send the girl into hysterics and then out of them again into awed silence.

"Sallie," said Jennifer humbly, "if you will only be quiet and not cry I will give you my turquoise locket; I had a little rather that you did not pray either, aloud; I think it might be a very good thing for both of us if we prayed in our souls. Ask Mohammed to help you with the boxes; your master will not be home before six o'clock; Mohammed is a good kind creature, and you must overcome your dislike for his complexion, which is surely no more than a healthy coat of tan. I feel absolutely certain that he would defend us faithfully and with his life against any dangers which might attend our journey. Pray give me the books on my dressing-table, and raise the blind perhaps three inches. Thank you; I shall not need you again this morning."

"Oh, my dear Miss Jenny — I should say Madam, as more respectful — but is it tigers or savages that you have in mind?" cried the unhappy girl, wringing her hands while her voice again ascended in an increasing wail to heaven.

Jennifer held out her breakfast tray with a gesture of appeal; this occupied the wildly fluttering pink hands which were causing her such inward disquiet; her next words sent an increased colour into Sallie's plump cheeks, from which fear had removed the Devonshire roses, leaving a strange skim-milkiness in their stead.

"My girl," said Jennifer in a very small voice, but with profound dignity, made the more striking by the fact that she lay helplessly recumbent in a royal bed several sizes too large for her narrow limbs and the sorrowful ivory oval of her face, " my good girl, I am forced to speak with a severity which distresses me; you must positively manage to control yourself at once; hysteria can serve no useful purpose in the terrible situation in which we find ourselves at this moment. Prayer — silent prayer, you understand — I strongly recommend; industry never comes amiss to a disturbed spirit. You must pack the boxes directly; if you feel the absolute necessity of crying I must beg you to go down into the kitchen; I forbid you to scream within the limits of the garden. I am sorry to issue such rigorous commands, but I must at all costs compose myself; it is my first duty to my husband. Oh, my dear Sallie, I am indeed heartbroken to have to scold you; I have never before spoken to you so sternly; these are hard words, I am aware."

She lifted her large eyes to ascertain for herself the effect that such unwonted harshness had produced; they were swimming in tears that spilled over and hung like diamond pear-drops among her curls. Sallie's round blue eyes were also wet; she fell down on her knees beside her mistress's bed, moving silently and with great gentleness for all her impetuous and lively strength of body. She took Jennifer in her arms and kissed her; her soft West country voice was another caress. "I'll do as you say, ma'am; I'll be good," she said with the docility of an affectionate child.

"We must strive for unshaken fortitude under misfortune . . ." Jennifer began bravely, and then subsided into quiet despair against Sallie's pink calico bosom. They clung together like sisters, and now the stronger one consoled the weaker.

"I'll take care of you, Miss Jenny; never fear; it's cruel to carry a poor lamb like you into this Babylonian wilderness, but I shan't let a single savage and ravening beast come nigh you; no, not if I have to fight them like the Christian martyrs in the pictures, and they in their night-gowns with their hair down their backs being suddenly aroused, I dare say, by their cruel persecutors, which by their faces I should judge to be foreigners and natives. But, oh, please leave off saying those dreadful long words, just like the master, which always make my blood run cold and will wear you to a frazzle speaking them with a tiny little mouth such as yours which was never meant for anything sourer than strawberries and pretty songs and other sweet things which perhaps I shouldn't mention. Now cry if you've a mind to, and a nice clean apron's better any day than a lace pocket handkerchief, so here's mine, still smelling lovely of the lavender which Mrs. Mattock gave me the day I left home all sewed up in beautiful cheesecloth bags as neat as neat."

If Sallie's spirited harangue was somewhat lacking in tact, the missing quality was amply atoned for by the exceeding kindness of her words; Jennifer kissed her with a gratitude which might have been considered unbecoming, in the eyes of the conventional observer, in one of her superior station; luckily the two girls were alone save for the presence of a small flame-coloured macaw in a silver cage; his judgment of their conduct was presumably lenient, as he was deeply attached to them both, and would perch upon the shoulder of either, eating sugar from her lips without a thought of the difference in social position between the mistress and the maid. If he indulged a preference it was for Sallie, since she possessed a more immediate access to the store-room and pantry than Gerald's domestic theories ever accorded his wife; Jennifer, nevertheless, still occupied a high place in the affections of this charming and sagacious bird; he would sit for hours upon the gilded eminence of her chair-back, while she sang, to the accompaniment of her spinet, the delicious strains of Corelli and other famous composers.

The two girls drew apart; Jennifer dried her eyes delicately upon the starched frill of Sallie's apron; Sallie used the back of her hand for the same purpose. She picked up the little lacquered breakfast tray, which she had deposited in a somewhat precarious position on the dressing-table, and prepared to leave the room. Her eyes were red; an embarrassed smile made a dimple at the corner of her mouth. She bent down again, quickly, to smooth her mistress's tangled locks; these lay scattered over the tossed pillows of the bed, in a curiously detached and careless brilliance; framing the pathetic triangle of her face almost as the quiet countenance of death is crowned incongruously with bright and living hair.

" An orange now, or a little slice of melon? " asked Sallie in a wheedling tone.

" No, thank you, you excellent and devoted creature," replied Jennifer. "May I have my books, if you please? There is my prayer-book on top; it is that which I especially wish to read. And now my mirror, and the smaller flask of Cologne water; that will be all. You are a very good girl."

" If you would like me to brush your hair, ma'am — " began the faithful servant, but Jennifer squeezed her hand gratefully and pushed her from the bed with a gentle but determined obstinacy.

" No, my dear Sallie; the books at once, if you love me; and do you go and pack the boxes, taking care not to tire yourself; I shall dine in my room at twelve; you need not prepare my bath before eleven; that will give you two good working hours in the coolest part of the day."

Jennifer lay back upon embroidered linen, straightening the scalloped border of the sheet on either side; she sniffed at the Cologne water and examined herself with sympathetic interest in the quicksilver depths of the mirror; she looked pale and fatigued, but admirably calm. Next she opened the fat prayer-book, which had been her grandmother's; the robin's-egg blue of its cover had faded to aquamarine, its aureate cross was but an indentation flaked with gold-leaf. The yellow pages clung together; even the tapering finger-tips of this fairy child had trouble in disengaging their gilt edges.

"And dost subdue the raging of the sea . . ." Ah, no; that was all wrong; that was for the Bay of Biscay; she ruffled the leaves impatiently. "From lightning and tempest . . ." That would include thunder-storms, of course; that was better. "All who travel by land and by water." That was what she wanted. "From plague, pestilence, and famine; from battle, murder, and from sudden death."

The words rang ominously in her ears; they were not by any means wholly reassuring, but they appeared appropriate. "All prisoners and captives . . . and young children." It had said young children; a woman of seventeen was not a child. . . . "Now lettest Thou Thy servant depart in peace, according to Thy word. . . ." In peace; in darkness; in the shadow of death. "And to guide our feet into the way of peace." Peace was a beautiful thing.

She let the prayer-book fall upon the floor, and lacked the energy to pick it up again. It was too sad; sadder than Clarissa Harlowe.

The next volume which came to her hand contained the works of the poet Collins; Gerald had recommended the Persian Eclogues to her attention.

"You should read Petis de la Croix's translation of the 'Zafarnama,' if you are sincerely interested in the home of your ancestors," he had informed her gravely. "It is rendered into very

pure and graceful French, and should constitute no strain whatever upon your understanding, my love; if, however, you feel
inclined to begin with something lighter, I should suggest these
Persian pastorals of Collins; they are not of course either in-
formative or correct, but they convey to the mental palate a slight
flavour of Eastern poetry in a diluted form which may appeal
to your taste; at least you will derive no harm from their perusal."
She looked at them now in languid appraisal of their length;
she did not feel inclined, since coming to Calcutta, to pursue any
amusement except sleep for more than ten minutes at a time.
She dropped the book; it fell open in another place, where a
marker had lain for years.

As a matter of fact, the bit of mauve silk ribbon had belonged to Lady Camphile; she had once owned a shady hat
trimmed with long violet streamers, one of which she had
snipped off with her garden shears to mark a certain poem in a
book which her young son's tutor had but lately brought down
from London; the incident occurred shortly before her death,
which calamity seemed to distress the quiet middle-aged bachelor
so keenly that he actually resigned his position the following
spring and departed for Philadelphia, where he joined the
Quaker sect and taught school for many uneventful years. He
did not, however, survive the excitement of the American
Revolution.

Jennifer tossed the ribbon to one side, and fixed her attention
upon the leaf which it had marked; the compact form of the
poem and the assurance that it occupied no more than two
printed pages encouraged her to read further. " Ode to Evening "; it was a pleasant title.

She repeated it to herself with exquisite precision, shaping
the syllables with her lips as she sighed them forth in a single
expulsion of breath. In spite of the peacock-blue jalousies the
room was inordinately hot; a variety of exotic flowers dangled
their bells or spread their cups to fill the air with fragrance;
the floor was striped along its entire length by thin white lines
of an excessive brightness from the murderous dazzle of the
sun without. The bird drooped in his cage; below their bubble
of engraved glass the gold-fish seemed expiring; the very jungle-

born plants appeared to faint, rising to fall again like fountains of warm green water; the smooth forms of the jars which contained them, hammered from that flaxen-blonde bell-metal of Murshidabad which has more silver than brass in its composition, illumined the darkness like lanterns of primrose-coloured silk, candle-lit within.

Jennifer flung the heavy fleece of hair away from her shoulders and began to read, saying the words aloud but very low:

> " Or upland fallows grey
> Reflect its last cool gleam . . .
> And hamlets brown, and dim-discovered spires,
> And hears their simple bell, and marks o'er all
> Thy dewy fingers draw
> The gradual dusky veil."

" The gradual dusky veil." Her eyelids closed; her whisper was an evocation.

Through the transparent tissue of her eyelids the darkness was tinted with red; in Calcutta a thousand temple bells were ringing with tongues that had no silver at all in their composition; in Devonshire the Lent lilies were over.

She did not sleep, nor could she call to mind with any degree of conviction the wet April woods at Cleverly-Neville. If she evoked any memory, it did not belong in her own life. To a superstitious person it might be a matter not entirely lacking in elements of awe to know that she perceived quite plainly the picture of a grey-haired lady with a book in her hand who sat upon a stone garden bench and gazed with pensive eyes over a wide prospect of purple downs; in the twilight between sunset and moonrise; she wore Gerald's amethyst signet-ring upon her middle finger. The landscape was too young for April; the misty beech trees belonged to a backward March or a mild soft February without frost; it was a very tranquil evening.

> " Now teach me, maid composed,
> To breathe some softened strain."

The poem was, after all, a form of prayer; Jennifer certainly derived great benefit from its recitation. She lay still as a mouse until eleven o'clock, when Sallie knocked guardedly upon the door and announced her mistress's bath as ready and waiting; in its shallow receptacle of the best Cornish tin the water looked clear and inviting; it was scented with the expressed essence of the yellow jasmine, and either Mohammed or Sallie had thoughtfully sprinkled it with a handful of yellow rose-leaves and sprigs of verbena; an exhaustive search of the little chamber failed to reveal the presence of a single cobra or scorpion. Nevertheless, as Jennifer stepped through the crystal surface of the bath she felt cruelly disappointed; it was warm as new milk or human blood, and she had wished it to be colder than the moonlit air of a winter night at home.

8

THE TOMB OF JAHANARA

THE EVENING was deathly still; after the heat of the day, a certain clammy mist enveloped the garden, which suffocated the lungs and touched the flesh with a perfidious moisture; Jennifer wandered from the crowded drawing-rooms into this sinister fog; her gauzy dress hung limp as the wet leaves around her; the ringlets above her brow were curled like the tendrils of dishevelled vines. From some obscure spot where the servants waited drifted the scent of Indian tobacco, impregnated with melted sugar and rose-water and with the heavier odour of narcotics, smelling of eternal sleep.

Within the house the talk and laughter drowned the music; single notes were borne to her upon the flood of grosser sound like little flowers on a muddy stream. She had been dancing steadily for three hours; she dropped suddenly, like an escaping creature struck with a lethal shaft, upon the vague white coping of a lily-pond; before her eyes the stagnant water spread a mirror of black glass; a ray of light from the house flawed it from side to side.

Her next door neighbour had a Hindu gardener, a young Bengali with enormous earrings and pointed nails, thin, agile, pretty as a marmoset is pretty; though no more than fourteen years old his eyes were always drowsy with opium. To him she had sometimes talked, as he clipped his mistress's side of the hedge and she pricked her fingers plucking sprigs from her own in the freshness of early morning; she had a great curiosity as to his religious convictions, and the delicate hauteur of his demeanour conformed to her theories of good breeding; she found Mohammed's scorn of the boy quite inexplicable, in which opinion Sallie concurred; Gerald was never consulted upon the subject, and remained always in complete ignorance of the youthful Brahmin's existence. She thought of the strange gods whom this child worshipped; in her mind the name of Shiva repeated itself like an incantation.

Out of Mohammed's outraged wrath and horror, out of Sallie's tittering reports of the same, a vast equivocal figure had lifted its head to stare blindly into her face; now it confronted her in the dark looking-glass of the lily-pond. Shiva the terrible, the adored; Shiva the saint of solitude, of murder, and of suicide; Shiva who had married two wives, whose names were Idleness and Death.

"Shiva the Terrible!" It is probable that she spoke the words aloud; they were immediately answered.

"May I inquire, madame, why you, who are so obviously one of the little lambs of the good God, should address yourself to this pagan and repulsive deity?"

She raised her eyes; she seemed to rise slowly and painfully from mysterious and dreadful profundities, like a diver who has dived too far and feels the weight of water obstinate to subdue his head. The acrid perfume of a very strong cheroot filled her nostrils; she saw its burning end like a vermilion planet that dappled the fog with light, and faintly illuminated the face of the man who held it; she marked clearly the veined and corded hand which prepared to cast it into extinction.

"Oh, please do not throw your cheroot away, my dear sir," she said quickly. "I like it; it makes a little star in the darkness."

"I retain it then, with your kind permission, madame, the more gladly because the wicked insects do not love it overmuch," replied the gentleman with a strong French accent; he bowed low, and then straightened to a prodigious height against the mist; save for a decided stoop, he might easily have out-topped Gerald himself; his thinness amounted to emaciation.

Jennifer could see him more clearly now; his features were well cut along lines of aristocratic distinction, but the tight-drawn skin over his hollow temples and high cheek-bones was dark and dry as old leather; his nose, if inferior in point of size to Gerald's, surpassed it in the extreme slenderness of its aquiline form; its bridge was hardly broader than the curved edge of a knife, and seemed to threaten its parchment covering. His hair was pure silver-grey, neither snow nor pepper and salt, but burnished to the authentic brightness of a new shilling. He wore extremely short, close-clipped whiskers, which fairly glittered against his lean brown cheeks. Under his prominent eyebrows his coffee-brown eyes glittered too; they were singularly brilliant in their deep bony setting; his closed and colourless mouth was almost invisible, but when he smiled his face was scored with laughing wrinkles; his teeth were very white. His expression was at once sad, chivalrous, and amused; his voice was vivacious; Jennifer loved him on the instant.

"My dear child and honoured hostess," he continued, "I cannot allow you to lie upon this damp and contaminated marble; every breath you draw of this miasmic air is potent to destroy. Permit me to assist you to rise; that is better, if you will accept my arm for a moment it may be better still. As I bowed over your hand this evening I noticed that it was hot; it is now quite cold; this is not well. You do not remember me; my name is Saint Amond; I am by nationality French, by profession a soldier; my little star is Mars."

His teeth flashed in a smile as he tightened them upon his cheroot for a single pull; Jennifer admired the way he held it away from him, his fingers fastidiously bent like the claws of a proud bird.

He had drawn her to her feet; she leaned against him and listened; the face of Shiva had receded, but the outer fringes of the night were still full of menace, and she did not care to speak.

"I am at the present moment the guest of my kind friend.

M. Chevillard at Ghyretty House; he as you know is the Governor of our province of Pondicherry. It is a pleasant country spot, not five miles from Chandernagore; to an exile like myself it is almost a bit of France mercifully transplanted to build an oasis in the desert. My month's leave will be over to-morrow; I walked in this garden to struggle against despair, perhaps to hope for a blessed visitation of cholera or typhus. I was very wicked; I am a Christian, and as such I do not importune Shiva; are you not also a Christian, madame? You have the face of a young martyr who must perish at the first turn of the thumbscrew; you would be safer in a shrine, I think, than in this execrable place. I have watched your countenance to-night, and I do not like to see the little lambs of God so sorrowful. For me, it is sufficiently fitting; I have deserved it; my folly has demanded it; sorrow is my meat and drink. For you it is as poisonous as that thick and fatal water at your feet; flee from it, madame, before it is too late." He was still smiling, but his voice was urgent and incisive.

"To-morrow you go to Delhi!" he cried in a higher key, his accent becoming more marked as his excitement increased. "Do you at all realise what that means, in this country, at this season? The doctors are mad; your husband is a dangerous lunatic. Your pardon, madame, for the speech's impoliteness; its truth is evident. Your friends are perhaps guilty of no more than criminal negligence; from your parents you are sundered by immense distances. It remains for me, madame, a stranger, old enough to be your father, gentle enough to be your confessor, to rescue you from this insanity. Return with me to Pondicherry to-night; my kind friend Chevillard will receive you with all due honour; his wife will assume a mother's rôle until we have taken steps to convey you to England in health and safety. You trust me; your eyes tell me as much; will you not come?"

Jennifer shook her head voicelessly; she was without hope. Her curls fell forward over her bended brow and swung back and forth like little bronze bells, silent with doom. The Frenchman sighed profoundly; he was too wise to entertain any doubts of the finality of her decision; her very lethargy was more unconquerable than the most determined combativeness.

"If it is not to be the shrine, it must then be the other thing," he muttered to himself, knowing that she was not listening; he saw her stretched upon the rack, but his dry and sunken eyes refused to yield a tear to the atrocious spectacle; he was perhaps too great a fatalist to be wholly a Christian; he read too much Seneca, and his heart was broken.

"*Adieu, madame,*" he said sadly, taking her hand very softly between his harsh and roughened palms. "I wish you better fortune; it may be that a worthier one than myself will be sent to rescue you. I have been a soldier of France, I have sometimes fought well, but always my impetuosity has been my undoing; it has brought undeserved disgrace upon an honoured name. I am happy only in possessing loyal friends; I must assuredly die an exile. Doubtless I have many weary years to survive; you will not believe it, my child, but I am only forty-six; every fever in India has burned me in its fire, and yet I was not consumed; the snakes have splintered their fangs against my hide to small purpose; I am, I grieve to say, invulnerable. I am an officer of cavalry; I have the singular misfortune to be military instructor at the court of Hyder Ali. The success of the young Tippoo Sahib in the invasion of the Carnatic was largely due to my teaching; I have made him a clever leader of horse, but I cannot change his reprehensible character, in which, as in Nero's, levity and the most savage lust for blood are monstrously combined. God help the next victims of his rapacious cruelty, and forgive me my sin in having trained it to effective use. Adieu, madame, once more; I wish you a nobler rescuer than my poor self." He loosed her hand and prepared to depart; until this moment Jennifer had not spoken a single word.

With a swiftness truly amazing to him, who had felt the lax droop of her shoulder against his arm during the whole of his monologue, she caught him round the neck, standing on tiptoe and clinging to him with the feeble force of her desperation. Her gauzy draperies tore upon the gilt buttons of his uniform; her hair was a wet tangle under his chin. He was too tall; she dropped her arms and raised them again to bury her face in her hands.

"I cannot go with you; I cannot possibly go with you," she said. "But in the name of heaven I entreat you to stay with me; do not leave me; I cannot bear you to leave me. You are kind; you are apparently very wise; I am sure you will not leave me. You are the first person whom I have seen since quitting Devonshire who was in the least like my father; you have a nose like my father's; you are tall; your hands are brown like his; you are very kind. Would you not by any chance accompany us on our journey? I should feel so much safer in your presence; oh, sir, I do with all my heart entreat you not to leave me alone! "

The unhappy man begged her to come with him instead; he would have carried her away in his arms but for the proximity of the house and the certainty of detection. But her cowardice was like adamant; she would not go, though he asked her on his knees. Finally he left her; he was distraught, and contracted a severe fever in consequence of the night's adventure, a fever which he survived for twenty exiled years. Jennifer never forgot him; she soon, however, lost the memory of his tortured face, and retained only the recollection of the pressure of his kind and withered hands upon her hands.

It is quite useless to attempt an adequate description of the amazing journey to Delhi; its splendours, dangerous escapes and incredible adventures are best left to the imagination of the reader. Jennifer preferred the motion of her luxurious palanquin to the swaying insecurity which might have purchased her the superior position occupied by her husband upon the back of an elephant; she never forgot the astonishing spectacle of Gerald, straight as a lance and stiff as a poker, accommodating himself in some uncanny fashion to the swinging pace of the monstrous animal; his face remained as immobile as a carven Buddha beneath the green umbrella which he habitually carried. In the hands of any other man this article would beyond peradventure of a doubt have appeared ludicrous in the extreme; Gerald, with his air of an ambiguous god demanding silent tribute from an unmannerly universe which he had just succeeded in taming, made the umbrella as awful as a sceptre and as ornamental as a lotus-flower. He disdained to carry an ankus; if a bearer prodded the hinder parts of the great beast now and then, it was not in Gerald's elevated province to be aware of the circumstance.

Enveloped in a fawn-coloured cloak of heavy Chinese silk, with his pale face burned by the sun to the exact shade of a delicately toasted biscuit, and his yellow hair bleached by the same powerful agency to approximately a like tint, he was a curious and commanding figure, the incarnation of some ivory idol of remote antiquity. His simple dignity far transcended that of any mere modern image of an eastern deity; the gates of Lhassa would assuredly have fallen before his majestic and inexpressive countenance.

Save for the green umbrella, he condescended to no covering for his erect and narrow head; the natives regarded him with increased respect and fear after the passage of the first noontide over him without the faintest sign upon his part that his brains were boiling in his skull preparatory to death by sunstroke; when he failed to topple from his lofty station in the manner which they had so confidently expected their reliance upon their own judgment was naturally shaken, while their belief in his superhuman qualities was as inevitably augmented.

To relate the history of Jennifer's private experiences upon this pilgrimage would of necessity entail so long a list of fears, tears, fainting fits, smelling-salts, cambric handkerchiefs steeped in lavender water, sleeping potions and chincona pills that the interest in such a tale of suffering would infallibly flag; suffice it to say that she survived to behold the great wall of Delhi rise at last against the seemingly interminable turquoise distance. It is probable that Sallie was largely instrumental in saving her mistress's life by her unremitting attentions and her great skill in concocting cooling beverages from fruits according to the directions furnished her by Mohammed; she had a much lighter hand than the manservant, attributable perhaps to her experiences as a still-room maid upon her first introduction into the household at Cleverly-Neville at the age of twelve.

Gerald did all that lay in his power to mitigate the horrors of the journey; he always insisted that champagne was more refreshing than sal volatile, and had the good fortune to be able to present Jennifer with that strange and sumptuous curiosity, the skin of the rare black and white Bengal tiger, a superb specimen of which wonders he shot early one morning in a jungle so profoundly sunk in green depths of vegetation as to render it far darker than a starry midnight in open country. Jennifer, hearing the shots and assuming at once that they portended dangers, buried her eyes in the pillows and refused to move during the entire day, which she spent in a state of comparative insensibility; by evening, however, she was sufficiently recovered to be induced to listen to Gerald's stirring account of the whole affair, which he followed by an enthusiastic dissertation relative to his wife's imagined loveliness at some future time when the tiger-skin should be properly cured and mounted and Jennifer suitably arranged upon its surface in a pose and costume worthy the pied magnificence of their couch.

At a much later date this spoil of victory certainly formed a prodigiously fine floor-covering for the small music room which its owner constructed for its especial reception; a piano of polished ebony, totally without decoration, a few ebony chairs, and several exquisite examples of black and white Wedgwood completed the furnishings of this fantastic apartment. The room was circular in shape and attained no little celebrity in the London of the Regency under the title of Camphile's Magpie Chamber.

As the travellers passed through the parched and arid suburbs of Delhi, Jennifer perceived in the distance a noble building of rose-coloured sandstone inlaid with white marble; it stood in a terraced garden, the whole surrounded by an embattled wall, with watch-towers and four defensible gates. Farther away, crimson against the azure sky of waning afternoon, a monumental column out-topped all visible erections; its gigantic plinth was a polygon of twenty sides.

Jennifer's words were smothered in her mouth; the heat was intense, but her awe at beholding these stupendous sepulchres and towers was largely responsible for her inability to breathe. Gerald had dismounted and walked beside her, holding her hand; Mohammed carried the green umbrella. Her husband's long fingers were firm and slightly chilly around the limpness of her own; his amethyst signet shone cool as a grape frosted with autumnal bloom.

" These, my child, are the graves of your deceased relatives," he said, bowing politely in the general direction of the huge buildings. " That roseate fortress is none other than the tomb of Hamayun, second of the Mogul dynasty." His forensic manner was perfect; of the gravity of his secret mind she could not feel so certain.

"I confess I fail to comprehend you, Gerald," she said with a feeble peevishness, rendered forgivable by the fact that the heat was undoubtedly very enervating. " I do not consider it fair to tease me when I am so exceedingly tired. I have never under-stood in the least your motive in saying that I have relatives in these wild places; would to God that the thing were true! " And she began to cry in contemplating the vast comfort which might imaginably have been derived from the presence of a great-uncle or an acidulous aunt within those looming walls; she would have kissed her most scornful Lorn cousin with rapture.

Gerald, pacing noiselessly through the thick red dust of the road, appeared to ruminate before replying.

"Have you forgotten your descent from the great Tambur-laine? " he inquired with surprise. " I cannot credit such a lapse of memory upon your part; I myself can only claim a drop of bastard William's blood, yet in my youth I stood upon the battle-ments of Falaise with my very heart in my throat and my eyes so dazzled that I could not see the spring fields of Normandy spread below me like a flowered petticoat left to dry on the river bank by my fair ancestress when love called her up the steep and winding stair to bed with her overlord; my Plantagenet strain is rendered questionable by the confusion of the Crusades, yet think you that I scaled the crumbling sides of Château Gail-lard and mounted breathlessly to its summit without a fierce and passionate pride in Richard of the Lion Heart tearing at my breast-bone? To be sure, I was no more than nineteen at the time; ten years have taught me a sterner and more controlled deportment; nevertheless I believe that if at this moment I were passing, as you are passing, into the ancient city conquered in 1398 by my honoured forebear Tamburlaine the Tartar, I should be much tempted to fall on my knees and kiss the reverend ground, at once hallowed and made bloody by his victories. But enough of sentiment; he was no kin of mine, and for you I fear the exertion might prove fatiguing."

With which considerate words he ended his oratory, and stroked her hand reassuringly while mopping his brow with a white silk handkerchief, a precaution which appeared quite unnecessary owing to the amazing circumstance of his face having retained, during the whole of this eloquent speech, the calm detachment and pallor of a fine slice of cold chicken.

"I should be most happy to do as you suggest," his wife replied in a very shaky voice, "were I not convinced that there are snakes in the dust."

"Quite possibly there are, my love," said Gerald kindly. "The karait, famed as the deadliest snake in India, inhabits just such dust as is now so unfortunately furring my boots; the heel must be well shod which is to be set upon that fellow's head, I assure you. Yet he is no bigger than a pretty green garter snake which would scarcely succeed in frightening an English lady planting lilies of the valley in the shade. Life is obscure; the event is inexplicable always to the asking mind."

He stooped and deliberately rummaged in the dust at his feet, as if searching for the squirming threads of death it might contain; then he straightened himself, smiling a little, and carefully wiped his thin fingers on the handkerchief; against the bright silver sheen of the new silk the marks of his finger-tips were red.

At this period Shah Alam had reigned in Delhi for perhaps two years; his rule was a mere pretence on the part of the Mahrattas; the true power lay in the hands of their leader, Sindhia. The Shah was permitted to retain to a certain degree the state and circumstance suitable to his exalted name; Gerald made sure of being royally entertained at the court, and indulged no doubt of his own ability to soothe the sentiments of the Shah in the little matter of Kora and Allahabad, which Hastings had somewhat high-handedly transferred to the Vizier of Oudh over the head of Clive's contrary transaction with the Mogul prince. He was not disappointed; the monarch fell upon his neck with protestations of undying friendship, and though his brow darkened at the mention of Hastings' name, it was wiped smooth again by the first of Gerald's quiet compliments, coincident in point of time with that masterly player's third move in a game of chess which the two were indulging in after the evening meal; it was an amazingly clumsy blunder, and Alam beat him with ease.

Jennifer slept for a week, waking only to partake of delicacies conveyed to her with the respectful homage of the Shah; Gerald experienced no ill effects whatever from his protracted travels. At the end of that time his wife arose, greatly refreshed by the savoury and cooling remedies of the Shah's *cuisine*. Attired in white, and veiled almost like a bride in frail Italian laces against the heat of the declining sun, she accompanied her husband and their royal host upon a complete tour of the palace of Shah Jehan; the Hall of Public Audience pleased her with its golden dome and engrailed arches, but the Hall of Private Audience amazed her almost to tears, and she declared, to the Shah's secret amusement and Gerald's even more secret annoyance, that she would very willingly spend her entire life within its confines, if she might have all the sherbets and candied limes that she wished and a stringed orchestra to play Scotch ballads and Italian opera when she was melancholy.

Forthwith she began to sing Miss Elliot's beautiful Lament for Flodden; it is probable that no stranger vision was ever devised by destiny than that of Jennifer Lorn standing in the exact centre of the miraculous pavilion of white marble and lifting her mournful little voice to cry, "I've heard them liltin' at our ewe-milkin' . . . The flowers of the forest are all wede away."

Around her upon every hand were flowers innumerable of serpentine, lapis lazuli, and red and purple porphyry; they formed a delicate design upon the arches and patterned the silver ceiling above her head. Repeated in each panel over the narrow arched doorways at the ends of the hall, ran a scrolled inscription in Persian; Alam courteously translated the words to his lovely guest, bending low to whisper in her ear:

"If Paradise be on this earth, it is this, it is this, it is this."

"It is certainly the most delightful room that I ever beheld;

I should like to live in it forever, and I am shockingly tired of travel," replied Jennifer.

"Ah, but you must see Agra," Gerald whispered in her other ear; Jennifer bowed her head beneath the jewelled trellises of constellated flowers and leaves.

"It is a pity that the Peacock Throne no longer embellishes your palace," said Gerald to Shah Alam; he felt distinctly displeased by the latter's very marked attentions to Jennifer during the course of their stroll, and he possessed to perfection the art of snubbing without offence. "It is a great loss; the larger hall looks somewhat bare without some such decoration; I wonder if the tale be well accredited which places it in Persia at the present time. I have always believed that it was borne off among the spoils of victory after the regrettable invasion of your charming country in '38; the conquerors of Karnal and the plains of Peshawar must have been put to some slight trouble in order to convey it through the Khyber Pass, but I make no doubt that it is now in Shiraz or Isfahan. Perhaps you and I, Jennifer, my child, may have the pleasure of viewing it when we visit Persia, a course upon which I am irrevocably determined. The French jeweller Tavernier, who saw the throne in the latter half of the last century, reports it as being of amazing richness and exquisite beauty, the expanded tails of the two peacocks being so inlaid with sapphires, rubies, emeralds, and other precious stones of appropriate colours as to represent life; upon the pearls encircling the twelve columns and the canopy he set an even higher value."

The Shah clutched at the diamonds upon his breast, and cast his eyes to heaven; the vividness of the picture drawn by Gerald was painful to him, but he could not resent the perfect courtesy of his guest's conversation. He did not miss the hint, so deftly introduced, of an English embassy to Persia, and this point gave him pause in his cogitations; he had thought of sending an embassy to Persia from his own court of Delhi, and he asked himself whether the King of England, the Governor-General of India, or his old friend the Honourable Gerald Poynyard had been accorded by providence a devilish power of reading the hidden minds of Eastern princes. Jennifer looked up at the two faces; the dark and the pale were equally impassive; behind its mystery the Shah's topaz gaze smouldered a little, but Gerald's eyes were cold as pebbles in a brook.

"We are unable to remain much longer to trespass upon your munificent hospitality," continued Gerald with suave but vigorous decision. "It is unfortunate that we must return to Calcutta before taking ship for Bushire; I should have preferred to follow the path of Nadir Shah through the stupendous passes of those mountains which in ancient Sanscrit are well christened 'Snow-Abode'; the low temperature would be a delightful change. But needless to say I must consult with His Excellency before taking my departure on a mission so important. If you will make it possible for my wife and myself to visit Agra under the most favourable conditions I shall esteem it as a mark of sincere kindness; pray do not put yourself to the trouble of accompanying us, as the journey would but weary you; besides, affairs of state demand your presence here; your adoring people need you. I should like to behold the Taj once more under the rays of the full moon; my almanac tells me that ten days from this date she will have reached her supreme moment of splendour. I have a fancy, my love"—he turned to Jennifer—"to see you stand mirrored in the waters which surround that Titanic bubble blown in mother-of-pearl; I have a fancy to see you etched like an exquisite impertinence against that background of mortal grief conjured into still solemnities of marble; you must wear your white satin with the very full hoops, and Sallie must dress your hair as if you were about to dine with the Dauphiness; I trust the girl has not neglected to bring a supply of powder."

When the Shah seized the opportunity of suggesting that the court metal-workers immediately prepare a quantity of gold and silver-dust ground finer than rice-flour, Gerald informed him with polite contempt that he used only the best French brands, citing a certain shop in the rue Saint Denis as the only true source of tonsorial elegance to be found under heaven.

"I do not really care for Eastern cosmetics, my dear friend," he concluded, permitting a discreet flavour of honey to tinge the acid of his voice, "I do not approve of the use of kohl;

henna I deprecate; I have never been tempted to dye my beard blue." And he stroked his smooth chin, smiling at Jennifer; she tried to picture him in a turban, with a perfumed mass of hair curling about his narrow jaw. It was hard to imagine; once imagined, it was horrible; the yellow waxen mask above the beard of indigo evoked abominable things.

Upon the last afternoon of their stay at the court of Alam, Gerald rode with his wife to the ruins of old Delhi, where stood the gigantic tower of ruddy sand-stone whose plinth was a polygon of twenty sides; the sunset overlaid it with a stronger sanguine. Gerald, for once, was slightly wearied by antiquity; he sat upon a fallen column of monumental size; its capital bore the ancient honeysuckle with bead and reel ornament, but he did not trouble to examine this. Having taken the wise precaution of carrying a book in his coat pocket, he was speedily immersed in the comedies of Terence; of these he was inordinately fond.

" I am heartily sick of Tartars and Barbarians," he announced. " I had rather see the Coliseum by moonlight than twenty Taj Mahals; I wish we were in Rome. There, my dear, would be a good background for you, if you like, classic and magnificent; you are not exactly in the grand style yourself, you are rather the Clytie of Annibale Caracci engraved by Signor Bartolozzi, but by that token you would be the more engaging with the ghost of Rome howling above you, its thumb implacably subversed over your loveliness. Wander among these stones if it amuses you; I will resume my reading. Terence is perennially charming to my mind; Montaigne applies to him the phrase of Horace, '*Liquidus paroque simillimus amni*'; it is well deserved." He turned to his book; the slight wave of his hand was sufficient dismissal for Jennifer.

She walked slowly away from him; it may be that she felt a little lonely. She found a hidden grave some distance from the others; harsh dusty grass grew over it, the inscription upon its worn surface was scarcely legible, its stone was coarse and crumbling. Jennifer could not read the chiselled words; she wondered what they meant. She sat swinging her little heels; waiting for Gerald to finish his book; under the shadow of the Minar tower she was no bigger than a gauze-winged fly. Below her silken ruffles the epitaph spoke silently in stone to this effect:

"Throw only a few blades of grass upon my tomb; that is all which should conceal the last seclusion of the humble.

"Here sleeps the unfortunate and ephemeral Jahanara, daughter of the Emperor Shah Jahan and pupil of a poor fakir."

Jennifer Lorn

BOOK III: *THE PRINCE*

1

THE RED EARTHEN BOWL

On a summer's afternoon of the most exquisite and entranced loveliness, two men sat upon a pink marble bench in the back garden of Kerim Khan's palace at Shiraz; the moveless atmosphere about them was saturated with the scent of roses; rose-petals, yellow or delicately flushed with the colours of a shell, lay unregarded at their feet; the shadow of an oak tree formed a circular pool upon the grass, blue and distinct as the royal fish-ponds farther down the slope of emerald lawn. In this refreshing shade their limbs felt cool and relaxed as if it were indeed water instead of air which supported them; their faces were smoothed to an almost inane contentment.

They conversed in low unhurried voices, and at the same time they sipped delicately some amber liquid contained in little sherbet cups of pale-green porcelain; a large blue platter of transparent glass was set between them, and this was heaped with gigantic cakes of a curled and crackling thinness, liberally sprinkled with powdered sugar and slightly burnt along the edges. Above the sherbet cups there rose a fragrance poignant and ethereal; the cakes, hot from the oven, steamed with spice and honey.

"Mirza Abbas," said the older of the two, patting his companion on the shoulder with a gesture at once fraternal and fatherly, " for the twentieth time I take pleasure in assuring you that no one but yourself has ever been permitted by an indulgent providence to attain complete perfection in the art of baking elephant's ears; these in particular . . . ah, my boy, not any of the seven tongues which I speak with such faulty fluency has words wherein to praise them as they should be praised; four of these languages are living and three of them are dead, but were these mighty dead to arise and unloose the mouths of Homer and Vergil and King David himself from the grave, their eloquence could never . . ."

The rest of his speech was rendered unintelligible by reason of his rapid consumption of the cakes, which he folded skillfully into compact squares and inserted between his strong white teeth in a somewhat absent-minded manner.

He was a singularly handsome man, tall and vigorous; his complexion was fresh and sanguine, his features possessed a symmetry so striking that they suggested the Hermes of Praxiteles turned a light-hearted forty. He was attired in a great Arabian cloak of camel's hair, in which an approximate and evidently intentional sable hue had been produced by varied dyes, now showing strange tints of green and purple under the influence of sun and rain. His thick and curling locks half concealed a small portion of his scalp which might have been either an incipient baldness or a neglected tonsure; the profusion of his dark brown hair, touched here and there by grey, hinted at the latter explanation of this phenomenon.

His broad torso and brawny shoulders moved under the heavy stuff of his mantle with the deliberation of tremendous strength; beneath the sun-burned skin of his bare calves and ankles the muscles flowed like waves. His hands were disproportionately small, with short blunt fingers and square nails; the arches of his feet stood up from the grass as if they had been builded out of stone by a clever engineer. Around his classic lips there played a smile of sly and humorous mockery; his eyes were of a most brilliant sapphire blue, and their amazing size was made conspicuous by the length and blackness of the lashes; the colour and clarity of their gaze was like that of an amiable infant. He looked affectionately at the young man seated beside him, whose appearance presented so surprising a contrast to his own.

"My son," he said kindly, "have another drop of my apricot brandy; it goes grandly with your confectionary, and it will do you no harm, being about as potent as barley water, and fitter, I think, to perfume a lady's handkerchief than to warm the cockles of a prince's heart."

His companion, a slim and languid youth of perhaps nineteen or twenty indolent Persian summers, frowned vaguely and bit his lip with his little sharp teeth before replying; his right hand, inordinately slender, and noiseless as the air through which it slid, poured a few drops of golden liquor into the cup at his side; his left hand lay negligently upon his narrow knees; his large dark eyes were fixed upon the pearly clouds above the tree-tops.

"I should not; I consider it sinful," he murmured sadly. The drops united to form a trickle; the cup brimmed; he raised it to his mouth and sipped the brandy with melancholy appreciation.

"I think it is very good, my dear friend; I find it quite strong enough, too; my dissatisfaction is with myself. I violate my principles as I drink." He drained the cup, and set it down with a gesture of quiet despair.

"You talk like a Sunnite," replied the other with good-humoured contempt. "I cannot conceive where you discover these principles of yours, my son; to the descendant of Ismail they should be abhorrent; to the poetical dabbler in Magian necromancies they should be fatiguing; to the Christian you are soon to become they should be ridiculous. For the present, let us grant that you are still a Mohammedan, but has your advanced Sufism room for these petty prejudices? They are positively Turkish."

The youth regarded him with dignity; he raised his eyebrows, but his voice remained low; a quality of weariness crept into it as he spoke.

"It is not a question of inherited principles; it is a purely personal matter, between my own conscience and myself. I do not entirely understand my feeling; I am simply convinced that for me it is wrong to indulge in alcohol. My mother has striven for some years to overcome this unhappy prejudice, as you call it; she would agree with all you say; my eccentricity has caused her much pain. But — I am what I am."

He drank another cup of brandy, then sat silent, with compressed lips and folded arms. Save for the tragic expression of his countenance, he was in all particulars the complete prince of an Arabian Nights entertainment; a dandy, a troubadour, a silken sprig of extravagant royalty.

He was clothed in a shirt of fine cotton cloth, lavishly embroidered at the throat with minute flowers in threads of white and gold; his loose trousers, of the same material, terminated in narrow slippers of thin grass-green morocco; the extreme slenderness of his waist was defined by a broad black belt of varnished leather, the clasp of which was a solid mass of magnificent emeralds. His garments were like snow; his whole person breathed of clean linen and rose-water; his neatness was superlative. A short tunic, patterned like a Cashmere shawl in black and violet and green, was flung upon the trampled rose-leaves at his feet. The crown of his head was shaved; above his ears the dark hair was drawn forward into two love-locks which encroached upon the smooth pallor of his cheeks. If he wore no beard, the omission represented no deliberate disregard of Persian fashions; he was very young. The faintest possible penciling of down sketched a tentative line along his upper lip; his eyebrows were traced in scarcely visible curves. His features were delicate; what they lacked in decisive chiselling was more than atoned for by the perfection of their finish. His long brown eyes might have belonged to a little brother of Semiramis; his finger-nails were filed into sharp points.

" My dear boy," said the elder man solicitously, replenishing the small cup with a generous hand, " I entreat you not to fall into another fit of despondency; it cannot fail to ruin your digestion. See, it is a delectable afternoon, and you are talking to the most agreeable if perhaps the most ignorant person in Persia; your task for to-day is over; to-morrow's will of necessity be light, since the declining health of the Shah gives him so great a partiality for simple broths and stewed fowls; your talented assistants are quite competent to deal with any culinary problem which may arise during your most protracted absence. You are young; you are charming both in mind and appearance; you display real genius in the art to which your life is dedicated; why should you repine? It grieves me to witness this waste of your happiest years; only the suspicion that sorrow is a great delight to you restrains me from weeping with you on every possible occasion. Come, my lad; eat, drink, and be merry; to-morrow the Shah may die, and I may have the pleasure of assisting you to ascend the throne of Abbas the Great."

The young Persian smiled sadly; slowly his brown eyes filled with tears. He lifted one hand; for a moment a spectral sceptre hovered in the air. Then he crumpled his fingers together with a gesture of disgust.

" No, Father O'Donnell," he said somewhat haughtily. " No, such vanities are not for me. I am not a conqueror " — his lip curled slightly — " I am an artist."

" Well, well," replied Father O'Donnell amiably. " Just have it as you like. . . . I merely thought that you might enjoy the palace, and the patronage of poets, and such trifles; I was not advising you to conduct a campaign against the Ottoman Empire; in fact, I should strongly deprecate the course. But the bauble shall be taken away, by all means and immediately, my son."

" These cryptic assurances of yours are a little trying now and then," murmured the youth. " To what do you refer, pray, if I may ask? "

" Criminal records of the past, dear lad. 'Tis ignorance on my part; ignorance and sheer emptiness of mind. Things float in and out of it; 'tis the mind of an infant before whose eyes bright and curious things are continually dangled in a daze. I should have been a scholar; my parents treated me very ill in the matter of my education. However, no more of that for the present; 'tis your story and not mine that shall be told to-day, as you promised faithfully over the last batch of peach brandy I distilled in the dovecote."

A changed smile flickered like sunlight over the melancholy countenance of Prince Abbas; the smile of a man about to speak of himself; he appeared almost jocund. The late sunlight was indeed thrusting long fingers of faint and gilded rose colour through the dark leaves of the oak tree; earth and sky seemed unsubstantial as tints and fragrances of flowers.

"If you so desire," he said gently, inclining his head a little and lowering his eyes.

"My life has been a sad one, as you know, dear friend," he began in a controlled but slightly fatigued voice; the prismed sparkle of a tear was distinctly visible among his lashes. "My life has been a sad one," he repeated in a corroborative whisper to himself.

"The sadness is not in your life, 'tis in your own heart, my child," said Father O'Donnell. "You have a fine life compared to many poor devils around these very premises who are laughing and roaring all day and all night; to be sure these are mostly Kurds or even Ethiopian slaves, but their happiness is evident enough in spite of that. You have grand clothes and yet grander viands; drink you can get by a word to me or a visit to old Ismail the fruiterer in the new bazaar whom I've converted to the Christian faith and whose vineyards yield the best grapes to be found in the environs of Shiraz. Life's a strong fluid running from the conduits of heaven into our veins; pipe it through a little glass tube like yourself and the pressure is bound to be painful; the speed and spate of it will maybe crack you. Your chemists and elderly magicians hereabouts have many such tubes of azure glass, sapphire like this plate or the colour of sea-water; pretty as jewels they are but not so durable; they are all very well for measuring and testing and pouring a gold drop here and a silver drop there, but fill them up with harsh new wine and they'd burst like bubbles. An old earthen pipe like myself is dry and thirsty and so a most voracious drinker of life at its source; I'm no more to be split by the vital stream than if I were stone or steel. Stone and steel you'll find, slender and inflexible or ragged with moss like an ancient well; copper twisted like the worm in Ismail's still; bright wheaten straws through which a tiny trickle may meander. I've seen great souls bearing rivers heavier than those which flow along Roman aqueducts; they'd no more mind or indeed notice the vast weight of water than if it had been the dew of a summer evening such as this. But your pardon, my boy; I have as usual interrupted you; your pardon, pray continue your narrative at once."

"I am the last hope of the Safawid Dynasty," remarked the

youth, with a pensive pride which ignored the interruption. " I am practically the final Haidari. My unfortunate cousin Shah Rukh enjoys a pathetic shadow of power under the protection of the chief of the Abdali Afghans; blinded by the atrocious orders of the head Mullah at Meshed, rendered half-imbecile by many indignities received at the hands of Jiafir the Kurd and Mir Alam the Arabian, his state is hardly enviable. His royal blood is tainted by an admixture of the robber blood of Nadir; only upon his mother's side is he a Safawid. Poor puppet king — I can but pity him! "

" You are talking in blank verse, my lad," cried Father O'Donnell warningly. " Your sympathetic sentiments concerning your unfortunate relative are very edifying, but I wish to hear more of yourself, and more especially of your boyhood, and the influences which swayed you in your choice of a profession. In spite of my complete ignorance of history, the subject has long delighted me; it is a satisfying thing to know that you are of the noble Haidari, the Lionine, the House of Ismail, whose warriors cast their armour to the winds with disdain of other protection than the great cry of Shiah. So, my little cream-coloured cat of Isfahan, you are indeed a lion-cub by inheritance. Strange, strange, strange; and your father was a poet, and you are a cook! Ah, child, I wish you could collect the energy to climb, with the help of God and his poor servant Francis O'Donnell, upon the throne so soon to be vacated by the providential death of Kerim Khan. He is long past seventy, and you have exceptional opportunities — "

" What? " shrieked Abbas, in a voice of hysterical horror. " Are you suggesting poison? " Cold beads of sweat stood out upon his smooth brow; his lips assumed a greenish hue.

" Is this attack attributable to professional honour, or is it merely an ethical scruple? " inquired Father O'Donnell with cool and kindly scorn. " Curious to observe," he went on placidly, " with what malign persistence these suspicions dog the footsteps of the Companions of Jesus. Your question was worthy of the young Puritans of Port Royal; you are a coward, my child, and did I not know your mind fairly well, and love its innocence and its absurdity, I should be angry. I shall not trouble for my own sake to explain away your fears; in order to calm your agitation,

I shall condescend to assure you of the benignity of my intentions towards that worthy Paynim within the palace. He is a harmless old man; if he has too many wives, the same may be said of Solomon. I meant no more than the simple truth of his extreme age, and your own popularity in Shiraz. I was about to remark that you possess exceptional opportunities for reaching your people's hearts through their stomachs."

Abbas swallowed hard once or twice; slowly the colour returned to his arrogant little face; a dark flush succeeded his pallor. He glanced with secret misgiving at the face of his friend; it was not wickedness that he now feared to find; it was ridicule. But the profile of Father O'Donnell was lifted to the appearing stars; it had the pure gravity of an antique cameo. The prince sighed with relief; he felt slightly faint, and, finding that nothing except a delicate scent of apricots lingered in the flask at his side, he plucked a rose and crushed it in his hand in order that its sharp sweetness might revive his soul.

" Forgive me, my dear friend and second father," he said humbly. " The fault was mine, yet if you knew how distressingly frequent are the plots, counterplots, poisonings and other malpractices, in the vicinity of this court, you would not wonder at my passing thought; such things are common here, and congenial to the Persian character; perhaps I was less shocked than you believe. The truth is this; the contemplation of so great a crime, not against the body of a senile usurper, but against the very spirit of my art, that exquisite and fragile spirit whose every ingredient is a divine inspiration, shook me to the foundations of my being and induced a momentary giddiness which is now, I am happy to assure you, rapidly passing away." He ate a roseleaf, and appeared completely restored.

" If I knew! " exclaimed Father O'Donnell with considerable indignation. " And who, may I inquire, is so likely to know of these doings as myself? 'Tis not that I hear a large variety of confessions as yet; that will come in its own time, when I have vanquished the indulgent image of Mahound in many hearts. But this to me — who have lived at the festering courts of Spain and France and Italy! Let me inform you, presumptuous boy, that your secret diplomacy is not nearly so discreditable as you seek to represent. You will never make a statesman, so much is evident, but that is no reason why you should not make a very pretty king. Ha! Haidari! " His mighty laugh made the moon-silvered oak leaves shake like aspens upon the air; between them the moon trembled in the unmoving blue.

" Did you ever hear tell of the Borgias, now, or the Medicis? I've a special fancy for Cæsar myself," he went on ruminatively. Abbas smiled.

" Naturally I am not ignorant of the famous characters to whom you refer," he said in a patronising tone, shrugging his shoulders. " The last mentioned is often celebrated in terms of praise by our Eastern poets; he ranks with Timur and Iskander. I am not a child."

" Indeed? " inquired the other in a voice of gentle amazement. " 'Tis because you wear no beard that I'm apt to forget your age, I suppose. But to your story; I wish to hear of the child you must once have been."

" As all Shiraz remembers," began Abbas, in a languid manner touched by pale forensic fire, " I am the only son of that prince whom the Afghan robber Nadir murdered at the age of ten; I mean, of course, to say that the bandit believed my poor father to have been murdered, whereas he was in reality smuggled from his prison, in a large hamper of dirty linen, by certain devoted servants of our family, descendants of those same Turks whom Timur freed out of compliment to my reverend forebear at Ardebil during the fourteenth century. I have often heard my poor father complain of the frightful suffering inflicted upon his sensitive and fastidious soul by the necessity of lying quite still with his face under the red cotton neckerchief of some one who was either a stable-boy or a camel-driver, and who should have sent his neckerchief to be washed several weeks prior to the date of my poor father's escape. The little sufferer survived the terrible experience, however, being more fortunate in this than his cousin the son of Tahmasp, who had been given a choice of conveyances owing to his superior rank. This ill-fated child decided upon a wine-jar, and the jar being full owing to gross neglect and stupidity on the part of the servants, perished miserably by drowning. Though he was a scion of the reigning branch of the family, and my poor father but a crownless prince, it was well known at the time that Nadir desired the death of the latter most ardently; my father was precociously gifted with poetic genius, and was in addition the grandson of my ancestral namesake Mirza Abbas whom the dying Suleiman would have set upon his throne in place of the cowardly Hosain, later victim of that inhuman monster Mahmud." He leaned back panting and fanned himself with a small illuminated book drawn from the embroidered pocket of his blouse.

Father O'Donnell examined him with sympathetic interest. "And has the little cream-coloured cat of Isfahan so much of the lion blood in him after all?" he said, more to himself than to the exhausted prince at his side. "But no more of that; tell me now how did you come to take up cooking?"

The eyes of Abbas grew dreamy upon the dreaming prospect of lawn and pool and moonlight; he plucked another rose and sniffed it peacefully before replying. "You admit, then, that it is an art?" he said, turning upon his friend with a perfectly perceptible defiance stiffening his languor. "Because if you do not, I'm not prepared to argue the point with you; I feel too deeply, I may even say too painfully upon the subject to air it to an unsympathetic listener; my heart-strings are involved and wound up in this matter, and I would not willingly open my heart to a mocker." He stared, pale and suspicious, into the other's face.

"Do I? But do I not, indeed?" cried Father O'Donnell with enthusiasm, slapping the prince upon the back with so hearty a kindness that the boy reeled where he reclined in the corner of the pink marble bench. "And now to our fat-tailed sheep, my lad with moon on forehead and star on chin!"

"Such ornamentations of the face with gold-leaf have long since gone out of style," Abbas remarked in parentheses. "But this is the way it all came about, in the beginning. My poor father was a great poet; there is no manner of doubt to be entertained in the matter, and the critics of Shiraz will all corroborate my statement. But, as in the case of many of our most exquisite singers of an older day, Fame came not to his hand during his lifetime; the jewelled bird preferred to perch among the bowers of Paradise, eating sugar from the lips of Jami and Hatifi. My father was of a warlike and noble mind; the battle-chants and historical romances which he composed are among the most vivid and spirited of which our land can boast. A goldsmith of Jerusalem, himself a poet of no mean attainment, said openly in the bazaars and market places of Shiraz that my father made songs to ring with a rare and spicy music evoked from seemingly casual words. Another poet and critic of this city compared my father's work to glittering tapestries and clear-voiced bells. It was very gratifying, but my father was not content with all this praise. He wished, in short, to be a king. You will observe that I have not inherited his tastes in this respect; I am more like my mother. She experienced great terror as a child in witnessing the massacres of Mahmud; the effect upon my father of these scenes of horror was very different; though but a babe in arms his anger and holy indignation knew no bounds, but my mother's infant soul was deeply scarred by fear, and she has never since been able to view even the mildest form of assassination with any degree of composure. She was quite convinced that any effort on my father's part to regain the throne would result in his immediate murder; I have no hesitancy in accepting her opinion.

"My poor father pined and grieved for danger; his poetry became increasingly superb and bloody, but the pecuniary gain was small, and in spite of the warm encouragement of the before-mentioned critics and fellow-craftsmen, he faded away and died, in the belief that his honours would never become commensurate with his achievements. But prior to his sad demise, he had left strict directions as to my education, and the bitterness of his mind and heart caused him to expressly forbid me to learn or practice any of the fine arts. I could not be a poet; no more could I seek relief for my overflowing soul in the pipes and strings of dulcimer and lute; painting and the art of illuminating and engrossing manuscripts was to remain a closed book to me, a book whose exquisite cover and filagree clasps caused me the most excruciating longing. Sculpture, even ceramics, the trades of the gold- and silversmith, the architects' magnificent skill in calling airy towers to life in the sky, all these were denied me. My father had forgotten nothing. I was in despair; my health and spirits suffered from this enforced deprivation; my dear mother was at her wit's end.

" Upon how small and seemingly unimportant an event the entire happiness of a lifetime may depend! " he continued with fervent interest in his own story. " Has that reflection ever occurred to you, Father O'Donnell, or is it but the fantastic whimsy of a poet's son? "

" It has, and 'tis not," replied Father O'Donnell with pleasant brevity. " Go on with your story, my lad. We'll soon be reaching the elephants' ears."

" It was the morning of my twelfth birthday," Abbas pronounced solemnly, " a gleaming day in mid-most June, when the heavens seemed God's own countenance smiling upon his children. I ran about the kitchen, somewhat sad at heart, but very hungry, for my dear mother had been so busily occupied in the preparation of a vanilla birthday-cake and a strawberry sherbet for my supper, destined to be shared with several young Haidari cousins, that she had forgotten to give me any breakfast. I skipped, I strolled, I pottered about the large airy kitchen with its earthen floor and rows of turquoise-coloured pots and copper pans. I ate a raisin here and a morsel of citron there, and still I was starving, but of course respect and courtesy forbade me to make my dear mother aware of her innocent omission of our morning meal."

" You must have been an uncommonly polite child," said Father O'Donnell. The prince shook his head slightly in deprecation of a statement with which he evidently agreed.

" At last I possessed myself of a crust of stale bread, and a bit of cheese; these were deposited within a little pink wooden box, decorated with brightly burnished wire, which lay in a remote corner of the room. I have since come to a realisation of the distressing fact that this was none other than a mouse-trap, and the knowledge has caused me qualms, but at least I have no cause to think that it had ever contained a mouse. The thing was conspicuously new and shining, and my dear mother's absent habit of mind makes it practically certain that she had forgotten to set it."

" There should be a lesson in all this, if only we were clever enough to discover it," said Father O'Donnell. " It sounds like the beginning of a moral tale out of a French primer. But proceed, my prince."

"Just as I was biting into this dry fodder," the youth went on in growing excitement, "my dear mother spied me, and rushed upon me with cries of mingled pity and terror. Clutching with both hands at her luxuriant curls, her still girlish face flushed by the exertions of cookery, she looked like a moss rosebud in a fit of hysterics, the resemblance to this flower being heightened by the fact that all this pretty hair was dyed a brilliant emerald green, setting off her pink cheeks and hazel eyes to much advantage. My mother was very pious, you must know, in those days; she certainly would not have conversed with a Christian with the toleration which she now bestows upon you. The tradition that Hezret-i-Fatima, the wife of the Prophet, will tear out by the roots every white hair she sees upon a woman's head was accepted by most Persian ladies of the past generation. My poor father's death had been a great sorrow to my dear mother; one white hair shone henceforward among the clustering brown locks which had always been the admiration of our small circle of friends. 'Little gazelle, do not dye that fawn-coloured fur of yours,' my grandmother entreated. 'You can easily pluck out this one white hair without the assistance of the severe Fatima; I shall cherish you so that no other will appear until you are yourself a grandmother.' But my dear mother was firm; she felt it in the nature of a religious observance and a tribute to my poor father's memory, and beside, she had always wanted to have green hair. It was really very becoming, and lightened the effect of her heavy mourning most charmingly."

"Your mother is a charming woman, indeed," said Father O'Donnell. The prince bowed as if he thought the remark had come better from his own lips than that of his friend. He had a very royal manner.

"Presently, after she had snatched the bread and cheese from my hands and thrown them out of the window to rejoice the hearts of the nightingales, she gave me a saucer full of candied rose-leaves; then perceiving that my disappointment was still keen though admirably controlled, she exclaimed that though she couldn't in the least remember what in the Prophet's Paradise we had breakfasted upon, she was sure it must have been something flimsy and unsustaining, as she herself was hungry and I was nothing but a pair of large eyes staring at the saucepans upon the stove. Presently she snatched from the stove a small skillet, in which about a cupful of chicken broth was already bubbling pleasantly, and with all the ardour of maternal love and her own impulsive nature she added thereto a lump of fresh butter, a few sprigs of saffron, and a pinch of those dried herbs, aromatic and appetising, which are yearly gathered upon the slopes of Mount Sinai and sold to religious housewives throughout the East. Not content with these consoling activities, which were already causing me the most ecstatic pangs of hope, she proceeded to lift the cover from well-nigh every saucepan simmering above the fire, thereby releasing vapours of amazing fragrance while she deftly ladled a spoonful of this and a morsel of that into the fortunate skillet.

"I stood spellbound, swaying a little in a species of etherial intoxication as the delicate fumes mounted to my brain. Had the outcome been much longer delayed, I should assuredly have swooned; through a haze of thin steam I saw her flourishing bright cannisters of salt and pungent peppercorns. Then I was drawn gently to the round blue table under the rose-veiled casement. I sat down; my mother thrust a silver spoon into my hand, and placed before me a simple red earthen bowl, long associated in my mind with milk and rice and similar innocencies of childhood. Now all was changed; before my face wavered an incense cloud the like of which I had never smelt. No terrestrial porridge could produce such perfume, worthy of the Prophet's Paradise, nor have I ever understood by what divine chance my mother's careless touch had created such beauty. Laugh, my friend, if you will, but I tell you that authentic beauty rose in spiritual exhalation from that earthen bowl, even as the goddess rose from the Grecian wave. Do you believe me?" His voice trembled perceptibly.

"I believe you, my boy," said Father O'Donnell kindly. He was not smiling; the prince thought his mouth was rather grimly set for that of a sympathetic listener.

"Of course I realise," the royal youth continued stubbornly,

" that my extreme hunger would have rendered any food savoury at the moment, but after making all due allowance for the weakness of my flesh, I still maintain that the scented smoke which ravished my senses fed a famine far higher than any I had before experienced. No perfume expressed from the white or yellow jasmine, no double-distilled rose-water of Fajhum, nor sugar of violets, no musk or ambergris, could rival it in purity and distinction. In that instant, and without tasting the inspired concoction, I decided to dedicate my life to the art of cookery. My poor father, in his poet's ignorance of the world, had never thought to forbid my entering the temple of art through that particular portal; I was free to follow what I now perceived to be the way of my dreams. I sat long and silently in front of the blue table, now become an altar to all loveliness. I did not touch the food; as it congealed and became unsightly I gently closed my eyes and motioned to my mother to remove the dish.

" She was in despair; her solicitude leaped to the conclusion that I was ill, nor could my pale and exalted looks serve to dispel so natural an illusion. She was, after all, a woman; she could not understand the miraculous radiance upon my brow, my distracted speech, and the appalling solemnity of my eyes. She wept, and though I strove to comfort her, my efforts were in vain.

" The remainder of the day passed like a tranquil and beatific trance. I remember lying in my narrow white bed between the sandal-wood scented sheets, watching a pallid sky chequered by fantastic patterns of quince and apple blossoms; I remember thinking that their April fragrance, enchanting and elusive, could be captured and enhanced in the jellied essences, coloured like roses or cloudy amber, which their fruit might yet yield to my hand. I remember the clamorous voices of my Haidari cousins on the little lawn below my window, and my mother's pretty pitying face as she brought me rice and milk instead of the festal sherbet and sweetmeats. And I remember saying to her, a bit impatiently I fear, ' Ah, mother, with a hint of nutmeg and a suspicion of orange flower water, this might be made quite palatable! ' Strange, beautiful, unreal hours — dreams and mysteries — mysteries and dreams. Though it is full seven years ago, my friend, I remember; but how I remember! "

His soliloquy subsided in his throat with something akin to a sob; Father O'Donnell frankly envied him his capacity for pleasurable melancholy.

" As you know," the boy said proudly, " there is something ascetic in my spirit; I have never cared very deeply about the actual taste of my work. Let its essential odour satisfy my mind and senses, and I am content. I rarely judge by the grosser test of actual gustation, and then only when the higher faculty has warned me that an element is lacking or a flavour overstressed. For myself, a handful of dried beans, a few lentils, a spare crust of bread, these suffice. Wine — ah, that is different! I think I see you smile, and yet you must know that I am speaking the truth. I admit that my affection for the juices of the grape and pomegranate is a shame and a sorrow to me, but wine in its very nature is less mundane than food; the madness of its fumes is etherial though evil. But, in cooking, to create a masterpiece for the nose alone — that is exquisite, that is Art! "

" 'Tis your nose that's bigger than your stomach, then," remarked the older man amiably. The prince looked puzzled; with one hand he drew tighter the varnished belt encircling his wasp waist; with the other he casually caressed the bridge of his small straight nose.

A silence fell between the two friends, keeping pace with the soft descent of darkness and dew which was turning the red rose black and the white rose moon-coloured. The moon herself was no more than a phosphorescent feather among the oak leaves.

2

THE BYZANTINE IMAGE

At length Father O'Donnell drew forth from beneath his vast and enveloping mantle a minute lantern of the finest Persian workmanship, struck light with all the violence of superb and unnecessary muscular power, and deposited the thing, glowing like a handful of gems, upon the seat beside him. Its top was a clear mosaic of rainbow sparks; its four sides stained the flame within to pink or amber, emerald or blue. By this fantastic illumination he prepared to open a small breviary of incredible age and shabbiness, but before he had adjusted its crumpled pages to his satisfaction, the prince interrupted him.

"When may I see the Virgin?" he inquired timidly.

Father O'Donnell sighed, and regarded the youth with a satirical lift of his brows. "Never, in this world, unless a miracle is vouchsafed you," he said conclusively.

The prince frowned angrily, but bit his lip into an ingratiating smile before answering. "As you are well aware, I only refer, and that with the utmost deference, to the Byzantine image," he murmured.

"Ah, you mean the little ivory picture of Our Lady that I found in the new bazaar this morning! Or perhaps it's more of a statue than a picture, only I couldn't say, because of my profound ignorance of the seven arts, and all else under heaven. However, I'm convinced at least of this much," he went on in a low and rapid articulation which the prince experienced great difficulty in following, "the work is of the fifth century, or maybe just possibly of the early part of the sixth, executed I should judge by a Greek or Syrian of the utmost skill, for though the general treatment of the figure is like all Byzantine *bas-relief* somewhat flat and conventionalised, the masterly modelling of the hands and arms, carved quite free of the background, and the exquisite though impersonal beauty of the face betray a superlative artist. I lean towards the theory of Syrian workmanship when I remember the great angel of the balanced pinions and the intent countenance which I once beheld in the shop of a Syrian carver in Constantinople, but there's this to be said for the Greek, that the hair and the halo are of purest gold, and what's that but the true chryselephantine . . ."

He paused for a reply, and receiving none, continued with evident interest in his own words, " 'Tis the central portion of a small triptych; the marks of hinges are plainly visible upon the back of the panel."

"Am I not to be accorded the privilege of beholding this

marvel?" Mirza Abbas inquired with gentle acerbity. "Do you perhaps consider me too bloody a paynim for such an honour?"

"By no means, dear boy," said the priest pleasantly. "Look, now, and see what a treasure it is I've had the luck to discover."

From the inner recesses of his robe he produced an oblong package of worn black brocade; this he unfolded slowly and with the most meticulous care, until at last its contents lay upon his broad palm exposed to the prince's avid gaze. The object thus displayed was indeed beautiful; the boy caught his breath and clenched his hands in excitement as the yellow lantern light fell clear upon the image.

The ivory panel was perhaps six inches long and slightly more than half as wide; as Father O'Donnell held it the figure of Our Lady appeared to be recumbent yet alive, lifting little hands which implored rather than blessed. The delicately cut face, no larger than the prince's finger-nail, looked innocent and vaguely troubled; shallow scallops of gold hair framed it beneath the folds of the ivory mantle; behind the head were spiked rays of gold. The lantern's amber glass made the ivory itself only a paler gold.

The prince turned the lantern until the image was drenched in green light. "See, she is drowned," he said sadly, "she has returned to the sea; she has taken to herself its cold colour, she is asleep in the sea."

He turned the lantern again. "But no, she ascends to the Seventh Heaven; she floats in its azure space; her wings are folded, yet she flies in Heaven."

The priest laid his hand upon the boy's wrist; he was frowning. "You are a curious young idolator, and I doubt that I'll ever make a Christian of you. Give over your Magian lantern play; you are irreverent." He reached for the lantern, but the prince was too quick for him; in a flash the ivory seemed to melt into human flesh in auroral light from the rose-coloured glass set in the lantern's fourth side.

The prince threw back his head and laughed joyfully; the image smiled at him. "Ah, behold your miracle!" he cried. "She lives, she breathes, she is made mortal before my eyes. She is a woman who wakes in the dawn and smiles in the flush of the dawn; she is a woman who smiles into the face of her beloved! "

Father O'Donnell was very angry. With the calm of undisputed strength he removed the lantern from the prince's grasp and cast it, extinguished and shattered, far down the slope of the lawn. Then he painstakingly returned the panel to its wrappings of black brocade. His eyes were inexorable.

"With God's help, I shall hold that sacred object hidden from your impious gaze forever," he said sternly. "It was my intention to give it to you on that auspicious day when you were actually received into the Church; now I fear that your soul is lost beyond my power to save it; I believe you are mad." There were tears in his indignant eyes; the prince was weeping openly and at his feet.

He placed his brown hand on the boy's shoulder; he was more moved than he cared to admit. "There, take heart!" he exclaimed suddenly. "I was too rough with you, poor lad; there's more silliness than sin in you, any day; that's plain enough to be seen. We must be patient with each other; if you'll ask Our Lady's pardon, I'll gladly ask yours for roaring at you like a wild bull, and you bleating like a sheep for penitence."

The prince looked up gratefully at his preceptor; his expression was angelic. "You have forgiven me, then? You will not visit your anger upon me any longer?"

Father O'Donnell looked down at him quizzically. The boy knelt in the dewy grass, knelt upon one knee in the attitude affected by mediæval pages, with a conscious grace reflected in the pathetic glances of his long-lashed eyes. There was little of the true penitent in his look, but much of the child and something, even, of the sentimental spaniel; the priest's heart was melted.

"You know I'm not the only one who has to forgive you, Abbas," he pronounced at last in a subdued voice. "You are strangely perverse at times, but it's my duty to remember that you're a Persian and a poet; I can't expect you to behave as yet like the good stupid little Belgians of Bruges. I think I may safely promise you, after all, that if you will but attend to your studies you'll have what you wish."

"The Byzantine image!" cried the prince with happy animation.

Father O'Donnell jerked him roughly to his feet and shook him vigorously. "No!" he thundered. "Never while I live! Faith was what I meant, and decent behaviour, and purity of mind!" For the first time his national accent was plainly audible in these emphatic words. "Are you not forever saying that you want to be a Christian, that you must be a Christian, that you'll make any sacrifice if only you can be a Christian?"

"And a Jesuit," the prince amended carefully.

"Yes, that's what you've got at the back of your head all the time! A Jesuit! For all it conveys to you, it might as well be a Mullah or a Mage — 'tis simply your precious idea of personal aggrandisement. Have you any notion, my lad, of what it would mean? Poverty — Chastity — Obedience — the Sacrifice of the Intellect!" He finished on a note of withering scorn.

The prince drooped slightly, but did not wither. "I have rejected the doctrines of Sufi," he said with dignity, "I have dabbled in the Magian mysteries of Zoroaster; I have investigated the teachings of Buddha and Confucius. Thanks to your good offices, I am not wholly ignorant of the superstitions of the Greeks, or the cynical pretences of the Romans. I have concluded, not that I wish to become a Christian, but that I have already attained that state. Touching the other matter, I beg you not to disturb yourself with doubts and indignations. I am poor " — he lifted his head — "I am chaste " — he folded his hands — "I am obedient " — he inclined his brow with an immense haughtiness, raising it to exclaim — " and I am willing to sacrifice my intellect to God!"

"Stupendous!" replied the priest with irritating urbanity. "But I fear you'll have to be content with becoming a mere Christian; had I been able to spirit you into some retreat five years ago, when first you fell into my hands, your ambitions might have been realised, for you were at that date exactly fourteen years old, the proper age for a novice. But Persia does not boast a Saint Omer, and even had you been in Europe, the colleges and houses were one by one closing in the most tragic confusion. I have told you of my heart-breaking departure from

Spain, and the incredible gloom of my existence in Corsica, where for a brief but dreadful period I lodged, for my sins, in the house of the most detestable people I have ever met, a young married couple called Buonaparte. The woman especially was to be condemned as a termagant and a scold; she had one little boy, Giuseppe, the object of my sincerest pity; I wonder if she ever bore another child to beat and starve."

"I do not know and I do not care," said the prince crossly. "Besides, you have told me all this before. I like better to hear of your journey to the East, of your sanguinary adventures and miraculous escapes, and of the success of your secret mission to the Caliph of Baghdad. Ah, but you were superb . . ." and he clapped his hands in admiring delight.

"I did not wholly fail to deserve the confidence with which my superiors had honoured me." Father O'Donnell spoke with becoming modesty; absently he fingered his stained and ragged robe. "I have never regretted my choice, for I was, indeed, by a curious combination of circumstances, left free to choose between the luxury of Frederick's court and this outlandish exile. In the case of the illustrious Frederick, the Society has been singularly fortunate; more fortunate than the world suspects. You know, of course . . ." He checked himself, and continued thoughtfully, "I realised that my humble talents were better fitted to overcome the barbarous Mahound than the more attenuated Anti-Christ of Sans Souci. Though for that matter, you have perhaps heard that Voltaire . . ." Again he checked himself, to murmur under his breath, "But he, to be sure, was converted by a Dominican!"

"And the image, what will you do with it now?" the prince ventured timidly. He dreaded a renewal of his friend's unaccountable anger, but curiosity overcame his fear. To his vast relief, the priest answered with perfect mildness.

"I shall not keep it," he said without regret. "I have no right to possess so beautiful a work of art, rendered trebly valuable by its sacred nature and extreme antiquity. Now that you have shown yourself unfit to be its custodian "—the prince shuddered and closed his eyes in mingled remorse and cupidity — "I shall, if possible, send it by the hand of a trusted messenger to one of my friends in Europe, one who will revere it and treasure it always. I have in mind, as possible recipients of this gift, an elderly scholar in Madrid, a very great lady in Paris, and a poor widow in Ireland. I have not yet decided among the three."

He was silent, seeming to meditate. The prince nodded his smooth dark head in mournful acquiescence; within his head were a thousand plans for discovering the identity of the messenger and having him waylaid and robbed; he hoped that there would be no necessity for resorting to murder. Father O'Donnell knew precisely what the boy was thinking; he sighed, and when he spoke again his voice was gently minatory.

"Your possessive instinct is over-strong, my dear child," he said. "Oh, jerk your eyebrows and shrug your shoulders if you please, but it's true, all the same, and you should study to eradicate the fault, which will bring you nothing but unhappiness. Of course it's largely the result of your mother's unwisdom in anticipating your every wish, but nevertheless I think you are somewhat to blame in the matter. Observe the absurdity of your aspiring to become one of the Clerks Regulars of the Society of Jesus, when you are the owner of no less than fifty-one pairs of morocco slippers, four dozen shirts of the finest embroidered cotton, and twenty-seven tunics of Cashmere wool."

"My mother —" began the prince perfidiously, but the other man paid no heed to the interruption.

"While I" — he went on, indicating several of the more conspicuous patches upon his disreputable robe — "while I, having lost my habit the very night I landed at Bushire, am thankful enough for this rough Arabian cape, the harsh texture of which would flay you alive like the unlucky victim of Apollo's wrath were it ever to come in contact with your oiled and pampered limbs. I believe it belonged to a celebrated horse-thief," he added, reflectively enlarging a ragged hole.

"So its appearance would certainly indicate." Mirza Abbas sniffed disdainfully, as if offended in another sense than sight. His delicate nostrils quivered.

"As for my breviary," the priest said, flicking open the shabby pages with affectionate care, "I have really no right to that, either, having grown unduly fond of the book. Only, I believe after all that the difficulty of securing another, in Shiraz, justifies me in retaining this one. I hope I am not wrong in this opinion." It was clear that he doted upon the thing.

"You could easily have it copied in the Bazaar," the prince suggested spitefully. "I know of a number of excellent penmen who would gladly undertake such a commission for a small sum, even enriching the volume with illuminations in colour and gold leaf, and binding it in embossed leather. I will take the book to the Bazaar to-morrow." He extended his slim hand.

"No," said Father O'Donnell with finality, "I cannot afford gold leaf." He hid the breviary in the wide sleeve of his Arabian cloak.

The crescent plume that lit the deepening sky floated softly down until it hung among the heavy-headed roses; the ground absorbed its unsubstantiality like rain. The night was dark, yet trees and flowers were translucent as black glass to the star-light; they glittered like black glass. Waves of pure sweetness flowed strangely, unhastened by any wind, from the white roses and the warmer wine-coloured roses, around the two figures on the marble bench, who now sat with all the immobility of marble in the centre of this softly stirring obscurity. The cold, aqueous scent of pond-lilies mounted like mist from the fish-ponds of Kerim Khan.

Across this tranquillity there suddenly flashed the startling trail of a light, somewhat shrill voice, like a small rocket of sound scattering vivacious and unnecessary notes upon the air. The prince jumped in his seat.

"Abbas, my child!" called the voice in cultivated Persian accents; "Abbas, I have been searching for you high and low; where are you hiding yourself, my little golden hawk?"

"It is my mother!" exclaimed the prince in surprise. "What can have brought her into the garden at this hour? Her voice betrays considerable agitation; I trust nothing untoward has taken place." And he began to tremble a little, presumably from excitement.

A plump but agile figure became visible, at this instant, ascending the slope with remarkable speed considering the circumstance of its being swaddled from top to toe in a large dark cloak. As the figure approached, two eye-holes glittered in the sombre material covering its face; its voice repeated " Abbas, Abbas, answer me at once! " and both men rose simultaneously from the marble bench.

" I am here, mother; is anything the matter? " Abbas inquired anxiously in his native tongue. Then relapsing once more into English, he added, " Father O'Donnell is with me, but from him we have no secrets."

" No? " said the lady politely, but with a rising inflection; her English was remarkably correct. " Good evening, Isauvi; I trust that my son has not been sitting long upon this chilly stone seat, for the night air at this season of the year is particularly dangerous, and I observe his tunic upon the grass." She stooped to recover the tunic, at the same moment attempting to test the degree of moisture which had so far penetrated the soles of the prince's slippers. He eluded her with a plaintive cry, only suffering her to drape the tunic across his shoulders.

Father O'Donnell bowed with grave courtesy. " Good evening, Madam," he replied. " I think the boy has come to no irreparable harm."

" You are aware how easily he catches cold — " began the fond parent, but her son interrupted her with an agonised plea for information concerning her errand.

" Very well," she said resignedly. " I was coming to that in good time. I have a strange piece of news for you. Some of the Banou's atrocious Turcoman relatives have captured a young Circassian girl of great beauty; she appears, however, upon the point of death, and pending the outcome of her present state of insensibility, she has been placed in my care. The Banou does not wish to alarm or incommode the other occupants of the harem while there remains the slightest fear that this person will turn into a corpse before morning; the women do not like corpses, even pretty ones. Meanwhile, my dear," she addressed her son respectfully, " if it would not too much trouble your sensitive spirit, I should like to consult you in the matter of diet. The poor girl is shockingly emaciated; we must see what we can do."

" Perhaps a dish of young lamb *à la crème,* or sweetbreads

stewed in milk of almonds — " suggested the prince hopefully, his whole mobile countenance alight with interest.

"But no, my child; nothing so elaborate will be advisable at present. Rather, if I may venture to counsel your admirable skill, I should prefer the patient to drink a little of your famous saffron broth, with a wafer baked in the silver oven. I leave it entirely to you, of course — but — " it was evident that she did no such thing; the prince nodded in filial assent.

"First, we should make sure that the vital spark has not escaped from the body of this unhappy creature," the voice of Father O'Donnell, at its most solemn depth, reminded them. "It is possible, even, that she may be in need of spiritual succour at my hands."

"Surely, Isauvi, you do not suspect this unfortunate of being a Christian?" The little lady was sincerely shocked; within the eye-holes her bright eyes rolled in alarm. "Oh, that cannot be, I assure you! She is beautiful, she is richly dressed, she has all the marks of high birth and breeding!" The prince's mother had her inherited prejudices, but she was a kind woman at heart, and at a warning glance from her son she concealed her horror with commendable speed.

"Let us all proceed together to my dwelling," the royal youth said, graciously linking his arm in that of the priest. "Mother, if you will permit me to escort you — " and he possessed himself of her arm also. Father O'Donnell and the Persian gentlewoman eyed each other, across his slender form, with the mutual confidence of a spoiled, aristocratic Oriental cat and a noble but impatient Irish wolf-hound. Abbas was perfectly happy.

Jennifer lay upon a large divan in the principal apartment of the little house. The couch was heaped to a luxurious depth with cushions of blue and silver, purple and velvet black. Above her, a round silver lamp, bright as a mirror and filled with fragrant oil, shed its moonlight radiance upon her motionless figure. The room, hung with long shadows and vaulted with incense-smoke, had the look of a *chapelle ardente*. The sleeping child was attired in a thick shawl of cream-coloured Chuddah wool; a fine veil, its white silk traced delicately with a pattern of gold threads, covered her from head to foot. Her face was invisible; her thin hands, flung to the right and the left of her body, moulded the silk perceptibly.

To the three persons entering the room she appeared already dead. A pretty marriageable girl sadly cut off in her youth, thought the lady. A white rose fallen to mortality, thought the prince. A slaughtered innocent, thought Father O'Donnell, more intensely. His energetic stride outstripped the others: before either could protest, he had torn the veil from Jennifer's face and flung it upon the tiled floor. Her lovely little face lay revealed, framed in shallow scallops of gold hair below the ivory folds of the shawl. She looked innocent and vaguely troubled. As Father O'Donnell bent over the couch, her lips stirred and she lifted her hands imploringly.

" The Byzantine image! " whispered the boy; he fell upon his knees and covered his eyes with his hands.

While his mother sprinkled the girl's brow with rose-water, Abbas remained kneeling, crouched at the foot of the divan; he was trembling uncontrollably. Father O'Donnell, re-entering the room with a small gold-speckled glass of some potent liquor, patted him kindly on his shaking shoulder, but he paid no heed. A terrible emotion, seemingly extraneous to himself, and yet strong as demoniac possession, convulsed his body and soul to an agony such pampered flesh and spirit could ill support. As Jennifer opened her large distracted eyes, the prince raised his own for an instant and looked her full in the face; then his eyelids closed, and he fell forward with his forehead against the foot of the couch and his arms hanging helplessly, like those of a broken marionette; the jewelled bangles on his wrists tinkled like a flight of little bells.

In response to the mother's wild cry of alarm, Father O'Donnell lifted the boy from the floor, and found him to be, if not unconscious, yet apparently dazed and deprived of the power of speech. Dragging a few large cushions from the couch, he threw them into a corner and deposited Abbas upon their comfortable thickness, where he lay supine, his head supported by a gigantic pillow of black velvet, and his eyes immovably fixed upon the face of the exquisite creature recumbent upon the couch. Even the brandy which the priest poured liberally down his throat did no more than elicit a glance of grateful recognition; of his mother's anxious presence he appeared completely unaware.

Presently, by some unaccountable chance, connected perhaps with the search for further restoratives, the enamoured boy found himself alone with his divinity. Instantly assuming a more dignified posture, and holding his head proudly erect, he fixed the girl with a brilliant yet dreaming glance, and inquired in poetic Persian as to the precise identity of the daughter of a peri, the celestial vision in ivory and gold, the jasmine-flower of immaculate sweetness, who had honoured his house by her presence. Receiving no reply, he addressed her as Venus Anadyomene in very fair Greek, and was proceeding to employ the Latin tongue, of which he knew little save prayers and holy exercises, when her gentle voice preserved him from blasphemy by murmuring weakly, " Where am I ? "

At these unmistakable English words the prince's amazement knew no bounds. " Who are you, little beloved ? " he cried breathlessly. Her long look of pitying and pathetic kindness calmed his extreme agitation like a cool hand laid across the fever of his eyes.

" I am a young English widow," she said with touching dignity. Her hands and eyelids fluttered feebly, but she contrived to assume a manner of mild and courteous composure, at once gentle and aloof. " As such I hope to command the chivalrous respect of all true gentlemen."

" And I am a disinherited prince," said Abbas, profoundly impressed, yet happy to be able to counter with so romantic a statement, " as such I hope to deserve your confidence and to serve you faithfully forever."

Jennifer found him charming, though her feeling for foreign royalty was tempered by a quiet scorn. " I am the daughter of a Scottish peer," she added a little haughtily.

" The daughter of a Scottish peri ! " the prince repeated after her. He was completely enchanted, floating in a glamorous daze through regions of forbidden sorceries. " Are you one of the Sidhe ? " he inquired with respect.

" No, I am one of the Lorns," said Jennifer quite simply. " One of the Lorns of Carterhaugh. My mother was a Cleverly-Neville, and " — she paused, but concluded that she owed it to herself, since the boy was plainly a prince — "I am a descendant of Tamburlaine the Great."

The lad was electrified; the statement placed a crown upon the glittering eminence which her words were rapidly building in his imagination, a species of Moorish castle in Spain executed in the material of dreams; the spun-sugar palace of his innermost ideal, spangled with candied violets and silver comfits. Approaching Jennifer with infinite awe, he set his lips to her little hand. "Then I am indeed the fortunate inheritor of your friendship!" he cried, and he explained very clearly to Jennifer the legend of the famous meeting at Ardebil between their renowned forebears; she on her part soon made the prince acquainted with the romantic history of Lady Helena Lorn and her noble Persian husband. An immediate bond was thus created between the two sentimental children; Father O'Donnell and the princess, upon returning to the room, observed nothing but the shyest and most demure looks in the faces of the young people, but the seeds of a profound affection had already been planted in the bosom of each.

3

ROSE-WATER OF FAJHUM

THE PRINCESS SHEKERLEB, for such was the charming Turkish name of the prince's mother, had removed her disguising outer garment, for though she was mentally incapable of comprehending Father O'Donnell's character of Christian priest, she was fully persuaded that he was not exactly a man, and so felt no embarrassment in unveiling her face before him. He, on his part, did not often encourage, save in those cases where diplomacy demanded, the curious Mohammedan prejudices of his potential flock in Shiraz. He knew precisely with what degree of speed the enthusiastic little lady would follow her adored son into the Church; meanwhile he humoured her, and avoided treading on the toes of her slippers even when she left them outside the Mosque.

Princess Shekerleb was the daughter of a Turkish lady; her

father had been a Shirazi of excellent but impoverished family, with Turkish affiliations. Her upbringing had been strictly orthodox; the green coiffure had been a direct compliment to the Prophet's fondness for that colour. But her growing boy had long since shamed her out of these opinions; under his guidance, she had become a devout Shi-ite, and her abundant hair was now as blue as indigo could make it. She was prettily attired in purple and gold, and Jennifer was immediately attracted by her charming face and figure. The poor girl felt that she had found an ally.

Strange to relate, such was indeed the truth, for Shekerleb, though possessing in full all the natural jealousies and misgivings of a devoted mother, was nevertheless of so romantic and indulgent a disposition that she was invariably moved by the sight of beauty in distress; furthermore, she could refuse her son nothing. She had not failed to note the prince's emotion, nor had her vivid imagination delayed in supplying both cause and cure for this phenomenon. While sincerely regretting the all-too-evident fact that her boy had fallen in love, she was not entirely averse to the idea that Abbas, rather than the reigning monarch, should enjoy this lovely and desirable bride.

" Elderly, bearded, and excessively-uxorious Kurdish goat! " she muttered indignantly in Persian, at the same time casting an appreciative glance at the fine countenance and graceful form of the reclining prince, who appeared to slumber.

Meanwhile she busied herself with a hundred small kindnesses in restoring Jennifer to consciousness and ameliorating her fatigue; wine, hot chicken broth with rice and raisins, and refreshing snow-chilled sherbet were prepared by her own hands and offered with many expressions of sympathy to her young guest, whose murmured gratitude was weak but continuous. The meal ended with a mutual embrace, and a few tears by way of seasoning.

After a somewhat prolonged absence, Father O'Donnell entered with an air of discouragement; his brow was grave, his lips compressed. " I can do nothing," he informed the princess. " The head eunuch is our friend, but his efforts to persuade the Banou are quite unavailing. She repeats, with characteristic obstinacy, that her cousin Aslan Sultan, the Turcoman chief, captured this poor child for the especial benefit of Kerim Khan, who has been rather dull and moody of late, according to the gossip of the court. This unspeakable woman is apparently too old to dread the dominion of another favourite; she merely wishes to supply an ironic travesty of a toy to the monarch's second childhood. Our only hope lies in the fact that the Banou is willing, for the present, that the girl should remain in your care; she says that the degree of emaciation to which the poor creature has been reduced renders her repellent to the sight, and she bids you to lose no time in administering the most fattening diet that your son's skill can provide. It is long since I have seen a European lady, but I think that the extreme slenderness of our young friend is perhaps natural, as it is certainly pleasing and appropriate to her years."

Jennifer opened her eyes and gave him a look of intense gratitude, and then folded her hands upon her breast and composed her features to classic calm, lightened by an expression of great sweetness and resignation. She was still so sleepy that she had heard no word of this alarming conversation save the Banou's insult and the priest's kindly compliment.

"The Banou is a corpulent Turcoman, and has no conception of true Persian elegance," said the princess, complacently tightening the clasp of the jewelled girdle which encircled her trim figure. "I consider this young lady to be a model of grace and breeding." She bowed to Jennifer, who nodded her head feebly in reply. "And what, my dear," continued Shekerleb, absentmindedly continuing to speak English, "is your nationality, if I may ask? Are you a Circassian or a Georgian, or even, by any chance, a Greek? I have heard that the young Greek women of fashion are very beautiful," she added politely.

Jennifer smiled; she seemed to absorb the flattery while rejecting the suggestion. "I am a native of Devonshire," she replied with engaging simplicity.

"Holy Mother of — ! " cried the priest in blank amazement.

"Allah! il Allah! " echoed the princess shrilly, naturally assuming, from his tone, that Devonshire must be some region of wild and terrifying wonders, like the abode of Eblis or the horrible mountain of Kaf. She stepped back from the couch in considerable alarm. "Where is this country, O'Donnell Baba?" she asked.

"It is a portion of England," the priest explained, "celebrated, I believe, for its luxuriant beauty, and especially for the superior quality of its cream and its roses."

"Celebrated, above all else, for the exceeding beauty of one white rose!" said the prince in an intense and thrilling whisper. He sat up and stared about him as if aroused from a profound trance.

His mother looked at him with a certain asperity brightening her hazel eyes. "If you are sufficiently recovered to speak, my son," she said with unwonted severity, "I suggest that you retire for the night; you must be in need of rest. It is not suitable that you remain any longer in the same room with our guest."

Abbas appeared to be overcome by an access of fatigue; he lay back against the cushions and closed his eyes. "I think I will stay where I am for the present, mother," he answered. "I do not see any immediate necessity for going. Besides, I consider myself affianced to this lady; I shall marry her to-morrow, and remove her from all danger of indignity." His tone was final; he did not even trouble to open his eyes.

"Not so fast, my boy," Father O'Donnell warned him; at the same moment the plaintive voice of Jennifer was clearly audible from the couch.

"I cannot marry you, my dear prince," it said gently, "until the customary year has elapsed. I fear it is not in the best of taste to discuss such matters with so recent a widow as myself. My chief care at present," she explained with mild disapproval, "is to procure some suitable mourning. The costume I am wearing, I realise with pain, is shockingly inappropriate. Dear Gerald was always so scrupulous concerning such points of taste and etiquette; his judgment was perfect." Her eyes filled with tears; she wept quietly, but with an air of deep and hopeless melancholy.

Father O'Donnell stooped over her and took her fingers, white and limp as the scrap of lace handkerchief crumpled between them, in his hand. He addressed her in a firm voice which was nevertheless soft and reassuring. "Are you a member of the Church, my child?" he asked her.

Jennifer stopped crying, and looked up at him with startled eyes; he thought he had never before seen so lovely or so pitiful a face.

"I am, of course," she informed him, more tranquil now that she had beheld the benignity of his intentions clear upon his ample brow. "Are you a priest?" This choice of words, the result not so much, perhaps, of the nuns' training as of the fact that the rector at Cleverly-Neville was a very High Anglican, with an extravagant wife and a wistful longing for celibacy, was the innocent cause of a misunderstanding which may have affected Jennifer's future to the brink of the grave and more mystically beyond. It did not occur to Father O'Donnell that she meant a priest of the Church of England; for her own part she had forgotten that any other church existed.

"Yes, my dear," he told her; she felt, suddenly, that he was her father. She liked him better than the rector, who had prepared her for confirmation, and considered her unforgivably feminine and slightly Evangelical. His wife had loved the girl; Jennifer wept anew, remembering the vivacious countenance of Mrs. Prothero framed in blue taffeta under a blonde lace veil.

Soon, however, she dried her eyes and looked about her; a glance, wan and sympathetic, passed between the prince and herself, then, with the prettiest deference, she addressed her words to the princess.

"You will marvel, Madam, at my presence in your country and more particularly at the strangeness of my appearance," she said humbly, unable to realise that her attire was infinitely more suited to her surroundings than the extreme of fashion represented by a Parisian riding-habit and plumed *chapeau,* or even the coveted crêpe veil of her present desires. "I must explain the circumstances which brought me here, and also assure you that I am an English lady of good family, who presumes upon your hospitality only because her destitute condition renders her helpless. My parents are in England, my husband" — her eyes dilated with grief and horror — "has been most atrociously murdered by the same band of robbers which conveyed me to this city. He was sent as a special envoy from His Majesty's government in India to the court of Kerim Khan — in what tragic and untoward fashion do I now find myself at the precise destination to which our journey tended! Our party landed at the Port of Bushire, where the heads of the British Factory showed us every conceivable kindness, at the same time encouraging us to expect a like cordiality from the Khan, with whom they had always maintained the pleasantest relations. They said much of his intelligent interest in commerce and agriculture, and of his sincere regard for our own great and enlightened civilisation. It was with the happiest and most fervent hopes that we set forth for Shiraz."

She ceased, and lying back among the pillows allowed a few quiet tears to trickle along the ivory of her smooth thin cheeks; her hair had fallen in light dishevelment across her brow, and she tossed it back with a faintly hysteric gesture before continuing her narrative.

" During the first days of the journey gaiety and good humour prevailed; my husband and I were mounted upon horses, while our servants and guides rode excellent mules; a large number of these useful animals carried the impedimenta of travel so that we lacked for nothing, and were exceedingly comfortable and contented. My dear husband was a superb horseman; his knowledge of history was amazing, and his fund of anecdote inexhaustible. As a travelling companion, and indeed in every other relation of life " — she explained with a loyal little sob — " he was the most superior person whom it has ever been my privilege to know."

" Your husband must have been a great Giaour lord," said Shekerleb consolingly. " It is always an honour to have been married to a superior husband! " and she sighed without bitterness.

" Her father is the Emperor of Scotland, and her mother is a peri — " began Abbas, but the princess silenced him with a wave of her hand; she was well accustomed to the extravagance of her son's imagination.

" But as we approached the lofty and difficult mountain passes which lie to the south of Shiraz," Jennifer went on unheeding, with faster speech and lightning-flashes of excitement from her expanding eyes, " as we drew near to these dangerous and depressing regions we became aware of a certain uneasiness among the servants; inquiries resulted in the disclosure of the fact that a famous band of outlaws, the terror of the entire countryside, was known to be lying in wait for us, impregnably entrenched within the highest pass of all. My husband's indignation knew no bounds, but, with characteristic British courage, he determined to press onward. I own to a far lesser fortitude; in fine, I was well-nigh distracted with fear. The reassurances of my dear Gerald and the ministrations of my faithful maid somewhat restored my spirits, but when, upon a dark and thunderous evening, made yet more sinister by a crimson sunset and the icy portent of extreme cold, we prepared to ascend this pass prior to pitching our camp in the adjoining valley, I found myself a prey to the gloomiest forebodings.

"Alas, my worst fears were but too soon to be realised!" she continued, the shaken eloquence of her voice rising tremulously above the sympathetic comments of all three listeners. "Scarcely had we traversed the little plateau which lay below the pass itself, and observed those grim pinnacles of calcined stone closing down on us like the jaws of some mythological monster, than we were made aware, by a very bedlam of the fiercest cries and imprecations, of the sudden advance from above of a great company of barbarians, clad in rude cloaks and wearing sheep-skin caps; one and all were armed to the teeth. A shower of arrows fell about our heads, while our small party huddled together in the utmost consternation and dismay. Only my husband, as ever heroic and composed, rode to meet the murderous horde."

Jennifer flung her arm across her face and shuddered violently; then a natural and reviving pride strengthened her voice to firmness.

"Never, while the breath of life animates my bosom, shall I forget the magnificent spectacle of his solitary figure, tall and straight as a pine tree, riding forward alone to the combat. Perhaps a certain slight obstinacy in his otherwise quite perfect disposition accounted for the apparent foolhardiness of the undertaking; perhaps scorn of our cowardly servitors drove him to desperation. For my own part, I am convinced that a noble self-confidence supported him in the belief that he could vanquish these miscreants single-handed. He was attired in white linen, as was his invariable custom when travelling, but over this he wore, owing to the unseasonable cold, a mantle of rough white wool, which, if it somewhat impeded his movements, added much to his impressive appearance. He rode a splendid snow-white Arabian steed; he was armed only with a pair of pistols and a malacca cane."

" A sword-stick was it, now? " asked Father O'Donnell with cordial interest. Jennifer shook her head.

" It was merely a silver-headed malacca cane," she said distinctly. " He had the habit of strolling beside his horse, sometimes for miles at a time; he was an indefatigable walker. The cane he found useful for this form of exercise, and for keeping order among the servants." She paused, allowing the others to digest their surprise; she looked very proud.

" He assumed his station upon a large rock which lay athwart the path, reining in his horse with one hand; the other held his pistol. As the savages surrounded him, he emptied his weapon into their midst, and flung it squarely at the head of their chief, whom it momentarily stunned. The villain fell crashing to the ground, while his followers renewed their savage warfare on every side. My husband calmly took the other pistol from his belt, and discharged it at very close range, in the convulsed and hideous faces of his enemies; a number of lifeless bodies soon strewed the rocks at his feet. Then, with the most intrepid composure, he lifted the cane in ironical salute, and laid about him, like a fencer, with astonishing grace and skill. The wretches were so far amazed by this exhibition of courage that they actually drew back a few paces, watching him with awestruck looks and muttered imprecations. ' The mad Giaour is wearing the invisible armour of Eblis! ' they cried, and forthwith began to pray; some went so far as to kneel on the sharp stones in the very extremity of terror.

" My husband was indeed a figure of almost supernatural power; I was irresistibly reminded of Richard Cœur de Lion among the Paynim hosts, or of King Arthur withstanding the onslaught of his unhallowed foes. I dared to hope — as with what agonised fervour I prayed — that right would triumph, and a deserving Christian gentleman be accorded a miraculous escape from death. But no; it was not to be.

" At that moment the chief of the Turcomans awoke from his

swoon; jumping to his feet, he loudly abused his men for their timidity, at the same time beating them unmercifully with his spear. Drawing his terrible long bow and fixing therein an arrow like a dagger, he let the deadly shaft fly straight at my husband, whom it struck squarely in the breast. Gerald swayed, as if with the impact of a blow, then, leaping lightly to the ground, he dismissed his horse to safety, and stood alone and unattended upon the summit of the rock. A screaming press of spears and darts was immediately loosed at his shining and uncovered head; he fell to earth pierced by twenty arrows."

"He sold his life dearly," said the priest with satisfaction. "He was a brave man; God rest his reckless spirit."

"They feared him even in death," Jennifer answered slowly. "They buried him then and there, on that black and solitary peak, weighing down his body with stones and rubble, and driving a stake through his heart."

"So, there is little more to tell," she went on; her voice was low and exhausted. "The rest of us were made prisoners; my dear and faithful maid, Sallie, nearly lost her life in attempting to defend me, but she was quickly bound and gagged and flung across her captor's saddle-bow. Mohammed, my husband's body-servant, too late repenting of his cowardice, made some efforts to save my person from such indignity; finally I was permitted to ride my own horse. This man was a Musselman, and by virtue of his green turban and grave bearded face, the robbers seemed to grant him a certain immunity from physical assault. He was an accomplished barber, and promised them, with the most abject expressions of respect towards their chief, a complete shaving of crowns as soon as their encampment should be reached.

"Our eyes were now blindfolded, and for upward of an hour we rode along steep and apparently winding paths; at the end of this time I was lifted from my saddle, and the bandage being removed from my eyes, I beheld a small valley filled with the black tents and sturdy flocks of the Turcoman band. I was henceforth treated with sinister consideration; my ghastliest fears were aroused by this parody of kindness, and I allowed myself to be led into the women's quarters and supplied with food without daring, even, to beg for mercy from my savage jailers. Sallie I saw no more; poor girl, I tremble for her life, and for all that the good creature held still more dear.

"I was forced to eat a little supper of tough mutton stewed with onions and dates, and to drink a bowl of sour milk so liberally salted that I perished for thirst during the remainder of that long and torturing night; the darkness into which my tent was plunged was as noonday compared to my spirit's black despair.

"In the morning, an old Turcoman woman performed my toilette with some care; I was bathed, my hair was brushed and braided, and I was clothed in the garments I now wear. My arms were loaded with heavy gold bracelets; a barbaric necklace of gold was clasped about my throat, almost throttling me by its enormous weight. Finally, I was swaddled like an infant in shawls, and placed upon the saddle-bow of the chief's gigantic Khorasan horse. All day, through terrific alternations of heat and cold, through high and intricate defiles and burning plains, my husband's murderer and I rode onward in complete silence. By nightfall we were at the gates of Shiraz.

"The weakness and apathy of a condition without hope and without help now descended upon me; I permitted myself to be carried into the palace, neither opening my eyes nor displaying any other sign of consciousness. The Chief's strong arms relinquished me to a soft and infinitely repellent grasp; I knew that a woman held me. I heard her voice, guttural and thickly sweet, like an asthmatic pigeon, above my head; she was evidently quarrelling with the man, but I could not, I would not, open my eyes to look into a countenance which I instinctively felt could fill me only with horror and disgust."

"You were right, my dear," said Shekerleb sympathetically. "The Banou is both corpulent and abandoned; I consider her hideous. At that moment, too, in spite of her contralto dove-notes, she was furiously angry; she was quite capable of scooping out your eyes with her long finger-nails had you had the temerity to open them."

"Be careful, *Khanum,* you are frightening the child," said the the priest in mild remonstrance, while Jennifer blanched perceptibly at the lady's suggestion.

"The Banou was angry," continued the princess volubly, "because she thought that her cousin Aslan had brought her a corpse; you looked remarkably dead, dear madam. Of course you have an extremely white skin, and doubtless the shawls were suffocating; certainly I despaired of reviving you. You are fortunate to have fallen into my care; the Banou might even now be shaking in your poor little face the dried skin of a female hyena and feeding you with pills made from a monkey's liver, merely in order to make you more attractive to the Shah. She is an ignorant and superstitious person, inordinately cruel, and of a very low grade of intelligence. I do not believe that she has read a single ode of Hafiz, and any camel-driver in Shiraz can recite more classical verse than this illiterate creature."

The contemptuous tone in which the princess pronounced this statement apprised Jennifer of the fact that Shekerleb, like her own mother, was a voracious reader of poetry; the circumstance seemed a happy augury of friendship, and she closed her eyes with a contented smile. The princess, looking down at her, began to chant, in a delicate soprano, the three hundred and thirty-first ode of Hafiz, wherein occurs that lovely line, " A baby fallen from the moon."

" She is asleep," said Shekerleb at last, and was silent.

" She is asleep," said Father O'Donnell; he rose and prepared to leave the room on tiptoe. " I shall ponder the matter carefully, my friends, and with the help of prayer, I may yet arrive at some solution of our difficulties." He raised his hand in a brief gesture of benediction, and departed.

" She is asleep," said the prince in an hypnotic whisper; he approached the couch and stooped over it in a dreaming tranquillity of awe. Then he lifted Jennifer's hand to his lips and kissed it with infinite gentleness.

He moved towards the door, which brimmed with spangled blue darkness; as he stepped across the threshold, his mother spoke to him in a clear voice.

" Do you love her better than you love me? " she asked nonchalantly. Her son turned and looked at her intently; his dark eyes, soft as a pair of velvet butterflies, skimmed lightly over the undisturbed surface of her face, avoiding her own eyes with swift and exquisite dexterity.

" Of course not," he said firmly and mendaciously. He passed, without a sound, into the blue and silver night.   .

Five minutes later, the prince had flung himself face downward in the dewy grass, under a dripping canopy of white roses. He was weeping, but not bitterly; it is doubtful whether his tears contained any appreciable quantity of salt; certainly they were innocent of either blood or gall. Their composition was not unlike that of the purest Fajhum rose-water; they mingled without sharpness with the dew upon the slumbering flowers.

4

THE HERON'S FEATHER

THE FOLLOWING morning, Jennifer awoke to a chorus of birds and the sweetness of shaken honeysuckle. She felt secure and almost happy; the princess, entering, seemed a comrade. Their clear eyes met in an unguarded glance.

Shekerleb carried in her hands a small tray of hammered brass; upon this were laid forth, in the most appetising manner, a fine sugar melon of Kashan, a plateful of little brown cakes, and a glass of white Kismischean wine. " Drink this, my dear," said the princess encouragingly, " the Banou is coming to see you, and you will need nourishment."

At this terrifying news, poor Jennifer began to cry; she hid her head under the folds of her shawl and refused to be comforted for some minutes. At the end of that time, finding her young friend still in tears, Shekerleb said philosophically, " After all, child, you are affianced to my son, and the Banou cannot harm you." There was not the slightest foundation for this boast, but both ladies believed it implicitly; the princess sighed, and the girl looked up at her gratefully.

" Do you really consider an engagement is proper, at present ? " she inquired.

" Under the circumstances, yes," Shekerleb replied with resignation. " My son is extremely young, but he has set his heart upon you, and if you are slain, or even delivered over to the caresses of

Kerim Khan, I fear that the boy will suffer in health and spirits; such an incident might seriously disturb his peace of mind and interfere with his education. He is very sensitive and impressionable." She brooded for a moment in maternal sadness, and then went on more cheerfully.

" After all, it might be worse; you are beautiful, and your birth and breeding are highly satisfactory. It is a pity that you are a member of a Giaour family, however prominent and respected in your own land. But of that, no matter; I hope I am incapable of petty prejudice where my dear son's happiness is concerned. It will be your cherished duty to protect him from the rough assaults of reality long after I am laid to rest in well-deserved weariness," and she began to weep at the picture thus conjured up, for though she was no more than fifty years old, she often indulged in the luxury of tears at her own imagined obsequies.

At this moment, a loud noise in the courtyard announced the arrival of the Banou; Shekerleb hastily set the tray upon a small table and began to arrange Jennifer's tangled locks in some semblance of order. The girl, her face like white glass and her hair like feathers of flame, had never appeared so lovely or so lost a thing as at the exact instant of the Banou's alarming entrance; she was a candle dying in the wind of wicked destiny.

The Banou was preceded by two enormous Ethiopian eunuchs; her own great bulk was sexless in its black wrappings. As soon as this covering was flung aside, however, her huge breasts and undulating haunches proclaimed her womanhood; she reeked of raw female. Scented, painted, and clothed with a gorgeousness at once rich and grotesque, she filled the cool room with an overpowering heat and odour; she steamed and bubbled like a cauldron of gross unguents. The fastidious princess hid her disgust under the gloss of perfect courtesy; Jennifer, too weak for pretence, lay limp and extinguished upon the couch; her heart had almost stopped beating.

" Is the girl dead? " the Banou asked in a throaty chuckle. She touched Jennifer's closed eyes with a henna-crimsoned hand.

" No, Banou; the child still lives," answered Shekerleb unsmilingly. She stood, a genteelly defiant little figure, facing the

Banou; it was abundantly evident that she had been born a lady and the Banou a Turcoman.

" The child lives," she repeated solemnly, " but I cannot answer for her survival of any alarm or disturbance; I must humbly suggest that she be left in complete isolation for a few days." Jennifer breathed again, but the princess continued more ominously, " I have the gravest fears for her life; in fact, I do not believe that even the combined efforts of my son and myself can save her from an early grave; her constitution has been weakened beyond hope of recovery. We must prepare for the worst." She shook her head dolefully, at the same time giving a sharp but reassuring pinch to Jennifer's arm, a form of comfort which the terrified girl was at a loss to understand.

" There is nothing the matter with her except starvation," said the Banou in a rich, greedy voice. " Observe her revolting state of emaciation; this wrist is like a little bone that has been picked by a yellow dog. Faugh — she sickens me; I shall lose my appetite for the mid-day meal if I look at her much longer."

She heaved with disgusting laughter, playing a tattoo on Jennifer's thin collar-bone with cushiony fingers. " But she has fine eyes and magnificent hair; put twenty-five pounds of human flesh on that ramshackle affair she calls her body, and she might fit very comfortably into the Khan's lap one of these evenings. I suppose my pretty Abbas fed her on three violets and a drop of honey; tell him that she must have sheep's tails smothered in rice and butter, thick soups, good greasy fricassees, and as much pure fat as she can stomach; I should strongly advise her to drink a mixture of cream and olive oil with her meals."

Jennifer fainted.

" It is hardly in accordance with correct Persian fashion — " began Shekerleb, who had a thorough contempt for the Banou's inelegant tastes. Then she noticed her young guest's condition; a hopeful light came into her eyes.

" I think you have killed her, Madam," she said respectfully; " she had a very timid nature."

" Nonsense," said the Banou angrily. " She's no more dead than I am; she has simply fainted from hunger. This is the fault of that wretched scullion Abbas; if he cannot fatten her into the semblance of humanity within the week I shall have him beaten with a poisoned knout and thrown into the fish-pond to nourish the carp."

The boy's mother felt no alarm at these threats, for she was well aware that the prince was far too accomplished a cook to be put to death by a notorious glutton; his famous eggs fried in sugar and butter would alone have saved him from the slightest possibility of danger. The Banou's next words, however, left the princess a little uneasy.

"As for the girl," the atrocious woman announced without shame, "I shall give her a week, and then, if she has not grown any fatter, I shall allow the Nubian slaves to administer the bowstring; afterwards, as a salutary lesson for Abbas, he may have the privilege of stuffing her with pistachio nuts and roasting her like a spring lamb for the Khan's birthday banquet; Kerim shall taste this delicacy in one form or the other." She laughed loudly and unpleasantly; Shekerleb perceived that she felt a certain annoyance on the subject of the monarch's senile amours, and while always thoroughly at ease in her character of procuress, still cherished a mild regret for her former profession of odalisque.

The Banou waddled from the room, diffusing upon the pure air of the princess's apartment a medley of egregious perfumes both foreign and domestic; a dreadful heat, like the slow combustion of decay, seemed disseminated from her person.

Shekerleb immediately opened a greenish crystal flask of orange-flower water, and began to fan Jennifer with a white heron's wing mounted in silver. The girl revived at once.

"Has she gone?" she inquired wildly, tossing from side to side upon the soft pillows like one in the throes of a high fever. "And, oh, my dear princess, do you truly believe me to be upon the point of death? In heaven's name, only tell me that you do, for then I shall be saved from the hideous future in store for me! Oh, madam, madam, could you but dream with what a passion of repugnance I have, since my earliest infancy, turned shuddering from the very thought of mutton fat! And now — actually to be forced to eat it! Better a thousand times a swift annihilation than such a torturing indignity! Oh, death, come quickly, and hide me in the security of any grave, from this disastrous fate!"

She shivered from head to foot in a delirium of fear; Abbas, entering quietly from the garden, his arms full of white and yellow roses, his slim figure clad in a cool harmony of white and fading gold, was horrified to behold the pathetic spectacle of her agony and grief. He rushed towards the couch, letting the roses fall unheeded upon the blue-tiled floor.

"Mother!" he cried reproachfully, turning on his innocent parent a look of stern rebuke. "What have you done to her?"

"I have done nothing except wait upon her faithfully since a quarter to nine o'clock," the princess answered tranquilly. "The Banou has been here, however, and seems to have excited her a little." She sniffed with exquisite refinement.

"I am probably dying," Jennifer said with gentle self-satisfaction. Her fear had largely subsided; the prince's presence in the room refreshed her fevered weariness like the shadow of a tree or the shimmer of a fountain.

"Never, my beloved, while the breath of life —" he began in a shaking voice, but his mother interrupted him.

"It might be a very good thing," she said demurely.

Jennifer nodded mutely, in mournful acquiescence, but the prince turned paler than his shirt. He stared at Shekerleb like one who discovers a ghoul among the flowers of his darling's tomb.

"What — did — you — say?" he finally enunciated with white lips.

The princess smiled with a pleased consciousness of perfect altruism; if she had ever secretly entertained any desire for the girl's demise, her mother's heart had long since overcome it. It was but too apparent that such an event would cause the prince intolerable pain, and from this he must be saved at all cost to her own feelings. She was, indeed, a devoted mother.

"You are a pair of silly children," she permitted herself to reply with a slight air of superiority. "Any clever person should be able to see at once that in some such direction lies her only hope of safety. Of course she need not really die" — Jennifer looked relieved, and Abbas bestowed a bright smile upon his mother which she deliberately ignored — "she need not really die; I have still a small quantity of that narcotic powder which my father purchased in Aracan. A dose of this very singular drug produces sleep so profound and lasting that the ignorant invariably suppose it to be death itself; the deep trance persists for three days, and the illusion is complete. Let us give the young lady one of these powders, dissolved in a little wine; after I have announced her death to the Banou we will convey her to a place of safety, on the pretext of interring her; our combined ingenuities should easily arrange the rest. It will be very simple," she finished happily, "and surely very romantic."

All three looked thoroughly pleased; they had the air of a pair of light-hearted conspirators preparing to kidnap an affectionate baby. They gazed at each other with large and excited eyes and drew closer in whispered confabulation. Without, the birds sang incessantly and the roses bloomed in rich profusion.

A sudden brisk knock upon the outer door brought Abbas to his feet with a nervous start.

"It is Father O'Donnell," he said, an expression of annoyance clouding his smooth brow. "I fear he will have some objection to offer; he spoke last night of the Patriarch of Antioch, and even of Armenia. It appears that a large Christian settlement surrounds the monastery of the Three Churches at the foot of Agri Dagh, upon whose summit, in bygone days, the ark of Noah rested from the waves. He is determined that my bride shall be among Christians; he is also extremely insistent upon the purely conventional point of the year's delay which English social custom has interposed between a widow, however young and lovely, and the happiness which her heart may demand. He is a very obstinate man."

Father O'Donnell knocked again, and louder. Abbas was trembling slightly.

"Go, my son, and admit your friend," said Shekerleb, "it is not necessary to acquaint him with our plan; it is entirely a family affair. He is a well-meaning person, but we need not ask his advice upon really important matters. He has served very nicely to teach you foreign tongues and history, he is even skilled in the intricacies of our own literature, but I have never trusted his judgment, and after all, he is only a Giaour." She laughed a little scornfully; the prince walked slowly to the door and admitted Father O'Donnell. The priest entered the room with a firm step and a lively expression of countenance; his handsome face looked fresh and care-free. He was visibly in the best of health and humour.

"I have been thinking of the narcotic powder your parents brought from Aracan," he said immediately to the princess, when he had given them all his greeting and benediction. "I believe that by means of that miraculous drug we may effect the escape and ultimate safety of this poor child; 'tis a thing which must be done and so shall be done, by the help of faith and our own faithful efforts."

Abbas and Shekerleb started guiltily and exchanged glances of confusion and alarm; Jennifer was too bewildered to understand a word of the conversation, whose meaning had for some moments eluded her fatigued intelligence, and which now became more and more impossible for her faculties to grasp. Fortunately her trusting nature, though severely shaken by the events of the past few days, enabled her to lie contentedly enough in a species of half-dream, while above her sleepy head the tongues of the others drove busily back and forth like shuttles weaving light or darkness for her future wear.

"I will leave the business of the hypnotic draught to you, Khanum," Father O'Donnell was saying eagerly, "but will myself undertake to break the news of her supposed death to the Khan; I am in fairly good odour with the old gentleman at present. I will then explain that, as the daughter of a great Giaour lord, her noble birth entitles her to Christian burial, and that in the renowned Armenian monastery of the Three Churches there exists a crypt or vault precisely suited to this purpose. Of course that is not strictly true, as the monks would never admit even a dead woman within their walls, but our problem demands desperate remedies, and our consciences may be clear. I shall then convey the apparent corpse to Armenia, and leave our young friend in the kindly charge of the wife of one of the leading citizens of the pleasant village of Gavmishlu. There, recommended to God and Saint Gregorio, she may pass her first year of widowhood in a peaceful and decorous manner; at the end of this period I, for one, can see no objection to the marriage which my pupil here so ardently desires."

He smiled indulgently at the prince, who covered up his sulkiness and impatience as best he could, by nibbling rose-leaves, kicking his mother surreptitiously under the table, and darting veiled but impassioned looks at Jennifer. Shekerleb began to protest a little, in her impulsive way, at this prospect of un-necessary delay in the matter of her son's happiness, but she soon grew silent under the painful promptings of his green morocco slippers. Father O'Donnell talked on imperturbably; the ob-ject of their mutual anxiety had relinquished her will to a most profound and dreamless slumber.

The benign influence of sleep fell more softly than the moted sunbeams across her innocent face, colouring it with tranquillity and the serener tints of childhood. Thus, relaxed and untroubled, she appeared no more than twelve years old, her brow untouched by weariness or terror, her beauty impersonal and transparent as the air itself. She seemed drained of the denser stuff of hu-manity, like a crystal cup too lovely to pollute with wine. Her very bloodlessness suggested merely a bodily purity and grace; Father O'Donnell alone had the wisdom and common-sense to pity so exquisite a creature.

The princess sat congratulating herself upon the very evident refinement of the girl's small features; she thanked Allah that her grandchildren would be able to count upon straight noses and short upper lips. The prince clenched his hands and closed his eyes in an ecstasy of spiritual greed; he was an admirably virtuous youth, but his possessive instincts were unduly strong, and his heart-strings were racked and torn asunder by several painful emotions as he contemplated the living and beloved image of his ideal.

When Father O'Donnell had at last departed, after appointing that evening for a further discussion of plans, the prince turned to his mother in some agitation.

"Surely, surely, you do not mean to be influenced by his opinion in this affair?" he inquired peevishly; his nerves were but too evidently shattered by excitement and suspense; he had the greatest difficulty in controlling his voice and the movements of his slender hands. His mother looked at him sympathetically; she saw that he was in no condition to be opposed or angered.

"Certainly not, my child," she replied soothingly, laying her plump little palm upon his thin and twitching fingers. "Set your mind at rest on that score. I do not approve of long engagements, and beside, the Banou will never allow the Isauvi to steal the girl like a sheep before her very eyes. He is a kind man, but simple-minded in the extreme; he has no gift for diplomacy." Her tone of good-humoured contempt fell like balsam drops healing the wounded fury of the prince's thoughts; he saw his mother as a strong and beneficent creature, capable of coping with a dozen licentious monarchs and cowardly priests.

The light of happy expectancy which now chased the thwarted frown from his brow penetrated the secret places of his mother's heart like wine. She felt exalted, appeased, and prepared for immolation on an immediate altar.

"You shall marry the girl at once," she cried superbly. "I will go fetch a priest of our own persuasion, and by dispensing with some of the less important ceremony, the wedding shall be solemnised this same night. Do not worry; I will arrange it all; only be calm, my little enameled falcon, and you shall have your desire." She ran from the room, scattering tears and smiles like pale and rosy flowers in her path.

The prince sat up, drying his eyes and arranging his love-locks with an air of dreamy abstraction. Then he turned towards the couch; it was empty.

He leapt to his feet with an exclamation of horror, and gaining the doorway in a single graceful bound, snatched Jennifer from its very threshold; the girl stood swaying in the sunshine, dazed and blinded by its sudden brilliance, and shaken like a spray of white blossoms by the hot south wind. Meekly she surrendered herself to the prince's care, but when he had laid her on the divan and covered her up with a shawl as a vague precaution against harm, he saw that she was weeping uncontrollably.

"I will not be strangled, I will not be stolen like a sheep, and I will not, no, not even for you, be married by a Pagan priest," she sobbed breathlessly, displaying an unwonted vivacity in her protesting cries. "I will not be forced to eat fat mutton, and I will not wear these hateful and improper clothes another minute!"

She made a brief and ineffectual attempt to rise; the prince pushed her gently back against the pillows, and asked solicitously, "Shall I not bring you a glass of iced wine or a cooling sherbet? I think you are feverish."

Jennifer screamed faintly, and caught at his hand. "No," she implored him; "I beg of you, my dear prince, not to poison me or administer a narcotic powder. I am terribly frightened, and I want very much to go home!" At this point her sobs became so poignantly heart-rending that the emotional boy was himself completely overcome; they lay helpless, she upon the couch and he half-kneeling beside it, while an unreasoning passion of despair descended upon them both, violent yet essentially slight and evanescent as an April storm.

Jennifer recovered herself first; she leaned over the prince and patted him with timid and affectionate pity upon the top of his head.

"Don't cry; please don't cry," she said gently. "I am not really afraid of you; I am simply a little hysterical because so many and such curious things have happened to me recently. But pray believe that I am not really afraid of you." She looked long at his sleek dark head with its shaven crown; he continued to hide his face against the edge of the couch, and she to stroke his hair with her finger-tips each time his shoulders were shaken by a sob. Finally she added, in a small voice, and greatly to her own surprise, "I love you."

"But as a sister; purely as a sister," she amended a moment later under the too ecstatic impact of his response. "I do not wish to marry any one at present. Neither do I wish to go to Armenia, and as for staying in the vicinity of the palace, I should very shortly perish of trepidation and suspense in so sinister an environment. I appeal to you, beloved and desired though but lately discovered brother of my heart, to rescue me from this triple dilemma. I think, perhaps, that we had better go back to Devonshire at once; my parents will welcome you as friend and kinsman; you will be as another son to their old age, and should our affections ripen into something more than fraternal sentiments, they will bless our union and watch over us always. It will be delightfully quiet in Cleverly-Neville after so much danger and distress; I am sure that you will find our simple country life congenial and soothing in the extreme. The soft climate of Devonshire is very tranquillising to the nerves," she ended complacently, " and I have no doubt that my dear father will put the little dower house in perfect order in the event of our marriage; its situation is charmingly retired and peaceful." Mentally she withdrew to the seclusion of the dower house, closing white doors and settling flowered curtains against the fiery present.

" I wish I might conceal you in the fabulous caves of Kashan," said the prince tenderly. " Legend relates the existence there of a magical well, deeper than the hills are high, at the bottom of which bloom perpetual gardens of enchantment. But I am afraid the idea is not entirely practical." He sighed.

" Do not allow yourself to be disheartened by our apparent difficulties," said Jennifer kindly, rather relishing the sensation of being, for once, the wise and capable woman of affairs. " I am sure that, by taking a little thought, we can arrange everything quite simply and pleasantly. It is only a question of escaping from Shiraz and reaching England as soon as possible; I do not believe that England can be so far away as Armenia, for example; it is not in the least that sort of place. I have always observed that civilised countries are more accessible than savage ones," she remarked profoundly. " Of course we cannot return by way of Bushire and the sea; the Turcomans make the mountains quite impassable, and as for the sea, I am unfortunately a wretched sailor. But I feel assured that if we travel north by easy stages we shall eventually find ourselves in France, or, at the very worst, Germany, and from these comparatively homelike regions almost any one will be able to direct us to Devonshire. I trust that we shall not be required by providence to leave Cleverly-Neville again; I am tired of travelling." Indeed, her exhausted looks bespoke the truth of this very moderate statement, but her eyes were startlingly illuminated by hope, and her bright hair seemed to play like dancing flames above her lifted brow.

The prince was impressed; he felt that the daughter of a peri and the descendant of a Tartar king could accomplish many miracles forbidden to ordinary mortals. From that instant he laid his slight and changeable will in her white incompetent hands, with a pathetic trust in their superhuman powers. His wearied little soul forgot bewilderment and fear, floating in the hollow cloud of a heaven almost attained.

"What shall I do?" he asked humbly; although he was at most times a coward, he was sincerely sorry that there existed no necessity for sacrificing his life in her service. His eyes mirrored darkly a dumb unquestioning devotion.

"I suppose we must first procure horses, and food for our journey," said Jennifer seriously. She felt her responsibility deeply; in some dim fashion she realised that henceforth she must be the leader of their adventurings, and for the first time in her life she was conscious of a desire to be strong and bold. In a word, all her care now was to protect and comfort her young comrade while contriving a mutual safety for their lives and fortunes.

"I have plenty of horses to ride," began Abbas with a royal air. "Of course, strictly speaking, they do not belong to me, but since I am the rightful prince of this country —"

"No, no, my dear," Jennifer interrupted gently, "we must not dream of stealing anything; it would really not be right. Have you no horse of your own?" The circumstances of her life had led her to assume that every well-bred human being possessed at least a dozen horses.

"I have a beautiful little grey donkey," the prince admitted at last, rather shyly. "He is growing old, but his strength is really remarkable, and he is the most docile creature imaginable. If you would not despise such an animal —" the boy was silent, lowering his eyes before a vision of the white-maned, silver-tasselled steeds of his desires. "He is perhaps not very suitable for your perfection," he murmured, sorrowfully kissing her hand.

Jennifer took both his hands in hers and held them against her heart; he could feel its unstable tripping beat under the white shawl. She looked at him with extraordinary tenderness and surprise. "I love donkeys," she said in the voice of a young mother whispering her child to sleep. There was compassion in her voice, and a certain composed and dedicated quality of lovingkindness.

"There is also the question of disguise," she continued. "Perhaps it would be well for me to don masculine attire like my ancestress Lady Helena, for the singularity of my present costume cannot hope to escape attention. If you happen to have —" She stopped, blushing deeply and hanging her head.

"I have," said the prince, exhibiting symptoms of a like embarrassment; "I believe that my garments of two summers ago will — will be quite practicable. I was not so tall at that time, you understand, and —" The remainder of his words died still-born; he mopped his brow with a printed silk handkerchief, and looked appealingly at Jennifer.

She had already assumed an expression of courageous calm; her small hands were clenched, her eyes dilated. "If you will fetch them, and leave me for a space, I will effect the necessary change," she answered bravely.

The prince sauntered from the room, attempting to look unconcerned; when he returned, singing a little Persian folk-song under his excited breath, he bore a hastily folded bundle of fine silk and cotton stuffs. With an air of well-bred abstraction he brought forth from the corner his mother's silver ewer of sweet-scented spring water; a fleecy Turkish towel was flung negligently upon the couch; a huge bowl of sapphire glass appeared mysteriously from nowhere. He rummaged among his mother's possessions and produced, with the manner of a sleep-walking conjuror, various fragrant powders and fascinating perfumes, from the macerated roots of orris to the heavier attar of rose. Then, wordlessly, he drifted from the shadowy chamber like a breath of wind.

Had Bernadin de Saint Pierre's celebrated romance of *Paul et Virginie* been completed at that time there is no doubt whatever that its conclusion would have been favourably endorsed by Jennifer; the novelist, for his part, might have received valuable and edifying hints from the demeanour of the girl upon the present occasion. She made fast the lock of the door and drew yet closer the slats of the blue *persiennes* at every window; she surrounded the basin and ewer with a tall screen, pierced and painted like a lady's fan. Finally, her ivory pallor suffused by the colour of natural delicacy, she approached the bundle of silk and cotton stuffs, and, with trembling fingers, untied the knot whereby its contents were secured from view.

Half an hour later, the prince, leaving the little rose-hung stable where he had been engaged in saddling his donkey and providing the faithful animal with a generous meal of oats, topped off by a fragment of sugar candy and a fine Demavend apple, noticed with dismay that the shadows were already lengthening upon the emerald lawns of the palace garden. He hastened his light step, and arriving at his own door, was preparing to knock, when the door flew open in his face, revealing a slim and lovely boy attired with princely magnificence. White, tarnished silver, and thin traceries of black and scarlet combined to produce a costume of startling elegance and distinction. The exquisite and ambiguous creature confronting him bore in one hand a mirror; the other clutched a long strip of black silk which the prince immediately recognised as a turban. A torrent of unconfined and shining copper hair fell about the shoulders of this amazing apparition.

" Will you be good enough to arrange my turban for me? " Jennifer asked him without a trace of her former embarrassment, at the same time regarding the mirror with steadfast satisfaction. " I cannot manage it, because I have such quantities of hair, but I believe that it will be very becoming if properly draped, with perhaps a simple jewel among its folds."

Her face was intent and fixed upon her image in the mirror; vanity had superseded shyness in her innocent mind. At once, her childish eagerness put the prince completely at his ease.

A moment after, she had seated herself before the large silver looking-glass suspended above Shekerleb's dressing-table; the prince stood behind her. " How well these fantastic garments suit my peculiar type of beauty! " she prattled on happily, piling her hair into a twisted coronet with careless hands. " Dear Gerald would have been enchanted; his taste was always for the fanciful and singular, though chaste and delicate, in art." Her countenance clouded with soft regret, and then flashed into ecstasy as the prince wound the turban above her milky brow and set a heron's feather, misted with tiny brilliants, in the centre of the black folds. Quick as imagination, he pulled two springy tendrils of bright hair from beneath their covering, and let them lie coiled, like rings of golden wire, against her clear temples and smooth cheeks. Then he stepped back, with the air of a magician, and clapped his hands silently, as if summoning fellow-sprites to admire a peri's loveliness.

" Oh, beautiful! " they breathed with simultaneous awe, contemplating the picture in the mirror as if louder words could shatter it to crumbs of quicksilver and glass.

Then, as Abbas flung a cloak of black Kermanshah weave over her scintillation, Jennifer rose slowly to her feet, and remarked, examining her little slippers of red morocco, " And only think, if it were not for these shoes and the small scarlet flowers on my tunic, it would really be half-mourning, and so admirably adapted to my present needs." It was plain that she extracted a certain mild comfort from this reflection, though she would have discarded the red slippers with extreme reluctance.

The prince, who was totally unable to understand her train of thought, was content with her obvious pleasure, fondly believing that the subtlety of her etherial mental processes transcended his grosser mind; he still regarded her as a supernatural being. It must be admitted that her appearance fully justified this extravagant supposition.

" Come; there is no time to be lost," he said with gentle firmness, taking her hand in his. He was actually so exalted and transformed by the power of love that he forgot to look at himself in the mirror after donning his own cloak of heavy violet wool; fortunately its graceful folds fell obediently into lines of classic beauty about his slender limbs. " My mother may return at any moment, with a mollah, or Father O'Donnell may come back with a map of Armenia and a quantity of good advice. I am weary of arguing with old people; let us be gone at once, my silver dove."

" Will not your absence cause your mother considerable alarm? " Jennifer asked, looking faintly troubled; her thoughtful nature ever shrank from causing pain.

" Possibly," admitted the prince with some impatience. He

seized a scrap of vellum and drew from his belt a pretty gilt pen and a diminutive ink-horn. Although forbidden by his father's will to practise the art professionally, he was an accomplished amateur draughtsman and writer of elegant script. "I will leave a little note for her, and decorate its margin with an amusing design; I think a picture of our two hearts — so —with a slightly malicious caricature of Father O'Donnell attempting to separate them will be certain to appeal to her sense of humour. Then an affectionate message from us both, and an assurance of a happy if distant reunion; she cannot fail to be satisfied." He executed the writing with hurried skill and, depositing it upon his mother's pin-cushion, drew Jennifer swiftly from the room.

An hour later, under the diffused and amber rays of the declining sun, a small grey donkey might have been observed traversing the northern environs of Shiraz; on either side of the patient beast strolled a slim and languid youth of princely bearing. The taller of the two wore a violet cloak; the other was enveloped in a black mantle of unrelieved and sombre richness.

5

THE SERPENT IN PERSEPOLIS

Whether owing to her sudden but none the less sincere affection for Abbas, or to the enlivening effects of her outward change of character, a vague and mysterious metamorphosis appeared to take place in the spirit of the child Jennifer from the very instant of her escape from Shiraz. From languor she passed to the lightest vivacity; her temper became merry and wild in the extreme; she was all at once a tease, a tomboy, and a witch. Each sign of fear or weakness was soon dissipated in the full illumination and speed of her humour; she danced, she sang, she pulled down fruit from every tree and tasted the water of every wayside spring. She refused to burden the silvery back of old Rhustum the donkey with the inconsiderable thistledown of her body; her feet skipped and shied among the lights and shadows of the path, but her soul flew above them winged and darting like a dragon-fly. She climbed an almond tree and pelted the prince with green astringent husks; she threw her cloak to the wind and turned a mad spontaneous handspring as the crescent moon appeared between the higher clouds and the sun dropped like a pomegranate into the cool blue valleys lying to the west of Mosella.

Upon the banks of Rocnabad they sat down to supper; spreading their cloaks upon the grass and reclining against a mossy shoulder of rock the better to enjoy their simple fare; the stars sprinkled their bread with fire and the dews diluted their wine with enchantment. In addition to these delicacies, Abbas prepared a salad of the most ingenious charm, reciting meanwhile the loves of Megnoun and Leilah with thrilling intonation, as he mixed in a thin porcelain bowl the eggs of little birds, cream, citron juice, slices of cucumber, and the inner leaves of various delicate herbs.

"I am so happy!" sighed Jennifer, dipping a wild strawberry into her wine. "I have never been quite so happy, not even in Devonshire." She pulled off her turban, allowing her long hair to drown the sleeping hyacinths among the grasses in a veritably hyacinthine flood of light and colour. She began, very softly, to sing the Lament for Flodden; her extreme happiness made her voice more than ever mournful and forlorn.

"I, also, am reposing in a state of perfect happiness," said the prince in a hushed whisper. "I am afraid to breathe, lest the sharp breath snap one of my heart-strings and I die on a note of harmonious praise. Let me calm the clamour of my breath to silence; then it will rise without offence to your ears, like incense before the ivory shrine. And again, let the incense be invisible, nor interpose the impertinence of colour between the purity of the air and the more ghostly purity of your soul. But, I pray that the frankincense of my love may be sweet in your nostrils." He kissed the tarnished silver fringe upon Jennifer's tunic.

The girl experienced a pang of tenderness; his words, though pleasantly melodious, conveyed almost nothing to her mind, but the sound of his voice, and, above all, the sight of the slight ripple in his smooth hair as he bent his head lower and lower until it rested at her feet, caused her heart to contract with sudden pain. She put a timid hand against his cheek; then, when she had felt his tears cold upon her hand, she drew him closer until she had hidden his tears under her hair and dried them with the little warmth and comfort of her breast.

So they sat for perhaps an hour, sundered by immensities, yet bound together by a hundred common ties of childishness and vanity and weakness; innocence had not left them, nor human love approached too near. Their mutual affection was like one of those beautiful blue butterflies of Cashmere, so rare and so elusive, which exist in the upper regions of the air but seldom present themselves to mortal view.

At last, the prince rose, and, stooping over Jennifer, kissed her with the most reverential composure. Their lips met scrupulously and in silence; as she closed her eyes under the tented bower of eglantine which shielded her from the sky, she saw him walk quickly over the summit of a little hill and disappear among a grove of tamarisks. The moonlight was shed like water from his moving figure, and he was gone. In absolute tranquillity and trust she pulled the cloak about her shoulders, laid her cheek against her folded hands, and slept.

For twelve days their delightful journey continued, uninterrupted save by playful excursions through the fruitful fields and vineyards of the adjacent country, and by the night's welcome and uneventful repose. The large panniers which swung on either side of Rhustum's saddle were constantly replenished with fresh vegetables; grapes from the vines, and a variety of wild and cultivated fruit was always within the reach of their most idle wish. The wine-shops, or as the romantic prince preferred to call them, Magian convents, were numerous and good, but the young companions preferred in the main to drink water enhanced by flavorous citron or sharper lime. Their food was simple but sustaining; eggs, milk, and butter were purchased without difficulty from the complacent peasantry, and now and then a tumbling hilly stream afforded trout or royal salmon to the prince's skill. Game birds abounded; golden pheasants, snow-cocks, black partridge and iridescent doves hid in every wood, but the children were too tender-hearted to harm these beautiful creatures, and, moreover, they lacked the means no less than the will to slay them.

At the end of a week of this jocund and salutary life, the pair had completely lost their pallid looks and languishing manners; they were as bright-eyed and agile as the hares and slim gazelles which frolicked in the deeper forests. In addition to this charming outward alteration, their natures had enjoyed a comparable improvement; Abbas was no longer spoiled and peevish, nor Jennifer vain and melancholy. A benignant miracle had been performed in the very substance of their flesh and spirit; they were not merely like two pining birds suddenly released from the gilt cruelty of their cage, they were, it appeared, a pair of expensive but sickly little pigeons hilariously transformed into meadow larks.

As they walked one golden morning through the vineyards of Khullar, the boy turned to his companion to inquire, "Would you not like, my star of dawn, to visit the strange city of Istakhr, perhaps better known to you by its antique title of Persepolis? It lies a little to the east of our ideal course, but well warrants a short delay in its fallen but enormous splendour. What say you, my imperishable rose?"

"I think it sounds an excessively charming plan," cried Jennifer with enthusiasm. "Let us not waste too much time over the ruins, my prince, but find some cool and quiet spot wherein to enjoy our fruit and salad; while you recite a sweetly pensive ode, or give your exquisite imitation of the Persian singing-birds, I can employ myself in mending that rent in your mantle. If you are not too tired, you might make a few pancakes; I will beat the eggs and whip the cream with pleasure. It will be utterly delightful; have we time to reach Persepolis to-day?"

"I think not," said Abbas kindly, smiling in spite of himself at her youthful frivolity. "I think not, but we can easily cover the distance by to-morrow afternoon, and that without undue haste. I heartily agree with you, my pearl of antelopes, in your distaste for the dull science of archæology; Father O'Donnell wearied me well-nigh beyond endurance by his insistence upon its dusty detail. But history " — his eyes lit with luminous points of gold — " and above all ancient history, especially when it is admittedly untrue — ah, that delights my soul, even as such fascinating subjects as judicial astrology and the higher branches of advanced necromancies."

Jennifer thought him very clever, but she was accustomed to cleverness, and soon beguiled him, by way of a brief discussion of the character of Zoroaster, into a game of hide-and-seek among the grapevines. Her influence over the prince's mind was a constant source of wonder to the girl, who had invariably played the part of feathered shuttlecock to the obstinacy of others. Her husband had always appeared completely unmoved and imperturbable; she marvelled incessantly to behold her curious power in regard to the temperamental Abbas, never doubting, however, in view of his revived condition, that her power was no less benign than strong, in which faith she was, in all probability, correct.

Towards sunset on the following afternoon the two young travellers approached the terrible ruins of Persepolis, which soared among the tinted clouds of evening with an effect of majesty hardly inferior to the heavens themselves. Abbas was irresistibly reminded of the fabulous cities of Shadukiam and Ambreabad, abodes of peris, and capitals of legendary Ginnistan, while to Jennifer the imposing spectacle forcibly recalled her first sight of London. They clutched each the other's hand in an ecstasy of bewilderment and awe; their eyes widened and their faces paled before the unbelievable vision of Istahkr, city of Solyman and spoil of Alexander, standing naked and noble as the skeleton of all past greatness still challenging oblivious eternity.

The children insensibly drew closer; they lacked the courage to ascend the vast flight of steps leading to the terrace of the minarets, those lofty columns each consecrated to a star, which Solyman ben Daoud had lifted from the earth to support the impious elevation of his own mind. Above them, carven from the black marble of the hillside itself, the graves of the preadamite sultans preserved a sinister repose.

Tethering Rhustum to the lower limbs of a thunder-blasted tree, the two huddled under the shelter of a projecting rock; a few violets and other pastoral flowers flourished in this hidden place, where the rays of the sun were caught and held and the wind could not enter. The prince kindled a little fire, and Jennifer brought forth their small store of fruits and ingenuous herbs;

they were quiet, but composed and happy in each other's company. Having eaten sparingly, they remained crouched on the grass, in perfect silence, and clasped in a close and infinitely affectionate embrace. Their gaze was fixed upon the terrace; their hearts, accelerated by a vague trepidation, beat together consolingly.

Suddenly a voice, clear and chilly as the atmosphere above the distant mountains, smote upon their astonished senses. From between the gigantic watch-towers a tall figure emerged, clad from head to foot in white linen. A dark attendant followed in his steps, carrying a travelling-cloak of heavy white wool and a furled green umbrella. The man in white linen was far above the common height, thin and straight as a ramrod; his carriage and manner were dignified to the point of stiffness, yet he bore himself with such an air of elegance and pride that the very column lowering over his mortality seemed somewhat dwarfed by the perfection of his poise. His face was colourless and almost without expression; his features, and particularly his narrow high-bridged nose and pale arched brows, bespoke the extreme aristocrat. In one long pallid hand he carried a little volume richly bound in tree-calf; his other arm hung in a white silk sling. His slightly sallow skin appeared bleached and transparent; his countenance was somewhat lined and drawn, and one lean cheek displayed a neat thread-like scar.

Withal, he had the air of a man invincible in strength and courage; it was impossible to associate him with weakness or failure. The prince, observing the form and size of his admirably shod feet and the set of his head upon his shoulders, concluded that he was at least a king in his own country. Though evidently a foreigner, the man was completely well-bred. The smoky yellow sunset crested this personage's sandy hair with flame as he spoke again in a cold, ringing voice.

"And ride in triumph through Persepolis!" said Gerald clearly. The slight satirical smile which played around his compressed lips excused the words for their grandiloquence, but in reality he was amused rather by the words themselves than by his use of them, for though he had read the Elizabethan dramatists at an early age, owing to the exigency of his father's library, they had more often moved him to ridicule than to admiration, and at the present moment he was inclined to laugh outright at the barbarous quality of Mr. Marlowe's blank verse. Hastily muttering a fine acrid sentence from Seneca to rid his mouth of this bombastic taste, he paused upon the brink of the black marble stairway to survey the scene before him.

He was accompanied by a short stout man, dressed in the height of Persian fashion, whom Abbas recognised as a provincial governor of some importance. The poor fellow was rendered half invisible by Gerald's august presence; he kept nodding his head with great servility while gazing upward into the face of his companion, who noticed him no more than courtesy required.

"The ruins of the Archæmenidæ," continued Gerald with suave hauteur, "are of the most immediate interest to any student of mankind; the successive monarchs which this spot has exalted and consumed are a wise commentary on the futility of existence. Their boastful inscriptions and their arrogant sarcophagi — what are these but ashes in the mouths of the astute?"

"Quite so, your Excellency; your Excellency is abundantly right," panted the stout Persian at his elbow. Gerald went on unmoved.

"How singular is the consideration," he murmured, more to his own soul than to the receptive ears of his companion, "that my virtuous and beautiful Jennifer has joined the ranks of the unreturning dead; she sleeps with Darius and Artaxerxes, while I once more tread the dust which contains her loveliness and their magnificence. Singular, indeed, that I am alive at this instant, who was buried quite as thoroughly by my Turcoman friends as the spiced and bitumined occupants of these tombs. I have not told you, sir, of my miraculous escape from death in the passes below Shiraz," he said, turning to the other man with an air of polite condescension. "You are aware, of course, that I have had the profound misfortune to lose my young wife." He pronounced the words with icy calm, and paused for a full minute, during which he kept his eyes fixed and remote upon the remote horizon.

"As for my adventure among the savages," he went on courteously, "it was perhaps sufficiently curious to merit a brief recital. You must know that after the wretches had apparently slain me and cast me into a deep pit with a number of stones cracking my ribs and breast-bones, they took the precaution to drive a stake through what they erroneously supposed to be my heart, but which was in reality no more than the left lapel of my cloak; my side was barely grazed in the process."

"Such are the advantages of possessing an elegant figure," said the Persian with an envious glance at Gerald's refined anatomy. The Englishman bowed gravely.

"My faithful servant here," continued Gerald, indicating Mohammed, who looked miserably embarrassed, "is no less accomplished as a surgeon than as a barber. He was captured by the tribesmen, but succeeded in eluding their vigilance the next day. Returning at once to the spot where they had interred me, he managed to remove the stones from my body, and found me to be still alive, though desperately wounded. He was not surprised; he knew me very well, and had not supposed that I could be slain with any particular ease. Not to weary your patience with lengthy explanations, I will content myself with saying that he concealed me in a commodious cavern upon a bed of wild thyme and basil, and tended me with unremitting care until my wounds, which numbered no less than seventeen, were practically healed. My health had really benefited by the enforced rest, and as soon as we had procured by strategy a pair of horses belonging to our late captors, we proceeded direct to Shiraz, where I was met by the sad news of my wife's death at the hands of the Turcoman hordes." He paused again for a decorous space of silence, meanwhile fixing the Persian with a cold and forbidding eye, under which the unfortunate man dared not venture a single expression of condolence.

"That this city of Istakhr is one and the same with the Persepolis of more remote antiquity has been known beyond dispute since the time of Pietro della Valle, who visited it in 1621," concluded Gerald, changing the subject with calm finality. He descended the steps and disappeared among the colossal ruins of the plain, followed by his two companions; presently the sound of horses' hooves, rapidly diminishing in the distance, came to the stunned and aching senses of the two children crouched under the grass-grown slab of stone which had hidden them from view.

"It was my husband," said Jennifer in a breaking thread of voice. "It was Gerald. I tried to call out to him, but I could not. How very tall he is, and his eyes — did you notice the colour of his eyes, Abbas? They are like ice over black water, and yet they are pale, like his face. But how tall he is! I suppose I should be happy to know that he is alive, and yet — " She fell silent, hiding her face against the prince's shoulder.

"I knew he must be a great lord," Abbas replied in a tone of unwilling admiration. Then, in a burst of confidence, " He frightens you, does he not, my darling? I do not wonder at that; he frightens me also; I believe he is a Djinn."

"But how is it possible that Gerald should frighten me; is he not my husband? " asked Jennifer in amazement, lifting her enlarged eyes, which brimmed with tears, to the prince's look of grave solicitude. "Nor can I admit the least resemblance to a Djinn, in one who is so obviously the fine flower of English gentlemen." She pronounced the words with steady lips; she was, however, shivering so violently that Abbas, believing her to be cold, drew his cloak about her tremors. She accepted the attention passively and without comment.

"He is precisely like one of the more malignant Djinn," said the prince stubbornly. "He also resembles the lost angel Harud, who stands head downward in the burning Babylonian sand, teaching sorceries to the misguided. I shall not allow you to see him again, my silver gazelle; he would assuredly devour you with his long yellow teeth." He kissed her cold fingers, and endeavouring to warm them, laid her hand against his cheek.

"My husband is a remarkably handsome man," Jennifer persisted primly. "He has beautiful teeth, and would never, under any circumstances, stand upon his head. He bears not the slightest likeness to a lost angel; I have always thought of him in connection with King Arthur, or possibly the Black Prince." The innocent creature had never heard the moral character of the Black Prince impugned; she regarded Abbas with increasing indignation.

The boy, on his part, displayed considerable obstinacy; he was, perhaps, a little jealous, and that for the first time in his life. In addition to this disturbing emotion, he was conscious of a growing sense of uneasiness in a world which contained himself and the tall gentleman in white linen.

"I think we had best be continuing our journey; we can reach one of the small villages lying north of this melancholy spot by nightfall, and the sight of a few simple human faces would be cheering to my spirits; I should also be extremely thankful for a glass of wine, as I am very tired," he said nervously. Nevertheless, he felt hopeful; Jennifer had rarely failed to respond sympathetically to complaints of fatigue. He leaned back against the rock in an attitude of exhaustion, closing his eyes and permitting the fine pallor of his face to plead for itself; his mouth was set in lines of patient suffering. He waited.

Jennifer drew herself away from him; she sat up very straight and stared at him haughtily. He was fortunate to escape the expression of outraged propriety which filled her eyes with darting and indignant lightning.

"You are an excessively silly boy, Abbas," she enunciated crisply. "If you were not so young and inexperienced I should regard your proposals as insulting to my honour; your ignorance of the world alone excuses you in your impertinent folly. Are you not aware that I am the adored and devoted wife of the heir to one of the oldest baronies in England, who is also an invaluable civil servant and the favoured friend of the Governor of Bengal?" She paused, to give her words their full and devastating effect; the prince had covered his face with the folds of his mantle, and now lay motionless. He made no answer whatever.

"I must at once request you to allow me to return to Shiraz," Jennifer went on; her manner was becoming more and more formal and chilling; it is a pity that the poor child was denied the opportunity of practising her new-found airs of courtly disdain in some more populous spot than the ruins of Persepolis. They would have gone very well in the salon of Madame du Deffand, for example, where she had cut so timid and shrinking a figure during the preceding winter. The urbane and unremitting efforts whereby Gerald had sought to turn his wife into a woman of the world were now at last beginning to bear fruit, fruit bitterer and less digestible than Dead Sea apples between the teeth of the unhappy prince.

He lay grinding his teeth in agony and rage, at the same time forcing back with considerable difficulty the tears which stung his eyelids like imprisoned wasps. His pride, his love, his highest and most dearly impossible hopes had fallen to a destruction no less complete, if slightly less impressive, than that which Alexander, assisted by the invincible battalions of Time, had wrought upon Persepolis. His emotions deprived him of strength and almost of life itself; his hand at that moment lacked the force to crush a worm, yet, such was the concentrated and quintessential fury of his spirit, that he would unhesitatingly have consigned the entire universe to destruction with no more pity than it cost him to crack the shell of a hazel-nut. Though he could never rise to the illustrious distinction of the Macedonian conqueror, it is probable that Abbas excelled even Alexander the Great in royal anger and tormented pride, as he lay half-fainting under the shadow of the Forty Minarets.

Jennifer rose, without another glance in his direction, and began to pack their few possessions in a shawl, which she strapped securely to Rhustum's back. The panniers were refilled with their load of fruit and cresses; the fresh eggs and pats of butter were laid carefully upon these. Then after arranging her disordered hair and smoothing out as best she could her crumpled and fantastic garments, she shook the prince gently, at the same time requesting him, in a polite but distant tone, to rise and accompany her without delay. Her eyes were like black stars ringed with amber; her uncovered head flung its fires upon the rainy wind.

At the touch of her hand upon his sleeve, the prince shuddered and appeared to sicken as if at the approach of some venomous reptile; then he struck at her hand, feebly, but with hectic violence. Jennifer started back; her eyes filled with brief tears which the wind instantly sucked from her lashes, leaving her eyes wide, and clear as dark crystals.

"An English gentleman never strikes a woman," she said with sweet composure.

As it was obviously out of the question to persuade Abbas to move before morning, Jennifer resigned herself to spending the night under the same roof with him; the roof was merely a low rocky projection, and the shelter it afforded slight and uncertain. Wrapping herself in her inky mantle, she lay down at some little distance from her companion; the cold wind and scattered drops of rain which sprinkled her couch she bore with perfect fortitude, but it was long before sleep visited her pillow. The fact that her pillow was a large fragment of flint may partly have accounted for this insomnia, but the confusion and infelicity of her emotions were undoubtedly its chief cause. Abbas lay as one dead, his face turned to the blank unanswering rock, his cloak drawn over his head. From time to time she looked at him; an icy pressure constricted her heart, but her mind was firm, cool, and empty of all save a sense of decorum.

Towards morning they both fell asleep; the wind increased in cold and velocity, and the sky was overclouded. Impelled either by a desire for warmth, or by some deeper and more pathetic instinct, the two unfortunate children turned to each other's arms in the profound unconsciousness of slumber; the chilly dawn discovered them clasped in a mournful embrace, their common pillow, of which the prince had appropriated the major portion, wet with pitiable tears.

The sadness and ironical contrast presented by the homeward journey, as compared to the idyllic fortnight which preceded it, are too melancholy to bear a prolonged description. Let it suffice to relate that for every happy hour of the first innocent pilgrimage, the reversed and tragic path of the return was marked by a like period of depression, pride, and well-nigh intolerable longing.

The low mud walls and huddled roofs of Shiraz appeared at length against the southern horizon; as they passed the tomb of the poet Hafiz where it lies embowered in roses upon the confines of the city, the prince and Jennifer were both weeping inconsolably. The name evoked tender memories in the mind of each, and now they had not addressed a single syllable one to the other during the past three days.

It was very late when they entered the palace garden, under a green and gibbous moon; a deathly silence prevailed, and the dew upon the grass was pale as ashes. Near the prince's cottage they paused, regarding each other inimically; then they spoke together, their voices cold with estrangement.

"Where are you going?" asked Jennifer and Abbas in one breath.

The prince answered first; he had the better opportunity for causing pain. "I am going to my mother," he said quietly. "I shall not see you again, I think. May I inquire as to your own destination? Shiraz is notoriously dangerous at this hour of the night; perhaps the Banou would have the charity to shelter you."

The girl, a mere ghost in a ragged cloak of darkness, could turn no paler than the last few hours had left her; her voice, however, now seemed withdrawn into her heart as the blood from her cheeks had been. In a moment she contrived to summon it; her whisper was distinct. "I am going to find my husband."

Abbas knew that she was going to her destruction; he suspected that she was going to her death, but he was deeply offended, and proud as only a prince can be proud. "I wish you happiness," he said, elaborately. "Good-bye."

"Good-bye," Jennifer replied softly; the little word, shorn of every title of endearment or courtesy, fell through the air like a bird without wings.

Abruptly, without a look or gesture of forgiveness, they turned from each other in the black and terrible night and were gone, their light and rapid footsteps rustling the grass for an instant and then passing into an echo, and thence lessening to oblivion.

6

THE GROVE OF CYPRESSES

When the two eunuchs carried Jennifer into the harem, the Banou was still awake. Parting the curtains of carnation-coloured silk that separated her own apartment from that of the other women, she peered into the obscurity with angry reddened eyes, then, observing the nature of the burden borne by her henchmen, she smiled and licked her lips with satisfaction. The Khan had been ill-humoured of late, and here was a tender if unsustaining morsel for his ailing appetite.

The Banou had grown hideous in the service of sin and the indulgence of her own body, but her boldly curving nose, large brow, and sensual lips still possessed a trace of heavy symmetry and raddled bloom; only her prominent eyes, lashless and red-lidded, were beyond the help of kohl or antimony to brighten or conceal. She was dressed as usual in a profusion of rich untidy garments; the variety and pungent strength of the unguents she affected were powerless to destroy the odour of sweat which enveloped her, as her jewels were powerless to lend grace or distinction to her vast heaving limbs and bosom. To the girl, still struggling desperately in the grasp of the eunuchs, the face of the atrocious creature emerging from between the thin folds of carmine silk seemed the picture of ultimate and perfected evil; at that moment hope died within her labouring heart, and she ceased every attempt to resist or escape the fate which awaited her.

Open-eyed, her lovely countenance still vivid with the terror in her blood and the living worm which devoured her soul alive, Jennifer suffered herself to be bathed in a great pool of black marble, in water scented with the essence of every flower; her eyelids were painted with purple antimony and her pale cheeks tinted with Egyptian rouge. The magnificent lengths of her hair, washed in the wine and the juice of lemons, were dried by Abyssinian slaves wielding great fans of peacock feathers; it spread itself upon the perfumed air like waves of sunlight made substantial. Her lips and finger-nails were coloured like coral against the white transparence of her skin.

" She is pretty even now; when she is fat she will be prettier," said the Banou unctuously, pinching Jennifer's pointed chin. " She is not my favourite type, I confess; she has neither salt in her complexion nor spice in her mouth. But she will make a very wholesome breakfast for Kerim Khan; he is too old for highly seasoned dishes." She laughed long and horribly.

" Now, my love-bird," the woman continued, dangling an equivocal object before Jennifer's dilated eyes, " look carefully upon this neat plaited cord, cleverly woven from silk and cat-gut; it is none other than the renowned bow-string of romance, improved and modernised by my own ingenuity! I am proud of this little invention. Behold, I hang it above your couch; sleep well, my porcelain treasure. Should you attempt to escape, this intelligent machine will automatically descend to encircle your slender throat with a clasp more virtuous than the Khan's; its embrace, however, though impersonal and chaste, is invariably fatal. Good night; may your slumbers be tranquil and refresh-ing. At dawn I shall return with the Khan." She went out, ex-tinguishing the three great lamps of golden filigree whereby the room was lit, whose lights were sanguine garnet and cornelian.

The girl lay quiet, but tense and ringing, as it were, with the rush of invisible winds and rivers; within her veins the whistling blood deafened her with its thin insistence, while the entire darkness of the place moved past her in a slower, deadlier mo-tion, dragging her gradually onward and downward with a dreadful patience and precision. She was a minute and whirling star, turning ever upon its own axis and singing as it turned, singing without volition or delight the music of its swift destruc-tion. The room was a channel for elemental fear and horror; around this larger circle she swung endlessly, as the planets swing about the sun. Surrounded and at the same time pierced through and through by several deaths, she was nevertheless awake and alive in the bright fever of every vein and nerve. At last, she lived; now she knew she must die.

The screen of mother-of-pearl and sandal-wood which hid the eastern window of the room appeared suddenly set with larger and more luminous disks of iridescence; the dawn came through these little orifices white and pure and pearly as globes of snow-water. Then, from very far away, a tiny sound pene-trated the gorgeous screen; it seemed to fall upon the ear with a tone as vague and delicate as the colour of the dawn upon the eyelids. The girl thought it must be the voice of a wild bird, waking in too bright dawn, and lost and frightened at the instant of its waking.

The voice drew nearer, and all at once it ceased to cry like a bird; it called, and its voice was human. It was the voice of the prince calling to his love; calling and crying to his silver gazelle and his imperishable rose of ivory, who now lay dying in the very early morning with the bow-string above her head and the innermost vein of her heart broken in two forever.

Jennifer moved upon her pillows with a violent effort of will; she leaned upon her elbow and listened. Then she lifted her head and looked straight at the bow-string; it writhed before her eyes like a green and golden snake. She sat bolt upright among the crimson pillows and called to the prince in a clear melodious voice. " My dear," she called, "my dearest love, I am coming! "

As she leapt from the couch the bow-string fell softly down; she felt its silken touch upon her throat; its touch was gentle, like a caress. Then she tore at the silk and screamed; her throat and hands were all entangled in the silk and still she screamed and screamed. " Gerald — Gerald — Gerald! They have murdered me! "

So, in death, her husband possessed her completely; she died with his name upon her lips.

This circumstance would without doubt have been a source of the keenest satisfaction to Gerald, had he been aware of it; he could not, however, hear his wife's expiring words, being at that hour peacefully asleep in a distant wing of the palace. He never, therefore, had the felicity of realising that she had called to him with her dying breath. The full comprehension of this fact was reserved for the unfortunate prince, who, standing beneath Jennifer's window, heard her cry distinctly.

For a moment his limbs failed him, and he would have fallen had he not put out his hand to grasp the lower branches of a magnificent damask rose-bush; the flowers, being full blown, quietly detached themselves and wavered to the ground as he touched them. He stood swaying in a shower of sweetness, his face like thrice-refined wax, his eyes round holes through which a darkness seemed to pour like smoke. Then, dragging his feet along the dewy grass, his head bent as if a millstone hung upon his breast, he went home to his mother, passing thin and shadow-like across the bright mirror of the breaking day.

An hour later the Banou, entering the room where Jennifer

lay dead, perceived at once what had occurred, and smote her swollen hands together in frank annoyance. The bow-string, doubtless shaken from its hook by the girl's sudden leap upward, had dropped upon her throat; she had perished of its silken string as surely as if the noose had been fanged or poisoned. She had died of pure fear; extended upon the crimson couch, unclothed save for one garment of clear white lawn, she looked as if some hidden wound had pierced her heart and drained her body of mortality, the colour of which stained the very bed upon which her body slept.

"The Khan will be angry; that cannot be avoided," said the Banou philosophically to her favourite Abbyssinian. "Luckily the Georgian virgin whom my cousin captured yesterday is extremely handsome; prepare the bath at once."

She left the chamber of death, and walked, as swiftly as her huge bulk would permit, in the direction of the prince's cottage. She knocked loudly upon the door; then, receiving no answer, entered at once and without permission.

Abbas had flung himself down in the corridor; the cold blue tiles below his brow were no colder than the hand his mother held between her own. Since he had returned to the house he had not spoken, nor moved save to draw away his hand once or twice; finally he gave up the struggle and lay still, allowing Shekerleb to chafe his fingers; this she continued to do with a certain timid obstinacy. Father O'Donnell stood at some distance from the pair, gazing sadly at his pupil's motionless form; the lines in his face drooped, and it was evident that he was very tired. Each time that Shekerleb attempted to address her son, the priest shook his head without speaking.

"Good morning," cried the Banou in a thick, jocular voice, shoving Abbas's body a little to one side with the toe of her tight Turkish slipper. "How is my little cook to-day, and his lady mother, and O'Donnell Baba the distinguished diplomat? I have missed you, dear prince; your assistants are wretched bunglers one and all. We have not had a decent meal since you left on your pleasure jaunt; I know you will welcome the immediate opportunity of relieving our starvation. To-night, as his loyal subjects must be well aware, the birthday banquet of our beloved ruler takes place; I expect you to exhibit your most poetic skill upon this festive occasion. I have even a small suggestion to make. Do you not consider that a little English lamb, tender and toothsome, might tempt our Kerim's failing appetite? Display your genius, dear Abbas, to-night if ever; dress your lamb with sweet herbs and pistachio nuts, roast her in your silver oven; the Khan will give you half his kingdom for a slice of that delicate flesh! "

The princess turned aside her face and groped blindly for her smelling-salts; Father O'Donnell became very pale, but rather with anger than disgust; his eyes were blue daggers pointed at the Banou's bosom. He strode quickly across the narrow corridor and caught her wrist in an unmerciful grip; his fingers were like metal still hot and convulsive from the fire, but they hardened around her wrist into cold steel. She whined as the fat bulged between their edges.

"How dare you come into this house to torture a helpless child, having already slain one within the hour?" he said terribly, as he alone could speak. "Begone, before I arrogate unto myself the privilege of a higher power; God will deal with you according to your deserts. Go; do not tempt me longer, for I was born a violent man, and have with difficulty subdued my nature."

The Banou looked at him; though unbelievably abandoned and lascivious, she was a brave woman. But Father O'Donnell appalled her; she departed without another word.

"I am afraid she will have you executed immediately," said the princess in a low, sympathetic whisper. "Luckily for me, my dear son is safe from her vengeance; no one can even boil an egg to her gluttonous taste except the boy. She knows my personal innocence; my grief and amazement on learning of my son's abduction were too plain for suspicion of pretence or complicity. The Banou was almost kind, and seemed to understand my feelings very well, considering the coarseness of her nature; I am horrified at her cruelty to my darling child."

She leaned weeping over Abbas; fears for his reason, for his life even, shook her to the foundations of her little being. The priest looked at her, profound pity making his fierce blue eyes gentler than her own eyes bended on her son.

"Do not disturb him, Khanum," he said softly. "The poor boy's fast asleep. It's no wonder, and he that weary with grief and bewilderment. Put a pillow under his head and leave him be; I'll speak with you in the kitchen."

They stood together by the kitchen table; Shekerleb's preparations for her son's untasted breakfast were pathetically scattered over the well-scrubbed surface; a large sugar-melon had a silver knife still plunged into its rind. The princess looked at Father O'Donnell defiantly; her voice was excited and slightly shrill as she addressed him.

"You know, of course, that I do not consider Abbas in the least to blame," she began, keeping her gaze turned persistently upon the floor. "The girl was far more experienced than he; it was a case of abduction, pure and simple; even the Banou recognised that. My son is the soul of virtue and innocence; of this young woman we know nothing save that she was reckless and impatient, and is now, by reason of her folly, deceased. For my own part, I shall not pretend to a sorrow I cannot feel; I have my child again, and if I may be granted the happiness of restoring him to health and sanity, I ask no more of heaven. I trust, however, that you will assist me in all things; may I count upon your friendship not to disturb or agitate the boy by undeserved reproaches or regrets? We must never speak of this again in his presence; he cannot bear it."

Father O'Donnell looked thoughtful and sorry as he replied; he probably loved the prince with a love nearly as great as a mother's, but he could not always indorse the lad's conduct with an equally warm approval. He considered an instant before saying firmly, "I am afraid I cannot consent to that to-day."

"You will kill the child; is his life nothing to you?" cried Shekerleb indignantly, her eyes full of tears. The priest smiled bitterly.

"The life of a child is always worth something," he said with sad brevity. The princess did not in the least understand him until he went on, his voice recovering its careful kindness.

"Even the life of this poor girl who now lies dead within

the palace is worth a little sorrow, which his youth must inevitably make fleeting, on the part of your son. Had he trusted to my wisdom, which, though faulty, has been ever at his service, he might have been spared the few tears which I shall require him to shed. An hour after I left your dwelling, on the day of the children's disastrous flight, I had learned that the girl's husband was alive and in the hands of a faithful attendant; my opportunities for informing myself as to such matters are, as you know, exceptional. At that very moment you were engaged in persuading the mollah to marry these infants according to the rites of Moslem, and Abbas himself, urged quite as much by his own desires as by the importunities of another, was flying northward in forgetfulness of both his mother and his friend. Fortunately I have been able to curb the gossip of the anterooms; the Khan has received the Englishman in full divan, and the most cordial relations prevail between them. Had this gentleman, who I must assure you is a personage of invincible will and well-nigh unbounded power, the faintest conception of the truth, your unlucky country would be plunged into a war with one of the world's greatest nations. The results of such a conflict would be ruinous to your state; England would absorb it like a lion swallowing a honeycomb. You perceive the approaching fate of India; Persia, more helpless and more effete, would fare even worse."

The princess contrived to detach her mind for an instant from the question of whether or not she should risk disturbing her son's slumbers in order to cover him, as a precaution against draughts, with her richest Cashmere shawl. She looked up at Father O'Donnell, a worried frown wrinkling her pretty brows.

"Oh, I hope that you will avoid any trouble with the English envoy," she said hastily. "Though but a babe in arms at the time, the horrors of the Afghan invasion left their indelible print upon my soul, if not upon my memory. You will be seriously to blame, O'Donnell Baba, if you allow this war. And now, if you will excuse me, I think I shall prepare a little chicken broth against the hour of my son's awakening; it will sustain him in whatever discipline you see fit to impose."

She turned from the priest with every mark of polite disapproval; Father O'Donnell, refraining from even the faintest shrug of the shoulders, such as his long European residence might amply have excused, left the house with a quiet murmur of farewell. In the corridor he stooped over Abbas; the boy was sleeping peacefully.

The priest proceeded slowly across the glittering lawns and between the avenues of oak and cypress; his lips were moving, and from time to time he shook his head so that the thick brown locks were flung from side to side like a savage mane. His blue eyes brooded darkly on the darkness of his own spirit; he was nearer despair than he had ever been before. He was not praying; his moving lips repeated again and again the same words.

" My fault, utterly my fault from beginning to end; I love him, and so I never can believe he is a coward; I might have known; I might have known; I might have known."

In spite of his remorseful bitterness of mood, Father O'Donnell went directly to the doors of the palace and there presented himself with a composed and smiling countenance; he was once more the diplomat. He was received with the utmost courtesy by a certain distinguished official; as the pair passed along the marble corridor the priest glanced curiously at the portals of embossed and gilded wood which concealed the Khan's private council chamber. The official looked important.

" He is closeted with the British Envoy," he whispered. " A charming man, though somewhat cold and formal. He brings us the most pleasing assurances of his government's good intentions. In the event of any trouble with " — he dropped his voice to inaudibility — " we could, I feel certain, count upon their aid."

After a brief audience with another distinguished official, and a consultation with the head eunuch, the priest left the palace by a side entrance, and returned to his own humble dwelling, where he spent the long languorous June day in fasting and prayer, his thoughts laying the severest chastisement upon him. Finally, towards seven o'clock, he rose from his knees, and walked wearily and, it seemed, unwillingly, in the direction of the prince's cottage. Arrived at the blue-painted door, he hesitated for a moment; his knock when it came was curiously indecisive.

Shekerleb opened the door almost immediately; she had an

air of self-importance and placid obstinacy. She looked remarkably pretty; her cheeks were pink and her hazel eyes clear and contented.

"You cannot possibly disturb him now," she said at once, as if she had rehearsed the words, which somewhat lacked her usual urbanity. "He is still asleep. I have given him a little wholesome food and put him to bed; he never really waked, even when I made him get up and go to his own room. I do not believe he remembers a single distressing detail of his terrible experience; exhaustion has mercifully made his mind a blank. I am very thankful for this, though naturally anxious as to his recovery, but the excellent and devout physician whom I have consulted assures me that I have no cause for real concern. He must be kept absolutely quiet, and shielded from the remotest suggestion of anything unpleasant."

Her manner was more eloquent than her words; her look exceeded courtesy in its contempt. The priest sighed deeply; the sigh was one of obvious relief.

"Very well, Khanum," he answered, "it shall be as you say. I will not importune you for a sight of him until you send for me; count upon my friendship in all things, and be content. If he talks of me, assure him of my unchanged affection."

The princess drank the humility of his words like sweetened wine; she smiled, bowed without speaking, and closed the door with extreme though careful finality.

The priest departed through the sapphire dusk with a firm step; his erect shoulders seemed loosed from some deadly burden, his forehead was lifted broad and white under the sky's serenity. "I'll do it; it's all I can do for her now, and I'll do it," he said aloud, adding softly, under his breath, "Poor boy; I'm thankful he was sleeping. I'll manage somehow; who knows? Maybe an angel will appear to be my acolyte."

To the prince, waking suddenly in his familiar bed, the night was full of noises and portents of despair. The crying of a hungry dog, the unseasonable crowing of a cock, the questioning note of a sleepy bird in the vines without his window, all struck upon his heart in a rush of cold fear, while the wind ruffled his hair and dried the dampness of his brow. Then with horrible and resistless force his memory returned to him; the atrocious truth blazed in the night like lightning, and he buried his head under his pillow to escape, for a moment's suffocating darkness, the ineluctable reality. Then he sprang shivering from the bed, and flinging a thin cloak over his fine white cotton garments, he opened the window, and, cautious only for silence and the terror of delay, jumped lightly to the ground and ran like a madman in the direction of the palace.

His bare feet made no sound upon the shaven sward; even the longer grasses barely rustled behind his flying heels. Like a madman, like a ghost, like a lost and bewildered bird, he skimmed the surface of the earth, threading the air as if his limbs were of its very substance, and but a swifter portion of itself. He had nearly reached the locked doors of the palace when a light, silvering the obscurity of a cypress grove, made him pause to wonder and perhaps to fear.

Father O'Donnell had erected a small altar in the middle of the cypress grove; upon the altar two great candles were burning behind the mass-book and the bell. The priest had saved from the wreck of his material fortunes only the most magnificent of his vestments; no robes of black or purple remained to him. He stood, tall as a golden tree among the trees of darkness, clad from head to foot in cloth of gold and sumptuous laces, with golden stole and alb and golden chasuble; the cross upon his back was wrought in threads of solid gold. His face was calm and beautiful and sad above the gothic splendour of his raiment; he was a figure from the deep mystery of the middle ages, superb and barbarous and holy. The altar-cloth was entirely composed of Irish point lace, yellowed and elaborate, studded with thick roses; the candlesticks were of gold. Below the altar the ground was very black along a narrow space; the prince thought he was looking at the shadow of the altar, and then he knew that what he saw was a little grave, open and empty and humble in the enormous earth. Beside the grave, and still more profoundly shadowed by the altar, Jennifer lay in her coffin.

It was no coffin, but merely a shallow chest of fine cedar, with a hinged lid, and faint arabesques of blue and gold colouring

its grain. Narrow and shallow as it was, it held room for the
child's still fragility and repose. The prince, fallen to his knees
in the dark night, could distinguish the small face, like the wax
mask of a doll, and the shining hair laid in stiff Byzantine folds
about it.

The priest's voice, clear and resonant as a vast bell, swung
upward in the words of the Mass.

" Et introibo ad altare Deo, ad Deum qui laetificat juventutem
meum — "

The prince lay motionless in the deep grass, while above him
the great voice swung like a wave-rocked bell high above the
head of a drowned man. Like the whisper from a dead throat
the response came faint and drowned.

" Ite, missa est." Father O'Donnell turned from the altar;
he closed the lid of the coffin and lifted it as easily as if it held
only the body of a little bird. Yet he trembled, for he was not
sure who had spoken the responses.

He lowered the coffin into the ground which he had blessed;
flinging back the wide lace sleeves of his vestments, he took a
new spade in his hands and shovelled the earth upon the coffin
lid. The loose earth fell so lightly that the prince did not even
hear it fall. Father O'Donnell set the sods carefully back in place,
and knelt to pray.

To him as he knelt, crawling through the grass like a hurt
animal, came the prince. The priest put his hand for an instant
on the boy's shoulder; they knelt together as he prayed.

When Father O'Donnell rose, his great height growing up
and up like a gold tree in the darkness, the prince still crouched
upon the grave. The priest leaned down to ask him a question.
" Leave me," said the prince.

With a gesture more of despair than of benediction, the priest
moved away; then returning, he put something into the boy's
hand. " If it were any comfort to you, my child — " he said in a
voice of little hope and much tenderness.

His tall and sumptuously attired form strode away between
the cypresses; he disappeared like a great gold sun among their
gloomy trunks and tiered and drooping boughs.

The prince lay stretched at his full length upon Jennifer's grave, his face pressed against the sods which had a faint fragrance of the earth about them. The candles upon the altar were extinguished by the wind and the cypresses appeared to press closer about the grave.

The prince lay face downward in the grass, weeping tears in which a cruel venom of blood and gall were mingled. In one hand he held the Byzantine image of the Virgin, which Father O'Donnell had put into his hand for a little grain of comfort.

Along the avenues of oak and cypress, and across the shaven lawns came strolling a very tall slender man, dressed entirely in white linen. His uncovered hair shone pale and silvery in the starlight; his face was colourless and composed as marble. In his long thin fingers he held one perfect rose, in whose petals white and cream and pink were subdued to pearliness; as he walked he sniffed at the rose delicately and with an air of abstraction. His head was lifted the better to observe the spiked and glittering stars and to hear the nightingales' voices scattered like fragrance from the blossoming trees of the Khan's garden.

Gerald walked slowly through the lovely darkness; his senses were ravished into a divine calm by its happy influence. He entered the cypress grove with silent footsteps, and stopped, perplexed by the strange sight presented to his view.

Upon an obviously new-made grave lay the body of a young man; he lay as if dead, face downward in the grass. Beside the grave stood a small altar richly furnished with all the appurtenances of the Roman ritual.

Gerald stooped over the young man, and ascertained that he breathed, indeed, but faintly, and with uneven speed. His right hand, relaxed and inordinately slender, held a little object, vaguely distinguishable as a carving in ivory. To Gerald's discerning eye, the thing appeared to be both rare and valuable. He stood for a moment looking down at the pathetic figure of the prince; he lifted his high nose disdainfully to witness the very evident weakness and prostration of the unhappy boy. He fingered his pocket pistol, a small but deadly weapon of beautiful workmanship, and even, moved perhaps by the romantic and historic associations of the spot, considered with sober amusement the possibility of strangling the unconscious youth. Then, succumbing to one of his rare impulses of pity, he leaned over very quietly and detached the ivory image from the prince's limp fingers with the utmost gentleness and care, taking pains not to waken or in any other manner distress or alarm one so patently in need of repose.

Gerald departed as softly as he had come, meanwhile examining with lively interest the little object which he had just acquired. Its charming face, smaller than his smallest finger-nail, looked up at him; its expression was innocent and vaguely troubled.

"I believe this to be a Byzantine carving of great antiquity," said Gerald to himself complacently as he stepped from the cypress grove into the comparative brightness of the rose-garden. "The face bears a distinct resemblance to my late dear wife; this alone would render it valuable to me, but it is, quite apart from this consideration, an exquisite work of art. I am most fortunate to have procured it at the cost of so little expense or pain."

Wrapping the ivory carefully in a handkerchief of fine white silk, he consigned it to his pocket, and strolled onward, humming an old French air, through the dark and redundant beauty of the palace gardens.

Within the darker shadow of the grove, the prince lay sleeping; his breath against the grass blades stirred them with scarcely perceptible motion. His breath subsided as the moon rose, and finally, as the cold green moonlight touched his body, ceased altogether to disturb his perfect rest.

THE

VENETIAN GLASS

NEPHEW

WITH A SPECIAL PREFACE BY
CARL VAN DOREN

TO

WILLIAM

WITH MY LOVE

The Venetian Glass Nephew

PREFACE

*In September 1924 Elinor Wylie wrote to me from the
MacDowell Colony about The Venetian Glass Nephew.
" It goes on fairly well, and I believe you'll like it. I shall
have the first part completely finished for you to see
when I come back, and the rest mapped out quite clearly.
It's not another Jennifer — but perhaps that's as well."
She had told me, before going to Peterborough, only
that the new book was to be a kind of moral fairy tale
of the eighteenth century. I was prepared for the witty
moral if not, entirely, for the glittering beauty which I
found in the first third of the manuscript she brought
with her to New York. Although contributor and editor, she and I were friends, and we conspired to let the
Nephew appear as a serial in The Century Magazine.*

*The conspiracy had its little perils, dramatic now but
disturbing then. She needed money. " Can the Venetian
Glass Nephew help me at all, as yet? " she asked in a
letter from New Canaan early in October. " I find I*

*have unexpectedly to pay the interest, as well as the pay-
ing off, on the mortgage. There is a difference, though
it takes an expert to understand. . . . Of course I hope
you can manage this advance, but if you can't, don't
picture me as suicidal in consequence. It is my reprehensible nature to welcome excitement and change, and the
idea of being melodramatically foreclosed and forced to
find another — and of course a better — place to live is
in itself attractive to my mind. But one must do one's
duty, hence this letter."*

*I arranged with the publishers of the magazine to let
her have the whole amount she was being paid for the
serial, without telling them that two-thirds of it were still
to be written. As we both wanted it to appear as soon as
possible, we ran another risk. The first part was in type
before there was any second or third, and it was assigned
to its month in the Century at a time when neither of us
could be certain that the rest would follow at monthly
intervals. What was most perilous, Elinor Wylie made
only one copy of each part, which, exquisite and unique,
came from New Canaan to New York and then went to
the printers in New Hampshire. There were breathless
weeks until the last proofs reached my office. Although
I was troubled by the danger that the manuscript might
be lost, I could not refuse to share a hazard which was
so much more hers than mine. To her the risk was tonic.
I think it kept her waywardly excited to realize that her
sharp and shining prose had to take its chances in the*

mail and that the loss of it would be tragic to her plans.

Gay, erudite, precise, The Venetian Glass Nephew reads like a joyful holiday. It was written under stress. In her second novel Elinor Wylie felt she had to prove, to her exacting self even more than to others, that Jennifer Lorn had not been an accident. She must repeat the triumph to justify her turn from verse to prose. Hurt by the charge that she had deserted poetry, she must make it plain that she was novelist as well as poet. She had debts and bills to meet. Everything seemed crucial to her sensitive, proud nerves. At New Canaan, where she carried out what she had sketched at Peterborough, she had a household with three small stepchildren to look after, and she could write only when they were at school. Yet the manuscript of the Nephew might almost be a fair copy, typed with sure fingers, hardly a single slight change or correction to a page.

No outer confusion could seriously disturb her inner will. When dejected, she was still gallant and humorous. " Did we not," she said in a letter the next year, " make a fine mistake in our youth — which was so very nearly contemporaneous — in becoming what . . . the Peterboro servants call creators? *What a noble shoemaker — to choose a trade at random, or because shoemakers are always liberals — would not you have made, and I how excellent at contriving artificial flowers or the peep-show scenes inside Easter eggs! You will say that these also savour of creation, but our present trouble . . . springs from our stubborn attempt to utilize our wretched minds, to make unpleasant greyish convolutions work for us instead of trained and agile fingertips and the beautiful rhythmic strength of habit. How lovely is benign stupidity! — as no-one really ever wrote. Two years ago the New Republic would have had a poem from me on the subject. Now you must put up with a dull letter. It is hard on you, and I hope it is hard on the New Republic." Volatile as her temper was, she was actually as indestructible and resolute as water. She had a level of her own from which no circumstances could dam her long.*

This strong native level of her mind cuts through the fantasy of The Venetian Glass Nephew. It is a fable of the marriage of Art and Nature, specifically Christian Art and Pagan Nature. Virginio has been made not born. Even though Casanova himself (as Chastelneuf) has had a hand in the making, something less than natural blood runs in Virginio's mild veins. He may satisfy his uncle the Cardinal, according to whose pious desire he has been shaped, but he is not enough for his bride Rosalba, Nature's lively daughter. He can love, he cannot play. If this were a romantic plot, the ending might be happier and simpler, with the boy of Art adapting himself to the girl of Nature. Realism is sadder if truer. In the conflict between Art and Nature it is Nature which must yield. Rosalba, despairing, takes the advice of Casanova, who knows there can be no compromise, only one conclusion.

*She enters a furnace at Sèvres and comes out porcelain.
At last she is the right bride for a Virginio.*

Elinor Wylie was too much a poet to let her moral
stand like bare bones in a vacuum. She chose Venice for
a setting and spun the story as if her language were
ductile glass. Rosalba, her poet could make English say,
" was a flame whose consummation may be bitter, but
whose promissory blooming is tenderer than apple blossoms. To the five senses of an observer she was indeed
imagined flowers to breathe, as she must have been velvet
to touch, cream to taste, the crescent moon to gaze upon,
and, to the listening ear, a melody repeated by a mocking-bird." Here are formal words fixed in a schematic
pattern but glinting with the light which they catch and
throw off. The whole book is built with the lovely,
amused formality which this sentence has, and every
paragraph flashes erudition.

Few novels so short and smiling can ever have been
so learned. " The gondolas were black, but all their
canopies were coloured like the parterres of a prince's
garden. The sunlight smelled of musk and peppermint;
although the day was warm, a lady carried a muff of
panther-fur; she was followed by an Ethiopian in scarlet
livery, bearing a letter sealed with Spanish wax. A naked
child, an Eros cast in gilded bronze, drank from the sea-
green shell of a melon, held high above his lips." Or
again: " Peter Innocent breakfasted on a large bowl of
chocolate and a very small piece of marzipan, of which

he was inordinately fond. The other cardinals sprinkled spices in their cups, or drank coffee sweet with sugar and brandy; they ate a great many little birds, roasted with bacon and red pepper, and they had strawberries from Passeriano and peaches from Algiers. Every one ate what he preferred; Braschi Onesti had candied chestnuts and champagne." Or again, within the drier field where erudition usually works: " The chevalier, whatever his peccadillos, practised only the higher forms of transcendental and divine magic, as opposed to nigromancy and goetia. . . . Here was no place for the Ahriman of the Persians, the Typhon of the Egyptians, the Python of the Greeks, the Croquemitaine, the obscene deity of the Sabbath. Let it be remembered that Isis was impeccable in her widowhood, that Diana Panthea was a virgin; that Apollonius of Tyana never yielded to the seductions of pleasure; that Plotinus of Alexandria was ascetic in the manner of his life; and that Raymond Lully was the victim of a hopeless passion which made him chaste forever. Vesper, not Lucifer, blazed now in the pentagram upon the marble pavement."

Such erudition may be decoration, but the decoration of The Venetian Glass Nephew seems intrinsic in it. If Elinor Wylie had been as curt as a fabulist or as abstract as a moralist she would have told her story to the intellect, not to the eye. Her story as she did tell it is all pictures. Everything in her Venice is brightly visible, from the blue balloon of the opening paragraph to the whipped cream and wafers of the ending. She had ransacked a decade of history for images that could be wittily drawn and beautifully coloured. Curiosity will some day trace the historical facts she used to the books in which she found them. The list, headed by Vernon Lee's Studies of the Eighteenth Century in Italy and the Memoirs of Casanova and of Carlo Gozzi, will not be too long. Elinor Wylie was already full of her favourite century before she set herself to imagine Venice in its age of tinsel. Scrupulous as she might be about dates and streets and churches and costumes, her older memory was her major source. And her older memory served her less than her pictorial imagination. The Nephew was to be a poem as well as a moral tale. With a frolicking invention she enriched and confirmed the fairy story, giving it such a look of life as Casanova and Alvise Luna gave Virginio, glass within, almost flesh and blood without.

In one of her letters Elinor Wylie quoted something she had read: " He liked the flavour of an imperfect world and the preposterousness of peccant humanity." " That's the principle," she added, " upon which I write my own immortal works! " It was the principle which made The Venetian Glass Nephew both laughing and tender. It gave the novel its charming justice by which, in the strife of Art with Nature, sympathy is on the side of Nature but skill is on the side of Art.

CARL VAN DOREN

The Venetian Glass Nephew

CONTENTS

BOOK ONE: *PETER INNOCENT*

BOOK TWO: *VIRGINIO*

BOOK THREE: *ROSALBA*

The Venetian Glass Nephew

BOOK I: *PETER INNOCENT*

"And then he wept a little, and fell to talking of magic and macaroni."
Prince de Ligne.

1

BLUE BALLOON

PETER INNOCENT BON was about to return to the Republic of Venice; although he had that very day entered upon the eighty-first year of his age, his eyes, blue as veronica flowers, were even now full of a child's tears. His heart was lighter than a flower; indeed, it danced so high and airily, and teased the tenuous cord of his mortality with such persistent malice, that he conceived of it as a toy balloon, an azure plaything in a pantomime, caught by a thread of gold to stable earth, and germane to the sky.

It will be unnecessary to explain to minds versed in such matters that Peter Innocent Bon must by no means be confounded with John Bona of Mondovi, a misapprehension imaginable in the ignorant, since both were cardinals and both distinguished scholars. But wider far than the mere century of time separating the lives of these holy men is the gulph that sunders their natures and their activities. Consanguinity there may have been, in reason, but the two were never spiritually akin. Peter Innocent undoubtedly possessed the Antwerp edition of his cousin's works, published in 1777, and the devotional treatise "De Sacrificio Missæ" was often in his hands; a few marginal notes attest to application saddened by bewilderment. To those desiring to achieve a better comprehension of the character of Peter Innocent Bon, cardinal priest and cardinal prefect of the Congregation of the Propaganda, the historian recommends a careful study of his poetical writings (Venice, 1790) and his notes upon liturgical subjects (Parma, 1794). His memoirs, surveying as they did almost the entire length of the eighteenth century with a bland and illuminative eye, must have contained matter of the highest interest; this valuable document was unfortunately destroyed by Madame de Staël in a passing fit of temper during the composition of "Corinne," merely because it contained a simple unadorned account of the coronation of Corilla Olimpica.

On this eighth of May, 1782, Peter Innocent, clad in the grey-brown garb of the Franciscan Friars Minor, stood dreaming among delicate grotesques in the porch of his titulary church of St. Bonaventura. It was evening; the Roman sun had lost its imperial savagery, and tempered light lay tenderly upon the cardinal's brow. His face, that had beheld the secular world for eighty years, was lifted to the more transparent heaven; forgetting Rome and even the Vatican, he regarded the Holy City above the horns of the new moon. He looked affectionately yet familiarly into the little loopholes of the stars, with none of the bitter hunger of the returning exile; to Peter Innocent the bread of earth was never salty, nor the stairs of heaven too steep. As a boy may see at evening the lighted windows of his mother's kitchen, he saw without surprise celestial preparation for his home-coming through a bright chink that may have been Aldebaran. Tugging at its gilded thread, his heart danced over him, a blue balloon in deeper aërial blue.

Above the chiselled silver of his head, his heart danced, expanded by happiness and an exquisite gratitude towards all humanity and the Son of God made man. In particular, his heart blessed the new pope, Pius VI, for although Giovanni Angelo Braschi had ruled Christendom for some seven years, Peter Innocent never thought of him save as a handsome innovation, superseding with the suavest courtesy the cardinal's dead patron and beloved friend, the Franciscan Clement XIV. Now this same Pius, whom Peter Innocent a little feared, the more that he was beautiful and brilliant and vain, proposed for reasons of his own to visit the green lagoons and golden palaces of Venice, having among his suite, again for reasons of his own, Peter Innocent Bon, cardinal prefect of the Congregation of the Propaganda.

The cardinal did not concern himself with reasons; he thought of Venice, and the bright thread pulled hard upon his heart. He had not seen that city for nearly thirty years; not since his brother Nicholas Bon was banished to the monastery of Venda by the Council of Ten and the Inquisitors of the Holy Office. In that same year Paul Dona was confined in the fortress of Palma, and five years later the noble Angelo Querini was imprisoned in the castle of St. Felice at Verona.

For a time the spirit of Peter Innocent suffered a faint infusion of bitterness throughout its milk and honey; he began to believe in spies and politics, and found himself disliking the Dominicans without feeling any particular love for the Jesuits. But he managed with admirable tact to hold himself aloof from all dissension, and it is certain that his veined patrician hand was not among those which upheld the fainting resolution of Lorenzo Ganganelli as the pontiff traced the momentous syllables of the brief, *Dominus ac redemptor* and signed it Clement, servant of the servants of God.

But this was years, and happy years, ago, and to-day Peter Innocent could remember that all these brave and liberal senators had been set free either by death or by the reforms of '63, and that Querini had travelled in Switzerland and become a valued friend of Voltaire's. The cardinal had long ago forgiven Venice, and upon this Ascension Eve his heart was a blue balloon because it was going home.

He thought of himself as a child upon other Ascension eves and morrows, in a past not dim at all, but radiant as a double dawn in sky and water. He saw the *Bucintoro* setting forth from Santa Lucia, a gilded barge arrayed in cloth of gold, with winged lions, tritons, nereids, painted with gold and burnished by the sun, with the great standard of the republic crackling like lightning overhead. He thought of the ancient glory of Venice, and of the Lion of the Evangelist. His grey habit of the Seraphic Order fell from his shoulders, and he was a child again, in a coat of sapphire velvet, with a silver feather in his cap.

Softly, very softly, the supple folds of dun-colour descended once more over this remembered magnificence, and Peter Innocent felt the worn, warm fabric about his fragile bones. Here, too, was cause for gratitude, for the new pope had permitted him to continue in this ingenuous disguise, first granted him by the generosity of Clement, so that he alone of the pontifical family went comfortably impoverished, clad in the mystic tatters of Assisi. Within a remote wing of the Vatican a wardrobe of ebony and figured brass guarded vestments of white and red and green, of violet and black and the more curious sheen of metal, with robes and rochets of a less sacral character and rich liturgical gloves and stockings, intermixed with honorific decorations.

Peter Innocent loved best to drift, elusive as a skeleton leaf, along the streets of Rome, recognized by all, but accosted by none save an occasional German traveller or English milord; the legerity of the French mind made the Gallic visitor quick to comprehend his desire for solitude, and the very transparency of the masking rendered it invulnerable. Whether or not he believed himself effectively disguised remained a mystery to the last. He spoke but little; indeed it was a common saying at the time that Clement had forgotten to unseal his mouth; his smile, however, impressed even the most impious as a small flame burning perpetually within the silver shadow of his countenance.

At the conclusion of Vespers, he often knelt in a sculptured recess of the Church of St. Bonaventura, while the words *O salutaris hostia* were borne upon the wings of ancient music towards the benediction. As the priest, his shoulders wrapped in the humeral veil, lifted the monstrance from the lighted altar and with it described in that already consecrated air the sign of the cross, the tears of Peter Innocent aspersed like holy water whatever evil might survive within those walls, beneath that vaulted nave.

2

CONSIDER THE LILIES

NEAR St. George in Alga, upon an iridescent morning of mid-
May, the Doge and Signory of Venice received the pontiff and
his suite, conveying them thence to the monastery of St. John
and St. Paul, where they were sumptuously lodged. As the lacquered barge imposed its fan of ripples, like a peacock's tail,
upon lagoon and narrowing canal, the visitors vied with one another in expressions of awe and contentment; they moved in the
heart of a pearl whose orient skin was outer space. Peter Innocent alone was silent; his youth overwhelmed him as though
every immemorial wave of the Adriatic were poured upon his
pensive head. He bowed his face upon his folded hands; when
he lifted his eyes again, they were dazzled by the great palaces
of the Venetian patriciate, all arabesqued in marble and embossed by emblems. Here burned the silver torch of the Morosini;
the silver ladder of the Gradenigo scaled the heavens; the five-
leaved roses of the house of Loredan endured in frosted stone so
delicate that it appeared to spread a perfume on the air.

The gondolas were black, but all their canopies were coloured
like the parterres of a prince's garden. The sunlight smelled of
musk and peppermint; although the day was warm, a lady carried a muff of panther-fur; she was followed by an Ethiopian in
scarlet livery, bearing a letter sealed with Spanish wax. A naked
child, an Eros cast in gilded bronze, drank from the sea-green
shell of a melon, held high above his lips. Peter Innocent remembered that the Italians of an elder day, while yet that day was
young, made melancholy synonymous with wickedness, and gave
to the verb to "think" the sense of to "be sad." He took the
meaning, but without a heavy mind; his heart's indulgence was
poured like a libation over Venice and absorbed in her waters.

He remembered his old friend, the priest called Testa, the
Diogenes of the spiders' webs, who shared his straw pallet with
a familiar rat, and lived on mouldy bread and lentils. And he

remembered, also, that other eccentric, the ancient with the iron bell, who was used to stand upon the quays and bridges, crying out with his own outlandish tongue and the bell's clapper, crying upon all men to be happy, in the name of God. And although this person was a Moor and an infidel, he was nevertheless a philosopher and a lover of humanity. Peter Innocent thought of him with kindness, preferring him, perhaps, for a reprehensible moment, to the Christian priest, and wondering if he were not the wiser man. For Peter Innocent, flying through sunlight followed by a peacock's tail of foam, attired for once in all the splendour relative to his spiritual and temporal state, had not forgotten that long before he had assumed this purple he had fared very happily as one of the jongleurs of God. So, like the Moor, he rang continually a little bell whose tongue was not of iron, but of gold, and bright and silent as a flame.

The cardinal Peter Innocent was at all times silent, since Pope Clement had neglected to unseal his mouth; now he was hushed into a profounder stillness by his private felicity, and by the high and rapid speech of those about him. The Doge and the Procurator Manin were engaged in conversation with their illustrious visitor Pius VI; although preserving every indication of reverence for his Holiness, the Venetian nobles did not hesitate to address him with fluency and animation. The pope's nephew, the blond and arrogant Braschi Onesti, grandee of Spain and prince of the Holy Empire, stared somewhat haughtily upon these self-possessed patricians; he wore a coat of carnation velvet, and the little finger of his left hand was all but hidden by an emerald of fabulous value. At his knee the Abate Monti crouched like a beaten hound. " Consider the lilies — " and the pope's device, cut on a hundred monuments in Rome, was an heraldic wind, blowing down lilies like waves of the sea! This, too, was inscribed on marbles by Canova and the recovered classical remains of Herculaneum; yet Solomon in all his glory had no finer coat than young Braschi Onesti, nor could his seal have utterly outshone that green intaglio graved with the head of Agrippina. So thought Peter Innocent, and as the thought was, for him, faintly malicious, his smile flickered for a moment like a flame that has had a pinch of salt sprinkled upon its clarity.

For here, and suddenly, a small regret, an obscure discomfort, touched the cardinal with a pain no more important than may be inflicted by a kitten's ivory claw. So slight a blow it was that his mind scarcely recorded it; the glancing scratch cut the thin skin of his soul a little, as always, and if this same skin had been a visible thing, the closest scrutiny might have revealed a vast number of similar punctures, microscopically bleeding. This was the recurrent thorn in the clean flesh of Peter Innocent; this was his cross: he had no nephew.

So far as he knew, he was the only cardinal suffering under a like deprivation. He could not but consider the circumstance as a direct chastisement at the hand of God, yet he could not for the life of him decide wherefore the divine anger had so visited him; he examined his conscience, and found no really adequate sin. Nieces he had in plenty, the pretty flowering of Nicholas's romantic marriage; his sisters, having entered convents in early youth, might not, according to his code, be expected to serve him save by the efficacy of prayer. So far prayer had proved singularly inefficacious.

For his own part, he had prayed and fasted and made pilgrimages; there had been a period of hair shirts, but these had been forbidden by Pope Clement and his physician as merely a protracted form of torture of dubious virtue under the peculiar conditions.

Sometimes Peter Innocent wondered very vaguely and benignantly at the number of nephews possessed by some of the more powerful cardinals; it did not occur to his charity, however, to regard these youths as a commodity procurable by other means than the help of God and the wedded happiness of one's brothers and sisters. Of late he had been pricked to a certain reverential envy by the pope's very evident satisfaction in the society of the magnificent Braschi Onesti, haughty, negligently handsome, a prince of nephews indeed, and, more lately, a prince of the Holy Empire. Peter Innocent might himself have preferred a gentler nephew, a creature malleable and engaging to the affections of a mild old man, but at this moment he was immensely taken by the carnation velvet coat and Cæsar's signet-ring.

It is conceivable that he may have permitted himself a passing dream of parenthood — conceivable, but unlikely. The extreme chastity of his body extended to his spirit, or perhaps it were juster to say that the body and spirit of Peter Innocent was in this eighty-first year of his age a single amalgam, made from two substances of equal purity. This much is probable; that returning at a jocund season to a home of such miraculous loveliness as flowed and floated in the waves and clouds of Venice, he felt within the stiff and sanctified chrysalis of his flesh a lively movement as of uncurling wings, such exquisite and painted films as a moth hangs down to dry from the under side of a linden leaf. And he would have provided with joyous gratitude an opportunity to any saint to slit him down the back like a locust, if thereby might be freed a younger, fairer, and, to his humility, more perfect being than Peter Innocent Bon, perishing for this mystical offspring with all the fervour of the elder phœnix.

So thinking, or, more precisely, feeling, Peter Innocent passed into the monastery of St. John and St. Paul, whose venerable porch was a cavern dripping with refreshment after the full and golden glare of noon.

3

RITORNO DI TOBIA

The next day dawned like a crocus, and all the lilies of the pontiff's suite arose in green and silver and vermilion.

Peter Innocent breakfasted on a large bowl of chocolate and a very small piece of *marzipan,* of which he was inordinately fond. The other cardinals sprinkled spices in their cups, or drank coffee sweet with sugar and brandy; they ate a great many little birds, roasted with bacon and red pepper, and they had strawberries from Passeriano and peaches from Algiers. Every one ate what he preferred; Braschi Onesti had candied chestnuts and champagne.

Presently the pope called Peter Innocent into his particular chamber. Pius was sitting up in bed; his beautiful ivory face looked grieved and weary under a canopy the colour of pot-pourri, heavy with a like perfume. Across his knees lay Sanaz-zaro's *Arcadia,* stamped with the dolphin of the first Manutius. At his elbow stood an engraved goblet of clear water.

"Peter," he said in a soft voice, "after I have received the Doge and the assembled signory and granted audience both public and private to various bishops of the Venetian territory, I shall be very tired. Yet, even so, I must assist, together with the Patriarch Giovanelli, at a *Te Deum* rendered by the voices of the ducal choir, accompanied by fivescore instruments under the baton of Pasquale Galuppi. I am ill; the journey has exhausted and the republic's arrogance annoyed a mind already languid with affairs. May I count upon your friendship to support me in this hour of trial?"

Peter Innocent was overcome by pity and amaze at the pope's condescension. He fell rustlingly to his knees, and picking up the pontifical slipper, which reposed upon a silken drugget by the bed, he kissed it with reverence. Pius smiled indulgently, extending his fine hand in a gesture of release to indicate a comfortable armchair plumped by pigeon-down. The cardinal regained his feet rather shakily and sank among these cushions, breathless.

"Holiness," he whispered, "what singular good fortune makes me capable of serving you, and in what essential does such service lie?" Privately, he prayed the business might not be connected with the Inquisition or the liberal opinions of his brother Nicholas.

"Merely this and thus," replied the pope, closing his eyes with an air of elegant fatigue. "This respectable choirmaster, Galuppi, has composed a cantata for five voices in my especial honour, and on the words of Gaspare Gozzi; it will be performed at the Incurabili this afternoon. Ludovico Manin pays for it, and it will be a very pretty compliment, but of course I cannot attend in person; the *Te Deum* will consume my extremest energies; my vitality can support no further burden. As the eldest prelate in my suite, you will make an acceptable substitute for the father of Christendom; as a Venetian, your presence will confer satisfaction, as, I trust, your sensibilities will receive pleasure; these men are your compatriots. May I rely upon you, my kind Peter?"

The cardinal was deeply touched by these proofs of confidence; he was also overjoyed at the prospect of hearing the musical result of a collaboration between two beloved friends of his early manhood; he fancied he might meet them again and kiss their frosty cheeks. He had heard news of this cantata; its subject, the Return of Tobias, impressed him as being even more appropriate to his own obscure instance than to that of the sovereign pontiff. And he thought of the fresh virginal voices of the Incurabili, which had been taught to weave vocal harmonies as painstakingly as the fingers of less fortunate orphans are instructed in the intricacies of lace-making.

" Yes," he contrived to breathe, and " Gratitude," and " Holiness," and so was about to depart, when Pius stayed him with a gesture of white hands.

" Peter," he said affectionately, "if you are wearied by this ceremony, I will permit you to absent yourself from the festivities of the evening. Do as you please, my dear good fellow; you must have youthful affiliations to rebind, old memories to renew and cherish. I shall understand; this night is your own, unhampered by any duty to me. And, you know, — " he smiled very sweetly, — " a higher power is vested in my unworthy person; you may do as you like, Peter, for to-night, without fear of the consequences." His smile grew more indulgent, and he laughed with a peculiar tenderness as Peter Innocent kissed his scented ring and left him.

4

CRYSTAL MONSTERS

BLUE dusk, thicker than fog and tinted with expressed essence of heaven along the falling colour of the dew, enveloped Peter Innocent as he slipped from the lighted doorway of the Incurabili; the music prolonged itself through other channels than his ears, and seemed to influence the hue of the most distant star and the perfume of the nearest pomegranate flower. He was happy, but a little loneliness, even a little fear, tinctured his mood. He had been unable to identify either of his old friends, and had found himself too shy to ask for them among the brocaded crowd of notables. Unobserved, he had sought the consolation of the twilight; he loved to be alone, but to-night his tranquillity had somehow failed him. He felt cold and rather tremulous as a touch fell upon his shoulder.

It was Alvise Luna, the glass-blower of Murano. He had grown very old, and his pale eyes were sunken in a face blank and dusty as a bag of yellow meal. Peter Innocent was shocked by the man's appearance, and greeted him sympathetically.

" Eminence," said Luna in a voice threaded by a whine, " I had not hoped to be recognized, nor, if recognized, acknowledged as an acquaintance by your Eminence. I have fallen upon evil times. I, whose ancestors worked in crystal for the great Duke of Buckingham and visited Tuscany at the invitation of the munificent Cosimo Second, I have not, to be frank with you, one copper coin wherewith to brighten another, I have drunk water for a fortnight, and the things I have eaten are not fit to be mentioned in your eminent presence. I am reduced to working for the infamous Giorgio Barbaria, who wishes to manufacture black glass bottles on the English lines; I have, as you may remember, considerable knowledge of foreign factories, and he pays me a dog's wages to instruct him. I am starving; my wife and children are starving; my little grandchildren are already dead from malnutrition. May I humbly beg your Eminence to aid me in my undeserved and dreadful trouble? "

This Luna was a liar and a sorcerer, and the Holy Office was already upon his path, which led through some of the most unsavoury cellars of Venice, marked out by a slimy brilliance like the track of a snail. But Peter Innocent did not know this, and had he known, he would not have understood it. He saw that the man was frightened, and he believed that he was hungry. As a matter of fact, Luna had plenty of money and merely wanted more; at the moment an enormous supper of polenta was distending his greasy waistcoat. But he was a dyspeptic, and his wry neck and hollow eyes looked wretched enough to move a more obdurate heart than Peter Innocent's.

" Of course," said the gentle old man, " of course, my poor friend, I will do what I can to help you."

An hour later, Peter Innocent was picking his slow, uncertain way down a damp and noisome corridor; Luna followed him, holding a candle as high as the dripping ceiling would permit. They descended a worn flight of stone stairs, and found themselves in a low-vaulted chamber whose debased Byzantine arches were dimly illuminated by a pair of ship's lanterns dependent therefrom.

This apartment was but too evidently a cellar, for a good three inches of water, cold and ambiguous, polluted the embroidered clocks upon the cardinal's stockings. Nevertheless, certain portions of the walls were covered by tapestries smouldering with the rich fancies of the Renaissance, and a number of carved cabinets and tables showed surfaces inlaid with brass or panelled in exotic lacquer. At one end of the chamber's secretive length, a small furnace filled with wood ashes made a spot of expiring rose-amber in the gloom.

Luna walked to the centre of the room, and, rapidly waving his guttering tallow back and forth, ignited in a flash a score of white wax candles cupped in coloured glass. Peter Innocent saw that a superb chandelier hung from the highest vaulting of the roof, a fantastic thing of flowers and icicles and silver bells, tinkling in the midst of squalor. And now, with a tinted radiance flooding every corner of the cobwebbed cellar, a hundred graceful and preposterous shapes sprang into the enchanted view: winged and maned and dolphin-finned, griffins and lions, stags and peacocks, and monsters fabulously horned and taloned.

The cardinal perceived in addition to these savage and exquisite creatures the accustomed implements of the glass-blower's trade: pontils and blowpipes, pincers and wooden battledores. Upon a platform, raised above the pervasive dampness of the stone-flagged floor, stood the workman's chair, with its rigid parallel arms suggesting some rude instrument of torture. Seated within this strange machine was a mysterious stranger, wrapped in a black cloak, and wearing a small mask of black velvet.

Peter Innocent at once became aware of an element of masquerade in the appearance of this person. Having himself long ago assumed a disguise, albeit an holy one, he readily observed the same quality in the dress of others, and as readily ascribed it to the most innocuous desire for privacy. He took the gentleman to be a person of simple and retiring disposition, and acknowledged courteously and at once Luna's gesture of introduction. The stranger rose, displaying an impressive figure, tall and muscular. He wore a quantity of beautiful lace, and his rings were diamonds of the first brilliance; save for these elegant details, his clothes were of a uniform sable hue. His head was covered by a short chestnut peruke, and through the slits of his mask his eyes glinted very dark and bright. The skin of his face and hands was swarthy and faintly lined; the cardinal judged him to be past his first youth.

"Your Eminence," said Luna in French, which he spoke fluently, having, for several disgraceful reasons, been much in Paris, "permit me to present M. de Chastelneuf, Chevalier de Langeist." The latter title was pronounced in the German manner, and the cardinal was at a loss to conjecture the stranger's nationality until he spoke. His manners were courtly, if a little antiquated and florid, but he conversed with a strong Venetian accent, and Peter Innocent had no doubt that he was a native of the republic.

The chevalier kissed the cardinal's hand with immense politeness, and began at once to speak of the prelate's poetical works, displaying a quite remarkable knowledge and acumen. In this way, and through the use of copious quotation from the classics, the gentleman contrived to convey an impression of learning and respectability, and Peter Innocent felt sure he must be a person of consequence.

Such, in a measure, was indeed the case, for M. de Chastelneuf, as this narrative must continue to call him, had at one time or another attracted the attention of almost every court of Europe, and on this very evening no less a notable than Messer Grand himself had given our gentleman much good advice not unconnected with the miasmic quality of the Venetian air, and the superior salubrity of Munich or Vienna. And since it was the chevalier's invariable habit to travel in a superb English carriage, emblazoned with the arms of a ruined lord, and as, moreover, he seldom travelled alone, he had been faced with the disagreeable necessity of selling his diamonds and his point d'Alençon without delay. Save for the fortunate intervention of Luna, who knew the cardinal's simplicity was good for at least a thousand sequins, M. de Chastelneuf might have been forced to part with his cross of the Order of the Golden Spur. It is not surprising that his happiness in greeting Peter Innocent was unfeigned and infectious.

Presently the cardinal found himself ensconced within the glass-blower's misshapen armchair, with dry slippers upon his feet, and a couple of hot bricks under these. A glass of excellent Levantine Muscat warmed his vitals; the long room appeared less cavernous, and the crystal apparitions which filled it glowed like jewels in the renewed stream of his own vivacity. His two companions were persons of wit and esoteric learning, and his admiration for Luna increased as he examined one by one the marvellous progeny of the workman's art. As for the chevalier, the delicacy of his mind was equalled only by its ascetic and fastidious grace: Peter Innocent was soothed and enraptured by this refined society.

The chevalier removed his mask, and his face showed handsome and aquiline, almost Oriental in its dusky tints, yet all Venetian in the liveliness and valour which informed its every smile. He had a nose like a falcon, and his deep-set eyes were black and gold. He told Peter Innocent that he had, in his youth, been honoured by the friendship of Benedict XIV, who had once taken his advice upon some little matters of no importance.

Suddenly M. de Chastelneuf rose to his very considerable height, at the same time making, for the benefit of Luna's eyes alone, an enigmatical sign whose nature it is impossible to describe. Luna also rose; the pair appeared to move in unison to some unheard and rhythmical injunction; salt and spices were destroyed upon the fire, and their smoke permitted to dim the purer radiance of the candle-flames. Then, at an unintelligible word pronounced by the altered voice of Chastelneuf, the incredible came to pass.

Peter Innocent beheld a golden griffin lift his wings to fan the air; a stag, of azure glass dappled with the same gold, stepped with a fairy pride across the expanse of Chinese lacquer which separated him from his mate, and the two, meeting, caressed each other with delicate gestures of affection. A humming-bird, with feathers blown in pearl-colour and crimson, flew from his perch, alighting on the leafy chandelier; the spray that received him bent and swayed, and from its largest rose a petal drifted to the floor.

There is not the slightest use in pretending that Peter Innocent was shocked or even very greatly surprised. His mind moved happily in an atmosphere of miracles, and the charming nature of these phenomena precluded any suspicion of evil. He felt like a child who perceives at his first carnival a blue sky flowering with confetti, or who is presented at Christmas-time with one of those delightful German toys called Christbaum, bright with silver foil and tiny scarlet candles. So, without uncomfortable amazement, he stared enchanted at the delicious marvel of awakened life.

5

PIAVOLA DE FRANZA

It was Luna who finally crossed himself surreptitiously before addressing the cardinal in hoarse and lowered tones.

"Eminence," he whispered, "you have seen what our combined skill can accomplish; this, however, is only the beginning. It is very pretty to watch these insects and atomies, but what would you say to a flying horse able to transport your Eminence to Ecbatana; or a Cameroonian gorilla, blown in the best *mille fiori* and capable of strangling, with thumb and finger, persons inimical to your Eminence's peace of mind? I have, too, an extremely practical Indian serpent, the poison fang ingeniously supplied with *aqua tofana.*" And he laid his hand upon the lock of a great chest, bound with copper, which occupied one corner of the room.

Peter Innocent turned pale as milk; in another moment he would have been constrained to believe evil of Alvise Luna. But Chastelneuf observed the old man's uneasiness, and, stepping forward with an air of well-bred piety, he refilled the cardinal's empty glass and reverentially saluted his cold hand. Then he spoke very softly and persuasively.

"Monseigneur," he said, for despite his marked Italian accent he continued to employ the French language, "you must not be offended by the rough jests of my poor friend Luna; he is a stupid fellow, but good as bread, and of a simplicity truly pitiable in these wicked times. See how he has been persecuted by the Three, those sinister officials who deprived your noble brother of his liberty, and who have been the death of innumerable worthy citizens of Venice. Consider his industry, and talent, and then reflect upon his wretched circumstances and the sufferings of his devoted wife and children. I am sure you will consent to help him, Monseigneur; he asks no charity, but merely that you will patronize and encourage his beautiful craft by the purchase of one or two little articles of undoubted utilitarian and æsthetic value. This, for example — "

He made as if to open the iron-studded door of an inner chamber, but Luna stopped him with a clutch upon the arm and an imprecation. Chastelneuf smiled imperturbably and proceeded, flicking invisible dust grains from his satin sleeve:

"Your Eminence will graciously refrain from considering me presumptuous when I make clear the extent of our success in manipulating Murano glass; we are able to vitalize not only dumb animals, but even, with God's help, creatures formed in the divine image. It is a great responsibility, but I trust we acquit ourselves worthily as custodians of this sacred mystery. Monseigneur, you are ever in the company of the elect, but I, who am like your Eminence of a certain age, know all too well that the pangs of loneliness sometimes invade the most profoundly religious heart, and that our declining years, in their hallowed progression towards our Father's house, must needs require now and then the pitiful grace of human companionship, in salutation and farewell. If, then, the presence of a little being compact of modesty and sweetness, at once a daughter and a loving friend, blonde and ethereal as the ivory ladies of Carriera, could solace some spiritual hunger — "

He broke off, and silencing Luna by an imperious movement of the hand, walked firmly to the iron-studded door and opened it. Within, stiffly disposed upon a small gilt chair of French design, Peter Innocent could discern, though dimly, something like a large doll or a little girl; the creature appeared about sixteen years old, and wore a pale pink dress, trimmed with feather flowers in the best possible taste. A quantity of silvery-yellow hair fell to her shoulders, and her fair complexion was transparent and tinted like a shell. Her eyes were closed, her face tranquil and pretty. The cardinal was forcibly reminded of the Poupée de France in the Merceria, and, less vividly, of his sisters attired for their first ball, which was that given by the Morosini for Count Oldenburg in 1708, when he himself was six years of age. Since that time he had not particularly observed female clothing, except now and then in shop windows, and always rather to admire than to approve. He felt obscurely ill at ease, and although his heart was wrung by a certain air of pathos conveyed by the little figure propped on its gilded chair, he did not want to look at it any longer. He was distinctly relieved when Chastelneuf closed the closet door, which swung to with a ponderous clang of metal. Yet he was aware of a slight sense of cruelty towards the curious doll; it must be very lonely in the dark, behind the iron door.

"I should have no use, I am afraid, for this interesting example of your art," he said somewhat timidly to the two men, who regarded him with scarcely concealed disgust in their veiled and greedy gaze. "I should really find myself at a loss to care for so complicated a piece of mechanism. The — ah — the young lady looks so alarmingly fragile, and I fear I do not understand the requirements of such — ah — such rarities. But I trust you will be careful to find a purchaser in whose kindness you can confide this poor — ah, child; she seems a mere child." He paused, interrogating them with his anxious blue eyes; they nodded in gloomy affirmation.

It is said by adepts, who may or may not be fitted to pronounce upon the subject, that when a man relinquishes the love of women from his infancy he condemns his predestined virgin to eternal violence wrought upon her by the demons of debauch. It is hardly reasonable to suppose that this young person artificially formed from Venetian glass can have suffered a like fate, but it is an unfortunate fact that Alvise Luna sold her, within the next fortnight, to an elderly senator of atrocious morals and immense wealth. He did not find her fabric durable, and perhaps she had no soul.

The chevalier was the first to break the uncomfortable silence;

he was at once his suave and animated self. The cardinal felt better immediately.

"I quite understand your scruples, Monseigneur," he cried with enthusiasm, "and oh, how rare it is, in this material age, to discover virtue so sensitive or sympathies so warm as yours are proved to be! But surely, surely, there is some elegant trifle, some elfin toy, which might serve to remind you of Venice and of your youth within her occult circle of lagoons. A little greyhound, perhaps, or a talking parakeet; we have been particularly successful with parakeets."

At this instant the stupendous plan struck Peter Innocent like a falling star. He was dizzied by the glittering impact, and swayed in his chair, but his gentle voice was perfectly clear and steady as he answered: "Monsieur de Chastelneuf," he said, "and you, my old friend Luna, there is indeed something which I have long wished to possess, and with which your truly admirable skill may be able to supply me. Do you think, by any fortunate chance, that you could make me a nephew?"

Luna, who knew Chastelneuf to a hair's-breadth of precise disillusion, started in alarm as the other parted his smiling lips to reply; the glass-blower could have informed you to a semicolon of the exact witticism fluttering upon the chevalier's tongue. To his overwhelming relief, the pungent butterfly was swallowed without the faintest grimace, and the words which actually emerged were models of chaste sobriety. A perfumed handkerchief passed across the mouth, the ghost of a sigh, and Chastelneuf's expression matched his speech. He was decorous, and only Luna knew the measure of his stoical abstention.

"Your Eminence," said the chevalier, bowing, "does us too much honour thus to admit us into a consultation on family affairs. But, happily, we are most excellently fitted to advise and aid you in this respect; we have, I may say, made a specialty of nephews." And he reminded Luna, with the toe of his buckled shoe, that a cheerful demeanour was indicated for this occasion.

Alvise Luna was more than a little troubled; he had not bargained for so extensive an order, and would have preferred to undertake a contract for a dragon or a Hyrcamean tiger any day. He was a religious man at heart, and although he was strongly predisposed by nature and inheritance towards chicanery and murder he viewed with profound distrust the extra-natural and Hermetic practices of his companion. To him there was something infinitely alarming in the idea of pre-empting the power of Deity to shape a being human at least in semblance, if not in soul, and he would rather have made a dozen manticores than one small baby. Nevertheless, he fixed his mind upon the heavenly shimmer of a thousand sequins, and entered with tolerable good grace into the current discussion.

6

AVEEVA VADELILITH

PETER INNOCENT had no difficulty whatever in obtaining from the pope full permission to absent himself for an indefinite number of hours upon the third night after the strange adventure just related. This latter night was that of May nineteenth, the date of official departure for the pontifical suite, but Pius bade the cardinal do as he pleased, and if he chanced to be too late to join the other prelates upon their leaving Venice, he might easily overtake them, said the Holy Father, during the journey of the following day, which must be made by water, and slowly, as befitted so illustrious a progress. He conferred his blessing upon the grateful old man, and, with the same indulgent smile, embraced him.

The season was Pentecost, and the water running in the veins of Venice appeared like wine under the transmutation of the sun. Pius VI, attired in the extreme of liturgical splendour, celebrated Mass at the church of St. John and St. Paul. Passing out into the Campo he imparted his benediction to the multitude from a high platform whose timbers were heavily overlaid with varnishes of gold. No sooner was this ceremony accomplished than Peter Innocent, his heart no longer a blue balloon, but a swinging censer of holy and aspiring prayer, hastened towards that equivocal quarter of the town in whose bowels the mysterious cellar lay concealed. He wore once more the indistinguished dress of a Franciscan friar, and as he walked, his eyes were fixed upon the pages of a little book whose covers bore the cruciform symbol of his faith.

Meanwhile Alvise and the Chevalier de Langeist awaited him in the vaulted chamber of their secret activities; Luna was observably nervous, but Chastelneuf was calm and majestic, the very picture of courtly self-possession in his coat of gold brocade and black velvet breeches, with a jewelled order tangled in the rich laces upon his breast.

"Rely upon my diplomacy," said this personage to his shivering companion. "I have learned much since the days of Mme. von Wulfe and the grand operation. I alone of all the adepts of my acquaintance have survived the wretched effects of Balsamo's petty larcenies. Saint-Germain is dying in Hesse, under the unpleasant pseudonym of Zaraski. Cagliostro has incurred the rigours of imprisonment and poverty; he has abundantly deserved a severer punishment. I saw him first at Aix, in Provence, a mere boy, sewing cockleshells on his black oilcloth coat, while his young wife stood at his elbow, holding a great crucifix of some base metal coloured to resemble gold. She was adorably pretty, but depraved. That was twenty years ago, and I am wiser now; if my peculiar talents have languished, my judgment has ripened and matured. I am entirely satisfied with our preparations for to-night."

"That is all very well," sneered Luna, "but I have had all the hard work. My lips are cracked, and my hands flayed by such unexampled labours; I have performed prodigies; my lungs are old leather, and my windpipe scorched macaroni, yet you grudge me a glass of your precious *monte pulciano,* and I suppose I am to have a very dog's share of the money compared with your lion's portion. So it always is. Poor honest fellow that I am, I never manage to look out for my own interests, and yet I am the best glass-blower in the known world." And he began to weep in sincere self-pity.

"Quite true," said Chastelneuf, with careless good-nature, "and a lovely bit of work you've done to-day; your masterpiece, I cordially assure you. We could get an enormous sum for this juvenile Apollo from the director of the opera; he would make an ideal soprano, and both sexes would go into indiscriminate

ecstasies over him if he appeared, shall we say, in the latest production of Cimarosa or Mozart? Of course I should have to alter my
plans a little, but he should have a golden voice, I promise you.
Only, I think our ingenuous prelate is, in the vernacular, the lucky
draw in the lottery; he will not talk, and as he is by nature close-
mouthed, he will have to pay through the nose."

"Are you determined upon waiting until after midnight to
perform the undertaking?" asked Luna, with an anxious scowl.
"I should have thought Thursday the more suitable date, and
Thursday has yet three hours to run. Surely the thing you are
about to do may be described as a political and religious operation;
I have been reading your copy of Paracelsus, with its interesting
marginal notes, and Paracelsus says very plainly that Friday is a
day exclusively reserved for amorous works. I cannot see the
connection, although it is quite like you to try to turn the most
serious occasion into a common love-affair."

"Common, do you say?" cried the chevalier, indignantly.
"*Cospetto!—Che bella cosa!* Is it a common occurrence in my
life, I ask you, to refrain for three entire days from all human
enjoyments, to confine myself to a vegetarian diet, and to eschew
intoxicating liquors? A pretty regimen for a gentleman of my
faculties! Then, too, I have had the trouble of burning, upon
rising and retiring, a costly perfume composed of the juice of
laurels, salt, camphor, white resin, and sulphur, repeating at the
same time the four sacred words. I beg to remind you that I am
no longer an amateur, as in the past; *Paralis* has advanced. As for
the matter of the amorous operation, of course it is precisely that.
Do you imagine I could send this poor innocent forth into the
world improperly equipped to deal with his fellows? Friday it
must be, or I'm a Turk!"

"As you please, as you please," grumbled Luna, resignedly.
"I merely thought you might look very fine in a scarlet vest-
ment, with a wreath of oak, poplar, fig, and pomegranate leaves;
also I happen to have some ambergris, balm, grain of paradise,
macis, and saffron lying idle about the place, which I understand are the correct perfumes for Thursday. But I was purely
altruistic; for my own part I wish sincerely it were Tuesday, so
that we might inaugurate an appalling work of vengeance. I

fancy the blood-coloured robe and the magical sword and dagger. There is a beautiful picture of them in Paracelsus."

His face was alight with eager satisfaction, but Chastelneuf silenced him with a haughty sign of disapproval.

"Nonsense!" he said impatiently. "You know nothing whatever about it, and I advise you to keep your long nose out of such dangerous matters; these instruments of precision in the hands of the ignorant are lethal to the soul. Now, if you have prepared the inner chamber according to my directions, all is ready; but first let us have a look at the boy."

Luna could not suppress a grin of pride as he led the way to a heavily carved cupboard in the farthest corner of the room; the thing was a veritable cathedral in miniature, gothic and grotesque, with a hundred saints and gargoyles leaning from among its wreaths of fruit and flowers. He opened the door of this piece of furniture to a cautious crack; Chastelneuf peered over his shoulder. The two smiled joyously at each other as Luna closed the cupboard door with care.

"Miraculous!" shouted the chevalier, slapping Luna on the back in a transport of enthusiasm. "Divine! And even now he seems to live: Alvise, do you know you have given him a distinct look of his reverend uncle: a sweet touch that; and oh, the delicacy of the thing! The hair, the eyelashes, the very finger-nails! O marvellous Luna!"

"It was a good thought that, to patronize your own tailor, though it has cost us a pretty penny," began Luna, handsomely, when a timid knock upon the outer door apprised the friends of Peter Innocent's proximity.

While Luna engaged the cardinal in more or less agreeable conversation, Chastelneuf disappeared into the inner apartment. The time passed rapidly, and Peter Innocent had just finished his third glass of wine and persuaded a pair of coral-coloured crystal love-birds to perch upon his forefinger, when the all but inaudible strains of a flute or violin recalled him from a waking dream. Guided by Luna, he passed into the other chamber, whence these sounds proceeded, and there beheld a scene of ceremonial enchantment.

Let it be clearly understood at once that the chevalier, whatever his peccadillos, practised only the higher forms of transcendental and divine magic, as opposed to nigromancy and goetia; otherwise he could have done nothing in the presence of such holiness as Peter Innocent's; the cardinal moreover carried upon his person a crucifix and a Book of Prayer, infallible talismans against the evil one. Here was no place for the Ahriman of the Persians, the Typhon of the Egyptians, the Python of the Greeks, the Croquemitaine, the obscene deity of the Sabbath. Let it be remembered that Isis was impeccable in her widowhood, that Diana Panthea was a virgin; that Apollonius of Tyana never yielded to the seductions of pleasure; that Plotinus of Alexandria was ascetic in the manner of his life; and that Raymond Lully was the victim of a hopeless passion which made him chaste forever. Vesper, not Lucifer, blazed now in the pentagram upon the marble pavement, and Peter Innocent stepped forward without fear.

The chamber, which was both larger and higher than the anteroom, was hung with charming tapestries of rose and green, and the chevalier was robed in vestments of sky-blue silk; a crown of violets encircled his chestnut peruke. His ring was enriched by a magnificent turquoise, and his clasps and tiara were of lapis-lazuli and beryl. The walls were covered with festoons of roses, myrtle, and olive, and the atmosphere quivered with the emanations of innumerable spices.

Upon the Parian floor there stood an altar of perfumes, and upon this altar there lay an unblemished lambskin, and upon this lambskin was traced in pure vermilion a pentagram with one point in the ascendant. It had been sprinkled with holy water, and dried by the smoke of myrrh and aloes, and over it Chastelneuf had uttered the names of the five genii, which are Gabriel, Raphael, Anael, Samael, and Oriphiel.

The adept towered above the tripod of evocation; he bore in the centre of his breast a copper talisman with the character of Anael traced thereon, together with the words: "Aveeva Vadelilith."

Luna withdrew into the shadows, where he waved slowly an enormous fan of swan's feathers.

7

CONJURATION OF THE FOUR

PETER INNOCENT came forward into the light, which fell with an effect of moonshine from the sacred lamp. He had no sense of fear and, what is more singular, no sense of sin; this appears to be indisputable proof of the beneficent quality of the ritual employed by Chastelneuf, upon this occasion at least. The cardinal never told of that night's wonders, and had he done so he would certainly have been burnt by the Holy Office; but his conscience remained immaculate throughout. He had his private theories, however, concerning the Christian and supplementary ceremonies proper to the undertaking, and he held his book and his crucifix very firmly in his two hands as he confronted the chevalier.

Chastelneuf lifted in the air the true and absolute magic wand, which must not be confounded with the simple divining-rod, or the trident of Paracelsus. This was composed of a single perfectly straight branch of the almond-tree, cut with a golden pruning-knife at the exact moment of its flowering; one of the extremities was fitted with a triangular prism, and the other with a similar figure of black resin; this end of the wand was gilded, and that silvered. A long needle of magnetized iron pierced the entire length of this consecrated instrument, which was the verendum of the magus, too occult to be shown to uninitiate eyes; the chevalier was probably unwise to employ it in the presence of the cardinal and Luna, but he was a brave man, and very vain of his attainments.

" As this creature to whom we are about to impart the privilege of living is composed of natural elements, I purpose to invoke the spirits of these components, which are the Four: air, water, fire, and earth. He who is about to be born was formed from sand and holy water, fused in extremest heat and shaped by human breath. Through the agency of these powers, a spirit shall enter into this bodily image, but whether mortal or elemental I cannot tell, nor does it greatly matter."

Chastelneuf spoke thus with an authentic dignity, which deepened as he proceeded with the exorcisms. And now the cardinal perceived behind the altar an object of funereal character, resembling a bier; it was covered by a white cloth whose folds conformed in some measure to the outlines of a corpse decently disposed for burial. The thing had been invisible a moment since; now the rays of the lamp were concentrated upon its ominous quiescence.

Tracing their symbol upon the air with an eagle's quill, the adept now intoned the prayer of the sylphs; he exorcized the water by the imposition of hands, and by mingling with it a little consecrated salt and the ash of incense. The aspergillum used was formed of twigs of vervain, periwinkle, sage, mint, and basil, tied by a thread expertly abstracted from a virgin's distaff and provided with a handle of hazelwood from a tree which had not yet fruited. The prayer of the undines was then recited with proper solemnity, and afterward the prayer of the salamanders, so soon as the fire had been suitably exorcized by the sprinkling of salt, white resin, camphor, and sulphur, and by calling upon the kings of the sun and lightning, the volcanoes, and the great astral light. Lastly, the earth was exorcized by efficacious means, and the gnomic prayer pronounced. The chevalier then lifted successively the sword, the rod, and the cup, and proclaimed, in a loud voice, the conjuration of the Four.

"Caput mortuum, the Lord command thee by the living and votive serpent! Cherub, the Lord command thee by Adam Jotchavah! Wandering Eagle, the Lord command thee by the wings of the Bull! Serpent, the Lord Tetragrammaton command thee by the angel and the lion! Michael, Gabriel, Raphael, and Anael! Flow, moisture, by the spirit of Eloim! Earth, be established by Adam Jotchavah! Spread, firmament, by Jahuvehu, Zebaoth! Fulfil, judgement, by fire in the virtue of Michael! Angel of the blind eyes, obey, or pass away with this holy water! Work, winged Bull, or revert to the earth, unless thou wouldst have me pierce thee with this sword! Chained Eagle, obey my sign, or fly before this breathing! This, by virtue of the Pentagram, which is the morning star, and by the name of the Tetragram, which is written in the centre of the cross of light! Amen."

At this moment the white cloth covering the body seemed to move of its own volition, rising slowly until it floated free of the bier; its corners were drawn apart, and the fabric violently divided into four quarters. Upon a narrow trestle Peter Innocent saw the figure of a young man; he appeared very tall and slender in his complete immobility. He was dressed in the fantastic extreme of fashion, and his costume was the more singular in that it was entirely white. He wore a white velvet coat embroidered with silver spangles, a velvet waistcoat to match, white satin breeches, white silk stockings, and shoes with diamond buckles. His linen and lace were exquisite, and on one hand was placed a curious ring consisting of a large crystal set over white satin.

The cardinal stared intently at the face of this elegant creature, but could distinguish little save the suggestion of a straight nose, arched eyebrows, and the glimmer of pale hair over a paler brow. The eyes were closed, the hands relaxed and quiet.

Meanwhile, above the tripod, the mystery thickened with the perfumed smoke; there came a loud command, a moon of radiance appeared, dissolved, and vanished, and with the most startling celerity the young man bounded from his couch and gracefully abased himself before the venerable prelate, in whom he seemed to recognize a father or a friend. At the same instant the chevalier stepped forward and affected an introduction between the two, mingling simplicity with polished ease of manner.

All were visibly moved by this happy consummation of their ritual, and even Luna permitted a few tears of relief and cupidity to trickle down his dusty cheeks. Chastelneuf was laughing, shaking hands, and offering choice wines in slim Murano goblets to the cardinal and his nephew. The boy smiled, bowed, and sipped with the most lifelike gestures of politeness; but Peter Innocent stood silent in a tranquillity like stone, bewitched and awed by his felicity, and gazing at his nephew with infinite love and wonder in his eyes.

8

CREATURE OF SALT

UPON the most minute examination, Peter Innocent failed to discover anything in the appearance of his young kinsman — for as such we must henceforward consider him — which could suggest an abhuman origin or composition. True, the boy's skin was so fair as to seem almost translucent, and the luminous flax of his abundant hair had the fragility of spun glass; but these details merely served to give distinction to his undoubted beauty. It is possible that Luna had employed, in weaving with his breath these miraculous lovelocks, a secret method by which his ancestors had produced *vitro de trina,* or crystal lace, of such spider-web delicacy that it shattered at the vibrations of an angry voice or the too poignant wailing of a violin. The long gold eyelashes matched the hair; the eyes themselves were the colour of sea water, the pure Venetian aquamarine.

As opposed to the very ornamental lightness of his physical equipment, the young man's manner was composed and firm, and his perfect self-possession might have contained a hint of patronage had its affability been less pronounced. He ignored Luna with charming good-humour, condescended to the chevalier without offending him, and put Peter Innocent at his ease with equal facility and despatch.

" My dearest uncle, my more than father," he cried with fastidiously restrained emotion, saluting the cardinal on both cheeks with the utmost tenderness, while two bright glassy tears, volatile as quicksilver, fell shining through the air. " Chevalier, that's a sound wine, though heavy to my particular fancy. You don't happen to have such a thing as a *viola de gamba* about, do you? A little music would not be amiss — I am sure you sing — that sweet duet of Cimarosa's, let us say." And he began to hum, in an enchanting tenor, the words:

> " *Prima che spunti*
> *In ciel l'aurora . . ."*

The cardinal put out his hand, and softly touched the white satin sleeve of his new nephew.

" Dear boy, it gives me the greatest satisfaction to witness your careless happiness," he said timidly, " but there is one thing, one slight precautionary measure, which I hesitate to omit, much as it grieves me to interrupt your singing. I wonder if I might trouble you for a little clear water? " he continued, turning to Luna with a courteous smile.

The chevalier bounded forward, eager to serve, with the stoup of holy water from the evocative altar; but Peter Innocent shrank hastily away as he shook his silver head in refusal.

" Not that, I think, my kind friend. Believe me, I am very grateful, but if I might have only a cupful from the spring which I observed in the adjoining cellar, I should prefer — Ah, you are goodness itself; I thank you."

Peter Innocent took the water which Luna brought him in a cracked china cup; holding it very carefully, he blessed it according to the Roman ritual, thus establishing its potency against evil spirits. This was a different consecration, indeed, from that surrounding the furniture of the chevalier's altar; this blessing, uttered in the old man's quiet voice, was spoken with another and an holier authority.

" . . . that wherever thou art sprinkled every phantasy and wickedness and wile of diabolic deceit may flee and leave that place, and every unclean spirit. . . ." Thus was exorcized the creature of salt lurking invisible in the broken cup, and likewise the creature of water . . . " that thou mayst avail to uproot and expel this enemy with all his apostate angels, by the virtue of the same our Lord Jesus Christ."

Now was the water become a creature in the service of God's mysteries for the driving out of demons. In a whisper so low as to be well-nigh inaudible even to the boy, who at a sign had knelt upon the pavement with instinctive docility, Peter Innocent repeated certain formulæ of blessing especially efficacious against devils and invocative of divine protection. Clear drops of water fell upon the bowed and shining head.

Chastelneuf was secretly annoyed.

" That was quite unnecessary, I assure you," he said rather

stiffly. "There is not an ounce of harm in the boy; the prescription calls for the purest ingredients, as Luna can tell you, and, for my own part, I have used the best magic known to the ancients. However, as you will. I suppose we all have our prejudices."

"I was sure you would understand an old man's anxiety," replied the cardinal, pacifically. "And now I will not trespass longer upon your kindness, save to give you this little wallet with my profoundest gratitude, and to wish you both a very good morning."

It was morning, and between the cracks in the jalousies pale blades of light were driven like angelic swords.

"Where are you taking the boy, Eminence?" asked the chevalier with renewed cheerfulness, playing a lively tune upon the jingling wallet, whose chorus was five thousand sequins. "Remember, he's scarcely used to a rough world as yet, and his finger-nails may be brittle for a day or two."

"We are going to the Church of St. John and St. Paul, my friend, where this poor child must receive the sacrament of baptism," Peter Innocent said slowly. He looked with pity and something perilously near adoration into the smooth, transparent countenance of the boy, who clasped his arm and smiled in meek response.

Mounting a short flight of steps, M. de Chastelneuf flung open an iron-barred door, and suddenly dawn flooded the room like a river of golden water loosed upon it. Without, the canal still preserved a sleepy colour, neither grey nor blue, but the house-tops were painted in extravagant tints of rose and flame by a sun new-risen from the Adriatic.

"What name will you give the boy, Monseigneur?" inquired the chevalier. "I feel a certain proprietary interest in his fortunes, which under your auspices must be uniformly happy, and I should like to know his name."

The cardinal mused, considered, and replied.

"I believe I shall call him Virginio," he said, his eyes tracing the exquisite and ingenuous outlines of his nephew's half-averted face.

"A pretty name, but I trust it may not long be strictly appropriate; I have spared no pains to make our young friend a com-

plete work of art, after the best natural patterns," answered the
Chevalier de Langeist, with a not unpardonable pride, bowing
deeply as Peter Innocent and his pale and luminous companion
passed into the morning, and so were gone like a black pearl and
a white, melting within a chalice of honeyed yellow wine.

END OF BOOK ONE

The Venetian Glass Nephew

BOOK II: *VIRGINIO*

"I had had an affair with the moon, in which there was neither sin nor shame."   *Laurence Sterne.*

9

OF SAPPHO LITTLE, BUT ALL ROSES

In Angelo Querini's classical garden at Altichieri there stood a summer-house dedicated to the goddess of Folly; this charming structure was, paradoxically enough, presided over by a bust of Marcus Aurelius and decorated with a motto from Montaigne. A more apposite taste had graced the dovecote with a Grecian Venus, and raised an altar to the spirit of tranquillity in the midst of abundances of sweet basil, lavender, and thyme.

Midway between an Egyptian sarcophagus and an Etruscan monument, both heavily overgrown with deep viridian moss, a marble bench disclosed its rosy veining to the September sun, and seemed to invite a languorous repose in keeping with the season. From the door of the shadowed summer-house a young girl presently emerged; her lively glance surveyed the autumnal lawns and arbours, and instantly selected the carved and coral-coloured seat as most benignant to her mood. She carried an armful of books; these she disposed within reach, herself reclining in the sunnier corner of the bench. She was soft and inscrutable as a Persian kitten.

A black kitten among the bright and gilded trees, with hazel eyes transfused with gold, and hair so dark that only at the temples a darkening golden tinge survived in smoky black. Her dress was black as soot; such a dress, decent, and austere, as clothed Querini's admired and admirable young friend Fulvia Vivaldi in her Genevan retreat; too black, in spite of the clear muslin kerchief and the silver chain, for Rosalba Berni on her eighteenth birthday.

This was, then, the celebrated Rosalba, better known among the Arcadians of Italy as Sappho the Younger, or to the more affectionate few, the Infant Sappho. This child was an orphan by report, and by profoundly proven faith the ward and adoptive daughter of the noble and liberal Angelo Querini, ex-senator of the Venetian patriciate and valued comrade of Voltaire. It was openly declared that she was a descendant of Francesco Berni the poet, to whose sparkling blood she owed her marvellous wit and the inventive lightness of her mind; other more insinuating murmurs attributed these qualities to an equally effervescent source: the whispered name of the Cardinal de Bernis was a veritable Arcadian diploma of mental grace, and Rosalba's eyebrows were distinctly French.

She had these brows, arched forever in a delicate amazement, drawn upon a smooth forehead; her dark hair grew in a point; and her eyes were large between black lashes; their expression was calm, but impertinent. Her mouth was curled like a scarlet petal in some early frost of irony; her skin was white as the rose of her baptismal name. Across her slightly tilted nose a score of golden freckles made her human; for the rest, in form and elegance of gesture, she was Artemis.

Yet not the Artemis of ivory or of quarried stone, however exquisite. Rosalba was more vital than opening roses or ripened fruit; she lived and moved and burned within the chilly greenery with a palpable warmth; she was a flame whose consummation may be bitter, but whose promissory blooming is tenderer than apple blossoms. To the five senses of an observer she was indeed imagined flowers to breathe, as she must have been velvet to touch, cream to taste, the crescent moon to gaze upon, and, to the listening ear, a melody repeated by a mocking-bird.

It was all to the credit of M. de Chastelneuf that the five senses of this particular observer were so poetically acute; the young Virginio leaned upon a mossy column, while love for Rosalba Berni whirled over him like a fragrant wave, and left him drowned in those same waters from which the mother of such love arose.

"'O bianca Galatea!'" said Virginio, politely, quoting Metastasio.

"My name is Sappho," Rosalba replied rather crossly. "I do not care for Italian verse; I prefer the classics, and, above all, Ossian. I am at present busy, very busy, with a translation of the latter, for the benefit of those unfortunate people who are unable to read it in the original Gaelic."

"Is it not written in English?" Virginio inquired timidly. "And have I not heard that Signor Cesarotti —"

"Be silent, if you cannot converse intelligently."

Rosalba pronounced these words with perfect calm; she was imperial rather than rude.

"Precisely," Virginio returned, with a gentle smile; she was suddenly aware that he was far more beautiful than any Adonis in Querini's garden. He reminded her of marble. Or was it marble of which he reminded her? Something more translucent; crystal, perhaps.

"I am reading, as you see," she said more kindly, "but I can spare you a few moments; I dare say you would like me to show you the books I have this very morning received from my kind friend and guardian. Approach, young sir; the gate is unlocked, and if you will wear white shoes, you must expect the dew to spoil them."

Virginio drew near her as one who visits, in simple reverence and awe, the shrine of an immortal; she laughed, and made a place for him beside her on the bench, among the richly bound volumes which surrounded her.

"Here, my poor boy, are the 'Confessions' of Rousseau; I suppose you have never read them. For my part, I have been familiar with their pages for years; this rose-coloured levant is merely a new dress for an old and adored companion. Here is the 'Cecilia' of Signorina Burney, published this same year in London; it will be so much Greek to you. Here is some real

Greek; a manuscript copy of the Codex Palatinus, or Anthology of Cephalas; the original is unfortunately locked up in the Vatican library."

"Where could it be safer, or in the company of so many equally holy treasures?" asked Virginio in mild surprise, which turned to actual terror as Rosalba whirled upon him with the silken savagery of a little panther. It was now evident that, who-ever her father, her mother must have been Italian.

"Are you a victim of superstition, and dare to enter these sacred shades?" she cried in honest indignation. Her eyes were burning amber, and the crisp tendrils of her hair appeared disturbed and shaken. Virginio trembled; a faint cracking sensation menaced his expanded heart.

"I am a Christian," he contrived to enunciate; he was very pale, and looked more than ever transparent. Rosalba was touched in spite of her convictions.

"Do not be distressed; I am myself a deist," she cried generously. Virginio put his cold hand over his sea-blue eyes; bright glassy tears fell into the air, and lay like silver on the yellow linden tassels at Rosalba's feet. "My poor boy, we have all made mistakes," she told him, seriously; she found his emotion curiously disturbing. "Look, I am often very silly myself; I have wasted half my birthday morning in re-reading a peculiarly childish novel by Carlo Gozzi. I am ashamed to admit that his fairy-stories have always had an attraction for my mind. Listen; it was this that I found so absorbing, this nonsense." And she proceeded to read the following passage from a shabby little book bound in coloured paper, and furnished with a marker of green silk ribbon.

"'A lady, adorned in the Venetian fashion, with a Florentine petticoat, and a blue satin vest, apparently fresh from the mercer's, trimmed with sleeves of the finest lace; she wore rings and bracelets of the richest gold, and a necklace set with Indian diamonds.'"

10

POESY RING

ROSALBA's voice died into quivering silence; she hung her supercilious head, and the contemptuous petals of her lips parted to sigh. " The ' Cecilia ' was given me as a special concession to feminine frivolity; it may also serve to improve my English," she murmured with apparent irrelevance. " It is a delightful book, I am sure. And next year I am to have the Encyclopédie, if I am diligent. Has not my dear Jean-Jacques a beautiful new dress, the exact shade, would you say, of a pink geranium? "

Virginio's shining flaxen brows stirred faintly to a frown.·

" Would you not prefer a beautiful new dress for the adornment of your own divine beauty? " he inquired with respectful interest. " I do not think a geranium pink coat particularly suitable to the charms of M. Rousseau."

" Oh, but I would rather have yellow," cried Rosalba, in spite of herself — " Pale yellow like a frosted leaf, or rosier, like the sunny side of peaches."

She stopped, sincerely sorry she had not been inventing pretty images for a poem about philosophy or the ringlets of a child. Shame tinted her cheek more delicately than imagination can contrive to colour it. Virginio's veins were molten with love and pity.

As a matter of stern, immutable fact, Rosalba was hardly a fit object for pity, although love enveloped her in a natural shower like sunlight. In the Venice of her time, and indeed throughout the whole of Arcadian Italy, she had from her precocious childhood been petted as a tenth and darling Muse; flattery had been her painted rattle, and early fame her skipping-rope. Yet since no visible laurel had enwreathed her hair, and since her dress was sombre with decorum, Virginio saw not Sappho, but Cinderella.

A blush suffused Virginio's face; the blood showed clearly, like wine that stains a pearly glass. From his hand he drew the curious ring which the Chevalier de Langeist had given him. It was a large crystal set over white satin; the band was gold, engraved with an English motto.

"Will you accept this trifling gift upon the fortunate occasion of your natal day?" he asked, with a graceful inclination of his luminous head.

"Yes, and most gratefully," Rosalba replied, with a smile of simple pleasure. "This is precisely what I have longed to possess; this must, I think, be an Indian diamond."

"Nearly, but not quite," Virginio admitted. "However, it is, as you see, very singular and charming; that is magic written on the gold. The words are possibly in cabalistic Hebrew; I know at least that they are secret and in the highest degree potent for conjuration."

"That is not Hebrew; that is English, I believe," said Rosalba, pondering the inscription. "It says — but this is extraordinary — it says, 'Fear God and love me.' The sentiment is elevated, and the language extremely choice; the whole forms an appropriate motto for a deist."

"The first words, yes; these are intended for the deist," explained Virginio, who did not have the slightest conception of the meaning of this mysterious term. "The rest — that enchanting phrase, if I may be permitted to repeat it; that legend, 'Love me,' this is addressed to the woman, the goddess, the eternal, unattainable Diana. Accept the prayer; put on the ring, O loveliest." He affixed the bauble, with a kiss, upon her middle finger, where it hung a little loose; it had fitted his own slender ring finger to perfection.

"I shall give you a guard," he said, "a guard of Indian diamonds." Rosalba laughed for joy.

"Touching the comparatively unimportant matter of my presence here to-day," Virginio continued suavely, retaining, with an air of negligence, Rosalba's hand within his own, "I must explain that I bear a letter to the noble Angelo Querini; it is upon the part of my revered uncle and benefactor, Cardinal Bon. These two were comrades in their season of tender youth; their hearts preserve the innocence of that vanished aureate age. My uncle desires to intrust me to the occasional kindness of his friend; he hopes I may be now and then allowed to visit Querini in his hallowed seclusion. I require, it seems, a certain amount of rustic air; my constitution is unfortunately fragile." Virginio did his charming best to appear pathetic, and succeeded admirably in the attempt; against the light his lifted hand moved in a crystalline transparency.

Rosalba frowned at the name of cardinal, but Virginio had already learned to prefer a frown to a smile in such an instance; as a cardinal's nephew he was accustomed to many and repellent smiles upon inimical lips. He was rather grateful to the girl for her look of gravity; it was his profoundest wish to be taken seriously, and persons of both sexes were but too apt, in his brief experience, to credit him with a mental lightness commensurate with his physical mould.

" Why are you not in Rome? " Rosalba questioned somewhat accusingly. Her manner revealed fastidious distaste, and Virginio was deeply grieved by her intolerance.

" I am too ignorant as yet for Roman society," he said quietly. " My uncle has arranged for my education at the Academy of Nobles in Venice. The age of admission is only eleven, but I am very simple-minded, and, besides, nobody can be certain of my exact years. I have, for my own part, a strong conviction that I am not less than nineteen and not more than twenty."

" I should say you were tall for nineteen and remarkably silly for twenty," Rosalba answered cruelly. Then, as he stood silent and very pale, she put out her hand again and touched his fingers in impulsive pity. Her hand was warm and vibrating with life; Virginio's hand was cold and thin, and as she clasped it, an ominous cracking startled her with strangeness, she felt as if his fingers were so many brittle icicles.

" Be careful, Signorina; you may injure yourself," said Virginio, sadly, examining his hands with the minutest care.

Rosalba looked at her own palm, where a tiny scratch showed scarlet; she could have sworn that a splinter of glass still clung there. Suddenly she was afraid; she stared at the boy in an enchantment of horror. The sun shrank up into a savage polar star, and the heavens were another colour than blue. The trees had tongues, and when she shut her eyes, she could hear the shuffle of their heavy feet upon the protesting grass; its blades were presently to be reborn as serpents.

Then two bright glassy tears, volatile as quicksilver, fell shining through the disfigured day, and as they splashed upon Rosalba's little breast, she drew Virginio beyond her fear and comforted him in the security of innocence.

So, with the utmost simplicity, Rosalba Berni was constrained to fear God and love Virginio all in the space of five seconds, yet this thing, so quickly done, was not to be undone within the memory of that generation, and when the dark and the flaxen head were frost and silver, the event remained unchanged.

11

CALMON THE PHILOSOPHER

" I TRUST that the noble Angelo Querini will approve our engagement," said Virginio in a tone of practical good sense, after a brief and iridescent cloud of unreality had enveloped them for a time in silence, whose mist dispersed too soon. " I think we should hasten to make known to him the history of the past fifteen minutes; he has been as a father to your girlhood, and he should be told of our betrothal without delay."

" H-m," and " M-yes," replied Rosalba, doubtfully; she was not certain that she wished to be betrothed; still less did she desire to acquaint her noble guardian with a fact so subject to the alterations of fancy. " Oh — shall we? " she inquired with a notable lack of enthusiasm.

" It is our duty." Such was Virginio's obdurate opinion; Rosalba accepted it, to her own surprise and considerable indignation. Dimly, as an inauspicious providence perceived through wizard crystal, she began to be aware that her lover was incapable of bending, however cruelly a clumsy world might break the refinement of his substance. In a prophetic flash she realized that she must henceforward and always, as the ancient Venetian proverb has it, handle him with white suède gauntlets steeped in rose-water.

Gentle and grave, and by her footfall half reluctant, she passed from the sumptuous autumnal sunlight of the garden into the chilly corridors of Querini's country house; the floors were paved in lozenges of grey and yellow marble, and upon the walls a long processsion was frozen in magical decay, which had once issued like a rainbow from the fresh and glittering palette of Carpaccio.

At her side Virginio stepped delicately and very proudly, in shining contrast to her austere black silk and bloodless lawn; he wore his white satin coat with silver spangles, and the lace upon his shirt might almost have purchased Constantinople from the Ottoman princes.

To Angelo Querini, in his pillared library, frescoed in faintly gilded russet and religious blue, and presided over by a bronze bust of Lord Verulam, the boy was an apparition from the fabulous other side of the moon.

This impression was the more amazing, in that Angelo Querini believed in neither apparitions nor fables save as the results of an imperfect digestion and an inferior intellect. His was a mind so purely rational that it had long since demanded and received absolute divorce from his naturally impetuous heart, which was thereby set at liberty to be as affectionate and foolish as it pleased without disturbing in the slightest degree Querini's mental conviction as to the profound selfishness of all human action. In this way his head was enabled to breathe the invigorating airs of philosophic disgust, while his heart enjoyed to the full a lifelong orgy of benevolence; Minerva might have sprung from his reasonable brow, but the daughter of his breast was Charity.

Therefore it was a foregone conclusion that the liberal cynic would overlook the irregularity of Virginio's birth, and the kind old man receive him as a son. Rosalba, until this moment free as a humming-bird nourished at the Muses' hands, felt the meshes of a sudden net envelop her in its invisible gossamer. Being herself a philosopher, she reflected sagely that the disquieting fact of her capture being now quietly accomplished, there was no further wisdom in revolt. Besides, in her innermost soul she no longer desired a freedom vacuous of Virginio, and as she took her guardian's congratulatory kiss, she succumbed for the first time in her life to the warm, delightful luxury of complete unreason.

In this delicious mental condition, she listened ravished to Virginio's account of his supernatural origin; neither the boy's simple confession nor Querini's kindly satirical smiles disturbed her in the slightest degree. Personally, and counter to every conviction which had so far upheld her brilliant intellect, she was inclined to credit her lover; but the whole question appeared to her of trifling importance compared with the exquisite grace wherewith Virginio expounded it, and she cared very little whether he had emerged from an Arabian orange or flown to earth upon the wings of the celebrated Green Bird, so long as he had come to her at last.

"This is a romance worthy of the invention of your friend the Count," said Querini, answering her thought. He was benignant, he was even tender, but Rosalba recognized the sceptical amusement in his eyes. She blushed, then blushed again more vividly, ashamed of blushing.

"The Count must be right, after all; this story, of whose accuracy I can entertain no doubt, must prove him right," she said firmly, opening her own eyes very wide in a glance of calm and arrogant assurance. No longer need she conceal her predilection for fairy-tales, nor fear to admit that her favourite author was, after all, not M. Jean-Jacques Rousseau, but Count Carlo Gozzi. Magic was justified by experiment; it was become a verity, true, rational and possible, like mathematics or the rights of man.

It is regrettable to be obliged to confess that the noble Angelo Querini did not share Rosalba's belief in Virginio's narrative; he felt quite certain that the handsome youth was the blue-eyed flower of Peter Innocent's wild oats. It is to the credit of his heart, however, that he viewed the supposed offspring of the cardinal's folly with the most solicitous compassion and respect. His mind emitted a private spark of laughter, reflected in his eyes, perhaps, but admirably absent from his grave and courteous lips.

"Curious, curious indeed," he ruminated gently, while joining their hands with a logical deistic blessing. "These little ones are the children of superstition and vice, yet how powerless has been the error of their parents to infect their intrinsic loveliness! Oh, nature, virtue, reason, and Voltaire! Oh, excellent Helvetius!

Philanthropically bestow upon these infants a ray of your own illumination! May their bodies remain pagan, their minds emancipated, and their moral qualities incorruptibly pure! " In his excitement he had almost pronounced " Amen," but caught himself in time to substitute a sentiment from the " Republic " of Plato.

12

UNCLES AND SONS

AT this very moment, by one of those pleasing coincidences more common in romantic fiction than among the ineptitudes of mortal life, the Cardinal Peter Innocent Bon, Count Carlo Gozzi, and the Chevalier de Langeist sat together within a turret chamber of the haunted palace of Saint Canziano; upon the countenance of each gentleman there brooded an expression of thoughtful melancholy. The lofty room, open to the four great azure winds of heaven, was festooned with cobwebs and dustily strewn with the count's famous collection of Arabian and Neapolitan fairytales. These volumes, in many instances richly bound in ancient levantine leathers, were fallen into a state of sad decay, repeated in the person of their owner, who had worn the same wig for twenty years, and whose silver shoe-buckles were broken. The door drooped upon its hinges, the window-panes were starred and splintered, and from the carven ceiling enormous spiders dangled mockingly above the absorbed faces of the three friends.

It can occasion no undue surprise to learn that Peter Innocent and Carlo Gozzi had been comrades since boyhood; the saintly and fastidious prelate and the aristocratic dreamer were spiritual kinsmen from their hereditary cradles. It is not generally known to history, however, that the patrician Gozzi and the adventurer Chastelneuf had even the slightest acquaintance with each other, and indeed it was the invariable care of both to conceal the circumstance; nevertheless, a sincere affection existed between them. It is possible that this mutual esteem was the result of a certain pamphlet, lampooning the Abbé Chiari, of which the chevalier was the reputed author. Such rumours had cost him dear in the opinion of the Council; they had, perhaps, rewarded him with the singular friendship of Carlo Gozzi.

Chastelneuf was splendidly attired in ashen-grey velvet; a silver-laced hat, a furred travelling-cloak, and a small white mask were flung upon a lamed and tattered chair at his elbow. Peter Innocent wore his severest habit; the slight disorder of its austerity suggested another journey, less luxurious than the chevalier's. Gozzi had wrapped his emaciated form in a ragged dressing-gown, apparently constructed from a bit of tapestry, in which the loves of Leda and her swan had been decently terminated by the sempstress; a virtuous pair of shears had shortened the fable with the garment, and left both the count and Leda colder for their loss. Two senatorial portraits by Titian and Tintoretto ignored the goblin chamber and its occupants with respective airs of proud detachment and opulent contempt.

"I had hardly expected to find my worthy — ahem — my interesting friend M. de Chastelneuf a member of our little company, Carlo," said Peter Innocent, timidly. He disliked very much the prospect of hurting any one's feelings, but he had come all the way from Rome on purpose to consult with the count upon matters of secrecy and importance; the chevalier's presence was a glittering blow to privacy, while his suave voice delicately divided silence, as one cuts a precious fruit. The cardinal, very kindly, wished him in Vienna.

Chastelneuf glanced at the count with smiling eyes beneath lifted brows; the latter answered the unspoken question at once.

"My dear Peter," he cried rather impatiently, " do you suppose the chevalier has travelled post from the Austrian frontier, and that at the gravest danger to his personal fortunes, for no better reason than to interrupt our consultation? On the contrary, it is he who shall resolve our difficulties; he has an excellent plan, and one which cannot fail to meet with your approval. But first let me ask you: did you furnish this vitreous young relative of yours with letters of introduction to Angelo Querini? "

"I did, without doubt," the cardinal assured him plaintively, " and at the cost, moreover, of several severe pangs of conscience. Querini is an estimable person in many respects, and my brother Nicholas was devoted to him. I cannot forget, however, that the man is an unbeliever and a Voltairian; he has insulted holy church upon various pretexts; he is a mocker and, I am afraid, a confirmed philosopher."

" ' Mock on, mock on, Voltaire, Rousseau! ' " muttered Carlo, who had seen the poem in manuscript among the papers of an eccentric English scholar of his acquaintance. " ' And the wind blows it back again! ' Where it listeth; true, very true. A detestable person, Querini; he cultivates plaster busts in his garden, which have devoured all the elves. But Chastelneuf says he has a pretty niece, a nymph by no means plaster."

The chevalier permitted himself to smile slightly in replying.

" Not a niece, my dear Count; a ward is surely another matter."

" Why? " demanded Peter Innocent with unwonted asperity; as an uncle, he resented the implied sneer without understanding it.

" Ah, Eminence, spare my blushes upon such a question! " Chastelneuf cried gaily; an impudent and evasive laugh puzzled the cardinal by its refined ribaldry.

" Do not quarrel, gentlemen," protested Gozzi, who was deriving a wicked satisfaction from this curious encounter between the powers of light and semi-darkness as represented by his friends. " We are all met to-day in order to discuss the future of two ingenuous young creatures in whom I, for my part, take the warmest and most fatherly interest."

" Two young creatures? " The cardinal looked pale with alarm. "Did I understand you to say two, my dear Carlo? Virginio has never been, so far as I know, anything in the least like twins."

" There is no question of twins, save in so far as the sweet affinity of lovers may simulate the natal bond," began Carlo Gozzi, but the chevalier interrupted him with something less than his customary politeness.

" Of course there can be no question of twins as yet," he said in a low, shocked voice, turning upon the cardinal a face congealed into dignified horror. " We are barely arrived at the point of arranging a match between Virginio and the niece of Cardinal de Bernis, and already your Eminence is talking of twins. The thought is perhaps a little indelicate, although we may all indulge such hopes in the intimacy of our devotions. But as to the match, is it not exquisitely suitable, and can you possibly withhold your approval when I explain — "

"Marriage! Virginio married! " exclaimed Peter Innocent, wildly; and, " Bernis! The niece of Cardinal de Bernis! " cried Carlo Gozzi with an almost comparable accession of surprise. " I thought he was going to study the Greek dramatists! " added the one, while the other ended, " And I, that she was the ward of Angelo Querini! "

13

SPIRITUAL FATHERS

" You were both quite correct in your conclusions," the chevalier reassured them.

" The divining crystal upon my watch-chain informs me that ·Virginio has this moment opened a folio of Sophocles, while the noble Querini is giving the best possible proof of his benevolent guardianship by conferring a double blessing and a modest competence upon the betrothed pair; his notary has but just entered the room; I believe he is about to draw up a new will. It is all very charming and idyllic, and I congratulate your Eminence most heartily upon a felicitous solution of your problems." He bowed, nor could the cardinal detect a look or gesture indicative of aught save urbanity and good humour.

" My problems were, after all, very simple, and you should not have come all the way from Vienna to solve them, Chevalier." Peter Innocent hoped he was not speaking too haughtily to this adventurous person; Carlo Gozzi healed whatever breach the gentle voice had made by laughing cynically and wiping his eyes upon a large bandanna handkerchief. It was impossible to say whether he was merry or sad.

" It was all my fault, Peter my dear," said Carlo Gozzi. " I have been melancholy of late; I miss my poor Truffaldino and his company of masks. In parting, we embraced, weeping bitterly. I had not wept since that mischievous lunar moth, Teresa

Ricci, flew away to the moon where she belonged, but now I cannot stay my tears. In vain have I attempted to be philosophical, which is merely to say heartless; my hopes have perished with the venerable comedy of Venice, which I must soon follow to undeserved oblivion. Meanwhile my one comfort has been the society of your delightful nephew; in him I have renewed my youth and experienced afresh the enchantment of fairy-tales and the ravishing pleasure of the impossible. I visited him in the sombre Academy of Nobles. In his black uniform, enveloped in a bright blue cloak, he was precisely like one of the disinherited princes of my own fancy; I loved him, and I longed to see him happy."

"I know you have been goodness itself to the boy, my Carlo; he wrote me of lessons in Arabic and antique Spanish. He cannot have been lonely in your edifying society, and now with these new excitements and adventures in the classics into which Querini is about to introduce him, his days will be overflowing with aureate dreams indeed. What more can the lad desire?"

"Don't you understand, Eminence?" asked the Chevalier. He gazed sternly at the cardinal, while true and generous indignation kindled within his smouldering golden eyes. His sinewy brown hand had sought and found his sword-hilt before it fell, still clenched, in recognition of Peter Innocent's silvered and benignant locks. "I beg your Eminence's pardon if I appear impetuous, but the boy, the poor boy, is, after all, very nearly human."

"Oh, I trust he is not merely human," interposed Gozzi. "There has been some talk of elementals, and I have always longed to meet an elemental. Virginio, with his translucent flesh, like flame made frost — Virginio is happily something better than human, or so I have believed."

"And is there something better on this inferior side of heaven?" Chastelneuf spoke with passion, and yet there was a perilous tenderness in his falcon look.

"We are all of us God's children, and fashioned in His image; we are moved by a breath of His divinity," said the cardinal, softly and somewhat fearfully; but Carlo Gozzi was not satisfied.

"Did you or did you not, M. de Chastelneuf, assure me, upon your honour as a gentleman, of this youth's supernatural origin?"

he demanded hotly. " I have loved him like a son, because I conceived him to be magic incarnate; am I to learn now that he is a common mortal like myself, and perhaps of baser clay? " He stared significantly at the chevalier, and his words were a challenge.

"Oh, no! Oh, no! " said Chastelneuf, wearily. " Calm yourself, my dear Count; your suspicions are unfortunately unfounded. The boy is all that you could wish him to be; he is an exquisite monster, a celestial prodigy, blown from the very air itself, and captured in an earthy net so fragile that its meshes could not withstand the violence of a mortal soul. I do not know to a certainty what spirit informs this mutable fabric; whether it be a creature of the elder world, nourished in the heart of a sapling or fallen from between the breasts of a cloud; only I think it lacks the roughness and the pitifulness of humanity. Be content, both of you; the cardinal may have his angel and the count his elfin prince; Virginio will never disappoint you. I have given him a ring; the same was given me in my youth by a beloved friend, and its influence is infallibly benign. If it should chance to light a little fire in that hollow heart, and set true tears burning in those glassy eyes, such marvels are not harmful, but salutary and kind. I, too, have felt for Virginio an affection fatherly and apprehensive; I have come from Vienna for the express purpose of promoting his happiness, and it is my prayer — yes, my profoundest supplication to my Maker — that this happiness is about to be consummated."

He fell silent; to Gozzi, who knew him well, it was an amazement to perceive a veritable moisture dimming the vehement colour of his eyes.

Peter Innocent was moved; his countenance, placid and humane as a sacred effigy, was turned toward the Chevalier in lenient concern, as Chastelneuf sat down and covered his face with his hand, shaken by some curious fit of ardour or revolt.

" I will consent to any plan, within reason, which can promote my nephew's ultimate happiness," said Peter Innocent, gravely.

Chastelneuf still bit his lip in tormented silence, but Gozzi burst forth into voluble rejoicing as he wrung the cardinal's hand with warmth.

"Oh, good! very good indeed! This is the best news I have heard in a twelvemonth. Peter, I knew I could rely upon your merciful heart when you were made to realize the boy's loneliness and isolation; Chevalier, my compliments to your invariable sagacity. Oh, it will be an extremely charming little romance, a fairy-tale come true, not desiccated and compressed within the pages of a book, but alive and kicking its scarlet heels, as the ancient Bergamesque proverb puts it. And the lad is actually a fantasy in Murano glass instead of vulgar flesh and blood! I myself could not have invented a prettier conceit, or one more gracefully in accordance with the best magical traditions."

Peter Innocent observed this enthusiasm with indulgence, but a natural anxiety led him to seek further enlightenment from his friend.

"And who, pray, is the young lady whom I am about to embrace as the bride of Virginio and, consequently, my own child? If I am not mistaken, the chevalier described her as a niece of Monseigneur de Bernis."

"Oh, niece if you like; that title does as well as another," said Chastelneuf, with recovered sprightliness. "And, indeed, I honour your scruples; nothing is more lamentable than lascivious gossip and scandalmongering. But in this case, it can do no harm to admit what your Eminence, as a man of the world, must already have suspected, in view of a certain prelate's profane reputation; the fact, in fine, and to make a long story short, that this lovely girl is a daughter of Cardinal de Bernis and . . ."

"But must you make it short, Chevalier?" interrupted Gozzi. He made no effort to conceal his eagerness, and his wintry eyes were bright with anticipation. "Your stories are always so entertaining, and never too good to be true; I am sure that Peter will join me in urging you to continue at your leisure with the recital of this mysterious amour. Eh, Peter, my boy, are you with me?"

14

NUNS AND LOVERS

PETER INNOCENT, whose eyes were blue as veronica flowers, and whose inmost soul was as a silver reliquary of chaste design, felt somewhat at a loss to conjecture whether or no he was, precisely, with Carlo Gozzi at the immediate moment. A doubt, insidious and sinister, as to the exact nature of the company filtered between the argent filigree of his reflections; he smelled brimstone as the count opened his tortoiseshell snuff-box, and observed with relief the normal outline of the chevalier's elegantly buckled shoes. When he replied, his speech was tempered by unaccustomed caution.

" Carlo, I cannot quite say that I am with you, but I hope I shall never be very far from such an old and trusted friend; no difference can sever us that may not be bridged by a clasp of the hand. Only I wonder a little. Is it, was it, entirely suitable for Cardinal de Bernis to have a daughter? "

Gozzi appeared slightly embarrassed, but Chastelneuf assumed the responsibility of answering without a trace of hesitation.

" Monseigneur, I feel sure your fears will be set at rest when I explain this affair; its complete suitability is perhaps its chief charm to a refined mind. The Cardinal de Bernis was possibly, in his youth, faintly inclined towards profligacy; he was brilliant and well bred, but flippant and occasionally unwise. Some of the ladies upon whom he bestowed his butterfly favours shared his weakness; one alone of all that rainbow number remained modest and virginal even under the intoxication of love. I knew her; it might have been my privilege to preserve her delicate illusions from maculation at the hands of beasts. She was unwavering in her faith, which, most unhappily for her, was pinned not upon the bosom of her God, but starrily, like a bright religious order, over the shifting heart of François-Joachim de Bernis."

" Proceed," said Gozzi. " This begins to be amusing."

" The tale is not truly amusing," said Chastelneuf, meditatively. "It is sad, I am afraid, and its only happy ending is Rosalba, who is herself not an end, but a beginning. For the French ambassador at Rome it is very sad; for a little Venetian widow it was, perhaps, sadder. I will tell it to you, if you like, but I cannot promise to make you laugh except at the ridiculous spectacle of my own tears."

"Go on, my friend," replied the inscrutable Gozzi. Peter Innocent was silent, but from an inner pocket he drew a fine cambric handkerchief, sweet with lavender.

"I am the villain of this piece, Eminence," the chevalier continued with a sort of melancholy pride. "When I have finished, you will find it impossible to condemn Bernis; your feelings towards the innocuous partner of his unwisdom can be no harsher than regret softened by commiseration. Ah, Caterina, if I had never led you into that select conclave of libertines, you might even now be a happy wife and mother, and I, content and honoured, the father of a lovelier creature than either Virginio or Rosalba! I may say without vanity," he added, "that in my youth I was not ill favoured."

"Proceed! proceed!" cried Gozzi, impatiently. "You were always as black as a Moor; Time has spilt no milk and roses from your leather cheek, over which you should waste your tears. Be good enough to stop crying, Jacques; tell your story."

"It is now nearly thirty years since I first saw Caterina," Chastelneuf went on. "She was but fourteen years old, and her little face had all the blameless brilliance of a child's. I loved her, but with a levity and cynicism incomprehensible to my maturer perceptions. I seduced her, but tenderly, for I had determined to make her mine legally and for life. We spent hours in the gardens at Saint Blaise, where we ran races together; the prize, which I permitted her to win, was a pair of blue garters. I was captivated; her candour, her ingenuousness, her vivacity, all contrived to make me her slave, for the union of beauty, intelligence, and innocence has ever swayed me.

"A parent, perhaps no crueller than her lover, but certainly for the moment more severe, immured Caterina within a convent at Murano; we were unable to meet, and had only the chilly comfort of smuggled letters, and the ambiguous tremors of hope, as sustenance for our reciprocal dreams. I gave her my portrait, commissioning a young Piedmontese to render it in the smallest miniature; he painted an exquisite Saint Catherine of the same dimensions, and a clever Venetian jeweller mounted them both in a ring. The patron saint concealed my countenance, but the expert craftsman had provided the fantastic setting with a hidden spring, and I fear that my pictured eyes often disturbed the devout eyelids of poor Caterina by hot and secular tears.

" This comedy continued for several months; I grew very thin and mournful, and lived miracles of faithfulness in the mere denial of my natural instincts. At last I made bold to enter the convent chapel; one of the novices was about to take the veil, and I knew I might pass unobserved among the crowd of visitors.

" After the investiture I walked into the convent parlour with the other pious spectators, and standing within four paces of my poor little love, I perceived her gazing at me in a species of ecstasy; happiness made wide her hazel eyes and parted her lips to suspire tenderness.

" Alas! I had no sooner conferred the fleeting joy of my smile upon this unfortunate child than I robbed her again, and forever; my heart, always elastic, rebounded from the small and shrinking form of Caterina, to fall with terrific violence at the feet of a tall nun beneath whose cool reserve a secret fire was visible, even as her coif disclosed an unlicensed curl of red-gold hair above a face fair to pallor and lovely to delirium. I was completely overcome; my head swam among singing clouds, and I should assuredly have fainted had not a kindly old lay sister led me into the sharp sea winds of the conventual garden.

" If ever I write my memoirs, which I shall refuse to call confessions, since that infamous rascal Rousseau has profaned the title, I may describe at leisured length the course of my infatuation for the nun, Mary Magdalen, and its legendary end; I may aspire to draw her portrait, more intimately even than my young Piedmontese drew it for me, naked upon a couch of black satin, demure and shameless behind an ivory medallion of the Annunciation fitted into the lid of a gold snuff-box.

" This refulgent lady was the friend of the Abbé de Bernis;

she had taken the veil out of pure caprice, and had the discretion
to conceal any unhappiness she may have felt. Her illustrious
birth and her extravagant liberality procured innumerable privileges denied to the other nuns; the tale of her amorous adventures
must not insult the laudable ears of your Eminence. Suffice it to
say that she and I between us plotted to debauch the peaceable
simplicity of poor Caterina; I gave my darling to the power of
the dog, and in a room of mirrors, lighted by girandoles and
candelabra of rock crystal and gilded bronze, Bernis took the child
in his arms and drank her frightened tears with feverish avidity.
I retired, laughing, to sup with Mary Magdalen in the adjoining
chamber; the nun was disguised as a handsome youth in rose-
coloured velvet and black satin, and we devoured oysters and
truffles from silver chafing-dishes and fine Dresden china. The
wines were burgundy and champagne; I remember that I was
excessively thirsty. I was mixing a salad of anchovies and hard-
boiled eggs when the door opened and Bernis entered, followed
by Caterina.

" Bernis was a man of forty; to my intolerant eye he was already a little worn, a little thin; his good looks were faintly tainted
by effeminacy. He was invariably dressed in the extreme of elegance; the beauty of his hands was proverbial.

" Now, with an air of the most polished courtesy, he offered
one of these miraculous hands to Caterina; he bowed, and I saw
nobility rise to his forehead, shaking back the perfumed flippancy
of his thoughts as a lion shakes back his mane. So I knew that
although I had abandoned my darling to the lion, the power of
the dog was dead. I am ashamed to admit that I was furiously
jealous of Bernis.

" I cannot tell you the truth of this matter because I have never
known it. What I conceive to be the truth seemed inconceivable
at that confounding moment; the room, with its vain and equivocal elegance, its exquisite depravity, its engravings by Meunius
and Toletana, the lovely epicene figure of the nun, the perverse
integrity of the ambassador's bearing, all conspired to render the
scene incredible. Caterina, attired in a childish gown of green
gauze, was composed and smiling; she looked up at Bernis, and

her gaze was limpid with faith. I was very angry; knowing a portion of my loss, I raged inwardly, and longed to kill the two; the deeper significance of their mutual glances was hidden from my eyes by a curtain of blood."

15

CAME FORTH SWEETNESS

PETER INNOCENT had covered his face with the lavender-scented handkerchief, but Gozzi remained satirical and unmoved. The chevalier brushed the back of his hand across his shining and dilated eyes, as if to dissipate the remembered darkness of crimson. He continued to speak in a measured and deliberate voice:

"I did not see Caterina again; she returned to the convent at Murano, and within the year her parents had married her to an honest Venetian lawyer, who adored and tormented her youth with an intolerable devotion. Bernis, as you know, was soon afterwards recalled to France; the nun Mary Magdalen and I were left to console each other with meditations upon infidelity. Our natures were but too similar; each libertine despised the other, and we parted without regret or charitable illusion, without prejudice, and without compassion for each other's spirits, subdued to such resemblance by the unloving flesh."

"Peter, if you can make, as the peasants say at Chioggia, either dragon's head or mermaid's tail of this unholy rigmarole, you are a cleverer man than I, and that I should be sorry to believe!" exclaimed Gozzi in exasperation, as the chevalier's recital drew to an apparent close on a note of profound repentance.

Peter Innocent raised his seraphic and bewildered eyes, enlarged by tears too scorching to be cooled by a cambric handkerchief; he did not look at Gozzi or at Chastelneuf, but straight into the sky, a deep, blue pool reversed, suspended, spreading like a tree, like a shade, like the shadow of a sapphire rock.

"I can make neither head nor tail of this tragedy, Carlo," he answered, "yet, for my comfort, the chevalier has made me believe it has a heart, and that not chimærical or devilish, but vulnerably human. I cannot understand, and yet, beneath the covert and obscure, I can feel the beating of a heart."

" You are a cleverer man than I, Peter," said Carlo Gozzi, who believed in elves. He said it in humility, for sometimes he believed in angels.

" You are right, Eminence; it is the heart of poor mortality which beats in my story, and echoes in your ears; the sound is the sum of human hearts which still vibrate in unison because, though broken, they have mended each other with love."

Chastelneuf spoke solemnly, but Gozzi questioned him with a quizzical scorn.

" Do you say love, O melancholy Jacques? "

" I say it," replied the chevalier; the habitual visor of insolence masked his face upon the word. " To clarify the matter further for your Eminence's comprehension," he went on, in a light and cursive voice, " I must remind you that Bernis had no sooner become a power in France than he had the unfortunate honour of incurring the enmity of the royal favourite. He had the temerity to suggest that the Prince de Soubise was not a fit person to command the King's armies; the Pompadour was majestically offended, and when the pope presented Bernis with a cardinal's hat, Louis bestowed it upon him with his own hands and forthwith exiled him to Soissons, where he remained for six years, a broken and embittered man."

" Lorenzo Ganganelli loved that man," said Peter Innocent.

" I know he did, and therefore his successor hates him, Eminence; when you return to Rome, you may do a kindness to a dying lion."

" Chevalier, I think you are wrong; I am very old, and I should only weary the Cardinal de Bernis," Peter Innocent replied modestly.

" Your nephew's sweetheart will not weary him," Chastelneuf cried with a curiously happy laugh. " Wait; do not believe me a madman. I have more riddles to elucidate if you can spare me the patience."

" I have a fabulous appetite for old wives' tales," Gozzi admitted rudely, and Peter Innocent was quiet and kind in his silence.

"Good," said the chevalier. "We were at Soissons, were we not? At Soissons in a cold December, with a northeast wind and seventy miles dividing it from the classic gaiety of Versailles. Here, among Gothic churches and darker mediæval memories of Saint Crispin the Shoemaker and Louis the Pious, here where Becket prayed and Abélard despaired, Bernis came alone and sorrowful, having put his trust in princes, and served his country better than his king's mistress.

"Imagine, if you are something kindlier than stone, the desolation of that Christmas season, when in Soissons the Gothic roses of Notre Dame were carved in snow, and the Cardinal de Bernis sat alone in his vast apartment. He had caused no fire to be lighted, no supper to be laid, and when the chimes, like stars made audible, began to pierce the midnight with rejoicing, he stopped his ears against their voices, and wept the burning tears of Lucifer fallen from heaven.

"At that moment, out of the darkness, upon the wings of the bells as it were, and feathered with snow like a little bird, Caterina came to him."

"Thank God!" said Carlo Gozzi, fervently. Peter Innocent said nothing.

"She folded him in her grey cloak, that was all feathered and furred with the snow, and she kissed his beautiful cold hands. It was the first kiss she had ever given him; she gave it to the lion who had delivered her from the power of the dog, at Venice, in the room of mirrors, on an evening of full carnival, when she was only fourteen years old."

"I am glad she came," said Carlo Gozzi, adding, after he had cleared his throat, "I suppose, then, that we are to understand that Rosalba Berni is the offspring of this interesting union!"

"Yes, you are to understand precisely that, my dear Count; I fear you are incapable of fully appreciating the poignancy of the situation, but the bare facts you are at liberty to understand," answered the chevalier with impudent urbanity. He finished the tale, turning his blazing eyes towards Peter Innocent, who continued to say nothing.

"When Caterina came to Soissons on Christmas eve, she was seventeen years old and a widow. At that time Bernis was past

forty, and tired by the vanities of a Dead-Sea dream, an ashy-
flavoured world. Six years later, when Rosalba was born in the
South, her father could laugh very lightly as he sprinkled her
with almond blossoms and peach blossoms and cherry blossoms
or tickled her lips with a pigeon's feather. Perhaps he was happy
because he had been recalled to court, where he had magnificently
rejected the seals of office; perhaps he was happy because he was
archbishop of Albi. Perhaps, on the other hand, he was happy
because of Rosalba, who had been born in happiness in the South,
in a farmhouse whose outer walls were covered with espaliered
peach trees, and whose windows were fringed with climbing roses.
Upon the day of her birth a golden peach knocked at the door
and a white rose flew into the window. Bernis ate the peach
and gave the rose to Caterina. To the child they gave the name
Rosalba.

" At Albi, the archbishop's palace is a fortified castle of the
Middle Ages, and perhaps it is not strange that Bernis loved better
the farmhouse with the espaliered fruit-trees. Here for five years
a golden age endured; a little world existed for a time, round and
smooth and perfect as a peach. A bitter stone was hidden in its
heart, but before Bernis set his teeth to that his felicity was absolute. Then, in the plenitude of summer, Caterina died.

" Bernis gave every rose in the garden to Caterina; she clasped
them with gentle indifference. In this same manner she accepted
his last kiss; he was glad enough to go to Rome, to assist at the
conclave which elected Lorenzo Ganganelli. He had a chill conviction of her forgetfulness.

" Rosalba was conveyed to Paris in the care of an impoverished
cousin of her father's; this gentlewoman was amiable, but frivolous and injudicious. Having acquired a little wealth through the
generosity of her kinsman Bernis, she repaired to Versailles, taking
the child with her. There, in the midst of that sumptuous, but
effete, civilization, Rosalba was remarked by Madame Necker for
her wit and beauty and selected as a playmate for that lady's
precocious little daughter.

" Thus, while yet of tender years, the girl was made free of
the best *philosophe* society; by the time she was twelve she was
among the shining ornaments of Madame Necker's Friday re-

ceptions; the Mondays of Madame Geoffrin, the Tuesdays of Madame Helvétius, were incomplete without Rosalba's elfin grace. Her cousin desired above all else a fashionable marriage for her protégée but beneath brocaded petticoats the child's silk stockings, though gossamer and clocked with lace, were already obstinately blue. She refused, by impertinent implication, a round dozen of silver-gilded youths; Versailles was a blown Easter egg, excessively sugared, and she cared only for political reform and the awards of the Académie française."

16

DIVERSIONS AT FERNEY

"Intolerable imp! " exclaimed Count Carlo Gozzi in disgust. "It is this same horror, this unfeminine baggage, this most ungentle lady whom I have laughed to scorn in all my charming plays! She is the Princess Turandot, who utters riddles in the tone of an academician; she is Barberina, who has read Holbach while Carletti was dressing her hair. I had hardly realized the extent of her folly. However if you, Chevalier, say she is pretty — and you do say so, do you not? "

"And good? You have assured me of her virtue? " faltered Peter Innocent.

The chevalier regarded them with skilfully displayed contempt; he elevated his eyebrows the polite fraction of an inch.

"Eminence," he pronounced, " it is even possible, as the French pastry cooks have it, to put too many perfect ingredients into a pound cake. Enough, they remind us, is better than dyspepsia. Yourself and the count may live to regret the fact that Rosalba has never had a cold in the head or an illaudable impulse. Such things are, perhaps, disfiguring for the moment, but they humble the spirit of the young. Rosalba is not humble."

"Is she proud? " said Peter Innocent.

"Not in the least, Eminence," Chastelneuf replied. " She is merely perfect. You may be completely at ease in her company; she has the simplicity of the truly great."

Carlo Gozzi snorted indignantly, but Peter Innocent perceived no cause for annoyance. His simplicity excelled Rosalba's.

"And her friendship with Voltaire?" he went on a little nervously in spite of the chevalier's reassurances. "I have wondered, do you know, whether that were quite desirable. Of course its results were most fortunate; there can be no doubt that Querini has sheltered her from every tempered blast. But Voltaire as the intimate companion of a child of twelve — no, I confess the reflection has troubled me."

"Monseigneur, as I said to M. de Voltaire after reciting thirty-six stanzas of that divine twenty-third canto of ' Ariosto,' describing the madness of Roland with the most dreadful accuracy, — when I had finished, I assure you, the philosopher fell upon my neck, sobbing; tears were in all eyes, — but, I repeat, as I said to him at this affecting moment, you are too satirical, *cher maitre;* be human, as now, and like Ariosto you will be sublime! Oh, I remember it very well! Your Eminence is right; there was a vein of irony in the man which I must be the first to deprecate. And yet, he had intelligence; I think Rosalba was attracted by his intelligence. Then, too, you would not have her guilty of ingratitude, and he was kind to her."

"He stole her from a convent, did he not?" inquired Gozzi, who was beginning to be bored by the continued amiability of his two friends. To his relief, Peter Innocent looked shocked; the chevalier remained incurably good-humoured.

"Oh, quite!" the imperturbable chevalier cried. "But such a convent! Really, I cannot, in your Eminence's presence, attempt to explain; there were, however, circumstances too distressing to recall. I should hardly go so far as to say he stole her; rescue is the appropriate word, surely. The affair was shrouded in mystery; some said she had been immured by her ambitious cousin for refusing to wed a one-eyed marquis; others that she had incurred the enmity of the Neckers by embracing the free-trade principles of Turgot. Still another version, and that which I am myself inclined to credit, ascribes her abduction to the machinations of a rich Englishman, Milord Camphor or Camphile, who returning widowed from the East, beheld and desired, within the chilly inspiration of a single breath, Rosalba's loveliness and warm vivacity. It is but natural that the squire of Ferney, who had heard all of these stories in their most exaggerated forms, should have hastened to free this adorable creature from the chains of tyranny and vile superstition."

" And the name of this convent? " asked Peter Innocent, rather apologetically.

" That, Eminence, I am not at liberty to divulge; another time, perhaps. You see," the chevalier added, " it was the same convent from which M. de Voltaire had previously rescued Philiberte de Varicourt."

" Oho! Belle et Bonne! " exclaimed the count, who evidently saw. Peter Innocent did not, but his modesty prevented him from demanding an explanation.

" Precisely. And here, very luckily for little Rosalba, our good friend Querini appeared upon the scene. He came to pay his last respects to Voltaire; the fatal journey to Paris had already been discussed; ' Irène ' was well-nigh completed, and the patriarch experienced, within his venerable breast, a lively and determined longing to visit once more the country of his birth. The noble Angelo Querini found the household at Ferney more or less at sevens, elevens, and thirteens, as the school children say; Rosalba was crying in the boot closet under the stairs, and ' Belle et Bonne ' was biting her nails in her boudoir. M. de Voltaire and the Marquis de Villette were locked in the study drinking English punch and suffering from profound depression."

" What had occurred to disturb their philosophical serenity? " asked Gozzi, with an air of quiet satisfaction.

" Nothing; nothing at all, save that the Sage of Ferney had committed the trifling indiscretion of addressing Rosalba as ' Plus Belle et Plus Bonne ' in the fascinating presence of Philiberte. Our little friend had just completed a very creditable Horatian ode, entitled ' To My Heroic Champion '; this she recited, wearing a neat new frock of dark blue merino, with her hair arranged in becoming ringlets. The result was curious, and, to a man of eighty-four, disturbing. I have sometimes suspected that his decease was hastened — but, no, these ladies' dainty and frangible shoulder blades must not be burdened by so deplorable an event as the death of Voltaire! He perished of a surfeit of coffee and academic honours."

"Unrepentant," said Carlo Gozzi with intense and pleasurable conviction.

"Perhaps merely discourteous," said Chastelneuf, kindly.

Peter Innocent said nothing; he was absorbed in silent supplication for the immortal soul of François Arouet de Voltaire. The Deity's replying silence appeared to him an unconditional consent to his request for leniency. The softened airs and mistier hues of the Venetian afternoon surrounded this moment with a mild halo of salvation, and Peter Innocent felt sure that the sage was forgiven.

Far away, across the melancholy marshes of Altichieri, Virginio and Rosalba, fantastically cloaked and masked, had seized the same propitious moment to ascend the steps of the chevalier's elegant English carriage. They bore a large portmanteau and a couple of bandboxes, and the noble Angelo Querini, as he slammed the emblazoned door upon their smiles and blushes, wished them God-speed with all the prayerful emotion of his foolish heart, while his sagacious brow condemned them for a pair of young lunatics whirling in spangled frenzy towards a riddle and a doom.

END OF BOOK TWO

The Venetian Glass Nephew

BOOK III: *ROSALBA*

"But some, and these the elect among gardeners, will always prefer China Roses."   *Christopher Warren.*

17

GOLDEN BRIDE

" And now," murmured Chastelneuf with obvious regret, gazing dreamily over the housetops, which the descending day had diapered with a changed and more intricate design of shadow — " and now, I repeat, my patient friends, there is little left to tell. You have been indulgent; the hour grows older, and matures into a time more suited to adventure than to these vague reminiscences. In a word, Querini adopted Rosalba upon the spot; he conveyed her to Venice, and encouraged her in the study of the arts and sciences. Poetry was her natural voice; the Arcadian Academy received her with acclaim, and forthwith fell down and kissed the abbreviated hem of her schoolgirl's gown. The Infant Sappho was baptized in Castalia, and shaking the fountain drops from her juvenile curls, she lifted up her throat to sing. The rest you know; it cannot take me above five minutes to recount the principal events of Rosalba's Venetian career. You must remember — "

" But is it quite necessary, Chevalier? " Gozzi inquired with

284

plaintive scorn. "We have all heard too much of the Infant Sappho; some of us, impelled no doubt by morbid curiosity, have even read her verses. We recall very vividly and with peculiar pain the ridiculous festivities which marked her coronation at Rome, and all the nauseating verbiage, which, with the bad luxuriance of a weed, has kept her reputation virulently green. If you desire to converse further about the past, I must beg you to confine yourself to your own memories; why not favour us with an account of your escape from the Leads?"

Chastelneuf smiled; he was well aware of the count's savage irony, but he turned to Peter Innocent with bland composure.

"If his Eminence wishes; I am always at his disposal."

"I should be charmed —" began the cardinal; but Gozzi interposed in sincere alarm.

"For God's sake, Peter, do not encourage the rascal; the story will be an affair of hours, and we have much to accomplish before nightfall. Did you succeed in procuring a suitable gown for the girl, Jacques? You are accustomed to these matters; you have seduced several milliners, and your taste is impeccable."

"I have arranged for everything; I have ordered the supper, and bespoke the best string quartet in the four hospitals. The casino is in readiness; I have not yet relinquished its key to the new tenant, and my own servant has seen to it that there are fresh fires on the hearths, fresh candles in the girandoles, and fresh white roses in the crystal urns. I considered jasmine, I mused on lilies of the valley, but I knew I was wrong; there must be only white roses for this wedding-night. Am I not wise, your Eminence?"

Peter Innocent was at a loss to reply; his blue eyes were clouded by fatigue and bewilderment.

"Wedding-night?" he faltered, suddenly afraid. "Is it Virginio's wedding-night?"

"That is for your Eminence to say," the chevalier replied with courtly mendacity. "Also, it were only proper to await Virginio's own decision as to this momentous business; having seen Rosalba, I cannot question its affirmative nature. Carlo Gozzi and I have been planning a little surprise for the young people; a fête, *un petit diner à deux*, quite simple, you compre-

hend, but complete in every detail. It is Rosalba's birthday; since
the noble Angelo Querini adopted her, her garments have been
fashioned with a severe disregard of the prevailing *mode,* and
frivolity has been absent from her life. Even at her coronation
she was permitted no greater magnificence than a Greek robe
of virgin white; the material was velvet, I believe, but the cut
was antiquated. The Arcadian Academy has adored her manner of dressing, so chaste, so austere, so truly classical; but
Rosalba has been unhappy. ' This was well enough for Ferney,'
she has said, ' but for Venice, no! I can be young only once;
am I never to have a single little stitch *alla francese,* not even
a plain lemon-coloured Milordino with cloth of silver incisions,
or a modest mantle of gold-green camelot lined with Canadian
marten? I love my guardian with profound devotion, but I am,
after all, a woman, and it is sad not to possess a robe of Holland
poussé, trimmed with Spanish point! ' Oh, she has wept, your
Eminence; she has grieved in secret; we must endeavour to
console her. What do you think; are you for flame or peach
or girlish primrose? I am convinced it must be yellow. Tell me,
do you agree? "

Around the cardinal's frosty and abstracted head a dozen
rainbows seemed revolving in vertiginous arcs: colours of sun,
of harvest moon, of comet's tail and hell-fire streamed out upon
the increasing violet of dusk, and lit all Venice with their fer-
vency. He hesitated, and Gozzi answered for him.

" That is a problem for you and the milliner's apprentice to
determine ecstatically between yourselves; it does not concern
Cardinal Bon. Peter, we have indeed hoped that our little festival
in honour of these children might result in a wedding; for me
there must ever be the happy conclusion to my fairy-tales, and I
think to-night's performance will be the ultimate fantasy which
I shall prepare for any stage. I do not care for the girl save as
the inevitable partner for the prince; it is sufficient that she is
pretty and not too intolerable a fool. But for Virginio I desire
happiness, and over and above that good measure, a little pleasure running down, like shining bubbles, like golden grains. I
had thought, myself, that what with music and dancing and a
small quantity of very light wine to enliven them, the babes

might frolic until dawn, and then we could all hire a gondola —
for mine is at the pawnbroker's — and, proceeding to the church
of St. John and St. Paul, allow Peter to pronounce the blessing of holy church upon their union. Then, perhaps, another
gondola, and an *al fresco* breakfast upon the sands of the sea
or in some rustic grove. What do you say, Peter?"

This time Peter Innocent was at the trembling point of reply,
but the chevalier sent him back into silence by an ejaculation of
surprise.

"Good heavens! What an insanity is this, my dear Count!
Surely the marriage must take place before supper; it is only
right and *convenable* if the young people are to dance together
all night. I could never countenance such indiscretion; I am
sincerely shocked. 'Frolic until dawn' indeed! But of course
his Eminence will not permit it even for a moment."

"Confound you!" cried Carlo Gozzi. "You know perfectly
well, Jacques, that I did not mean — "

"What?" said the chevalier, demurely.

The count looked at the cardinal; then he sighed deeply,
and returned to its decaying sheath the jewelled Florentine
dagger which his hand had for a moment caressed.

"Never mind; nothing. I meant nothing, since Peter Innocent is here; but beware how you annoy me, Chastelneuf."

"Oh, I intended no harm!" the chevalier assured him gaily.
"I am possibly a trifle over-scrupulous about the conventions,
but you must contrive to forgive a finical old friend, Carlo. We
must all be very kind to-night; as for the marriage, I leave its
hour to the choice of Cardinal Bon, and its subsequent good
fortune to the benevolence of Almighty God." Casting a triumphant glance at Carlo Gozzi, Chastelneuf bowed his head
in double humility to higher powers.

"If Virginio must really be married, I do not think it matters very much whether I marry him before or after supper,"
said Peter Innocent, gently. His delicately chiselled face was worn
by anxiety, but his voice was firm as he continued: "I had
hoped, as Carlo understands, that my dear nephew might find
a conclusive felicity in the charitable embrace of the church,
as I have done. My earthly joy has so nearly approached the

heavenly, I have so thirsted for the peace of God and have been so thankfully appeased, that I had prayed for him a like simplicity of rapture. But if Carlo here, who has seen much of the lad's expanding soul, concludes that the complications of the secular life are indispensable to his content, so be it. Further, if the chevalier's account of young Rosalba Berni is but half so veracious as his proven honour must guarantee, I am well satisfied of her worthiness to be Virginio's wife. Therefore I will not withhold my consent from these nuptials; my heart awaits the lovers. Only, since it is better to avoid a too precipitate deed, however valid, let us follow Carlo's advice; the wedding shall take place to-morrow morning at the Church of Saint John and Saint Paul, whose benisons be upon these children."

The tower room was trembling in the violet dusk, like an island pinnacle invaded by the tide; the tide was evening, which rose rather than descended, flowing softly, smoothly, and invincibly from the deep lagoons, without the lightest undulation of a wave, without a sound, yet influential as the sea itself. Blue-violet and grey, red-violet where the sun informed it, the evening drowned the room in tinted darkness, until the faces of the three friends floated like nebulous ocean monsters in the gloom: Peter Innocent's face was coloured like a dead pearl, Carlo Gozzi's gleamed phosphorescent yellow. The chevalier's nervous hands wavered, brown as water weeds; his countenance was obscured.

The stairs which mounted to the tower chamber were crumbled and hazardous, yet upon their peril some one climbed, a footfall tinkled suddenly, incredibly tiny, a scampering as of winged mice, a skimming as of swallows. The rumour neared; heels or hoofs clicked upon stone at a fawn's pace; feathers or gauzy fabrics rustled and flew. The rusty latch cried out, the leathern door creaked in a draft, and Rosalba was within the room.

By some perverse vagary of the evening clouds, the sun and moon crossed swords above her head; under this pointed arch of light she ran into the room. The sun's long final ray was rosy and dim; the moon's first ray was silvery green and poignant. But Rosalba was pure gold from head to foot; she was brighter than the swords of light. A chaplet of golden leaves confined the burnished shadow of her hair; her sandal thongs were gilded; her gown, an Arcadian travesty of Diana's, was cut from cloth of gold. Her face was clear and pale, and her little freckles powdered it tenderly, like grains of golden dust. Her eyes were gold made magically translucent.

Her quick glance swept the apartment in a single scintillation, then, uttering a wild and joyous cry, she rushed upon Peter Innocent with all the ardour and velocity of a shooting star.

He was afraid. She was throttling him with her slender arms, and yet her lips were soft upon his cheek, and somewhere, in the profoundest caverns of his heart, love moved and wondered, answering her from a dream.

"Darling, even if you are a cardinal!" she said, "and lovely, even if you are an Eminence! Oh, you are beautiful, and like Virginio; I knew you at once! I shall adore you, and obey you always!" And she fell to kissing his hand. The fragility of those unresponsive and chilly finger-tips struck lightly yet insistently at her happiness, and she drew back in alarm, crying sadly:

"Oh, but you too, you too! You shiver and break when I touch you! Are you made of ice, that you cannot bear the little weight of my hand?"

Carlo Gozzi, to his own amazement, made a small sound of pity; the chevalier stepped forward and took the girl's hand between his own. He kissed it gravely and essayed to speak. At that precise instant the door swung open, and Virginio, sheathed in a silver cloak, came softly into the room; he entered like the twilight, and Rosalba was quenched within his arms.

18

TOO MANY PASTRY COOKS

"INEVITABLY ruin the meringue, as they say in Vienna!" the chevalier concluded lightly, closing his tortoise-shell snuff-box with a sharp click.

"Ah, you are right; the whole affair is whipped cream, and

we are endeavouring to turn it into good solid butter." Carlo Gozzi agreed; his face was thoughtful and surprisingly humane upon the reflection. " What is man? A fantastical puff-paste, as Webster truly remarks."

" I implore you not to be forever quoting the English trage-dians, my dear Count; it is disconcerting, to say the least, in this enlightened eighteenth century of ours. If Shakspere and his barbaric kin could have been gently licked into shape by the suave cat-tongue of Addison, they might have been endurable. As it is, I beg you to consider my earache, which is troublesome in November, and cannot brook a Gothic brutality of syllables. Touching the puff-paste, the simile is just enough, if Virginio is a man. I thought, however, we had determined him an elemental."

" H'm," said Gozzi, drily, " quite so, quite so. But, to my romantic fancy, an elemental moved among thunderstorms and whirlwinds; its least conceivable spirit was a snowfall. But Vir-ginio is animated by the soul of an icicle or a small, pale skeleton leaf. I have no patience with him since he carries his arm in a sling."

" Come, come, my friend," cried Chastelneuf, " you are too hard on the boy. Rosalba is, after all, very impulsive; her danc-ing is hoydenish, and she is addicted to running races, like Atalanta gone mad. Look, there she is, at the end of the cypress alley; she seems to be indulging in a game of tag with his Eminence."

The scene, precisely etched in slender lines upon a clear green west of early winter, was the garden of a small casino near Venice; the hour was sunset. A delicate chill flavoured the atmosphere with a perfume of frost and fallen leaves; the chevalier wore his fur pelisse, and the count was wrapped in a Bedouin cape of camel's hair; his head was covered by a scarlet nightcap.

Over the lawn, powdered with blown yellow petals, the noble Angelo Querini approached; his grave and judicial garments reproved the perished flowers. He seated himself upon a marble bench by the side of the two friends, first spreading a shawl of Scottish plaid against the frigidity of the stone. His eyes sought the distant figure of Rosalba, which flitted unquietly along the vistas of the garden, exquisitely strange and savage in a cloak of tawny velvet lined with foxes' skins.

"She used never to be so wild a creature while she shared my roof," he said sadly. "She was always so studious, so docile, so domestic! God knows what possesses her poor little body; her tranquillity is turned to quicksilver. She runs like a rabbit, like a deer, to and fro within the confines of these walls, and at night she is very tired. I think she cries. She is afraid of Virginio."

"But Virginio is afraid of her!" cried Carlo Gozzi, rather angrily. "Rosalba is not afraid; she is a brave child. The boy is afraid; look at him now, leaning against the wall, as white as pumiced parchment, and as limp. He is a coward; how can he be afraid of a little woodland fawn like our Rosalba?"

It was true; the slim form of Virginio appeared crucified upon one of the stucco walls of the inclosure. His feet were crossed; his fair head drooped and fainted; one arm was outspread among the vines; the other hung in a black silk sling. There was an agony of weakness in the attitude; his transparent hand was clenched upon a broken tendril of vine.

"She is afraid of Virginio," Angelo Querini repeated obstinately.

"I believe you are both of you right; they are afraid of each other," said Chastelneuf. "Our experiment has not been wholly successful: two mild substances are, in the intimate fusion of marriage, beginning to effervesce; there are signs of an explosion. It is a pity, but the case is by no means hopeless."

Both Querini and Carlo Gozzi continued to stare indignantly at the pathetic spectacle of Virginio's despair. Querini felt a truly paternal solicitude for Rosalba, and Gozzi, upon learning that the girl was a confirmed admirer of his fairy drama, had quickly altered his opinion of her character and intellect. She appeared to him now the very embodiment of inner grace, and he reflected angrily that Virginio was a poor atomy to mate with this burning and spiritual child of love, who wore a wild beast's pelt above a heart more vulnerable than a little lamb's.

"The incident of the broken arm," drawled the chevalier,

himself regarding Virginio through half-shut eyelids, " was, you comprehend, somewhat alarming to our young friend here. He is timid and fears to repeat the experience; his wife is impetuous and inclined to be careless. It is true that she did not actually touch him; they were running along the laurel alley, and he stumbled and fell. I was able to repair the damage, but it has shaken him seriously. Apparently he blames Rosalba; she, for her part, is proud, and in the consciousness of innocence, wounded to the soul by his implicit reproach. Neither will speak; their silence is like a darkness over them, in which suspicion flourishes."

" What does Peter say? "

" Nothing, in words; evidently he grieves, however, and I think he holds us responsible for the failure of his nephew's happiness. He feels certain that a monastery, rather than marriage, is Virginio's natural haven. Rosalba he has forgiven, but he cannot look upon her without pain."

" Forgiven her! And for what fault, may I ask? Is it a crime on this unlucky infant's part that we have incontinently wedded her to a glass mannikin instead of decent blood and bone? God pardon us for our unholy meddling, for we have hurt the loveliest thing alive! "

Marvellous to relate, along the ancient leather of Carlo Gozzi's cheek a single glabrous tear moved slowly downward; the others observed it with awe, not attempting to answer until he had removed it with the sleeve of his burnous. Then the chevalier cleared his throat and spoke briskly.

" I share your indignation, my dear Count, but the fact remains. Peter has forgiven Rosalba; you know we cannot prevent Peter from forgiving people even when they have done no harm. He is incapable of harbouring resentment, but he must have the comfort of an occasional absolution to uphold him; he has remitted Rosalba's non-existent sins against Virginio. See how tenderly he addresses the elusive child. She shrinks, she starts like a doe transfixed by an arrow, yet Peter's shaft was feathered by compassion; he let fly from the strings of his heart. He is a saint whose silver niche should never know these invasive anxieties; I have erred in giving him a nephew."

Virginio stirred and wavered against the wall; languidly he straightened his slight limbs to glide across the grass toward his wife. He was very pale, and his beautiful face appeared mute, and blinded by mysterious sorrow; its smooth, pure contours were immobile as a mask of gauze over the countenance of one lately dead.

19

BURNING LEAF

"It is a pity Rosalba is late; she is always so fond of *perdrix au choux,* and François has surpassed himself this evening," Chastelneuf commented reflectively, emptying his champagne goblet for the twelfth time.

The salon of the little casino was brilliantly, yet softly, illuminated by innumerable candles, and the Murano mirrors which formed its walls steeped the repeated lights in cool sea-coloured distances. The pyramid of grapes upon the table seemed moulded from the same silvered glass, and the flowers themselves were a fountain of crystalline spray. Peter Innocent, Carlo Gozzi, and Angelo Querini stained the pale, bright chamber with their black and rusty-brown attire; the chevalier's crimson startled it like a blow; only Virginio, resigned and pallid in pearly satin, fitted into the setting like a clear jewel clasped by a ring. His air of fragility was heightened by a cold and fearful lucency upon his brow; he looked ill, refused all food, and drank nothing save iced soda-water. He did not speak, but occupied his visibly shaking hands in the manufacture of little bread pellets. These were not grimy, as are the bread pellets of ordinary mortals; they appeared to acquire an added whiteness from the touch of his delicate and listless fingers.

"I overheard her tell Lucietta to repair the grey and lemon lutestring for to-night; one of the silver tassels was amiss, I think. Without doubt, she intended to dine with us; her absence begins to be alarming." Chastelneuf frowned into his replenished wineglass.

"I will go search for her," cried Querini and Carlo Gozzi

with simultaneous eagerness. Gozzi was already upon his feet; Querini was rising majestically from his carven chair. Peter Innocent said nothing; the silence of Virginio became appreciably more profound.

"Your pardon, gentlemen; I believe I am best fitted for this embassy." The chevalier's voice was authoritative, and he was at the door in three great strides. "There is a bonfire in the garden," he threw back over his shoulder, like an irrelevant glove, as he passed from the room. The challenge, if challenge it were, seemed flung directly into Virginio's bloodless and impassive face. The boy was whiter than white glass, more quiet than fallen snow; his long, fair eyelashes were lowered over his chill cerulean eyes.

Chastelneuf ran hastily from the lighted house into the obscurity of the dusk; behind him the windows made tall parallelograms of radiance, tinted by curtains of rainbow silk; in front a stranger colour tore the darkness into ribbons and flew upward in fringes of scarlet. "Merely the leaves, which the gardener is burning," the chevalier told himself in reassurance.

Nevertheless his buckled shoes leaped over the ground like the hoofs of a stallion, and he reached the end of the laurel alley three seconds in advance of Rosalba, who had danced into his vision on the instant, lighter, brighter, and more insensate than a burning leaf. Her cloak of fox skins opened into wings, the air upheld her, and she floated into the heart of the fire.

In another second she was safe; Chastelneuf stood over her on the smoking grass and stamped out the sparks with his buckled shoes; he knelt, and crushed between his sinewy hands the little ruffle of flame which scalloped the edges of her crumpled gown.

"Why were you so wicked, so cruelly wicked?" he cried. "Why did you not tell me that you wished to die? Do you understand that I am always here to give you whatever you want? Yes, even if it is death, I will give it to you; but sweetly flavoured and in a golden box. I will give you the death of these others if you desire it; I will give you life such as you have not imagined save in heaven.

"My child, my child, you have observed that I love you, but have you comprehended the quality of my love? It is such as you will never discover in the hollow veins of Virginio or among the noble ganglions of Querini's intellect; it is love, lust, passion, humility, and wonder; it is human, not divine, not animal, but the love of mortal for mortal; it is at your service. I love you; I have loved many times and in many fashions, but this love is all your own. Use it as you will; I have no expectation that you can return it in kind. I have done you an irreparable wrong; forgive me; I entreat your forgiveness, my darling. I believed that I loved Virginio, for he is the fair product of my ingenuity, but in attempting to provide him with those things needful to happiness I have sacrificed you, who are worth a million pale Virginios. You are the true child of my heart, and its ultimate affection; I will even love you with a father's love, if I may not love you with a lover's. I will subdue my spirit to your least command if you will promise me to live! "

The chevalier spoke with the most impassioned fervour, and Rosalba smiled among her tawny furs to see him so perturbed. In the midst of her own despair, she perceived nothing save cause for mirth in the agitation of one whom she had always regarded as a benevolent elderly gentleman, respectably conversant with the Italian classics and the court circulars of Europe.

Chastelneuf experienced a pang of extreme humiliation; he felt Rosalba's eyes, wild and acute as those of a trapped vixen, transfix his chestnut peruke and pierce to the silver stubble beneath it. The wrinkles upon his face were deepened as by acid, and his falcon look grew weary with the recollection of unrestful years. Rosalba, innocent alike of cruelty or compassion, shifted her gaze without speaking, and then cried aloud in the voice of a prisoned creature tardily released. Virginio, so veiled in twilight as to appear no more than a moving part of the invisible, now glided from the obscurity of the garden.

Rosalba shot upward like an impulsive flower nourished on subterranean flame; she ran, a pointed blossom of the dragon seed, straight to Virginio's heart. She might have been a dagger in that heart; the boy drew himself erect, closed his eyes, and stood swaying in an agony apparent as a wound. There was another and a sharper cry, an echo and a confused murmuring; the two slim figures clung together for an instant. Then they were again divided; the blue translucent dusk flowed between them like a narrow river; they stretched their hands to each other, and their tears fell into the swift and narrow stream of time and were lost.

Chastelneuf forgot his own sorrowful anger in a sudden pity; he was intolerably saddened by the spectacle of the lovers' frustration. He wanted nothing half so much as to see them happy and at peace under the evening stars; their youth was darling to his senses, like the smell of flowers or the flavour of wine, and he observed it without envy. He relinquished the luxury of self-commiseration, and reminding his vanity how easily he might have been Rosalba's parent, he cleared his throat, straightened his chestnut peruke, and spoke.

"My children," he said in a tone admirably paternal and concerned, "I am inexpressibly grieved to witness your distress; I am forced to conclude that all is not well between you. Trust me to understand your reticences, but trust me yet again, and further, to resolve your problems in my larger experience. If you will confide in me, my dears, I can convince you of my ability to assist you in any dilemma."

Even as he pronounced the words with such judicial calm, his mind was troubled and his bowels wrung by a dreadful premonition; pity grew fierce as anger in his soul, and his heart gnawed at his ribs.

Dimly as he now discerned the two figures confronting each other across the profound spaces, coloured more ambiguously than twilight, of their mutual and mortal fear, he was yet aware of a difference in air and attitude, which made Rosalba, to the peculiar pattern of his own mind, the sadder by an infinity of pain.

Virginio stood silent and curiously withdrawn; his white satin shoes were rooted to the ground, but he swayed in the windless atmosphere, and the rustle of his garments and the glimmer of his flaxen hair made a faint music and a fainter illumination, like the stir of a sapling birch tree in the dark.

"Virginio?" said Rosalba, softly.

The rustle of silk and the glimmer of silvery gold appeared, to the chevalier's watchfulness, to assume a new quality; the one had the tinkle, the other the sheen, of something cold and glassy. The sapling birch tree wore no leaves; its slender branches were incased in crystal, and at the tip of every twig a smooth bright icicle hung tremulous.

"Virginio?" said Rosalba again, and again softly, but now she said it with despair.

The girl fluttered restlessly about; she was light as thistle-down or dancing flame. Her little hands, emerging from the loose, voluminous wings of her mantle, were lifted continually towards Virginio in a gesture of supplication, mockery, and compassion. Although, in her brilliance, she was fire to Virginio's crackling ice, the chevalier remembered suddenly that the essential substance of that element is delicate and tender and more malleable than the very air, whereas ice is denser even than water, and often hard as stone. And he reflected truly that it was Rosalba's spirit that must inevitably be wounded in this unnatural warfare, however brittle Virginio's bones might prove.

"Have you no word to say to me, my children?" he entreated, and at last Rosalba answered him. She turned from Virginio with recovered composure, and faced Chastelneuf with a look of great dignity and sedateness.

"I shall be most grateful for your support and guidance, Chevalier," she said politely. All tint or tremor of the fantastic had fallen from her aspect, and she was nothing stranger than a slight, elegant girl in a velvet cloak, who strove to appear haughty despite her evident fatigue, and whose pale and pretty countenance was wet with ingenuous human tears.

20

SPIDERWEB TANGLE

"I AM willing," cried Rosalba, "to do anything; anything, everything, or nothing; I am the servant of the chevalier's advice."

"Anything within reason," amended Querini; his ward interrupted him with quite unfilial scorn.

"Oh, but anything, within or without, or far from reason as

the moon from sirocco or I from Notre Dame de Paris! Reason is for old gentlemen, like you and M. de Voltaire; the chevalier understands my determination."

Chastelneuf, thus suddenly made free of the dedicated insanity of youth, smiled into the fire of cedar logs, pervaded by a sweeter, more scented warmth than theirs.

"Reason is not the goddess of emergencies." Carlo Gozzi spoke sententiously, ruffling his thin hair above a corrugated brow. Peter Innocent said nothing.

The little apartment was charming with its fawn-coloured *boiseries* and rose-garlanded carpet; the books behind their gilded lattices enriched the walls by a soft and variegated pattern of their own. The room was called the *study,* after an English fashion; its air was warm and intimate. Every one, with the exception of Virginio, preferred it to the pale and mirrored salon where he now sat alone, nibbling a long green strip of angelica and idly perusing the pages of Frederick Martens' " Natural History of Spitzbergen." "There grows an Arctic flower," he read; but his tranquillity was now and again shattered by the heat and hurry of voices from the open door.

" It is the only solution," pronounced the chevalier. His passing glow was fled, and melancholy possessed him, hollowing his eyes and parching the accustomed glibness of his speech. " I had forgotten my youth, I think," he continued, subdued to shame. "I remembered love, for that still lives in my breast, but I did not remember the races which I ran with Caterina in the gardens of Saint Blaise; my rheumatisms obscured my mind. Virginio can embrace his wife in comfort; his body is attuned to marital bliss. I arranged for that; it was in my opinion of the first importance. But I totally neglected to provide for the lighter contingencies of courtship; he cannot support the rigours of hide-and-seek or the excitement of a bout of blindman's-buff. A handspring would be the end of him. He is a perfect husband, I assure you, but he can never be a playmate for this poor child. When you are older, my dear, it will not grieve you; the domestic pleasures of the *foyer* will suffice."

He ceased; Rosalba was weeping uncontrollably.

" No! no! " she murmured through her tears, " it is too difficult; I cannot bear it! Better a thousand times some violent change, some mad and excessive sacrifice! I lie in his arms at night; my breath is stilled because I love him, and his kisses close my lips over my laughter and my eyelids over my tears. But in the morning, when there is no more moonlight, and the sun is shining with the insistence of a golden trumpet made fire instead of sound, when all the red and yellow cockerels are crowing and the larks fly upward like particles of flame, then when I wake and look at him he is afraid. He trembles; when I spring up in the sunshine he trembles at my side; when I run to the window, he pulls the covers about his ears; when I fling the curtains apart to let the light rush in, he faints upon his pillow; the delicate vibration of the dawn afflicts him like a thunderstroke. I tell you, it is too difficult; I cannot bear it, and I would rather die than have it so."

" This is intolerably sad," said Peter Innocent. " The girl is not to blame, yet perhaps we shall have to put her into a convent."

But, " Never! never! never! " cried his three companions with an equal rage, and Rosalba fell upon her knees before him and anointed his hands with her despair.

"There is nothing for it, after all, but the magic," the chevalier repeated solemnly. With the utmost gentleness he raised Rosalba to her feet and conducted her to the shelter of a winged armchair near the hearth.

Reflected firelight rose and fell in rays upon her face, so that it shone unquietly between golden pallor and the colour of blushes; so also her ringlets were transformed from bright to dark and back again to brighter. The gauzes of her dress were disarranged, and among their folds hung here a pink and here a scarlet leaf, and here a frosty flake of ashes. Always she seemed to move and waver in the leaping light, stirred partly by its changes and partly by the shaking of her own heart, and although she was slight and shaken, her look was brave and vibrant and alive.

"Yes, the magic by all means," she said eagerly, quickened to fervour by a radiance above and beyond the cedar flames. "I am not afraid; it will not hurt me if I am not afraid."

" Non dolet! " cried Angelo Querini in a terrible voice, shielding his countenance from view.

" But you can assure us that it will be purely beneficent, or white magic, my dear friend? " asked Peter Innocent, with anxious concern; he was shocked by the violence of the chevalier's reply.

" I can assure you of nothing so absurd, your Eminence. The Deity may justly approve of the affair of Virginio; He cannot seriously object to the vivification of a few handfuls of harmless Murano sand and a pipkin of holy water. But it is another and a very different matter to deprive one of His creatures of the delights and powers bestowed upon her by Himself; we shall require the devil's aid in murdering Rosalba."

" Murder? Surely we are not talking of murder! " Peter Innocent made the sign of the cross, shivering visibly in the blast of horror invoked by the loud and bloody word.

" Ah, not officially, perhaps." The chevalier's bitterness was profound and quiet; absently he lifted Rosalba's warm, sunburnt little hand to his twisted lips. " We shall, indeed, leave her the privilege of living; possibly, in her new and chastened state, she may be duly grateful. But of this Rosalba, this child who sits before us clothed in light and eloquent with the breath of God — of this Rosalba nothing will remain. Yet, if you prefer, we need not call it murder."

" Remember that it is my own wish; the cardinal would have sent me to a convent."

The girl spoke gently and without irony, but Chastelneuf bowed his head as if a millstone hung upon his breast; what depth of water closed above that head, or whether tinged with salt or vinegar or gall, it were worse than useless to conjecture.

" It is your own wish; I will not dispute it," he said humbly. " I am, in point of fact, responsible for the plan; I myself proposed it, and, indeed, it appears to be the only unravelling, save the convent, of this deplorable tangle. Of course I could always rescue you from the convent," he added hopefully and under his breath to Rosalba. The girl did not heed him; her eyes were fixed upon Peter Innocent, and she addressed that venerable prelate with the desperate courage of a suppliant.

" I am no more afraid of black magic than of white, Eminence. In the whole world there is only one thing of which I am afraid, and that thing is Virginio's fear. Let me suffer this ordeal, whatever it may prove, and live thereafter in peace and contentment with my beloved husband; this is all I ask."

"A sacrifice proffered in such tenderness cannot come amiss to the mercy of God." Peter Innocent put forth his veined, transparent hand in a gesture of reassurance, and Rosalba thanked him with a pale, but valiant, smile.

"I shall have a word to interpose in this matter," said Angelo Querini. "I do not believe in magic, either black or white; it is not rational, logical, or decent. I do not wish Rosalba to be mixed up in necromancy and kindred follies."

"I believe in magic, and that so religiously that I cannot countenance such practices as the chevalier proposes; the danger to a simple child like Rosalba is appalling. It is well enough, when I write of it, for the negress Smeraldina to be dipped into a cauldron of flame, emerging whiter than a clay pipe, but for this little firebird to be caught and frozen into lifelessness, that is another story altogether, too tragic for my perusal. Let us turn her into a fawn or a vixen or a tawny panther, and set her free forever."

21

METHOD OF THE BROTHERS DUBOIS

"There is a villa at Strà, upon the banks of the Brenta, whose aviaries contain eagles from the Apennines, and whose fenced inclosures hold captive a hundred stags, wild roe, and mountain goats. Do you believe, because the hornbeam is green and the myrtle fragrant, that these creatures are happy? Rosalba, enchanted into some savage form, would wound her bosom against thorny walls, and find herself a prisoner among invisible labyrinths. She would still be bound fast to Virginio, to run like a hound at his heel, or flutter falcon-wise to his wrist. This were no freedom, but a strange refinement of pain. Rather let her shrink into a china doll and have done with feeling than that she should assume wings prematurely broken or a hind's fleetness without liberty of heart!"

" You are an orator, M. de Chastelneuf; allow me to congratulate you upon your eloquence." Thus spoke the noble Angelo Querini, one time senator of the Republic of Venice. " It might, however, be employed in some worthier cause than the wilful deception of a young girl. We have none of us forgotten Madame von Wulfe and the cruel farce of *Quérilinth*."

" I thank you for the compliment, my dear Querini; your approbation is ever welcome. For the insult I forgive you, even as I hope Madame von Wulfe has forgiven me. In the present matter I can have no motive other than altruism, and I assure you of my good faith. Nevertheless, it is for Rosalba to decide whether or no I now embark upon what must prove for all concerned a solemn and hazardous undertaking."

" I wish it; I demand it," Rosalba answered firmly. " Desperate as the means must be, it is my only remedy for torment. I am prepared to incur the equivalent of death in order to achieve peace for Virginio."

" The child is one of God's elected angels! " cried Peter Innocent in awe. " If she should unhappily perish in this dark adventure, she must in common fairness be canonized. Meanwhile I wish I had her safe among the Poor Clares of Assisi; she is too saintly for this secular arena of mortal life."

" Nonsense! She is nothing of the sort; she is merely a luckless girl who loves a glass manikin instead of kind, consoling flesh and blood! " the chevalier retorted with sardonic insolence. It was plain that his own flesh and blood were racked and poisoned by revolt.

M. de Chastelneuf was very pale. His eyes were sunken in his head, and his face was ravaged like a starving man's. Yet, worn and sharpened and intolerably wrung, he still maintained, despite this betrayal of his body, a certain victory of spirit, a simple affair of courage, perhaps, and accustomed coolness against heavy odds. And again, it was plain that he did not suffer for himself alone.

" Above all, we must be practical," he said, recovering perfectly his manner of impudent composure. " There is a method — not my own, I may say, but that of the celebrated Brothers Dubois, late of Vincennes — whereby young ladies are rendered harmless to the tranquillity of others and permanently deprived of their surplus emotions. Quite frankly, it is magic of a vehement and painful variety; the subject is ultimately transformed into fine porcelain, but the process is not agreeable, and the result, although miraculous, is somewhat inhuman. I have known fathers who submitted their daughters to the ordeal, husbands who forced it upon their wives, but never, until this hour, have I known a woman to desire the torture of her own free will. It is an agony more incisive than birth or dissolution; I dare not veil the circumstance with pity."

" And may a woman undergo this terrible ordeal and live? " Carlo Gozzi alone found voice, and that the thinnest whisper, to inquire.

" Yes, she may live, and flourish, and be fair and decorous and delightful." Chastelneuf ground his strong white teeth upon the words. " She may, to all appearances and outward seeming, remain a mortal woman; for aught I know to the contrary a purified soul may burn peacefully within the pretty fabric of her body. But — she will be porcelain; fine porcelain, remember, and no longer clay. In a porcelain vessel filled with clear water a rose may live for a little while, but out of clay a rose may rise alive and blooming, set on the roots of elder roses. There is a difference, but it does not matter."

" Nothing matters except Virginio," said Rosalba, softly.

Even as the chevalier drove sharp nails into his palms and bit his lip until he tasted blood, even as Peter Innocent bowed his lovely silver brow in sorrowful acquiescence, Virginio entered quietly and sadly, like the softer echo of Rosalba's voice.

None who looked upon him then wondered afterward at the fabulous chivalry of the girl's devotion; the lovers looked into each other's eyes, and their eyes were tender, pitiful, and afraid. Virginio wore a quality of pure translucent beauty, unwarmed by earth, the beauty of an element like sea or air, or that refined and rarefied sunlight mirrored by the moon. He wore this beauty meekly, and with a slight and delicate timidity he approached his wife and folded her within his arms. Felicity hovered above their bending heads, flying nearer, yet never alighting; the wings of felicity were so nearly visible that to Carlo Gozzi they appeared feathered like those of the pigeons of Saint Mark, and to Peter Innocent like the Holy Ghost itself in the shape of a silver dove.

Furthermore, to Peter Innocent, whose mind was a missal book of sacred images, Virginio figured as the young John Baptist, wandering immaculate in the desert, and Rosalba as a small golden lioness, of equal virtue and simplicity, but pagan and untamable and shy.

So, like a pair of legendary children, they came to the cardinal where he sat musing by the fire, and, moved by one impulse, sank upon their knees before him and inclined their bright locks to his blessing. The flaxen and the darkly burnished head bent side by side beneath his hand, and Peter Innocent's musings were made audible as prayer, and in the silence smoke rose like incense from the crumbling cedar logs, ascending through the chimney to the frosty night, and thence perhaps, to heaven.

22

PÂTE TENDRE

" IF you were hard paste, we should have to send you to Meissen," said the chevalier, smiling and alert in an elegant new travelling-cloak of bottle-green broadcloth. The midday sun lay yellow along a vast map spread upon the writing-desk, and although it was November, the windows stood open to sweet and jocund breezes. An atmosphere of nervous gaiety pervaded the study; a strapped portmanteau and a Florentine dressing-case occupied the settee, and seven large bandboxes were piled in a corner.

Upon the mantelpiece two crystal vases exhaled a mist of jasmine, and between these were set a number of china figurines of exquisite workmanship. A fantastic bellarmine grimaced at a Bow cupid, and a delicious Chelsea group of the Four Seasons, modelled by Roubiliac, and glowing with every floral tint, contrasted curiously with a fine white Derby biscuit statuette of Queen Charlotte and her children.

" Yes, Meissen for hard paste," repeated Chastelneuf, cheer-

fully, " and from that grim fortress you might come forth with a
rosy Saxon complexion and no sensibilities whatever."

" And no freckles? " asked Rosalba, with a pardonable feminine eagerness.

" No, my love; you would be as pink as a sugar-plum and as
smooth as whipped cream. However, Meissen is far too Germanic
for your peculiar mentality, and you could never survive its furnaces. It must be either Sèvres or Marseilles, since Hannong of
Strasburg has been dead these two years, and you are averse to
visiting England."

" I cannot forget that I am a Frenchwoman." Rosalba spoke
with a faint trace of hauteur, gazing rather wistfully at the Chelsea figure of Spring, attired in a vernal dress of apple green and
pearl colour.

" I should like to see you in white Marseilles faïence," said the
chevalier. " I once beheld a shepherdess in biscuit-porcelain, made
in the factory of the Duc de Villeroy at Mennecy, which was almost worthy of you. Nevertheless, I believe we shall be wise in
selecting Sèvres. It was the scene of the Brothers Dubois's amazing discovery; they were subsequently dismissed for drunkenness
and the practice of venomous magic. They came to me with letters from the Prince of Courland, whom they had greatly assisted
in the search for the philosopher's stone. I was able to resolve the
slight difficulties they had encountered by means of my infallible
compound of Hungarian crystal and native cinnabar. Overcome
with gratitude, they presented me with the secret recipe associated
with their name. Since then I have ever been in a position to turn
ladies into porcelain, but I have not often availed myself of the
opportunity; the process is opposed to my principles and natural
proclivities."

" Dear Chevalier, I am quite familiar with your sentiments,"
murmured Rosalba, sympathetically and a little shyly. " But you
will surely not refuse to aid me, upon this occasion, in my search
for happiness. I have understood you to say, have I not, that you
are capable of complete and single-handed success in the absence
of the Brothers Dubois? "

" But yes, and fortunately, since the Brothers Dubois are at
present inaccessibly situated in purgatory or some even less salu-

brious region," Chastelneuf assured her. " I need no help in the matter, save that of such skilled workmen as are to be found in any porcelain factory, augmented by those supernatural agencies which I must not scruple to employ."

" I am glad it is to be Sèvres, when all is said and done." Rosalba gazed reflectively into a tortoise-shell mirror, comparing her image therein with the countenance of an enchanting china figure, sculptured by Clodion in the classic taste, which the chevalier, bowing, presented to her view, poised daintily upon the palm of his hand.

" Oh, it is undoubtedly your *genre!*" cried Chastelneuf with enthusiasm, touching the girl's pale cheek with a respectfully tentative forefinger. " The true Sèvres, the soft paste of the old régime, not this stony stuff they have derived from the Germans. You are the finest *porcelaine de France;* I know the ingredients." And he began to chant a medley of words, in which Rosalba was at some pains to distinguish syllables analogous to " Fontainebleau sand — pure sea salt — Aliante alum — and powdered alabaster." Certainly the chevalier was a gentleman of various and esoteric learning, whose knowledge of humanity was both profound and nice. Rosalba resigned her will to his, and faced the future with mingled fortitude and acute curiosity.

" It is decided, then, that the cardinal accompany us, while Virginio remains with Querini and Carlo Gozzi, perfecting himself in the study of Greek, Latin, Arabic, and antique Spanish. He will thus be enabled to compare philosophies with fairy-tales, and to contemplate life with the stoicism of the one and the insouciance of the other. I have also suggested that he become proficient upon the flute and engage a really good fencing-master," said the chevalier, divesting himself of his travelling cloak and taking a pinch of snuff.

" We depart in an hour's time," he continued lightly, consulting a sumptuous jewelled watch, " and you will doubtless prefer to make your adieus to Virginio unattended by the most affectionate friend. I withdraw, therefore, but shall await you, with restrained impatience, in the adjoining apartment. I am sure we shall have no cause to regret our decision in the matter of factories." His smile contrived a positive frivolity, and Rosalba experienced a thrill of gratitude.

"The cardinal makes me feel that I am setting forth upon a penitential pilgrimage," she said plaintively. "You are less alarming: allow it to remain a mere affair of millinery. I could almost believe that we were going to Paris to select a costume for the carnival."

"But that, in a way, is true enough, my child," cried Chastelneuf, retiring. As he went, he coughed thrice behind a fine lace handkerchief, and wiped his eyes.

Presently Virginio knocked gently upon the door, and entered like a cloud of cooler air.

"Adieu, Virginio, my darling," whispered Rosalba.

"Adieu, adieu, my heart's beloved," the boy replied. Their voices were too low for audible trembling, but their hands, clinging together in the final instant, shook like thin white petals in a hurricane.

"Virginio, good-bye."

"Good-bye, Rosalba."

"I am going."

"I know; good-bye, my love."

"Virginio —"

"My dear —"

"Good-bye."

They embraced; bright glassy tears fell upon Rosalba's breast, and upon Virginio's cold hands Rosalba's tears fell quick and glittering as sunshower drops, and warm almost as the kisses wherewith they were mingled.

The great door closed at last between the lovers, leaving no sound; its painted panels confronted them severally with Pan's cruel nonchalance and Medusa's uncomfortable stare.

Virginio examined his finger-nails; they were quite uninjured, but the least finger of his left hand appeared to have suffered a slight sprain.

Rosalba, drawing on her white suède gloves, observed without surprise that both her wrists were faintly flecked with blood, as though a bracelet of thorns had lately clasped them.

23

ORDEAL BY FIRE

THROUGH a landscape lightly strewn with snow, and rendered graciously austere by long, converging lines of leafless poplars, the three strange travellers approached the neighbourhood of Paris.

The chevalier's English carriage was commodious and softly cushioned, and the discomforts of the journey had been negligible; nevertheless a ponderable sadness was bound upon the shoulders of the adventurers, as if indeed they carried ambiguous packs too heavy for their spirits. Their chins were sunk against their breasts, and even Chastelneuf strove quite in vain to dissipate this burden by companionable chatter.

" Paris must wait," he observed to Rosalba. " Afterward, when our affair is concluded, it will be time to think of the *trousseau,* which only Paris can fitly provide for a Frenchwoman. I consider you too fine for our Venetian barbarities of fashion, which tend ever to the extravagant and the capricious. You must see Bertin, of course; the queen swears by her, although the little Polignac, always so demure and so chic, is of another opinion entirely. But you will choose for yourself; it is the prerogative of Venus."

Rosalba raised her satirically penciled brows the least reproving shade, and the chevalier subsided into a conversation with Peter Innocent, who remained immersed in his breviary, vouchsafing now and again an absent-minded nod or a grieved monosyllable in response to the other's volubility.

" While I warmly second your decision as to the preservation of the strictest incognito, Eminence, I can assure you that no such peril attaches itself to our activities in this enlightened land of France as we should inevitably incur at home. In Venice we should have the Holy Office upon our tracks in a twinkling; here we need only fear the unfriendly attention of the Academy of Sciences.

" Instead of the Three and their spies, we must shun the associates of Bailly and Franklin. They are about to disturb the magnetic afflatus of Mesmer, but he, you know, is a charlatan."

"Yes?" said Peter Innocent, clutching his rosary.

They drove through the Forest of Meudon; beyond lay the park and the two châteaux. The sun was setting somewhere over their left shoulders.

"Have you heard that the duc de Chartres is cutting down the magnificent chestnut alleys in the Palais-Royal?" inquired the chevalier.

His companions preserved a silence unbroken save by sighs.

Presently they reached the outskirts of the ancient town of Sèvres; at a little distance from the factory, whose dark bulk rose upon the river-bank, a curious tower was conspicuous above a clump of nameless trees.

"Private workroom of the Brothers Dubois," the chevalier explained in hushed, oppressive accents.

"But they are dead, and the place is evidently deserted!" cried the cardinal, his voice vibrating to the chill along his spine.

"True; only too true," said Chastelneuf.

Perhaps the vitreous tiles which roofed the structure possessed a coppery glaze, perhaps the doors and windows were bound with this red metal, or perhaps the setting sun performed a sinister miracle of transmutation, and turned the tower into blood and flame. Its shape was very singular and menacing against the holy evening sky, where upon a field of violet a few small stars were visible. The carriage halted at a word from Chastelneuf, and came to a standstill at the mouth of a clearing in the clump of trees; feathery grasses, tipped with snow, had overgrown the path. The horses stamped their feet in the stillness; steam floated in thick clouds about their heads. The chevalier's Spanish servant, shrouded to the eyes in a sombre cloak, awaited his master's instructions with an air of taciturn complicity in some questionable design.

"Monseigneur, you will proceed to the inn at Versailles, where a fire, a feather bed, and a roasted fowl are in readiness," Chastelneuf declared, fixing the cardinal with an hypnotic eye. "Rosalba and I must now go on alone."

"On foot?" Peter Innocent asked in a weak voice.

"On foot, but not far; Rosalba will have ample opportunity to dry her slippers before the night is out." The words were significant and sharp; the cardinal shuddered.

"I am not afraid," said Rosalba, for the thousandth time, in a pitiful whisper. "They do not throw salt into the furnaces any more, nor use pulverized ox-bones, as they do in England."

"She need not suffer a second firing," said Chastelneuf. "I have concluded that no glaze is necessary, though, for that matter, the modern glaze is no longer by immersion, but by sprinkling, as in Christian baptism. But we shall leave Rosalba in the simple biscuit state. Console yourself, Eminence; your responsibility is heavy, but she shall be saved."

Peter Innocent found a slight support for his swooning spirit in the religious flavour of these final reassurances; he watched the pair depart through tears, and made his every breath a prayer as the trees met over the chevalier's haughty head and took Rosalba into their equivocal embrace.

For one brief instant the tower was split by a streak of brightness, and all the vehemence of fire outraged the tranquillity of the twilit wood; then the door closed, the smoke dispersed, the fumes faded in air, and with their going Peter Innocent was borne like thistledown, by the swift agency of two black horses, along the lonely road to Versailles.

24

SILVER CORD

In the ancient Satory quarter of Versailles, under the very shadow of the new cathedral of St. Louis, there lay a little tavern whose sign bore the symbol of the Silver Bowman. In the only parlour the narrow place afforded a clear fire had been kindled, before whose consolatory incandescence the Cardinal Peter Innocent Bon now warmed his hands and meditated upon the wonders of the world.

The eighth of these, to his enchanted thinking, and which had but this moment vanished in a visible smoke from between his fingers, was not the greater nor the smaller Trianon, nor yet the palace itself, nor the gardens nor the orangery. The thing had been more marvellous than these, both magic and geometric; a flower inclosed in a carven frame, a lovely formal pattern. A flake of snow, fallen from the dove-coloured skies of France, had melted in the heat of the fire.

Although Peter Innocent had often found the Roman winter of a severity too poignant for his anatomy to support without pain, he had rarely encountered the mysteries of frost and snow, and now his recollection wandered to the Christmas season of 1716, when he had seen Venice no longer blue and gold, but muffled and masked in whiteness. Oblivion like sleep had come at first upon the town, and then a bitter wind, and finally, when the sun shone again in the heavens, the palaces and church towers had flashed and scintillated beneath a covering of quicksilver. All this was memorable to Peter Innocent after many years, and he could picture the wine shop, even, where his father had taken him for a glass of malvasia from Epirus. He had been fourteen years old at the time, the malvasia had tasted warm as imagined Acroceraunian spring.

Since then, and so for uncounted Christmas seasons, Peter Innocent had forgotten the miracle of snow. Now he was enraptured, and opening the casement against a stubborn blast of the north, he filled his hands once more with the intricate crystals.

Yet all too soon the crystals dissolved again to icy moisture, and Peter Innocent considered beauty's evanescence as typified in those spilt drops of snow water.

A thin white wine of France stood in a green decanter by his elbow, but he foretasted it as cold astringent stuff; he wished Rosalba would return to brew him a glass of negus, with nutmeg in it, and the grated rind of a lemon.

A small volume bound in creamy vellum lay by the decanter, in a pool of green reflected light; he knew it for a copy of Rosalba's poems, printed at Pisa less than a year ago as a gift from Querini to his ward.

An absurd medley of quotation sprinkled the title-page with tags from Seneca and Catullus. Here cried the unchristian wastrel to his strumpet: "Remains to be slept the sleep of one unbroken night." Here the virtuous philosopher remarked, with equal gloom: "We are kindled and put out." Peter Innocent found the poems themselves hard to decipher in the failing light.

He picked up a fine Venetian edition of Theocritus, but the book fell open at an unknown line, and this is what he read: "The lamb is gone, the poor young thing is gone . . . a savage wolf has crunched her in his jaws, and the dogs bay; what profits it to weep, when of that lost creature not a bone nor a cinder is left?"

Peter Innocent poured out a measure of the thin white wine; the goblet was full to the brim, and a little wine was spilled upon the pages of the book, for the cardinal's hand was trembling. He shivered, huddled in his worn habit of the Friars Minor; he wished very heartily that he had indeed borrowed the chevalier's luxurious dressing-gown of quilted purple silk, as Rosalba had more than once suggested.

The streets of Versailles were veiled by falling snow, and the wheels of the few cabriolets and chariots which passed beneath the window of the inn were noiseless in their revolutions; only the occasional crack of a whip shattered the frosty silence. Peter Innocent was very lonely.

Almost, he believed, he would have welcomed the arrival of those visitors whom his shy secretiveness had so far avoided. His incognito had been studiously preserved; even the curious eye of Louis de Rohan Guéménée, Cardinal Grand Almoner and Archbishop of Strasburg, had failed to mark the elusive wearer of the grey-brown garb of St. Francis.

With the benediction of Assisi's name, there came into Peter Innocent's mind a sudden longing to be comforted, and he turned, like a bewildered child, to the dear protection of his patron saint. His fingers sought and found the leaves of another book, wherein his own scholarly Italian hand had traced certain passages from the life of Francis. His sight, under the encroaching dusk, grew dim; then he saw plainly what was written in the book.

"O brother fire, most beautiful of all creatures, be courteous to me at this hour, knowing how well I have always loved thee and ever will for His love Who created thee!"

Upon the instant, the fire upon the hearth appeared to lift its terrible head in anger and spring like a tiger at his throat; he put up his feeble arms in a defensive gesture, and dropped them again in despair. The portent was revenge from heaven.

For even now, at his advice, at his desire, Rosalba was giving her body to be burned. " Be courteous to me at this hour — " The hour was struck, and the jaws of the furnace had received the child.

He caught up the decanter of wine, and flung it, a bubble of green glass, into the burning fangs of the fire, where it was destroyed in a moment. Then he fell upon his knees, and would have beat out the flames with his hands; but his strength failed him, the monster leaped upward with a roar, and Peter Innocent felt its teeth fasten in his shoulder; then he fainted.

He was revived by the chevalier's voice and Rosalba's touch upon his temples. The window stood open to the snow, which blew inward, golden particles emerging strangely from an infinity of blue dusk; a handful of snow was sprinkled over his eyes, which throbbed with fever. The fire still raged within its bars, but as Rosalba stooped to tend it, he could have sworn that she spoke in a low, caressing tone, and perhaps admonished it by a sign; presently the flames sank down and seemed to slumber.

The chevalier's cloak was wet with snow, and his face confessed a weariness and lassitude most carefully excluded from his speech.

" All is well, Eminence," he said, flinging his laced hat upon the table with a long-drawn sigh of fatigue. " She has survived our ministrations; a diabolic ordeal has served its purpose, and she has returned to you alive. Of her courage I cannot speak; her present composure may speak for her, even in silence. Yet perhaps, of her charity, she has a word for those who have wronged her."

Rosalba leaned at ease against the window-frame, and the snow blew past her lifted head and powdered it with particles of gold. There was about her an air of perfect calm; she was poised, composed, and quiet, yet without stiffness; her attitude had the grace of a bird arrested in flight, a flower flexible, but unmoved by wind. Peter Innocent knew instinctively that her spirit was unstirred by any pang that may not be suffered by an exemplary child of seven.

Her face was exquisitely clear and fresh in every tilted line and smooth velvety surface; her hair was miraculously symmetrical, and its thick scallops had the quality of gilded bronze. Her mantle fell about her in delicate sculptured folds.

"God give you peace!" said Rosalba to Peter Innocent, with a gentle candour unaware of pity and its intolerable demands.

25

INTERIOR BY LONGHI

How delicate a contrivance of language must lull the imagination to repose before it may sing or picture to itself, while half asleep, Rosalba's home-coming!

This must be spoken in a whisper, dreamed in a meditation, drawn in the palest colours of pearls, set to an accompaniment of reverential music, veiling silence with a silver veil.

In that hour when the shadows flow like clear blue water along the golden sands of day, in the mildness of afternoon, in a place profoundly quiet, Virginio and Rosalba met and kissed.

Their very garments were awed into submission, so that silk dared not rustle or flowers shed their fragrance; the heels of their shoes were dipped in magic, so that they made no sound, and a dimness like the smoke of incense obscured the shining of their hair.

Nothing else in the world was ever so soft as their lips and the clasp of their hands; these were softer than the wings of grey moths or the frosty feathers of dandelion seed.

A little brush, smoothing thin pigments on a polished cedar panel, may trace more lightly and precisely than any pen the figures of Virginio and Rosalba, the wedded lovers of a fairy-tale, who now live happy ever after, in Venice, in a world of porcelain and Murano mirrors.

It has been said, and that upon distinguished authority, that Pietro Longhi survived, in the amber peace of a mellowing century, until the age of eighty; the statement is difficult to refute.

For those who would believe it, there exists in support of this theory a small painting, bearing the artist's signature not only in the mere syllables of his name, but, more convincingly, in every curve and colour of the scene itself.

The hand of a very old man is evident in the fine performance; the lines waver, the colours are subdued and etherealized. The hand is the hand of Longhi, and he was an old man when Rosalba returned to Venice in the amber twilight of a dying century.

This twilight fills the picture, and is reflected from the mirrors of the background; the faces of the lovers emerge like stars from this profundity of twilight. The figure of Peter Innocent is there, quiet as a carven saint in his niche; he wears the grey-brown habit of the Friars Minor, and his veined and fragile hands are folded upon a cross. That noble brow and faint ironic smile can only be Querini's, and Count Carlo Gozzi looks impish and melancholy in a new periwig and the rich mantle of a patrician. The chevalier is absent; it is said he has retired to Bohemia.

The faces of the lovers are most beautiful and pure; the gentle and elegiac quality of their love appears unmarred by longing. Having forgotten fear and the requirements of pity, their tenderness becomes a placid looking-glass in which each beholds the other; the mercurial wildness which no longer moves them is fixed behind this transparent screen, lending brightness to the mirrored images.

At any moment they may awake; Virginio will put on his pearl-coloured greatcoat and wrap an ermine tippet about Rosalba's throat, and the season being winter and very clear and cold, they will hurry to a fashionable pastry cook's to eat whipped cream and wafers.

THE

ORPHAN ANGEL

WITH A SPECIAL PREFACE BY
STEPHEN VINCENT BENÉT

TO WHOM IT MAY CONCERN

The Orphan Angel

PREFACE

Genius comes among us in many ways, but sometimes as suddenly and sharply as a new star. The course of the average writer — even the very good writer — is, often enough, fairly easy for the critics to plot, looking backwards. There are the first attempts and the juvenilia, the fumblings and false starts, the slow or swift development into strength. To be blind to this process is to sentimentalize art — to complain of it is to complain of the apple-tree because it bears leaves and flowers before it bears fruit. Only sometimes, as I say, it happens otherwise. The tree grows before our eyes like an Indian magician's — we look at the familiar patterns of heaven and there is a new and burning dust between Rigel and Altair.

It was so with Elinor Wylie. It is true that she had written before, it is true that she had published privately and suppressed a small book of verses before "Nets To Catch The Wind." But when that book appeared, in

319

1921, the usual critical adjectives reserved for first books of verse simply did not apply. It was not " promising " or " interesting " or " creditable " — it was the work of a scrupulous and inimitable artist. And " Jennifer Lorn," with its complete command of style, its extraordinary wit, beauty and finish, is as different from the average " first novel " as if it came from another world.

In the eight, packed years of her writing life, Elinor Wylie wrote four novels. Of these, " The Orphan Angel " is the third, the longest, and the only one that has an American background. It was, to its author, a very personal book, for in it she drew at full length the mortal image of that one of the English poets to whom she gave an entire devotion.

I have heard people speak of that devotion as if it were a pose, a hobby, or a blind worship. It was none of these things. She was entirely sincere about it but she was also entirely mature. In " The Orphan Angel " she could and did show her hero, Shiloh, as sometimes pedantic, sometimes naïve and often difficult. She could laugh at him a little with no diminution of love and make of him no less an immortal because he was sometimes preposterous. As a result, in a work of fiction, a work entirely and necessarily outside of the real events of his life, she has probably come nearer to the essential character of Shelley than any of the critics. For that, too, is genius, that clairvoyance that sees beyond fact and circumstance into truth.

There are three strands woven together in the fabric of the book — a spirit, whose ruling passion is a passion for liberty in a world where liberty is the unpermitted thing — a knight-errant, whose fatal habit it is to rescue princesses from dragons, with no thought whatever of the necessary dangers of that pastime after the dragon is dead — and that lost America of rivers and forests, of wild turkeys and buckskin riflemen and the red shape in the wilderness which lies somewhere at the back of all our minds.

The whole search for Sylvie La Croix is a green-and-silver arras that could hang in a long chamber at Knole or Amboise and be taken, from a distance, for some hunting-tapestry, woven these many years. For the style is not " modern," in our contemporary sense — it deliberately employs the full resources of a language — and the architecture is nearer Wren than Wright. And yet, the first glance would undeceive the eye. These hounds and horses are of another breed, they are not the King's or the Duke's — these riders and runners and walkers have the high cheek-bones and the drawling, salty voices of a new world. The sun may hang in the heavens like an heraldic shield and the evening fall softly as a fall of snow whose flakes are shadow instead of shining crystal, but when we come to the feast, there is baked ham and roasted turkey, pot-pie and custard-pie.

" ' Fiend, I defy thee! With a calm, fixed mind, all

*that thou canst inflict I bid thee do,' said Shiloh, bravely,
but in a rather faint voice.*

*' Which remark don't butter no parsnips,' replied
David, with some impatience, ' First place the bastard
can't hear you and second place it wouldn't do no good
if he did.' "*

*The tone of the book is a little exaggerated, in those
two speeches, but they are very characteristic. They give
an inkling of that mixture of luminous beauty and wild
earth which gives " The Orphan Angel " its peculiar
charm.*

*For the book is fine and ghostly as a tea-clipper under
its cloud of white sail, but as solid and seaworthy, too.
Beneath the incantation and the spell lie an admirable
knowledge, an admirable craftsmanship. Elinor Wylie
was a great lyric poet — she could also have been a great
scholar, for she had many of the scholar's gifts, including an extraordinary patience and thoroughness in research. We are all of us familiar with the sort of people
who profess such extreme devotion to a cause or a personality that they cannot bear to have it tainted by fact.
They lie in the warm, relaxing bath of their own emotions and murmur, " Oh, don't tell me who wrote that
beautiful thing — don't tell me he limped or was married — you are spoiling my dream."*

*Such an attitude is one of the marks of the permanent
adolescent. It was not Elinor Wylie's. She knew every
small incident in Shelley's life as thoroughly as any com-*

mentator, she knew what he ate and drank and how much money he had in his pocket, but she knew these things without dryness or pretense. She knew them, not as one knows a lesson, but as one remembers a past. She would talk of them as casually as of a personal reminiscence. And, similarly, the whole journey of Shiloh and David, across the continent, from Boston to San Diego, may seem to the reader, at times, like a fantastic fairy tale. But every stage of that journey could be plotted on a map of the period — and each stage would be right and probable, down to the number of days it took to traverse it and the means of locomotion used. The transmutation of the material is magic; but the little details of food and drink and gear that make a past live again were sought for and gathered from a hundred sources by a mind that seemed to know by instinct where its necessary victual lay.

The pilgrimage in search of Jasper Cross's sister across the America of the Eighteen-Twenties is the twisted silver plait that holds the book together. On this are strung the bright and diverse beads of adventure and incident — the river-ark and the rifle-match, the wilderness-wedding and the Indian stake. And, always, there are certain ladies who appear, from Melissa of the small clear singsong, Shiloh's most touching worshipper, to Anne the singular child with hair like a magical bronze bell who would have felt such genuine pleasure in giving Shiloh the head of his enemy, if Shiloh had only wanted it. And always, as there are ladies who appear, so there are ladies to be left. With exquisite courtesy, with amiable recollection, sometimes even in sheer though by no means unmanly panic, but, nevertheless, to be left. For ladies are, somehow, inconsonant with liberty, and yet, the instinct to rescue persists in spite of the facts.

" ' But I am afraid that I am an excessively poor hand at rescuing people,' said Shiloh and opened his eyes upon reality." And yet, with the next lady, he forgets, though his author does not. The book ends, and ends in grave beauty, but the soul's comedy is unfinished. It cannot, indeed, be finished — for its essence is the disparity between an ideal and the world.

Here is a head-dress of eagle-feathers taken from an Aricarax chief and a volume of Condorcet, read by candle on a flatboat. Here is The Missouri Intelligencer *and Tom O'Bedlam's song. And here, in a frame that has the hard bronze of Latin within it as well as the silver, is the picture of a lost America and, wandering through it, two strange companions, a Yankee boy called David Butternut and another who walks as swiftly as the West wind. Here are many adventures and one that is always the spirit's. And here is a prose that was unique in our time.*

I have written around and about this book and yet, it seems to me now, I have told little of it, though I hope I have said enough to make the reader impatient to be through with this preface and beat out of Leghorn har-

bor with the Witch of the West. *But, perhaps, on my part, such a course was inevitable, for the look of the printed pages is bound up in my mind with certain recollections and the sound of a voice, reading, a little hastily, a little scornfully, as if impatient with beauty and fire themselves because they were not a beauty beyond all mortal conception, a fire that fed on something lighter and more pellucid than air. I have heard that voice many times. It had the accent of greatness. I shall not hear it again. But the words remain, and these were some of the words.*

STEPHEN VINCENT BENÉT

NEW YORK CITY, 1933.

The Orphan Angel

CONTENTS

327

The Orphan Angel

I

WESTERN WAVE

On the eighth of July, 1822, at half past six in the evening, the American clipper-built brig *Witch of the West* was beating out of Leghorn Harbour, close-hauled upon the increasing wind. She was a smart little vessel; beneath the varnished black of immaculate paint a new copper bottom glittered bravely as she leaned over nearly upon her beam-ends in the racing glass-green sea.

In place of the dried codfish, furs, and Virginian tobacco with which she had put forth from Boston seven weeks before, the pretty ship now carried a luxurious cargo of wine, olive oil, and candied tropic fruits; her shining surfaces and slender compact proportions concealed an appropriate core of honeyed essences and spice. Yet, as she struggled under naked and singing shrouds against the force and violence of the summer hurricane, she wore an air no less valiant than graceful, like the aërial composure of a cloud.

"If we spin her round upon her heel, as we oughter, and put back to port, you'll hang, Davy, or I'll eat my oilskins," said the skipper, a red-haired Yankee from New Bedford; he spat an impatient expletive and a thin stream of tobacco juice within an inch of young David Butternut's excellent sea-boots. The captain had shipped upon an old-fashioned whaler, in the capacity of cabin-boy, during the most formative period of his youth; his manners were often rough to the point of boorishness, but a soft heart beat under the horny tarpaulin of his seaman's coat.

"You'll hang, I calculate," repeated the skipper pessimistically. " And mebbe you'll burn too, for you boys picked the quarrel in the porch of a church, and that's what these Eyetalians call sacrilegious, I reckon. You've attracted the notice of the authorities, and I doubt that I'd have power to help you, my lad. We got our clearance papers just in time to save your skin, otherwise I'd never have sailed into the jaws of this dirty weather."

"I know it, sir," replied the youth with becoming modesty, "and trust me, Cap'n, to be properly grateful." David Butternut was a tall muscular stripling from the coasts of Maine; the changing fortunes which had uprooted him from a forest to set him upon the slanting deck of a brig appeared to have fitted him into his surroundings as neatly as any shipbuilder transplants a pine-tree to carry spread of sail. " Not that I'd have you drown the other boys along of me; I don't see as there's such an almighty difference betwixt hanging and drowning, after all. Go back if you've a mind to, sir, and don't never bother about me; I'm not worthy of any such kindness, and I don't rightly know as I'd rather not hang; it's a fine dry death, when everything's said and done."

"No, no, Dave my boy, you're wrong there," the captain insisted with an indulgent smile, " as you'd realize full well if ever you'd been strung from the yard-arm, like I was once in the good old days. Cut down in the nick of time, by the special intercession of the first mate, but my throat was sore for a week, I do assure you. No, it's a damned uncomfortable death, lad, and I hope it's not necessary that you should hang this voyage. Jasper Cross was a nasty customer, for all his pleasant gentlemanly airs, and there's some of us as knows you only acted in self-defence; yet the law's a pretty crank thing to handle, and I'd not give a wooden dollar as the price of your neck in Leghorn to-night."

David shot an appreciative glance towards the captain, in whom he had long recognised a true if an untender friend. "Thank you kindly, sir, I'm sure," he whispered huskily, brushing the sleeve of his pea-jacket across his ingenuous blue eyes.

"Now, boy," said the captain in a brisk business-like manner, "seeing as you've left us kinder short-handed with that there fist of yours, mebbe you'd better attend to reefing the topsail, and quit worrying about murders."

Butternut turned cheerfully enough to this change of employment, and good Captain Ffoulkastle remained for a moment lost in reverie, gazing out over the tumultuous sea, where all the elements of sublimity and terror raged unseen behind a descending veil of darkness.

Suddenly, with the amazement of a thunderclap, he beheld a human countenance emerge from this sinister obscurity to float upon the dark like a drowning star, without mortality or substance.

"Man overboard!" cried Captain Ffoulkastle in a tremendous voice; he spoke to himself in an awe-struck murmur. "Strike my timbers if I didn't think it was that sarpent Jasper, come aboard to pester us, but here's Jasper's corpse still a-rolling in the bloody scuppers, lads not having time to tidy up along of this blasted storm. Still, I'll stake my soul it's Jasper's ghost I seen . . ." whispered the captain nervously. Another great wave lifted the mysterious face well-nigh to the level of the vessel's plunging side, where it shone brighter and whiter than before in a flash from the larboard lantern.

"Man overboard!" shouted the captain a second time, and in response to his call young David Butternut leaped from the mast as from the summit of a swaying forest tree and sprang into the blackness of the ocean.

"Didn't even wait to kick off them heavy boots of his," observed the captain philosophically. "Well, there goes another of my able seamen!" Aloud he bellowed "Ready about!" and "Helms down!" and was about to add "Lower the boat!"

when he perceived that David, by some miracle of superhuman strength and agility, and by the material aid of a rope flung by his affectionate comrades, had indeed regained the deck, bearing in his arms a singular and unearthly burden.

"It's Jasper's attendant angel!" breathed the captain, surprised into a momentary pang of pure mysticism.

The scene was solemn to the extremity of awe; upon the deck, illuminated by the faint glimmer of a lantern, lay the blood-stained corpse of Jasper Cross, and above this tragic indication of impermanence appeared, supported in the arms of David Butternut, a veritable image of the same figure, but brighter, clearer, fairer, as if from the blessing of another planet. The creature's eyes were closed, but its countenance wore a look of beatitude and innocence infinitely touching to behold, and the composure of the brow was childlike and serene.

"Cap'n, I don't know what I've snatched from the fury of the waters," said David simply, "but I do know this: it's something good and something beautiful, and if I've preserved its body from destruction, I think it's saved my soul from everlasting death!"

In his own face was mirrored a reflection of the preternatural light shining upon the stranger's forehead, and as he gazed from one to the other of these curious visions, this the secular portent of mortality, and that the embodiment of spiritual grace, he trembled and wept as if he had that moment come naked into a legendary world.

"Give Davy a tot of rum," said the captain compassionately. "The poor boy must be chilled to the bone. And some of you lazy lubbers look to the stranger and see whether there's any life mixed with the sea-water in his innards."

Captain Ffoulkastle had satisfied himself that the unknown was a human creature, and as such singularly innocuous, but to the superstitious sailors he was still an object of fear; not until the blustering second mate had led the way with a laugh and a brutal jest did any dare to lay his hand upon the body, now lying tranquilly along the blood-stained deck.

"Our Jasper's twin, by the pretty face on him," cried the mate with a coarse chuckle. "And both of them deader nor doornails, damn their silly eyes; we won't pour good Demerara after stinking sea-water down the throats of no drowned men, will we, boys? "

He was about to spurn the motionless form with the toe of his great tarry boot, but David Butternut sprang forward in time to prevent this act of cruelty, and the indignant murmurs of the men soon warned the mate that such sentiments were unsuited to the hour and the grave occasion. Swallowing a curse, he applied himself with tolerable interest to the problem of ascertaining whether or no life yet lingered in the stranger's breast.

"Gone, I do declare," said the mate casually, dropping the cold hand and shrugging his shoulders. "Well, reckon there's nothing to do but pitch him back into that pesky tea-cup where he come from."

"But, by graminy," cried David in horror, "we're a-going to try to bring him round, ain't we? I know in my heart he's some kind of messenger from God, and if we reject him now, indifferent-like, what's to become of us all? I asks you honest, is that the face of an angel, or ain't it? " None cared to contradict him; without another word he unscrewed the flask of rum which the captain had given him and attempted to pour a few drops of the fiery liquid between the colourless lips of the unconscious stranger.

Presently the captain's repeated cry of "All hands ahoy!" left the young sailor the sole occupant of that retired portion of the deck, but still David knelt devoutly beside the mysterious visitant, forgetful of the storm and its attendant pandemonium, and searching with an agonized attention the peaceful face of the unknown.

Meanwhile his mind was full of confused prayers and images, in which the continued life of this mortal, snatched by his strength from the blackness of annihilation, seemed the dear embodiment of something lost and infinitely cherished.

"To make up for Jasper!" he muttered to himself with a shaking mouth, " oh, to make up for Jasper! Please, please, come back, and I shall be forgiven! "

2

As if in answer to David's low entreaty, the stranger stirred, and, opening large blue eyes, gazed with an expression of innocent bewilderment straight into the small blue eyes of his preserver.

With a cry of joy, David caught the living creature's hand in a strong salty grasp, and, to his own and the other's extreme amazement, covered the cold wet fingers with religious kisses.

"Thank God!" he cried, while the tears mingled with the bitter spray upon his cheeks. "Thank God you've come back! Now everything will be all right, I reckon; I thanks you with all my heart for coming, and I bless you for ever and ever."

"Where am I?" asked the stranger in a very faint voice; his voice seemed to travel from tragic distances, and yet he was smiling a little at David's vehemence. "And where is Edward, and what has become of that poor boy, Charles Vivian the sailor?"

"I am that poor boy David Butternut, a sailor and a murderer," declared David with fierce humility. "Leastways, I reckon as I'm a murderer, though not going for to do more than bust his head for him when he ups and draws a knife on me. But I've a goldarned heavy hand, more's the pity, and there he lays as cold as so many pounds of salt cod, and 'twas me as killed him, and I won't deny it; no, never to you, whatever tale I tells the police when we lands in Boston. Can you be friends with a murderer, young fellow? 'Cause I want for you to be my friend, and yet I'm a terrible sinner to ask for friendship from the likes of you."

"The likes of me!" repeated the stranger softly and ironically. "The likes of me will not refuse your friendship, David Butternut, nor fear to shake the hand which all unwittingly has sent another man to unravel the ultimate enigma of the grave." He essayed weakly to offer his own right hand to David, who took it with a cry of gratitude.

"You know I was so lucky as to save your life, don't you?" asked David a moment later with renewed cheerfulness. "Yes, stranger, I hopped into that there dirty old sea, and I pulled you out as easy as rolling off a log in the Kennebec. But now tell me, seeing as we're friends, are you an angel or a man, and are you any kin to Jasper there? for you're alike as two peas, only he's a rotten black pea and you're a brand-new silver one. Who are you, young feller, and what might be your name, and do you happen to come from heaven or anywhere along those coasts?"

"No, not precisely," answered the stranger gently and a little sadly. "I do not come from anywhere along those coasts, nor am I any kin to Jasper there, save as all men are brothers. As for my name, it is . . ."

But here the stranger's voice failed him so completely that David Butternut, bending low, could with difficulty distinguish any sound, and that perplexing and dispersed upon the wind. At the same time he noticed with alarm that the other's countenance had assumed an excessive and sorrowful pallor, and that his large blue eyes were closed as if in sleep.

"Are you all right?" he inquired sharply, a chilly sensation contracting his heart almost to suffocation. "Hey, there, young feller, are you all right, or are you a-going to die after all?" And he shook the other by his thin shoulder, as one who rouses an obstinate and beloved dreamer from oblivion.

A slight smile was discernible upon the stranger's pale and composed lips, and he contrived to enunciate, slowly, but with exquisite politeness, a few words of amused reassurance.

"I am exceedingly sorry to constitute myself a nuisance, and I would not for the world have you distress yourself upon my poor account, but I believe, my dear David, that I am about to solve the great mystery of dissolution."

Apparently suiting the action to the word, he lay relaxed and motionless upon the deck, while David, with a loud cry of dismay, ran headlong towards the lighted cabin.

The captain, in dripping tarpaulins and very high boots, was filling his pipe by the fitful illumination of a brazen lamp sus-

pended from the ceiling by chains and shaken violently by the
motion of the ship. Under the falling alternations of flame and
shadow his weatherbeaten face was intent and tranquil.

"Well, what is it now?" he called testily, in response to
David's frantic knock and immediate entrance. "I calculate those
lazy dogs are skeered of this capful of wind, and want me to
sing them to sleep. But who in hell told you to come in here?"
he demanded irascibly, recognising his visitor.

"Oh, please, sir," David began in agitated accents, "that
there young stranger has been and died again on deck, and I
want for you to come along and look at him, and mebbe give
him just a drop of that special peach brandy that we had on
the Fourth of July. Aw, Cap'n, I'd be that grateful if you'd spare
him just a little drop!"

"Come, come, Dave my lad," said the captain calmly, presenting to these agonised entreaties the impassive front of a
carven storm-scarred fragment of hickory wood, "keep cool and
I'll spare you a minute for this business, though it's sheer waste
of time fussing over a dead boy with all you kicking live ones
on my hands. It's the time and not the brandy that I grudge him,
Dave, but it's worth it if we can bring him round and put him
in the starboard watch to take Jasper's place. And that reminds
me," said the captain indulgently, his eyes on David's simple
honest countenance, "I have a fine scheme for saving your
precious neck, my lad, when we land in Boston."

David paid no heed to his remarks, watching instead with
the most fascinated attention the decanting of a minute quantity
of peach brandy into a thick blue tea-cup, which feat the captain
performed with amazing delicacy and skill. Without another
word the two sturdy sailors made their way through unnoticed
prodigies of wind and thunder to that part of the ship where the
mysterious stranger lay entranced or dead.

To the captain, and in a far greater degree to David, there
appeared something obscurely moving and magical in the scene
now presented to their view. The ultimate curtain of the sky
was split at intervals by hieroglyphs of lightning and the immense profundities of cloud seemed audible in thunder. Above
their heads, the rigging of the ship was plucked to an intense

thin music by the hurricane, and driven sheets of green and silver water drowned them in cold and phosphorescent brilliance.

Upon the slanting deck two figures were disposed, miraculously still in the midst of this delirium. Jasper, with the bruise darkening at his temple and blood upon his brow, stared upward with an angry questioning insistence, but the other lay as if asleep, with quiet eyelids and dark hair drenched with spray, and the locks of hair were folded about his forehead like a spiked and ghostly crown.

3

"They both look just about equally dead as drowned rats," said the captain, shaking off the atmosphere of supernatural awe with an impatient movement of his massive shoulders. " But I reckon as this one can be revived with a little judicious encouragement, and a mite of creature comfort. Then," said the captain briskly, for he was after all an eminently practical man, " you'll be safe as a landlocked harbour, according to this plan of mine. Once get this fellow on his sea-legs, and slushing down the mainmast from the royal-mast-head," said the captain with anticipatory gusto, " and you won't be able to tell him from Jasper, and no more will the Boston police, or my name ain't Abner Ffoulkastle! " And he gave David a hearty punch in the ribs before kneeling down, with becoming gravity, to feel the stranger's pulse and to force between his lips the entire contents of the thick blue tea-cup.

" There's life in the young dog yet," he informed David, who waited breathless in an agony of fear. "Yes, he'll be hauling at a hawser by to-morrow morning, with his ribs lined with good salt beef and sea-bread. Now, Dave, I want you to understand that it's all to your profit to learn him the ropes, as they say, and make a useful sailor out of him, for by this means you'll save yourself from the gallows and the other boys from a deal of extra work. Do you catch on, my lad? "

" Yes, sir; I think so, sir," murmured David in confusion. " You want for me to learn this stranger to take Jasper's place on shipboard. . . ."

"Yes, and on shore too, when the time comes," said the captain with a kindly chuckle. "Jasper was an orphan, and a black sheep, from some God-forsaken high-and-dry hole out west, and I hardly look for much trouble from his relatives. If we can satisfy the port authorities in Boston that we come home with the same crew that we shipped on sailing, that'll be enough for your purposes. Your mates won't split on you, and as for this young fellow, he seems by his face to be a gentle obliging sort of chap, and one that would be glad enough to help a friend in a little emergency. Wouldn't you, my lad?" he added, with a smile at the unknown, who at this moment opened his eyes and gazed inquiringly about him.

"I shall be most happy to help my friend David by any honourable act which lies within my powers to perform," he answered at once, in a firm if somewhat far-away voice, with a quick surprising flash of blue from his large intelligent eyes. At the same time he essayed to rise, but the captain thrust him down again with a brief peremptory gesture.

"No, you lay there, stranger, till we've done our little transformation act," he said cheerfully. "Here, you David, run and fetch Jasper's Sunday clothes, while I strip these wet rags off this lad and shove 'em overboard. But no—I've a brighter idee than even that—we'll rig Jasper out in the stranger's suit, and then if any body is found, by bad luck," said the captain with a jovial laugh, "they'll think it yours, mate, and nobody's likely to suspect our Davy of killing *you!*"

While David hurried below in search of Jasper's Sunday outfit, the captain busied himself in peeling from the stranger's slender limbs the cold and dripping garments which had clothed them. A pair of black pantaloons, a short black jacket, somewhat the worse for wear, a white shirt unbuttoned at the neck, and the customary quantity of underlinen completed their number, and by the time that David arrived with the necessary covering, the unknown youth lay naked and shivering in the chilly wind, protesting feebly against the captain's forcible removal of his property.

"Please be careful of the books; I do entreat you to be careful of Keats and Sophocles," he cried faintly, but the captain heeded him not at all, and proceeded calmly upon his course, stripping Jasper's body and methodically reclothing it in the short black jacket and the shabby pantaloons.

"Never saw such a pair of fools as you two boys in all my born days," he grunted contemptuously, seeing David's averted face and the stranger's wild and stag-like eyes shaded by a thin cold hand, and hearing their united murmurs of horror and surprise. "Are you scared of poor Jasper's dead corpse, David Butternut, you that had the guts to strike him down, and are you, my lad, who lately faced the raging ocean without particular signs of fear, hiding your eyes from a mere harmless murdered body? For shame, I say to both of you; your conduct's unworthy of men and sailors. Turn to, and help me, David, for Jasper's a damned dead weight to heave over, I can tell you."

At last, and without the aid of his young companions, the captain's self-imposed duty was completed, and, lifting Jasper's corpse in his mighty arms, he carried it to the rail, and balanced it there above the turbulent and racing sea.

"My Keats, my Sophocles!" cried the stranger in an agonized whisper. "Oh, I do beg of you not to throw my Sophocles into the ocean!" His large blue eyes were full of tears.

"He means the books he has in his pockets, sir," explained David. "Leastways, they're Jasper's pockets now, I suppose, but the books belong to the stranger, and I can see he sets great store by them."

"I can't be bothered with no books!" shouted the captain with magnificent scorn. "Now David, I'm going to shove your messmate overboard, and if you want to bid him good-bye, here's your last chance. Well, I can't stand here all night waiting for you to make up your mind, my lad; here goes, Jasper Cross, and may the Lord have mercy upon your soul!"

The body descended through the darkness into the whirling pit of the waters, and its phosphorescent track was a moment visible and then no more. The captain and David removed their caps; the stranger closed his eyes and seemed to meditate or pray.

"I could find it in my heart to desire for this poor fellow's mortal remains a more classic dignity of requiem," he said at length with some emotion. "And yet is it not, after all, singularly fitting that a sailor's clay should be thus committed to the vaulted caverns of the crystal wave? I have frequently observed . . ."

"And I have frequently observed that you young rascals talk too much," said the captain shortly. "Moreover, you're shivering fit to shake your teeth out, and if David doesn't hustle you into those dry warm clothes you'll take your death of cold. Now, Davy, look alive, and let's see how this lad appears in a proper outfit. Rub him down a bit with this here bandanna, and button him up smart in them Sunday togs, and I dare say he'll be a decent enough looking chap when you've done with him."

4

THE storm had by now somewhat abated, and an occasional gleam of tarnished moonlight lit the swift procession of the clouds. By this illumination, and by the rays of the larboard lantern, David Butternut noticed with compassion the stranger's pallor and evident exhaustion, and with the utmost neatness and dispatch he proceeded to clothe him in the comfortable garments from Jasper's locker, and to chafe his frozen hands into a condition distantly resembling warmth.

"When you've finished, bring him along to my cabin," called the captain, disappearing down the deck. "Get the cook to dry Jasper's old clothes in the galley, and they'll do him for every-day. I'll see that he gets a drop of hot grog from the steward, for he looks as if he needed it."

"How do you feel now, stranger?" asked David solicitously when the two found themselves alone.

"Oh, I shall do very well, I think," returned the other evasively, as if unwilling to be led into complaint. "I shall probably be none the worse for my experience, after a crust of bread and a good night's sleep. But tell me, David, was Jasper a wicked man?"

"Not what you'd really call wicked," replied David charitably. "He was a queer mixture, was Jasper, with a face like a choirboy's, half the time, and half the time like a devil's; with beautiful manners, gentleman's manners, and no book-learning at all, savage and revengeful, in a way of speaking, and yet with a soft heart for any woman as cared to fool him; free with his money, when he had any, and a good enough friend when he was sober. But he was hardly ever sober," added David with a burst of honesty, "and he was so ignorant, stranger, if you'll credit me, that he couldn't hardly write his own name. Funny, to think of your books in poor old Jasper's pockets, down there where even the great fishes ain't got no eyes! "

The stranger shuddered a little, but David went on unheeding, driven by a painful excitement into the appeasement of confession.

" 'Twas his craze for women killed him in the end, you might say, though I suppose I killed him right enough with this fist of mine, only I never meant for to do it, I'll swear on a stack of Bibles —and God strike me dead if I'd lie to a friend, a kind friend like you, and you believe me, don't you, Shiloh? "

" What is that curious name by which you have just addressed me, David? " asked the stranger, a look of keen intellectual curiosity lighting his wan countenance.

" Shiloh? Why, Shiloh out of the scriptures, to be sure; 'twas you yourself told me to call you that just before you fainted. Then I knew for certain what I had somehow suspected all along; that you were sent by God to save me from damnation. I can't explain it, but I know your coming has made it all fair and square about Jasper, and because I raised you up out of the devouring sea I'm no longer a murderer, praise be to heaven! "

" But who was Shiloh? " persisted the unknown. " I seem to have encountered the word repeatedly during my career; Byron called me Shiloh before he called me the Snake, and I know of course that the name occurs with frequency in the Scriptures; but I retain a strong impression that Shiloh is a place rather than a person."

" Sometimes it's a place right enough," David admitted. " But don't you remember the chapter in Genesis where old Jacob is a-scolding of his sons, and almighty mean the old man is to some of them, how he says as the sceptre shall not depart from Judah until Shiloh come? That's you, stranger, I reckon, and you knew it yourself a while ago, but has most likely forgotten it on account of being cold and tired and sorrowful. Come with me now, Shiloh, my dear friend Shiloh that has saved my soul, and I will find you food and a place to sleep, and to-morrow I will teach you to be a sailor."

So saying, he very tenderly assisted the stranger to rise, and the two young men stood face to face in the intermittent moonlight, and tall and slender as twin pillars of some temple of the sea. The stranger swayed a little, but David stood strong as stone, and where the other's blowing hair was darkness shot with silver, David's was close and curly like a golden cap, and where the other was pale, David was ruddy like his namesake, and his blue eyes met the wilder, wider eyes with infinite humility and trust.

"Just about my height, you are," said David happily. "And now catch a-hold of my arm, and come along to the captain's cabin for a nice glass of hot grog."

Captain Ffoulkastle looked up with frank curiosity as the two companions knocked and entered. Without a word he waved his hand towards a locker, where they seated themselves side by side in attitudes of respectful attention and courteous patience. He handed the stranger a large glass of steaming rum punch, which the young man regarded silently and with apparent disapproval.

"Drink it up, son," said the captain in an authoritative voice. "Orders is orders aboard the *Witch of the West,* and you're ordered to drink that toddy without making any ungrateful faces. Don't be dainty, but get it under your belt double quick; now, then, down she goes with a yo-heave-ho, my hearty!"

The stranger obeyed, swallowed the scalding drink with an expression of acute agony, and leaned back rather limply against the panelling, exhausted by the unnatural effort.

"Take the glass from him, Davy; I don't want it broken," said the captain. "Pour yourself a nip from that jug on the table, and then go out on deck and wait there until I call you. I've got this Jasper business to attend to with our young friend here, and perhaps it might embarrass you a bit; also he may have family affairs to discuss with me, and for that we need privacy. Run along, and don't sit there gaping like a stuck pig."

David, his eyes fixed admiringly upon the stranger's dreaming countenance, sidled slowly from the cabin, closing the door cautiously behind him, and the captain turned to his guest with a brisk and kindly question.

5

TEN minutes later, Captain Ffoulkastle realized with sincere regret that he was shouting the fiftieth of these questions, briskly indeed, but not at all kindly, into the pale and distressed visage of the weary and bewildered unknown, who remained unknown in spite of a number of polite, painstaking answers with which he had met the captain's inquiry. The poor young man had visibly reached the end of his powers, and his sad self-command was the more surprising inasmuch as he looked quite ready to weep, to faint, or to expire in the event of further confusion; yet, withal, his dignity remained somehow unimpaired.

" Oh, hell," cried the captain at length. " You're plumb worn out, and so am I, and all to no purpose so far as sense is concerned. It comes to this, in the main: you say you're so and so, and frankly, I don't believe you, but even if it were true — and mind, I'm not admitting that it is — I couldn't put back into the port of Leghorn for all the poets in Christendom, nor for all the philosophers in heathen parts, nor for all the wives and children in Italy. Understand that, and take it as final; my first and only duty is to the owners of this ship, and they're already sick of waiting for a clipper that's been as slow as molasses in January. So back to Boston we must go, and you must come along with us, working your passage as best you can, since you have no money, and submitting yourself to my discipline as I think fit. Davy will help you; he's a good-hearted boy, but it's a hard life, and you must make up your mind to it."

" It is not the hardships which I anticipate with dread," said the stranger gently. " It is rather the thought of the suspense and terror that my absence must engender in the hearts of my loved ones, and my own extreme anxiety as to the fate of my friend Edward, under which my spirit sinks to desolation."

" As to the fate of your friend Edward," said the captain with

inexorable firmness, " you may well feel regret, but anxiety is unnecessary; by now he is comfortably drowned. The same thing
applies to this sailor chap, Vivian; I have already told you that
your escape was a damned miracle, and there isn't one chance in
a million that the others were snatched up by any similar providence. Be a sensible lad, now, and accept the plain truth from a
man old enough to be your father; the others are dead, and you're
alive, and bloody lucky, if you ask me, so give thanks to God for
his manifold mercies and be prepared to haul on a rope with a
stout heart and a strong pair of hands."

The stranger stared at his slender hands, which were sufficiently sunburnt and sinewy to have attracted the captain's favourable attention; then, with something very like a stifled sob,
he covered his stricken face and leaned mute and trembling
against the wall.

" How can I believe that Edward is dead? " he demanded presently, in a broken voice. " He, the best and bravest of men, the
kindest, cheerfulest creature under the broad sky? Such an one
should never pasture the abhorrèd worm . . ."

" It's not worms, but fishes, as will make a meal of him," said
the captain consolingly. " And now, to turn to brighter subjects,
how about this here murder business? The case stands, roughly,
like this: here's Davy, a good boy if a bit hasty, has killed Jasper
by means of a clip on the head, not meaning for to do it, but along
of impetuosity and a heavy fist, as you might say. Jasper got ugly
back in Leghorn, because Dave give a coral necklace or some such
fal-lal to a young Eyetalian girl with whom he was keeping company, for Jasper was a brass sarpent with the women, and he'd
had his weather eye on this little craft ever since the day he
landed. But she preferred master Dave, and they walked out together very nice and proper every Sunday afternoon, quite as if
the piazza had been Boston Common, and she took him round to
supper with her folks, and everything was all serene. Until last
night, that is, when Jasper picked a quarrel with David just as
he and his girl were coming out of one of these popish churches,
and the boys went at it hammer and tongs, and the Eyetalians
begin to chatter like monkeys, and a couple of women had hysterics, and then before you could say Jack Robinson there was a

crowd of these little gibbering policemen on the scene, and I had hard work getting my lads back on board without a spell of jail for one or both of them. I knew Dave was fighting mad, but Jasper seemed cool enough until six o'clock this evening, jest as we were beating out of the harbour in the dusk; suddenly he was on top of young David like a tiger cat, and I saw the glitter of one of them thin Tuscan knives as he whipped it out of his pocket and struck to kill. I'll swear to my dying day that Jasper struck to kill, and Dave hit back at him in honest self-defence, as you or I might do, stranger, if six inches of steel was a-tickling of our ribs. Well, sir, the blow cracked Jasper's head like a bloody walnut-shell, and there he laid on the deck, deader'n mutton, and there warn't nothing to do about it, as I could see, and I says to the boys, 'Swab down the deck, and straighten out Jasper,' but just then the storm come up, and I reckon you know the rest as well as I do."

6

"Certainly the sympathies of any just and virtuous person must be entirely with David," said the stranger meditatively. He had perfectly recovered his composure, and had listened with a kindling glance and a brightening cheek to the captain's recital. Seen thus, with the swaying radiance of the lamp dispersed over his countenance, he appeared to be about twenty-five years old, very slim and graceful, with a deceptive air of delicacy veiling an uncommonly strong and active body.

"Clipper-built, or I'm a flying Dutchman," said the captain to himself with satisfaction. "Worth any two of these broad-beamed fellows ballasted with too many pounds of plum-duff."

The stranger's face was now illuminated by a pure healthy colour, and a fine sunburn somewhat obscured the inherent transparency of his complexion. He wore the unmistakable air of one who has lived companioned by the elements, and his dark blue eyes had the clarity and brilliance of a sea-gull's gaze.

"Pretty coat of tan he's got," said the captain to himself with increasing approval. "And sailor's eyes; sailor's eyes if ever I seen any."

" Now David Butternut," the captain continued aloud, " runs considerable risk of being hanged unless you'll consent to my proposal. Briefly, the plan is this: that you should try your luck with the rest of the boys for the remainder of the voyage, and that you should land in Boston in the character of Jasper Cross for the simple purpose of saving Davy's neck. After the port authorities are squared, there's no need for you to hang around any longer, and you can ship for Leghorn on the first ship that offers, or take passage like a fine gentleman if you can find the money. If you can't, you'll be a fairly able seaman by that time, and can always get a berth on your merits, and my recommendation. By this means, my lad, you'll be rescuing a comrade from a disgraceful death, and at the same time earning an honest living. Don't forget, either," added the captain impressively, " that David has already rescued you from death by drowning; seems to me that the least you can do in return is to be obliging, and help him out of this very tight hole in which he finds himself, which is neither more nor less than the hangman's noose, my hearty."

" Since you plead so eloquently for this excellent young man, I know not how to refuse your humane request," answered the stranger with an air of mild perplexity. " Yet the circumstance of a voyage to the New World at this particular moment may conceivably embarrass my future, as it certainly complicates my present state. Nevertheless I should be overcome with humiliation, in withholding from David the brotherly aid which on his part was so generously expended in the preservation of my life; I therefore cannot longer hesitate in consenting to your proposal, and here is my hand upon the bargain."

" Then you'll do it, and keep mum? " said the captain in some confusion, feeling himself adrift in a tidal wave of words. At the same time he took rather gingerly into his own broad palm the other's outstretched hand, examining its nervous shape and flexible sinews with professional interest.

" Stick these arms of yours up to their elbows in a tar-bucket, and they'll look more like it," he said with a judicial squint. " Still, it's done a lot for you, even the make-believe business of navigating that pretty toy which has just capsized. Crank as an egg-shell, she must have been, but at least her ropes have hardened your hands into a proper sailor's, my lad, and I reckon you'll be a real addition to the starboard watch."

"I trust so, indeed," the stranger replied politely. "But one stipulation I must make before undertaking my duties: that you will regard the relinquishment of my will to yours as a voluntary act, honourably based upon a desire to benefit a fellow-being, and not merely as the compliant submission of a coward and a weakling. Superior strength shall never daunt the independence of my spirit — while tyranny . . ."

"Easy now with that there talk of tyranny, my young cockerel," said the captain with good-humoured authority. "There ain't no tyranny aboard the *Witch of the West,* so long as you obey orders and keep a civil tongue in your head. Do your duty like a man, and you'll fare well enough; so long as we pull together, you'll find me a clever fellow, and if the second mate is a bit rough in his methods sometimes, you'll live to thank him for his trouble one of these days. Now, boy, I'm going to call Davy; have you anything more to say to me?"

"Only this: that since you doubt my identity I should infinitely prefer to be addressed by some name other than my own," said the stranger softly and rather haughtily. "I suggest therefore that I be known as Shiloh; David already believes that such is my true title, and the word pleases me with its curious antique music. And now, Captain Ffoulkastle, I have the honour to bid you a very good night, and to assure you of my devotion to the welfare of this noble vessel, of my loyalty to yourself, and of my disinterested friendship for David; farewell."

Shiloh, for thus must our narrative continue to know him, rose to his feet upon the completion of this speech, bowed slightly, and then, assuming an attitude of dignified detachment, stood with folded arms awaiting the captain's further commands. He looked very tall under the low beams of the cabin, very slim and strange and foreign to the scene, with his preposterous elegance, his romantic grace, and the aristocratic attenuation of his frame. At the same time, he wore the indubitable air of an athlete; even the captain's critical gaze granted him muscle and bone, agility and strength and lightning quickness of the faculties. His face was bronzed, save where the exceeding whiteness of the forehead betrayed itself under the tumbled hair, whose dark eccentric exuberance was flecked with silver.

"Queer, about his hair," thought the captain. "For the lad don't look a day over twenty-five. But it's his eyes that make me wonder; sailor's eyes, and something more that I can't rightly recollect; seems as if I'd dreamed about them, mebbe, or heard tell of them in a tale."

"Davy," he called aloud; and then to Shiloh, "Well, my lad; so long; Davy will look out for you." Moved by a sudden impulse of pity, he laid his great hand familiarly on the stranger's shoulder. "Don't be downhearted, boy; you'll see the Fortezza Vecchia again before six months are out."

"Perhaps," said Shiloh, as one who dreams a dream, and that intolerably sad, "perhaps you are right; who shall foretell the future? To my own eyes it is shadowed; I am no prophet, but my heart is singularly shaken by foreboding, and my mind is troubled. Yet I say again to you, perhaps you may be right, for doubtless you are wiser than I, and I am very tired."

7

"You'll do now, Shiloh; you haven't at all the look of a green hand," said David a few moments later, giving a conjuring and peculiar twist to his friend's black silk neckerchief. "We must manage to shear away some of those crazy locks of yours, but otherwise you've a decent cut to your jib, and them things of Jasper's fits you like a second skin."

Indeed, David Butternut might well feel proud of his handiwork, for he had contrived to create the illusion of custom in Shiloh's appearance; the trousers, belted tightly about the narrow loins, and hanging loose and baggy around the feet, the checked shirt negligently ample, the low-crowned varnished hat, shiny and black, with half a fathom of black ribbon falling over the left eye, all these details confessed the master's touch in their arrangement.

"Shove your hat a mite farther to the back of your head, son, and we'll go below," said David with lively satisfaction.

"David, have you ever seen an albatross, and have you read

The Ancient Mariner?" asked Shiloh as they proceeded to the hatchway. " I have called Coleridge a hooded eagle among blinking owls, but perhaps he is rather . . ."

" Shiloh, for pity's sake stow that talk about reading until we're alone," whispered David in desperation. " There's some of the boys ain't never learned to read, and they'll think as you're putting on lugs. Of course I seen lots of albatross when I was rounding the Cape, but it don't do to mention them silly things too much on shipboard. As for ancient mariners, you're a-going to meet old Zebulun Cary in a minute, and he's so ancient that they say he's got barnacles growing on his . . ."

But before David could conclude this curious exposition of natural science, the two had reached the steerage, where the starboard watch slept. It was now past eight o'clock and, the second of the dog-watches being over, the men were preparing for rest. There were no berths in the steerage, and very little light; the scene was one of indescribable confusion to any unaccustomed eyes. Mattresses, chests, blankets, and boots seemed mixed inextricably upon the tilting floor, with coils of rigging, spare sails, and ship stores not yet stowed away. A pervasive fragrance of bilge-water clogged the brain as the darkness obscured the vision, and the low growling murmur of speech was equally confusing to the senses. David had a sudden misgiving; he glanced anxiously at Shiloh, but in the heavy twilight the stranger's face was admirably composed and clear. Curiosity, and the eager friendliness of simple good breeding, informed his luminous gaze and the quick question of his smile.

" It's all right," said David immediately, as much to himself as to the other. " And now, Shiloh, you take my mattress for the present; this roll of canvas will do for me. Mates, this is Shiloh, that you seen me fish out of the water a while ago; he's come to take Jasper's place in the starboard watch. I'm going up to the galley to get him a mug of tea and molasses and a hunk of bread, for I reckon he's almighty hungry; say a word to him, boys, to make him feel at home, for he come damn near to laying down to-night along with the bones of poor drowned sailors in the depth of the sea, and mebbe he feels sort of strange and lonely-like among us."

The sailors subjected Shiloh to a prolonged scrutiny, in which inquisitive wonder was mingled with suspicion and doubt; nevertheless one or two of them made shift to address him in kindly rallying tones, and even to slap him on the back with rough jocularity. These advances he accepted in a spirit of happy simplicity; he was palpably both tired and hungry, and he yawned frequently and rubbed his eyes with a childlike lack of self-consciousness, yet all the while he was alert and shining with a sympathetic interest in his queer surroundings. He talked little, but when he did he was frank and outspoken like a well-conditioned boy, and presently the sailors perceived his essential good-will, and smiled at him in spite of themselves.

"Not a bad youngster; better than Jasper, if you ask me," said old Zebulun Cary, and a subtle spirit of peace pervaded the steerage, warming poor Shiloh's soul as the hot tea was even then warming his vitals.

"What very excellent tea, and what truly magnificent bread you have brought me, David," he said at last. "Thank you for the loan of your case-knife, but I do not believe I shall require any of Mr. Cary's plug tobacco. And do you tell me that this beverage owes its superior flavour to the introduction of molasses? I must remember that, I must indeed. Water bewitched, I perceive Mr. Cary calls it; a charming name, and one most germane to my fancy! But I must no longer detain you from your slumbers; I trust that you will not stand on ceremony, and as I am myself amazingly sleepy, perhaps I had better bid you all good-night. Good-night, my best David, and a thousand thanks for your unprecedented kindness. For my own part, I was never more comfortable in my life, and I feel sure that the morning will discover me completely restored. Good-night; no, I would not dream of taking your other blanket, David; no, not on any account. Good-night, good-night to you all."

"Does the poor innocent imagine that he's going to be let to sleep the long night through without a hail?" inquired old Zebulun Cary of David. "I fear he's got some sharp surprises coming to him, along of Mister Murdoch and what-not. Pity he's not in the larboard watch, for the chief mate's a kindly gentleman and a true sailor, but Murdoch's a different story, and this lad's just the sort of high-mettled youngster he loves to come it over. Did you warn Shiloh, David, or is he still unsuspecting-like as the babe unborn? God knows he looks a perfect infant a-laying there! "

"Shiloh's kind of worn-out at present, what with being drowned and everything," said David with an almost paternal pride, " and of course he doesn't look very old, I'll allow, but he's quick and strong as they make 'em; I seen him stripped, and I do assure you, Zebulun, he's like a young Indian brave from the primeval forest. Mister Murdoch, with his precious belaying-pin, had better not try any of his tricks on Shiloh, or he may find he's roused a proper wildcat. Yes, sir, Shiloh's an uncommon sort of fellow; you can see that with half an eye. What's more, the cap'n said as how he could sleep till seven bells in the morning, and there ain't nobody going to wake him while I'm around, not all the Mister Murdochs this side of hell! "

"Easy now, Davy; don't get excited," the old man replied soothingly. "Cap'n's orders is cap'n's orders, and Murdoch's not the kind of fool to dispute 'em. He'll leave Shiloh sleep till morning, I make no doubt, and then have his revenge subtle-like and sly with a kick in the ribs or some such deviltry. I advise you, lad, to hold hard and steer keerfully, and not be asking for trouble; you'll be a better friend to Shiloh in so doing. Oh, you young stripling limbs of Satan are altogether too rash and mutinous by nature, too prone to contention and revolt, for a peaceful man like me! Now for God's sake let me get a mite of rest, and quit tucking up Shiloh like a blooming baby; you'll only wake him, and that would be a pity, seeing how tired he is."

"I don't think he'll wake," said David, preparing for repose. " He must have had an almighty lot of liquor, first and last, before the cap'n and I were finished with him, and he has the look of a very sound sleeper."

So saying, he turned upon his side, and closed his eyes, but slumber eluded him, and against the darkness the stranger's countenance still floated like a drowning star. The roll of canvas under his head was hard enough, and his thick woolen garments were clammy with salt and spray, but David, in the admirable vigour of his blood, remained profoundly indifferent to these things. Rather he was disturbed by a vague melancholy abnormal

to his mind, a hint, an evasive whisper of despair. He knew with
the clarity of intense conviction that Shiloh's presence was his
own release from guilt, that Shiloh's life atoned obliquely for
another's murder, and that in saving Shiloh he was himself
delivered from a deeper annihilation of the soul. Now suddenly
he felt that perhaps he had been less than kind in his insistence,
since Shiloh was so very tired.

"Seems lunatic and outlandish, but I keep on asking of myself
if he wouldn't of rather drowned," whispered David in the darkness. "He was so peaceful, and I made him come to me; I cried
to him to come, and he heard me. Well, mebbe I've done wrong;
mebbe by now he'd be in some high gold house in heaven, laying
asleep between fine white linen sheets, with the moon and the
morning stars singing together outside the window like birds
upon a bough. Mebbe I've asked too much of him, mebbe life'll
be too hard for him to bear. But I'll try to make it up to him; I'll
do my level best; I'll be like one of these here faithful dogs you
hear of, running at his side through the world, loving to him, but
fierce as a wolf to his enemies. And that," said David with his eyes
on the dim radiance of Shiloh's forehead, "and that, I reckon, is
what they call a vow."

Afterwards he slept, until the cry of "All starbowlines ahoy!
Eight bells there below; do you hear the news?" roused him from
dedicated and heroic dreams to stagger up on deck with the rest
of the starboard watch. The skies were clear as black crystal now,
and the toppling waves slid by in glassy brightness. David drank
the cool winds as if they had been the waters of some airy spring,
and the taut ropes wetted with spray quivered under his hand like
the sinews of a flying horse, winged and monstrous and unreasonable, which sprang ever towards the west along a smooth white
valley of the sea.

The Orphan Angel

II

PURE ANTICIPATED COGNITION

" SEEMS as if I'd like to climb a hill, along about moonrise to-night, and see the earth spread out below me," said David to Shiloh upon the last evening of the voyage. It was a tranquil twilight hour, and the crew were sitting on the windlass or lying comfortably on the forecastle, smoking, singing, and telling curious yarns. A violet sky contained a few frosty stars, and from the quarter-deck the rhythmic footsteps of the captain and the first mate sounded small and far-away upon the measureless quiet of the atmosphere.

The two friends were momentarily occupied with a large tin pot of tea and a kid of salt beef, and the calm of appeased hunger had lately descended over their spirits like a pleasant cloud. David's ingenuous face wore a look of the liveliest satisfaction, and ever and anon he turned his curly head to stare proudly at his companion, whose long slender limbs were disposed in an attitude of easy grace upon the forecastle's weather side.

" It certainly does beat all, the way you've looked up aboard ship," remarked David parenthetically. " I remember when I first seen you, Shiloh, I thought as how you was sort of an unearthly critter, but now there ain't none of us can touch you for nimbleness and spunk. To see you on a yard I'd swear you'd been bred to the trade of knotting a reef-point, and you swing down them shrouds and back-stays like a blooming monkey. And my stars, how the victuals seem to suit you, Shiloh; you're hard as hickory and cat-gut, and brown as a copper penny! Cap'n says . . ." continued David boastfully, but Shiloh stopped him with a brotherly hand upon his arm, and David saw that the other was blushing furiously under the clear bronze colour of his cheek.

"Really, David, your partiality is so kind that it overwhelms me with a sense of my profound unworthiness," said Shiloh, laughing. "You must not praise me so warmly, my dear friend; your admiration is far in excess of my modest capabilities. Yet it is true that I have succeeded beyond my most sanguine anticipations in performing my duties on shipboard, and I have rarely experienced a keener joy than in the reefing of the fore-topsail during the last storm. The frenzied elements appeared obedient to my hand, and in the howling of the gale I heard the voice of a baffled host of kings. But I fear I have interrupted you, David; pray go on with your meditation upon mountain-peaks."

"Oh, I was just saying as how I'd like to climb a hill to-night, and watch the moon rise over the spread-out land," said David rather shyly. "You see, Shiloh, I was born down in Maine, and there's plenty of hills in them parts, sightly places, standing tall above the pine-trees. Sometimes I don't hardly feel that I was meant to sail the seas; I get so homesick for the hills, and I asks myself: *David, what are you doing on this lonesome waste of waters?* Shiloh, if you would come with me, I believe I'd go stepping westward, to the great mountains that I've heard tell of ever since I was a child."

"David, do you know that you have unconsciously quoted Wordsworth?" asked Shiloh eagerly. "That is a most interesting example of a naturally poetic impulse informing a simple mind. Now if you would only try your skill at composing even the least elaborate hymn to Liberty, I feel sure you would be miraculously repaid. Your noble country must inevitably inspire such vehement longing to express in words. . . . But forgive me, I perceive that I am boring you with my enthusiasms. We were speaking of the hills."

"Yes, we were speaking of the hills, and I was wishing that you'd come with me to climb them," cried David earnestly.

" Wouldn't you admire to be a pioneer, Shiloh, like that wonderful and famous old codger Colonel Boone, and seek out strange places full of wild bears and buffaloes and mountain lions, and kill 'em with your naked hands, mebbe, and trap the eagles, and hunt the savages? I don't want you to think me downright bloodthirsty," said David timidly, " but ain't you ever sort of hankered after them things, Shiloh? "

" Assuredly I have desired these things, David," said Shiloh with his customary gentleness. " I love all waste and solitary places, as I have affirmed ere this; power dwells apart in its tranquillity. Could you have come with me to the vale of Chamounix, to behold Mont Blanc . . . ! But enough; we will have adventures wilder, holier even than this. Bear with me, my friend, for a little while, and we will perform prodigies together."

" Shiloh," said David suddenly, in an agitated whisper, " there's something that I feel I'm bound to tell you; something that troubles me turrible at times. I hadn't exactly meant to tell you, Shiloh, you being so good and kind to me, and I not wanting to bother you with foolishness. But it's this, Shiloh: Jasper had a twin sister."

Shiloh turned his large blue eyes towards David with a look of mild surprise, for the lad's voice had broken upon the words, and an expression of superstitious fear convulsed his lips and brow.

" A twin sister! " and " Jasper! " cried Shiloh blankly. Watching David's face, his own grew rather pale, and his gaze widened as upon a vision and a mystery.

"Yes, Shiloh; Jasper's sister," David answered slowly, staring into the other's eyes. " And I feel in my bones a most powerful conviction that I must go west to rescue her; it's the least I can do for poor old Jasper."

" But is she in any imminent peril? " inquired Shiloh, an expiring gleam of worldly wisdom contending with the chivalric fever of his mind.

" Well, I don't know exactly as you'd call it peril," said David candidly. " But I'm sure she's in constant danger of being stolen by the Indians, and then of course she's almighty poor; poverty-stricken and forlorn. The girl's an orphan, too, and with her brother dead and done for, I can't help feeling that she's sort of unfortunate. Mebbe I'm too soft-hearted, but the thought of that girl has haunted my dreams, Shiloh, and I've about made up my mind to wander out west in search of her."

"But don't you know where to look for this interesting young creature, David?" asked Shiloh in amazement. "To employ a homely simile, would not your quest resemble the hunting of a bright silver needle in a savage subfuscated haystack? By what shining clue do you propose to unravel this riddle?"

"Funny, your calling her a silver needle," David commented thoughtfully. "Because that's the name that Jasper used to give her: Silver. It's a queer name, and I reckon she's a queer girl; more like a sperrit than a mortal woman. But beautiful; Jasper always said she was very beautiful. He loved his sister, did poor old Jasper, and he never showed me her portrait without tears in them angry eyes of his, and a shake in his voice."

"Silver, Silver, a silver sister in a valley alone," repeated Shiloh dreamily, his eyes upon the arch of the evening sky.

"I don't think she lives in a valley; Jasper always spoke of mountains. But I know her name was written on the back of her portrait, and mebbe it tells where she lives too; I'll look for it in Jasper's ditty-box."

David rose to his feet and hurried toward the steerage, but Shiloh appeared indifferent to his errand; indeed it is doubtful whether or not he had remarked his friend's departure. He lay very still, his slender hands clasped behind his head, his gaze profoundly fixed upon the stars. At intervals he murmured to himself the name of Jasper's sister. "Silver, Silver," said Shiloh to his own heart, whispering the word aloud like an hypnotic incantation.

The violet sky, withdrawn as it darkened, was pierced now by innumerable stars, its purity of colour holding an even intenser purity of light, so that the luminous distance trembled like water, and was no more stable than the sea; yet in the moving, wavering brightness was composure, and the clear dignity of peace. This brightness and tranquillity fell from the air like dew, and echoed in the absence of any sound, to lie cool and musical upon Shiloh's spirit.

2

PRESENTLY David returned panting, a little parcel clutched tightly in his sunburnt hand, and the close gold rings of his hair dishevelled by haste.

"Here it is!" he cried triumphantly. "I found it between a pack of cards and a velvet prayer-book, laying next to Jasper's big Spanish pistol. All that truck is just like Jasper, a crazy mixture of good and bad, but here's the little portrait right enough; and now tell me what you think of Silver, Shiloh, and whether or not I had better go in search of the girl."

Shiloh took the little object carefully in his slim brown fingers; he regarded it with a rapt and dreaming attention while unfolding the crimson handkerchief and opening the shagreen case. Within, the portrait lay revealed; he stared at it in silence, his eyes large and preternaturally radiant in the starlight.

"Silver," he said again, very gently, "must we go in search of you, Silver? What do you say, *animula, vagula, blandula,* little soul like a cloud, like a feather?"

The starlight was no more than twilight, and the ivory oval upon Shiloh's palm glimmered uncertainly, as if faintly lit with inner phosphorescence. The pictured face was small and pale, the shining hair was silvery pale, the eyes alone were full of a soft darkness, like the patterned eyes upon the wings of moths.

"You see, David," said Shiloh with a curious smile, "Silver has told me that we must come and find her; she has told me with her eyes, but very plainly, and I dare not disobey."

"Oh, Shiloh, that's what I've been a-hoping all along, only I dassn't ask you myself, it seemed so kind of unreasonable! But if you come too, we'll be bound to find her, I'm certain sure of that, and the poor girl will welcome you like a brother, you being the dead spit of Jasper, and him no more. Not but what you're far finer and stranger than Jasper, somehow, but with a sister's partiality she may be forgiven for taking note of the likeness. Yes, it'll be a wonderful happy day for Silver when you ride out of the east on a wild pony, with your eyes like saucers of blue sea-water and your hair like a capful of north wind. Oh, I know I'm talking kind of crazy; forgive me, Shiloh, but I'm so pleased that I reckon I'm nearly out of my mind, and I can't keep a-hold of the sense of what I'm saying! "

Indeed, the honest fellow's eyes were full of tears, and he wrung Shiloh's hand with fervent and tempestuous joy. Shiloh sat up, restored the portrait to its case, and, wrapping it in the crimson silk handkerchief, slipped it into his own pocket.

"Very well," he pronounced calmly, "that is quite settled, then; we travel west in search of Silver. I have other duties, other dear and necessary devoirs to perform, but this comes first, as it is the most poignant and burning cry of all. By the eloquent patience of those lips, by the deep entreaty of those eyes, I swear that I will come. Silver, do you hear me, even across the world? I swear that I will come."

He ceased, and thereafter was silent for so long a time that David grew restless, teased by a thousand questions of how and when and where, and longing for the warm reality of words. Nevertheless the boy preserved a laudable peace, out of respect for Shiloh's hushed and exalted countenance and the enchanted fire of his eyes.

It grew darker; eight bells were struck, the clear notes dividing the quiet atmosphere with measured cadences. The log was hove, the wheel relieved, and the other men of the starboard watch went below, but still Shiloh lay upon the forecastle, his eyes importuning the stars, and in each of his eyes a fire brighter than a star was pointed and apparent.

"Shiloh," said David at last, "Shiloh, didn't you hear the watch going below? It's your trick at the wheel to-night, Shiloh, and you ought to get some rest while there's time. Furthermore, if we land to-morrow there'll be an almighty lot to do, and we've a long journey ahead of us, a long journey into the west. Better come below, Shiloh, and try to sleep."

Shiloh rose quickly and noiselessly, and with admirable docility followed David to the hatchway. He ran his long fingers through his blowing locks, lifting his face to the heavens with a look half bewildered, half entranced.

" Do you really believe that we shall land to-morrow, Davy? "
he asked in a voice of wonder.

" I do," said David decidedly, " unless Boston has taken a
running start and jumped back into the tall timber. Yes, we'll see
the three hills by to-morrow at sundown, and I'll show you the
sights of the town, and we'll eat a proper meal of good fresh beef
and onions and apple pie and cheese, washed down with punch
and Philadelphia porter. That's something to hearten your innards, my boy, after all these weeks of scouse and biscuit."

" David," said Shiloh with profound solemnity, " David, I
wish to ask you an important question." His bright eyes transfixed the other with a piercing scrutiny.

" Ask away, Shiloh," replied David valiantly. " You know I
ain't so very learned in history and such-like subjects, but I know
Boston was discovered from the Indians by Cap'n John Smith,
and I've heard tell of the tea-party and Paul Revere, and I visited
the Old South Church and two distilleries last time I landed. I
reckon I have a pretty fair idea of the town, and I'll answer you
honest to the best of my powers."

" David," said Shiloh with an increased solemnity, and his
words were audibly shaken by some obscure emotion, " David,
tell me only this: do you believe we shall be able to buy penny
buns in Boston? "

3

NEXT day the *Witch of the West* passed Castle Island as the sun
was setting, thus terminating a swift and prosperous voyage with
peculiar fitness, along a smooth broad path of molten gold. Shiloh
sniffed the mingled fragrance of the land with rapture; he
smelled freedom in the abstract, and more particularly his romantic senses detected spices from the India Wharf, while his fastidi-
ousness noted soap and candles from Boston Pier and his country-
bred nose was aware of the distant aroma of new-mown hay.
As for his eyes, they were full to overflowing of new visions
and revelations, so much so indeed that they spilled a little
of their brightness in tears upon the altar of liberty, and the

gilded pine-cone crowning the State House dazzled them like a flame.

Later, as the ship lay alongside Hancock's Wharf, her riding-lights yellow against a fine blue dusk, Shiloh and David sat in Captain Ffoulkastle's cabin and shyly discussed the future. Without, under a constellation of lanterns, the men were already breaking bulk, for a consignment of candied fruits and Chian claret must reach the hands of a certain Salem merchant on the morrow. Captain Ffoulkastle had been with the owners in their magnificent warehouse on Broad Street, and Shiloh, in the character of Jasper Cross, had casually wandered ashore and supped with David in a waterfront ordinary without attracting a notice more peculiar than that which must inevitably be accorded to any tall young sailor with large and luminous blue eyes. The police had betrayed no interest in him, but several pretty girls in simple calico had gazed upon him kindly, and a benevolent white-haired gentleman had offered him a glass of excellent cider.

Therefore he felt at peace with the whole world; he leaned back against the mahogany panelling of the cabin, his long legs stretched out in front of him, his hands clasped loosely in his lap, his face composed to a delicate mask of pure tranquillity and good will. The captain detected a slight relaxing of discipline in this nonchalant attitude, but Shiloh was so clearly innocent of offence, so friendly and so exquisitely courteous, that it was impossible to find tyrannical or bitter fault with him. David, divided between loyal apprehension and admiring pride, kept glancing from one to the other of his two companions; the captain looked at Shiloh, and Shiloh looked at the ceiling as if it had been hung with stars.

"Well, my lads," said the captain at last, "I'm sorry that I can't dissuade you from this wild-goose chase. Nobody can say as I'm a hard-hearted man, and I feel most tenderly towards Jasper's poor little orphan sister, but you can be of no practical use to the child, not even knowing where she lives, and you'll be wasting precious time over plain foolishness. You young rapscallions should stick to the sea, and not go rampaging over the western prairies, running after a lost girl that neither of you never saw. Davy here's a smart fellow in a gale, and Shiloh has done wonders considering what a green hand he was when he come aboard.

Now take my advice, and sign on with me for the return voyage. Leghorn's the port for you, Shiloh, if you've got a wife and child down Lerici way."

At these words David emitted a curious hoot of laughter, causing Shiloh to turn to him in mild annoyance and the captain in unconcealed surprise. He blushed, and ducked his head in embarrassment, as the others stared at him.

" Beg pardon, cap'n, and you, Shiloh old friend," he mumbled, " but it always makes me laugh something cruel to think of Shiloh there with a wife and baby. Why, he's only a baby himself in a manner of speaking, for all he says that he's twenty-nine years old, and it don't seem hardly proper for him to be a husband and a father and have all this ballast of duties and sacred obligations, as he names 'em. There he sets as if sweet butter wouldn't melt in his mouth, and he's always pitching me yarns of mud turtles and sarpents and supernatural monsters, and yet he says he has a wife and child; it's plumb ridiculous, and I don't believe him! "

" Nevertheless it is true," said Shiloh with gentle dignity. " It is true, David, although to a boy of twenty-one it may seem strange. At your age I had been already twice a father; a fortnight ago I celebrated my thirtieth birthday amid the profound solitudes of the Atlantic, and these silver locks above my brow may attest my absolute veracity. It grieves me that you should not accept my word, David; but some day you will understand."

David, speechless with shame, held out his hand with a look of imploring apology, and Shiloh took the hand and its amending message with a smile.

" I'm sorry," said Shiloh; " I didn't mean to scold you, David. You see, I am somewhat weary of being taken for a child, since the years have taught me so much of sorrowful wisdom."

" Then, my lad," the captain interpolated briskly, " why don't you apply a bit of that wisdom to the present case? If you keep on this wild western tack you'll be calmly deserting your wife, who you tell me is a lady of breeding and sensibility. How can you reconcile that with your conscience, Christian or no Christian? I was raised a good Calvinist, and never had no dealings with Unitarians nor free-thinkers, so it's hard for me to take your meaning, but why should you think it necessary to run off after this here Silver girl when you have a lawful wedded wife at San Terenzo? "

4

THE DELICATE mask of tranquillity upon Shiloh's face was shattered in an instant; he became very pale, and his brow was troubled above darkened eyes. A singular look of apprehension crept into these eyes, tired, yet painfully alert and brilliant. He had all at once the air of a hunted thing, a wild deer, fragile and untamed, and the brightness of his eyes was amazing.

" I must decline to discuss my domestic affairs with a stranger," he said in a tense contemptuous voice, and as he spoke his whole slight body trembled. Captain Ffoulkastle was surprised to perceive that the boy was both wounded and angry, and forgave him the more readily inasmuch as Shiloh had never before given evidence of either of these regrettable states of mind.

" Steady," said the captain in a warning tone. " I didn't intend to pry into your private life, my lad, but I hate to see you behaving like a fool and a knave without a mouthful of friendly advice from your elders. I know you're a good boy, I might almost say a very good boy; you're brave as a lion in the face of danger, and you've a soft heart for any sort of trouble among your mates; I've watched you, and I know. But you're inclined to be hot-headed and what the schoolmasters call idealistic, and that never did nobody no service," said the captain with a comprehensive sweep of the arm.

" I wonder," said Shiloh softly. He had completely regained his composure, and was at all points his charming self, save for a slight pallor and a fainter shadow upon the eyelids.

" You must understand," he continued with a sweetly reasonable air, " that I have been much persecuted at the hands of authority, and I am therefore unduly sensitive to any hint of despotism. I was mistaken in my resentment, and I entreat your pardon. Touching the matter of my return to Italy, the case is strangely complicated by circumstance, which, being assured of your benevolent intentions, I will here pause to elucidate."

"Shall I go on deck, Shiloh, and leave you and the cap'n alone?" asked David rather miserably, torn between curiosity and the desire to spare his friend at all cost to himself. He was immensely relieved by Shiloh's permission to remain, implicit in a quick gesture of the hand.

"Know, then," said Shiloh to Captain Ffoulkastle, "that my situation is one of peculiar difficulty and peril. I speak not of bodily peril; to that I am indifferent, as you have rightly judged, but of those spiritual dangers and blights which beset the soul upon the slopes of time, and to which I am particularly susceptible. I am not certain," said Shiloh in a shaken voice, "that my wife desires my return."

"Fiddlesticks!" cried the captain, and "Oh, rats!" ejaculated David with the same accord. Indeed, Shiloh's evident grace and distinction, his nervous strength, and the strange deep colour of his eyes rendered the thing incredible. He was too completely the bright embodiment of an ideal to be unwelcome in reality, and both David and the captain rejected the notion with simultaneous scorn.

Shiloh accepted the interruption as the compliment it indubitably was. A sad smile played for an instant about his expressive lips, and his face was grave again.

"Yet it is but too true, my friends," he assured them with gentle melancholy. "Nor is it so unnatural a suspicion as you appear to believe. I am not one profoundly to engage the affections of a feeling heart, I fear, nor has nature bestowed her choicest workmanship upon my form and hue. I have long perceived that my presence was wearisome and my faults offensive to her whom you have named; let us not name her again, but dash the tear from the eye and the memory from the mind of sorrow. My present thought is this: that I should indite a letter to this lady, and dispatch it by the faithful hand of Captain Ffoulkastle, thus insuring its certain and immediate delivery. In less than a month it will be in her possession, when she can come to a decision at leisure and free from the agitations of soul which must inevitably attend my personal reappearance. In a word, I shall permit her to choose, untrammelled by aught save her own desires, between a future of complete independence and one spent by my side amid the austerities of the new world."

"A pretty rough choice for a lady, my lad," the captain replied thoughtfully. "Is your mind entirely easy on this point, taking into consideration the stormy passage, and the foreign land, not to mention Indians and snakes and such vermin as the females never precisely cotton to in America? Because you must remember there's a sight more sows' ears than silk purses west of the Alleghanies."

"My determination is irrevocable," said Shiloh with proud simplicity. "I shall never return to that theatre of tyrannies, the continent of Europe, and my greatest content would be to retire with my wife and child to some cabin in the wilderness or solitary island in the sea, and, utterly deserting all human society, to shut upon our retreat the flood-gates of the world. Nevertheless, as I have said, the decision rests with her; if the die be cast against me, henceforward I must live alone, and devote either to oblivion or to future generations the overflowings of a mind which, timely withdrawn from the contagion, shall be kept fit for no baser object."

"But Shiloh," cried David in honest distress, his heart wrung by the sad nobility of these words and the resignation of the broken voice which pronounced them, "you won't never need to be alone; you'll have me always, and mebbe you'll have Silver too."

"'Tain't likely, far as I can see, that you'll ever find that girl," said the captain with crushing common sense. "But then, it's just as well, what with one thing and another, and you being a married man, and David no more than a silly boy. For silly you are, Davy, to leave this ship that's been more than father and mother to you, and go r'aring and ramping over the earth with this atheistical son of Belial. Oh, I've said he was a good lad, and I'll stick to it that he is, but only look at him there, a-shutting of his eyes — and them sailor's eyes at that — to all save vanity and the chasing of rainbows! I've no patience with neither of you," said the captain explosively, striking the table a resounding blow with his great hairy fist.

"And if I may make so bold," he went on presently, with heavy sarcasm, "I'd like to inquire what provision in money you've made for this poor lady that was unlucky enough to marry you some time back. I suppose you'd thought of that, even in the midst of your precious plots and plans for improving the world."

"Assuredly I had considered that question," Shiloh answered with imperturbable politeness. "And since I perceive your interest to be an unselfish one, unsmirched by vulgar curiosity, I may inform you that I shall suggest in my letter the simplest of all solutions: namely, that my own income be transferred to my wife in the event of a separation. Does this arrangement meet with your approval?" he asked, with light and amiable irony.

"That's fair enough, I'll allow," the captain grudgingly admitted, "and I reckon it might even be called generous if the whole crazy scheme were not so damnably unnecessary. What's all this talk of a separation? I don't credit for a split second your notion that your wife's grown tired of you; why should she, for the Lord's sake? You're a handsome young devil, quick as a catamount, and them eyes of yours might strike any girl plumb silly. I'm weary, bitterly weary, of your foolishness, and I wash my hands of the whole affair."

"And that, if you could but comprehend it, is precisely my wife's sentiment in the matter; she is weary, bitterly weary, of my foolishness. But, washing your hands like Pilate, you will not stay for an answer, and as the whole subject is infinitely painful to a sensitive mind, I suggest that we abandon it forthwith and for ever. The letter I will presently compose, counting upon your friendly offices for its safe delivery into the lady's hands. For the rest, I need not further assure you of my unalterable esteem for yourself, nor of my never-ending gratitude for your benevolence."

"Oh, shucks," protested Captain Ffoulkastle, touched in spite of himself by the other's evident sincerity, "I don't deserve none of them fine phrases, having done no more than my duty by you, boy. You've been a clever lad about the ship, too, and worth your salt beef with the best of 'em. And that reminds me: since you're both so stubborn sot in your ways about going west, here's your rightful pay, Dave and Shiloh, and a little extry something to help you out of the tight holes you're bound to fall into now and again. Oh, a dollar or two more or less won't break me this voyage, and I don't want no thanks for it, only I hope to find you two young idjits a-languishing here on Boston Pier when I return, waiting and thankful to be signed on again. Meanwhiles, the *Witch* will lay alongside Hancock's for another fortnight, and you can bring me the letter any day, Shiloh; you know it's safe in my keeping. Mebbe the answer will be a mite more cheerful than you seem to calculate."

"I trust so, indeed, but my mind is a prey to the gloomiest forebodings," replied Shiloh with an ambiguous shake of his romantic locks, and a glance of darkling fire.

"Now, lads," the captain continued pleasantly, "you can sleep aboard the ship to-night if you've a mind to, only give me a hail in the morning before you're off for good or bad, as the case may be. If I'm not here, I'll be over with Mr. Russell in the warehouse, or in the Broad Street ordinary across the way. Run along now, and lend a hand with them crates, and mind you don't go feeding candied citron and Chianti to the flounders, you young scalawag of a Shiloh."

When Shiloh and David had departed, the captain sat for a while lost in profound reflection; sometimes he frowned, and several times he laughed aloud with a robust guffaw, but in the main his look was puzzled and indignant, and he rubbed the hair above his brow into a veritable cockatoo's crest of flaming interrogation in unwonted agonies of thought. Finally, with a portentous shake of the head he sought his couch, nor did slumber in the least enlighten the baffled course of his obscure ruminations.

5

"First things I want to buy me are a bottle of cherry brandy, a yeller silk neckerchief, and a new jack-knife," cried David cheerfully, jingling a double handful of coins.

"And I," said Shiloh, with a deeper, dreamier fervour, " must purchase a loaf of fresh bread, a few raisins, Calderón's *Magico Prodigioso,* and, if possible, the works of the Greek dramatists in pocket editions."

It was a flawless morning of mid-August, and the docks presented a picture of the liveliest activity under an amber superfluity of sunlight. The breeze was sharply flavoured with salt and the exotic fragrance of spices from the India Wharf, and overhead the bland white clouds of summer preserved a stately leisure of their own. The splendid warehouses of Broad Street were bright with white and pumpkin-coloured paint, and far away the State House dome hung like a shining bubble above Beacon Hill.

"How passing fair the world appears to-day," said Shiloh in measured accents. "The senses alone, unaided by the mind, might discover in this scene a new world, unsullied by the blots which disface the elder. The very countenances of the people unite a Republican simplicity of morals with that politeness and delicacy of manners which render virtue amiable. The good cloth coat habits the man; calicoes and chintzes adorn the modest unassuming beauty of the woman and the blue-eyed babe. To crown my happiness, I observe none of those livid wretches, covered with rags who in Europe, soliciting our compassion even from the foot of the altar, seem to bear testimony against religion and the order of society. With what pleasure do I contemplate this enchanting town, and enjoy the spectacle of liberty where nature, education, and habit have engraved the equality of rights upon the hearts of the multitude!"

"Boston's a sightly spot, I'll allow," agreed David with a moderated ardour. "Not but what there're prettier places down in Maine, if you know where to look for 'em. I ain't much of a hand at stringing words together, such shiny words as I'd need to make you see it as it is, Shiloh, but believe me that it beats this city hollower than an old snare-drum. Yes, sir, you ought to see them mountains setting right up out of the bright blue sea, Mount Desert and Isle au Haut and Grand Manan, covered with a kind of pearliness in the distance, and mebbe with another range of hills a-floating over 'em in the heavens. Mirage, they call it, same as mirrors, I suppose, and sure enough there's a looking-glass colour about it all, wavy and clear as water. Oh, I can't put such notions into speech, but I wish you could see them mountains in the evening, under the moon, rising up out of a smooth sea."

"I wish I could, indeed," said Shiloh rather wistfully. "But

I suppose there is no possibility of finding Silver in the hills of Maine. Yet I would dearly love to see your home, David, and share the golden pageant of your childhood's memories."

" We have an elegant house in Castine," said David, " a fine modern house, painted white like these here Boston houses. But when I was a little shaver we used to live in a log house; a fort, it was really, for fighting Indians. The British burnt that place in 1812; I was only eleven, but I was almighty mad, and I know I went for the sergeant like a crazy wildcat. My daddy was to sea at the time, taking part in the war, you understand, and I had my mother kind of on my mind. Well, mebbe it was all for the best, as the new place is so neat and tasteful, but I think I liked the log house better."

" It was consecrated to you by the blood of your ancestors, who had fought for freedom, and bedewed the lintel with their sacred lives," suggested Shiloh.

" Some were scalped, but not a one was ever killed," David confessed, " so I reckon they fought to save their precious skins. French used to give 'em a sight of trouble, too, and they say the French love freedom. But I guess they were different in those days."

" A happy augury of the perfectibility of the human mind! " cried Shiloh. He had removed his varnished black hat, and the fresh breeze from the harbour lifted the dark abundance of his hair and made the silver in it shine like the rippling silver on the under side of willow leaves. He strode along with an amazing airy speed, and his bare brown throat and brighter forehead were washed to coolness by the wind of it.

Presently he began to intone the words of some high incantation of the soul, by which the names of oceans and elemental storms and the processional seasons of the year were influenced to music. And this chant resounded with an illimitable and solemn exaltation, so that it was no mere artifice of speech, but deserved rather to be numbered among the natural and vital forces, like a whirlwind or a meteoric flame.

So speaking, or perhaps singing, Shiloh passed along the clean and sunny streets of Boston, and all who beheld him marvelled at his beauty and the singular triumph plain upon his brow. Some thought him mad, but few forbore to love him, and into the hearts of several his image entered that morning to remain always, the bright wound of an arrow pointed by a star.

"I ain't never heard that hymn before, Shiloh, but it's real uplifting," said David at his side.

Suddenly Shiloh darted into a small grocer's shop and emerged with a loaf of bread and a twist of brown paper. He looked more triumphant than ever as he shook a dozen raisins into David's hand.

"Sustenance for the inner man, Davy," he cried. "Not by bread alone shall he live." And he made a pun upon a certain passage in the Testament, which, being Greek, was doubly Greek to David.

Nevertheless David was supremely happy; he purchased his yellow neckerchief and his jack-knife, and, as a temporary substitute for the cherry brandy, some fine ripe peaches and a great sheet of gingerbread. On this simple fare they made their noonday meal, seated under a tree in Franklin Place.

" 'Tain't exactly my idea of a square meal, but I suppose we must get used to roughing it," said David, philosophically, swallowing the ultimate crumb of gingerbread. He drew the jack-knife from his pocket, and began to carve a peach-stone with meticulous care.

"Can do mighty pretty things with cherry-stones, but this ain't the season for cherries," announced David, squinting at his intricate handiwork.

Along the shady turf, Shiloh had composed his graceful limbs as if for slumber, but suddenly he sat up with a start, and, producing pencil and paper from some unapparent hiding-place, he prepared to write.

The grassy square, chequered in amber and emerald by the lengthening afternoon, was very quiet; only above the neat red roofs the plumes of smoke were set in motion by the air, but all else was tranquil in a plenitude of light and warmth. David sat with his curly golden head bent over the carving; and the sun fell upon him like a stream of sunny water, but Shiloh lay in shadow, and the shadow too was coloured like water, the deeper colour of the sea. Each after his peculiar fashion was absorbed by the work of his hands and brain to forgetfulness of all else, and the hours slipped swiftly by into the west, and the work went on, in delicate periods of creation.

At last David rose and stretched himself with a yawn, his flushed face burnished to copper by the sunset. Shiloh rose also; he was pale, and the locks of his hair were disarrayed as though by prodigies of invisible speed.

"You look kind of like you'd come from the moon," said David laughing.

"That was a good long lazy afternoon," he went on. "We didn't do nothing, of course, only sit and fritter away our time like a couple of truants out of Sunday School, but it was pleasant, wonderful pleasant. And there's your paper all covered with squiggles like the acrostics in the *Advertiser,* and here's my peach-stone, carved with a funny little face. Shall I chuck it away, Shiloh, or save it to give to Silver when we find her?"

"By all means save it, David," Shiloh said gravely. "I shall save my squiggles, as you call them, to give to her also. They are magic squiggles, only waiting to sing her to sleep with the voice of a Mediterranean wave and a Tuscan nightingale. I wish they might sing myself to sleep, and at once, for I am amazingly tired."

"I know you are, by the way you blink your eyes and ruffle your hair," replied David in surprise, "but why you're tired beats me completely, for you've done nothing but rest for three mortal hours! However, most likely you're hungry and don't rightly realize it; come along with me and get a bite of hot supper under your belt and you'll feel better. You can't expect to live on dry bread and raisins in a free country, my lad, whatever you may do in Italy. Steer for the Broad Street ordinary, and I'll set you up to a steak and kidney pie and a pint of porter."

6

LATE that night, in their modest lodgings, Shiloh sat long in meditation by the light of a single candle. In the near-by bed,

David slumbered below the cheerful rainbow of a patchwork quilt, and sounds without were hushed to the tranquillity of darkness. Finally Shiloh opened the little attic window and leaned out under the stars; he shivered slightly in the keen wind from the sea, and the brightness of his eyes was full of tears as he looked eastward.

Afterwards he wrote a letter to his wife, sitting hunched over the rickety table and seeing the great shadows flicker like ghosts upon the whitewashed walls. The quill pen trembled in his hand, and its feather made another flying shadow above his head. A tear fell upon the sheets of the letter, and he brushed it away in anger at his own weakness, for he had ever studied to be brave, and now he had need of all his faculties of courage. Beyond the four white walls the greater shadow of a greater wing engulfed the sky.

At last the letter was finished; Shiloh sealed it carefully with red wax, and leaned back exhausted.

" It is finished," he said aloud, with a vague recollection that the words were not his own but another's.

He leaned against the whitewashed wall, below the steeply sloping roof of the attic, and he was so tired that he forgot to think or even to suffer. The deep conviction that he was unloved had entered his soul like mortal iron, but now the agony was past, and he was only a little breathless and confounded and faint as he sat and listened to the strokes of midnight falling through the air and watched the candle burning to its end.

Before its uncertain light had reached the socket, he had found the hidden portrait of Jasper's sister; he turned to it in his weariness as a scolded child turns to a picture-book. Indeed its cool pure colours and gentle looks were a consolation to his drowsy mind, and suddenly he knew that he could sleep.

" A silver cup of cold water," said Shiloh to himself sleepily. With infinite reverence he kissed the small pale lips of the portrait.

In another moment he was slumbering by David's warm and comforting humanity, under the homely rainbow of the patchwork quilt.

The Orphan Angel

III

LOVE IN DESOLATION

" Shiloh," asked David, with his mouth full of johnny-cake and fried ham, " where is it that a man is half horse, half alligator? "

A lion-coloured sunlight enriched the long pine tables at the Broad Street ordinary, gilding their beeswaxed surfaces with an imperial varnish. Curtains of scarlet cotton fluttered against a clear blue sky, and the gaiety of a good breakfast pervaded the air. It was impossible to be melancholy after the third cup of China tea, and Shiloh looked up with an enchanted smile.

" ' Dog-headed, bosom-eyed, and bird-footed,' " he murmured reflectively, spreading honeycomb on a slice of new bread. " But your image is even stranger, David, and your monster of a more prodigious brood. Is he a riddle, or the beast out of Revelations? "

" He was Jasper," David explained gravely. " Leastways, that was Jasper's manner of speaking about his friends. If I could only remember what part of the country had a name for rearing such unholy critters, we might chart our course for Silver."

" For that matter, there is a vast variety of charts and atlases in the adjoining room," said Shiloh helpfully. " I observed them this morning while you were bargaining with our host, and I was especially attracted by a seventeenth-century map of the Caucasus. But I believe that there is an American geography among them."

"Then we'll lose no time in finding it," David said firmly, finishing his porter in one prodigious gulp. "The missis won't mind your admiring her parlour, since you've already made yourself civil to her, and old man Fernald has often told me I might inspect his library. He's proud of them books of his, and he likes us to take an interest in them. He's all for educating sailors, and some of his books is French."

"Seems as though I'd know the name when I see it," he went on a moment later, in the hushed seclusion of the front room. It was a pretty little chamber, panelled in white; the walls were hung with coloured maps, and upon the chimneypiece, within bubbles of bright glass, bloomed a profusion of delicate wax flowers.

"Now," said Shiloh, depositing a large atlas upon the round mahogany table, "here is an opportunity for refreshing your memory. This map represents the states and territories of your noble land. Here must the monster dwell, among these impenetrable forests or upon these sublime and awful pinnacles of rock."

"H'm," pondered David, knitting his brow. "'Twas mountains where he lived, I'll take my oath, but then, why the alligator? Stands to reason an alligator means water of some sort, a lake or a river. Keep a sharp lookout for a country of hills and rivers, Shiloh, where a man might run like a horse over the upland and dive like a fish into the valley swimming-hole. That's the country where we'll find Silver."

"I wish it might be the Rocky Mountains, David." Shiloh's nose was within an inch of the map, and his voice trembled with eagerness. "As for a river, I cannot be satisfied with a lesser flood than that of the Father of Waters, as the redskin names the Mississippi. Unfortunately that mighty river flows at some considerable distance from the peaks of the Rockies, and we cannot hope to discover a junction of their several immensities. It is a pity, but there are other mountains in America. There are mountains in Virginia, mountains in the Carolinas."

"No, no, it wasn't none of them ladies' names, Shiloh," David protested impatiently, turning over the leaves of the atlas with a determined hand. " It was some fine queer word that I always liked, some Indian word it was, that sounded kind of rough and brave to me. I remember that Jasper used to say this place was once the common hunting-ground of many tribes of Indians, and that even now these savages, driven from it long ago, have a sad lamenting song to remember it by. But the name; what was the name? "

" Was it New Connecticut, or Ohio? " asked Shiloh. " Was it the Illinois? " David shook his head disconsolately, thumbing the broad pages of the book.

" Was it Indiana? " Shiloh persisted. " Was it Indiana, or Kentucky? "

" By jiminy, you've got it! " David leaped from his chair in strong excitement, and slapped Shiloh upon the back with such triumphant violence that the other's slight form swayed like a sapling in a September gale. " Trust you, Shiloh, to strike the very word; you're the smartest chap alive, I do believe, and any-one'd think you'd been raised down East, for you've got proper Yankee brains and gumption! Yes, by cracky, that's it! Kentucky, old Kentucky, Jasper's old Kentucky! Now it's all plain sailing to the port of this Silver girl, and shall we start to-day, Shiloh, for we've a fair wind setting from the sea? We'll tell the captain where we're going, and be off."

" By all means let us go to-day, David," Shiloh answered, closing the atlas with a light gesture of finality. He rose to his feet; the fingers of one long brown hand ruffled his hair into the blown feathers of predestined speed; his other hand sought and found the miniature of Silver. He stared at the shut shagreen case as if it had been an holy talisman.

" ' And the souls of whom thou lovest walk upon the winds with lightness! ' " said Shiloh, and with this surprising remark, glided swiftly from the chamber into the volatile golden airs of noon.

2

" LET us never go west with a deacon again! " cried Shiloh, escaping from the vicinity of the meeting-house with a sigh of relief. The bright-plumed birch-trees closed around his flight, and he turned to David panting a little, and vehement with laughter.

"The privilege of riding in an excessively heavy waggon is hardly worth the dangers of the prayer-meeting, Davy; another minute, and those gloomy portals would have received us with a groan! Here, in the forest, we are safe, but the peril was appalling, and we have need of sustenance to restore our shattered nerves."

From his pocket he drew an apple and a hard-boiled egg, and, seating himself under a lofty festoon of blackberry vines, he proceeded to devour this ingenuous fare with neat celerity, plucking his dessert from the darkly jewelled garlands above his head, and refusing David's flask with exquisitely courteous obstinacy.

"No; a crystal spring must soon be forthcoming, if these sylvan vistas redeem one-tenth of their promissory charms. You'll make a drinker of me yet, I have no doubt, amid the parched and desiccated horrors of the plains, but these lovely honey-flowing hills and valleys quench my thirst with falling dews and deep cool springs of atmosphere. It is enough; such hunger as I still can feel involves the soul alone. But why did we ever deliver our bodies into the hands of the Westchester deacon, Davy? "

"Because he offered us a lift up a long hill, and we was tired, and the sun was hot," said David reasonably, demolishing an apple-core with a thoughtful air. " Truth to tell, he warn't such a bad old codger, Shiloh, if you'd have let him stick to the history of his rheumatiz, and hadn't got him started on religion. Of course its being the Sabbath sort of druv him on, but folks doesn't mostly expect sailors to go to meeting; it ain't natural, and 'twas your being an atheist got him enraged-like, and set on saving you from hell-fire. If I was you, Shiloh," said David with feeling, an imploring look in his small blue eyes, "I'd go sort of easy, leastways with deacons, on that there atheist tack of yours."

"I shall endeavour to amend my conduct according to your kind suggestion, David." Shiloh's docility was complete and disarmingly gentle; he continued to eat blackberries and to smile into the azure distance between the delicate colonnades of birch-trees.

"One thing the old catawampus told us that come in handy for our health, leaving hell out of the question," David went on, "was that news of his about their having yaller fever in New York; we can go round by the ferry to Hobuck, and run no risk of catching it, but 'twas an almighty fortunate providence as sent him along with the tidings. Yaller fever's no laughing matter; I've seen it in New Orleans and the Indies, and I don't want to see it no more. We'll cut across Jersey to Pennsylvania like greased lightning and be in the high Alleghanies, out of harm's way, before you know it, but I should have hated to leave your bones a-bleaching on the Battery, Shiloh."

"Nevertheless, I question whether we are morally justified in avoiding the plague-stricken city," said Shiloh with stubborn meekness. "My own best content would be rather to venture boldly among its cankered multitude, in an attempt to alleviate somewhat the rigour of their agonies. Surely this were the part of that humane and charitable valour by whose impulse we would seek to live! Can we hesitate, when expiring voices call?"

"I can," replied David with commendable decision, "and I'm not a-going to let you catch the yaller fever, Shiloh, not for all the expiring voices in the whole tarnation town of New York. Besides," he added hastily, observing the fanatic brilliance of his companion's widening eyes, "don't go forgetting Silver, for pity's sake; what would Silver do if you were dead, Shiloh?"

"True; she might have some cause to regret my premature demise," Shiloh admitted in tones of marked disappointment. "Yet it seems a base and cowardly dereliction of duty to preserve our own lives at the expense of our brothers' suffering. I cannot forget those hollowed eyes I might have closed in peace, those fevered throats I might have slaked with cold fresh water.

For Silver's ultimate happiness, it must be so, but I shall turn sadly enough towards the wholesome summits of the hills."

"Well, I can't say as I will," said David cheerfully. "I'll be all-fired glad to climb a mountain again, and to get a breath of good pure air after all that stuffy sea-fog."

Ten days of wayfaring had set a deeper tint of bronze upon our young friends' faces, and put a lengthier swing into their step along the sun-powdered road. A smell of September was in the air; Michaelmas daisies and a feathery saffron flower unknown to Shiloh bloomed profusely in the hedges, and a rose-red plume upon a maple confessed to a glitter of frost at daybreak. Nevertheless the weather was incomparably fine; Shiloh had seldom beheld such sunsets, even in Italy, and the winds were perfumed with wild grapes and apples. Indian grass was fragrant in the marshy hollows; scented fern and juniper were fantastically sweet upon the hillsides. All the thickets were ambrosial with blackberries, and the outcroppings of granite among the higher meadows were savage gardens of blueberry-bushes, warm between walls of rock. There were very few mornings when David did not find a handful of mushrooms for breakfast.

They walked in the vivacious early hours, and through the long delicate decline of day; the stillness of noon surrounded them until they lay moveless as flies in amber under the profoundest shade. David was of a piece with the landscape, indigenous to its trees and stones; he was a chip of these blocks of hickory and granite. His colours, too, were manifest in every field; if you had to match his eyes with the blue mountains you need go no farther than apples and pumpkins for the honest brightness of his cheeks and hair. But Shiloh shone exquisitely alien to the earth; you looked for wings upon his heels, and his mercurial rarity was so marked that the very dust silvering his shoulders might have been the eccentric metal of another planet. Yet none the less he appeared the stronger for this singularity; he had shed lassitude and dejection like an effete and heavy mantle flung from tameless speed. And, although his eyes were still the stars of a wilder heaven, he was brown and ruddy as David; his tints were fiercer, partaking of the subtlety of flame, and his feet burnt up the long white miles like magic.

On rainy nights they found a tavern, if no hospitable barn threw wide its hay-loft, but such nights were happily infrequent, and their customary slumbers were sheltered by ricks and the woven trellises of trees. Sun-warmed hay is notoriously sweet, and while few leaves had fallen, David covered the bare ground with balsam boughs and springy heaps of fern, and they slept soft enough even in the forest. The hour before dawn was cold; David burrowed deeper into his rustic couch, and if Shiloh woke shivering, he had only to lift his eyes to the sunrise to be kindled into divinity again.

Besides the seasonable fruits of the earth, bread and cheese and beer were cheap at every tavern; on frosty evenings David might sup on ham and johnny-cake, and Shiloh indulge a fancy for a well-peppered mutton-chop.

"It is an infallible remedy for muscular fatigue," he would say gravely. "I had the hint from Peacock, years ago, and it has stood me in good stead under a variety of circumstances." And he would call for blueberry pie and pineapple cheese to follow in a fashion which, for him, was well-nigh imperious.

That Sunday afternoon, as the ferry carried them towards the Jersey shore, they both confessed to a tender sadness in abandoning New England.

"It's home to me," said David. "Though Maine's the top-notch part of it, Connecticut ain't so bad. Even wooden nutmegs taste kind of good on custard pies."

"It is a fair land, New England," said Shiloh sighing, "and the cradle of the infant Liberty." He dashed a tear from his eye, moved perhaps by high imaginings of freedom, and perhaps by the thought of his own child.

3

IN the quiet town of Philadelphia a Quaker boarding-house received the two companions; the good woman who kept it had been upon the point of refusing lodging to the dusty ragged sailors, when a glance from Shiloh's large blue eyes had effectually softened her heart, and wrought the miracle of much broadcloth and fine linen. Upon the brick pavement of Mulberry Street a pretty lady in a leghorn bonnet and a white merino shawl had smiled at the pair; a kindly shopkeeper, lounging under his great striped awning, had offered them hot cinnamon buns and coffee at the price of a penny roll. The city seemed a pleasant place in which to linger, and Shiloh would fain have seen the celebrated waterworks at Fair Mount, with their catalpa trees and marble naiad, but the sultry weather and the advancing season alike suggested haste, and David advised an immediate flight into the cooler hills.

"No use dodging yaller fever to pick up malairy here," he said, and the friends went forth into a region of stone farmhouses and rolling meadows.

"Blow the man down!" sang David a little later, in the teeth of the west wind, but Shiloh sang another song, of his own making, as he sped like the shadow of a cloud across the golden land.

"You could do your thirty miles a day regular even on a corduroy road, I truly believe," said David admiringly. "Flying Shiloh; that's what I call you to myself. Like a ship, you are, close-hauled upon the gale; I do admire to see you go so fast and nimble, even when I'm near breaking my neck to keep up with you."

The length and agility of Shiloh's legs, and David's dogged determination not to allow the lateral rolling of his own step to interfere with the general pace, had indeed resulted in a very fair rate of speed for the journey. Trusting to shoe-leather and human sinew, the pair had proceeded almost as rapidly as if they drove a light buggy or shandrydan, and although they accepted with gratitude an occasional lift from a friendly waggoner, such interludes were rather in the nature of delays, for the companions could easily outwalk any brace of cart-horses hitched to a lumbering van. By the time they crossed from Pennsylvania into Maryland they had found themselves under the necessity of purchasing new hobnailed boots, but their muscles were in superb condition, and they had learned to sleep peacefully under the hood of the heaviest waggon that ever rattled over rocky streams or stirred the thunders upon covered bridges.

They arrived in Cumberland excessively ragged and brown; their spirits were buoyant as the bright autumnal air, and their bodies had hardened into thin contrivances of fiddle-strings and steel. They had managed, by Sabbath-breaking and audacity, to make nearly seventy-five miles for every three days of their pilgrimage.

"Can't go lickety-split up them mountains like you'd want to, Shiloh," said David, eyeing the sober beginnings of the great National Road. "Mebbe we can't even beat the stage-coach into Wheeling, unless we sprout wings like a turkey-buzzard."

"Oh, stage-coaches be blowed!" cried Shiloh robustly; association with David had enriched his vocabulary with several vigorous expletives. "Stage-coaches are for old women suffering from elephantiasis and a plague of bandboxes; we need not concern ourselves with such chimæras. My only regret is that we must descend to the level of a common steamboat on the Ohio, instead of continuing this wild free existence in an Indian canoe or pinnace, along the lucent waters of *la belle Rivière*."

September among the Alleghany hills wore deep transparent tints of auburn and amber, veiled in azure haze; the maples and the sumachs showed the colours of roses, and Shiloh went drunk with loveliness and new cider. The nights were delicately chill, but the sunburnt days were hot and sweet at the core, and wholesome as apples. Sometimes a deep green Pennsylvanian valley invited them to slumber beside a chuckling mill-wheel or a spring-house comfortable with cream; sometimes a level meadow in Virginia lay above the evening clouds, hiding a stone cottage bright with candlelight and firelight. There were breakfasts of coddled eggs and waffle cakes, and suppers of wild turkey and mountain venison. The land flowed with milk and melted butter and honey in the comb.

Shiloh was happy, taking no thought even for the most auspicious morrow, vivid and careless as the wind itself. The money that the captain had given him seemed inexhaustible, because the more earnestly he pressed it upon the farmer's wife or the country storekeeper, the more darkly and profoundly must his blue eyes speak to their inmost hearts with a peculiar spiritual grace, so that they were constrained to refuse payment

for their hospitality. And not infrequently he would draw forth
his little books and read to them before the fire, while David
chopped kindling by lantern-light in the back yard, or helped the
hired man with the milking.

The books which he had bought in Boston were ever in his
hands; he attained a high degree of proficiency in perusing them
while he walked, without in the least moderating the rapidity
of his step, and David soon became familiar with the sublime
mysterious rhythm of certain scenes from Sophocles, owing to
Shiloh's habit of declaiming them aloud upon the summits of the
loftier Appalachian hills.

4

" GOLDARN it, Shiloh, you're enough to make a sea-cow laugh,"
cried David one radiant afternoon, as the two descended into
the cool emerald depths of a mountain valley. A slight eccentricity was indeed observable in his companion's appearance;
the bright bronze column of Shiloh's throat emerged from the
tattered collar of his blue cotton shirt, his pantaloons were secured about his slender waist by part of an old saddle-girth, and
his fantastic locks were crowned by a wreath of scarlet Virginia
creeper. He seemed half fawn, half panther in his grace and
savagery.

The ashen-coloured peaks above them were covered with
a profusion of azalea and rhododendron bushes, intermixed with
the lacquered viridian gloss of cedar and hemlock, and the coppery luxuriance of oak and beech. A variety of mosses and creep-
ing plants carpeted the ground with woven leaves, and fruits of
blue and crimson dangling from the wild vine and the brier
rose were lovelier than flowers. Below, the clear waters of the
Monongahela, fringed by romantic piles of rock, mirrored a
golden picture of the scene.

A shadowed pool lay deep under the shelter of a cliff; Shiloh
cast his dusty garments from him with cries of joy, and leapt
into the cold revivifying stream. Afterwards he sat naked upon
a broad black stone, reading Herodotus in the waning rosy light.

" A practice," said Shiloh, " excessively refreshing in the hot weather." And presently he laid down his book, and began to twist a bit of brown paper into the mimic likeness of a boat, whose sail was a gossamer skeleton leaf.

"You're real handy at that, Shiloh," David commented admiringly. He drew forth his own jack-knife, and busied himself about the manufacture of a very superior type of willow whistle. "Silly, for two grown men," grinned David, slipping a section of pith from the smooth willow bark with exquisite precision. He put the whistle to his lips and blew one long shrill note.

"A voice," murmured Shiloh dreamily, "heard from some Pythian cavern in the solitudes where Delphi stood. Your flute is extraordinarily Hellenic, Davy. By its music we are transported to the banks of Peneus, and linger under the crags of Tempe, and see the water-lilies floating on the stream. We are with Plato by old Ilissus, under the sacred plane-tree among the sweet scent of flowering sallows, and above there is the nightingale of Sophocles in the ivy of the pine, who is watching the sunset so that it may dare to sing."

"That there's a catbird," said David, "and this here's not a flute but a plain whistle. Still, you do talk most beautiful, Shiloh, and the sound of them words is like bees around a locust-tree at noonday. I do admire to hear them Greek names; tell me some more, out of that old boy Hummer, and a hummer he was, I reckon, in his own time, too."

Thereupon Shiloh, sitting naked like an image of bronze above the golden pool, subdued his voice into the whispering of waves among sea-weed, and stretched it taut into the very cord of Apollo's bow, which vibrated and sang. And David listened entranced, unmoving save when now and again he blew a single note, clearer and shriller than a bird's, upon his willow whistle.

A small moon rose over the treetops; the night was warm, and the tranquillity of the forest was unbroken below the falling dew; the pool turned slowly from gold to silver under the moon, and a tender wind stirred the water into flakes of brightness.

Suddenly, on the extremest margin of the farther bank, a dim ethereal figure was visible in opalescent mist; the figure was slight and wavering, and its floating garments were without colour and apparently without substance.

"By golly, it's a girl," cried David, "and she's a-going to jump into the river if we don't get to her in double quick time. Scramble over them stones, Shiloh, as lively as ever you can, and I'll swim to her in a jiffy."

He was already kicking off his heavy boots, when the more impetuous Shiloh passed him like a long bronze javelin flung into the broken pool, and in another instant David saw him attain the opposite bank and emerge dripping with moonlight upon its terraced rocks.

"So it done some good my chucking him head-first into the Susquehanna," thought David as he dived. "I knew I could teach him to swim, if he only give me a chance, and he struck out real pretty across that creek."

Meanwhile Shiloh had gained the side of the young girl; he stood before her charmingly unconscious that his only garment was a glamour of silvery light, and his eyes were grave and luminous with solicitude.

"Please do not think me impertinent if I assume that you are in distress, and so inquire," said Shiloh with a slight chivalric bow, "whether or no I may have the felicity of assisting you."

The young girl fixed her gaze upon Shiloh's large and radiant eyes; the element of the unconventional in his appearance doubtless for this reason escaped her notice, and she spoke without surprise, in a voice of considerable emotion.

"Pappy tried to choke me 'cause the hoe-cake wasn't crisp," said the young girl, and began to weep bitterly, covering her face with a pair of small pale hands.

Her face, when at last she lifted it, was also small and pale; a quantity of soft dark hair surrounded it with shadow, under which the grey glimmer of enormous eyes was evident through tears. She appeared to be about fifteen years old; her beauty was immature and fragile, but exquisitely refined. She was no more than skin and bone, but the delicate texture of the one and the graceful proportions of the other made them sweet as the stem and petals of a slender flower. A gown of thin white muslin, frosted by moonlight, showed fresh and pure in spite of several fantastic patches and rents; her little feet were bare among the cold green tendrils of the ground pine, and as she wept she shivered like a silver leaf.

"For the land's sake, Shiloh, take these if you're a-going to talk to a lady," David cried in an agony of shyness, hastily divesting himself of his own pantaloons and diving back into the pool. The chilly water cooled his blushes, and Shiloh calmly proceeded to don the borrowed garment, meanwhile continuing to address the weeping girl in tones of affectionate and consoling warmth.

"You must really stop crying, my dear young lady, and tell me more about your cruel parent," he said at last, fastening his belt with a business-like air, and hanging a magnificent garland of Virginia creeper around his gleaming shoulders in lieu of a shirt. "While David and I are near you, no man dare lay a finger upon your safety, and if you will but confide in me as a friend, I feel sure that I shall be able to relieve your immediate melancholy." And he took her hand between his own beautiful strong brown hands.

5

"Stranger," said the child, in a soft little drawling voice, which was at once illiterate and delightful, "if you don't mind I'd sort of like to sit down on that big log, and lean against the chinaberry tree, for I've got a heap of queer things to tell you, and Pappy shaked me so that I'm all of a tremble. They's been powerful dark doings to-night down to Pappy's cabin, and even now that he's rode off to the Dutchman's tavern at Little Washington I don't hardly dare to breathe above a whisper. Yes, I'll be right glad for you to hold my hand, for I'm cold as early morning and scairt as a rabbit."

Shiloh, with his air of romantic courtesy, led the child ceremoniously towards the mossy log; they seated themselves upon its crumbling surface, and as the china-berry tree was hard and narrow, Shiloh's shoulder seemed a more natural resting-place for his companion's curly head. She settled herself thus with a sigh of tired contentment, closing her eyes, upon whose fringes bright tears still glittered in the moonlight.

"My name . . ." began the child, in her soft slow drawl, but Shiloh gently interrupted her.

"Is Silver; surely it is Silver, and we have found you by enchantment," he said tenderly, raising her hand to his lips.

"No, sir; I'm mighty sorry, but my name is Melissa, Melissa Daingerfield," said the child apologetically. "Pappy comes from a grand family, kin to all the quality in Virginia, but he's shiftless, is Pappy, and he won't work when he's in liquor. Ma was a lady, a lovely lady like a lily as I remember her, but he bruk her with his cruel ways, and she fell down into the dust and died, jest like a lily that you've trod into the dust. I was only seven years old when she died; I went with her into the green yard and we laid down in the shade of the laurels; she couldn't bear to stay in the cabin, 'cause it was full of smoke and dust and smashed whisky bottles, and she smiled at the sun between the green laurels, and pretty soon I knew she was dead. I kissed her, and I cried, and Pappy come raging and swearing into the yard and looked down at us both, and then he flung hisself on the ground beside Ma and cried fit to break his heart for a long while, but when I put out my hand to comfort him he pushed me away and cursed me with an awful curse. Since that day he's always hated me, and he's been powerful unkind to me for seven weary years. Oh, sir, I beg as you will help me, for Pappy's a bloody-minded man when he's been drinking, and I'm scairt most to death that he'll murder me some day."

During this tragic narrative Shiloh's countenance had become pale with horror, and his eyes appeared supernaturally large, and brilliant with agitated light. His sensitive and passionate nature was ever profoundly moved by the thought of cruelty, and now he had difficulty in commanding his voice even to a shaken murmur of pity and reverential affection.

"Did you but hear her, David," he demanded in a firmer tone, turning to his friend, and at the same time clasping the child Melissa more closely to his furiously beating heart, "and do you stand by unmoved by this recital of unprecedented suffering, or is your soul convulsed with indignation like my own?"

David had returned by way of the slippery rocks, and waited in respectful silence at some little distance from the others. He wore Shiloh's pantaloons and his own shirt, and carried Shiloh's shirt carefully over his arm.

"I reckon I ain't exactly what you might call unmoved, Shiloh," he protested with considerable heat, kicking violently at the inoffensive ground. "In fact, if this young lady will give me her kind permission, I'm moved to go to Little Washington and wallop her parent good and plenty no later than to-night. The infernal swine, if I may say so, of course meaning no discourtesy, to lay his dirty hand on a pretty little slip of a thing like her, God blast him, and I hope you'll excuse me, Miss, as he's your father, but I never, no I never in all my born days heard tell of such wickedness before, and her with no mother, and such beautiful hair, and no man could bear it calmly without busting loose, and oh, damn, damn, damn!"

With which unwonted ebullition of feeling David subsided once more into silence, broken only by an occasional cough or a suspicious snuffle. Shiloh made no attempt to conceal his tumultuous emotion, and tears shone in the profundity of his eyes as he turned again to Melissa.

"You see," he said with a reassuring smile, "you see, my dear child, that you have two very brave champions, who will nevertheless do nothing to alarm you."

"I sure is glad to hear you say so, stranger," Melissa answered solemnly, "for Pappy kin break you gentlemen like a couple of sticks of kindling if you rouses him to wrath. Pappy kin spit further, curse worser, and hit heavier than any other man around these parts, and I don't want him to bust your head nor black your handsome eyes for you."

To Shiloh's amazement, a very true pride was apparent in Melissa's words, and she raised her curly locks from his shoulder and faced him with a flashing look of defiance.

"Do not appeal to my cowardice, my dear," he said rather haughtily. "It is at best an uncertain quantity." The irony in his voice was lost upon the child, but she saw that he was hurt, and caught at his hand in a gesture of humility.

"I asks your pardon, stranger, if I spoke hasty," she whispered, bending her head against his breast. "I'm kind of fond of Pappy, and it riled me to hear you talk of champeens like you was pugilists and Pappy jest nobody at all, him that has knocked out heavyweights from Kentuck and Missoura. I reckon you can't fix a man's hog-meat and mush fer seven years without gitting mighty attached to him, spite of being banged about a bit when the corn liquor's extry powerful in his sperrit. Forgive me; it's jest family pride and filial vanity, I reckon, but Pappy's a gentleman born, and you should see him lift my grandaddy's old flintlock musket jest by sticking one finger into the barr'l of it! "

"You are a darling child, and a very loyal daughter," said Shiloh, touched to the soul by the girl's simplicity. " But you know you really must not run about the country at night attempting to drown yourself; I shall never have a moment's peace of mind if you do not promise me to desist. Furthermore, I shall consider your future as my especial care; I must lose no time in arranging for a suitable education for one of your undoubted talents, and your material welfare must be secured immediately. Your charm and fragility demand certain refinements; true taste hires not the pale drudge luxury, I admit, but you need a sufficiency of simple food and a pair of pretty slippers at once."

At these words, spoken with exquisite sympathy and respect, Melissa clapped her little hands in ingenuous delight.

"Oh, glory, glory! " she cried, jumping to her feet and executing an impromptu saraband upon the ground pine. "They's the beautifulest slippers in Wheeling, like Miss Marianna Grimes wore at her wedding, and that's no more'n twenty miles away, and we kin walk it in one day, I reckon! Oh, glory hallelujah, stranger, I thanks you with all my heart for them kind sentiments, and mebbe you kin knock Pappy out if you tries hard enough, and oh, you are the generousest gentleman in all the world, and I love you! "

It was impossible to help laughing at her pleasure, and yet her pleasure was curiously pathetic. David made a peculiar grunting sound; Shiloh's large eyes brimmed alike with tears and laughter, as he received a glancing kiss of gratitude upon the tips of his fingers.

"One moment, my dear friend," he said to David, drawing him aside into the shadow of the china-berry tree. "The thing I am about to propose may in all probability surprise you, since it runs counter to my declared convictions, yet I believe that for once instinct must prompt a charitable action, setting logic at defiance. Much as I abominate the galling customary chain of matrimony, I am nevertheless aware that a journey to Wheeling in our company might involve Melissa in embarrassments both painful and humiliating, unless one of us were in a position to protect her from flagitious calumnies and insulting abuse. I, as you know, am already wedded, but you are fortunately free; in brief, had you not better marry the poor child? "

"Who? Me?" cried David in sincere alarm. "Now, Shiloh, you're never a-going to make me get married just for the sake of buying a girl a pair of slippers! That's plumb plain foolishness, that is, as you'd know if the moon wasn't shining and Melissa didn't have such pretty curls. Besides, I'm already half promised to little Bianca over in Leghorn, what with walking out with her Sundays, and even lambasting Jasper all on account of her, and then," David concluded, blushing furiously the while, " and then, Shiloh, you see there's always Silver."

Shiloh, his face pale as a dawn of moonlight in the shadow of the china-berry tree, remained for a long moment without answering; his voice, when at last it broke the silence, was noticeably strained and weary.

"True, David," he said gently. "There is, indeed, always Silver; I had not forgotten, but she shines to me ever as a holy sister, and I suppose I am a fool. I had not perceived, I had not imagined, that you felt . . . but no matter, I will speak no more of this madness. I am sorry; the fault is my incurable simplicity. Help me now to contrive some more pragmatic scheme, serviceable to employ for the relief of this young creature, fallen so strangely, and as it were from the clouds, upon our casual mercies."

David, feeling himself touched upon the tenderest strings of his heart, blushed more hotly than before, and stammered in confusion.

"Oh, well, I guess we can manage somehow without marrying her, Shiloh, though I have no wish to treat the poor thing mean, nor be stingy with our money, if it comes to that. We ain't spent hardly anything lately, what with folks along the road being so hospitable and open-handed, and I should calculate as we might be able to spare her five dollars anyway, even if we can't have the fun of knocking down that rotten father of hers and stamping on his ugly head, like I'd admire to do. And mebbe we can find some kind lady hereabouts as'll bring the child up like a Christian, and see that she has shoes and stockings and her hair in decent braids. The Lord knows I don't want to desert a fellow mortal who's in trouble, but marry her I won't, and that's final," said David with emphasis.

"My dear David, let us say no more about it, I beseech you," Shiloh replied in a low pained voice. "Above all, we must not allow Melissa herself to overhear our discussion; imagine the mortification of a sensitive spirit under such circumstances! Melissa, my child," he continued, turning to the girl his most winning look of gallantry, "since you are to accompany us to Wheeling, have you no relatives in that town who may, while unluckily depriving us of the joys of your society, nevertheless supply a more fitting refuge to your inevitable fatigue than our poor though devoted efforts can achieve?"

Melissa laughed merrily, and reseated herself upon the log, curling up her little bare feet under the tattered ruffle of her muslin gown.

"Stranger, you do talk a heap of furrin words, don't you? I reckon I knows pretty well what you're trying to say, all the same, Ma having spoke French something beautiful, and Pappy hisself being a powerful fine scholar when he's sober. So I answers you, yes; I've an own aunt in Wheeling, my Ma's second sister, only I've never laid eyes on her along of Pappy swearing to murder me cruel if I did, but Aunt Juliana her name is, and she's a Sunday-school teacher in the First Methodist Church!"

"Dear me," said Shiloh regretfully, "I am indeed sorry to hear you say so; I should have preferred a secular schoolmistress for the instruction of youth. However, all now depends upon this lady's personal character, and since we have no cause to credit aught but good of your beloved mother's close relative, we must hope for the best. To-morrow we go to Wheeling; it shall be my dearest care to place you unharmed under the protection of this excellent female. Meanwhile I suppose we must part until the morning; the forest will afford sufficient shelter to David and myself, and doubtless your father's cabin may serve as your asylum for a single night."

"Oh, Lordy, yes," Melissa answered cheerfully, "I reckon I shan't take no harm from another night under Pappy's roof, though if he catched you there he'd kill you same as he would a fly. But he don't never leave the Dutchman's tavern till daybreak, and you-all had better come along home with me and git a bite of corn-dodger and mebbe a mite of bacon. Plenty of clabber there is, too, and liquor for them as likes it. Then you can sleep in the corn-crib, and be ready to start at sun-up, before ever Pappy gits back from Little Washington."

"Don't sound extra safe to me," said David cautiously. "But then again, I'm goldarned hungry. Guess we might as well go with the young lady and get a proper supper; I'd rather risk having a skinful of buckshot than starve to death, and we had nothing but apples at noon. Only, I never could abide clabber, and the liquor's real good in these parts," he concluded plaintively, with a glance at Shiloh.

6

HALF an hour later the three were seated about a square pine table in Mr. Daingerfield's cabin; a fire of oak logs had smouldered into rosy ashes upon the hearth, where several dishes of coarse blue and grey crockery companionably steamed. The table was spread with a clean chequered cloth, and upon this was set a generous platter of fried pork, a pint bowl of apple sauce and another of pickles, and a vast pile of corn-dodgers. There was also a saucer of fresh butter, two pitchers filled respectively with buttermilk and new cider, and a large honeycomb. A water-bucket and a jug of whisky were placed with admirable impartiality side by side upon a bench in the corner of the room.

"I don't generally git time to eat," said Melissa happily, with her mouth full of honey and corn-dodger, "'cept when Pappy goes off on a bust, and then I'm mostly so lonely that I cries all night and hasn't the heart even to swallow a bite of mush. Now this is mighty different; it does me good to see you-all tuck in your victuals, and I could sing for joy to see your faces a-smiling at me so kind and grateful-like. Oh, glory be to God, I'm so joy-ful that I could fall down on my knees and pray, 'cause I've got two loving friends, and I'm going to Wheeling to visit my aunty, and buy me a pair of prunella shoes!"

A tallow candle stuck in a green glass bottle illuminated the table; by its light Melissa appeared lovelier than ever, with vivid cheeks and small vermilion lips. The grey of her enormous eyes was shot with emerald and amber, in a complicated maze of colour, and Shiloh thought of her honey-sounding name, and wondered whether Silver's eyes were hazel or pure brown, like the patterned eyes upon the wings of moths. And he remembered another pair of hazel eyes, which might even now be mournful by the shores of the Gulf of Spezzia, and he sighed profoundly, above his cup of new cider. He did not perceive that the girl was watch-ing his own face, his own luminous eyes, with an adoring con-centration, and he flushed shyly when she said good-night to him, standing on tiptoe and lifting her mouth to be kissed as if she had been a child of seven years.

"I reckon I like you best, Mr. Shiloh," she whispered. "David's a right sweet boy, and I wish he was my brother, but they's some-thing about you I love with all my heart. I reckon it's your eyes, Mr. Shiloh; you've got powerful pretty eyes."

"Good-night, Melissa," said Shiloh, kissing her as gently as if she had been a child of seven years. "Please believe that I love you too, and that I shall endeavour to serve you, by virtue of that love." And he went very softly from the house, without another word or backward glance, and the small silver moon, which hung over the western hills, was like an aureole about his head as he departed.

"Good-night, Miss Melissa," said David, following him, "and thank you for an elegant supper, not to mention the finest drink of corn whisky as I've had in Virginia." And he too disappeared into the night, fading as a glimmer of yellow hair and the sound of a strong young voice singing "Blow the man down."

The two went at once to the corn-crib; it was quite dry and comfortable, and within five minutes they were both deep in dreamless slumbers upon rustling mattresses of corn-stalks. The moon dropped down behind the hills, and in the darkened night their tranquillity was unbroken even by the shadow of a dream.

Melissa said her prayers as usual, to her mother's portrait, which hung in an obscure corner out of reach of Mr. Daingerfield's familiar wrath, with a pink calico curtain artfully disposed over its pensive countenance. Then she curled herself up in her little low truckle-bed, and at first she wept, because Mr. Shiloh had such powerful pretty eyes, but at last she fell asleep smiling, because in the morning she was going to Wheeling, to buy her a pair of prunella shoes.

7

THE MORNING dawned cold and rainy; an equinoctial gale seemed to smell of the sea even among these inland hills, and the twenty miles to Wheeling stretched sinister and clammy with mud under the inundation of the clouds. Melissa waked her two friends at five o'clock; in the pale unnatural light her small face glimmered like a sick pearl, and she appeared unsubstantial as the dim etheric double of the jocund creature who had laughed over the supper-table. Even David felt a chilly stiffness in his magnificent sinews, and Shiloh, although he would not for the world have mentioned the circumstance, was suffering from a slight attack of neuralgia in the left temple. Nevertheless, they greeted each other with affectionate cheerfulness, in which a faintly plaintive quality was mingled, and the sight of a superb fire leaping upon the cabin hearth warmed them all three into smiles again.

"They's roasted eggs in them ashes, and coffee in the big tin pot," said Melissa quickly. "And now, gentlemen, I'm afeared we must hurry jest a mite, so's to be gone afore Pappy gits back from Little Washington. I wish I could 'a' cooked you a sure-enough breakfast, with wheat bread and chicken fixings, but mebbe I kin do that when I gits to my aunty's house. Make out the best you can with hoe-cake and hot coffee; they's a cupful of cream on the table. You look kind of froze, Mr. Shiloh, so sit down by the fire and warm yourself while I bring you your breakfast. David, put another log on the fire so as Mr. Shiloh kin warm hisself nice and comfortable while he drinks his coffee."

Melissa was attired in a man's drab woolen greatcoat, worn over a short frock of faded indigo and yellow homespun; even these shabby garments failed to conceal her delicate prettiness, but she looked the most pathetic of orphans as she trotted about the cabin, her little bare feet blue with cold against the hard clay floor. Shiloh stared ruefully at his own stout shoes; at last he took them off and set them side by side upon the hearth. Now Shiloh had beautiful narrow feet like an Indian's, but he was six feet tall and his shoes had been made by a country cobbler, who was incidentally a Dutchman. The shoes seemed absurdly large ever to be laced over Shiloh's aristocratic insteps; as a substitute for the prunella slippers they were preposterous.

"Do you think," asked Shiloh, in a humble, doubting voice, "that you could possibly wear my shoes, little Melissa? I should say Cinderella, for the notion is obviously farcical, now that I observe the minute proportions of your toes, and yet I cannot reconcile my mind to the prospect of miles of mud, with the winds of autumn howling about your slender unprotected ankles. Will you be so good as at least to make the attempt, out of the charitable kindness of your heart?" And he stooped and lifted the shoes from the stone hearth, as though they had been some novel form of sacrifice and he the acolyte of a new religion.

"Oh, Mr. Shiloh, indeed and indeed I couldn't!" cried Melissa in sincere distress, falling to her knees by his side; her spirit laid oblations counter to his upon the fire-warmed stone, and she took the shoes very firmly from him and placed them before him on the hearth. He saw to his amazement that she was crying.

"It's not that they's a bit too big," she protested through her tears. "They's mighty fine shoes, Mr. Shiloh, a heap too fine for me. Put 'em on quick, Mr. Shiloh, and I'll lace 'em up for you; please let me lace 'em up for you! I love you, Mr. Shiloh, and I couldn't let you go barefoot in the rain!"

"If you refuse to wear the shoes, Melissa, I certainly shall not do so," Shiloh answered with gentle obstinacy, preparing to sling the clumsy contrivances around his neck by their buckskin laces. The two gazed at one another, drowned in mutual glances of admiration, and deadlocked in a stubborn self-denial.

"Can't you see the poor girl could never wear them things,

Shiloh?" David demanded with some impatience. "I'd be happy to lend her mine, for the matter of that, but look at the size of the brutes; fit for a giant. Seven-league boots they may be, but they weren't cobbled on a lady's last. Now put on your own like a sensible fellow, and we'll steer clear of this Daingerfield before he comes a-hollering after our blood for breakfast."

"You're a gentleman, Mr. Shiloh, but I'm jest a child that's used to running barefoot," cried Melissa, skipping along the road with rain-drops in her curly hair. She had tied up her slender hoard of treasures in a bright silk handkerchief, and it now dangled from Shiloh's stick beside a bandanna heavy with Greek tragedies and Albemarle pippins. She had left her father's great-coat behind, and her gown was kilted about her little waist with a leather thong. Hot coffee and exercise had warmed them all to merriment, and Melissa was as playful as a kitten and as innocent as a fleecy lamb.

She proved to be, as Shiloh prettily remarked, a heaven-born traveller; her small curvetting feet had no difficulty in keeping up with his long strides, even upon the ascending slopes of hills, or along their steep and perilous declivities.

"I'll allow the girl is goldarned nimble; nimble as a squirrel!" said David, and Shiloh laughed and spoke of the Acroceraunian mountains.

Melissa talked very little, but she sang a vast variety of hymns, in a small soprano voice in which the notes were clear and cool and pure as drops of rain.

> "God moves in a mysterious way,
> His wonders to perform;
> He plants his footsteps in the sea,
> And rides upon the storm."

Thus Melissa sang upon the mountain-tops, and as she sang she fixed her eyes upon Shiloh's countenance, while Shiloh in his turn stared radiantly into the valleys of the west, where the clouds were already lifting.

8

PRESENTLY the land began to fall away into rolling meadows and low hills; the road crossed a long succession of stone bridges, and there were farmhouses among the trees by the stream. They halted at noon before the door of a modest dwelling, whose mistress refused payment for a pitcher of milk and a bowl of pickled peaches. The travellers' pockets were full of cold bacon and corn-bread, and they made a sufficient if somewhat chilly meal under the shelter of an enormous apple-tree. When Shiloh returned the empty bowl and pitcher to the farmwife, she looked at him pityingly and offered him a silver quarter and a tin cup of whisky, both of which benefits he courteously declined.

The rain had now ceased, and as the afternoon lengthened the sun emerged from watery mists, coloured in the softest tints of rose and amber; a rainbow spanned the opposite heaven with an arch of flame. The hearts of the three friends were simultaneously lightened and infused by hope, and they paused upon a broad stone bridge to rest for a moment, and to admire the opalescent clouds reflected in the stream, which with the sky itself formed the two hemispheres of a circle of living pearl. Toward the west lay Wheeling, invisible as yet, but imagined vividly as a cluster of white spires and evening lamps, inviting the weary to repose.

Presently the hoof-beats of a horse were loudly audible along the road whence they had come, and Melissa clutched at Shiloh's hand in instinctive alarm, and trembled in some quick prevision of despair.

" It's Pappy; I knows it's Pappy," she breathed shudderingly, pale as the smallest dying rain-cloud in the sky. " He's borrowed Jesse Bryan's horse and he's a-chasing us with murder in his heart. I knowed it was too beautiful to last, Mr. Shiloh; to-day's been jest a dream to me, walking with you and David in the peaceful rain, and seeing the face of my Redeemer upon the high hills, and the rainbow, and the promised land. Now I reckon I've got to go back to Pappy's cabin, and git more beatings than ever because I tried to run away. Good-bye, Mr. Shiloh, my darling

Mr. Shiloh, and now run, run for your life, before Pappy catches you and kills you!"

Shiloh and David did not move; they stood leaning upon the low stone parapet of the bridge in attitudes of admirable composure, and only a faint reflection of Melissa's extreme pallor was apparent upon their faces. Shiloh's eyes were very bright; David had set his lips into a grim Puritan line; they stared along the muddy road, and each one hoped that the other could not hear the hurried beating of his heart.

Suddenly a horseman appeared around the turn of the road; he was bent forward over the neck of an iron-grey horse, and he rode as if for a wager, madly, and with loud and profane exhortations to his steed; he wore a red shirt, and his streaming sable hair was uncovered to the wind.

"It's Pappy; O sweet Jesus, help us, 'cause it's Pappy sure enough!" cried Melissa, collapsing in a little heap against the coping of the bridge, and hiding her eyes with her shaking hands.

At this instant the rider perceived them; he reined in his horse with a violent imprecation, and leapt to the ground beside the panting animal. Steam rose in wreaths into the moist air; the horse hung his head, labouring for breath, but the man showed no evidences of exhaustion, and he faced the two friends with a savage sneering laugh.

"So," he drawled in a husky voice, which was nevertheless that of an educated man, " you gentlemen have seen fit to run off with my little girl, have you? I presume you know the penalty for that in the great state of Virginia; I presume you know that I am about to shoot you down like the curs you are, unless you can convince me of your honourable intentions. Now pray explain yourselves, and be quick about it, for by heaven you have neither of you many minutes to survive if you've harmed a hair of this little angel's head. Image of her sainted mother, she is, and the sweet snow-apple of her father's eye! Now, sirs, I am waiting, as your most impartial judge, but, I have a shrewd suspicion, as your righteous executioner to boot."

He drew a gigantic pistol from his holster, cocked it, and stood regarding Shiloh and David with a cold distasteful stare. Mr. Daingerfield was a singularly handsome man; he had a fine thin aquiline nose, a quantity of raven-black hair, and a pair of magnificent grey eyes set under beetling brows. It was not difficult to believe that the best blood of Virginia informed the arteries of his splendid frame, but his temper appeared to be irascible, and he had the unfortunate habit of picking his glittering white teeth with his pocket-knife. He now produced this instrument, employing it in the manner described; Shiloh watched him in a species of sinister fascination, and for fully a minute there was no sound save the plashing of water under the little bridge.

" Well, speak up, sir, or you will compel me to shoot you unheard! " said Mr. Daingerfield irritably, caressing the trigger of the pistol with an absent-minded touch.

" My dear Mr. Daingerfield," began Shiloh politely, " I must emphatically assure you that you have mistaken our intentions. We are not curs; my natural resentment at this insulting term must yield to the respect in which I hold a father's sacred anxiety as to the welfare of his child, but I repeat, you have mistaken our intentions. Only the desire to be of service to this young lady has led us to accompany her to Wheeling, and it is our purpose to place her under the protection of a superior female relative when once our journey is accomplished."

" Then am I to understand that your purpose was not matrimonial? " Mr. Daingerfield inquired with perfidious calm; Melissa, peeping from between her cold fingers, saw his smile, and the manner in which he softly teetered back and forth on his toes, and she knew the peril imminent in the pistol-barrel.

" To my profound regret, I could not contemplate such felicity," said Shiloh with trusting candour. " You see, I happen to be already married."

In the next instant, three several events providentially conspired to save Shiloh from annihilation: Mr. Daingerfield's pistol flashed in the pan, Melissa rose from her apparent swoon and flung herself like a frail shield upon Shiloh's bosom, and David cleared his throat and spoke with portentous solemnity.

" It's me as wants to marry your daughter, sir," he said deferentially, turning his varnished hat in his broad muscular hands, and looking a veritable model of bashful and deserving love. " My friend here is just giving us the pleasure of his company as far as

Wheeling, so as to make it more seemly-like for Melissa and me until we get to Miss Juliana's. Melissa took a fancy to buy her wedding-dress in town, and she thought as how her aunt could advise her about biases and ruchings and such-like fal-lals, her being young, and unlearned in these matters same as me. I hope, sir, as you'll forgive us being a bit hot-headed and impatient, and not waiting for you to come back from Little Washington. Mebbe you'll come along with us now, sir, and give us your blessing when the minister of the First Methodist Church splices us up right and tight and proper to-morrow morning; we'd admire to have your blessing, Mr. Daingerfield, on our wedding-day."

Mr. Daingerfield appeared considerably mollified by this speech; nevertheless he looked rather regretfully at the slim aristocratic figure of Shiloh, who seemed to him better suited to any romantic rôle, whether of seducer or bridegroom, than the earthier David. Within the corded veins of his forehead the blood of the Daingerfields throbbed protestingly, but David was strong and comely and well-formed, and Mr. Daingerfield resigned himself to a plebeian son-in-law with a sigh of appreciation for an honest workingman's usefulness in the hog-pen and the corn-patch.

"I suppose you realize that you are scarcely a fitting match for my daughter," he replied proudly, twirling his opulent mustachios. "However, you are doubtless a worthy fellow, and although it is a pity that you are a common sailor and a Yankee, you have the air of possessing the domestic virtues, I will therefore consider your proposals for my little Melissa's hand, nor can a father's heart fail to be softened by the evident preference evinced by her maidenly confusion."

David's down-cast countenance turned slowly to a sumptuous copper tint; he glanced furtively at Melissa, and perceived that the girl's face was hidden against Shiloh's breast; she seemed half-fainting and completely forlorn. Shiloh supported her with the most reverential tenderness; he bent his head, and whispered words of comfort and advice above her tumbled curls. At that moment Shiloh appeared, even to his friend's simple eyes, as very knightly, very noble, very pale, polished to a scrupulous image of pure chivalry; David wondered miserably what high exalted arrows of unwisdom he was feathering for Melissa's little ears. Nevertheless, the devoted fellow felt a pang of happiness in considering that he had indubitably saved Shiloh's luminous existence from an ugly shattering death, and he felt that no sacrifice, not the very nightmare of an early marriage, was too painful in the light of this consummation. And, even now, he could not help hoping that he might himself be saved.

"Melissa, my little darling," said Mr. Daingerfield fondly, "why don't you raise up your lovely eyes and look your poor old father in the face? Don't be timid, my precious treasure; come to your daddy's arms and kiss him good-bye. I'm losing my one ewe lamb in losing you, but I can't destroy the pretty pastoral idyll of your love, or rub the bloom from your morning joy. And so I say to this exemplary young man, ' Take her, my boy, with a father's blessing and a father's tears, and may the brightest of good luck be with you both, my children! ' "

Mr. Daingerfield pronounced this edifying speech with a beaming smile upon the company; his consternation was extreme when his daughter lifted up her drooping head to say with surprising finality, "I've changed my mind, Pappy; I don't want to marry David nohow. I reckon I'd ruther go along home with you; seems as if I'd kind of lost my taste for matrimony."

9

SHILOH gave a low shocked cry of horror, but David's heart leaped up like a wild creature released from a trap, and as he looked at his friend his eyes were passionate with a mute entreaty.

Melissa gently extricated herself from Shiloh's absent-minded embrace, and walked bravely up to her tall father; her little face was as white as the plume of some lost impossible crusade, her eyes were shrines of a perpetual devotion.

"Pappy," she said in a small clear singsong voice, as if she were repeating an austere and delicate admonition of the soul, "Pappy, I reckon you'll have to take me home with you to-night; I reckon you'll have to keep me with you always. I done made a mistake 'bout loving David; I don't love him, and I won't marry him. I love somebody else, and there can't nobody git me to name his blessed name, but I reckon I love him forever."

"What does the girl mean?" demanded Mr. Daingerfield indignantly. "Is she moon-struck, or have you been taking her to religious revivals? This is either the language of lunacy, or that of salvation; in my experience the two come to much the same thing in the end."

"I ain't crazy, Pappy, and I ain't been a-follering no preachers," said Melissa with simplicity and pride. "I'll be a good daughter to you if you'll jest leave me alone to keep the counsels of my own heart in peace and quiet." She folded her small hands over some secret, locked in her breast below the shallow breathing, and looked imploringly at her father.

"Well, I am totally unable to understand the vagaries of the feminine soul," sighed Mr. Daingerfield, "but I suppose it is a lady's immemorial prerogative to change her mind; I can only apologise to my young friend here, and perhaps bid him not completely to despair, since your affections are still malleable and mobile. Doubtless in a year or two," he said consolingly to David, who writhed in an agony of embarrassment, "my daughter may be persuaded to look more kindly upon your suit; she is after all little more than a child."

"Yessir," stammered David, "yessir, mebbe so, sir; I'm sure I hope so, sir." The varnished hat revolved so rapidly in his hands that it threw off points of light like those scattered from the circumference of a Catherine's wheel.

"But, Melissa!" exclaimed Shiloh wildly, his blue eyes brilliant with amazement, "what is this insanity? In the name of heaven, pause ere it be too late; you cannot mean to plunge once more into the gloomy pool of solitude and fear which has engulfed your youth these many years! Oh, my dear little friend, consider well what you are doing, and even if you will not marry David, pray, pray be advised to seek the respectable aid of your Aunt Juliana!"

"Really, my good sir, you presume upon my leniency when you dare thus to address my daughter," said Mr. Daingerfield angrily. "Who are you, may I ask, and why do you make so curiously free with the intimate family cognomen of my deceased wife's sister? If you knew Aunt Juliana, as you call her with such singular impertinence, you would hesitate before advising an innocent child to cast herself upon the ambiguous mercies of as dark and bigoted a soul as ever crushed the resilient laughter from the heart of youth. Oh, sir, you speak very glibly of solitude and fear, but what is an honest occasional black eye or a stormy uncompanioned midnight compared to the monstrous panic of the revival or the saturnalia of the camp-meeting, where young creatures in the gay dawn of existence are seized upon by a sinister madness, horror-struck, and rendered feeble and enervated for ever? It was for this reason that I forbade my poor wife to hold any communication with her unhappy sister; it is for this that I have kept Melissa herself aloof and untrammelled in our mountain fastness, and, believe me or not as you will, you would abandon both her body and her delicate spirit to destruction, if you conveyed her within the power of that appalling woman!"

Mr. Daingerfield paused exhausted, and wiped the sweat from his brow; it was plain that he did not love his sister-in-law.

"I reckon as Pappy is right, Mr. Shiloh," Melissa interposed softly, slipping her hand into Shiloh's, and looking up at him with sad adoring eyes. "I reckon I better bid you good-bye, and go back to the cabin with Pappy. Aunt Juliana must be a holy terror, and I'd be scairt to death of her, worser than I am of Pappy. I'm powerful happy to have known you, Mr. Shiloh, and I won't never forget you s' long as I live, and ever after, if they is an ever after."

She put up her face to be kissed; she could not speak of the prunella slippers, nor of her love for Shiloh, which burned in her eyes like two perpetual tapers in a most single-minded shrine. The small face that he kissed was cold with tears, and for a moment he held her against his heart, but was unable to feel the little beating of her own.

Mr. Daingerfield had been busily dusting his great hip-boots with his heavy riding-crop; at last he seemed to steel his courage to some disagreeable duty, and he turned to Shiloh with a look of positive shyness in his fierce grey eyes.

"Sir," he began ceremoniously, "I owe you neither explanation nor apology; the fault lies entirely with you, and I am surprised at my fantastic weakness. The fact remains, however, that I feel a strong desire to assure you of my profound affection for my daughter, and of my recently taken determination to amend my ways for her benefit. She may have mentioned," said Mr. Daingerfield rather self-consciously, " that I am perhaps over-fond of the good corn liquor of my native state, and that my temper is at times uncertain. I marvel at my own folly, yet somehow I would not have you go from me without these guarantees of my good faith towards my child, and even — but indeed, I blush for my irrational dementia as I speak — and even, sir, I would fain shake your hand in parting, and call you, however foolishly, my friend. There's something about you, sir," said Mr. Daingerfield with unwilling warmth, " by gad, sir, I swear there's something about you that I like! Will you have a drink of whisky? " He produced a fine silver flask of Jacobean workmanship, and unscrewed the top with accustomed celerity.

" No, thank you," answered Shiloh, distaste chilling the words to faint hauteur. " I wish," he went on, " that you would not drink . . ."

" Corn liquor! " shouted David in the nick of time; Mr. Daingerfield's brow had darkened again alarmingly. " He has a fancy for French brandy, has my mate, and he won't never stop singing its praises, in season and out of season. He wants for you to take to that, Mr. Daingerfield; he thinks corn whisky's bad for the digestion. I tell him that's all moonshine, but he will have his little joke."

" How absurd you are, David! " Shiloh was slightly annoyed; he did not know that his friend had saved his life for the second time within half an hour. Mr. Daingerfield restored the flask to his pocket with an indulgent smile, wiping his lips upon a fine linen handkerchief.

" You young fellows are always silly about French kick-shaws," he said in a tone of pleased superiority. " Brandy may be all right for boys, but it isn't a gentleman's drink; it has no fire and passion in it. However, if you'll follow me into Wheeling, and meet me at the residence of my friend Judge Poindexter, I can promise you as pretty a glass of *fine Champagne* as was ever

smuggled out of France. Darkness has descended upon our conference, and I propose an adjournment to the Judge's hospitable
parlour. It is too late to return to my home this evening, and I
am sure my daughter must be considerably fatigued. I will furnish you with the Judge's address, and ride on with my little girl
upon the pillion of my saddle; you will follow me as soon as you
may find it convenient, and the remainder of the night may be
profitably spent in determining the relative merits of French
brandy and the rarest corn whisky in Wheeling."

Shiloh appeared aloof and pensive; he felt all at once very
tired, and he would have given his hope of supper for the privilege of sleeping under a hedgerow fresh with early moonlight,
but Melissa's eyes implored him, and David shook his arm and
muttered in his ear long eloquent prophecies of beefsteaks and hot
toddy. He had not the heart to disappoint them, although he desired with all his soul to be alone in the companionship of burning
indignations and fastidious dreams.

"Very well," he said wearily, "we shall be most happy to accept your friend's kind hospitality for to-night. To-morrow we
must depart upon other business, but for to-night I am at your
service."

10

LITTLE more than an hour later, Shiloh and David sat in the dim
and tranquil elegance of Judge Poindexter's parlour; oak logs
glowed between high brass andirons under the white mantelpiece,
and the wine-coloured surface of the mahogany table reflected the
subdued brilliance of the flame. It reflected in addition several
cut-glass decanters and steaming plates surmounted by silver
covers; the cloth had been drawn before the friends' arrival, but
Judge Poindexter had insisted upon calling for freshly broiled
chops and freshly opened Burgundy, and the stiff and foot-sore
travellers were expanding under the benign influence of his fire,
his generous food and drink, and his benevolent smile.

Shiloh, relaxed in the smooth fragrant depths of a great leather
arm-chair, regarded the judge with unconcealed approval; he was
forcibly reminded of his childhood's guide, the venerable Dr. Lind

of Windsor. The judge was tall and spare; his upright figure and the frosty abundance of his locks accorded well with a face of singular refinement and humane power. His low voice, warmly coloured by the accent of his country, charmed the listener no less by its quaint and pleasant modulations than by the high and fearless opinions which it so felicitously expressed.

It was clear that the judge entertained a distinguished regard for Mr. Daingerfield in spite of that gentleman's eccentricities and foibles; in the course of the conversation it became evident that the eminent jurist had been the devoted friend of Mr. Daingerfield's father, and that he still cherished this friendship's memory in preserving an affection for the son. Shiloh was amazed to observe the amelioration wrought in Mr. Daingerfield's manner and mood by the judge's society, and he thought of the perfectibility of mankind, and condemned himself for an impatient and undisciplined spirit.

Melissa had been sent to bed; she lay in the judge's wide white guest-chamber and dreamed, between waking and half-asleep, of Shiloh riding upon a mountain storm. She was neither happy nor unhappy; dimly she perceived that the variations of a single day had given her the ultimate sum of experience; the fact that this experience was of the soul alone troubled her tired body very little.

Both Shiloh and David were thinking of Melissa, as their minds grew drowsy under the gentle influence of the fire and the fragrant wine. Because they were each essentially generous and merciful, although in different spiritual degrees, each thought of Melissa tenderly, and hardly of himself, David because he did not want to marry her at the First Methodist Church, and Shiloh because he could not make her happy for ever in some golden sanctuary of immaculate innocence.

Presently they both heard with relief the judge's clear pronouncement of her name; they listened, and their drowsy careworn minds were suddenly at peace.

"Hector," said Judge Poindexter in his warm and cordial voice, "you'd better leave your little girl with me this winter. I'm lonely in this great house, and it must be lonely for the child in that wild valley of yours after the snow falls. I'll send her to a seminary for young ladies if you like, but personally I should pre-

fer to turn her loose in my library, with an occasional tutor to
help her over the hard places. My old 'Rastus and 'Mandy will
take care of her as if she were a spun-glass fairy doll, and I'll see
that she has companions of her own pretty age as well as my senile
devotion. You'd better do it, Hector, and make an old man
happy."

"The offer is like your invariable kind heart, Judge," said
Mr. Daingerfield, an added huskiness in his tones, "and for my
poor child's sake I shall accept it, without blinding my eyes to
its charitable nature. But from you alone such charity is not an
humiliation; rather indeed, when your hand confers it, do I
account it honourable alike to you and to me. Melissa is fortunate
in possessing such a friendship; it is the only legacy which my
dear father's poverty permitted him to leave, but it is more valuable than a miser's millions. Your health, sir, pledged in your
own soul-warming whisky and my undying gratitude!"

Mr. Daingerfield drained his replenished tumbler; he drank
whisky without stint while the rest of the company drank wine,
and sparingly at that. Shiloh had relaxed his usual abstinence in
compliment to the judge's gentle urbanity; a single glass of Burgundy had proved, together with the well-peppered mutton chop,
a perfect panacea for muscular fatigue, and since the natural mood
of his soul was universal benevolence and lovingkindness towards
all men, he now floated in an aureate cloud of contentment towards the haven of sleep. To be sure, he had not touched the
delicate amber decanter of French brandy which his host had set
at his right hand, and he watched Mr. Daingerfield's libations
with a sensitive shiver of alarm, but his mind was at peace concerning Melissa, and a delicious langour held him immovable
in the great leather chair.

David was no less happy; his supper had exceeded his most
sanguine expectations, and he did not share Shiloh's scruples
about the generous wines of France. He was warmed through
and through, and he felt almost sleek with pure comfort and the
consciousness that it was no longer necessary to marry Melissa,
or even to horsewhip her father. A lazy self-satisfaction made him
stretch his superb muscles and yawn deliberately into the fire.
He considered the excellence of the judge's *cuisine* and the ele-

gance of his old-fashioned parlour, and he knew that the child Melissa had found a safe anchorage and a sweet untroubled harbour.

Shiloh lifted his bright sleepy eyes towards the towering rows of books which lined the panelled walls; he perceived that the judge's library was well chosen, and he rejoiced for the sake of his little friend. Among the richly bound volumes he recognised the names of the French philosophers, and was happy in identifying the familiar bulk of *Political Justice* besides the *Republic* of Plato. He realised with poignant relief that the judge must be a person of liberal and enlightened views, and in spite of his extreme weariness he rose from his chair to draw from among its closely packed companions Locke's *Essay on the Human Understanding,* in whose pages he was presently profoundly lost.

" So, Mr. Shiloh," said the judge, smiling indulgently at his guest's graceful and fantastic figure and the intent beauty of his face bent upon the book, " I suppose you've come over here, as the ode puts it, ' From kings who seek in gothic night to hide the blaze of moral light.' Very right and proper for a fine young fellow like yourself, and if you have a fancy to establish yourself in Wheeling I can furnish you with some valuable introductions to leading citizens of our fair town. I hope you may decide to settle among us, sir, for you would be a delightful addition to our intellectual society, which is select, indeed, but unfortunately limited."

Shiloh shook his wind-blown hair in courteous regret; he looked a trifle wistfully at the richly ordered rows of books, the clear bright fire, the comfortable curtains of crimson brocade against the white-panelled walls, but his eyes sought a chink in the wooden blind through which a silver lancet seemed to pierce; he knew it for the thorny brightness of a star, and his heart tore at his ribs like something savage and imprisoned.

" Alas, no; I fear it is impossible," he said with calm politeness. " To-morrow we must prolong our journey still farther into the west; it grieves me that we must bid farewell to Melissa, but doubtless we shall return. Please believe us sensible of your kindness; I have no words wherewith to thank you."

He was palpably moved; the judge knew him to be weary, and

guessed him to be perplexed and sad. Indeed, melancholy had suddenly taken possession of Shiloh's mind at the thought of parting from Melissa; he was eager to be gone, and yet he longed to stay. He felt the familiar pity divide his heart, and he grew pale with the purely moral pain of it.

" I am sure that you gentlemen are ready for repose," said the judge humanely. "Come; 'Rastus will show you your bed-chamber, which I trust you will find comfortable and quiet after the fatigues of your journey. I have given orders that you are to be called betimes, and you will find breakfast prepared against your rising; I regret profoundly that the Cincinnati steamboat departs at so ungodly an hour, but you would be ill-advised to miss this opportunity of travelling by water along that beautiful natural avenue of traffic, the Ohio. I shall give myself the pleasure of joining you at breakfast, but I fear you must bid good-bye to Mr. Daingerfield to-night, as he is not an early riser. To Melissa I will myself convey your affectionate adieux; I know she will be sorry not to see you, but the poor child is sadly tired, and it will be more merciful to let her sleep until nature is restored."

Cheerful good-nights were exchanged between Mr. Dain-gerfield and the two friends; the judge followed them into the hall to see them safely into the respectful custody of old 'Rastus. They took their shining brass candlesticks from the table and ascended the low broad flight of stairs to the charming, old-fashioned room prepared for their reception. A cordial blaze welcomed them from its hearth; there was a bowl of late yellow roses upon the marble mantelpiece. Shiloh gave a sigh of un-conscious pleasure at sight of the embroidered linen sheets, turned down in a cool smooth triangle over the blue counterpane. His elevated mind abominated the luxuries of an effete civilisation, yet he had suffered all his life from an obscure unapprehended homesickness for the decorous comforts of his father's country house, and a long exile among the majestic draughts of Italian palaces had sharpened this ache to poignancy. The simple yet spacious amenities of the judge's guest-chamber were as balm and oil upon the throbbing of a neglected wound.

" I swan! " said David appreciatively, preparing for slumber.

"Now this is something like and no mistake. 'Tain't exactly pioneering, but it suits me down to the ground. Yes, sir, this beats cock-fighting, I do declare! So hurry up, Shiloh, and hop into that handsome bed, for you look clean tuckered out, and I'm so sleepy I could sleep standing up like a hoss, only thank God there ain't no need for such carryings-on in this elegant mansion."

11

SHILOH paid no heed to his friend's advice; he stood staring into the fire in an attitude of thoughtful melancholy. His brow, supported by his slender sunburnt hand, was shadowy with meditation; his eyes absorbed the flame into their burning blue.

"David," he said at length, "I must say farewell to Melissa."

"But you can't," David objected promptly. "You heard what the judge said about her being tired; she ain't coming down to breakfast to-morrow morning, and I for one don't blame her, seeing as we have to eat at the outlandish hour of four o'clock."

"I shall not wait until to-morrow morning," Shiloh answered with wild and dreamy enthusiasm. "I shall go to her to-night, alone, and in the very hush and suspension of mortality I shall give her a single parting kiss, thus mingling for a moment our extremest souls in hallowed chaste communion."

"Plague take you, Shiloh," cried David in a panic, "you can't mean them crazy words; I know you can't, not if you set a fippenny bit upon your life, with that rearing tearing Daingerfield right down the hall! Why, man, he'd shoot you full of bleeding holes as soon as he'd take a chaw of tobacco, and then there's this grand old codger the judge, that's used you like a prodigal son; you ain't never going to abuse his kindness like that, are you? Goldarn it, Shiloh, it's too bad, that's what it is, and I wouldn't have believed it of you."

"Precisely what is it that you do believe of me, David?" asked Shiloh gently. "Do you think that I would lay a finger upon this innocent save in an exalted reverence of love?"

"Of course not, Shiloh; I couldn't think ill of you, never," replied David blushing hotly. "I didn't mean nothing wicked;

I know blooming well as you're a kind of saint, and you wouldn't harm a mosquito, much less a little orphan like Melissa. But there's such a thing as common sense, and there's such a thing as caution, and you haven't got neither. What would those two gentlemen imagine, I ask you as a sensible man, if they caught you coming out of the child's room?"

"I am unable to conjecture," said Shiloh proudly. "I prefer not to probe the corrupt and pitiful suspicions which convention engenders in maggot-broods within the human mind."

"Then are you really set on going?" David inquired desperately. "Because if you are, I shall come along, just to see that you aren't shot without a proper trial. I'll stand outside in the passage, and if I hear any one coming I'll whistle a bar of ' Shannandore' to warn you. Why, man alive, there's no earthly use in your arguing; I'm not a-going to let you be murdered all by yourself, so hold your hush and leave me come with you as I say."

Shiloh proceeded along the passage with quick and noiseless steps; David followed him in a more hardly achieved silence, the floor creaking beneath his stockinged feet.

Outside Melissa's room they paused; Shiloh entered, leaving the door slightly ajar, while David waited in miserable anxiety, leaning against the wall of the passage, and listening to the jovial voices from the parlour, and to the heavy beating of his own pulses as the darkness weighed upon his heart.

Moonlight floated like a frosty bloom upon the white guest-chamber where Melissa lay; the wide white couch was spread with a delicate coverlet of moonlight, and beneath this thin silver Melissa slept, and woke, but not to cry, and slept again to dream. Now she awoke from happy sleep to a consciousness of peace, and she saw Shiloh plainly, and without surprise, as he approached her softly along a path of silver.

"Melissa," said Shiloh simply, "I have come to kiss you good-bye." He leaned above her in the moonlight, and the flood of silver poured from his shoulders in feathery flakes like the bright cataract of archangelic wings.

Melissa lifted up her lips to his kiss, with an invisible lifting of the heart; she did not speak, and although her enormous eyes were open, she still appeared to move in some miracle of sleep. She permitted him to take her small cold hand in his, without the faintest pressure of farewell, and he could not be sure that she had recognised his presence, or returned his kiss. Yet in that instant, in that soft and fleeting breath, the perfect essence of her soul went forth, to be drawn like a little pulse of sighing air into Shiloh's breathing, and set free again into nothingness.

It was not that she died; it was not even that she grieved, aware of any deprivation. She remained indeed singularly tranquil and composed, and when at last Shiloh passed gently from the room, she lay unmoving in a meek passion of relinquishment, tranced in accepted sorrow, and dedicated to the wonder of her loss for ever.

Afterwards she slept; when the pearl-coloured fogs of the eventual morning interposed their veils between her slumbers and Shiloh's departing form, she lay unconscious of his going, her cheek upon her folded hands. So was she to sleep, peacefully enough and perhaps even happily, throughout the long superfluous nights of the years to come; these were nevertheless not interminable, having a limit and a consummation set to their loneliness, and it were futile to affront the dignity of that consummation by prophecies of pity or of hope.

The Orphan Angel

IV

BROTHER LIZARDS

DAWN found the travellers among the river wharfs of Wheeling; David stared rather scornfully up at the vast luxurious shape of the steamboat *Lady Washington*. He had never plied his trade upon a power-driven vessel, and he did not scruple now to display a true sailor's contempt for such new-fangled devices.

"With all due respect for the judge, who was surely a grand old Roman, I don't think much pumpkins of that there top-heavy plaster ark," he said, eyeing the towering eminence of fresh paint and gilded curlicues with strong disfavour. "May be all very well for rivers, but you won't get a clumsy tub like that to beat a Salem clipper at sea, like they claim some of them have done. No, sir, she'll waddle along like a blooming mud-turtle all the way to Cincinnati, and by graminy I don't like the look of her. But come aboard, Shiloh, and we'll get our bearings; we don't have to decide yet for certain, for I see she's still taking on cargo, and she can't sail for another hour at least."

Shiloh followed his friend on board the steamboat; while David explored the possibilities of its lower deck the other leaned upon the rail, and watched the morning break over the noble bluffs which fringed the Ohio. Autumnal foliage glowed richly in the augmented light, and every withering tree bore a brief enchanting harvest of pure rose-colour under the sun's ascension. The river, flushing to responsive red, was thronged with curious and outlandish craft, keel-boats, broad-horns, and French batteaux, mingled with flimsier canoes and dinghies. An unsubstantial but populous city rose from the shining water; there were floating shops, floating taverns, and floating gambling-saloons, and from the stove-pipes of innumerable house-boats domestic plumes of smoke suggested coffee-pots and bacon and the pleasures of family life.

In the cabin above his head ladies and gentlemen were sitting down to an early breakfast; the savours of beefsteak and Mocha were wafted upon the freshening air, and David reapproached, unwrapping the large packet of sandwiches with which the judge's kindness had provided them.

"We did eat so goldarned previous," he explained apologetically, setting his broad white teeth into the generous layers of bread and butter and Virginia ham.

Shiloh was nibbling an apple, and watching the faces of his prospective fellow-travellers with admiration, wonder, and alarm. Here for the first time he perceived something vaguely approximating to his provisional hopes of a mighty race of pioneers inhabiting the primæval forests of the west. Shiloh had never beheld such a magnificent redundancy of beard as decorated the countenances of the men; even Trelawney's corsair mustachios faded into sparsity by comparison. Nor had he previously imagined that there was so much tobacco grown in the whole luxuriance of the New World as seemed necessary to these worthy persons' satisfaction; every whiskered cheek contained a formidable section of plug-cut, and the surface of the dark and narrow deck was not the cleanlier in consequence. He managed to curb a quite undemocratic disgust by a private meditation upon liberty, and while gently withdrawing himself into a less maculate corner he was consoled by a quotation from Lord Byron, which enabled him to finish his cool sweet apple in comparative peace of mind.

"Certainly they are surprisingly dirty, but then, 'corruption could not make their hearts her soil,'" thought Shiloh, still loyal to his dream of freedom.

His reflections, which contained perhaps the faint flavour of bitterness lacking in his apple-core, were somewhat rudely interrupted by a loud cry from David, who had seized his arm, and was endeavouring to drag him towards the rail under the influence of strong excitement. Shiloh feared for a moment that a suicidal impulse had overcome his friend's reason, and he attempted without success to oppose the forceful and persuasive grip of David's hand, but presently he realised that the latter's emotion was pleasurable in nature, and he discerned, among the swarm of river craft, the object of David's pointing forefinger and of the delighted scrutiny of his small blue eyes.

"Looky there, under our bows, Shiloh," shouted David ecstatically. "Now that there vessel's the spit and image of what a river-boat should look like, leastways according to my notion. By thunder, ain't she pretty, built on that elegant log raft, with her stove-pipe sticking up so pert and chipper out of her deckhouse, that's like a real little pioneers' cabin a-floating down the stream? See the men with their fowling-pieces, Shiloh, and the kegs that I calculate must be full of whisky and gunpowder, and the good old yaller dog laying asleep in the sun! Oh, that's the vessel for us, matey, and we're going aboard her this tarnation minute, 'stead of pottering about on this ornamental mausoleum for three-four enduring days! Come along, son, and we'll be signed on before you've cotched your breath."

Indeed, Shiloh was quite breathless with surprise and hurry by the time they had reached the wharf, and he permitted David to hire a row-boat from a negro boy and to pull out into the current of the stream without a single word of remonstrance. Finally he reached for the second pair of oars and placed them in the rowlocks with dexterous rapidity.

"Very well, David," he said with a laugh. "If you like the river-boat better, I can agree unhesitatingly with your romantic choice. I did not find the *Lady Washington* in the least degree prepossessing, and I shall welcome a change with all my heart. I have a shrewd suspicion that we are about to encounter adventures more manfully in keeping with our intentions than any by which our travels have been previously enlivened. But

here we are under the bows of the noble ship; let us try our
luck with her commander."

A few more vigorous strokes brought them alongside the
raft, which was formed of gigantic logs most durably lashed
together, and covered by a timber flooring; in the centre of this
rectangle was a sort of cabin, built of scantlings and planks, and
provided with an arched wooden roof, which gave it a grotesque
resemblance to the ark of biblical mythology. At the sides this
superstructure was almost flush with the edge of the raft; rude
wooden fins projected from opposite apertures into the water,
and served to navigate the clumsy craft in the absence of a tiller;
both fore and aft the plank deck extended for some distance beyond the cabin.

An excessively lanky individual with a short dust-coloured
beard lounged upon the forward deck; another and younger
man, clean-shaven and with a look of the scholar in his deep-
set grey eyes, sat hunched beside him, a fowling-piece across
his angular knees. A nondescript yellow dog dozed near them,
his wet black muzzle twitching in the sun. The scene was almost idyllic in its implications of leisure; a primitive checker-
board occupied the top of an inverted keg, and several tattered
books lay within reach. Shiloh noticed with heartfelt relief that
both of the men were smoking corncob pipes; although not
himself addicted to the use of tobacco, he was aware of the
impracticability of smoking and chewing at the same time, and
the evident enjoyment wherewith these persons inhaled the
fragrant fumes of the Virginian weed seemed an earnest of
their preference for the more agreeable habit. The clothing of
the pair was reduced by exposure to the elements to a uniform
earthen tint, their locks were long and untidy, yet withal there
was something of queer distinction in their appearance, and
their calm and thoughtful eyes interrogated the newcomers with
a frank and cordial curiosity.

In response to David's jovial hail the elder of the two rose
and leaned from the side of the ark; Shiloh saw that his warm
brown eyes were surrounded by a network of amiable wrinkles, and when he smiled similar wrinkles involved his entire
countenance in a map of pleasant past amusements and tolerant

scorns. He removed the pipe from his mouth with extreme deliberation.

"Well," he inquired affably, "what do you youngsters want aboard the *Prairie Flower?*"

David, for whom this pretty name had a pronounced appeal, nudged Shiloh surreptitiously and replied in his best able-seaman manner.

"Beg pardon, sir," he said respectfully, "but me and my mate was a-wondering whether you mightn't have a couple of berths for us aboard your vessel; we'd like to sign on regular, but if you don't need no extra hands we'd be ready and willing to pay anything as you might say in reason for our passage to Cincinnati. We're real strong and handy about a ship, sir, and you won't never regret it if you take us on, I do assure you."

"I couldn't take you as far as Cincinnati, my lad, for we are ourselves abandoning this noble galleon at Limestone," answered the unknown gentleman with the warm brown eyes; his wrinkles charted promises of excellent good-humour. "My friend the professor here, who is incidentally both first and second mate, happens to be betrothed to a young lady of Louisville, and it is our intention to strike across country to that Athens of the west without wasting time in other exploration. I am myself bound for distant Illinois, but a desire to be present at my learned colleague's nuptials has led me to accompany him to Kentucky. If you wish to come with us to Limestone, I have no objection, and as captain of this ship I believe I can guarantee an equal complaisance on the part of my crew."

He grinned humorously at the younger man, and Shiloh had a swift conviction that the nondescript yellow dog was the crew in whose friendly spirit the captain reposed such confidence. As if to affirm this supposition, the yellow dog opened one amber eye and winked with slow and indolent facetiousness.

"And couldn't you use us, sir? We're goldarned useful in a gale," said David eagerly; he had taken an immediate fancy to the captain, and his fingers ached for the touch of tarry ropes.

"Well, I'll be delighted to have your services in the arduous matter of agitating those oars about once in twenty-four hours," the captain replied. "They are solely for the purpose of steering, and we rarely trouble to employ them unless our craft is completely reversed by the current; I believe our stern is a trifle blunter than our bow, albeit I have never verified the point. For the rest, you will discover little to do beyond the ordinary domestic duties customary for the preservation of life; I trust that one of you is a passable cook, for indeed neither myself nor the professor is precisely skilled in that branch of science. Your nautical knowledge will, I fear, be somewhat more esoteric than is strictly necessary; we do not sail or steam, we simply drift, and I would rather you played a good game of checkers aboard the *Prairie Flower* than that you were past masters in the knotting of reef-points. But tie your boat to that staple, and swarm up the side, both of you, and I'll show you our beautiful vessel."

Shiloh and David lost no time in complying with his request, and a moment later they stood on the broad planks of the *Prairie Flower,* examining their new surroundings with an ecstatic and uncritical excitement.

"This," said the captain politely, "is Professor Lackland from Pennsylvania; he has recently been instructing the youth of the country in mathematics at Washington and Jefferson College, and is at present honourably employed as my first and second mate. I am Captain Appleby from Massachusetts, brevetted by the double virtue of a British rifle-bullet at New Orleans and my current command of this ship. And now whom, in your persons, have I the satisfaction of addressing?"

"My name's David Butternut, and I come from Castine in the state of Maine," replied David with equal courtesy, "and this here's my friend Shiloh; we're both able seamen, and we purpose to be pioneers. We're prospecting through the west in search of a messmate's sister that we fears is in trouble, and we're in a tarnation hurry to reach Kentucky. Any way as we can be useful aboard of the *Prairie Flower* suits us elegant, and we hopes as you'll find us proper sailors and clever fellows at checkers. About cooking we don't rightly understand so much, but we can try, can't we, Shiloh?"

"Assuredly we can try," said Shiloh with his frank disarming smile, which was so electric a matter of large blue eyes and universal benevolence.

Captain Appleby and Professor Lackland examined their guests with interest; they had from the first been favourably impressed by David's ingenuous countenance, and now they revised by a shade their initial observation of Shiloh, granting him less eccentricity and a greater degree of distinction. The captain noted that his body was a model of athletic lightness worthy of the Grecian heroes of antiquity, and the professor was aware that his brow was loftier and more illumined than that of a stoic philosopher or an Athenian poet. Each was conscious of a strong personal self-congratulation in the thought that henceforward the stranger was to be the companion of his voyage.

"As David says, my name is Shiloh," he informed them pleasantly. "I am a poet, and an adventurer upon the face of the earth. My native land has most unhappily of old been the enemy of yours, but time has healed the poignancy of that ancient wound, and my own convictions are so liberal that they cannot clash with your devotion to freedom. Much as I deprecate my country's conduct, so much so indeed that I have long sought relief from oppression in the kinder Italian clime, I nevertheless will not insult your patience by apologies; let our own friendly and untrammelled relations be sufficient earnest of our mutual good faith. I am honoured, sirs, in your acquaintance; the fact that one of you is a scholar and the other a soldier of unvanquished liberty adds exaltation to my delight."

"I thought you were an Englishman, by your accent," said the captain smiling. "Well, we shan't agree any the worse for that circumstance, my boy; I'm getting along in years, and in spite of the ounces of British lead in my game leg, I have to-day an admiration for your country probably considerably in excess of your own, which you tell me is non-existent. You are young and uncompromising, but the day may come when you'll be glad enough to go home and settle down in the Thames valley or the Weald of Sussex."

"How under the sun did you know . . . ?" began Shiloh rather wildly, but the other interrupted him with a paternal laugh.

"Never mind, my boy; don't agitate yourself about it, I beg of you. I haven't the faintest notion who you are, except that you're a man of breeding and cultivation; I've never visited your ancestral home, and if I made a lucky shot it was a sheer fluke, I assure you. I have no desire to pry into your personal affairs; forgive me if I have said anything to disturb the tranquillity of your spirit." He extended his lean corded hand in a gesture of deliberate kindliness.

"Excuse me, but are you not a graduate of Oxford, sir?" asked the professor in a dry precise voice. He was a thin young man with a pallid intelligent face and a pair of singularly piercing grey eyes, and there was something about his narrow elongated nose and the domed benignity of his forehead which reminded Shiloh of William Godwin.

"Not a graduate; I spent a couple of terms at Oxford in my unseasoned youth," replied Shiloh with dignity. "I was, as a matter of fact, expelled from the university owing to a boyish prank which was," explained Shiloh blushing, "of a purely intellectual character."

"We shan't like you any the less for that, son," said the captain. "We're sick of all colleges, aren't we, Lackland? But we're not sick of scholars and gentlemen, I can tell you, and you'll be a veritable godsend to the poor professor if you can talk Greek with him on the long autumn evenings; I'm sadly rusty since I took to navigating an ark among the snags and planters of the Ohio."

"Is that a volume of Condorcet which I perceive upon the deck?" asked Shiloh of the professor with companionable eagerness. "Because, if it is, I should be infinitely obliged to you for lending it to me for a few hours."

"It is," said the professor with all the warmth of which his curiously frigid voice was capable. "Take it, by all means, and keep it as long as you please. Captain Appleby is disposed to be facetious when he speaks of my fluency in the dead languages; I am unfortunately a wretched Greek scholar, but I am not wholly unlearned in the higher mathematics, and I have amused myself occasionally in my leisure moments with metaphysics and the philosophies of the elder civilizations. If you find any of these subjects in the least amusing, I shall be most happy for your company."

"But what radiant and incredible good fortune!" cried Shiloh in delight, seizing the professor's whitey-brown hand and wringing it with fervour. "You shall teach me the more advanced branches of mathematics, in which I am sadly deficient, and I shall be overjoyed to impart to you all that I know of the divine language of Hellas, although I dare say that your knowledge is not in truth inferior to my own. Oh, this is indeed felicity, to come upon such treasures of wisdom and philanthropy in the very wilderness itself! David, is not this amazingly lucky, that now we shall be able to talk about the calculus of variations?"

David eyed the pale professor with some suspicion; he was obviously relieved when the captain clapped him on the back and addressed him with a jovial laugh.

"I'd far rather that you learned to make flapjacks, for my personal convenience," said the captain decidedly. "Come now, David my lad, and I'll show you the rest of the noble ark of the covenant, as I call her. We have a superb state cabin amidships, and our kitchen is provided with a real hearth of mortared bricks, to say nothing of a Dutch oven and the largest iron pot and skillet this side of Pittsburgh."

Shiloh was soon deep in the professor's dog-eared volumes; he speedily abandoned Condorcet in favour of Cauchy's new treatise, and an expression of reverential pleasure made his blue eyes luminous as the kindled brain behind them. The professor's colourless and desiccated features glowed pallidly with a transmitted spark of this same fire, and the silvered darkness of one head and the rough and dusty-flaxen fairness of the other were bent in a single fascination above the mesmerising page.

2

MEANWHILE the captain and David explored the deck-house together; David was enchanted by innumerable miracles of ingenuity and convenience, and presently the captain had drawn from him the shy admission that he used to be quite a hand with the frying-pan and the hunter's kettle away back in the Maine woods before he run off to sea like the goldarned scalawag he was, by graminy.

"We'd ketch trout and fry 'em with a bit of bacon," said David reminiscently. "And in the big kettle — sugar-kettle as Ma had thrown out it was, really — we'd have mostly just plain stews, such as mebbe a good chunk of bear-steak or venison, with a rabbit or a pa'tridge or a brace of quail to make it tasty-like, and a handful of scallions for seasoning. That was simple and easy, but kind of good all the same, and when we didn't have no venison we'd fix up a mess of chowder with nice fresh cod and onions and potatoes, or mebbe if we'd find a few extra lobsters in our pots, that we didn't need to sell, we'd cook 'em on the rocks in red-hot sand and sea-weed. You'd laugh, sir, I suppose, at such childish notions, but it ain't so bad when you're real hungry and the lobsters is young and tender. You eat 'em with potatoes roasted in the ashes."

The captain's lean countenance assumed a look of positive starvation, and he regarded somewhat ruefully the arid un-succulent bags of coffee and corn-meal, which, with a quantity of dried apples and about half a bushel of smoked sausages, composed the entire stock of comestibles aboard the *Prairie Flower*. He laid his hand caressingly upon the consoling ro-tundity of a five-gallon keg, and addressed David in tones of measured firmness.

"My boy," he said with decision, "you and I must form a defensive alliance aboard this ship, in sheer self-preservation. I think I perceive in your friend Shiloh certain qualities only too familiar to me from my acquaintance with the excellent profes-sor; the chaste and abstracted intellect of the scholar refuses to concern itself with material considerations, and the mind flourishes at the expense of the emaciated frame. This would be all very well if the professor alone were involved in the priva-tion, but while he is perfectly content to gnaw a fragment of bacon-rind or a morsel of dried apple, I am reduced to a state of semi-starvation which is far removed from my natural desires and appetites. I feel sure that you have experienced similar suf-ferings as the price of your affection for the poet Shiloh. I be-lieve that an English singer of like convictions has noted the

phenomenal fact that chameleons feed on light and air; very
probably they may, poor little creatures, but ordinary mortals
cannot follow this ethereal example without a tragic diminution
of their vital force. David, let us conspire together against these
children of a sunnier star; let us insist upon a sufficiency of
food! "

David's face brightened conspicuously upon this suggestion;
at the same time his loyalty to Shiloh was too complete to permit him to give an unqualified assent to the captain's critical
remarks.

"I don't think as you hardly understand Shiloh as yet, sir,
if I may make so bold as to say so," he said modestly. " Shiloh's
a most surprising feller, a thundering wonder in more ways than
one. He's what they call a genius, I reckon, and he just plumb
forgets to eat now and then, but oh sir, it isn't as he's disapproving or superior like I guess the professor might be, judging by
the long sniffy shape of his nose. He's humble as a child, is
Shiloh, and he's tarnation thankful when I remind him to eat
his dinner, and so pleasant and gentle-like about it all that it
fair brings the tears to my eyes to think of it. 'Twould be so
goldarned easy to cheat him, and by jiminy I wish I could have
the everlasting licking of the man as tried it! Now the professor,
I calculate he's different; he has a look of my old schoolmaster
back in Castine, and I reckon he could be real nasty if you blew
the dinner-horn just as he was a-studying out a terrible problem
in arithmetic."

"You do not entirely do justice to the manifold excellences
of my friend the professor," replied the captain. " There is some
truth in what you say, yet he is undoubtedly a most amiable
young man, as well as an elegant and distinguished scholar.
Your temperaments may be somewhat uncongenial, David, but
you will soon learn to like as well as to respect him, and his
companionship will be a boon to Shiloh, I feel sure."

"Mebbe," said David dubiously; he found it hard to believe
in a fervent passion for the higher mathematics, and he was
glad when the captain began to talk of venison hams and mallard ducks.

"I'll tell you what you must do, David," the captain explained

eagerly. "You must take the skiff and row back to shore, towing
that hired tub of yours behind; then you can visit the markets
and select everything we require, the best of everything, my
boy, and plenty of that. Spare no expense; I intend to reform the
culinary mechanics of the *Prairie Flower*. Here's some money;
you'll find it ample, but if you prefer to contribute something towards your passage to Limestone, let it be in provisions; a nice
pair of chickens, say, or a few dozens of fresh eggs. We already
possess the more ordinary utensils, but perhaps you'd better lay
in a proper assortment of plates and spoons; the big lead spoons
are the best, and that Pittsburgh Liverpool ware is cheap and
durable as well as pretty. Now off with you, and don't forget
butter and cheese and milk, to say nothing of sugar and spices
and preserved fruits. I would prefer to have a share in the expedition, which is after my own heart, but I fear that our studious
young friends might sink the vessel upon a sawyer during my
absence, in some fit of sublimity or intense contemplation."

3

WHILE David rowed back to the wharf, the captain again sought
the deck where Shiloh and the professor sat absorbed; he lounged
idly against the rail, smoking his corncob pipe and scratching
the yellow dog between the animal's drowsily twitching ears.

"The principle of virtual velocities," Shiloh was saying
gravely, "employed by Lagrange to elucidate his theory of the
libration of the moon . . ."

The captain listened dreamily, lulled almost to slumber by
the chanting eloquence of Shiloh's voice; he smiled as the
professor's dry clipped tones cut sharp across his reverie.

"But my dear sir, I know little or nothing of astronomy, yet
surely I am right in believing that in Laplace's memoirs published
in the volumes of the French Academy, it is demonstrated that,
independently of any save the most general consideration as to
mass, the mutual action of the planets could never largely affect
the eccentricities and inclinations of their orbits."

The captain now perceived that Shiloh held Cauchy's treatise in one hand and in the other an open quarto of Lagrange, while the professor was similarly burdened with Gauss's *Disquisitiones arithmeticæ* and the third volume of Laplace's *Méchanique céleste.* While the one discoursed pedantically of planetary mean motion, or surveyed with a glazed grey eye the theory of probabilities, the other contrived to varnish with romantic glamour even the chilly calculus of finite differences, and to make of mechanical truth a lucid and harmonious revelation of serene and rigorous loveliness.

" The elimination of the unsatisfactory conception of the infinite from the metaphysics of the higher mathematics . . ." said Shiloh with passion, and the captain observed that his eyes were like portions of the midnight sky itself burning through the hollow sockets of a noble mask of exaltation; the mask was pale as snow or stone, but the eyes were bright pieces of infinity.

" Good heavens above! " cried the captain appositely, " what a precious pair of theorists you are, and how thankful I am that I have the delightful David to support me in my more ponderable incarnation of hungry flesh and blood! I realize that I am the basest of materialists, yet I own to a lively curiosity about the component parts of my dinner. But here comes David with the skiff full of charming provender; I discern a pair of my favourite mallard ducks, and, as I live, I believe he has succeeded in obtaining the venison ham of my Lucullan dreams! "

It was true; David bounded to the deck with his arms full of bundles and his face aglow with simple triumph, and as the captain praised him warmly for his sagacity and initiative in discovering so many rare and exquisite viands in the markets of Wheeling, Shiloh came forward with an air of generous and unselfish pleasure lighting his abstracted brow.

" My dear Davy," he said affectionately, " I have missed you even in the midst of the intellectual raptures of the last hour, but I have excellent good news for you, my friend. I had feared that you would be unable, owing to your unfamiliarity with the French tongue, properly to appreciate the rich and delicate satisfaction prepared for us by Lagrange and Laplace, yet behold, the professor has but just informed me that several of the latter's most celebrated works have been translated into English by a

Mr. Pond. See, here is one of them; shall not the professor explain it to you, David, so that we may all three share the delights of this mental ecstasy?"

David appeared so ridiculously alarmed by this kind proposal that the captain took pity on his distress, and sent him off to the kitchen, much to Shiloh's disappointment. The latter was far too polite to protest, but he gazed rather wistfully after his friend's departing form, sure that David had been cheated of a sublime and fearful joy, and his eyes were sorrowful as he listened to the captain's excuses.

"I quite understand that it is necessary to serve mallard ducks with an accompaniment of hominy and currant jelly," he said at length with extreme seriousness, "and I am certain that my good David possesses a skill capable of dressing these dishes to perfection, but might he not have had a moment's leisure in which to taste the true Pierian crystal? But no matter; he is too magnanimous a creature to repine, and I will not dull his bright example by spiritless complaints. I dare say, sir, that your experiences in the army have made it difficult for you to comprehend that boundless liberty of the soul which gives even a poor sailor a right to the treasures of high research, although you yourself fought with such valour to preserve that very liberty for the least of your countrymen. I crave your pardon if I am too severe in my strictures upon the discipline to which David has been subjected; I rely upon your honourable and charitable heart to forgive me, and to release David from his duties as soon as it is humanly possible to do so."

The captain contented himself with a courteous inclination of the head and a humorous and twisted smile; he presently joined David in the warm seclusion of the kitchen, where culinary operations of the most elaborate description were immediately begun. The two did not appear again until dinner-time, and then as the victorious heralds of so inspired a repast that even the scholar and the poet were startled into enthusiasm by the refined perfection of its flavours.

"Speaking of geniuses, David, Vatel might own a natural master in you," said the captain cryptically to his flushed assistant. "We should have had wild rice for the ducks, but this hominy is really very palatable. Shiloh, will you have a little more of the currant jelly? It is put up in glass jars by a worthy old lady of Wheeling, and upon my soul it is nearly equal to my own dear mother's delicate concoction."

The afternoon was flawless; as the ark drifted softly between the towering bluffs of the Ohio, the four companions lounged upon the deck in different attitudes of contented relaxation; the yellow dog dozed on the warm pine planks, and Shiloh dozed also, his head in a patch of sunlight. The others sucked sleepily at their corncob pipes; David and the captain had begun a game of checkers with red and white corns, but presently they grew too lazy to play, and there was no longer any sound except the lapping of water against the moss-grown sides of the *Prairie Flower*.

The season was the honeyed heart of Indian summer; the trees upon the lofty banks of the river were sumptuous in all the colours of the nobler metals, with here and there a higher plume of sanguine or of flame. Shiloh stretched himself as he dozed in the sun, and in the golden twilight of his drowsy mind a strain of music shaped itself in words, lucid and harmonious as the calculus of variations, and sumptuous as the processional colours of the forest.

He put his slim brown hand into his breast pocket, and very quietly drew forth pencil and paper, and there, while the others dozed, he wrote down certain words in a certain magical order of his own contriving, and put the paper back into his pocket, and slept, with his head in a bar of golden twilight.

The ensuing days were truly idyllic in their gentle progression; a life of idleness and innocent duty endured upon the *Prairie Flower,* and both Shiloh and David flourished in its fostering sunny air. Perhaps the very fact that the unhurried ark was drifting with the current instead of plunging forward animated by wings or the impetuous breath of steam, may have laid a profounder peace upon the spiritual atmosphere; it is certain that this peace existed, and that it was beneficent and dear.

David and the captain pacified the actual hunger of the body by a succession of almost incredibly savoury and appropriate meals, and Shiloh and the professor laboured untiringly in the starry vineyard of the higher mathematics to distil such wine as must appease the extremest mortal thirst of any soul.

Their material wants were few, and liberally satisfied; their duties were definite and simple, and the performance of such communal operations was drudgery to no one. The captain and David did the marketing, rowing ashore every second day for the purchase of provisions; the more prosperous hamlets along the river-banks furnished an endless plenty of fresh eggs and butter, chickens and ducks, and the kindly cultivated fruits of the earth. In their capable hands reposed the responsibility for sending these delicacies to the deck-house table well dressed and seasoned, a task most cheerfully and successfully accomplished. Upon Shiloh and the professor devolved the business of occasionally and violently agitating the vessel's gigantic oars; this they appeared to regard rather as a jocund form of sport than a serious employment, and often the professor's arid chuckle echoed upon the chime of Shiloh's fiery laughter as the two pulled desperately at the great leather-bound handles. They compared the callouses upon their palms with pardonable pride, and had there been even an ounce of superfluous flesh to pad their muscular slenderness, it must have been consumed like candle-wax in the flame of this singular exercise.

Theirs, too, was the slight innocuous toil of sweeping the cabin floor and tidying the primitive wooden berths with which this apartment was provided. Each was by nature fastidious and active, and their quick dexterous performance won the admiring praise of David and the captain. On the whole the domestic arrangements of the *Prairie Flower* were above reproach; a democratic peace and good-will reigned in all the labours of its daily life, and the four companions became firmer friends with each rising and setting of its rich autumnal sun.

The long amber afternoons were spent in recreation; Shiloh and the professor wandered happily among planetary perturbations, while the captain and David played at checkers or indulged an ingenuous taste for marbles. And not infrequently it came about that these enthusiasms grew vocal with excitement, and a curious chorus of strophe and antistrophe made musical the aureate descending hour.

" Knuckle down! " David would shout in his agreeable baritone. " Toy bone! Go to baste! " and the captain's booming bass
would roar its answer like replying cannon, " Man-lay! Clearings!
My first, I believe! " until the bluffs of the Ohio echoed with
innumerable Titanic voices, as if a monstrous warfare lay concealed behind the copper ramparts of the forest.

At the same instant the lighter, less substantial tones of Shiloh
and the professor might be lifted in ethereal cries concerning the
commensurability of the mean motions of Jupiter and Saturn,
or in sudden poignant exposition of the nebular hypothesis,
spoken in a thrilling whisper that trembled with its own intensity.

One day the several sciences of astronomy and marbles discovered a definite point of contact in the shape of a charming
sphere of azure glass, whose orbed circumference was interlaced
with mazy convolutions of pale and silvery threads. David had
won this lovely bauble from the captain in honourable combat,
and Shiloh, perceiving it, had desired it passionately, because of
its beauty and its vague resemblance to a universe in miniature.

" But I could not deprive you of your delightful plaything,
David," Shiloh protested nobly, with a veritable longing in the
large blue eyes that gazed at the large blue marble. " I really
should not consider it right to accept the gift of your unselfishness,
much as I admire this enchanting toy. See, it is indeed the universe, the true colour of heaven, streaked with wandering planets
and divine emanations; the wonder of it is that it has grown so
small that I can balance it upon the palm of my hand."

" Oh shucks, Shiloh, I want for you to have it! " said David.
" I can buy me another in the next village. I'll learn you to play
if you like, though them big ones ain't so good as the little black
alleys."

Shiloh and the professor rejoiced not only in their mutual
passion for astronomy and metaphysics; they spent many profitable hours in the discussion of ancient and modern poetry, and
the professor brought to birth a very pretty talent for the composition of classical odes in the Augustan manner. Shiloh was
continually busy with a pencil and a scribbled fragment of brown
paper; the product of these activities went into his breast pocket,
where various folded sheets lay secret against Silver's likeness.

He had already showed the little ivory oval to the other, in compliment to the professor's amiability in exhibiting the portrait of his own fiancée, the lovely Miss Rosalie Lillie of Louisville.

Professor Lackland wore his lady's picture in a flat locket of engine-turned gold, suspended by a black silk ribbon over the region of his heart. Shiloh was never weary of marvelling at this circumstance, nor at the apparent opposition existing between the professor's calm and chilly deportment and the internal temperature of this heart. In a thin precise voice more suitable for the expounding of algebraic functions the lover grew eloquent in praise of Miss Lillie's virtues and the splendid velvet of her eyes, until Shiloh longed to behold this paragon of tender brilliance, and stared rather wistfully at Silver's pale and evasive smile and the moth-wing darkness of her gaze.

The professor took a not unnatural delight in his Rosalie's accomplishments, and he informed Shiloh with vicarious pride that she was a gifted poetess and an elegant performer upon the Spanish guitar. Both Shiloh and David were determined to dance at their friend's approaching wedding, even though David should be capable of no more than a sailor's horn-pipe, and Shiloh of some airy and improbable *pas-seul* of his own invention.

At night the ark was invariably moored to a convenient tree; such storms as visited their voyage raged exclusively during these intervals of inactivity, and so hardly constituted a real annoyance, much less a danger or a problem. The tie-rope was admirably reliable, and the studious pair of steersmen developed a curious instinct for avoiding snags and planters among the waters of the majestic stream.

It is clearly impossible to give a detailed account of all the batter-cakes and biscuits, eggs and fried ham, steaks, stuffed chickens, and mysterious puddings produced by David and the captain with the aid of the Dutch oven and the enormous iron pot and skillet; suffice it to say that their quantity was unequalled by the stock of an average Covent Garden stall and their quality unsurpassed by the masterpieces of an exceptional Parisian chef. David grew sleek as a comely gold-curled ram that has feasted on honey-flowers and thyme, and even the lean dust-coloured captain blossomed into new vigour, and his twisted smiles were like a surprising pattern of foliage upon the dry stick of Aaron's rod.

The yellow dog basked in sunlight within a circle of beef-bones; the professor had rescued him from an unhappy Pittsburgh slum, and the creature believed that the river ark was a canine paradise created for his particular benefit. He was a placid contented beast, and everyone called him Log; the captain said that this was the diminutive of Ship's Log, but the professor insisted that it was obviously a contraction of Logarithm. David, whose vocabulary was racy of the soil, was convinced that Bump on a Log was the proper appellation; neither Shiloh nor the animal itself ever ventured an opinion on the subject.

Now all too soon the darling argosy approached its haven, and upon a softly melancholy evening of pale clouds and pearly river mists the *Prairie Flower* drew near to its destination, and the travellers beheld the lights of the little town of Limestone gleam faintly through a thin curtain of rain. Even the professor, who would presently be in the bright company of his beloved, owned to a mood of sadness; the others were frankly despondent, and the yellow dog whimpered in sympathy, a brute Adam dispossessed of paradise.

"You'd far better come with me, boys, and settle down in Illinois," said the captain, sucking pensively at his corncob pipe. "Then Shiloh can send for his wife and child, and David can marry Miss Silver and found a Butternut family in the productive soil of Pike County; this will save me the trouble of begetting any sons to be the comfort of my declining years; yours can maul the rails for my fence and hoe my truck-patch in the spring. I'll gladly turn over a part of the bounty lands I've bought up to any brisk young fellow who'll consent to populate the west in the interests of patriotism. Here's your golden opportunity as the servant of mankind, Shiloh, and do you, David, meditate upon your duties as an American citizen and perform what is required of you by a loving country."

Both Shiloh and David laughed in rather an embarrassed fashion; they shared in common a curious childlike innocence of speech and thought, and the captain's kind suggestion appeared slightly indelicate to this mutual taste for modesty. They did ample justice, however, to the complete benevolence of his intentions, and only an unswerving devotion to Silver prevented them from accepting his magnanimous offer. They shook their heads with stoical decision; the captain and the generous bounty lands of Pike County pleaded in vain against the sorrowful entreaty of Silver's eyes, which were after all no more than shadowy blots upon a small circle of ivory.

"David, David, how can I contrive to exist without your beautiful cooking?" cried the captain despairingly. "Here was I, beginning actually to take on flesh and to feel the replenished blood sparkle in my veins like April sap, and now I suppose I must go back to bacon and dried apples, with an occasional dreadful experiment in corned beef and cabbage. Lackland will miss his mathematics, I have no doubt, but his bride will be on hand to console him, and after all there is very little succulence in the integral calculus. My case is much harder, yet I will not weary you with my lamentations; I only hope that we may have a good supper to-night, to prepare us for the morrow's parting."

"But you are all coming to my wedding; I insist upon your presence at my wedding," said the professor eagerly, adding in a faintly dubious tone, "I am convinced that Rosalie would desire it above all things; she is the soul of hospitality, and my friends are to be her friends always, and by her own heartfelt wishes."

"We'd be rather a ruffianly crew to introduce into a lady's parlour, Lackland," the captain objected; he had small faith in Miss Lillie's ability to be friendly with a trio of ragged tramps. "You must remember that we can none of us afford new clothes, and although Shiloh's so particular about shaving his practically non-existent beard, David and I have somewhat the air of minor Hebrew prophets, and we're all disgracefully tattered and weather-worn. Your fiancée must be a remarkable girl if she can consent to receive us."

"She is a remarkable girl," explained the professor proudly. "She is a talented, liberal, lovely creature, and her father's financial reverses have unfortunately familiarized her with poverty, and softened a heart which adversity was powerless to shatter. I believe that the family is at present residing in a species of log cabin in the remote environs of Louisville, and although they have been since birth accustomed to the niceties and refinements of affluence in that metropolis of the west, I know that their hospitality is as exquisite when dispensed from four rude walls of unhewn timber as when the noblest mansion on Third Avenue sheltered its grace. Come, my dear comrades; my Rosalie will welcome you with joy, and her charming parents will endorse the pleasure of their child in your acquaintance. Surely you will not permit a few sartorial deficiences to cheat us upon this auspicious occasion."

"By graminy, Shiloh, I agree with the professor," said David. "I don't see as we look so tarnation terrible, anyway, and Cap'n and I could borrow your razor and smarten up a bit before the wedding. I'd admire to meet the professor's young lady, and I think a fine old-fashioned reel or country dance, with a few fancy liquors, would do us all a power of good, loosen our joints like, and put ginger into our spirits. Myself, I'm real handy with a needle, what with being raised a sailor and all, and I reckon I can set a stitch here and a stitch there in these wild raggedy garments of ours as'll spruce 'em up considerable in a brace of shakes. Then Shiloh and I can borrow a cake of that elegant brown soap and wash our shirts in the river like we did last week; I fetched the collar off'n mine pounding it with a big rock, but it was goldarned clean when I had done with it. At the same time we'll have a chance to scrub ourselves most particular, and I warrant we won't disgrace the professor when once we gets to the party, will we, Shiloh?"

"Certainly we shall endeavour to make ourselves presentable in honour of our friend's felicity," Shiloh answered gracefully. "If Miss Rosalie Lillie will allow us to pay our respects to her, even in this woefully dilapidated condition, she must indeed be the daughter of nobility and gentle tolerance; Professor Lackland is profoundly happy in uniting his fortunes with one so virtuously gifted and so sweetly bred."

"Well, I dare say we shall not actually invalidate the ceremony," said the captain with a philosophic yawn. "And yet I confess to a flavour of scepticism in my faith in your fiancée's liberality, if that liberality must embrace a bearded villain like myself. However, I will investigate my stock of outmoded necker-chiefs and antique flowered waistcoats, and we will all come forth like the celebrated Incredibles of Bonaparte's Directory. I believe my lieutenant's uniform is in the large portmanteau under my berth; when I was brevetted a captain in 'fifteen I steadily set my face against the purchase of a new set of regi-mentals, in spite of my poor old mother's tears, and her only con-solation lay in embalming the war-worn remnant of the other in a superfluity of gum-camphor. Shall I resurrect its glories, pro-fessor, in compliment to your nuptials?"

Shiloh and David warmly seconding this proposal, the cap-tain was persuaded to repair to the cabin in search of his uniform, and presently he emerged in the full magnificence of threadbare blue broadcloth laced with tarnished gold. The sword which clanked against his long bony thigh seemed the pattern of his own soul turned to steel, slender and fine and durable, yet rusty, and sad-coloured with disuse.

"A captain's sword, you see," he said, smiling cynically. "I managed to afford this dainty lethal instrument, although I could not afford a new uniform. My choice was perhaps unwise, since the fighting was over, and a prosperous coat covers a multitude of follies."

"I swan, Cap'n, you're a perfect picture in them clothes!" cried David delightedly. "I calculate as how you'll clean knock their eyes out at the wedding, a-swaggering in with that grand pair of gold epaulettes on your shoulders, and that sword a-rattling by your side. I'm proud to know you, sir, and you'll be a credit to the professor in the eyes of his stylish friends, I'll bet my bottom dollar as you will!"

"You do indeed approximate closely to my conception of the ideal warrior," said Shiloh in an awe-struck voice. "You are aware, Captain Appleby, how irrevocably I am fixed in my disapproval of bloodshed, but there are certain struggles, like the present conflict in Greece and the lofty strife in which you won your own well-merited laurels, to which no ordinary standards may fitly be applied; their very nature exempts them from con-demnation. You are doubtless familiar with Wordsworth's noble poem upon the Character of the Happy Warrior; I think I can recite a portion of it from memory, if you will permit me to do so in salutation to a soldier of freedom."

"It's more than kind of you, my boy, but I beg you to spare my blushes," replied the captain laughing. "You regard me through the medium of your own romantic mind; the only part of that very fine poem which applies to me is the line about the unfortunate person who was left unthought-of in obscurity; that's my portrait to the life."

"Good heavens!" cried Shiloh in distress, "how can you possibly suggest anything so supremely ridiculous? The moment you strode out of the cabin door, looking so tall and exalted, you reminded me forcibly of the line, 'Happy as a lover, and attired with sudden brightness, like a man inspired.'"

"And that," said the captain rather bitterly, "is because, my dear Shiloh, you are an incurable idealist. But perhaps," he added quietly, stroking the hilt of his sword, "you may have the right of it, after all."

And indeed the captain was a sufficiently splendid figure, as he stood upon the deck of the *Prairie Flower* with the expiring glimmer of a rose-red evening piercing the pearly river-mists to paint his shabby coat to the colour of dragon's blood; forgotten lions raged suddenly in his untidy earth-tinted hair, and his beard was tawny in the sunset. It is somewhat more than possible that Shiloh may have had the right of it, but since the question involves enormous mortal issues, it is not the privilege of this simple tale to attempt to disentangle them.

4

Next day the travellers set off through a wild region of bear-brakes and thickets; the roads were a succession of corduroys and mud-holes, and although no more than a hundred miles divided them from Louisville, they could not hope to make the journey in less than six or seven days. They had abandoned the *Prairie Flower* at the rude riverside wharf of Limestone; David and Shiloh had bedewed the worn planks of her deck with actual tears, and when the captain succeeded in selling her to an old gentleman who was contemplating a trip to Cincinnati to visit his married daughter, they regarded the good silver dollars of her price with shuddering horror as a sinister kind of blood-money. Nevertheless, they were greatly refreshed and comforted by an excellent dinner at the Limestone tavern, and they set off in company with their friends in a state of subdued cheerfulness and determined hope.

The captain wore his uniform, since they travelled light, and were able to carry only such luggage as each might tie within the compass of a large pocket-handkerchief. The professor's suit of mouldy black broadcloth looked oddly out of keeping with the luxuriant savagery of the forest scene, yet his spare and wiry frame was capable of supporting exertions and fatigues which might have caused a giant to complain. David strode crashing through the underbrush with a superb contempt for fallen logs and mud-puddles, and his hair was like a golden fleece in the sunlight, but Shiloh appeared almost a part of the wilderness itself in the fantastic simplicity of his tattered garments and the bright profusion of his uncovered locks. He sped swiftly forward like a natural force, a sapling tree made animate, a wave, a moving cloud, and such an exaltation made his blue eyes luminous that the others wondered to behold him, and forbore to protest against a pace most difficult to follow.

"Mebbe I can beat you on the highroad, Shiloh," said David with an admiring grin, "but there ain't never been nobody could walk on broken ground so fast as you."

The yellow dog loped at their heels, and his joyous barking echoed like laughter through the forest aisles. Now and again he would turn aside from the path to chase a muskrat or a rabbit, and then Shiloh would reason with him gently and with logical precision on the subject of clemency and the duties of the strong towards the weak, supporting his brilliant argument by morsels of brown sugar, of which the animal was inordinately fond.

Towards nightfall they approached a settler's cabin; it occupied a clearing in the dense timber, and was neatly and picturesquely constructed of rough logs. A field of Indian corn surrounded this rude sylvan retreat, and a potato-patch lay close to a tiny orchard of peach- and apple-trees. Tall sugar-maples shaded

the dooryard, and in this sheltered spot a thin young woman sat
spinning, her sombre eyes fixed upon the ground.

At the sound of the travellers' footsteps she looked up
startled; a painful flush dyed her cheek with duskier crimson,
and she put her hand to her breast in a gesture of alarm. Three
ragged children who were playing in the dusty grass at her feet
drew closer to their mother's knee, and all four stared at the newcomers with the wide frightened eyes of defenceless animals.

Shiloh stepped forward with his most engaging smile, and
a simple word of reassurance; the woman immediately lost her
look of terror, and the children came shyly nearer to gaze in
fascination at the stranger, whose consoling beauty shone through
rags as humble as their own.

" Land sakes, how you skeered us," said the woman in a flat
lonely voice; Shiloh noticed that her wide defenceless eyes were
full of lost and lonely darkness.

" Reckon you can have some bacon and pone; I can't accommodate you with no chicken fixin's," said the woman sadly in
response to their courteous request for supper. Nevertheless, she
provided them with an ample and not unsavoury meal, and the
interior of the cabin proved to be comfortable and clean. The
woman seemed to take a mournful pride in her domestic effi-
ciency; she smiled at Shiloh's compliments to her plump pretty
children, and explained that their ragged attire was merely a concession to their preference for making mud-pies.

" Can't keep 'em decent nohow," she complained. " They've
got good linsey and cotton dresses that I wove with my own
hands, but they wear 'em out like so much cobweb. Same with
stockin's; it's knit, knit, knit all the time and naught but holes
to show for it. As for shoes, I tell my old man that we ought to
get 'em shod like Tom and Jerry there; they wears out a heap
of sole-leather in a year, and my old man gets sick of playin'
shoemaker."

" But think of the priceless dower of independence which
you will leave to them, and to your children's children," cried
Shiloh fervently, and the woman flushed with pleasure, and allowed that that was true, and presently she was telling proudly
of her marvellous success at candle-making, and of the very

superior quality of her maple sugar, which Shiloh tasted with keen appreciation. And while the captain and the professor praised the livestock and the noble growth of Indian corn, Shiloh and David sat on the floor in front of the fire of cedar logs, and David gave the boy his willow whistle, and showed him how to whittle jackstraws out of wood, and Shiloh made a brown paper boat for the two little girls to launch in their mother's washtub.

"Lordy, if here ain't my old man back from the store already!" said the woman suddenly, as a fair-haired giant burst into the warm room, and stood transfixed by amazement at sight of its cheerfully crowded state. His six-foot-one of brawn and muscle was precisely measured to fit Shiloh's preconceived notion of a pioneer, and he was cruelly disappointed when this prodigy laid several neat parcels of tea and coffee upon the cabin table of unvarnished pine; the carcass of a bear flung down upon the hearth would have seemed so much more in keeping with the man's appearance.

Introductions were speedily performed, and the frown which marked the farmer's brow was dissipated in the general merriment, in which the capering children joined with spirit. Good feeling prevailed; the host produced a five-gallon keg of whisky, and his wife fried another round of fresh eggs and flitch for the entire company.

"Swapped that batch of butter and chickens for a heap of store tea and coffee and good liquor," said the man complacently. He explained that these were the only commodities which were not produced upon the farm itself, and the travellers wondered at the resourcefulness of this sturdy freeman, who squeezed from the primitive world about him such plain abundant plenty.

"But it's powerful lonesome, powerful lonesome," he admitted, with a searching look into his wife's serious dark eyes. "And we gits the aguey in the fall pretty regular, me and Susan, though the young 'uns are right healthy, and we manage to struggle along. It's full twenty miles to the store, and further still if we wants to go to meeting; 'tain't often as we gits to see company like this of an evening, convenient to our own fireside."

Shiloh was in an ecstasy of admiration for the independence of this forest home; his eyes blazed brighter than the woman's best dip candles as he expounded his theories of freedom and enlarged upon the joys of privacy. The farmer and his wife exchanged occasional glances of scepticsm or surprise, but upon the whole they were immensely flattered, and so encouraged that they talked for an hour past their customary bed-time about the possibility of purchasing another cow and entertaining the preacher during the next revival.

The travellers slept on the floor in front of the comfortable embers; their kind host and hostess would not hear of their occupying the corn-crib. The following morning, after a generous breakfast of mush and milk and frizzled bacon, the wanderers set forth once more upon their journey, with manifold expressions of gratitude and esteem. Shiloh left a veritable flotilla of paper craft floating upon the soapy bubbles of the washtub, and the children's round blue eyes were full of tears as they kissed him farewell.

"But you must really have these young people instructed in the simpler branches of knowledge, such as reading, writing, and ciphering," he said solemnly as he shook the farmer's horny hand in parting.

"I won't have no child of mine hurtlin' away his time like that," answered the man with good-tempered scorn. "Now, honey," he admonished his elder daughter, patting her corn-silk curls, "say good-bye to the gentleman nice and polite, and don't act like a little scairt rabbit. No, sir," he went on decidedly, "the boy kin git a bit of book-larnin' later if he keers to, but my gals ain't never gwine to be high-larnt if I kin help it; nothin' spiles a woman for marriage like larnin' how to read."

"I am myself somewhat weary of the intellectual woman," confessed Shiloh, thinking of Jane Williams's delicious ignorance, and of the calm grey-eyed frigidity of his own domestic bluestocking; at the same instant he experienced a pang in wondering whether those eyes were dark with loneliness by the shores of Lerici Bay.

5

THIS shadow fled like a blur of smoke across the golden mirror of Shiloh's mind, a shiver of impermanent sorrow leaving laughter in its wake, a ripple on sunny water. For the day was too lovely to be marred by regrets or forebodings, and Shiloh dreamed happily of a time when his grey-eyed Mary should have joined him in the primeval forest, and of the delicate flotilla of fairy ships, folded from her finest cream-laid, hot-pressed notepaper, which should set sail for their child's delight upon a washtub full of rainbow bubbles, under the cloudless sapphire sky of freedom.

There was no peace in Shiloh's mind; its nature was a changing brightness, and often its agitations were divine. That morning, as he trod the forest paths, his spirit was quickened by a singular certainty of joy; a species of angelic possession set fiery lightnings round his brow. As he went forward through the trees this emanating fire was made actual in words; he spoke them scarcely above a whisper, and yet their echo filled the woods to overflowing.

Indian summer still prevailed under the impenetrable leafage of the forest; here no storm could blow, although the sun might filter down in motes of amber to warm the lower air. But overhead, where the tall tree-tops took the full rigour of the west, there was continual sound and movement, like the multitudinous hurry of the sea, and the rich profundity of autumnal colour was radiant in the wind.

Along the broad buffalo-streets, and through the tangled bear-brakes, between walls of white oak and tulip-trees, the four friends proceeded to the professor's wedding. A holiday mood possessed them; each sang such songs as memory and use made possible, so that while David roared with sonorous lungs of Greenland and the whale-fish, the captain hummed meditatively of The Pride of the Valley, and the bridegroom himself apostrophized Beauty's Eyes in a thin tenor. In this curious symphony Shiloh's voice was audible as a single taut and glittering string, drawn to a thread of sound, vibrating yet never broken.

At intervals the jocular yelping of the dog rattled from the underbrush like the bark of a snare-drum.

As evening rose in azure smoke from the trodden leaves of the forest, the professor found that his own and Shiloh's swifter pace had carried them somewhat in advance of the others; he paused to listen for the footsteps of his companions, and was suddenly aware of the words of Shiloh's song.

> "The golden gates of sleep unbar
> Where strength and beauty, met together,
> Kindle their image like a star
> In a sea of glassy weather!"

"A bridal song," said Shiloh smiling: "I made it in celebration of the mutual happiness of most beloved friends; its words are a good augury, yet I will make you another for yourself alone, before to-morrow."

They camped that night by a ford of the Licking, which shimmered among small white stones as numerous as a Milky Way. Winter was in the air at last; the great fire they builded warmed a darkness brittle with frost. The flame, nourished upon fat pine and cedar, grew upward in a formidable splendour like the trunk of another tree; its solid column stood between the oaks and beeches, touching the moss and ivy berries with coraline light, and seeming to support upon its summit a canopy of arching boughs tufted with mistletoe.

"Seemingly ain't a goldarned Injun left around this neck o' woods," lamented David as he cast a pine-knot upon the blaze. "This is a sightly spot for an ambush, and this fire can be seen for miles around, I reckon, yet here we sit as safe as a passel of old wives at a prayer-meeting. It's plumb ridiculous, Cap'n; even a bear would liven things up a bit, but I ain't seen nothing bigger than a jack-rabbit since I quit Boston."

"Personally, my young friend," said the captain, thoughtfully impaling a slice of chipped beef upon the point of a stick, "I can well dispense with the excitements of crushed ribs and cloven skulls. There may indeed be a bear or two in the cane-brake behind us, if you care to investigate its recesses, but the

Shawnees and Piankeshaws are happily shyer than in Simon Girty's days. I wish I might accommodate you with a supper of pemmican and parched corn, but you must be content with these substitutes." He straightened the tin coffee-pot upon its stones, and gave his attention to the sizzling beef.

Shiloh was pleasantly weary; a league of Kentucky mud-hole and buffalo-trace was more strenuous than the thirty smooth green miles between Marlow and London. He leaned against a fallen tulip-tree; the coffee in his tin cup was boiling hot, and sweet with maple sugar. A lazy suspicion persisted in his mind that David had laced it with fiery liquor from his flask; in calm defiance of his principles he did not greatly care. He ached with sleep; there was a musical confusion within his brain with whose falling rhythms he was half familiar.

"It is the sound of the sea," said Shiloh to himself, closing his sea-blue eyes against the electric brilliance of the flame. He had forgotten the steady rushing of the wind among the tree-tops, which indeed were far removed above the hollow where he lay. Now it appeared to him that waves instead of withered leaves were moving over him upon the currents of the air.

"I must write it down before it blows away," he said to himself absurdly; with one long hand he groped among the fallen leaves for the bit of brown paper which had contained the maple sugar. His head ached a little with sleep and the imminence of the music; he leaned upon his elbow in the extreme firelight and scribbled on the scrap of paper, to which a few moist amber crystals still adhered.

"There, Lackland, is your Epithalamium," he said presently; he slipped the folded paper into the professor's hand with a shy secretive haste, and turned upon his back with a sigh. In five seconds he was fast and profoundly asleep; the professor looked at him and wondered how he could slumber so peacefully in the radiant heat from the cedar logs, whose sanguine colour made the silvered locks of his hair into a fantastic wreath of flames.

"Looks like a salamander, or maybe a chameleon, doesn't he, Lackland?" said the captain with a queer smile. He stood staring down at Shiloh, and twisting his rusty beard with meditative fingers.

" Read, Lackland, and see what the chameleon has to say about marriage," he proposed at length.

The professor unfolded the paper and read, pausing first to admire the pretty drawing of a forest tree wherewith the manuscript was embellished.

" It is — rather an astonishing production," he murmured uncomfortably. " As a poem, I should pronounce it to be of the highest merit, but I should hardly care to show it to Miss Lillie upon the eve of our wedding."

The captain took the paper and perused it with reflective care; instead of returning it to the professor he deliberately put it into his own pocket-book.

" I'll keep this for the poor boy," he said with decision; his eyes were again upon Shiloh's sleeping figure, and both David and the professor observed the curious melancholy of his look. He had been wearing his ragged army greatcoat slung nonchalantly over one lean shoulder; now he removed it, and with a brusque embarrassed gesture tossed it upon the ground.

" Tuck it round the confounded critter, Davy," he exclaimed irritably. " Damned long legs of his, stretching miles from the logs; probably freeze before morning. Yes, that's more like it; I suppose his hair won't catch fire while he's asleep. And now, brother lizards," said the captain with a stupendous yawn, " let's to our rustic couches, because for my part I'm abjectly sleepy and crosser than David's mythical bear."

Nevertheless, the captain lay awake long after the others were absorbed in their respective dreams of Shawnee warriors and rose-red brides; at intervals he unfolded Shiloh's bit of brown paper, and reread it carefully by the light of the diminishing embers. At such times his face was illuminated by a brightness which seemed reflected from the uneven lines upon the paper, commensurate with something clearer and stronger than a dying flame, and his look, as it strayed to Shiloh's slight and motionless form, was full of grave affection and concern. At last he slept, but not before he had determined to venture into the delicate and mysterious reticences of the other's mind with a salty cordial of excellent advice.

" For," argued the captain sagely to himself, " even if he isn't the particular mad crusader I believe him to be, he'll never last in this wilderness; the first bout of chills and fever will shake him into kindling-wood."

With which kindly but mistaken foreboding the captain turned upon his side and slept, while the words of Shiloh's Epithalamium made an ocean music in his dreams.

6

"Shiloh," asked the captain in the crisp beginning of the next day, "why on earth don't you go home to your friends?"

The translucent clarity of early morning was in the sky; it filtered milkily among the tree-trunks, blanching Shiloh's countenance to a waxen mask. The captain was amazed to see how the increasing light scooped hollows around the shining eyes and set lines upon the corners of the lips.

"No," said Shiloh sharply and rather angrily, "no; I shall not go home until I have done what I set forth to do."

Then he stared suddenly at the other, stared with those bright and hollow eyes, and spoke again in a changed and gentler voice.

"But how is this — home to my friends?" demanded Shiloh. "Are not you and Lackland my friends?"

"Of course, my dear fellow," the captain assured him kindly; a pang of compunction visited his heart upon the instant, in observing how his question had altered Shiloh from yesterday's creature of warmth and hardihood into a pitiful difference and pain. He knew that there was suspicion and revolt in the variable brilliance of the eyes, and he wondered what hateful trap had closed upon the brain behind them. He was sincerely sorry that any careless words of his should have rendered this contrivance effective and set Shiloh wincing from the clutch of invisible fangs, and now his one desire was to undo the evil work.

"Of course we are your friends, with all our hearts," he repeated. "And for this very reason we have sometimes feared that you must be lonely in a new land, that you must often grieve for the older friends you've left in Italy and all the rich amenities of your former life. I know little enough about it, to be sure, but either it's made you what you are, Shiloh, or else you've shaped it like a bright shell to fit your soul; in either case it's better than the dog's life you've been leading here."

Shiloh stared at the captain incredulously; his astonished gaze shifted from the captain's solemn face to the comfortable antics of the yellow dog; he looked at the fluttering colour of the camp-fire and at the powdery hoar-frost melting on a scarlet leaf.

" It does not seem to me a dull or arduous existence," he said softly. " As for my past fortunes, they have been happier than I deserve; my regrets are all for my own shortcomings. Neverthe-less, you are wrong about my soul; it has clothed itself in no rain-bow shell; rather has it stifled in something narrow as a coffin, and obscure. This was of my own shaping, and by heaven I have lived withdrawn into its shadows like a tortoise under his horny shield; often I have felt the outrageous weight of the world upon my back. A sudden cataclysm split that armour; I emerged into a new element, a volatile compound of sun and sea-water and eccentric liberty, and in this I have contrived to swim and fly and scramble across half a continent, to the immense benefit of my health and spirits. You speak of a dog's life; I am at a loss to understand you. We live like wild deer or a free company of eagles; a finer life it is impossible to imagine. Don't send me home, Appleby; I don't want to go home; I want to go to the professor's wedding."

" And that you shall, by graminy, or I'm a double Dutch-man! " cried David furiously, standing with clenched fists at the captain's shoulder. His face was crimson under the bronze; the visible muscles of his arms were like knots of copper cable.

Both Shiloh and the captain burst into a shout of laughter; the deep rumble in the captain's throat was thunder to the light-ning of Shiloh's eyes. The professor regarded the scene with decorous surprise.

" Don't murder me, Davy," the captain finally found breath to implore. " I promise to let him attend all the weddings west of the Alleghanies, and he needn't go home to his Italian palace unless he chooses. Shiloh, my dear boy, I admit I was mistaken; if you like us as well as all that, I have nothing more to say."

" I should hope not, Captain Appleby, sir," David interposed indignantly. "Fair made my blood boil the way you was bothering and hectoring of him, and him so humble and polite and asking your leave, by jingo, as gentle as a lamb. He hasn't to ask nobody's favour to go to no weddings so long as I'm on deck, and as for his turning back to them goldarned fever-smitten heathen climes, I'll break the neck of the man that says he must. Didn't I fish him out of the bloody ocean with my own hands, and him as white as a new sail in moonshine, and ain't I seen him come to life, and grow strong and spunky as a young catamount? Think he's a-going to be let fall back into whatever hell was hurting of him? Not while I'm here to learn the reason why!"

"David, David, moderate this ebullition of loyalty, or you will be the death of me!" the captain entreated through his laughter. "I have no intention of arresting your friend's natural development of mind and body; on the contrary I am unaffectedly fond of him, and far from condemning him to fever-smitten climes, I mean to force him to swallow several ounces of quinine before the day is out. In regard to the relative salubriety of the Bay of Spezzia and a Kentucky cane-brake, I dare say it's a malarial six of one to an aguish half-dozen of the other, but never mind; Shiloh shall dance at this wedding, and there shall be cakes and ale for everyone."

"In so far as the sadly limited means of Mr. and Mrs. Lillie may permit," amended the professor nervously.

Shiloh was quite helpless with laughter; he leaned against a tulip-tree and wept for mirth. David's loving ferocity, the captain's amiable sarcasm, and the professor's bewilderment appeared equally amusing. He had been vaguely and courteously grieved by the captain's good advice, but now all remembrance of reality was swept away in a warm hightide of animal spirits.

"Thank you, David," he said brokenly. "I am truly grateful for your championship, but I do assure you, my dear fellow, that the captain and I are not at daggers drawn as you seem to suppose. I won't ask you to apologize to him for your impetuous words; his feeling heart will already have forgiven you; I must, however, request you to shake his hand in amity before we eat our breakfast. That's my brave Davy; that's my seven-at-a-blow shepherd boy. Now give us all a smile and a cup of coffee, and we shall know you are yourself again."

David, his face still glowing like red metal above the emotional furnace in his breast, managed to clasp the captain's hand without rancour; he felt ashamed of his heat, and mortified by Shiloh's levity. He shook his thick gold hair in stubborn disapproval before he spoke.

"All very well to laugh and carry on like that," he muttered with an ominous frown, "All very well to laugh and holler like a fool, only where'd you be now if it weren't for me, and where'd your sickly skeleton bones be bleaching? 'Tain't often as I remind you of that, Shiloh, but you know it's give me a sort of right to look after you, and see as nobody harms you, and you don't plumb forget to take care of yourself. Storms and sharks I've saved you from before this, and deacons and yaller fever and Mr. Daingerfield on dry land, and now mebbe it's going to be Injuns and bears and murdering bandits. If I spoke hasty to the captain, 'twas a long of me being bothered about you, and afeared you'd slip back to your Eyetalian troubles if he didn't leave you be in peace. And then," said David gruffly, "you talked so pitiful about wanting to go to the wedding, like you was a little boy and the captain a cross schoolmarm, that by tarnation I just clean boiled over like a hot sugar-kettle!"

"I know, Davy, I know!" cried Shiloh consolingly, clapping him on the back. "Come now and eat your bacon; everyone understands and everyone loves you for your excellent impulses. Believe me that I am not unmindful of my debt to you; I only wish I might repay it in kind."

"Aw, that's nothing," grumbled David, deluging Shiloh's tin plate with an excessive quantity of bacon-grease.

"But seriously, Appleby," Shiloh said to the captain a little later, while they were scrubbing the dishes with sand preparatory to bundling them into their packs, "I am eager to convince you of my good faith; my heart is in the search which David and I have so romantically begun, but over and above the dream of finding Silver, our journey has been a singularly happy progress into that forgetfulness for which my spirit longed. I have explained to you the curious circumstances of my life; a letter may soon reach me through the Commercial Bank of Louisville, whither Captain Ffoulkastle promised to forward all correspondence. I think it is as yet too soon to hope for word from Italy, but a prosperous voyage may so expedite matters that I shall know my fate within a few weeks. God grant that it may not be a mandate sentencing me to lifelong solitary exile; if I dared to imagine that she will join me in the innocent wilderness! But enough of that; I must bear with fortitude those things which cannot be mended short of Utopia. For the present I am fortunate; I neither remember nor attempt to prophesy, but am content with the propitious hour. Be patient with me, my friend, and permit me to deceive myself in transitory peace."

"With all my heart; I'll worry you no more, Shiloh, with sage advice," answered the captain emphatically. "You know your own business best, I dare say, and even if you don't, it's none of mine. There's always fifty acres of bounty land waiting for you in Pike, if you care to join me there; otherwise I'll wish you luck and God-speed on your wild-goose-chasing, and say good-bye. But first there's the wedding; we must all be merry for that, and just to avoid the possibility of a funeral, do let me persuade you to sample old Doctor Appleby's quinine-and-whisky cocktail."

"Oh, very well; if I must I suppose I must," said Shiloh, laughing with a wry face as he swallowed the fiery bitter dose. "You're determined to make a drunkard of me in spite of my principles, but we must all render some slight sacrifices to friendship, so here's to your best health in sanative gall and wormwood!" He drained the cup and put a fragment of maple sugar into his mouth; its taste of spring melted tenderly against his outraged palate.

The Orphan Angel

V

REFUSE THE BOON

Miss Rosalie Lillie was seated upon the wood-pile in an attitude of negligent grace; her fine eyes were fixed above the distant tamarack-trees in contemplation of some winged chimæra of the mind. A gold pencil-case was suspended by a delicate chain around the lady's creamy throat; a notebook peeped from the pocket of her blue satin apron, and a gilded album lay within reach. Under a furred cloak her attire was frail and silken; she wore thin-soled bronze slippers, and her hands were encased in gloves of primrose kidskin.

Miss Lillie was a singularly lovely girl; her features were regular and her figure tall and classically formed. She had a rich abundance of chestnut hair and her velvet eyes were the colour of purple-brown pansies. She looked very expensive and unsuitable against a background of enormous forest trees and ragged rail fences; the smoky November sun picked out the Italian cameo upon her bosom and increased the splendid damask of her cheek.

The reversed fortunes of the Lillie family had subdued their material welfare to the level of a log cabin, but this cabin was both neat and commodious, and the hand of refined taste had set a few late-blossoming plants in its circular flower-beds and draped its narrow windows with ruffled muslin curtains. The expanse of turf before the house had been entirely cleared of underbrush, and a modest vegetable-garden lent an air of respectability to the back premises; nevertheless the scene offered a melancholy contrast to the suave and regal creature now rudely enthroned upon the wood-pile.

Miss Lillie lifted her Spanish guitar from an adjacent pine-knot; she smoothed out its scarf of yellow silk with a pensive hand, and then idly strummed the opening chords of some rhapsodic love-song.

"Heigh-ho!" said Miss Lillie aloud, in time to the music, "heigh-ho, alas, I would that he were come!"

Her pansy-coloured eyes suddenly overflowed with facile tears; at the bottom of her heart she knew that she did not call upon the professor in this apostrophe. Beyond the oaks and tamaracks the sunset flared ominously into crimson and then ebbed away in gentler fluctuations of light; Miss Lillie saw the forest as a vast tapestry from which a paladin upon a snowy charger must presently emerge; even now she could hear the iron harmony of hoof-beats approaching to her magical undoing.

She raised her head; her chestnut ringlets fell about the fine carnation blushes of her face. A sound was indeed audible; she knew it for a trampling of footsteps along the logs of the corduroy road.

The sky was luminous now, but its rose reflections had subsided into pallor. In the cabin someone kindled a lamp; its illumination fell like mild domestic moonlight across the fields of pumpkins and Indian corn. Rosalie held her breath, waiting for a dawn of miracles to divide the forest with its ecstasy.

She saw the thorny underbrush violently shaken; lamplight in golden rain fell from its leaves to confuse her. A yellow creature like a goblin fox ran from beneath the bushes and frolicked on the lawn; it lifted its tawny muzzle to the appearing stars and barked with a sharp hylactism, and the woods echoed with airy cynic mirth.

A tall figure strode from under the oaken archway where the corduroy road debouched upon the fields; the pupils of Rosalie's eyes dilated into velvet black, and her suave deep pulses skipped a beat, for the striding figure, which moved so quickly among the little wigwams of the gathered corn, was assuredly not her fiancé the professor. At first, and for no reason save that he walked so lightly, and that his head was bound with a coronet of hawks' feathers, she believed the man to be an Indian brave; the fear which should have followed upon this wild imagination was absent from her heart. Then, as he came within the radius of lamplight, she perceived the sunburnt fairness of his skin and knew instinctively that his dazzled eyes were blue. He stared straight into the bright windows of the cabin; he must have stumbled against the scattered logs of the wood-pile if she had not spoken, in a hurried breathless whisper without words.

"I beg your pardon, Madam; I had not observed you in the obscurity of dusk," he said at once with exquisite courtesy.

Miss Lillie was enchanted by his accent and by his easy grace of manner; it was clear to her that a disinherited prince stood among the monstrous flame-coloured fruit of the pumpkin-field. She saw with pity and passionate indignation that the royal garments were extremely ragged, and that the delicate nobility of the brow was stained with dust. Yet did the eminent nature of this gentleman emerge purely from the casual tarnish of misfortune, and to the girl's vision the rough hawks' feathers were a proper diadem. Along the corduroy road the footsteps of a company of courtiers drew near with an effect of multitude; in truth David's tread was constitutionally heavy, and the captain and the professor were sadly tired.

"Oh sir," said Miss Lillie with feeling, "I do not know who you may be, but you must not pass our humble dwelling without accepting its hospitality for your weariness! My father and mother would never forgive me if I allowed a distressed traveller to proceed into the unknown uncheered by such warmth and sustenance as we can offer. I do beg that you will share our supper, and even spend the night if your engagements will permit."

The gentleman bowed slightly, his long fine hand upon his heart; he laughed in a light-minded manner a little out of keeping with the air of romantic poverty which Rosalie found so tragically poignant.

"My dear Miss Lillie," he answered politely, "surely no other engagement of mine can rival in importance the charming necessity of attending your wedding ceremony."

Rosalie felt herself grow cold and faint with disappointment; she could not tell what fantastic hopes had painted arabesques upon her mind for a moment. She was silent in the dull vacancy of her thoughts; she looked at the stranger to see whether there was any mockery in his laughter, and realised through a queer stupidity of pain that his smile held nothing but good-will and ingenuous pleasure. At that instant the professor approached across the darkening field; she submitted to his embrace with stiff pretended gestures of affection.

Her voice to her own ears was thin and artificial with despair, but indeed she managed to enact surprise and delight so prettily that the deception was precise enough for truth, and both Shiloh and David shared the professor's profound belief in his proven happiness. The captain glanced keenly at the animated face of this handsome girl who was about to marry his friend; he and David were quiet while the other three chattered excitedly of the journey and the wedding and the wicked price of wax orange-blossoms in Louisville. David's mind was full of awed admiration for Miss Lillie's classic beauty and elaborate grace; the captain's reflections were more critical and perhaps more melancholy.

"But Rosalie, my love, how imprudent of you to sit perched upon a wood-pile this particular chill November evening!" cried the professor with ill-concealed approbation of such engaging eccentricity. "I fear that you will most certainly contract a severe cold as the price of your poetics. Of course it is all very complimentary to me, to find you thus disconsolate and longing for my arrival, but next time you are moved to song I trust it may be by our own warm fireside, dearest girl. Meanwhile here is Shiloh, who has himself some talent for original composition, and who will doubtless furnish an elegant extract for the famous album; eh, Shiloh, what say you to a little rhyme-capping after supper in honour of the glad occasion?"

A strange expression, compounded of ironic mirth and some graver, wilder pang, flitted across Shiloh's countenance; it was visible only to the captain, who believed he could unriddle its

secret with a mad conjecture. He said nothing, but he looked at
Shiloh as if he also, among the cloudier regions of the soul, perceived that gentleman as a disinherited prince.

" But la, sirs, of what am I thinking, to detain you here in the
bleak twilight while we chatter about literature? I protest I am
but a poor hostess, and my parents will scold me unmercifully
if I delay another instant to introduce you to them. Sometimes
I could swear I was moonstruck; I fall a-dreaming even over my
fancy-work, and Mama warns me that at this rate I shall never
finish the sweet hearts'ease slippers I am making for poor Papa's
Christmas. You are a poet yourself, Mr. Shiloh, and no doubt
you can feel for me in my sad giddiness; the comfort is, such
moods are partially divine, but you will not persuade my dear
mother to credit this heresy, least of all when I allow the wild-
plum marmalade to boil over upon her immaculate hearth, as I
did this very morning."

Miss Lillie addressed this lively monologue to Shiloh, turning
the velvet splendours of her eyes upon him as she led the way to
the cabin in a rustling hurry of satin petticoats. Shiloh's nerves
were clean and sensitive as a child's after the fresh ascetic rigours
of the forest, and he was painfully affected by the lady's musical
voice and by the scent of patchouli which pervaded her garments.
Of her discourse only two words were made evident to his senses:
the thought of wild-plum marmalade was innocently pleasing to
the imagination, but he chose the flower rather than the fruit as
truer cordial for the spirit.

" Hearts'ease is my favourite flower," he said pensively. " I
wish very much that I possessed a pair of slippers worked in
hearts'ease; my friend Hunt had such a pair once, I remember,
and they were extremely beautiful."

Rosalie caught her breath with rapture; the death-knell of Mr.
Lillie's Christmas hopes was sounded in Shiloh's idle comment.
Already in fancy she felt herself tenderly sorting the Berlin wools
suitable for the production of an artistic masterpiece; the violet
and the purple threads flowed softly through her fingers as she
dreamed.

The lighted doorway of the cabin swung wide to receive the
travellers; their host and hostess stood within its warm low frame

with a lavish fire behind them and welcoming hands reaching out into the shadows. Shiloh found himself drawn into a comfortably glowing room; he sank into the corner of a settle and stared about him rather dizzily. A small pretty lady was embracing the professor; a tall stately gentleman was pounding the captain upon his stiff rheumatic shoulder-blades. David stood sheepishly by the hearth; he was blushing hotly, and his eyes followed Rosalie with looks of fatuous delight.

Miss Lillie was not unaware of the sentiment she had awakened in the breast of this nautical-looking person in the pea-jacket; the fact that the sentiment burned in an unsuitable quarter failed to deprive it of its entire charm of incense. Her vanity was soothed, and while she watched Shiloh from the rolling corner of a fine dark eye, she did not scruple to enslave David by a variety of ladylike enchantments.

"Mama, this is Mr. Shiloh, who appears to have come all the way from Italy to wish us joy upon our wedding-day! " she cried with a nicely modulated trill of laughter. "Didn't Lackland tell me that your home was in Italy, Mr. Shiloh? Ah, how I envy you the noble treasures of art with which that country must abound! Now I am quite sure you must be shockingly fatigued after your long journey; Papa must mix you a sherry cobbler at once, unless you prefer to drink whisky, like our dreadful Kentuckians."

Shiloh rose and bowed to the small pretty lady, who was evidently Miss Lillie's mother; she took his hand very kindly in hers and looked at him with gentle curiosity; for a moment she did not speak, and he was grateful for the pause. Her silence made a fragile peace in the centre of confusion; he noticed that, although her colours were all warm and velvety like her daughter's own, her little features were quite different, soft and blunt and childishly unformed. When finally she spoke it was only to express some simple anxiety as to his immediate comfort. Her voice was low; her southern accent blurred it sweetly into singsong. Shiloh blessed her for an assuaging antidote to the conflict of impressions which surrounded him.

The room was large, and presented an anomalous appearance upon closer view; the puncheon floor was covered with braided rugs, and there was a buffalo-skin before the hearth. Along the whitewashed log walls were hung a number of water-colour views of the French Riviera; curtains of glazed chintz concealed a recess, and the gilded strings of a harp glittered in the firelight. A splendid pier-glass, its carven frame spotted with damp, occupied the space between the windows. A marble-topped table of vermilion boule was piled with sheet music; a fowling-piece was suspended over the rough stone chimney, and rows of books crowded the shelves on either side of it, their rich morocco bindings contrasting strangely with the unplaned yellow pine.

The air was full of the thick opulent fragrance of food and drink; Shiloh could smell sherry, and frying ham, and a queer tart flavour which he later recognised as pickled cucumbers. He felt unhappy; his strong desire was to be gone into the cold conventual sanctuary of the forest. He drifted back towards the fire and sat down in the corner of the settle; he closed his eyes and tried to think of the extremest peaks of Monte San Pellegrino. Rosalie's velvet stare was pressing heavily upon his closed lids; the scent of patchouli came again to his nostrils, and he stifled in its syrupy fog.

2

"BETTER drink this, Mr. Shiloh; it'll do you good," said Mrs. Lillie's light voice at his shoulder. She put a sherry cobbler into his hand and stood regarding him with a look of mild perplexity; it was plain to him that like a dutiful child she waited for his approval of her offering. Her presence was like a small tender screen between his perturbed sensibilities and the intensity of her daughter's lustrous gaze.

Shiloh took the drink with a murmured expression of gratitude; he sniffed at it suspiciously while pretending to taste it. He was very thirsty, but he would infinitely have preferred to slake this longing in a bright tin dipper of spring-water or a foamy measure of new milk. Nevertheless, being at the limit of his endurance, he drank.

The mixture was smooth and palatable; Shiloh was reminded

of the negus brewed by Hogg behind the charmed oak of University College. Its gracious flavour medicined his mind to an immediate calm; he thanked Mrs. Lillie again and more fervently.

"That's a sweet boy," thought Mrs. Lillie with sympathetic interest. She attached no importance to paladins and princes; there was an orphaned quality in Shiloh's smile which smote her malleable heart with a peculiar pity. "He needs a mother, poor lamb," thought Mrs. Lillie, who was at most some ten years Shiloh's senior. "Rosie shouldn't be casting sheep's-eyes at him; it's positively indecent, with Lackland in the room, and the dear innocent himself half dead with sleep."

Aloud she said simply, "Why, I'm certainly glad you like it, Mr. Shiloh; it's nice sherry cobbler. Mr. Lillie used the last of his manzanilla to make it, except a dozen bottles he's saving for the wedding. We don't have many luxuries nowadays; I wish we could have enjoyed the pleasure of your company in our old home in Louisville. This is a terrible change for us all, of course; not but what I sometimes feel there are compensations even in the direst poverty, but then, it's very difficult for poor Rosie; the child has such a fastidious nature."

Rosalie's attention was momentarily diverted by her fiancé's gift of an engraved thimble; the professor was explaining that the pretty implement had been his mother's, and the lady was experiencing no little difficulty in forcing her square rosy fingertip into its thin gold cup. Mrs. Lillie, with a soft mouse-like furtiveness of motion, slipped into the vacant seat next to Shiloh; through a vertigo of sleep he noticed the delicate frosty threads in her chestnut hair and the faint lavender fragrance of her grey merino gown.

"Sometimes, Mr. Shiloh," said Mrs. Lillie, clasping her small hands in her lap and talking very fast in her tender shadowy voice, "sometimes I'm truly thankful to be poor, for my own part; it saves me such a world of trouble and domestic care. I wonder whether a boy like you can possibly realise what it means to a woman to have a popular hospitable husband and a beautiful ambitious daughter just growing up; I give you my word, Mr. Shiloh, that in Louisville three years ago we seldom sat down to table under twenty, and that doesn't include birthdays and holidays and political entertaining, and although the society is very select and almost worthy of your European standards, you know what gentlemen are, and then of course the drinking too, not that I'm narrow-minded, but naturally one has to regard the china and napery as part of a good housekeeper's duty, and although I made it a point never to complain to Mr. Lillie, some of his friends were sadly inconsiderate, particularly as his port was famous from the Cumberlands to the Barrens, and even in a slave state service is very unsatisfactory, and I suppose it was a dreadful calamity to have forty-six banks fail completely, and God knows what the legislature will do, but for myself I regret nothing but the conservatory, and when I think of poor folks starving that appears sinful, and just before the panic of eighteen-nineteen no fewer than four duels were fought in Louisville on Rosalie's account alone, she has her father's aristocratic nose but I believe it's rather her lovely eyes that explain it, and this is a remarkably quiet district, and I have enjoyed the peace and tranquillity beyond words to express, and now it's to be the professor after all, and if she hadn't gone to school with Miss Fuller whose mother came from Wilkes-Barre it would never have happened, and perhaps it's all for the best, only when I let her go East last April I thought of someone a little more comfortably settled, but he has a soul attuned to poetry as she says and an uncle in Congress so I dare say it will end quite happily."

Shiloh had been dreaming of a famous port between the Cumberlands and the Barrens; he saw it as a glassy harbour of pure quicksilver, bright between devouring jagged jaws of headland. Peace and tranquillity; a quiet port in a storm; its delicious waters drowned him in their deepest blessing.

When Mrs. Lillie stopped talking, the amazing silence woke him with a start; he stared wildly about him, ruffling the hair above his brow into wisps of dark and silver. His fingers touched the coronet of hawk's feathers, and he snatched it off with an exclamation of apology; he felt all at once savage and uncivilised and grimed with dust. He looked helplessly at the stains of clay and leaf-mould upon his slender hands.

"You'd like a bath, wouldn't you, Mr. Shiloh?" asked Mrs. Lillie with clairvoyant lovingkindness; Shiloh heard the saving words with passionate relief.

"If there were any lake or sequestered pool in the neighbourhood, I should be most grateful for directions which might enable me to find it . . ." he began, but his hostess cut him short with a sound of gentle mirth.

"Good gracious, my dear, you'd catch your death," she said laughing. "All the ponds will have ice on them to-night, and I can't have my poor guests frosted to match the wedding-cake. There's a big laundry tub in the out-house, if you're no prouder than my husband's ruffled shirts, and I can have plenty of hot water for you in a moment. My last batch of soap wasn't particularly successful, but it's better than nothing even if it didn't come from Paris. Edmund," she called to the professor, whose Christian name was thus for the first time revealed to his friends, "you and Mr. Shiloh are going to have a bath in the laundry tubs before supper; please do the honours of our establishment to the best of your ability while I put the kettle on with the captain's kind assistance."

"Really, Mama, how excessively indelicate!" cried Miss Lillie in a fever of rose-red shame.

Among the curling azure steam-clouds of the out-house Shiloh relaxed in the luxury of cleanliness; the hot water and the harsh brown soap appeared almost wickedly effete in their perfection of comfort. He eyed the fresh linen laid upon a yellow-painted chair with sensuous delight.

"I feel like a Roman emperor, Lackland," he said happily, in the vigorous exercise of a rough huckaback towel.

"You look more like a red Indian," replied the professor with some asperity. He had observed the singular interest which Shiloh seemed to have aroused in Miss Lillie's maidenly bosom, and he was by no means pleased by this phenomenon. He was far too fair-minded to hold his friend responsible, but he was only human, and his voice was sharp with annoyance and chagrin.

Shiloh noticed nothing; his weariness was miraculously fled, and he felt preternaturally hungry and intelligent and cheerful.

An absurd fancy visited his mind; his recovered vitality forced it into lively speech.

"I should like for supper," said Shiloh ridiculously, "a large mutton chop and a lost fragment of Sophocles and a pretty woman."

"Ahem," answered the professor with an acid smile. "I should be inclined to think you had already acquired the latter commodity."

"Oh, you mean Mrs. Lillie," said Shiloh with such translucent innocence that the professor had perforce to believe him while swallowing a private pang of jealousy. "Yes, is she not a charming person? I really think she liked me; I perceive her nature to be simple, but exquisitely sympathetic, candid, and pure. It is a type but too infrequently met with in this brutal mechanical age; I think I shall ask her for some bread and milk instead of those large alarming cucumbers I saw set forth in a cut-glass dish. Will she be offended if I refuse to eat virulent green cucumbers?"

"Of course not, you idiot," the professor replied impatiently. "Those were only pickles and relishes; you're not compelled to eat them, but you'll find them very excellent if you care to try. Rosalie has frequently spoken of her mother's pickles; you may have watermelon rind or limes or young spring onions if you are afraid of cucumbers."

"No thank you," murmured Shiloh, a look of unearthly terror widening his eyes. "I had far rather not make the attempt. Curious, are they not, these customs of the country? You will scarcely credit it, but in Italy young women of good family actually eat *garlic* . . ."

"Disgusting!" said the professor. "And what, pray, has such a depraved habit to do with cucumbers?" He spoke as sourly as if the most astringent of Mrs. Lillie's conserves were already wrinkling his palate, and Shiloh permitted the subject to languish into silence while struggling with the Gordian problem of his bootlaces.

In the large room of the cabin their host received them with a fine sleek blend of mockery and pompous rhetoric, mingled smoothly like his sherry cobblers. He was cast in the noblest Roman mould, but bilious-coloured and arid as a desert sand-storm;

it was evident that his desiccated frame must require a constant stimulating dew of punch and negus. His mannered speech was suavity itself, but he had the hot and violent eye of an irascible elderly stallion. One pictured him within the mahogany precincts of the counting-house, or splendid in the senate-chamber; his well-shod feet appeared to spurn the puncheon floor with instinctive scorn, and all his gestures threatened to demolish the cabin walls into abject heaps of match-wood.

After a massive meal of turkey and ham and hot waffle cake, crowned by quantities of custards and tipsy-parson and enlivened by much witty conversation, the company gathered about the profuse comfort of the fire; a superb set of ivory chessmen was produced from behind the flour-barrel, and the captain and Mr. Lillie gave themselves up to the high intricacies of the Allgaier gambit.

The cold turquoise forget-me-nots of Rosalie's new thimble hovered fastidiously over the rich furry colours of the Berlin wool; Tyrian hearts'ease burgeoned upon slippers grown conspicuously narrow for a father's gout. Now and again her refulgent gaze slid with velvet demureness to Shiloh's feet; easy tears clouded her enchanted vision to perceive with how preposterous an elegance his ankles emerged from the dusty hobnailed boots. She hummed softly to herself, and bent her curls above her sewing.

Mrs. Lillie was netting a little purse of pearl-grey silk; minute and glittering particles of steel were looped along its surface like a fall of dewdrops. "Nothing to put in it except my lucky silver levy and some pennies," she said, laughing.

The professor had found his lady's album; a pinch of jealousy peppered his delighted pride as he exhibited its marvels to his friend. Shiloh was sympathetic, but sleep had once more enveloped him in a wizard's mantle; he was vague and pale, surveying the scene giddily from the platform of a dream, and his weariness was a visible veil across his eyes.

"Oh, charming, charming," he repeated, swallowing the yawn he was too courteous to confess.

"You see," said the professor, turning a leaf upon which a poem was freshly inscribed with a quill pen below a dainty vignette of a pair of children playing battledore, "this was composed upon the wood-pile this very evening; she copied it while we were at our — ahem — ablutions. Is she not a girl of truly astonishing talent?"

Shiloh blinked, sighed, and read; Rosalie, watching him closely, was soothed and flattered by the profound sadness of his face.

" Ah, she has called her poem ' Hearts'-ease,' after the slippers," Shiloh murmured politely, staring at the words through his Delphic veil of sleep.

> "Thy tender syllables suggest
> A Paradise denied to me;
> Within this wasted, wounded breast
> The heart awakes uneasefully.

> "Hearts'-ease! If Heav'n but hear my prayer
> Thy pensive blessing I shall have
> When, purple upon proud despair,
> Thy blossoms glow above my grave!"

" A very pleasing set of verses," said Shiloh without irony; his wild and delicate mind was singularly uncritical in such matters, and the simplest expressions of melancholy were ever germane to his taste.

" Won't you write something of your own, Mr. Shiloh? " asked Rosalie with unaccustomed timidity; she dipped the long quill pen in her best Indian ink and laid the open book upon Shiloh's knee.

Its gilded satin covers were plump as pincushions; Shiloh was quite sensible of their weight, and of the fact that their glossy fabric was impregnated with the scent of patchouli. His weariness seemed intolerably augmented by the task required of his imagination.

" Anything; something you've already written, and can remember," the professor added in humane recognition of his comrade's pallid and bewildered looks.

Shiloh stared down at the virgin page, and the quill trembled and shook in his hand as though it were still a portion of some aërial wing; then he lifted his eyes, which passed blindly by Rosalie's sleek loveliness to rest upon her mother's half-averted face. The quill was poised and eager, alert for a leap into immediate blue; suddenly Shiloh's hand relaxed, and the feather wavered to the floor.

"I am sorry," said Shiloh faintly; "I am too tired to invent rhymes; I trust you will forgive me. Perhaps I can recall an appropriate trifle; do you happen to understand Italian? This was composed for a lady's album; it is quite in the album style."

"Alas, no," Rosalie replied regretfully. "French and German I know very well indeed; I have always been complimented upon my French accent, and Papa has taught me a smattering of Spanish for my guitar. But Italian . . ."

"A little," said Mrs. Lillie; "Petrarch's sonnets; when I was a girl." Her shadowy drawling voice was so low that only Shiloh heard her.

He picked up the pen and began to write. When he had finished he handed the book to Mrs. Lillie with a smile; the orphaned quality of his smile was more than ever evident to her pity, and she immediately began thinking about blankets for the spare bed, and wondering whether or no the best linen sheets had been properly aired.

Nevertheless she felt a mild curiosity concerning the Italian words traced upon the album's page; she perused them carefully, pleased to find that she had no difficulty in deciphering their meaning. At her shoulder Rosalie's warm presence was somehow stormy and inimical.

"'Buona notte, buona notte!' — Come mai
    La notte sara buona senza te? . . .
    La notte quando Lilla m'abbandona. . . ."

"How sweet!" said Mrs. Lillie gently. "Thank you, my dear. And now I think we had better all go to bed. Edmund, will you conduct the gentlemen to the attic? Mind the ladder, Mr. Butternut; it's a sad makeshift, but I'm sure your sailor's agility can manage it. I hope you will sleep well, Mr. Shiloh; pleasant dreams to you; good-night, good-night."

3

THE rhythmic beat of rain upon the roof woke Shiloh; the corn-husk mattress whispered rustlingly beneath his slender restless bones, which ached with weariness along their tightened nerves. He lay still, marvelling at the darkness and at the singular imminence of the rain, whose sound was so contiguous to his mind that his fingers groped for drops against his cheek. He knew, through some exquisite cognition of the body, that it must be morning; he was puzzled by the thick obscurity, and alarmed by a sense of imprisonment. He felt that he was suffocating, and, thrusting the hysteric mists of terror from his face, he leaped up with a muffled cry. A mysterious engine clattered to the floor; both wood and iron echoed his surprise, and a faint light entered to explain the gloom.

"Knocked over the pitchfork, by graminy, and the old lady's best patchwork goes trailing in the dirt!" exclaimed David's reassuring bass; Shiloh perceived the dim glimmer of his friend's head upon a near-by pillow, and realised that he himself was shivering upon the edge of a large bedstead, rudely curtained by a succession of quilts fastened to the rafters. A ghostly dawn penetrated this screen, and showed the attic strewn with a curious agglomeration of objects; three chests, an old-fashioned spinning-wheel, and a number of reels and swifts crowded the space between the two mattresses occupied by the captain and the professor. Shiloh's bed was placed immediately below the peak of the roof, upon whose surface rain drummed continuously; the wooden frame of the bed was still covered with a sylvan grain of bark, and its twisted proportions seemed to have shaped themselves in a spontaneous miracle of growth. Shiloh thought it a fit couch for a dryad; he was faintly troubled by David's mighty limbs disposed beneath the blankets, and by the nautical air which his friend retained even among the arboreal convolutions of the bedposts.

"But it isn't an air, it's a smart gale," remarked Shiloh meditatively, wondering why David had never married a mermaid.

"Wet day for a wedding," yawned the captain, rolling over upon his side and dispatching a dusty boot in the general direction of the professor's head. "Not but what your prospective parents understand admirably the art of excluding cold and damp by means of spirituous armour, God bless 'em."

"Spiritual armour?" said the professor in a voice of sleepy wonder. "Oh, no, I am quite irreligious; mine is the scientific mind, you know. Besides, my people were all Presbyterians, and I was taken to church at far too early an age. But I've been reading the marriage service, and upon my soul the thing's poetry, Appleby; it's equal to Dryden. 'In the time of man's innocency . . . mystical union.' Is it not prodigiously fine?"

"Detestable shackles," Shiloh cried indignantly, "garlanded with the most tremulous and tender flowers of speech!"

"But I calculate as how there'll be fiddlers," added David. "And certainly you'll allow that the victuals and drink are elegant."

"Which remark blends with the welcome scent of Mocha to remind us of breakfast," said the captain, rising and shaking himself like a lean earth-coloured hound.

At least three out of the four companions bumped their foreheads against the low-hung attic roof, but presently by the light of a long twelve a certain state of order was retrieved from among the tangled heaps of coats and shoes upon the floor, and they descended the stick ladder into the warmth and bustle of the living-room.

Mrs. Lillie provided them with a large iron skillet and a quantity of boiling hot water and strong brown soap, and setting these cosmetic luxuries on a bench beneath the eaves of the house they contrived a mild degree of cleanliness in common. There were plenty of huckaback towels; Shiloh found a great silky square of fine damask tucked under his arm, and vaguely perceived that his hostess had placed it there.

"I embroidered six dozen especially for my Louisville guest-chamber, but the ciphers are very hard upon the eyes," she told him seriously.

He shaved with one of Mr. Lillie's beautiful slim French razors; he felt deliciously soothed and tranquillized as he saun-

tered to the spring between the soft cold curtains of the rain.
He knelt and splashed the water in his face, and then drank of
its chilly sweetness; it was a delicate and cordial wine, and he
loved it better than all the golden manzanilla borne on galleons
out of the Old World.

"And now if I might only have tea for breakfast instead of
coffee, I should be quite content," said Shiloh to himself as he
returned through silver November mists to the cabin door.

A thin and flowery fragrance saluted his ravished senses as he
entered; it pierced the bacon smell like a filament of crystal, and
Shiloh saw a round blue Canton tea-pot upon the table, and a
noble tea-cup flanked by jugs of cream. Wreaths of jasmine-
blossoming smoke ascended towards the ceiling, veiling Mrs.
Lillie's pretty countenance in a becoming gossamer.

"This is really too kind of you!" he cried happily, hastening
to her side.

4

MESSENGERS, in the nimble likeness of a regiment of ragged boys,
were immediately sent forth over the neighbouring country to
summon guests to the wedding; it was not until three days later
that a sufficient company were assembled to lend the affair its final
social and religious grace.

The skies were once more calm and brilliant; a last autumnal
haze, withdrawn before the cruel steeliness of winter, rendered the
horizon blue as heaven itself. The cold was as yet slight and
brittle, breakable by the noonday sun into splinters of air clear
as ice and sweet as sugar. It was early afternoon; an afternoon
formed by a benevolent god for lively pastoral rejoicing, for dance
and song and the innocent relish of creature comforts.

Happily all such were now at hand; no Venetian carnival or
Maypole dance upon an English green could have presented a
more vivacious motley to the eye. Here were fine gentlemen and
fair ladies from Louisville, in cashmere and velvet and rich seasonable furs; here were farmers from the next clearing and moun-
taineers from the distant Cumberlands, in coonskin caps and
buckskin gaiters, with their wives and daughters in linsey-woolsey,

and copperas and blue plaid homespun. Here was an itinerant Baptist preacher from Maine who looked like a starving Hebrew prophet, and an Episcopal clergyman from Cincinnati who looked like a corrupt Roman emperor. The gathering overflowed into the fields; the grass-plot before the house was pied and variegated like a tropical garden. Shiloh gazed about him in stupefaction; he hated the crowd and the clamour, and yet he was fascinated by the improbability of the spectacle, and by the wild beanstalk speed of its sudden growth.

On the sunny sheltered side of the cabin the fiddlers were already tuning their instruments, hugging the battered honey-coloured fiddles to their breasts and whispering affectionately to the tense and nervous strings. Within the firelit living-room a long table was laid with warm and heartening viands and generous bowls of punch and sangaree; Mrs. Lillie was babbling of syllabubs against her husband's reiterated insistence upon gin-sling and juleps. Shiloh had never in his life seen so many baked hams and roasted turkeys; he was visited by a fleeting recollection of the breakfast-table at Field Place during the Christmas holidays, and the ghosts of cold pheasants and visionary rounds of beefs rose vaguely in his memory.

The soft preparatory wailing of the fiddles charmed him; he remembered Hogg's little apologue of the interrupted country dance and the enraged musicians.

"Do you know," he said to David, who was staring wide-eyed at the impressive scene, "I have come almost to believe in the truth of this fable; my friend was eloquent in his account of how I devoured all the rosin which these poor fellows had provided for their bows."

"And you might have done so, at that, Shiloh," David assured him, grinning. "Ain't we all seen you eating spruce gum, or licking the tar off pine trees same as a cat licks cream?"

He heard a gentle voice at his shoulder; Mrs. Lillie was behind him, her small face pink with some secret poignancy of alarm. Shiloh saw tears in her pretty eyes.

"Oh, my dear boy," she said quickly, "I shouldn't ask you such a thing, I know, but I feel sure that although such a recent friend you are a true one, and you would have great influence over her if only you would be so kind as to try. Now if you'll just go back of the chintz curtain at the end of the cabin you'll find poor Rosie with her wedding veil on and in her white satin which has turned out better than one could have expected but crying her eyes out and I can't think why except that she says nothing will induce her to marry him but perhaps if you reason with her you can persuade her and oh, Mr. Shiloh, I do entreat you to make the attempt for her father and I can do nothing."

A preternatural brightness of fear flashed into Shiloh's eyes; he would more willingly have fought the fiercest beasts at Ephesus than have been called upon to penetrate behind the chintz curtain into the privacy of Miss Lillie's passionate distress. At the same time he had a painful conviction that it was impossible to refuse this request.

"I am afraid I shall be rather worse than useless," he said with desperate calm, " but of course, if you believe I can be of service, I shall be most happy to assist you to the best of my powers."

Shiloh lifted the chintz curtain with a visibly trembling hand; he tapped timidly at the whitewashed log beside it, and a tear-drenched contralto murmur permitted him to enter the little recessed dressing-room.

The window at this end of the cabin was so tiny that two tall candles of deer tallow burned above the makeshift dimity flounces of the toilet-table. Miss Lillie sat upon a low stool; she regarded herself steadily in the depths of a round mirror which hung like a circle of shadow between the candles. The tarnished gilt festoons framed a countenance no longer suave and smooth and rich with carnation blushes; Rosalie had been crying, and her eyelids were smudged and reddened by her tears; for the rest she was pale and by no means beautiful in her grief. Nevertheless Shiloh liked her better than he had before; he wished that she would not scent her garments with patchouli, but he was profoundly touched by her evident trouble and confusion.

"I suppose you have come to laugh at me," she said defiantly; Shiloh was convinced that this was the language of madness or delirium.

"Good God, for what do you mistake me? " he cried in sincere horror. "I have only come in the forlorn hope of helping you, of comforting you for a sorrow I do not in the least comprehend. It was your mother's thought; if I intrude, pray tell me so, and I will immediately leave you."

"Please, please do not leave me," said Rosalie in a voice of humble entreaty. "It is a respite; it is a passing interval of peace; if you have any pity, you will not hasten its inevitable conclusion."

Shiloh, with an involuntary sigh, seated himself cross-legged upon the floor and prepared to be patient; the tuning of the fiddles sounded enchantingly free and far-away, like a chorus of magical grasshoppers.

"Why do you not desire to marry my excellent friend Lackland?" he inquired politely. "I quite understand all the theoretical objections to matrimony, but in this case the partner of your life will be a man of such high conscientiousness and noble tolerance that I confess I am at a loss to account for your extreme agitation."

Rosalie turned her eyes upon him; their pansy-colour was darkened to a dreadful despairing intensity of black. She gazed at him fixedly for a moment, and the blood was congealed in his veins; he saw the amazing anger of her eyes, and they seemed to him the unlighted sockets of a dream of bedlam.

Suddenly Miss Lillie uttered a piercing shriek, and fell into a fit of violent hysterical weeping, crumpling the delicate laces of her veil against her vehement tears.

Shiloh remained crouched upon the floor; slowly the blood was withdrawn from his face, leaving him so pale that every freckle was distinct and surprising against the fairness of his skin. He was frightened half out of his wits, and his astonishment was somewhat in excess of his fear. His hands became very cold; he could not have stirred a finger to save himself from destruction. The noise and passion of the scene were infinitely strange and horrible to his shrinking mind; he would have closed his eyes if he could, but he was incapable of exerting himself by the quiver of an eyelash.

His relief was sharp and painful when Mrs. Lillie came into the room; he returned to life in her reassuring presence, the blood flowed agonisingly along his frozen veins, and his teeth chattered in his head.

"Rosalie, control yourself at once!" cried Mrs. Lillie with unaccustomed crispness. "Can't you see that you are alarming Mr. Shiloh? Dry your eyes immediately, and I will fetch you some elder-flower water in which to bathe them, for you look neither more nor less than a fright, and the rector has been waiting this half hour, having come all the way from Cincinnati to learn that you are an ungrateful girl, to say nothing of poor Edmund."

Rosalie had never before been addressed with an equal severity; the spoiled child was so far astounded by the Spartan rigour of her mother's tones as to find them an effectual tonic against the hysterics. She did as she was bid quite meekly, only casting toward Shiloh's motionless form a glance imploring and to him inexplicable.

"The unhappy creature is suffering under some furious visitation of acute mania," he thought sadly; the little dressing-room was very hot, and he longed hopelessly for fresh air and the cheerful company of fiddlers.

"Run along out of doors, Mr. Shiloh," said Mrs. Lillie pleasantly. "I should never have sent you in here in the first place. Rosie's upset you, and no wonder, but there's a nice cool west wind blowing and you'll soon feel better out there among your friends. Now don't sit there staring at me, but get along, like a dear boy."

Shiloh rose obediently to his feet, and without a word walked lightly, swiftly, and rather unsteadily from the enigmatic chamber into the blue and windy afternoon.

"So," said Mrs. Lillie to her daughter, "I suppose that is the explanation of your behaviour. Thank heaven he doesn't suspect a thing, poor lamb; I'm not so certain about Edmund."

"Mama," cried Miss Lillie tragically, "how can you be so cruel? It is positively inhuman for a mother to mock a daughter's desperate unhappiness. Cold words and cynical reflections: is this all you have to offer me in my hour of trial?"

"I have some nice elder-flower water, Rosie, and one of your father's clean pocket-handkerchiefs. Now, my dear little girl, stop crying and answer me one question. Do you really mean not to marry Edmund, since in any case you can't marry — somebody else?"

Miss Lillie considered this problem for the briefest possible instant; the colour deepened in her cheeks, and her eyes grew bright with a contrary fire. Her mother observed with satisfaction that pride was rapidly repairing the ravages of grief upon the damask of her fine complexion.

" Certainly I should prefer to marry Edmund, if only in order to leave this detestable spot," she announced decidedly. She thought of the amenities of the eastern seaboard, and of the Philadelphia Assembly, to which Edmund's maternal aunt had promised to introduce her. She determined upon peach-coloured silk of the best quality, and felt sure that the trustees of the college must inevitably see eye-to-eye with her in the matter of Edmund's salary. " I must have been mad; of course I will marry him," she repeated, looking all at once extremely handsome.

" You must have been mad, dear; now let me arrange your veil," murmured her mother sympathetically. Rosalie submitted humbly to a second sleeking of her profuse tresses; she caught sight of herself in the glass, and realised that she was beautiful again.

Indeed, something of veritable madness had tinctured the hope which she had recently indulged; this infatuate conceit had followed Shiloh from the room, and Miss Lillie now discovered herself to be in cool possession of all her faculties, yet burning with the additional lustre of emotion. Her loveliness appeared actually augmented; faint purple shadows lay beneath her eyes, and her cheeks blazed under the frosty laces of her veil. She arranged the wreath of waxen orange-blossoms above her untroubled brows with hands that trembled not at all.

5

ALTHOUGH Miss Lillie's fingers trembled not at all, but moved composedly in unison with her pulses, Shiloh had drunk the cup of trembling, and found it poison for the spirit. His knees shook beneath him as he walked lightly from the ambiguous chamber; he did not in the least understand the nature of the scene enacted there, but he was profoundly moved by a sense of something sinister and equivocal in the air of the little room, lit dimly by its two tall candles of deer tallow. The atmosphere had been but too literally exhausted, and he suffered a corresponding prostration of soul as he staggered into the clear immaculate wind.

David ran to him at once; the honest fellow's countenance was crimson with alarm. He caught Shiloh by the elbow and hurried him to the sheltered side of the cabin, where sound flowed liquid and honey-sweet from the hollow fiddles.

" What in tarnation have they been a-doing to you, Shiloh? " he asked angrily, " and where have you been hiding all this gol-darned time, and why do you look as if you'd seen a million mildewed graveyard corpses? Have you met old Jasper, or have you catched the ague, or has someone been hurting of you, just in order to get his skull cracked against this pretty little fist of mine? "

" No, David," said Shiloh mildly. " I am very grateful to you for your kindness, but it is quite unnecessary to crack any skulls this afternoon. Nobody has been hurting me, yet I have a hideous conviction, impossible to explain, that I have been hurting someone else. Let us not speak of it any more; let us leave for Louisville this very minute. Come with me now, David, while we are as yet unobserved; I have a great desire to push on to Louisville to-night, and the evening is beginning to fall, and I wish we were miles away from all these noisy and terrifying people."

" Aw, Shiloh, ain't we even going to wait for the ceremony or the Virginia reel? " David inquired with pathetic eagerness; Shiloh could not resist the dog-like entreaty of his eyes.

" Oh, very well, my dear fellow; of course we will stay," he said laughing, while inwardly his mind cried with weariness like a child confused by glare and clamour. " We will stay for the wedding and the country dances, and then, since that silver feather of a moon must be fire to-night, we will go forth into the forest together after dark. You will come with me, will you not, my best David? I wish we were alone again, and hastening upon our truer quest."

" That I will, by graminy, and with all my heart! " cried David exultingly. " I like the cap'n and the professor real well, but I'm getting almighty sick of 'em, I'm bound to confess.

Scared blue I've been that you'd kind of weaken, Shiloh, and go off to those blasted bounty lands in Illinois, to breed fine upstanding young republicans like the cap'n says you should. And then where'd I be, I asks you, and where'd Silver be, and where'd you be yourself but tied down to a log cabin and a truck-patch and a passel of squawling brats? Oh, that ain't you, Shiloh, and 'tisn't me neither; we're for the raging wilderness and a life of bloody adventure."

"I trust so, sincerely," Shiloh agreed with gentle gravity.

"But oh, looky, Shiloh, here she comes, looking brighter and shinier than the first run of Kennebec salmon!" shouted David in excitement, clutching Shiloh's arm and nearly breaking its narrow bones. "There's Miss Lillie, or Miss Rosie as I call her to myself, and I swan she's the prettiest lady I ever see in all my born days, by cracky!"

Rosalie indeed appeared a perfect idealism of a lovely bride; anger and elder-flower water had smoothed all trace of tears from her brilliant lips and eyes. She glowed and undulated across the lawn in a billow and froth of whiteness; her skin had the suavity of the glassy blossoms about her brow, but it was richly stained with blushes where these were blanched and cold. She looked unreal, yet solid and deliberate as a statue; she might have been a noble wax doll, fashioned to delight some giant darling of the skies.

"Ain't she elegant?" David persisted, and Shiloh nodded without speaking. He was deeply relieved by the evident re-establishment of Miss Lillie's powers of self-control, and the mysterious sense of guilt which oppressed his heart to physical pain was sensibly lightened by the fine spectacle of her magnificence.

"What's she coming out here for, 'stead of being married all proper in the parlour?" wondered David, echoing the question in many curious looks and whispered comments.

"I protest I must be married out of doors, Mama," Rosalie had said as she applied a final delicate bloom of rice-powder to her glowing cheeks. Her mother knew better than to dispute the fantastic point; the girl was sane once more, but a dangerous temper simmered below the polished surface of her calm.

"I'll see what I can do with your father and the rector; he

likes your father's sherry, so he may be amenable by now," said Mrs. Lillie humbly. " Of course you'll catch cold, but it's your own wedding, and I suppose you must have your way."

" In this, at least," replied Rosalie, with a bitter compression of her bright and curving lips.

When at last she crossed the rough grey lawn upon her father's arm, the guests acknowledged an admiration greater than their shocked astonishment. Edmund Lackland stood waiting for her, tranced in quiet idolatry; Rosalie had never been so evidently the vision which lies beyond all metaphysics and astronomies.

" ' Ever remain in perfect love and peace together. . . .' Might it not be true, Davy, and were it not beautiful if it were true? " asked Shiloh in an awe-struck whisper. He was, as always, profoundly impressed by elevated language; he had tried quite sincerely to detest the ceremony, but the pure high heavens touched with pearly light, the first flower-coloured evening stars, the music of the solemn exhortation, proved too much for his prejudices. By the time Rosalie and Edmund were pronounced man and wife, Shiloh was almost persuaded to be a Christian.

Nevertheless, his graceful presence was conspicuously lacking among those who embraced the bride at the close of the service, and the captain caught him gazing wildly at the pretty scene with the look of a slim and mettlesome horse who goes in scornful terror of the curb.

" What's up, Shiloh? " asked Captain Appleby, who knew, with precision and a certain wicked pleasure. " Don't you intend to salute the lady? I never thought to see you so ungallant; her eye is upon you, my boy, and a remarkably reproachful eye it appears to be."

Shiloh blushed, and endeavoured to edge his way through the crowd to a more retired portion of the field. His efforts were circumvented by Mr. Lillie, who invited him to join the country dances then in progress, at the same time courteously offering to introduce him to several charming girls from Louisville. Shiloh was apparently trapped; on one side loomed the stately proportions of his host, brandishing a sherry cobbler in either hand; on the other side at least six lusty young women fluttered and giggled alarmingly. Behind him was Rosalie; in front of him a row of corn-shocks and a rail fence presented various barriers to escape.

The events of the last half-hour had strung his nerves to the breaking-point; Shiloh suddenly decided to go free at all costs, and, casting convention to the four strong winds of heaven, he dived between the corn-shocks and vaulted buoyantly over the rail fence. Mr. Lillie stared after him in dignified surprise; the eyes of the six young ladies from Louisville were round blue moons of amazement at his heels.

Shiloh paused among the pumpkins only long enough to pronounce an exquisitely polite but somewhat incoherent speech of apology; then he caught sight of David in the charitable distance, under the shadow of brown winter oak-trees. Shiloh turned and ran; if he had been running for his life he could not have achieved so passionate an energy as now possessed him in the pursuit of liberty.

6

Liberty eluded him among the delicate tawny grasses of the field; it flew visibly, a slender streak of light like a running hare; it fled before his longing, incredibly nimble and divine. Its silver scut flashed between the furrows of the next field and was gone; Shiloh stood beside David laughing and out of breath. The lovely thing had escaped him for the moment; it had vanished along the narrowing meadows of the distance, but its trace would be phosphorescent in the moonlight, and he would follow it in an hour or two.

Meanwhile he was very happy; he looked back over his shoulder and beheld the wedding dwindled into a bad dream. David put a cold metallic object into his hand; he perceived it to be a large duelling pistol of antique design, newly primed and redolent of raw gunpowder. He grew suddenly conscious that he was in the midst of a group of ragged men and boys; David appeared to be the honoured comrade of them all. Shiloh was favourably impressed by the intelligent democracy of their demeanour; he was pleased by their rough garments of homespun and Kentucky jean, and by their thin hawk-faces, which, variously tanned and freckled by the sun, preserved a uniformity of feature and expression. They wore the aspect of a tribe of fair-haired savages; Shiloh knew at once that they were hardy, humorous, and daring.

"We're a-shooting at that there mark, Shiloh, and you can have the next try if you've a mind to," David explained kindly. "Osbert's gone back to the cabin for a deck of cards for targets; it's pretty good sport at fifteen paces. See, we stick 'em atop of that stake yonder; Dan'l here's the best of the lot so far, but I lay you can lick us if you like. This here's a fine family; Kilpatrick their name is, and they come from Barrens, and their father's known as Squire Johnny, and he used to be a schoolmaster, but was forced to quit on account of fighting such a power of duels. These pistols as Bob loaned me has killed several gentlemen back in Barrens. At first they said they was white folks and me a Yankee, using the word 'Yankee' kind of abusive-like, but we fixed that up quite friendly after a little argument, and now we're all serene. Come on and have a shot while it's light enough, for the sun'll set afore we know it."

At this instant Osbert arrived with a pack of greasy playing-cards; the ace of diamonds was inserted in a cleft at the top of the stick, and Shiloh assumed his station at precisely fifteen paces from the mark. With an air at once nonchalant and vague he took aim and fired; the card quivered upon its rigid stem, and David saw that the pip had been cut meticulously from its exact centre.

"Neat as if you'd gone and done it with a pair of scissors, by jiminy!" he cried with a whoop of triumph. "Always knowed you was a wonder, but I admire to see it proved public to the satisfaction of all and sundry!"

A stranger of distinguished and commanding appearance, who had been idly loitering upon the outskirts of the group, seized the opportunity to approach Shiloh and felicitate him upon this small victory of skill. The man had a splendid pair of black mustachios and wore a tall top-hat and an overcoat richly lined with astrakhan.

"Allow me to congratulate you, sir," he said in a mellow powerful voice. "You are a magnificent shot; I should like to try my own luck against you on a wager."

Shiloh, who knew that this tribute of praise was grossly exaggerated, accepted it as a simple instance of civility. He was slightly embarrassed; one of his transitory blushes imparted a look of touching innocence to his open brow.

"I thank you, sir; it is nothing, and I am convinced that you could easily excel me," he said shyly, in the manner of a schoolboy detected in some ingenuous piece of mischief.

The ingratiating stranger was convinced of exactly the same thing; as a matter of local history he had already excelled so many people in that particular neighbourhood that the advent of Shiloh appeared truly providential to his mind.

"How much are you agreeable to bet, sir?" inquired the gentleman in the astrakhan collar with unctuous eagerness.

"I have no right to wager money, from a common store subject to my friend David's modest necessities, upon so hazardous a chance as my poor proficiency at target practice," explained Shiloh politely. "I shall, however, be most happy to determine our several degrees of excellence by an amicable trial of skill."

He was completely unprepared for the corrosive flood of profanity which burst sulphurously from the stranger's writhen lips; if an actual volcano had spattered the sweet autumnal herbage with malignant fire he could scarcely have been more mortally appalled.

"I am at a loss to understand how I have offended you, sir," he said quietly; his sense of spiritual decorum was outraged, and he spoke with tranquil contempt, but inwardly he was shivering with distaste and indignation. He laid his hand upon David's arm in order to restrain him, and David was amazed at the iron strength of that thin brown hand, and at the energy of anger implicit in its touch.

"I'll bash your damned dirty little head in!" the stranger shouted raucously, advancing upon Shiloh with clenched fists; his face was distorted into a grotesque mask of fury, and its gargoyle shape was stained to the ugly purple of a bruise.

"I'll bash your dirty little goddamned head into a bloody pudding!" he yelled once more, and David drew back, ready to strike a swift defending blow.

He was too late; before he had doubled up his fist into an

effective weapon Shiloh had struck instead; the stranger lay in a bulky crumpled heap upon the ground, and Shiloh was examining his own knuckles with an air of astonished concern.

"I do assure you, David, that he seemed to run straight into my hand! " said Shiloh with a sweetly reasonable smile, opening his large blue eyes and looking fully as dangerous as a new-born babe.

"We hope you've finished him, young feller, and no mistake! " cried the Kilpatrick family in happy chorus, capering about the body of their fallen enemy. " We all of us jest naterally hated Simon Hanna, and he was the wickedest sneakingest villain around these parts, as our dad can tell you. Now he's dead, and the widow and orphan can begin to sit up and take notice. As for you, you're a real genuine public benefactor, and we crave the honour of shaking you by the hand that done the deed! "

Shiloh appeared much confused by these manifestations of popularity; he continued to smile and to blush, while exchanging cordial handclasps with all his new friends from lean gigantic Daniel to goblin Osbert. It was pleasant to be regarded as a romantic champion of freedom, but he felt faintly sorry for Simon Hanna, and the flayed knuckles of his right hand were excessively painful in the strong Kilpatrick clutch.

"Do you really think he is dead, Davy? " he wondered anxiously, while David examined the prostrate foe with quick ungentle competence. " I had no idea that it was such an easy matter to kill a man; I suppose I should be overcome with remorse, but he was such a disagreeable person, and his manner was so gratuitously rude, that I cannot entirely regret having struck him. I hope, however, that he is not really dead, though I shall be sorry to disappoint my young friends the Kilpatricks."

"Aw, Shiloh, of course he's not dead, the cowardly dog," grunted David disgustedly, with his ear to Mr. Hanna's loudly labouring chest. " Can't you hear him puffing like a grampus, and don't you see he's as red in the face as a drunken turkey-cock? Takes more than a tap from your skinny fist to kill a beast like that; not but what you landed him one in the jaw very neatly, and a pleasure it was to see you do it. Clever and handy you always was, and quick as buttered lightning; I could teach you a trick or two in no time that would learn you to box blue-fiery rings around a lumbering hulk like him. Now we'd better be clearing out of here afore he comes to; he's an ugly customer, and if we want to fetch Louisville to-night we must be getting under weigh."

" It does not precisely agree with my notions of fair play to leave a vanquished enemy unconscious upon the field of combat," said Shiloh with a troubled sigh. " It is true that I am very eager to be gone, yet I should prefer to feel certain that this unhappy creature remains in charitable hands. May I count upon the good-ness of your hearts, and will you not succour him if it becomes necessary? " he asked the Kilpatricks with a charming trustful smile.

" No, sirree, we ain't a-going to succour no rascals like Simon Hanna," Daniel announced with cheerful ferocity. " Kicks is all he'll ever get from us; he's lucky if he doesn't get a bullet between his shoulder-blades one of these fine winter evenings. We likes you and we honours you, but you're a plumb fool if you tries to be charitable to that kind of trash. He ought to be squatched out and wiped off the face of the earth; now leave him lay, and that's too good for him. If you'll come along home with us we'll give you some wholesome liquor and make you known to our old dad; he'd be proud to meet the man that laid Simon Hanna low."

" It's real good whisky this time, too, though a little raw and indigestible through being a new batch," added Bob hospitably, " but it does the job just as well for all that, and we'll have you roaring drunk by midnight, I can promise you, young feller. Dad's damned pleasant company in his cups; he knows a power of comical songs he didn't learn in Sunday-school."

" Oh, thank you, thank you with all my heart for your delight-ful invitation, but I must really be going to Louisville," said Shiloh in a low agitated voice, wringing his hands with nervous-ness and moving rapidly away in the direction of the deeper forest.

David followed him, making frantic signs of farewell to the Kilpatricks, who stared after the departing pair in speechless bewilderment. Daniel scratched his freckled forehead and spat; Bob trundled Mr. Hanna's top-hat along the dusty ground with the toe of a reflective boot.

" Well," said little Osbert at length, breaking a silence pregnant with dismay, " they was a couple of crazy lunatic Yankees that didn't know good liquor when it was offered 'em gratis, but I'll say this much for 'em; they knew how to punch people in the jaw, didn't they, Dan'l? "

A groan from the recumbent Simon Hanna seemed to attest the truth of the lad's statement; Daniel caressed his own chin, and whistled gloomily as he gazed after Shiloh's swiftly diminishing form.

"You hold yours, or I'll do it for you, young Osbert," said Daniel with dark emphasis; he had been immensely impressed by Shiloh's personality, and it took a vast quantity of whisky to wash away the memory of his disappointment.

" He was a raging murderer, and no mistake," he told his father in one of the evening's intervals of comparative sobriety. " Wild-eyed he was, when he rushed on Simon, and fierce as a regular Shawnee, but I took a powerful fancy to him, and I would of liked to call the man my friend. Oh, sir, he was a proper ring-tailed squealer, if ever I see one; I wish we had him here, though I reckon we'd seem pretty tame company to him after the foot-and-hand, tooth-and-nail, claw-and-mud-scraper, knife-gun-and-tomahawk sort of massacree as he's accustomed to. 'Tarnal death to me! But he was a gentleman, and his name was *Fight!* "

7

" DAVID, if I am called upon to drink any more whisky I shall inevitably go mad," said Shiloh with passionate solemnity as he sped across the rough ploughed fields towards the forest.

" Better steer clear of Louisville then, my lad," David replied grimly, making certain that his own flask was snug in its accustomed pocket. " Seems to me that your easiest smoothest course would be to learn to love the stuff like I do, but since you won't nohow be reasonable and human, my advice to you is to keep running wild in the woods like the b'ars and catamounts, and not go near no towns, where folks is naterally drunk and friendly in spirit. Darn it, Shiloh, I think the world of you, as well you know, but it beats me why your habits are so eccentric and savage-like sometimes. Not drink whisky! Why, man, it ain't even decent, the way you go on about liquor, and it ain't suitable to a brave lively feller like you, taking up this tarnation teetotal attitude, and by graminy I wouldn't hardly think it of you, Shiloh, and I blush for you, I swear I do. Ain't you never heerd of civilisation afore this? "

"Frequently," answered Shiloh with becoming meekness. "I have heard many hard things of it, and more of myself as its invincible enemy. But perhaps you do not fully understand, my dear good Davy, the stupendous difference between our present shocking industrial system, and the high golden age of Greece. That was civilisation in its noblest form; this is merely . . ."

"Aw, stow it, Shiloh," rejoined David crossly. He was bitterly chagrined at parting with his new-found friends; loyalty forced him to accompany Shiloh wherever that fantastic creature chose to roam, but at least half his honest heart was in the Kilpatricks' cabin, among the merry fumes of corn.

He repented of his asperity, however, when he saw Shiloh droop his head and wither visibly into sadness, and his next words were amiable and reassuring in proportion to his pang of self-reproach.

"You crazy little scalawag, don't look so goldarned miserable," cried David with a burst of laughter. "Mebbe I was kind of crabbed just now, but I was thinking as how we might have had a rare old time with the Kilpatricks to-night, 'stead of traipsing off to the wilderness. Still, that's what we come west for, I'll allow, and I ain't a-going to scold you no more, Shiloh. By jiminy, we've both of us been forgetting about Silver and all we was calculating to do for the poor critter! "

"I never forget," said Shiloh seriously. His eyes were luminous with that peculiar fire which invariably informed them at the mention of Silver's name; they blazed like mortal stars in the soft monotonous twilight, and David stared at him marvelling, and perhaps a thought afraid.

"I been forgetting all I owes to him," he whispered to himself. "I been forgetting Silver, and Jasper dead and gone along of me, and the strange salvation of my soul that come to me when I brought Shiloh back to life in place of him I'd murdered. God forgive me if I ain't forgetting my vow, to follow him faithful through the world. Well, I'll say no more of whisky and such-like luxuries, and by golly if he wants to drink water he shall, or I'm a double Dutchman!"

His small blue eyes were full of tears as he turned to Shiloh and slapped him jovially upon the back, and his loud voice was shaky with an emotion other than mirth.

"Too late to make Louisville to-night, my hearty," he said. "We'll find one of these here crystal springs as you're always talking of, and pitch our camp in the depth of the wood, to give you a chance to get your bearings, like, and fetch your breath in peace and quiet. You're plumb wore out with crowds and carryings-on; you wasn't never meant to mix much in society, I reckon, for all your pretty manners."

"I believe you are right, David," replied Shiloh, with an involuntary sigh of relief.

Nevertheless his conscience smote him in remembering Captain Appleby and the professor, and he realized that there was something of cowardice in this sudden dereliction of friendship. He thought of the happy hours spent over the pages of Laplace, and of the smiling bounty lands of Illinois, and for a moment he paused in his wild-swan flight, and trembled with indecision. Then another and more curious memory shook his mind, and he smelled once again the mingled fragrance of patchouli and melted deer tallow. The recollection rendered him quite faint; he hurried onward, quivering with alarm, into the cool revivifying solitude of the wood.

A singular circumstance now forced itself upon his vague attention: his footsteps were a lighter echo of David's ponderous tread, but ever behind these a second more insubstantial echo sounded, a noise frail as the rustle of a skeleton leaf, and far away. At first he thought that the faithful yellow dog had left the noble beef-bones of the wedding-feast to follow them upon their journey; then he knew that the rhythm of the delicate scampering was familiar and human. A woman was running after them through the forest; her footsteps were very small and pathetic under the infinite arch of the darkness.

"No matter who it may be, we must wait for her," he said to David with perfect firmness; his heart, however, tried its best to escape from his bosom and be gone into silence and safety.

"But who in thunder can it be, and why are you so scared, Shiloh?" asked David in perplexity. "You appear to be scared green, and yet it can't be nothing wuss than a woman that's following us; don't see why you're so almighty scared o' women."

They stood together beneath the vaulted canopy of trees, heavy with mistletoe festoons; Shiloh was shivering, and David caught him by the elbow to steady his evident trepidation. The footsteps approached; they sounded peculiarly soft and harmless in the gentle secrecy of dusk.

"What on earth's the matter with you, you crazy catawampus?" asked David somewhat impatiently. "Goldarn me if you're not the looniest lad this side of Bedlam, mixing up with Simon Hanna as calm as a summer sea, and then throwing a fine conniption fit of terror 'cause a poor weak woman comes a-lolloping after us like a rabbit. 'Tain't nothing but a plain ordinary woman, I tell you, you silly innocent, so quit shivering, and speak polite to the lady when she catches up with us, for she won't take it as no compliment the way you're going on."

"Good God, it's only Mrs. Lillie!" breathed Shiloh thankfully; he stopped trembling, and went forward with a courteous eagerness to meet the small dishevelled form of his late hostess, who now emerged from the mysterious forest aisles.

"Oh, Mr. Shiloh, I do hope you will forgive me for running after you so unceremoniously!" cried Mrs. Lillie in an exhausted little voice. "I do hope you will forgive me, my dear boy, and I quite understand your wishing to leave the wearisome confusion of the wedding, but I had one or two trifles that I had meant to give you, and I could not bear you to go off all alone like that without a word of farewell, so I took the liberty of following you along the southern meadow, and of course I know it is very unconventional, but you see you had forgotten your bundle, and I thought with the winter coming on, and you being accustomed to a warmer climate, that I had better in spite of appearances."

The poor lady was in a pitiful state of distress; her pretty pearl-grey silk was torn, and her small imploring face was streaked with dust and tears. She carried the dilapidated gypsy bundle in one hand; the other held a neat brown-paper parcel and a pair of red mittens.

"I knew that most of Mr. Butternut's belongings were in the pockets of his pea-jacket," she went on anxiously. "And then, he's used to roughing it, but with you it's different, and if any little comfort could possibly be helpful, I should be so very happy, though to think of your spending Christmas among the red Indians is almost more than I can bear, but be that as it may, I brought you a packet of tea, because I know you're fond of it, and a few of my cucumber pickles to remind you of our pleasant times together, and I think that's all except hard-boiled eggs and radishes, and oh, of course the muffler which is around my own neck because I had so much to carry and you do forgive me, don't you?"

Shiloh was overcome with gratitude and remorse; the thought that he had actually fled from this tender creature was almost intolerably pathetic. To be sure, he had feared another in the approaching footsteps, but now he sought by every means in his power to restore some measure of confidence to Mrs. Lillie's frightened spirit. He took the red mittens with a murmured word of thanks and stood gazing affectionately at their donor, who in her turn gazed up at him with large adoring eyes.

"I do appreciate, far more than I can express, your amazing kindness to a lonely traveller," he said gently; the orphaned quality of his smile was starrily apparent in the twilight, and Mrs. Lillie loved him with a double adoration.

"We've heard about Simon Hanna," said Mrs. Lillie humbly, "and it was exactly like you, and wonderfully heroic and brave, but I do hope you'll be a little more careful about the savages, and I meant to ask you whether you had plenty of quinine and calomel, because being so far from a doctor, and perhaps with a tendency to colds, and O Mr. Butternut, you will take care of him, won't you?"

"I aim to do so, ma'am, to the best of my powers," replied David rather haughtily. He was excessively bored by Mrs. Lillie, and a little jealous of her.

"And now good-bye, and may God have you in His holy keeping, my dear boy," said Mrs. Lillie in a breaking voice. She took Shiloh's slender brown fingers in both her small white hands; she looked as if she were going to kiss his finger-tips, but only an invisible tear touched them in the silence.

Shiloh was painfully affected by her unconcealed sorrow; he wished very much to comfort her, if it were possible to do so without abandoning his own pursuit of liberty and peace. He tried to think of some simple consolation, and his wild and worried blue eyes fell upon the neat parcel of provisions, which had dropped unheeded to the ground.

"Would you not like Davy to make you a cup of tea before you leave us?" he inquired solicitously. "Davy makes excellent tea, and it might refresh you for your long homeward walk. It is quite chilly in these woods; I am sure a cup of tea would be both beneficial and delicious. Have you the flint and steel, Davy? because I can collect enough dry sticks in a moment to make a very cheerful little fire."

"Ain't no spring in sight, far as I can see, and how can you brew tea without water?" grumbled David obstructively. He need not have taken the pains to discourage Mrs. Lillie; her spirit was already completely shattered, and she smiled wanly and shook her head in response to Shiloh's benevolent suggestion.

"No, no; I really couldn't; I have not a particle of appetite, and besides, I must be getting back to my guests, and supper at six, and most of them counting on my special apple pandowdy, and nobody understands the Dutch oven but myself," she murmured desolately, turning to go.

In the dusk she was no more than a silky grey wisp of farewell; David himself was moved by her pitiful futility, at point to vanish into even less.

"If a swig from my flask could be any comfort, ma'am . . ." he muttered shyly.

Mrs. Lillie paid no heed to him; she took Shiloh's hand again, but now a thin gossamer suggestion of hauteur had fallen insensibly over her manner, rendering it at once formal and childish, so that she was like a little girl bidding a polite good-bye to a birthday party of ogres and warlocks. Behind this veil of exemplary civility her soft unhappy hazel eyes glinted with a feverish desire to be gone into nothingness.

"Good evening, Mr. Shiloh; I wish you a very pleasant journey," she whispered; tears shone along the spider-web thread of her voice; the obscurity of night received her as its own.

She fled with the quiet scampering haste of a squirrel or a field-mouse; the rustle of her going was almost unbelievably delicate and brief. High among the tree-tops the ghost of an echo trembled in the pale remaining leaves.

"Poor lady! I have a melancholy suspicion that her life is overshadowed by some vague but painful tragedy!" said Shiloh sadly, seating himself cross-legged at the base of a gigantic oak. "It would have been impracticable in the extreme to have attempted to join her fortunes to ours, and yet I am not wholly satisfied with my own conduct in the matter; I do not entirely approve of Mr. Lillie as a husband for this vulnerable creature. It is very distressing; I wish we might have solved the difficulties of her future."

"Aw, shucks, Shiloh, 'tain't none of our business!" cried David robustly. "Women, women; I know 'em! Wanted to be a mother to you, I dare say; wrap you up in red flannel and feed you on calomile pills and Queen Anne, drat her. Sooner I get you away from all that kind of Miss Nancy hanky-panky the better it'll be for your everlasting good. Weaken your guts, that's what women do; it's women as have taught you to drink chiny tea instead of decent whisky. 'Take care of him,' she says to me, indeed, as if you was a baby; she must be plumb off her head, the silly old hen!"

"Really, David, you are unnecessarily severe," murmured Shiloh absent-mindedly, crouching upon the frosty fallen leaves and staring rather forlornly into the hollow darkness; he felt unnerved, and uncomfortably chilly. The knitted muffler was hunched ridiculously about his ears; his uncovered hair stood on end like the feathers of some tropic bird dismayed by cold and brutal winter.

"It's not women; it's people; it's the whole hellish society of men," he said bitterly. "How is it possible that one of so weak and sensitive a nature as mine can run further the gauntlet through this world of cool ferocious malice?"

"Your coat's just rags and tags; we'll buy us some hunters' leather jackets in Louisville," replied David tactfully. "Now you look around for firewood while I find the creek; I can hear it a-gurgling among the stones at the bottom of this little gully. Then you can have your blamed cambric tea and I can have my grog, and we'll see what Mrs. Lillie give us for our supper."

8

A FEW moments later the scene was fabulously altered: Shiloh perceived a pleasantly circumscribed paradise in the small warm cavern of firelight which his friend had conjured out of blackness and despair. The pine boughs flung crackling streamers of pure yellow flame against the dark; David was already weaving other boughs into a screen to windward. The night smelled of spice and balsam and burning leaves.

"Don't this beat all their grand goings-on to blazes?" asked David triumphantly as he affixed the battered tin kettle to a gypsy tripod of crossed sticks.

Shiloh unwrapped Mrs. Lillie's brown-paper parcel; it was full of hard-boiled eggs and slim ice-coloured winter radishes; there was the wing of a fried chicken, and a few translucent slices of ham. She had remembered the salt; she had also remembered the crumbly lumps of maple sugar for his tea. His eyes brimmed with tears as he beheld these evidences of her loving kindness.

"Sort of thin fare for a cold night," was David's ungrateful comment. He plunged his hands into the vast unfathomable pockets of his pea-jacket, and drew forth an enormous chunk of streaky bacon and the better part of a roast wild turkey.

"Is that mustard in the old lady's package?" asked David eagerly. "Good; devilled turkey legs ain't by any means to be despised as victuals, by graminy. You sharpen a stick, Shiloh, while I finish thatching this here shack agin a possible blizzard."

Shiloh was completely happy again; he sipped sweet scalding tea out of a tin cup, and the exquisite warmth of the fire flowed upward from his toes as the hot tea flowed downward from his throat. He nibbled a crisp icy radish, and allowed David to attend to the devilled turkey.

" I am amazed to discover that I am excessively tired; there was something peculiarly unrestful about the atmosphere of Mr. Lillie's home, although his hospitality was generous to a fault," said Shiloh mildly, masking a yawn behind his slender fire-reddened fingers.

" Didn't suit you nohow; that was plain to be seen from the very word go," David answered judicially. " Can't exactly figure it out, but there was something disagreed with you terrible in the air of that farm; you was getting all peaked and unearthly-like, same as when I fust seen you. Lord, you look another man already in this nice little snug neck o' woods."

After an excellent supper, Shiloh amused himself by turning one of the choruses from the *Antigone* of Sophocles into English lyrical verse; this exercise of the poetic faculties rendered him deliciously sleepy by eleven o'clock. He fell into a light doze, soothed by recurrent waves of music from the inner convolutions of his own mind, now ringing like a sea-shell with harmonious cadences.

He was quite unaware of David's protracted absence; he woke suddenly, disturbed by the loud approach of some great beast that shuffled through the underbrush. The thing was dark and harshly furry; its gigantic shoulders were humped beneath a sinister spiked dream of Burnham Wood. Shiloh was sure that the creature was a bear; he was pleased to observe how curiosity overcame fear in the confusion of his senses.

The beast drew near; Shiloh leaped to his feet, prepared to sell his life only at the price of the most desperate and determined resistance possible to his tense and active frame. A pair of grimly bearded arms embraced him; then all at once they were recognisably David's, and David himself was laughing under a shawl of shaggy hide.

" Thought we might kind of enjoy a good old buffalo-robe to-night; there's liable to be a regular black frost afore morning," cried David, flinging his savage burden upon the ground. It lay like a wounded animal; Shiloh could fancy it ambushed to spring with the springing flames.

" Reckon I skeered you, didn't I? " asked David cockily. Shiloh was slightly annoyed; he recovered his toppling dignity by the little effort of a smile.

" Did you kill it? " he inquired amiably. David was enchanted by this fantastic theory of his exploit.

" I'll be switched if I didn't shoot it with a pea-shooter, and it with an elegant felt lining and all! " he chuckled, displaying the thick glossy fur mounted upon dark blue cloth of the richest and most durable description. Shiloh was impressed, but he was also troubled.

" But if you stole it from someone, Davy, that person must presumably go cold to-night," he said with profound anxiety, staring at David with large and solemn eyes.

" Stole your gran'mother; borrowed it, you mean, my lad," his friend replied jauntily. " And that feller won't be cold to-night, I can promise you; he's laying dead drunk in Mr. Lillie's kitchen at this very moment, and there's a roaring fire not a foot from his coat-tails. More likely to be roasted, he is; it's a real act of charity to take this here contraption and keep it safe till morning. He drives the stylishest oxcart in the county, and this robe is one of a pair, one to cover the straw cushions and one to cover the folks as rides on 'em. Now don't you go wrinkling your forehead and ruffling your goldarned crazy hair, but into the shack with you, and roll yourself up in this grand old buffalo-hide, and you won't know nothing till you smell frying bacon at sunrise."

When they were actually within the balsam-scented warmth of the shelter, with the heavy fur drawn up to their chins, David spoke once more, but very drowsily.

" This beats cock-fighting, don't it, Shiloh? " he asked in the accents of an absolute contentment; in the firelight his countenance was like a copper mask of peace.

" Presumably the comfort and tranquillity of our present situation must indeed be far superior to that peculiarly stupid and barbaric sport," said Shiloh in a voice impregnated with the gentle lenitive of sleep.

He lay watching the lovely diminution of the flames; they flickered softly along the reflecting surface of the fallen leaves, which still held some of the colours of fire in their delicate decay. The night smelled of spice and balsam; the smoke of the burning leaves was sweeter than incense. Shiloh was very happy; he knew this happiness, and savoured it upon his tongue with the exquisite bitter taste of wood-smoke, before the hypnotic dark overwhelmed him in oblivion.

His mind fled lightly and dizzily in front of the advancing wave of sleep; he drew Silver's miniature from his pocket, and gazed at the shagreen case by the diminished glimmer of the pine logs. He was too tired to open the case, but he could see quite clearly, behind painted shark-skin made magically transparent, the small pale face and the eyes suffused with darkness, like the patterned eyes upon the wings of moths.

A few frail snowflakes floated nonchalantly down; the fire subsided into tender rose-red ashes, and Shiloh slept, his lips against the little shagreen case.

VI

PASTORAL GARAMANT

"Ain't we never going to have no adventures?" asked David plaintively the next morning as he finished the last bit of bacon. The weather was warm again; no faintest trace of snow lingered upon the tiger-coloured leaves about their feet, and the sun was an incandescent shield behind the eastern fringe of tulip-trees. The buffalo robe was flung to one side, and the friends were in their shirt-sleeves, stretched at ease within the thermal influence of the awakened fire.

Shiloh had plunged into the stream before breakfast; it had been vehemently cold, but its fierce electric iciness had washed the cobwebby worries from his brain, and now he felt clean and strong and sanguine as he faced the daybreak. The bright blood was sentient under the sunburn on his cheek, and all his muscles were confident and happy; his eyes were almost savage in their brilliance. It was impossible to imagine him disheartened or ill; David looked at him with unconcealed approval, and filled the tin cups with potent boiling tea from the kettle.

"You seem ready and willing to lick your weight in wildcats, Shiloh; when do you reckon we'll get a chance at a scrap?" persisted David stubbornly.

"Soon, I hope, since your soul is set upon it, Davy," said Shiloh with a smile. "But meanwhile I have a small piece of news for you, not wholly lacking in elements of excitement." He drew the miniature from his pocket and opened the case; instead of turning to the portrait his attention was engaged by the circle of gold wherein the ivory was mounted.

"You see," he explained at last, while David watched him fascinated, "the back of this setting opens like a locket; there is a bit of paper within the space concealed. I found it this morning, before it was really light; I wanted to see the picture, but in the obscurity I found myself staring at the other side, and then I observed a little crack along its edge; finally I succeeded in prying it apart with my thumbnail, and this is what I discovered."

He handed a torn fragment of paper to David, who seized it avidly, and squinted with furious curiosity at the blurred inky characters upon its surface.

"'Jasper Crooks,'" read David slowly, "'Bumbolow's Tavern, Louisville, Kentucky.' Yes, but who's Jasper Crooks? Our Jasper, that I murdered aboard the brig, was Jasper Cross; do you calculate as how this is the same fellow with another name, Shiloh?"

"Assuredly it is the same person, Davy," explained Shiloh eagerly. "In fact, I think I can perceive the origin of the change; Crooks means precisely Cross if you spell it in the Latin manner, C-r-u-x. Doubtless one or the other of Jasper's names was assumed, in some stress of danger or disgrace. It is all very romantic, and I was quite sure you would be pleased; this will simplify our search considerably, now that we have an actual address in Louisville."

"I should say it would, by graminy!" cried David jubilantly. "Well, if that isn't the goldarndest piece of luck that I ever heard tell of, and just as I was beginning to be kind of mad 'cause we had to go to Louisville to find your old Eyetalian letter at the bank and all! Not that it'll be there for a month of Sundays, by my reckoning, but that doesn't matter now, with clues and false names and everything fine and sort of secret-like. I declare, Shiloh, you're a regular bloody wonder; haven't I always told you so?"

"You have been more than kind in your appreciation of my

virtues, Davy," Shiloh replied modestly. " But in this instance it was merely a singular bit of good fortune which guided my fingers to the scrap of paper. And now, if you will return the buffalo robe, I will occupy myself in stamping out the fire and tying up our bundles; I confess I am unwilling to meet any of the Lillie family this morning."

" Guess I'll just drop it in the road where somebody's sure to see it, and not go near the house myself," said David uneasily. " 'Tisn't so much the Lillies as I mind seeing as Captain Appleby; I feel kind of ungrateful when I think of all his kindness, and yet I'll be switched if I want to go and populate Pike county, as he calls fathering a passel of babies. Do you reckon we've used him shabby, Shiloh, or is your conscience clear about the captain? "

" Not entirely, I must admit," Shiloh answered sadly. " I am heartily ashamed of my inability to go back to the cabin and bid good-bye to them all, decently and frankly; my only excuse is that I detest farewells and that I am convinced that an interview with our friends would so affect my nerves as to render me incapable of continuing our journey to-day. And that," said Shiloh pensively, " would surely be a thousand pities; I am certain Captain Appleby would forgive me if he understood my present predicament."

" You hate anything as cramps your wild free goings-on, don't you, Shiloh? " inquired David with sympathetic interest. " Anything like a cut-and-dried hide-bound plan makes you downright miserable, I can see. 'Tain't easy to put words to what I mean, but you seem kind of scairt and jumpy soon as anyone tries to stop you going where you want to."

" You are perfectly right, David." Suddenly Shiloh looked rather haughty and desperate; his eyes had the brightness of a fawn's, and yet there was something of the panther in his air of pride. " I know I am a fool, my dear fellow, but you are amazingly right; any infringement of my personal liberty makes me sick with revolt. Nevertheless, I confess it is a fault; I shall learn better, I suppose, before I die."

" Aw, Shiloh, but why should you? " protested David loyally. " I like you best this way; I like you being so spunky and owdacious. Shouldn't want to be the man to stop you to-day, by cracky; don't seem as if nothing could, the look you've got in your eyes."

Shiloh was accessible to the flattery of this honest praise; he had been more than human if his eye had not brightened and his brow flushed upon the word. He shrugged his slim shoulders, seeming to cast some burden from them as he did so, and stared up into the luminous blue; then he laughed and leaped to his feet.

"I go on until I am stopped, and I never am stopped," cried Shiloh rather crazily, beginning to stamp out the remaining embers of the camp-fire.

Sparks flew into the air and whirled around his head like a swarm of parti-coloured bees, golden and tawny and vermilion; he stood in the midst of the swarming sparks and laughed. He looked a creature of fire, a fierce and subtle flame; even his wild and tattered garments were transfused by a curious effulgence, and upon the locks of his hair particles of light had fallen from the cloud of burning wings.

2

THEY stopped at noon by a great beaver-dam to eat the ultimate scrap of turkey; David drained his flask, and rejoiced to think of the good distilleries of Louisville. Shiloh discovered an enormous grapevine, thicker than a man's arm, among whose withered leaves a few bunches of grapes were still concealed; these were sun-dried and sugary as raisins, and he found them a very palatable dessert. He was further enchanted by the appearance of a huge snapping-turtle; he seemed to detect a sinister wisdom in the reptile's gleaming hooded eyes which charmed his imagination to dreams of prehistoric monsters. The parakeets had flown south, but many smaller birds chattered in the genial warmth, and the squirrels and chipmunks leaped like streaks of silver and ruddy lightning along the branches of the poplars and tulip-trees.

Another four miles brought the friends to the first houses of the town; to eyes accustomed to the cane-brake and the tomahawk improvement, the courthouse with its portico and spire loomed splendid in the distance. They inquired their way of a civil stranger in broadcloth and a beaver hat; presently they stood upon the steps of the Commercial Bank of Louisville, looking savage and unkempt in the shadow of its neatly pointed brickwork.

"You could thump me round the earth with a crab-apple sooner'n get me inside that green door, Shiloh," declared David firmly. "It seems so kind of prim-like and respectable that it makes me feel like a mad yaller dog. Reckon I'll go hunt for this here Bumbolow's tavern, and come back for you in half an hour; I'll be setting on these steps waiting for you when you finish talking to the old codgers in there. Beats me how you got the guts to face 'em, in them trousers, but then you never did care nothing for appearances, as the saying is."

David sauntered off happily in the direction of a swinging sign setting forth the virtues of Hope's Celebrated Whisky, and Shiloh, with a somewhat nervous air of bravado, laid his hand upon the shining brass doorknob of the Commercial Bank. He was faintly embarrassed by the fact that his boots were in a shocking condition and his blue jean shirt in holes, but far more powerful was the fear that disagreeable news was ambushed behind the smart green paint of the door-panels.

He felt quite light-headed with relief when a supercilious clerk informed him that there were no letters for Mr. Shiloh; only a sense of duty drove him to demand audience with some higher official.

"My dear sir, I trust I invariably recognise a gentleman when I see one," said Mr. Townley, unbending in the chaste mahogany comfort of his private sanctum. It was true; he had offered Shiloh a rich black cigar before he even glanced at the note of introduction with which Mr. Lillie had insisted upon providing his young friend. Shiloh promptly declined the gift of the unctuous Habana, but he was touched by the courtesy of his reception. The leather arm-chair was very grateful to his ascetic bones; he knew he was in danger of falling asleep, lulled by the pleasant laziness of Mr. Townley's voice.

"Unfortunately it is quite out of the question that a letter from Italy should reach Louisville for another six weeks," said

Mr. Townley with a condoling shake of his fine iron-grey head.
" Of course the post will travel much faster than you have walked
a like distance, but then you must allow for the two voyages
across the Atlantic, and that, be your ship the swiftest Yankee
clipper ever launched, must inevitably take time. I'm sorry, my
boy, so far as you are concerned; tidings of your wife and child
are now your one desire, I know, and it grieves me to have to
dash your more sanguine expectations. My advice to you is to stay
in Louisville until the letter comes; our posts are excellent; in
fact nine mails arrive weekly and are distributed from the post
office. I would most gladly find you some employment in our
town during your interval of enforced inactivity; if it were not
an impertinence I might suggest private tutoring, since Mr. Lillie
says you are an elegant classical scholar. Also, if you liked, I could
put you into the Bank; I am sure you write a legible clerkly hand,
and are clever at figures, eh, Mr. Shiloh? "

" You are more than kind, but really I fear I am unable to
avail myself of your generous offer," murmured Shiloh diffidently; Mr. Townley thought him a very sensitive and mild
young man, but the fantastic creature's mind was inwardly vivid
with rebellion. He was determined not to be trapped in a counting-house or a schoolroom, and the thought of the Italian letter
was strangely hateful to his spirit.

" Is it possible that I do not wish to hear from Mary? " he
asked himself in honest horror; then suddenly he knew the truth,
and shivered in a nakedness of soul. He had never wanted to hear
from Mary; his cold dread of being scolded transcended all the
other and more romantic emotions which Mary's accusing grey
eyes could arouse in his bosom.

The knowledge neatly stripped a layer of self-esteem from a
soul always susceptive to the point of agony; Shiloh was visibly
shaken, and Mr. Townley thought him in the chilly fit of a remit-
tent fever, and unlocked the cellarette with humane intention.
His guest declined the whisky with determined politeness; the
chill was moral rather than physical, and its passing left a frosty
ache not to be warmed by creature comfort.

" Still a bit agueish, aren't you? This sultry autumn
weather has played the devil with us all," said Mr. Townley

kindly, swallowing a therapeutic draught with an appreciative grimace.

Shiloh stared appalled at the spectacle of his own soul; the sunny afternoon was black with grief and shame. Nevertheless he experienced a certain sharp relief in knowing the worst about himself, and he resolved to discipline his weakness with the utmost rigour and severity. He rose to his feet, wan but indomitable.

"'The Magus Zoroaster, my dead child, met his own image walking in the garden,'" said Shiloh solemnly; Mr. Townley was more than ever certain that the man was in the grip of a tertian fever.

"I shall remain in Louisville until the letter arrives," Shiloh continued resolutely. "All other business must give place to the sacred duty of providing for the happiness of those I love; for the happiness of those I love." He repeated these concluding words no less than three several times; Mr. Townley began to believe that his young friend's ague had already been modified by an enormous remedial dose of whisky.

Shiloh was filled with an honourable desire to make amends; he saw himself waiting patiently and soberly for Mary, while David took the adventurous future to himself. He wondered which of Mr. Townley's suggestions would inflict the most exquisite retributive justice upon his spirit; the thought of teaching Latin to children was distasteful enough, but he fancied that the endless columns of figures in the ledgers of the Commercial Bank might be the fitter trial of his fortitude.

"Can you really find me a position in the bank?" he asked politely, hugging the dreadful resolution to his heart as if it had been a wolf-cub; under cover of his pride the Spartan boy was torn and bleeding.

"I am quite sure I can; it may not be a position of responsibility as yet, but the dignity of labour is apparent in the faithful efforts of the humblest clerk in our employ," replied Mr. Townley guardedly; he had no immediate intention of trusting this eccentric stranger beyond the limits of simple computations with a quill pen.

"Of course," Mr. Townley continued with helpful eagerness,

" if you decide to push farther into the west your letter can be forwarded in time; I mean if you will leave a definite address, in some accessible part of the country. People," said Mr. Townley vaguely, " do go west, particularly in the spring. But undoubtedly your safest plan is to remain in Louisville."

"I know," said Shiloh with a sigh and a shudder; the invisible wolf-cub was devouring the very core of his heart, and the memory of Silver's ivory face was extremest torture. With a shock of amazement he realized that she might even now be in Louisville; nevertheless she seemed to his depressed imagination infinitely farther removed than when a quarter-world had sundered them by thousands of savage miles.

As a matter of ironic fact, no letter was on its way from Italy; no letter had reached the grey-eyed widow in her Pisan solitude. Mary still believed herself to be a widow. In her sleeveless gown of black velvet, cut low to flatter the lovely marble of her bosom, she sat like an immemorial effigy of grief in the midst of the noisy household of the Hunts at Genoa. Pisa and San Terenzo were places of the past; England shimmered distantly through sea-born mists, and the world was sorrowful. Captain Ffoulkastle was neither a knave nor a fool; he was merely dead. The *Witch of the West* had gone down with all hands aboard three days out of Boston Harbour, on the seventh of September, 1822, and Shiloh's letter to his wife had gone with her to be obliterated for ever in the bitter green depth of the sea.

Therefore the excruciating division of Shiloh's soul was all for naught; he need not have suffered as he did in resolving to remain in Louisville. He was free to depart; free to return to Italy, or, less commendably, to set forth upon farther travels even beyond the moon.

"I shall stay," he said rather breathlessly, turning to go. "I must find my friend, and acquaint him with this new decision, but in the morning I shall present myself at your door, prepared to accept whatever employment I can obtain. For the moment, then, farewell; to-morrow we shall meet again."

He spoke with some degree of agitation, and Mr. Townley still wondered what disorder of body or of mind might account for his singular behaviour. The banker took off his silver-bowed spectacles and rubbed them with a red silk handkerchief; when he put them on again his curious guest had disappeared.

3

SHILOH found David sitting upon the steps of the bank eating gingernuts; he looked flushed and cheerful in the rose-coloured light from the west.

"Good news, Shiloh!" he cried at once, offering Shiloh the choice of an apple or a handful of gingernuts from his capacious pockets. "Leastways, mebbe you won't call it good, on account of us having a little matter of another three hundred miles to go, but I've seen this blasted old curmudgeon Bumbolow, and spite of him being most god-almighty drunk on Jamaica rum he remembers Jasper plain, and Jasper's pa and ma, and Silver herself, when she was nothing much more than a yaller-haired baby. Jasper come here to Bumbolow when he fust run away from home, along of the old man being a family friend, like; he run away when he was fifteen, but they didn't none of them live in Louisville; they come from St. Louis. Now quit glaring at me with them blue saucer eyes of yours, and listen careful; I know it's kind of confusing to strangers, but I reckon we can walk it if we ain't got the steamboat fare, and for my part I'd admire to push on to something a bit wilder, for this town's too niminy-piminy prim to suit me nohow with all these here brick houses. Strike me silly if I've seen an Injun yet; bloody-wild ground they call it, but it's too bloody tame for me. Not but what the whisky's real good, which they say as it's our bounden duty to drink, with the water so downright poisonous; you must lay off that blasted tea as long as you're in Louisville."

"I dare say I shall do very well if I do not omit the precaution of Chincona," said Shiloh sadly; he felt that it would require more than an infusion of tea-leaves to hearten him against the cold flood of melancholy overwhelming him at the sound of Silver's name. "If the water is really so unwholesome, however, I may take a glass of white wine with my supper. But Davy, I don't understand; is Silver then in St. Louis, as you call it?"

" Well, so far as that old bellowing Bumbolow can reckon, she must be," David assured him; Shiloh had a horrid vision of his own image balancing the ledger in the Commercial Bank of Louisville while David went on a journey alone, with Silver at that journey's end.

" You see," continued David eagerly, " seems as how her pa was a Frenchman, a regular scoundrel he was and the perfect spit of Jasper, and he was some kind of a river pirate and robbed a power of honest folk, murdered some too I reckon, and then at last the Injuns got him, and served him right, but it was hard on his innocent wife and children, and so Jasper gone wrong, and Silver was left an orphan along of her ma dying of sorrow and starvation, and the poor lady was Spanish, and from foreign parts, and always homesick in St. Louis, and her husband beat her, and she never could get properly warm in winter, and her life was a perfect hell until death released her, and then here was little Silver all forlorn, and I calculate as how it's a tarnation lucky thing we come west."

" And Silver is really destitute and in trouble! " cried Shiloh; the blood beat in his pulses, and his voice quivered in accord with them.

" I should just say she was, by graminy! " was David's delighted rejoinder; it was plain that he accounted the circumstance of Silver's poverty in the nature of a personal triumph.

" 'Tain't that I want the poor girl to be unhappy," he explained in the next breath, " only it would seem kind of loony and outlandish if we'd 'a' come all this goldarned ways without any rhyme or reason. But now it's all straight sailing, and we know we done right to come, and there's nothing to stop us leaving immediate for St. Louis to rescue her from misery."

Shiloh was silent; he had not the heart to dash in the slightest degree David's golden and chivalric dream, and he felt a curious reluctance to admit in words that his own part in their adventures was over for ever. David noticed his pallor and dejection and ascribed them to hunger, by which natural pang these symptoms were undoubtedly augmented.

" Talk about sorrow and starvation! " cried David. " You're the living picture of 'em now; if you could see the face on you

you'd die laughing. Why, you crazy son of a musket, won't you never learn no sense about your victuals? Come and get something under your belt; you ain't had nothing all day but a scraggy neck of turkey. There's elegant venison at the tavern, and mutton chops sizzling as beautiful as music."

Shiloh permitted himself to be led in the direction of the tavern, which was not Mr. Bumbolow's establishment, but a nearer and more cheerful hostelry. In spite of his melancholy he was not wholly unconscious of the salutary effects of a hot supper upon his drooping spirits; the planed venison was very savoury, and the ham and beefsteaks, hissing from the gridirons, were excellently tender and cooked to a turn. He wondered precisely how wicked he had been in abandoning the Pythagorean diet while travelling; he took another small slice of venison and decided that the lapse was forgivable.

"Peacock always said well-seasoned," murmured Shiloh, wielding the pepper canister with no uncertain hand. "And perhaps after all I will have a pint of some very light white wine, since you assure me that the water is so pestilential; I have no desire to fall a victim to the hepatic complaint which the landlord informs me is most prevalent in this insalubrious clime."

There was no light white wine to be had; Shiloh was forced to content himself with half a bottle of Marsala, of which David consumed the major portion. Nevertheless he felt warmed and comforted; he began to speculate upon the post office facilities for forwarding letters from Louisville into the farther west.

"Time to be getting on to Bumbolow's; I told him we'd be there by seven," said David, fortifying himself and the Marsala with two fingers of neat whisky. It was the moment for explanations, but Shiloh said nothing; he cracked a fine walnut and finished his glass of wine in complete silence.

4

WITHOUT, the night was starlit, and sweet with tonic frost; a brisk pace was indicated by the freshening wind. David made his way with admirable precision through a tangle of lampless streets;

finally he knocked three times upon a sagging door, which was opened by an elderly man of sinister appearance.

"Come along in and set down by the fire, young fellers," said this individual in an unpleasant snuffling voice; his crooked smile disclosed long yellowish teeth, and the gleam of his eyes was vulpine under bushy brows. Shiloh felt an immediate antipathy to the man, which the touch of a cold claw-fingered hand did little to dissipate.

"Don't be turned agin him, Shiloh, for pity's sake, just because he ain't pretty," whispered David as they filed into the inner room. "He's been a pirate and an outlaw by his own account, and he don't pretend to no special holiness, but he's got the very news we want of Silver, and I reckon he ain't a bad sort when you come to know him."

A good fire of hickory logs burnt upon the cracked stone hearth, and the low-ceiled room was warm with candlelight. In spite of scaling plaster and cobwebbed shadows the place had an air of comfort after the darkness and the sharp whirling dust of the streets. Shiloh saw that two or three quiet drinkers were gathered about a small table in the corner; the settle by the fire was empty, and towards this pleasant refuge Mr. Bumbolow now led them, with a secret look and a portentous shake of his scant grey whiskers.

"Easy now, easy now," said the old man huskily; he shuffled to a cupboard and returned with two thick tumblers of whisky, which he placed in front of the friends. "Don't you go a-talking at the top of your blasted lungs about Jacques la Croix, like you was to-day, young feller, or you and me'll be in jail afore we can say knife. Christ strike me blind if I don't wish I had a dollar for every murder he done in his time; blood-money it would be and no mistake, and a bloody bastard I'll call any man as contradicts me. But drink up, young fellers, and ask your questions, and whether I'll tell you any lies or not depends upon how civil you speak and how well you hold your liquor."

"But the name's not la Croix, Mr. Bumbolow; it's Cross or Crooks, as I was a-saying this afternoon," began David, but Shiloh hurriedly interrupted him.

"It's all the same, Davy; I see precisely how Jasper derived his different pseudonyms from the original form. Please go on, Mr. Bumbolow; we are most eagerly awaiting your valuable information."

"Valuable indeed," cried Mr. Bumbolow bitterly; "yes, and I suppose I must part with it for nothing to a couple of lousy beggars who can't even pay for their drinks!" Tears came into his eyes, and he smeared them away with the back of his hairy hand.

"We can pay you well for the drinks," David reassured him. "We're poor, but not so poor we have to spunge on you for them, by graminy. As for the tidings of Jasper, if you was his friend you ought to be ready and willing to aid his sister to the best of your powers."

"Friend!" repeated Mr. Bumbolow still more bitterly. "Yes, I was a true friend to him, as God is my witness, and a true friend to his father before him, and all I ever got for my pains was cheating and abuse from the pair of 'em, curse their dirty souls to hell. Think of me, a lonely old man a-trying to earn my living in a strange unfriendly town, and Jasper probably master of a ship by now, without even the gratitude to send me a pound of tobaccy from foreign parts."

"Jasper's dead and gone, as I told you," said David solemnly. "It's little Silver as we're trying to find; won't you help us, if only for her ma's sake as you used to be so fond of?"

"Fond of her! Fond of her, d'you say, young feller? Chris'-a'mighty, that ain't no proper way to put it; I plumb worshipped her, I did, and if I ain't done all I'd 'a' liked to 'a' done for her little gal, 'tis along of my years and my poverty, and not for lack of heart! Oh, Dolores, how I loved you in them days gone by!"

Here Mr. Bumbolow placed his yellow-grey head among the whisky-glasses on the table before him, and gave way to un-affected grief. The spectacle, while it jarred upon Shiloh's keen æsthetic sensibilities, touched him nevertheless to an uneasy pity; the old man was drunk and ridiculous, but he was palpably sincere.

"I do entreat you, sir, to believe in our friendship and in our tender care for Silver; we have every intention of succouring her, if that assurance can at all console you," said Shiloh, nervously

patting Mr. Bumbolow's ragged shoulder. The old man heeded
him, and, raising a blotched and haggard countenance, stared
half incredulously into the other's large and innocent blue eyes.
His own eyes were rheumy with the slow difficult tears of dotage.

"You ain't a-figuring to do her no harm, young gentleman?"
he inquired slyly, moved to an unwonted formality of address
by Shiloh's courtly manner and that romantic air of his no
tatters could obscure. "You ain't a-figuring to ruin her, perhaps, or cast her into prison along of her daddy's crimes? 'Cause
if you is, old Tom Bumbolow'll have a word to say, I reckon,
that'll fair scorch the hide off you. But no, young gentleman,
you can't be so sinful as to aim to ruin little Sylvie; I can't a-think
it of you, with them blue-chiny eyes of yours a-looking at me,
and I'm a-going to trust you and to tell you all."

"Good God, Mr. Bumbolow, pray divest your mind of this
hideous suspicion!" cried Shiloh, pale and luminous with horror. Mr. Bumbolow was convinced, and smiled an incredibly
crooked smile.

"Well, young gentleman, Silver as you call her, or Sylvie as
her daddy called her, speaking it French-like, or Maria Solidad
de Sylva, as her ma called her and the priest christened her,
must now be twenty-one years old; when last I heerd of her
she was fifteen, but that's five or six years ago, afore Jasper
runned away to sea. At that time she was apprenticed to a
French milliner in St. Louis; the shop was on the rue Royale,
or Main Street as they names it now. Her father was a blasted
scoundrel, a Canadian trapper known as Jacques la Croix, who
made his money by piracy and murder; her ma was a Spanish
lady, some kin to Governor Piernas as I've heard tell; how she
come to marry so much beneath her has always beat me, but
marry him she did, and bore him a family of children what
mostly died in infancy; Jasper and Sylvie was the youngest and
the only ones as lived to grow up."

"Why did Jasper take the name of Cross on shipboard, and
call himself Crooks in Louisville?" asked David; the point was
one that continued to trouble him.

"Reason enough, young feller, reason enough, if you'll listen
and mark my words," replied Mr. Bumbolow with some asperity.

"In the first place, his daddy was a pirate, with a price on his head when the Injuns killed him; in the second place Jasper himself was no plaster saint, as I've been a-telling of you. Lit out with his sister's savings when he bid her good-bye, and then runned away to sea from this very tavern, with my cash-box under his arm; reason enough if ever I'd caught him! "

"Tarnation mean, I call it," said David indignantly; the reflection was soothing to a conscience burdened, albeit lightly, with Jasper's premature demise.

"God-a'mighty mean, I say," agreed Mr. Bumbolow with feeling, " and I for one can't hold it agin you that you cracked his skull by mistake; lucky kind of a mistake for all concerned. But Sylvie, little Sylvie, she's a different kettle of sugar; the black and the white of it, was that pair of twins, and even in her cradle she shined beside his sulky shadow like a star."

"And what," asked Shiloh, his soul vibrating with his voice, " what colour are Silver's eyes, Mr. Bumbolow? "

"Well," Mr. Bumbolow answered judicially, drinking up Shiloh's whisky with an air of slow satisfaction, " well, that's a bit of a poser, young gentleman; reckon you'll have to find out for yourself. Dark they was, leastways when she was twelve years old, but whether grey or brown or hazel I don't rightly know and I wouldn't like to say. She was as fair as corn-silk, and soft and bright, but about her eyes I'm uncertain; you'll have to see them for yourself."

"I cannot do that," said Shiloh desperately, looking at David; " I am unable to go to St. Louis." He closed his eyelids upon some darling vision, and set his lips into a narrow resolute line.

"Oh, Shiloh, what crazy lunatic idea has got a-hold of you now? " David's cry was angry and amazed, but not so lamentable as Mr. Bumbolow's.

"I knowed it! " wailed the old man bitterly. "I knowed you never meant to help her like you was pretending! Too much of a fine gentleman, I dessay, to mix yourself up in the affairs of a poor little orphan like Sylvie; leave her starve, you will, while you drink and carouse, and pass by on the other side of Jordan like Pontius Pilate! Yah, you lily-livered bastard, I know you!" He choked over the dregs of Shiloh's whisky in the hurry of his indignant speech.

Shiloh stared from one to the other of his two accusers; he was hurt and bewildered by the violence of the attack, and his consciousness of innocence was so strong as to render him inarticulate. He knew, with terrible clarity, that he was relinquishing his own desires in remaining in Louisville, and that this was the course of sacrifice and self-discipline; the trick of circumstance which made it appear otherwise was a sharp temptation, and his eyes were brilliant with pain as he replied.

"Really, David," he said at last, and haltingly, "you do me an injustice; it is not a crazy idea, but my simple duty; I must wait for the Italian letter. And you, Mr. Bumbolow, who have thought fit to shower me with vulgar abuse, you also are singularly unjust, since I seek only some means of benefiting Silver without abandoning my other responsibilities. Davy shall go to St. Louis in my stead; he shall take all our money, and do what he can to help this child to happiness; for my part all my dearest hopes go with him."

He ceased, and David was silent, knowing some portion of the fever in Shiloh's heart, compounded alike of childish disappointment and archangelic rage; Mr. Bumbolow was not so scrupulous, and his voice was once more raised in furious protest.

"Davy, is it, indeed, to go in your stead?" he asked sarcastically. "And a pretty plan, too, I must say, to send her brother's murderer to the poor gal, all unsuspecting as she'd be, and trustful, a-laying of her little hand in his blood-stained fist without a-dreaming of the dreadful truth. No, my fine young gentleman, it's you or nobody as goes to St. Louis, and if you doesn't go Sylvie will most likely perish of starvation, for her ma was always delicate, and she wasn't more'n a little whiffet of a thing as I remember her, God bless her golden curls!" He wept, and David looked miserably guilty beneath his lachrymose regard.

"Not but what it wouldn't be proper enough for this young feller to come along if you was there to break the thing to her gentle-like and explain as how he done it accidental and without malice," Mr. Bumbolow went on more mildly. "But now, sir, I ask you fair and honest, could you expect a tender-minded little thing like Sylvie to take money from her brother's murderer? No, no, young gentleman, you're the lad as must do the deed, if it's to be done; as an old family friend I have a word to say, and I say it plain and emphatic: it's you or nobody!"

"The old man's right, Shiloh; 'twouldn't be noways decent unless you was along," said David wretchedly; he looked so dimmed and disheartened that the very gold of his hair was tarnished, and Shiloh longed to kindle him into energy again.

"But that is prejudice and superstition," murmured Shiloh with white lips; the temptation was stronger now, and the child and the archangel wrestled mortally within him.

He was dizzy with conflict; he had two souls, and not to save them both could he have disentangled the soul of light from the soul of shadow. He strove upon a pinnacle above the world; some prince of the powers of the air had borne him there, and this creature was a burning part of his own soul. Above him the rays of the sun were spread like golden wings.

Now there were wings about his head, the wings of eagles and the darker wings of vultures; his own wings beat upward into flame. Below the broken clouds a lucent prospect floated half-revealed; this was the other side of the moon; this was the silent silvery reverse of sorrow, the lovelier thing than love. Below the mortal weariness of conflict the valleys of the moon lay deep.

He strove for ever upon the pinnacle, among wings of light and shadow; then a starry fire pierced his side, and he was falling, falling among stars. The archangel was fallen, and all the loosened feathers of his wings were stars that fell with him. The air was wild with stars; they were thick as snowflakes about his head, and he was falling into the other side of the moon.

He fell headlong, not into the other side of the moon, but into Mr. Bumbolow's tavern in Louisville. "Lucifer, son of the morning, how art thou fallen!" he said absurdly, and knew that David was shaking him by the shoulder and that the air was full of sparks and ashes in a sudden draught from the chimney.

"Wake up, Shiloh!" cried David rather crossly. "Goldarn it, man, you can't go to sleep now; you've got to decide. Are you going to St. Louis, or ain't you? Wake up, for the love of Moses, and don't sit staring at me like a loony or a ghost! "

"I have decided," said Shiloh from the hollow of his dream. His voice was cool and quiet, but inwardly he was trembling with exaltation. "I have decided to go to St. Louis, to find Silver. I was mad to doubt it; I must go, and go to the end of the world if need be, searching until I shall find her."

5

"Let us not lose ourselves in distant and uncertain plans, but rather systematise and simplify our motions, at least for the present. It would be very delightful, to be sure, to travel by water, but obviously the expense is beyond our slender resources."

"I reckon it's Shanks' mare for us, Shiloh, all the way to St. Louis," David replied regretfully, eyeing the steamboat *Independence* with unconcealed longing. "Don't suppose we'll have the luck to fall in with no more arks like the cap'n's, neither, and though I'd admire to try my hand at paddling an Injun canoe again, 'twould be a matter of months with the current agin us and all that. Yessir, we got to walk it if we're a-going to make it afore the New Year. Gawd, I wish we'd 'a' had the cash to go cordelling upstream! "

The river-front at Shippingport was bright with traffic; the cries from deck and pilot-house were musical in David's ears, and the November air was amber wine. Nothing appeared difficult or dangerous on such a morning; to swim, even to fly seemed natural to the brave, and Shiloh was on mercurial tiptoe to be gone. The two early miles from Louisville had raced along an excellent turnpike; the rapids lay like a dancing glacier in the dawn, and the friends had walked down Tarascon Street to the levee singing " Shannandore " at the top of their exulting lungs.

"Come, Davy; we'll cross by the ferry and be off into the wilds," said Shiloh, for whose imagination the northern road traversed a fabulous map of primæval forest. David lingered by the water-front; the names of the steamboats charmed him, and as he caught the flashing sunlit letters one by one, he pondered upon the relative nobility of these golden appellations, *Tamer-lane* and *Vesta, Eagle, Rifleman,* and *Rising State.* At the same time he looked with something like contempt at the wingless ships whose paths were fixed and narrow along inland waters, and for a moment he was homesick for the trade-winds.

The crossing of the river was over all too soon; they were on a broad clear road again, with the image of Silver at the end of it. In a little wood by the wayside they cut themselves sticks from the young and living trees; David's stick was hickory, and Shiloh's a straight black shaft of cherry, speckled like a snake. Their bundles swung light enough from these, and the yellow sunlight was warm upon their backs. Behind them, down the sparkling distance of the water, someone was singing a sad song in a high and merry tenor; the melancholy notes were bloomed with joy, as a bunch of dark grapes may be frosted with brightness.

> " Oh, love was the 'casion of my misery;
> Now I am bound, but once I was free! "

" Oh, once I was bound, but now I am free! " sang Shiloh like a mocking echo, altering the refrain to his own mind.

In the Commercial Bank of Louisville a snub-nosed boy was unfastening the green shutters while Mr. Townley arranged the documents and ledgers upon his immaculate mahogany desk. In the fly-blown parlour of the tavern, Mr. Bumbolow, who had breakfasted upon Jamaica rum, wept bitterly because he could not remember whether a child's soft eyes were shadowy brown or hazel under the silver-gilded tangle of her hair.

It was a day for auspicious adventure, a day of angelic crystal dreaming over innocent earth; it seemed a pity to Shiloh that the morning disclosed nothing more mythical than a travelling ped-lar and a lost liver-coloured hound. Nevertheless, a lively splendour informed the very air, and spiced the somewhat meagre buttermilk and roasted potatoes of their noontide meal in a farmhouse kitchen. The frugal repast was pleasing to Shiloh's fastidious conscience; afterwards he snatched half an hour's sleep above the pages of Æschylus, while the back-log crumbled in the chimney and the kettle hummed. He had an enchanting sense of laziness, as he sat there, drowsily aware that David was chopping wood for the farmer's wife in a frenzy of native skill.

"These folks is proper Yankees, from down Portsmouth way," he told Shiloh when the other joined him by the wood-pile. Shiloh rubbed his eyes, partly to dissipate the trance of slumber and partly in admiration for the gleaming antics of the axe, which smote the log and loosed upon the air a flight of chips as buoyant as feathers.

"Easy as cutting butter with a hot knife!" cried David with a magnificent scorn for his own prowess. The dazzling steel flashed down once more, and left the pointed end of the log as cleanly wrought as though it had been finished with a chisel.

The neat white houses of New Albany were left behind; the twelve cool windy miles to Greenville flowed smooth as water through the afternoon, Indian Creek and Blue River were crossed in falling sunshine, and even the long twilight road to Fredericksburg was comforted by a crescent moon. They were very tired when the first candles of the town shone warm and yellow under the lonely silver of the sky; they had walked thirty-four miles since daybreak, and the way had been stranger than the way between Marlow and London, or the steep and wooded trails among the hills of Castine.

"We was plumb fools to come so far, but I'll allow as you can lick the hide off us all a-walking," said David, collapsing under a giant sycamore tree and loosening the buckskin laces of his boots with a vigorous groan. "Dunno how you manage to keep it up so slick an' chipper, for I'm clean tuckered out myself. I wish we was to supper in that elegant shingled house a piece back along the road."

Shiloh dropped lightly down upon the golden leaves beside him; he knew he would be stiff and sleepy within five minutes, but this first instant of suspended motion was still volatile with speed, and he felt exquisitely cock-a-hoop, and livelier than a hawk compared to David's twelve-stone-twelve of solid weariness. A divine levity informed his mind; he wondered whether the stuff of his body were subject to the same laws of gravitation as oppressed the mortal earth, and rejoiced to fancy his very flesh and blood more subtle than terrestrial air.

"A certain form of uncaptive balloon," he murmured happily, aware that the sycamore leaves were comforting and warm beneath a frosty dust of dew. He put his bundle under his head for a pillow and abandoned his faculties to slumber.

"Don't turn back, Davy, it's an unfortunate omen, and quite unnecessary," he said; through a descending veil of sleep he perceived that his friend had risen and was about to reconnoitre the surrounding country. "I had far rather sup in a hovel upon the forward line of march than retrace our steps to yonder commodious mansion. Only, my dear good Davy, pray beg our prospective hosts not to prepare any pork for our entertainment; I am amazingly tired of pork, and even bacon begins to bore me a little. Shall I be very discourteous if I decline to eat bacon?"

"You do beat the Dutch for impudence!" grumbled David, moving off in the direction of the village, where dusk was coloured genially by kitchen fires.

Shiloh was stiff and cold as a winter snake when David waked him twenty minutes later; he crawled meekly enough towards the white clapboarded cottage which his friend pointed out to him in the twilight.

"I fear we have somewhat overestimated our capacity for sustained effort," he admitted sorrowfully. "Our wings are most effectually clipped; we cannot fly so far to-morrow; we are geese, and perhaps not even wild geese at that, Davy." He looked profoundly serious as he flapped his arms in a vaguely aëronautical gesture.

"I'm pretty damn wild when I smell that pot-pie," David replied with passionate conviction.

"Now see here, Shiloh," he went on, pausing upon the threshold of the humble dwelling, "these folks ain't in any ways grand or stylish, like Miss Lillie and all that, but they come from my own neck of woods in a manner of speaking, though it's more Vermont than Maine, and I'd thank you to be extra civil in your dealings with 'em. Not but what you ain't always polite and pleasant; you're gentry, I know that, only don't go mocking of 'em even in your heart of hearts, or I shall guess it somehow. You told me you wouldn't eat no pork, and naturally this give 'em the notion to start with that you was a Jew or a Papist or such-like, for I says my friend won't eat no pork, and they says is it religion or just plain dyspepsia, and laughed, so now you must show 'em that you ain't pernickity nor proud. You may have to swallow just a mite of whisky, just to be friendly, but it won't be much, and the pot-pie is elegant."

Shiloh stared at David in pure amazement; his mind was so innocent of the vanity of birth or breeding that he was actually unaware of this weakness; his prides were all of a nobler lineage. He could not conceive why David should warn him to be kind to David's kindred, and he looked particularly haughty as he replied.

"David, I shall endeavour to conform to an ideal courtesy," said Shiloh in the cool clipped voice of his ancestors.

"To explain a bit more about these here folks," continued David, his hand upon the latch, "Bartlett's their name, but their ma was a Miss Higgins from Maine, and they're regular Yankees to begin with, but Hoosiers along of living in Indiana. People around these parts are all Hoosiers and Suckers, Buckeyes and Corncrackers; funny set o' names I'll allow, but I reckon them as bears 'em ain't so bad neither. The proper southerners calls themselves white folks, same as if the Yankees was niggers, but they don't mean no harm by it; it's just ignorance."

"In the eyes of the virtuous, all men are equal," said Shiloh rather absently; he was very tired, and the fragrance of the pot-pie was rendering him very hungry also.

He entered like a brilliant wraith into a white-washed kitchen full of Bartletts and Higginses; if a ghost were made of fire instead of graveyard mist it might wear for one night the fierce and luminous grace of Shiloh's beauty. Wind and warm autumnal sun had burned him to a flame of energy; even in his weariness there was no languor, and its fever set a more savage radiance upon his lifted brow.

"Lord save us, it's a wild rampaging Osage," remarked

Mrs. Bartlett with admirable calm as she poured the gravy upon the smoking platter.

Shiloh was charmed by his reception; to be taken for an Indian chieftain seemed the perfection of compliment, and the Bartletts' lean and strenuous faces appeared quite gentle in the domestic firelight which flashed so strangely from the splendour of his different flesh. They all looked straight into his amazing eyes and loved him in spite of themselves; the younger Bartletts loved him ironically, because he was so slim and dashing and ridiculous, and their mother loved him bitterly, because he reminded her of her one black sheep, Benjamin, who had run away to sea.

She kept looking to see if it were really Benjamin, while she dished out the pot-pie with Olympian impartiality; she was secretly relieved to discover that the mole was lacking from the left cheek, and that the eyes were blue instead of grey. Benjamin was still her favourite child, but seven years are seven years, and Benjamin had never been respectable, even in Vermont.

Shiloh received a piercing glance from the old lady's deep-set agate eyes, and an enormous portion of pot-pie in token of her approval. He was grateful for her evident solicitude for his comfort, but the food was a dubious blessing; he was quite horrified by the fact that at least half a peck of onions, as well as four young pullets, had entered into the composition of the lordly dish. His hunger was a pungent sauce which made possible a very fair play of knife and fork, and the boiled Indian corn and pumpkin jelly were bland and innocuous to his taste.

"Genuine store tea; none of your spice-wood nor yarb stuff," said Mrs. Bartlett proudly as she tipped the great brown teapot over his empty cup.

"Oh, ma'am, it's done my heart good to eat a real downright old-fashioned meal like this," cried David, drenching his flannel cakes in maple molasses. He looked sentimentally at the custard pies upon the sideboard, and the memory of his home was like nutmeg and cinnamon in his nostrils.

Indeed, David might have been the youngest and the ruddiest of the Bartletts themselves, so plain a kinship stared out honestly beneath straight brows and hair the colour of pine shavings from these square Puritan countenances. Shiloh observed the company silently while he sipped his tea, and was himself observed by all of them, but more especially by one who was neither a Bartlett nor a Higgins, but a widowed daughter-in-law from the marshy bottom-lands down around the Shineys.

She was a delicate ash-blonde creature, with something of Silver in her big bewildered eyes; he looked at her once to learn if this miracle might be, and then looked away to forget her in arrowy and flying dreams.

She had never beheld such another; she trembled in her worn little shoes to see him burn among the stiff automata surrounding him. She had always believed that her husband's family were strong and handsome folk, but now they appeared to her like so many wooden figures with a live man in their midst. A live man or the mortal image of an angel; his eyes were like blue thunderbolts against her soul.

"Dunno what ails ye, Deborah," said Mrs. Bartlett that night, when the sound of sobbing waked her. But she knew very well, and although she had loved her tall eldest son, she did not blame his widow for her alien tears. Benjamin had been his mother's favourite child, and the burning blue-eyed stranger, now sleeping peacefully in the hay-loft, was marvellously like Benjamin.

"Poor Benjamin; he wasn't ever what you might call respectable, even when he was singing in the choir at the First Congregational!" sighed Mrs. Bartlett as she turned upon her tow-linen pillow. "I calculate, when all's said and done, that it's the Lord's mercy this young fellow isn't Benjamin, for the poor lad doesn't look any too respectable either! I must count the spoons in the morning; I must remember to count my wedding spoons."

6

"TWENTY miles to Lebanon and cross Silver Creek!" chanted Shiloh some nine days later, as they left Johnson's Settlement upon the first morning of December. The altered season was cold and pale under a pure translucent sky, and last night's dews were now a velvet bloom of frost along the fields. A rosy muffled sun hung low in the virgin east, and the distant trees were feathery as snow crystals against the horizon.

"Snow in the air," said David, and sniffed, buttoning his pea-jacket closer about his splendid chest. "You was a fool, Shiloh, not to buy a leather waistcoat off that Injun in Vincennes; you'll freeze before we fetch St. Louis, in them rags."

"Shall we be there by candlelight?" inquired Shiloh in ridiculous continuation of his chant. He looked romantic and a little mad in a faded blue flannel shirt and a vest of Kentucky jean with most of its buttons missing; a fine new bandanna handkerchief passed under his right arm and was knotted on his left shoulder. This eccentric decoration lent lustre to his poor attire without adding very materially to its warmth; nevertheless Shiloh was obviously pleased with himself, and the sunburnt colours of his countenance were clear and tropical in the winter scene.

"How many miles to Babylon?" chanted Shiloh perversely, repeating his question about candlelight.

"It's Lebanon, you crazy loon, and I reckon we'll get there before dark, seeing as it's a bare score of miles 'stead of the four-score and ten as you're a-hollering about," David replied severely. "Waste your cash on a red-and-yaller bandanner and sing like a certified idjit and catch your death when you could have had a proper Injun jacket for five dollars with beads and foxes' fur all complete!"

"I confess I was unwise to miss so excellent an opportunity to guard against the rigours of the increasing cold," said Shiloh with admirable meekness. "I detest winter; the severity of climate in these northern latitudes is uncongenial to my temperament and my health alike. I wish Silver lived in the south."

"Which I don't neither; blamed glad I am to feel some human Christian weather at last; Thanksgiving day might as well been on the west coast of Africa with that goldarned mugginess. Beats me why you like it hot; you're a funny son of a musket and sometimes I think you come from hell."

"Sometimes I am quite of your opinion, David," answered Shiloh with gentle gravity.

"Aw, shucks," grunted David, ashamed of his impatience. "You may come from hell, but you're a god-damned decent kind of devil. We can buy all the Injun stuff we want in St. Louis; it's a grand market for that sort of notion, and I'd admire to see us rigged out like a couple of genuwine trappers."

The week had slid by like a painted frieze of small adventures; there had been the amusing incident of the one-eyed Shawnee at Hindostan, and the exquisite evening when the star-reflecting waters of White River had been stirred by a deer's thin cloven hoof. Shiloh had gazed enchanted at the creature's soft fantastic eyes and at the incredible elegance of its ankles, seeing a lovely chimerical image of his own soul mirrored in the moving stream. He had drawn the last crumb of maple sugar from his pocket and approached delicately over the frosted grass; the wild thing had surveyed him for a wizard instant of indecision, and then fled sideways into the twilight.

"It laughed at me; you heard it laugh, Davy," said Shiloh, pensively eating the maple sugar.

There had been a solitary buffalo beyond French Lick, and innumerable foxes, blue, grey, and black, in all the woods along the way. There had been opossums in the gum-trees, and ground-hogs devouring the mast in oaken groves. There had been the thrilling scent of cucumbers which portends a rattlesnake, and once, at sunset, a golden elemental shape which must have been a wildcat had leaped athwart the path. Altogether, Shiloh had known some seven days of sharp elusive happiness; at times he had gone cold and hungry, but at the worst he had gone free, and he throve like a salamander in fiery joy of this. You had only to look at the tawny freckles on his cheek and at the singular colour of his eyes to perceive the strength of his vitality.

"You ain't really civilised, Shiloh, for all your quality ways and pretty manners. We was bloody fools to walk fifteen miles on fried eggs and johnny-cake," young David had grumbled, who resented his friend's innocent attempts at asceticism, and was beginning to weary for Egyptian fleshpots and dressed beef.

The eve of Thanksgiving had found them upon the outskirts of Vincennes; in David's ears the exotic name chimed with melancholy forebodings of starvation for the morrow.

" Don't suppose there'll be a turkey in the whole damned town; these French bastards ain't got no proper idea of religion," he said gloomily.

" What is it, Davy? Some idyllic form of harvest festival? " inquired Shiloh, picturing a village church in Sussex hung with burnished laurel and coraline rose-apples. The memory belonged to his fifth year, long before his prejudice against orthodoxy had crystallized into acute repulsion. He saw the silvery diluted sunlight lie like water upon the scarlet berries, and heard the music that he had not learned to hate flow upward in a cloud of sound.

" It's sermons in the morning, and all your aunts and cousins to dinner, and slews of elegant victuals, and most generally a bit of skating along about afternoon, if your folks ain't too strict and you live in a nice climate like Maine," explained poor David with nostalgic fervour.

" I don't believe I should like it; the skating perhaps; certainly not the aunts and cousins," said Shiloh, and fell silent and a little sad, thinking of Harriet Grove and the holiday parties at which she had danced in a brightness of dawn-coloured tulle.

" Cheer up; mebbe there'll be some Christian families in Vincennes after all," David had encouraged him kindly.

There were few Congregationalists upon the banks of the Ouabache, but David discovered that even Catholics are Christians, and his Thanksgiving did not lack the darling incense of a roasted fowl. His dark-eyed hostess listened to his mournful praise of home, and there was turkey for dinner; wild turkey, stuffed with corn-meal and sausage meat, and pickles and preserves, and beautiful brown pastry shells filled with pumpkin chips and maple syrup.

" French notion of pies, but blamed good, by graminy," David had said with his mouth full. Afterwards there was ratafia from New Orleans, and ginger out of a blue-and-white

Canton jar with a dull silver top. "Beats cock-fighting," said David, and Shiloh agreed with him, and left the sweet fierce liquor untasted in the glass.

He was glad enough to be on the road again, and never so happy as when his companion permitted him to dine upon dry bread and apples in a pause by the wayside. Nevertheless, it was fortunate that David looked to his material welfare; otherwise he might have been tempted to subsist entirely upon light and air, flavoured with the sparkle of frost and the fragrance of burning leaves.

"Get that under your belt, or you'll snap in two like an icicle one of these cold winter days," David would say sternly, pointing to some homely hospitable meal, set smoking on the kitchen table of the night's lodging. Shiloh would smile divinely at the people of the farm, and sigh in secret to his own soul, and meekly eat corned beef and cabbage, or flitch and potatoes, or fried chicken and mush, or whatever the woman of the house might put before him. He was a charming guest; sometimes he laughed, but more often he was shy and gentle and rather sleepy over his supper. His courtesy was admirable; he was loved for this, and for the transparent innocence of his gaze. He was seldom allowed to pay for the privilege of sharing the family repast and spending the long dark night in the chilly comfort of the hay-loft.

"Plenty of blankets and buffalo robes, if you ain't too proud to be beholden to the hosses," their host would tell them with a grin, and Shiloh and David were often thankful for the loan as they burrowed deeper into the meagre store of hay.

Shiloh might fall asleep half stunned with fatigue, to wake shivering in a bitter black frost at sunrise, but the amazing resiliency and lightness of his body and the stubborn gaiety of his mind bore him onward into each new day, and by noon he was always slightly drunk with the effervescence of his own triumphant speed. David strode methodically at his shoulder; against the pearly winter landscape the two figures marched like prodigies of nature, David solid as a moving rock beside a gilded frigate that flew under press of sail.

Now upon the ninth morning of their journey they both felt

garrulous and energetic after an excellent night's sleep and a breakfast of hot coffee and griddle-cakes. Only forty miles remained of the long road to St. Louis, and two days more would leave those miles behind them like a smooth and glittering wake. It was an hour for high and extravagant nonsense, and Shiloh chanted a succession of absurd nursery rhymes to a chorus of picturesque profanity in David's profoundest bass.

"'Tain't often as I cuts loose, as well you know, young feller," said David when they paused for breath. "But you can't be raised a sailor and talk pure Sunday-school in the face of a fine fresh breeze like this 'un."

> "All the spirits that stand
> By the naked man
> In the book of moons, defend ye . . ."

Shiloh cried the words aloud; you could not truly say he sang.

> "That of your five sound senses
> You never be forsaken,
> Nor wander from
> Yourselves with Tom
> Abroad to beg your bacon."

"God blast your vitals for a thundering bloody son of a gun!" replied David; he had exhausted the more pungent terms in his vocabulary, and his tone was casual and pleasant; "why in the name of all damnation do you have to walk so god-damned fast? My lungs are busted keeping up with you, and my ears are fair split a-listening to that lunatic chantey. Quit it, Shiloh, for cris'sake, or I'll lambaste you one in the jaw as'll make you hold your hush to hell and high purposes!"

Shiloh looked at him in mild surprise, and perceiving the friendly smile upon his lips, ventured an amiable protest against a violence of language of which he could not wholly approve.

"I do not particularly care for your choice of words, Davy," he murmured softly. "If you were to call me a catawampus, now, I should be overjoyed; 'catawampus' is such an enchanting epithet. But bastard, and — no, but really, my dear Davy, I

trust I am sufficiently unprejudiced, but really I had far rather
you called me a catawampus."

"Aw, shucks, have it your own way, you crazy bedlamite,"
agreed David with a roar of affectionate laughter. "You know
I don't mean no harm by it; if I did, you'd soon be glaring at
me like a mountain lion, same as you did at Simon Hanna
when he forgot himself and spoke uncivil!"

"His looks were wild, and devil's blood stained his savage
hands and feet . . ." said Shiloh, who was beginning to chant
rhymes of his own composition, and to misquote them at that.

Certainly there was a fine barbaric sting in the air that danced
along the veins like lightning; the legendary profile of a Piankashaw warrior, sharply cut against the pale horizon, lifted Shiloh's
heart with ecstasy. Here was the authentic type of freedom,
sprung from the secret womb of this new world like a sudden
flower of bronze.

Shiloh's knowledge of the noble redskin was largely derived
from the imaginative works of M. Châteaubriand; it is probable
that he had never heard of the Wyoming Massacre, or of Bryant's
Station, and the benevolent associates of Simon Girty. His brow
flushed with rapture to behold the Piankashaw brave, who bestowed a brief contemptuous glance upon the travellers, and
disappeared into the distance like a pillar of tawny smoke.

"What happiness," cried Shiloh with innocent enthusiasm,
"to observe the free intrepid mien of this man, and to contrast
it to its high advantage with the cowed submissive manner of
the negro slaves whom I have seen to my sorrow in Virginia
and Kentucky! Thank heaven we are now within the boundaries
of liberty; often in Louisville my spirits completely overcame
me in considering the debasing effects of such bondage upon
the human race!"

"'Tain't right, it stands to reason," said David, wrinkling
his flaxen brows with difficult thought. "Slavery's agin nature, as
I reckon it, but mebbe these here Injuns ain't so grand as you
make out, Shiloh; I calculate as how they might be mighty
ugly customers if you was to rile 'em. Besides, the niggers seems
more cheerful-like, and somehow they got a kind of freedom in
their souls, as comes out in their singing, which sounds so queer

and far-away on a summer's night. I've heard 'em in Charlestown and New Orleans, down around the water-front; it's blamed queer, Shiloh. Seems like they know about the birds of the air, and about the powers of the air, both good and evil. Reckon it's what they calls an incantation."

"That's beautiful, David; I wish I might have heard them sing that song. And they too could be fierce if you were to rile them, as you call it, and small blame to them if they were. But I refuse to hear my beloved Indians traduced; I shall believe nothing illaudable of them until they have actually scalped me!" and Shiloh laughed, and tugged at his abundant and untidy hair as if to make certain of its immediate safety.

All day the sun hung in the heavens like an heraldic shield, turning from rose to silver and from silver to gold; all day the pure cold atmosphere preserved the frost upon the grass. The travellers went swiftly and joyfully across the hours, which coloured the earth with changing magic and were gone. If any shape of fear or horror lay concealed under the yellow archway of the west, their minds were innocent of its betrayal. It was a very lovely afternoon, and the evening fell as softly as a fall of snow whose flakes are shadow instead of shining crystal.

Shiloh flew upon the pinions of a superhuman happiness; before he came to Lebanon he made a song about the powers of the air both good and evil, and this song was so beautiful that it should have been sung by Lucifer or one of the other archangels if it were sung at all. Shiloh can hardly have been said to sing it; he chanted it rather harshly as it came into his head, and he looked so ragged and barbarous a figure that the song seemed far too fine for him. He was like a savage hunter who has caught a star of heaven in a net spread for wild-fowl; now upon the pinions of an archangelic happiness he carried the star with him along the road to Lebanon.

The Orphan Angel

VII

WILD SPIRIT

They reached St. Louis at the end of the next day, having walked twenty miles under a striped grey sky that spat and clawed at them in feline warfare of rain and sleet. Their clothes were in ill case for such inclemency, and they were drenched to the bone and shivering with cold in the first hour of their journey. By all the laws of nature they should have contracted the severest of chills; perhaps the unreasonable speed of their progress may have saved David from a chronic rheumatism and Shiloh from an attack of pleurisy. By eleven o'clock they had their second wind, which strove quite successfully against the far greater one which issued roaring from the clouded north, and when at last the sunset lifted a few shaking spears of light athwart the gloom, they were no more than half frozen and completely cross as the result of this protracted battle with the elements of storm.

David was cursing between gritted teeth; Shiloh clenched his own teeth even tighter to keep them from chattering, and thought longingly of the Indian's leather jerkin. His flannel shirt was like wet sea-weed against his skin, which he imagined must have turned green and silvery as a fish's beneath the cruel fall of water from above.

His feet still moved swiftly and evenly along the streaming road, but his mind had lost its flying lightness; he felt numb and stupid with cold, and for a moment he hated the whole world. He saw it as a monstrous beast, lying drowned and weltering in rainy blood under an assault of arrows from heaven; he saw the world as a dead beast, and winter issuing dragon-like from the north in an armour of frosted scales. He knew not which he hated most bitterly: the carrion body of the world, or the dragon hungry to devour it.

"Oo, how I hate the cold!" he said in a thin voice that whistled like the wind itself. Then around a bend in the road he beheld the river; for a crazy instant he thought he looked upon the sea, but in that same instant the clouds lifted and the remoter shore was visible, far-away and wavering like a mirage in a veil of rain. Shiloh stood still and gazed across the river, which washed the monstrous image of despair from his soul in a torrent of noble calm.

Its calm was that of undisputed power; it was not smooth, for the storm had lashed it into turbulence, and yet it laid a strange tranquillity on Shiloh's eyes as it stretched before him in the evening light. It was coloured tenderly enough by this, and coloured too by all the miles of living earth which it had taken to its flood, so that it was neither grey nor brown nor ruddy, but something of all three, mixed and made faint to opalescence by the sunset.

They crossed in a small keel-boat managed by two Frenchmen; the fellows were fantastically clothed in brightly dyed shirts and fringed leather breeches, with blue woollen scarves wrapped around their long black locks, and as they talked and gesticulated they seemed as singular and savage as a pair of parakeets. Shiloh was very happy again; he stood upright in the bow of the boat and drank the flying spray with rapture. The wind lifted his hair to wings, and he was no longer cold; it was impossible to believe that he had ever been cold or tired.

Upon landing in St. Louis they repaired at once to Yostic's tavern at the corner of First and Locust streets; Mr. Bumbolow had given them a letter to its proprietor, and they were kindly received in spite of their disreputable appearance. Perhaps Mr.

Bumbolow had mentioned their remaining store of silver dollars; perhaps Mr. Yostic was the benevolent spirit which his outward semblance so heartily suggested. Be this as it may have been, before their drenched garments had dried by the fire they were provided with an excellent hot meal and a bowl of steaming negus, and when they finally set forth into the darkening town their hearts were high above a friendly warmth of creature comfort.

They were going in search of Silver's milliner; the address was written in Mr. Bumbolow's crabbed script on a bit of brown paper. "Madame Clothilde, rue Royale"; so it was written on the bit of paper, but the words "rue Royale" had been blotted out, and "Main Street" scribbled in their stead. Mr. Bumbolow was growing old, and it was often hard for him to remember that the streets of St. Louis had changed the ancient regimen of their names.

"I suppose we must learn to call her Sylvie, David; she will not wish us to call her Silver any more. But I shall always think of her as that, and Silver Cross is a lovelier sound than Sylvie la Croix."

"What's her real name, Shiloh? I mean the name her mother gave her; Spanish-like it was, and too stiff and stately for a little girl, same as if you was to call a pretty catboat 'Victory' or 'Constitution' or some such frigate-name."

"Oh, that was a very stately name indeed, Davy; stately and saintly too, and musical, but perhaps a trifle like the plaster statues of the virgin in a Spanish cathedral," said Shiloh laughing. "Maria Solidad la Croix y de Sylva; that's a ridiculous mixture of tongues, and fit for the Tower of Babel, and yet it's charming in its way, and pitiful. The child of a French Canadian cut-throat and a Castilian lady; how romantic and dangerous an heritage!" Shiloh shivered, as if this romance were a danger to his own heart. "Saint Mary Solitude," he said, twisting it into English, and suddenly the double meaning of the words smote upon his heart and turned him pale.

"Mary Solitude; Saint Mary Solitude," he thought dizzily, seeing the darkly wooded shores of San Terenzo as plainly as though they had been painted within his eyelids. The Italian letter fluttered from among the cypresses, winged like a dove or the little white owl called aziola. It passed the long wine-coloured waves of the sea, and the steep and glassy waves of land whose crests were mountain-tops. It hovered over Louisville, with an olive branch in its beak, and he was three hundred miles from Louisville, and dreaming of another Mary Solitude.

"But I shall always call her Silver Cross," he said aloud, and David wondered why his voice laid an audible sadness upon the words.

They had plain directions from the tavern, and they found Madame Clothilde's shop with no greater trouble than the re-wetting of their shoes in a dozen large puddles along Main Street. The milliner appeared in response to their repeated summons; she proved to be a tall gaunt woman with the ghost of a moustache upon her grim upper lip, and Shiloh was reminded of Eliza Hitchener and the Good of Mankind.

"Sacred name, is this a suitable hour at which to disturb honest working-people?" grumbled Madame Clothilde in the accents of martyrdom; it was no more than seven o'clock, but the travellers' appearance had quickly convinced her that they had no honourable intention of purchasing a Spanish lace shawl or a bonnet imported from Paris by way of New Orleans. She lighted a single disapproving candle in the gloomy cavern of the shop, and faced them with a very black frown.

Shiloh's blue eyes caught the beam and shone like two good deeds in a world of bandboxes and dusty bolts of ribbon; his face emerged clearly from the surrounding shadows, and the candlelight danced in motes of radiance over a delicate mask of supernatural gold.

"Name of God, what can two ragged leetle Yankee tramps want with a fashionable modiste? Is it perhaps an Indian muslin robe, or a Leghorn hat with ostriche plumes?" cried Madame Clothilde, and cast her eyes to heaven, but her ill temper was strangely fled, and she permitted them to question her concerning Silver with no further marks of indignation than an occasional groan, or a shrug of her angular and expressive shoulder-blades.

"Sylvie? The little Sylvie la Croix? But naturally I knew her; have I not often rapped her knuckles for taking such crooked stitches, and for never basting her seams? If you will believe me, she would not wear a thimble; what is one to do with a girl who will not wear a thimble when she sews?"

"It is impossible to say, madame," replied Shiloh diplomatically, thinking that by far the best course would be to kiss the pricked forefinger of the milliner's apprentice called Sylvie la Croix. "But what, precisely, have you done with her, all without a thimble as she is? It is to discover this that we have come to St. Louis."

"I have done nothing, except to scold her now and then, always for her soul's good, and to teach her to trim bonnets with taste and discretion," said Madame Clothilde with an air of conscious and acidulous virtue. "But what that wicked old man has done with her is another matter; you had better demand from Monsieur Saint-Ange an account of his stewardship, my little cabbage, and not come bullying decent milliners out of their beds." She wrapped the folds of a red flannel dressing-gown about her bony limbs in the manner of a Roman matron answering some calumny intended for Cæsar's wife.

Shiloh experienced a pang of horrid fear; the name of Saint-Ange must cover a very hellish angel of the pit if one half the suspicion in Madame Clothilde's tones were justified. A pulse began to beat in his temple as he asked a question in a cracking whisper.

"For God's sake, what do you mean, madame? Do not torture me, I beg of you, but tell me what you mean."

"Nothing, except that Sylvie has gone to California by Monsieur Saint-Ange's advice, and that for my part I cannot approve of the step," said Madame Clothilde with dignity.

2

"To California!" cried Shiloh and David in one breath of amazement; a slight quality of nightmare seemed to move the atmosphere of the little shop, and Shiloh felt his hair prickle with cold surprise. The figure of Silver was once more remote and tiny at the end of a long road; it shone minute and brilliant as some sacred doll in a niche above a vast cathedral nave, among a multitude of candle-flames. Tears of weariness and disappointment came into Shiloh's eyes, and made the true candle-flame prismatic and cruciform like a thorny star.

Even David was disheartened; he took Shiloh's hand in his, gripping it with kindly violence, and the two stood together in the silence of a bad dream.

"But it's real, Davy; it's only too real and ineluctable," said Shiloh at last, and David understood at least half of his bitterness.

"You see," explained Madame Clothilde, who herself saw quite plainly that they were blinded and confused by wonder, "it is the little one's rich relatives who have taken her so far away; a fine piece of luck if only they are good to her. I doubt it, in my sad knowledge of life, but of course there are occasional miracles. But then these excellent Coronels were always proud and overbearing, and poor Sylvie is so much their inferior in birth, with her blood of a river-pirate and a murderer, that they cannot help despising her be they never so Christian in intention. Ah, it is all very sad, and I advised Saint-Ange against it from the first, but what would you? He is a stubborn man, and the Coronels promised great material advantages for the child."

"But who is Monsieur Saint-Ange, and why had he authority over Sylvie's happiness?" inquired Shiloh with nervous indignation; he longed to discover an object for the holy and somewhat hysterical rage which was shaking him to the marrow.

"Ah, he is merely an old man with a passion for interfering in other people's affairs," said Madame Clothilde more mildly. "Indeed, I suppose he would be harmless enough, though sufficiently mad, if he had not acquired an ascendency over Sylvie's youthful mind which has resulted in her undoing. Would it not be better to be a milliner's apprentice in an honest hard-working household like this than a drudge in the palaces of the wicked aristocrats? The dogs! They will tear her to pieces between them, like as not, and gobble the poor rabbit up without grace before

meat; it makes my blood boil even to think of it!" Madame
Clothilde's principles were sternly republican; she had left
France as a romantic girl, while yet the Revolution was in its
unbloodied infancy, and her hatred of the rich was only equalled
by her high talent for securing them as customers.

"Perhaps I should do better to sell slippers, in case these great
ones should lose their heads one fine day!" she would remark
to her intimates; nevertheless she numbered the first families
of St. Louis among her patrons, and the bonnets she made
them were a subtle inducement to pride.

Now she spoke with such fire that Shiloh was alight in a
moment; the picture of Silver as a small snow-soft rabbit being
devoured by wolfish dogs was too much for his composure, and
he cried aloud upon all the powers of gentleness and courage
as he besought Madame Clothilde for news of Silver's present
home.

"Is it really possible that she is a drudge? That they may
beat her, or tyrannise over her mind with the nameless cruelties
of the strong against the weak?" he asked in an agony of angry
pity. His agitation was so extreme that Madame Clothilde tried
to make him sit down and drink a soothing cup of camomile tea;
she was truly distressed when he insisted upon striding back
and forth between the counter and the front door and wringing
his hands like a madman.

"Calm yourself, my poor child, I beseech you; you will have
a frightful migraine after such a crisis of the nerves," she told
him when he began to tear his hair; her firm tones tranquillised
him a little, and he summoned sufficient resolution to frame a
coherent question as to the actual circumstances of Silver's going.

"Sit down and cease wringing your hands, and I will tell
you all I know," Madame Clothilde promised him; he sank
into a chair and listened quietly enough, with his forehead
against his clenched fists and his elbows on his knees, but even
in the dim light it was very evident that he trembled.

"It was like this, but you will find it difficult to understand
all the family names," Madame Clothilde began. "You have
heard much of the infamy of Jacques la Croix, but perhaps you
do not know that Sylvie's mother was a distant relative of

Governor Piernas, and that she had cousins in Spain and cousins in California and cousins in New Orleans. These Coronels were no kin to the governor, nor yet to the de Sylvas; they were her mother's people, that is to say Sylvie's grandmother's people, and they have been settled in California for some hundreds of years, I believe. One of the daughters came to New Orleans and married a de Sylva; Sylvie's mother was the fruit of that union, or the flower, for she was far more like a white flower than anything so rosy as an apple or a peach. Both the de Sylvas and the Coronels cast her off when she in her turn married Jacques la Croix; of course it was a very bad match, but families should hang together, and for my part I hold that they were unnecessarily severe. Poor Dolores; his murdering cheating ways were too hard for her, and his death the final disgrace. At last she died of grief and shame, leaving Sylvie and that mad sheep Jasper to the mercy of myself and Monsieur Saint-Ange. That old fool claims to be of the same blood as Saint-Ange de Bellerive, the friend of the great Pontiac; personally I doubt it, but at least he and I were by far the most respectable of the children's friends, and we did all we could for them, which was not much, for we are not rich like the arrogant Coronels of California."

"Would to heaven she had never left your kindly sheltering roof! How could this Saint-Ange permit such a tragical mistake to involve a child that he has cherished?" asked Shiloh in a broken voice.

"Ah, you may well wonder; I think he regrets it now himself, particularly since he has come into a little legacy. He is a fool, but I pity him; he worries constantly about the girl now she has gone. It was Jasper's disappearance that decided him; he always said that he had failed with the boy, and how could he be sure that the girl was safe from disaster? She was safe enough in my shop, but he is a snob, and a sycophant, and when the Coronels sent word that one of her cousins was in New Orleans, and that we were to dispatch Sylvie to him at once, the old gentleman scratched the money together somehow, and sent her off by steamboat down the river. Poor rabbit, she looked very pitiful in the little hood and cloak that I had made her;

dark blue with a scarlet lining it was, and a good durable English cloth, but she was crying so bitterly that I was afraid she would spot it. One can never be certain about these smooth-finished materials, and of course as usual she had lost her handkerchief and had to borrow mine! "

"But you said California, ma'am; you ain't going to tell us that Silver's gone around the Horn?" asked David in a sort of terror; the picture of the dark blue cloak and the borrowed handkerchief turned all his bones to tears.

"Yes, you good-for-nothing, that is precisely what I am about to tell you," Madame Clothilde answered shortly; in spite of her democratic ideals her heart rejected David in favour of Shiloh's quality of the exquisite and the finely-bred.

"Assuredly she has gone around the Horn, unless indeed she is drowned," she continued relentlessly; then Shiloh's shuddering groan touched her to pity and she spoke more gently as she turned to him.

"Do not despair, my dear; I suppose she is in California by now, and alive and well, though probably homesick for her old Clothilde," she said with tonic cheerfulness. "Monsieur Saint-Ange can give you more information; you had far better go to him at once. There is no need to distress yourself so cruelly; all may yet be well, and it is useless to torture your mind with these forebodings. Go to him; he is kind, and no more a fool than most men of his age. I have not clearly understood what is your true connection with Sylvie, but I am sure that you are her friend, and that you intend her nothing but benevolence."

"We was her brother's friends, and we aim to help his sister if we can," declared David with perfect simplicity; Shiloh felt a momentary shock in considering the special providence which had removed Jasper from life, and he looked a little wanly at David's broad right hand clenched in its casual strength. Then he knew that David had the true inwardness of the matter clear as daylight in his ingenuous mind, and he was ashamed of his misgivings and of the fainting purpose of his soul.

"I hope that you may be able to do so; I care profoundly for the happiness of that child," said Madame Clothilde, still addressing herself to Shiloh. She thought that he might make a charming husband for little Sylvie if only he would settle down in some lucrative business, and earn a decent livelihood.

"For, after all, breeding is something, and he has such singularly beautiful hands," thought the republican Madame Clothilde as she bade him good-night with a curious and unaccustomed tenderness unloosing the steely ligaments of her heart.

3

"But look a-here, sir," objected David, with a shade of regret in his manly tones, "if the old milliner's just a plumb idjit, and if these grand Spanish relations of Silver's is so god-a'mighty rich and respectable, how the mischief could she be in any need of help from the likes of us? I'm blamed if I can make it out nohow."

A night and a day had passed since the conversation with Madame Clothilde and now Shiloh and David sat at dinner with Monsieur Saint-Ange in that gentleman's comfortable dwelling. A recent legacy from a nonagenarian aunt had made it very comfortable indeed; it was built somewhat after the style of Colonel Auguste Chouteau's mansion, with walls of solid stone surrounded by a wooden verandah, and although it was no more than a miniature copy of the other house its true amenities were equal. The black walnut floor of the salon was freshly beeswaxed to a mirror which reflected several charming bits of furniture in the Empire mode, and two exquisite urns of white Marseilles faïence adorned the mantelpiece.

They had discovered him in this delightful apartment when last evening's search had led from the shop straight into his impressive presence; he was courteous and kind, and when he bade them to dinner upon the following day his manner made them implicitly a pair of foreign ambassadors whom whimsical fancy had disguised in rags.

"But this should have been all for Sylvie," he had said, with a gesture which included his padesoy dressing-gown, his decanter of cognac, and his volume of Montaigne, "only for her

I should have selected sea-green silk, a thimbleful of anisette, and the latest romance by a pious Frenchwoman."

David had been quite frankly afraid to come to-night, but now he sat at ease, well-fed and flattered into loquacity by his host's attentions, and when he repeated his question it was put to a friend.

" Blamed if I can make it out," he said again.

" Ah, my dear boy, there are other needs than riches, in this little irony of the good God's which we have agreed to call life. Madame Clothilde is of course entirely mad, but she has reason in her fears for Sylvie's happiness. I should have kept the child with me, but I was poor as skim-milk, and how was I to know that I had the honour to be my aunt Alphonsine's residuary legatee? I let her go, because the Coronels are rich and well-intentioned, but now I am sorry, and since I am too old and too rheumatic to go myself, you and Shiloh must go to California. I hope you will bring her back to me; at least you must go, and find out how she is supporting her exile. Is it not so, *mon brave?* " asked Monsieur Saint-Ange, smiling at Shiloh, whom from the first he had treated with distinguished consideration.

During the past twenty-four hours he had acquired the curious habit of looking fixedly at the young man and murmuring, to the ghost of an operatic melody, the song of the minstrel Blondel: " *O Richard, ô mon roi, l'univers t'abandonne!* " It was plain that he, no less than Miss Lillie and Captain Appleby, regarded Shiloh in the glamorous light of a disinherited prince. Indeed, he would have begged to lend him the raiment proper to royalty if the other's austere simplicity of habit had not bundled all sarsenet waistcoats and delicate cambric shirts into one contemptible oblivion, and now his gaze was well-nigh adoring upon the spectacle of Shiloh's fastidious lack of interest in *poulet en casserole* and old Madeira.

" *L'univers t'abandonne!* " remarked Monsieur Saint-Ange sadly, perhaps apropos of Shiloh's really shocking boots.

" Is it not rather I who have abandoned the universe? " asked Shiloh, in his charming faintly Italianate French.

" Possibly, by escaping from its prison, which is a captivity of more than Mohammedan rigour," agreed the old gentleman.

"And that is a very excellent reason why you should not abandon Sylvie to the severity of the Coronel dungeon. Oh, I am by no means to be taken literally, and doubtless the child has plenty of bodily liberty and nourishing food, but in this fine household of her cousins she must of necessity be a sort of little Cendrillon. How can an old and stupid godfather — who, alas, is not a wizard — turn her tatters into spun glass? Do not hesitate, *mon prince;* she must be weary of waiting in the ashes."

"You have not forgotten that I am already married, my friend?" asked Shiloh somewhat nervously; he was pale with excitement, and the slices of chicken upon his plate were quite untasted.

"I have not forgotten, *mon prince,*" answered Monsieur Saint-Ange with mysterious brevity.

"I am no prince of chivalric legend, but a wretched creature without durable virtue, and the slave of an enchantment. Did you ever read *The Tempest,* monsieur?"

"No, my dear, I never did, and now I probably never shall. I do not admire Shakspere," said Monsieur Saint-Ange with an intellectual honesty truly Gallic.

"It does not matter; there is a creature in *The Tempest* . . . but how can my own poverty and incompetence hope to serve the lady of this fairy-tale?"

It was clear that Shiloh was profoundly depressed; he wore the air of an unlucky angel fallen into a pit digged for the toughest and most horny-skinned of fiends. His countenance was blanched as though he bled in secret from some mortal wound, and above the luminous pallor of his brow the tossed hair showed a silver side like stormy willow leaves.

"I wish you would eat your dinner; you may serve Sylvie far better if you have not first starved yourself into a consumption," said Monsieur Saint-Ange rather impatiently.

"I am sorry, monsieur," murmured Shiloh politely, and turned a trifle paler as he cut a slice of chicken into two pieces and neglected to eat either of them. The recollection of several lovely ladies had taken away his appetite.

Several lovely ladies; seven imprisoned princesses. Melissa of the honey-sounding name, and Silver sitting among the ashes of her California exile, made the seven of the fairy-tale, added to those others out of the past. Always he had meant to be so wise and valiant, but all the princesses were still in prison, and he was a wretched creature and the slave of an enchantment.

The first of the ladies was little and slight, a child, a school-girl truly; her face was veiled in such a manner that he dare not look at it. She was Harriet; he had intended to rescue her from parental tyranny and the horrors of Mrs. Fenning's school at Clapham. He had been nineteen years old at the time and a philosopher, so that he had a rational disdain for knight-errantry, but she had wept bitterly, and her tears had been April rain-drops upon apple-blossom skin. There was never anything else that did not actually flower in a garden quite like Harriet's face, but such flowers are perishable, and alas . . . his mouth grew cold with an approaching faintness, and there was the taste of river-water upon his lips.

Mary was another child; *thou child of love and light!* She was all white and flaxen, but lighted like an alabaster lamp from within, and the shadow of her dark-grey eyes was clear as light itself. He had loved her and he would for ever love her; he had meant to rescue her from a cruel stepmother in green spectacles, and from the loneliness of unfulfilled desire; he had taken her away, and at first she had been happy. Yet he knew that he had often grieved her, and of late there had been a silent anger burning at the heart of her beauty. At Lerici, by the shores of the bay of Spezzia, she had burned with silent rage, and her white and golden flesh could scarcely veil the flame. Translucent flesh, and too mysterious soul; doubtless he was a fool not to un-derstand, but this darkness was bitterer than the depth of the sea.

Claire was a child; a spoiled child once, and charming as a tiger-kitten. He had tried very faithfully to stand her friend, but her fierceness was untamable by any pity; it was not pity or friendship that might have tamed her heart. He had been gentle with her as a brother, and all to no purpose; he had been patient, though such was not the natural pulse of his blood, but patience could never content this Claire, for whom even love was lack-ing in flavour unless it were spiced with ferocity. Poor tiger-kitten, miserably trapped in the household of Professor Bojti at

Florence! Now he could never set her free to frolic up and down the parti-coloured jungles of a dream.

Emilia Viviani was a captive dove; *poor captive bird, who from thy narrow cage* . . . there was no profit in the memory of that illusion. *I think one is always in love with something or other; the error lies in seeking in a mortal image the likeness of that which is, perhaps, eternal.* So he had written of Emilia, but first he had written of her to another tune, the veritable music of the soul . . . *but true love never yet was thus constrained . . . it overleaps . . . like lightning with invisible violence . . . and makes free . . . makes free . . . the limbs in chains . . . the heart in agony . . . the soul in dust and chaos . . .*

It was impossible to eat the liver-wing of the chicken while he remembered Emilia. There were chains of deathly weariness upon his limbs, and he would have given ten years of his life for a breath of free heaven to cool his forehead. The room was very hot.

Jane's hands were always cool. That was the expression of her inmost spirit, a cool and delicate spirit, not profound, but sweet as cream in a dairy. This lady had never been imprisoned, or, if she had, so long ago that her smiles had forgotten it; it was Edward who had freed her. But suppose . . . of course it was all a vision and a mirage . . . suppose that somewhere within her spirit there had lain a secret of divinity far sweeter than clover-scented cream, a sleeping warmth, an unawakened Psyche. It was too late ever to know this thing; the Psyche must lie unawakened now, with cool hands folded over her secret.

Melissa of the honey-sounding name was still a child, and happily this child was safe in the keeping of her father's friend. She was the least of all the ladies; she was only fourteen years old. She was far safer in her present keeping; to free her would have been to cast her forth into premature sorrow, into a midnight ravenous with wolves. It was better to have left her quietly in the shining moonlit room, and to have come away without a word, with only the ghost of a kiss, a little pulse of sighing air . . . such kisses die . . . but live . . . *but live within the sense they quicken.*

He closed his eyes, those eyes of burning and incredible blue which Melissa had loved more than he might ever know, and without their singular illumination his face became no more than a thin trivial mask; a death-mask it might have been, white as plaster under the sunburn, with hollow temples and tormented lips. His beauty was put out like a snuffed candle; if one were critical one saw that his nose was slightly ridiculous and that he had a great many freckles.

Neither Monsieur Saint-Ange nor David was critical; the first observed that his young friend was looking profoundly fatigued, and the other that civilisation never did agree with Shiloh nohow, and that he'd be switched if he could figger it out, but the poor boy appeared to have the shakes and he reckoned they'd better take to the road again.

"Crazy goings-on," grumbled David aloud. "Leaves good victuals on his plate and sits there like a graven idol, and it's no time at all since he was tearing along a-hollering at the top of his lungs, strong as a hoss and stubborn as a mule."

"Do be sensible and drink your wine; you need not talk if you are tired, but it is a pity not to drink such excellent Madeira," said Monsieur Saint-Ange to Shiloh.

Shiloh did not answer him; he was thinking of Silver. Six lovely ladies had gone glimmering through his mind in twice as many minutes, and although they had faded very softly into oblivion he was shaken by their going. The seventh still inhabited the future; he could not deceive himself into a longing to return into the past. The past was fair but tragical; a sickness fell upon his heart when he remembered it.

The future was different; a clear heaven-coloured wind blew out of the west, and its stars were of a purer brilliance. This seventh lady was far away, but not in the tragical past; she was set in a niche of the future. Like a saintly doll she glittered in a niche of stars, and yet she was the little figure of the fairy-tale, with ashes in her silver-golden hair and tears in the moth-wing darkness of her eyes.

"But I am afraid that I am an excessively poor hand at rescuing people," said Shiloh, and opened his own eyes upon reality.

It is necessary to confess that Monsieur Saint-Ange cared

only for the immediate relief of Shiloh's melancholy; in the religious city of St. Louis he was a placid infidel, and he troubled not at all about marriage and Mary as he dispensed hot coffee and humane advice for the comfort of his young friend's spiritual prostration. He was a kind old man, but he had no child, and he was lonely among the good burgesses of St. Louis. Shiloh's courtesy and eccentric grace had won him beyond reason and morality, and now he was all for flinging Sylvie's bonnet over the windmill if the gesture were medicinal to his favourite's pain.

He was horrified to perceive the ravages of care upon the beloved countenance; he put a great deal of sugar into the bitter black coffee, and poured out a generous measure of cognac to fill the cup. He gave Shiloh a small portion of cream cheese and a peach preserved in white brandy; he would have given him the moon if that delicacy had been obtainable, and he had every intention of giving him his heart's desire, if that desire chanced to be Sylvie la Croix.

"You must go to Sylvie, *mon prince;* I cannot explain my conviction, but nevertheless I feel that you must go," he said with emphasis, eager to catch the returning colour of joy in Shiloh's face. It was forthcoming, with a kindling glance of animation, and Monsieur Saint-Ange continued, "If it seems that she requires a husband, why not our gallant David here? Name of a dog, is he not good enough even for a princess?"

To himself he whispered that it would be better to be Shiloh's mistress than the other's wedded wife, and that either were a happy fortune for the daughter of Tomahawk Jacques la Croix. Truly he was a kind old man, but he cared little for the opinions of a world which he had studied to despise, and Shiloh had shown a subtle and comprehensive knowledge of his adored Montaigne.

Shiloh only wanted the support of such an assurance; he forgot the spectral visions of the last half hour, and when he had drunk the coffee and eaten the peach he felt much recovered. In spite of his fierce liberty of conscience he was curiously dependent upon Monsieur Saint-Ange's approval, and now with a sigh of exhaustion he relinquished his mind to the counsels which he longed to hear and to believe. His body, ever sensitive to the agitations of his soul, relaxed to peace, and he sipped a little of the Madeira and stared drowsily at the rainbow flames upon the hearth.

4

" I ADMIT," said Shiloh, " that we are in a slight pecuniary distress."

The scene was unchanged; only the augmented fire and the pattern of frost upon the window-panes showed that the season had advanced. It was seven days later, and the three companions were once more seated about Monsieur Saint-Ange's hospitable board, whose polished walnut surface reflected a number of cut-glass decanters and an English earthenware tea-pot. Shiloh had at last persuaded his host to let him drink Bohea instead of Madeira or ratafia punch.

" But my dear boy, I have already explained to you that I shall permit you to go to California only as the guests of my late Aunt Alphonsine," replied Monsieur Saint-Ange; then, perceiving a slight but significant stiffening of the innocent contours of Shiloh's countenance, he proceeded more cautiously. " Oh, I know that you are very well able to go without that poor lady's assistance, but consider what an inestimable favour you will be conferring upon me in thus consenting to further your journey in some degree of comfort and safety, by means of the material aid which my deceased relative is so anxious to bestow. I know that you are honourable, and I suspect that you are obstinate, but surely you will not refuse to borrow the price of a pack-mule? "

" Then," said Shiloh, evading the issue by another question, " I take it that you and Davy have decided against the Horn."

" Aw, Shiloh, you ain't never done it, and you don't rightly understand how goldarned slow it can be," protested David. " I been to Valparaiso twice, and I'm sick of them lousy vessels a-wallering in Cape weather. I been through the mill, Shiloh, ground and bolted, and I don't want no more of it than I can

help. I come west to see Injuns and buffalo and such-like varmints; you don't see none of them rounding the Horn, no, not
so many as you'd meet right here in St. Louis. Let's go overland, for the love of Moses, and get some fun for our money."

"Of which precisely twelve silver dollars remain," said
Shiloh, taking them out of his pocket and placing them carefully
in the centre of the dark mirror of the dining-table.

"And you can't get a decent pack-mule for less'n . . ." David
began, but Monsieur Saint-Ange stopped him with a warning
glance. David filled his glass with neat ratafia and whistled
thoughtfully between his teeth, his eyes upon the silver dollars.

Shiloh was not listening; he too stared at the twelve silver
dollars and appeared to dream. His demeanour was noticeably
subdued; it lacked that sharp and charming hint of the fantastic which marked it at its animated best.

He was attired in a white linen shirt unbuttoned at the
throat and a suit of shabby black merino; these garments had
belonged to the days of Monsieur Saint-Ange's respectable poverty, and there still lingered about them a faint atmosphere of
gum-camphor and erudition. Their prim antiquated cut enhanced their present wearer's look of youth and pathos; David
was painfully reminded of the perishing creature whom he
had drawn from the sea upon the night of Jasper's murder.
Here was the uncanny phantom come again, in place of the
dashing scarecrow of every day; here was the sign, the portent,
the messenger of salvation. Even the crumpled collar and the
books bulging from the pocket were the same; the bright and
dark supernal attributes were dimmed by custom and
brotherly use, but David felt his heart grow cold with the recollection of his vow.

"I been forgetting," he said to himself, "I been forgetting
how I dragged him back from death to save my own etarnal
soul, when mebbe he'd 'a' rather died, when mebbe life's too
damned hard for him. Well, if he's set his heart on rounding that
there bloody Horn, I'll go with him; I'll go with him to the ends
of the earth, to fight, die, work, beg, or steal hosses for him, by.
graminy. He may make a dog of me if he likes, or a nigger, or

a back-log, or a dinner; I've took a vow, and I mean to keep it
in spite of hell and high purposes. But all the same I hope he
ain't set his heart on that there lousy old Horn."

Monsieur Saint-Ange regarded Shiloh with an affection quite
unmixed with awe; he vaguely regretted having lent him the
merino suit, since its cut was too scholarly for a prince. The
boy's shining singularity was tamed by its decorum; he wore
the air of nothing more miraculous than a young revolutionary
poet or a romantic student of the arts, and one saw that he was
suffering from a slight but annoying cold in the head.

"I do most heartily detest this cruel weather," said Shiloh
rather crossly, and poured out another cup of tea.

"Beats me how you can feel that way about it," replied
David. "It's just nateral weather for Christmas time, seasonable
and healthy, and I like it a sight better'n summer. Ain't you
downright thankful to quit sweating like a hoss and puffing like
a grampus, and hear the snow go scrunch under your boots agin
when you walk? St. Louis's an elegant spot to my way of thinking; we might sort of hang around here all winter, and light
out with the trappers in the spring, or mebbe we might settle
down in one of them holes in the mountains with some of Ram-
say Crooks' or General Ashley's men, and go west by way of
Oregon when the snow melts. A power of them has done it
lately; I was talking to one of these French bastards only yesterday, and they do have a god-a'mighty lot of larks in the
winter-time. Wisht you could see it like that, Shiloh; don't win-
tering in a hole in the Rockies appeal to you none at all, with the
cards and the drink and the singing, and an Injun wife if you
was to fancy her?"

Monsieur Saint-Ange began to laugh, very quietly and courteously; the picture conjured up by David's words was exquisitely humorous to his imagination. Shiloh did not laugh; he took
one of his host's fine linen handkerchiefs from his pocket and
gravely blew his nose; then he shivered slightly and shook his
head.

"No, Davy; I am sorry to appear selfish, but really I should
prefer to go south if it were possible. I hate winter, and the

American winter seems to be particularly severe. I have not been warm since I reached St. Louis, except of course by Monsieur Saint-Ange's charitable hearth."

"It ain't possible, Shiloh; leastways not except you mean the Horn. That's south, I'll allow, but I reckon you'd find it a damned sight colder'n St. Louis. Still," said David with a dedicated sigh, "if you've set your heart upon that lousy Horn, the Horn it'll have to be, by graminy."

"Do not be alarmed, Davy," Shiloh hastened to reassure him, "I have really no desire to round the Horn; my true preference would lead me south by way of Santa Fé."

"For cris' sake what are you a-talking about Santa Fé for, Shiloh?" cried David indignantly. "That ain't got nothing to do with California; you only show your ignorance when you talk like that. Far better get to Oregon in early spring, and take our chances of a Yankee schooner as would land us down the coast."

"Possibly," said Shiloh, not in the least as if he meant it. "But there are two Americans called Workman and Spencer who went from New Mexico to Los Angeles with a Spanish caravan, and who are now trading in Santa Fé. The road is open to the venturesome and, after all, the road lies south. I feel certain it must be comparatively warm in Santa Fé."

"Well, of all the plumb foolishness . . ." began David, but Shiloh interrupted him by drawing several folded newspapers from his pockets and spreading them upon the polished surface of the table.

"You see," said Shiloh somewhat diffidently, "I have endeavoured to inform myself by means of the public prints. Here are three copies of the *Missouri Intelligencer;* I found them at the tavern, and I have derived both pleasure and profit from their perusal. Allow me to read you this extract from the issue of October eighth; its tone is more optimistic than those of the preceding reports, which speak forebodingly of starvation and murder."

"'The arrival of the greater part of the company under the superintendence of Colonel Cooper from Santa Fé, happily contradicts the report afloat a few weeks since, of their having been robbed and left in a starving condition. . . . Many have also returned who comprised the party under the direction of Captain Becknell. Those of both these parties who remained at Santa Fé — among whom is Captain Becknell — may be expected in a few weeks.'"

Shiloh read these words in a tone of quiet satisfaction; he handed the other newspapers to David, and waited smilingly while his friend's slow forefinger followed the lines of print.

"Well?" said Shiloh at last, and in a voice of triumph.

"Well?" asked David with a deliberate lack of enthusiasm; there had been nothing in the letters from Franklin and Fort Osage to modify his low opinion of the Santa Fé plan.

"But Davy, surely you perceive the manifest superiority of this mode of travel!" cried Shiloh excitedly. "Only consider its numerous advantages; the economy, the novelty, the surprising adventures! 'It is becoming a familiar operation for our citizens to visit this capital'; thus the *Intelligencer* of September seventeenth, and I have myself heard the same tale from a member of Jacob Fowler's party, who returned to Missouri last July. This man is in St. Louis at present; he is an excellent fellow, and he assures me that the thing is possible."

He looked so absurdly impractical and mild in the black merino suit and crumpled linen collar, so delicate and gentle, so patient under the affliction of a cold in the head, and so preeminently unfitted to cope with the realities of danger, that David almost laughed aloud. The burning spirit who had travelled at his side across half a continent was obscured by the dull garments and the duller infirmities of civilisation, and David forgot the fiery impulse of Shiloh's body in contemplating its slight proportions, now immobile within a borrowed coat.

"You couldn't never do it, Shiloh," he exclaimed rather scornfully. "You're crazy if you think you could, but I always known you was crazy. Why, you idjit, ain't I heard about that trail from my friends of the Rocky Mountain Fur Company, who wouldn't go near it for a mint of money, and don't I know it's god-damned awful? Bare hills and howling blizzards, and deserts and sand, and murdering Mexican bandits and horned toads and grizzlies and Iatans and all such devilish varmints, and no water, and you get so's you're thankful to chaw the very mules' ears for thirst, and false ponds a-hovering in the skies, and all manner of horrors! Oh, you couldn't never stand it, Shiloh, never in this world! "

" But how ridiculous, Davy! " said Shiloh with an equal scorn. " Of course I could stand it, and what is more, I shall. It is my irrevocable decision to go by way of Santa Fé; you have been ludicrously misinformed as to the conditions of the journey, but doubtless the deception was unintentional. Perhaps you have received an erroneous version of Captain Becknell's attempt to cross the desert instead of following his former route to Saint Michael, but you must not permit such nonsense to prejudice you against a course upon which I am resolutely determined."

" But why, Shiloh, why in the name of all tarnation? " David was really angry; the good dream of the hole in the Rockies, with cards and whisky and Indian wives, had lain very close to his heart, and Ashley's men had been eloquent in praise of these things. What had this dreadful desert journey to reveal in exchange for the long months of idleness, the buffalo beef and trappers' butter, the mountain bread fried in a kettle of boiling fat, the winter lodges buried deep in snow, the pure spring waking in northern woods, spring woods alight with birches? David was really angry.

" Because I detest the cold, and should very much like to be warm again," said Shiloh calmly.

" You're a fool, a pesky little fool, and I'm sick of your crazy notions! " David told him violently; he had forgotten his vow.

5

DAVID's mind was burrowing into a hole in the Rockies, with a dozen of Ashley's men; he saw the pine logs clear upon the hearth, the clean decks of cards, the noble kegs of liquor, the bags of pemmican. He heard the roof creak under its weight of snow; he strode to the door, and the snow lay upon the world under another fall of moonlight. For months the snow possessed the world as the deep sea possesses a drowned continent; David

heard its whispering silence through the winter nights. Within
his dreaming mind months passed in a single minute; he was
drowned in winter, and then he heard the sliding rush of snow
upon the roof as warm rain touched it, and he knew that this
rain was spring. There might be violets and bloodroot in the
northern woods, such flowers as grow in the woods of Maine;
there might even be a flower whose true name is arbutus. The
people of New England have given it another name; David
called it mayflower, and his mind made it into a symbol of his
home.

" A pesky little fool! " he cried again, and smote the table
with his fist until the twelve silver dollars leaped like trout
above a dark pool.

" That happens to be an unwarranted insult, Davy, and I
look to you to retract it."

Shiloh rose to his feet and stared at his friend with cold
blue eyes.

" They are both of them fools, and children," said Monsieur Saint-Ange to himself. " As for ' pesky,' I do not know,
since the word has no meaning for me, but they are a delightful pair of fools, and I am afraid that they are going to quarrel."

Indeed, Shiloh and David were now regarding each other
with looks of anger and distaste; Shiloh's eyes were the colour
of midnight in the haughty pallor of his face, and David was
deeply flushed and panting. For the moment they were utterly
estranged; David's ruddy and flaxen countenance appeared to
Shiloh the very personification of detested winter, while David
beheld Shiloh as some hateful brother to the Gila monster and
the horned toad of the Cimarron desert.

David jumped to his feet and glared at Shiloh from beneath a
twisted knot of tow-coloured eyebrows; Shiloh threw back his
head, and the locks of his hair seemed to bristle like the fell of
some slender savage beast. They doubled up their fists; they began to edge very delicately around the table, at the same time
murmuring, in soft perfidious voices, a number of curious and
disconnected words.

" Snow," said Shiloh, " cold; hideous unnecessary cold. For
months on end; worse than England; worse even than Scotland.

Shut in a cabin, endlessly; cards and whisky; greasy Indian women; whisky and women and bacon-grease. An edifying spectacle; soothing to sensitive nerves. And incidentally, cold; the lowest circle of hell; eternal cold. Why did I go to Italy, David? Ah, you don't know, do you? Would you like me to tell you, quite quietly and politely?"

"You would, would you?" David replied with apparent gentleness. "Going down into a lousy desert and dying of thirst to cure a cold in your head! Sensible; that's what it is; nice and sensible, and the spit and image of a pesky fool. Snakes and grizzlies and Iatans, and worse'n that, and you the worst of the lot. Aw, come on, and quit staring at me with them crazy eyes; come on, I say, and I'll learn you a little about them bastard desert trails!"

"But how kind of you, David; how very, very kind!" said Shiloh sweetly. "Only do you really believe that you are fitted to impart knowledge to your intellectual superiors? Because, do you know, I am strongly inclined to question your ability to teach me anything. And 'learn,' of course, is an intransitive verb; not that it matters, but these barbarities of language must excoriate the ears of all persons of sensibility."

"Hold your infernal hush, you blasted son of a gun," answered David in a furious whisper. "Language, is it? How about your own language, which I'm sick to death of hearing of it, with all them everlasting long words and lunatic expressions as'd make a cow laugh and drive a Christian crazy? You're a pretty one to talk about language now; you could be took up anywhere and jailed for most of the verbs you uses in an hour."

"Hah!" said Shiloh with withering contempt, and prepared to strike, just as David said "Gr-r-hah!" and raised his mighty fist in a destructive gesture.

Monsieur Saint-Ange stepped between them with perfect composure; he laid his left hand upon Shiloh's breast, and his right hand upon the splendid muscle of David's shoulder, and he could feel the several beating of their two hearts, one light and rapid like the heart of a flying creature, and the other shaken by a heavier and stronger pulse.

"This imbecility is unworthy of you both," he remarked

pleasantly. "Besides, there is really nothing to quarrel about; Shiloh's plan is not so warm or David's so cold as you appear to imagine. I dare say the hole in the Rockies, properly unventilated, may afford a far more salubrious climate than you are likely to encounter upon the Arkansaw in December. Settle it as you please; the only intelligent solution is to remain in St. Louis until spring, and that of course you will not do. Only don't kill each other over the question of the points of the compass; leave that office to our friends the Iatans."

"Yessir," said David obediently; he dropped his arm and un-clenched his fist with a great sigh.

"I beg your pardon, monsieur," said Shiloh with an air of bewilderment; he blinked his eyes as if he had just been roused from melancholy slumbers by a word of command.

"Sorry, David," said Shiloh, and David answered him, "Aw, I'm sorry; 't's all right." They looked at each other shyly and rather miserably; Shiloh gave a short embarrassed laugh, and David began to whistle very loudly through his teeth.

"We'll go your way, Davy," said Shiloh suddenly; David stopped whistling for a moment and grunted a stubborn negative.

"You're the skipper, and Santa Fé's your port," declared David decidedly, and returned to his interesting interpretation of "Shannandore."

"My God, are you now beginning to quarrel the other way about, in the pursuit of altruism?" cried Monsieur Saint-Ange with a groan. "You may argue all night, I suppose, having determined to be unselfish, and I confess that the prospect bores me."

"By amicable debate we may soon arrive at a solution . . ." began Shiloh, but David had already taken one of the silver dollars from the table; he spun it glittering in the air, and spoke.

"We'll toss a coin for it, sir; reckon you're plumb sick of us wrangling, ain't you? No, Shiloh, we ain't a-going to argue it out by no god-damned light of reason; you got to try your luck on this here dollar, my boy, and look sharp about it. Now, then, here she goes; is it the bird or the lady?"

"Tails!" cried Shiloh as the coin flew upward; he said it partly from a generous desire to leave the goddess for David, and partly because he admired eagles.

"And tails it is, by graminy!" admitted David with commendable good humour, as the silver circle came to rest over its own reflection in the polished walnut.

"Chance," murmured Shiloh, "the merest chance. It doesn't seem quite fair to Davy," but he was glad when Monsieur Saint-Ange assured him that it was. Shiloh felt a passionate inclination to go south, and he did not really believe that there was black ice on the Arkansaw, or snow in the passes above Santa Fé.

"But you will have your winter, Davy, and plenty of it, and Shiloh must learn to wear a buckskin shirt and to button it properly," said Monsieur Saint-Ange laughing. There was an ironical spark in his sherry-brown eyes, and the surface of his mind was brightly rippled by hilarity, but in its colder depths he was afraid.

Monsieur Saint-Ange was a philosopher; he knew the limitations of his own will, and he made no attempt to dissuade his young friend from a project which his maturer judgment condemned as foolhardy. Nevertheless, even with an ironical laugh upon his lips, he stared rather unhappily at Shiloh as that eccentric creature drank his seventh cup of tea in a trance of quiet excitement.

"How obstinate he is, he who appears so mild and tractable!" said Monsieur Saint-Ange to himself. "And how reckless, he who appears so reasonable! I cannot keep him in St. Louis; I have neither the force to save him, nor the stupidity to believe he will survive. He will die upon these cursed trails between here and California; he will die of cold or thirst, of starvation or the tomahawk; it is a hideous certainty, and I can do nothing. I marvel at my own folly in encouraging him to think of Sylvie; I have sent him to his death. I cannot keep him here; I cannot even put him aboard ship; I cannot purchase safety for him. Well, I shall lose him, as I have lost my poor little Sylvie; it is my misfortune to have conceived an affection for a vagabond. And yet, one sees his superiority at a glance; the hands, the brow, the preternatural intelligence! It is a pity, but it is impossible not to love him."

"Be careful, *ô mon roi;* the heathen may truly cast you into prison this time," he said to Shiloh, and hummed the song of the minstrel Blondel in a voice grown dry and thin as thread-paper.

6

NEXT day the three friends set forth into the snow-bloomed brightness of the early afternoon; there was that ineffable frosty glitter in the air which belongs only to a winter season of full sunshine. It was pleasant to feel the feathery crystals crunch into ice under a heavy boot, and pleasant to perceive the quickened breath made visible in frozen plumes of smoke. David trod the new pavement of Main Street as though it had been a quarter-deck; he had neatly cleaned and mended his clothes, and he looked a very able seaman indeed beside the slighter figures of his companions. His breadth of shoulder and mighty chest would have split the borrowed great-coat which suited Shiloh so well and made him appear so elegant, so melancholy, and so austere. It was a distinguished garment of dark blue broadcloth, and Monsieur Saint-Ange insisted that the cut had always been too narrow for him; certainly it was quite unworn, and Shiloh derived great comfort from its excellent fit and from the warmth of its lining.

He carried a hat in his hand; it was a beautiful pearl-grey beaver, and he would gladly have consented to wear it as a tribute to Monsieur Saint-Ange's sense of decorum; unfortunately it was so much too large for him that its brim would have rested lightly upon the bridge of his nose. He did not honestly regret this circumstance in spite of the keen wind whistling through his uncovered locks; the sun was bright, his cold was better, and Shiloh had never been fond of wearing a hat.

"But I think I should rather like a coonskin cap," he said happily, thinking of his friend who had come from Kentucky with Jacob Fowler. "Jeremiah has kindly consented to sell me his squirrel-rifle; I have had remarkable luck with it in shooting at a mark."

"Yes, I'll say that one thing for you, Shiloh," growled David, who would have said a thousand at need, "you're a goldarned good shot; don't know how you come to be, potting at sticks with pistols, or killing these here preserved birds as you was telling me about when you was a boy; I don't blame you for not taking to it, for it always sounds to me like pickles and jam. But I'll be switched if you ain't a natural-born good shot."

"Oh, no; not particularly," Shiloh answered, but he was profoundly flattered, and he thought affectionately of the squirrel-rifle which Jeremiah had consented to sell him.

"We will buy many coonskin caps for this journey," said Monsieur Saint-Ange with an indulgent smile. "Yes, many coonskin caps and buckskin breeches, many moccasins, much powder and ball, and a superfluity of squirrel-rifles."

Monsieur Saint-Ange had never been a grandfather, but now he felt rather like one as he observed the flush of joy upon his young friend's countenance. He had always desired to give pretty things to Sylvie, trifles of ivory and tinsel and swan's-down, and he had always been too poor. Now that at last he had plenty of money, Sylvie was far away; she fluttered far beyond the power of silk and spangled nets to draw her back again, and the money was so much base metal, heavy and comfortless and dull. It was like the dusty straw in the fairy-tale, lacking a princess to spin it into gold; Monsieur Saint-Ange was thankful that Shiloh needed a coonskin cap and a quantity of powder and ball. The old man smiled his stiff ironical smile, thinking how strangely these barbarous things were substituted for the shining scented toys which he had always longed to give to Sylvie.

It was the end of the first week in December, and already a holiday spirit seemed to pervade the atmosphere. The sharp gaiety of the winter day was clear to every sense; the sun was an intolerable brilliance in the west, the sky was a blue sparkle over the paler sparkle of the snow, all sounds were mingled in a brittle music, and the sting of the frost was no more acute than the fragrance of burning logs. Somewhere within one of the great stone houses on Main Street a fiddle-string quivered, and there was a smell of cider royal in the air.

Shiloh realised that the scene was livelier and more changeful than any he had beheld since the black curtain of hurricane shut Italy from his view. He was pleased by the varied aspect of the crowd, where ladies and gentlemen of evident breeding appeared in curious contrast to lean trappers from the northern woods, and *coureurs de bois* wild as Pawnees. There were bearded men from the flatboats, and hunters from the Appalachian slopes; there were tall contemptuous Osages and Mandans from the upper Missouri.

"Extraordinary!" said Shiloh, gazing about him with very bright eyes, and walking so fast that Monsieur Saint-Ange found it quite impossible to keep up with him.

Shiloh's expression was grave if inquisitive, but in reality he was in the highest and most effervescent spirits at the prospect of the savage journey imminent upon the morrow. In the first place he was having his own way, which always agreed with his health; in the second place, he and David had lately removed their disreputable bundles from the tavern to Monsieur Saint-Ange's guest-chamber, whose simple luxuries had wrought miraculously upon his nerves to soothe them. He was utterly unconscious of his invariable need for bodily peace and comfort, but he was none the less benefited by the presence of clean sheets and hot water and a quiet library well stocked with the Greek classics.

He and Monsieur Saint-Ange had finally reached an amicable understanding about the practical details of the journey; for the sake of Silver, Shiloh would permit his kind friend to provide David and himself with the necessities of travel. His only stipulations were extreme economy and an admission upon his benefactor's part that the money was merely a loan.

"Mary must of course be in receipt of my income at present," he had said. "If she decides against America, I shall leave her in complete enjoyment of this sum, and manage for myself as best I can."

"We might go into the fur trade, you and me, after we've found Silver and fetched her back here," David had suggested hopefully, thinking of the northern woods.

"You might even attempt authorship, *mon prince;* it is not so profitable as peltries, but I should never advise a person of your fastidious tastes to weary his soul in commerce," Monsieur Saint-Ange had said, thinking of Aunt Alphonsine's inheritance and of the fact that he had no son.

Shiloh had blinked his eyes and ruffled his hair, and said, "Yes; yes; I quite agree," to them both with admirable impartiality, thinking of Jeremiah's squirrel-rifle.

Now as he walked swiftly along the new stone pavement of
Main Street, which rang like iron in the glittering cold, he was
thinking very happily of salt and dried corn and beans, of pack-
mules, and of the high advantages to be derived from a life of
danger and adventurous chance. Both his pockets were full of
clippings from the *Missouri Intelligencer* relative to the various
expeditions which had reached Santa Fé; his head was stuffed
with singular details concerning the habits of buffalo and the
best way of approaching an Arapahoe village. Jeremiah had been
charmingly communicative, and Shiloh had a passion for acquir-
ing knowledge, and an excellent memory.

"I wish you would wait," said Monsieur Saint-Ange, who was
sadly out of breath. Shiloh paused obediently and turned to him
with a smile.

"I mean until spring; I wish you would wait and start your
journey in the spring; it would certainly be much wiser to wait for
spring," explained Monsieur Saint-Ange rather fractiously; he
was tired, and the fear of losing Shiloh entangled the roots of his
mind in chill despair.

"Oh, really there is not the slightest danger," Shiloh assured
him with absurd mendacity. "The winter is a most favourable
time to travel; Jacob Fowler did not reach Taos until January,
and you know he reached it in perfect safety, and Captain Becknell himself, I am informed, intends quitting Santa Fé on the
return journey about the middle of December. Doubtless we shall
pass him upon the way; I shall be delighted to meet Captain
Becknell."

"You'll meet many less desirable characters than Captain
Becknell, I am afraid; the average Comanche is not an amiable
person," said Monsieur Saint-Ange pessimistically.

"Perhaps not, yet I cannot help honouring his tameless spirit,"
replied Shiloh, whose own spirit refused to be dashed from its
eminence of joy.

"You are aware that the Mexicans kept one of the McKnights
in prison for ten years?" inquired Monsieur Saint-Ange.

"Oh, yes, but the change of government has had a most beneficial effect upon their institutions; I understand that there is even

talk of a republic," answered Shiloh with an invincible ignorance of fear.

"It does beat me the way you have the whole blasted business at your fingers' ends, Shiloh," said David, who had been largely convinced by the later clippings from the *Missouri Intelligencer* and by Shiloh's native eloquence and energy.

7

By the time the three friends returned to a beechwood fire and a dinner of roast guinea-fowl, Monsieur Saint-Ange felt more than ever like a grandfather, and Shiloh and David had each acquired a complete trapper's outfit of clothes and weapons. The old man had insisted upon purchasing a beautiful new rifle for Shiloh, imported at great expense from a celebrated Philadelphia gunsmith, and provided with the curious innovation of copper percussion-caps.

"You'll probably always prefer your wretched squirrel-rifle," said Monsieur Saint-Ange philosophically, "but you will oblige me by accepting this pretty little engine of destruction; it has a grace and finish which appear to me appropriate."

Shiloh had heard of some Spanish mules which a returned trader was willing to sell at a reasonable price; he had also heard that they could undoubtedly buy their salt from Colonel Cooper at Boone's Lick for the sum of one dollar a bushel. It was truly amazing to realise what a variety of fascinating information Shiloh had received from Jeremiah, and David stared in wonder and respect above the generous comfort of the dinner-table.

"Well, it does beat cock-fighting, the way you rattle off all that crazy stuff like you was born to it, Shiloh," he said, and shook his head as he dispatched the second drumstick of the guinea-hen.

"Of course," said Shiloh, warming to his subject under the influence of China tea, "we might effect a great economy by following the plan of Jacob Fowler, who actually took no provisions with him with the exception of salt, depending upon the purchase from the Osage Indians of the necessary supplies of buffalo and antelope, dried corn and pumpkins. I understand it answered admirably in the case of his party, and the less food we carry the fewer mules we shall be obliged to pack. What do you think of carrying nothing but salt, monsieur?"

"I have a very low opinion of the idea, my child," replied Monsieur Saint-Ange firmly. "I would far rather buy another pair of pack-mules and be sure that you will have a reasonable certainty of beans and coffee. The game you must get from the Indians, or obtain by your own skill, but at worst you may have beans and corn-meal to keep body and soul together."

"I suppose," said Shiloh, "that they must be kept together, and by beans; at least the prejudice in favour of this alliance appears to be universally accepted."

"'Twould be a lunatic notion if they wasn't, by graminy," cried David with considerable heat, helping himself to a large sweet potato which was pleasantly browned and glazed with maple molasses.

"And to-morrow, or the next day, you will be gone," remarked Monsieur Saint-Ange with desolate calm.

"I sincerely hope so," said Shiloh radiantly, and then curbed his manifest glad excitement as he saw the old man's stiff and bitter smile.

"But I have every intention of returning within the year," Shiloh assured him with charming seriousness; it required all Monsieur Saint-Ange's cynicism not to believe the promise.

Monsieur Saint-Ange was tired and sad; there had been so many things to do, and he had found them fatiguing in the extreme. They had gone to the Bank of St. Louis, and to John McKnight's store; there had been long interviews with traders, and an excited colloquy between Shiloh and a stray Mexican on the subject of the break with Spain. Now he wished very heartily to forget his weary anxiety in sleep; the thought of the morrow was too mournful to be remembered without pain, and he closed his eyes in a quite unphilosophical pang of loneliness.

"At least you will let me provide you with horses; be reasonable, and consent to this trifling mitigation of your discomfort," he said irritably.

"Please don't think me ungrateful; I am most sensible of your

generosity, but really I prefer to go on foot," Shiloh replied with
mild composure; his manner was like velvet over the metal of his
obstinacy.

"Reckon we can do it, sir; you see we ain't exactly new to it,
having tramped clear from Boston in two pairs of boots apiece and
patches along the road," David explained. "Nobody can lick
Shiloh walking, and though I ain't no great shakes myself I generally manages to keep up with him somehow. Don't you bother
about us, sir; we shall fetch up in Santa Fé alive and kicking,
spite of all the Injuns and god-damned varmints in creation.
Hosses ain't necessary, and being brought up to boats I ain't extra
clever with a hoss."

"Neither am I, you know; my horsemanship is adequate, but
certainly not brilliant," said Shiloh modestly. "I am far better
afoot; I can do thirty miles over broken ground and experience
no ill effects whatever."

"Yes, yes," answered Monsieur Saint-Ange, "but that wasn't
friable soil; you're not accustomed to sand. Well, there's no manner of use in scolding you; you must find out your mistake for
yourself. You can always buy a horse of sorts from the Indians,
in exchange for powder and ball and blankets, and that is precisely what you'll do sooner or later. It is a pity, because I could
have found you a better mount in St. Louis."

All three sat silent for a time, beholding a variety of prophetic
visions in the coloured flames; Monsieur Saint-Ange perceived
only tragic pictures, while David grinned mysteriously at what he
saw, and Shiloh trembled with expectancy. Monsieur Saint-Ange
drank Madeira, David drank New Orleans ratafia, and Shiloh
drank China tea.

"Good-night, my dear children," said Monsieur Saint-Ange
at last. "We are none of us particularly amusing this evening; I think we had far better go to bed. Your candlesticks
are in the hall, and I have told Baptiste to light a fire in your
room."

It was impossible to speak of the fact that to-morrow night
they would be gone; Shiloh was amazed to find himself moved
almost to tears as he bade his host good-night. He was torn between pity and an intense desire to go free of all emotional obli-

gations; it was impossible to speak of going, but a profound relief to think that they would soon be gone.

He liked his room, with its air of decorous quiet; he liked the easy-chair before the fire and the little book-cases on each side of the mantelpiece. " But I have never greatly admired French heroic verse," he said to David, taking *Athalie* from its shelf.

Nevertheless he perused it idly, sitting in the easy-chair before the small and jocund blaze upon the hearth; it was diverting to murmur the classic periods to himself in the midst of a fantastic dream of painted Indian braves. He sat toasting his long legs before the beechwood fire and murmuring the solemn couplets of Racine, and all the while he was dreaming of Comanches and the Spanish peaks and the pass above Santa Fé.

The Orphan Angel

VIII

THINGS THAT SEEM UNTAMABLE

"THIS," said Shiloh three days later, "reminds me of our first journey across France. You know we left Paris on foot, with a little donkey to carry our portmanteau; the animal was so feeble that we ended by carrying both it and its burden; we were obliged to sell it at Charenton and purchase a mule in its stead."

"Aw, you mean the time you went with them girls," replied David rather ungraciously; the peculiar circumstances of the adventure had always puzzled and repelled his simple mind. "I reckon you told me about that; they was in black silk dresses, and you didn't have nothing to eat but bread and fruit, and you sprained your ankle and had to buy some kind of a cart to ride in; crazy goings-on, I call it."

"Yes, and I remember that I beguiled the tedium of the way by telling the tale of the Seven Sleepers!" Shiloh laughed; the recollection of his youthful folly amused him and his innocence was unaware of David's Puritan prejudices.

"Well, it's a blamed nuisance having these mules to mind all the time," grumbled David; Shiloh was by no means clever with his slim brown hands, and it fell to David's lot to adjust the Spanish pack-saddles and cinch the broad grass-bandages.

"You're pulling it too tight, Davy; it's cruel to torture the

553

poor beast like that," was Shiloh's invariable comment, and David as invariably answered, " Aw, shut up, Shiloh, and leave me be; I got to do it like that there Mexican shown me, ain't I? Quit nagging at me, and gimme a hand with this goldarned strap."

David's own fingers were meticulous and strong in the performance of all manual labour; in twenty-four hours he was neatly familiar with every operation connected with the small caravan.

"Reckon you was smart at knotting reef-points 'cause you just naturally liked 'em," he told Shiloh. "You certainly are goddamned clumsy with a mule."

"I suppose I can learn," said Shiloh sadly, and without conviction. The woven straps eluded his light touch, and he was better at feeding and watering the mules, while he murmured to them in the starry flowery Spanish of Calderón's *Autos*.

There were three of these pack-mules: two to carry Shiloh's and David's equipment and one loaded with corn for the animals' own refreshment. There would be very little fodder on the Arkansaw. The mules were small elegant creatures, half burro and half Spanish horse; the Arabian strain made them pleasing to the eye, but their dispositions were deplorable. Nevertheless they were growing fond of Shiloh; they submitted patiently to his ministrations, and poetry did not appear to worry them so much as it did David.

It required Shiloh's wild and vivid fancy to perceive resemblances between the harvest fields of France and this Missouri prairie rough with winter. If he had crossed it in midsummer the landscape would have been bright with briar-roses and musical with doves; now it was nothing but long grey grass and frozen clay. Yet a particular glory clothed the wide horizon and the rolling spaces of the earth; they had the simplicity and strangeness of the sky or the empty miles of the sea.

"Flat as a pancake and ugly as a mud fence," said David, but Shiloh shook his head and talked vaguely of nobility.

The weather was cold but fine, and the roads none the worse for being hard as iron with the frost. The ice on the streams was thin and brittle as yet; the Boone's Lick road followed the course of the river into the central wilderness of Missouri, and the road was passable and the fords not too dangerous. By the grace of good luck and their excellent new boots Shiloh and David made the hundred and fifty miles to Franklin in six days.

When they entered the little town everyone perceived at once that they were travellers bound upon some adventurous quest; it would be untrue to say that they strutted, but their mien was proud and cheerful, and they contrived to walk as lightly as though they had not been tired.

"Them two young fellers is certainly all sot up about them there outfits o' theirn," said several elderly on-lookers, and spat not unkindly in the general direction of the approaching caravan.

Shiloh and David were indeed a singularly well-favoured pair in their hunting-shirts of dressed buckskin and long fringed trousers decorated with beads and porcupine quills. Shiloh wore the coveted coonskin cap and David a cap of darker bearskin; their powder-horns and bullet-pouches were slung over their left shoulders, and through their leather belts were thrust large formidable knives in sheaths of buffalo-hide.

"Couple o' beaver trappers making south to the mountains," said some, but others differed, believing that the strangers had a load of steam-loom shirtings, super-blues, and pelisse cloth for Santa Fé. "Kinda late to start," they said, and wagged their beards pessimistically over their whisky.

"The yaller-headed one's a Yankee; easy enough to figger that out, I reckon," observed a much-travelled gentleman from Virginia. "He's what they call a regular down-east Yankee, and a powerful big one at that; I reckon he's been a seafaring man from the rolling walk on him. That there other lad's a heap harder to place; first I thought he was an Injun, the soft way he steps, but I ain't never seen an Injun with blue eyes and freckles. I've took a powerful liking to him, all the same; guess I'll just inquire his name kinda friendly-like and offer him a drop o' liquor."

"Shiloh, eh? That's a mighty funny name, stranger," said the gentleman from Virginia; he was cut to the soul when Shiloh declined a sip from his flask, and yet his powerful liking persisted even in the face of this rebuff, and at the end of five minutes' vivacious conversation he evinced no more than pitying surprise when Shiloh admitted a desire for a cup of tea.

"Well, he brews it mighty strong, anyway, strong as lye, it appears to be, like it would rot the guts out of a copper worm," he explained to his companions; they all confessed that Shiloh was eccentric but agreeable, and most of them were quite prepared to forgive him his peculiar taste in beverages.

"Seems like there's something savage in that lad, spite of him being so polite," said the gentleman from Virginia approvingly.

David overheard the words; he looked at Shiloh and nodded with an air of ingenuous pride. It was David's darling weakness to assume the credit for Shiloh's virtues as an adventurer; he experienced almost the creator's sense of power in contemplating this quick and vital creature whom he had saved. Shiloh, drawn moribund from destruction by David's strong right arm; Shiloh, shaking off the trivial harness of civilisation to run wild through a recovered world; these were intoxicating conceits, and sources of the liveliest vanity to David.

And indeed he might well be forgiven for indulging such reflections, since a magical change was evident in Shiloh whenever he went free to lead an active and primitive life. Trelawney and Williams had observed the same happy metamorphosis aboard that crank and erratic little vessel which had been their plaything for a summer at Lerici. Now, as David watched his friend even through the critical eyes of the citizens of Franklin, he wondered for the twentieth time if this bronzed and strenuous apparition were in truth the same Shiloh who had crouched so forlornly over Monsieur Saint-Ange's study fire in the double misery of a cold in the head and a borrowed coat.

"It's the talk as does the mischief," said David to himself; "the talk, and the fuss, and the bother about women; that plays hob with Shiloh. Good beds and decent victuals ain't a-going to do nobody no harm; it's the worrying about women as does it, and now, what with the mules and everything, he ain't got no time for women."

The two young strangers enjoyed a gratifying popularity during their brief stay in Franklin; David's prowess in drinking and in the honourable art of self-defence were both appreciated, and Shiloh's regrettable preference for tea was excused upon the grounds of his excellent marksmanship and his engaging

manners. It was generally conceded that David's baritone was
an addition to the evening's entertainment, and that although
Shiloh seemed kinda shy-like and retiring, he might probably
be a ring-tailed roarer in a scrap, and you never knew about
them soft-spoken fellers if you riled 'em.

" The big tow-headed Yankee is a mighty nice lad," said the
gentleman from Virginia, " but for a right smart regular devil,
give me that there little blue-eyed Injun every time."

" You boys is terrible fools to be figgering on getting to Santa
Fé on foot," said the oldest inhabitant, who insisted upon calling
the town by its original name of Boone's Lick. " Take my advice, which you're welcome to free gratis for nothing, and get a
couple of hosses for yourselves afore you reach the Arkansaw.
'Tain't no time of year to start anyways, and what's the sense of
acting foolisher than you can help? "

" Thank you," Shiloh replied with his usual courtesy; " we
will consider your suggestion." But in reality he was adamant to
such whisperings of caution, and every hour his aspect became
more eccentric and more elegantly savage, until the very porcupine quills upon his buckskins appeared to bristle with impatient
fire.

" Got to be going, or Shiloh yonder'll bust his boiler," grinned
David, who had been talking to a steamboat captain from New
Orleans.

2

THEY encountered a snow-storm upon the first day after leaving
Franklin; David tramped stolidly through its frozen sands, but
now and then he would turn and look at Shiloh to see how he
was liking it. If Shiloh felt a secret misgiving as the cold wind
whirled the sleety crystals about his ears, his outward semblance
refused to confess it. He had discarded his heavy boots in favour
of greased moccasins, and his blanket great-coat hardly impeded the stubborn rapidity of his stride.

" These here hides are handier than any tent," David boasted
late that afternoon as he stretched a couple of deerskins across
a frame of willow boughs; but indeed it was David who was

handy. The jack-knife he had bought in Boston was still the favourite implement of his skill; he carried a little whetstone in a rawhide case. To Shiloh it appeared that the shelter was constructed with no more effort than David would have given to the proper cutting of a willow whistle.

"Plenty of driftwood a-laying round down by the creek," said David. "Fetch along as much as you can manage, Shiloh; Satan finds some mischief still, I reckon, so don't go pulling the books out of your pocket until after the kettle boils."

The mules were hobbled in a patch of cottonwood, whose leafless tops provided both a wind-break and a supper for the sagacious beasts. "Saves corn," explained David làconically, "and mules seem to find this sweet-bark cottonwood real tasty."

The azimuth compass was in Shiloh's keeping; he derived great satisfaction from plotting their probable course upon a scrap of paper before the sapphire darkness fell across the snow.

"And you could 'a' got that turkey if you'd had your wits about you; now you won't have nothing but what you call everlasting bacon for supper, and lucky to get it," said David, shaping neat patticakes of cornmeal and water and tossing them into the sizzling fat in the pan.

"You are perfectly right, Davy," Shiloh answered penitently; "I could have got the turkey, and quite easily. My wits were sufficiently about me, but at the last moment my heart misgave me, and I forbore to slay the bird. I suppose I shall have to overcome such scruples if I am to provide our camp with fresh game."

"Yessir, you'll have to get over all that kinda nonsense, if you don't want to catch the scurvy," was David's firm reply.

"That particular fowl," said Shiloh with a thoughtful sigh, "had so haughty and aquiline an air that I was awed into a dereliction of duty; I promise to be more ferocious to-morrow."

Even without the luxury of fresh game, the meal was warmly welcome to the travellers; Shiloh had never been so hungry in all his life, and he revised his views on bacon-grease while devouring hot fried corn-cakes with the appetite of a young and impulsive wolf. Nevertheless, although a table was lacking, his table manners remained perfect; unlike David, he did not swear when he burnt his tongue, or confuse the functions of a knife and fork. He ate a quantity of bacon and drank a great many cups of very strong tea, and yet by some queer grace he contrived to do these things in a fashion fastidious and well-bred and incurably polite.

"You're bound as you'll keep your quality ways, and set a good example to the prairie squirrels, ain't you?" David asked with a guffaw. David would always eat with his knife, but after years of forecastle amenities he found his friend's deportment singularly pleasant as a sauce for wilderness bread and bacon.

After supper Shiloh returned to his plottings with a pocket compass, until, grown weary of this exercise, he began scribbling on the other side of the scrap of paper. Thus in a series of minute pot-hooks was mysteriously captured the pure solitude of the skies and of the round plain spread with luminous snow, and this in the brief space of an hour, by the camp-fire's uncertain brightness.

"I understand so well," said Shiloh when he had folded the paper and put it away, " why that red-bearded man in Franklin longed to build his farm in the wilds of the primæval forest; they warned him that he would be lonely, and he replied: 'I wish never to hear the bark of a neighbour's dog.' That, to me, is quite comprehensible, but then I have ever loved all waste and solitary places."

"Well, this must suit you down to the ground then, by graminy," David told him as he unpacked the blankets and buffalo-skins which were to serve as bedding. "It's a bit too lonesome for my taste, and still it's exciting and kinda nice to think about Injuns and such-like, and to hear the wind a-whistling through them cottonwoods. Good-night, you crazy catawampus, and don't forget you gotta kill that turkey to-morrow."

This was the night of the sixteenth of December; by Christmas Eve they had killed several turkeys and encountered a band of wandering Osages from whom they purchased a supply of antelope and buffalo beef. The savages appeared friendly, and Shiloh was deeply impressed by their impassive copper-coloured countenances, with domed and shaven brows and high gaunt noses. He was remarkably clever at making himself understood by means of a few words and many smiles, and he was privately flattered by a belief in his ability to fathom and perhaps improve the mind of primitive man.

"Well, this'll be the god-damnedest Christmas that ever I

spent, not forgetting the one in irons owing to a little mistake on the cap'n's part, and the drunken one in Rio," mused David as he plucked a fine turkey cock which Shiloh had shot for their dinner. "Seems like it's kinda blasphemous to eat this bird in such an un-Christian country, among all these murdering heathen; I wisht we had some cranberries for sass."

"But Christmas is really a pagan festival, Davy," explained Shiloh, who had read John Brand in his youth, "and you know what Pliny has to say about mistletoe."

"I'll be switched if I know a word of it; I ain't never heard the old codger's name before," said David. "I don't specially hold with mistletoe, but I do hold with pumpkin pies. We don't have no mistletoe in Maine, but even aboard ship you'd get a bit of plum-duff for your dinner."

It was a curious Christmas Eve; the stars were solemn tapers burning high above a vast tranquillity of snow, and Shiloh's sensitive spirit was touched to rapture by their influential light. There was a delicate smell of winter in the smoke from the burning driftwood; and the ice on the little creek glittered with specks of silver and gold in the glow of the camp-fire.

"Sightly, ain't it?" said David, with his eyes on the enchanted scene. "But somehow it don't look Christian; sort of ghostly, like there might be uncanny critters about."

"I'll read you a poem concerning such superstitious fancies, Davy," murmured Shiloh in a soft and spectral voice. "Oh, no, it isn't one of my own poems; it isn't in the least my sort of thing."

He took from his pocket a small octavo volume which Monsieur Saint-Ange had given him; most of its leaves were yet uncut, because Monsieur Saint-Ange loved Milton no better than he did Shakspere.

> " ' And sullen Moloch fled
> Hath left in shadows dread,
> His burning idol all of blackest hue,
> In vain with cymbal's ring,
> They call the grisly king,
> In dismal dance about the furnace blue;
> The brutish gods of Nile as fast,
> Isis and Orus, and the dog Anubis haste.' "

"'Naught but profoundest hell can be his shroud,'" intoned Shiloh necromantically; he spoke the words in a low unearthly chant, and David felt the hair rise upon his scalp as he listened.

If David had been a Catholic he would undoubtedly have crossed himself; being only a rather careless Congregationalist, he began to whistle between teeth which had a tendency to chatter. A dim and phosphorescent light crept upward from the snow, and along the star-powdered horizon certain figures moved in an ambiguity of darkness. Perhaps they were a company of Osages returning from a hunt; perhaps they carried deerskins and rough white bearskins across their arching saddle-bows. Certainly they appeared very vague and monstrous in the distance; their horses had the equivocal shape of a dragon-brood. Shiloh stared after them in wonder quite unflawed by fear, but David pulled him down into the shelter and swore in a fluent grumble. David had stopped whistling, but he could not stop the chatter of his teeth.

"God damn you, Shiloh, for skeering the hide off me," he muttered. "Them bastard Injuns is bad enough, but that there poem is a sight skeerier, the way you say it. This is the goldarnedest Christmas Eve I ever expect to spend this side of hell."

3

It took them twenty-five days to reach the Arkansaw, and these days were often difficult enough, chequered not only by the inevitable alterations of midnight and noon, but also by black frosts and blinding snows. Yet, taken all in all, the sum of these days was not unprosperous; good fortune flourished in the minds of the friends, a halcyon sunlight gilded the morning skies, and the camp-fire at dusk bloomed like a desert rose. If they made twenty miles before the evening halt they were lucky, since this distance must be traversed in a single span; if the mules had been allowed to rest they would have tried to lie down, and then there would have been no getting them to their feet again without unpacking the load. This apparent cruelty was the source of some anxiety to Shiloh; it troubled David not at all, and he calmly followed the Mexican rule-of-thumb in managing the beasts. It must be admitted that they preferred Shiloh, in spite of his absent-minded manner; he was especially fond of the little bell-mare, to whom he would recite portions of the *Magico Prodigioso* while secretly nourishing her upon his own midday repast of parched corn.

David was as resourceful in the discovery of creeks as though a perpetual hazel wand had burgeoned in his hand, and Shiloh developed a marvellous gift for placating Osages and Pawnees. Some cherub upon a flying star may have held the reins of their luck in his indulgent power, or it may have hung upon David's durable good sense and Shiloh's scintillant intelligence and courage; suffice it to say that this luck continued for twenty-five winter days, and that there was an abundance of sweet water and fresh buffalo beef during all that time.

They shot many turkeys, and once Shiloh killed an antelope and wept over its delicate carcass in the light of a waning moon. He felt less tender about buffalo, but nevertheless he more often elected to purchase supplies from the Indians, and his personal taste inclined to dried pumpkins and maize.

The strange face of this country, the rolling prairie, the limestone bluffs, the streams bordered with cottonwood and willow, had a wild monotony which moved the beholder to sorrow and delight. It was like a landscape seen in a dream, veiled in the loneliness of something lost and forgotten. The clear airs, the shining colour of the heavens, the sunlight flashing from the snows, were not sufficient to exorcise a spirit of melancholy that possessed the scene. Shiloh, who had known such pure extremity of beauty among the glacial pinnacles of the Alps, for whom Italian waters had revealed dead palaces and towers, was nevertheless aware that this broad dominion wore a wonder of its own. It belonged not to the savages who scoured its distance, but to greater and more barbarous powers; its conquerors were the lightnings and the frosts.

Sometimes as a troop of wild horses passed the travellers Shiloh would gaze a little wistfully after their flight, but for the most part he was content to journey as he had chosen, trusting to his human endurance and speed. The fact that these qualities approached the superhuman made his course less arduous; the wings upon his heels were invisible, but it was hard to believe that they were broken. The Indians he regarded with fearless curiosity; his amicable sentiments toward both Osages and Pawnees made him unable to understand their hatred for each other, but by a sort of cool and airy friendship he contrived to win the suffrages of all.

At length the Spanish Peaks floated in cloud upon the horizon, and they beheld the Arkansaw rippling wide and shallow between banks of white sand. Above the low bluffs with their growth of willow a few tall cottonwood-trees stood naked against the evening sky.

Shiloh and David camped that night on an island in the river, crossing by a crazy bridge of flags and rushes. An old Indian fort sheltered them from the increasing wind; it was circular in shape and builded of logs laid one upon another. About it a tangle of grapevines still held some dried and frozen grapes, and within the fort a rude spit had been erected over the ashes of ancient fires.

"I should like to live forever in this charming and romantic spot!" cried Shiloh with his eyes upon the shining mountains, but David wagged his head and looked nervously at a blue feather of smoke to westward.

At midnight a fantastic clamour tore through the tranquillity of sleep; Shiloh waked to a confusion pierced with loud and violent cries. There were sounds of horses splashing through the river, and a fitful shimmer of torchlight on the willow-trees.

"They've got the mules," said David in his ear, "and I reckon they've got us too. Grab your gun and keep quiet."

There was really nothing else to do; Shiloh crouched on the pile of buffalo-skins and watched the monstrous spectacle through the door of the fort. It was a brilliant nightmare painted upon obscurity; his senses were quickened by amazement, but he did not remember to be afraid. He caught sight of slim bronze bodies striped with firelight, of faces savage with vermilion and plumbago, of the bloody nostrils and insensate eyes of stallions prodigious against the shattered dark.

Then there was a sudden diminution of noise; long furious execrations of farewell faded into stillness, and a portent loomed in the low doorway of the room. Shiloh perceived that the creature was an Indian; his gigantic height and the rich trappings of his robe were manifest even in the shadow which hid his countenance from view.

"That there fellow's an Iatan, Shiloh; easy now, 'cause them's the worst of the lot," whispered David in a hurried breath.

Shiloh rose to his feet and advanced to meet the visitor with tolerable composure; he was not frightened, but a certain pulse of awe slowed the beating of his heart and made his hand cold upon the cold steel of the squirrel-rifle. He held out his other hand to the Indian, who accepted it without a word, and stood waiting in impassive silence; his clasp was iron around Shiloh's slender fingers.

"Greetings and good fortune to you," said Shiloh steadily, in a phrase he had learned from the Pawnees.

It is possible that the words annoyed the Comanche because they were spoken in an enemy accent; it is possible that he had intended from the first to murder Shiloh and David for the sake of their small possessions. He had just saved the mules from a band of Pawnee horse-thieves; the scalps of some of these were even now reeking at his warriors' belts. He stared haughtily at Shiloh as if the pleasant speech had been a blow; his face was still obscured, but the chill implacable anger of his soul was evident in the altered air. Shiloh felt the thing, quick and flickering as a snake's tongue; it brushed him, and he shuddered to the marrow of his bones. He was not afraid, but horror laid a light reptilian touch upon his spirit before he spoke again.

"Surely there is no reason why we should hate each other, you and I," said Shiloh politely. "I have done no harm to you, nor you to me; let us each go upon his way in peace."

The Indian dropped Shiloh's hand; the casual gesture was harsh with contempt. "You are a thief and the brother of thieves," he said insolently. "You have stolen goods from the White Father, goods which that great chief intended for me. If you do not make restitution I shall kill you, torturing you first as a punishment for dishonesty."

"But how ridiculous; of course you cannot mean what you are saying," replied Shiloh; indignation caused his eyes to radiate blue lightnings upon this savage who thought fit to insult a friendly stranger with absurd uncivil words.

"You shall see how truly I have warned you," said the Comanche with scorn; he seized Shiloh's arm in a grip of inflexible metal and twisted it with peculiar ferocity.

Shiloh fought like an agile tiger-cat to escape; his gun was torn from his grasp in an instant, and he strove with bare hands and the courage of a blinding rage. There was a sanguine mist before his eyes, and the blood beat in his head like a madman's hammer. He was dimly aware of David at his back struggling with a score of painted devils; the hellish picture caused him to redouble his own attack upon the giant Indian. He strained against a Minotaur; the odds were so unequal that it hardly needed the onslaught of a dozen other warriors to bring Shiloh to his knees. He struck wildly and yet more wildly; there was a strange sound in his ears, and he knew that he sobbed with fury and exhaustion. The pang of anger against himself was his last conscious thought; a darkness full of dizzy stars descended, and like a comet he was whirled into oblivion.

He awoke to a darkness without stars or firelight; his forehead was cloven with a cruel shattering pain, and he felt as sick as if he had been crossing the Irish Channel in a storm. By an effort of will he mastered the horrid vertigo and gazed about him; slowly his aching senses pierced the gloom, and he perceived David huddled in the farthest corner of the fort; his brow rested upon his folded arms, and he was swearing and weeping in the same desperate breath.

Shiloh sat up; the outrageous pain within his skull seemed to split it asunder as he moved. The sickness rose to overcome him like a cold green wave of the sea; his forehead was damp with its loathsome dew. He clenched his hands and fought it as he had fought the Indian, and luckily with more success; in three seconds he was able to speak in a voice which David recognised.

"I lost my temper, didn't I?" asked Shiloh with sincere interest. "Did they scalp us, Davy? My head feels precisely as if I had been scalped, and there is a quantity of blood upon my hair."

"Reckon you was tomahawked but not scalped this time," replied David in a hoarse and shaken whisper. "God damn them bastards to the everlasting pit, we didn't do nothing, and they've beat us to a pulp and took us prisoner, and now they're fixing to burn us or some such lousy plan. I told you how it would be if we come south among them varmints."

"I am extremely sorry if I have brought disaster upon us, Davy," said Shiloh with a sigh; he felt quite unequal to an argument, and David's vehemence increased the frantic throbbing in his temples. "I suppose I should not have lost my temper with that unpleasant person with the vermilion stripes upon his cheekbones, but really I could not support his impertinent accusations for another moment. When he caught hold of my arm I was unable to bear the indignity; his behaviour was most offensive, Davy, and I confess that I struck him. I hope you will forgive me for my natural exasperation."

"Aw, I don't blame you, Shiloh; you couldn't have done different, not with him talking sassy and calling you a thief and all that," David admitted. "Quit worrying, Shiloh; I reckon we was bound to hit something like this from the first. Mebbe we can manage to give them devils the slip; I've been figgering how we can do it, but I got such a goldarned crack on the head that I can't think very clear yet."

"Neither can I, Davy; everything seems to have acquired an annoying trick of circular motion, and certainly I have a shocking headache," said Shiloh; the travail of consecutive thought made him feel so ill that he lay down again upon the buffalo robes and closed his eyes. In five minutes he was asleep; his dreams were troubled and somewhat feverish, but the poignancy of his misfortunes was mercifully softened by these slumbers, and David forbore to wake him from his brief repose.

4

WHEN Shiloh awoke for the second time the milk-white winter dawn was staining the gloom with soft and delicate light, and David was sitting up and swearing loudly into the new face of the day. Shiloh's head still ached violently, and he was infuriated to discover himself so far prostrated by pain and loss of blood that the least exertion appeared laborious in the extreme. He would have preferred to leap to his feet with a spirited war-cry and rush into the Comanche camp like a mad avenger; by straining every nerve and sinew he actually contrived to lean upon one elbow and look about him.

"Well, I see you're not dead yet, y' crazy catamount," said David with a grimace which might have been a grin upon lips less cut and battered out of shape. "One of them lousy sons o' guns come in here a minute ago and turned you over with the toe of his moccasin, kinda contemptuous-like; I reckon he thought you was done for, and he went out again with a few tender words to me about how they was fixing to burn us along about breakfast-time if the fine weather holds. They wouldn't leave us be like this if they calculated as we could talk to each other, so don't go roaring like the bull of Bashan and bringing 'em in here to lambaste us."

Shiloh felt that it would be quite impossible to roar like a bull, or even like a sucking dove; the idea of being burnt before breakfast affected him with an unpleasant qualm of nausea. "'Fiend, I defy thee! With a calm, fixed mind, all that thou canst inflict I bid thee do,'" said Shiloh bravely, but in rather a faint voice.

"Which remark don't butter no parsnips," replied David with some impatience. "First place the bastard can't hear you, and second place it wouldn't do no good if he did; he'd go on piling that brushwood and driving that stake cool as a cucumber. You can hear 'em out there arranging things as bright and cheerful as if it was the county fair and trotting-races instead of bloody murder; we got to act quick if we don't want to be smoked like a couple of hams."

"What course would you suggest, Davy?" asked Shiloh. "I am willing to adopt any plan which recommends itself to your judgment, although I am afraid I shall not be much help to you, as I seem to be somewhat dizzy."

"Yes, and you got a right to be, by graminy," David assured him. "Looky here, my lad, don't you know as you've got a hole in your head as I could lay two fingers in and that you're the spit and image of Lazarus out of the tomb? You're doing mighty well to be alive at all, after the clip that devil fetched you when you busted him one in the jaw."

This remark had a tonic effect upon Shiloh; very softly he touched the wound above his brow and stared curiously at the blood upon his fingers. " It appears to be a considerable aperture," he murmured proudly.

"Sure it is, and you must have a skull like cast iron," David told him, and Shiloh felt much better, and equal to the chances of escape.

He examined David by the snow-reflected light which filled the room, and observed that his friend's sunburnt countenance was yellowy-white and streaked with dust and gore; a large bruise about the left eye was already assuming hues of azure and purple. Shiloh wondered how his own face showed in the pearly flicker of dawn; he concluded rightly that he was very pale, that his abundant hair was wildly disarranged and matted over his wound, and that a great deal of blood had trickled down his brow and cheek.

" We're a pretty pair, ain't we, and fit to skeer a Christian into fits? " asked David, laughing at Shiloh's inquisitive scrutiny.

"Well, at least we are amazingly cheerful under the circumstances," Shiloh answered; he marvelled that it should be so, and could not help experiencing satisfaction in the knowledge.

"You see, Davy," he said with a sudden flash of insight, "neither you nor I really believes that he is about to be burnt alive; if we did we could not regard the prospect with any degree of equanimity. We expect something to happen; some miracle from heaven or some surprising act of courage from ourselves. At the same time we are rather pleased by the romantic character of martyr and heroic victim; if they actually burn us we shall not like it at all."

" Reckon you're right, Shiloh, but we're a-going to make a try at getting away before they roast us, ain't we? " David inquired. " Now, my plan is something like this: let's you and me pretend to be sorta weak and discouraged-like when they takes us out of here and drags us towards the stake; then just afore they ties us up let's make a dash for it and hop into the river. Ten to one they'll get us with their god-damned arrows, but anyways we'll give 'em a run for their money."

" It sounds," said Shiloh, " like a truly admirable plan." He was strengthened by the slight promise of freedom; excitement stimulated him as brandy might have heartened a less volatile spirit, and suddenly he was animated and resolved upon escape.

At that moment a shadow fell athwart the doorway and a tall Comanche entered with noiseless tread; Shiloh sank back against the buffalo-skins and succeeded in appearing upon the tragic point of death. His extreme pallor and the bloody wound above his brow aided him in the deception; he was further served by the fact that he was still rather faint and agitated from the events of the preceding night. The savage regarded him with placid scorn; he grunted contemptuously and pulled Shiloh to his feet with a single movement of his muscular arm. Then he turned to David with a muttered word of disdain; Shiloh leaned against the rough log wall of the fort and shook with pride and furious defiance.

David rose and tottered to the centre of the room; he looked sufficiently ghastly to make his assumption of weakness quite convincing. He swayed drunkenly and clawed at the Indian's athletic shoulder; the man was completely deceived, and grunted once more in cold and grim amusement. A second Comanche appeared at the door; his comrade jerked his thumb towards Shiloh, and the newcomer strode over to the ensanguined and dishevelled figure which drooped against the wall.

Shiloh had not forgotten the plan of escape; the hope was clear and kindling in his mind, and he strove to overcome the anger which convulsed his soul and vibrated in all his nerves. If the Comanche had moderated by a hair's breadth his insolent demeanour, if the spark of contempt in his opaque dark eye had been a shade less evident, it is possible that Shiloh might have acted with discretion and restraint. But he had had no breakfast, his head throbbed with sickening pain, and the Comanche's manner was excessively rude; Shiloh was unable to support the intolerable instant, and he lost his temper with the blinding impact of an electric thunderbolt.

" Come with me, you cowardly little dog," said the Indian in his own language; Shiloh did not understand the words, but their meaning was hideously plain to him in every insulting inflection of the other's voice and in the snaky glitter of his gaze.

Suddenly, and with the most startling effect, Shiloh straightened his thin body to its fullest height and glared into the Comanche's chill black eyes with eyes of burning blue; his lips writhed in a haughty smile, and he walked swiftly and steadily across the room to the open door; the sunlight fell sharp and silvery over his wounded forehead as he went.

"Go to the devil," said Shiloh to the amazed Comanche. "I am perfectly well able to proceed to my death without your impertinent assistance, thank you."

"Aw, now you've done it and no mistake; the fat's in the fire now, Shiloh, and that's no figger of speech neither!" cried David in the accents of despair.

Shiloh knew that he had flung their chance of liberty to the wind; he saw it whirled away like a feather down that unreturning stream of air. He had been guilty of this delirium in order to save his pride intact from the hands of the savage; he did not really regret the madness now that it was accomplished.

"Sorry, David," he threw back over his shoulder as he stalked into the unclouded morning.

David did not believe him; he understood his friend too thoroughly to mistake the supercilious cock of the head and the inspired lightness of the feet, and he realized that the moment was one of peculiar felicity for Shiloh.

Shiloh paused in the doorway of the fort and surveyed the scene without; he saw that the little island was thronged with Comanche warriors, and that the near-by shores of the river were covered with a vast concourse of men and horses. The atmosphere was clear and cold; the Indians' particoloured blankets appeared as moving fires in the sun, and their weapons glittered and rang in unison with the choral solemnity of their gestures. Against the pallid tints of sand and snow and frosty willow-trees the barbaric pageant lay uncoiled like a gorgeous snake.

Immediately in front of Shiloh, and in the centre of a ring of painted braves, a great stake had been driven into the snow; brushwood and faggots were piled about its base, and its appalling significance seemed already to cry to the unstained and smokeless heavens.

In the midst of this prodigious show of cruelty and power, Shiloh stood composed and firm; his eyes were singularly brilliant, and about his lips a small delighted smile mocked and saluted the puissance of his enemies. He was still pale, but his very whiteness was a luminous challenge to the swarthy countenances around him; he carried the blood-stained colour of his brow like a chivalric banner. The human vanity which had revolted against insolence, the defiant pride which had rejected hope, fell from him in that instant; he was a spirit of pure courage as he faced the Comanche braves.

They recognised this fortitude and respected it; he was actually permitted to walk unattended through the circle of warriors and to reach the dreadful stake alone and in silence. He had forgotten the brutal throbbing of his wound; he felt strong and triumphant and happy. He told himself that he was about to die, that certain minutes of execrable pain must be endured by his defenceless body, in which mortal pang his soul need have no part; he was glad to know that he was not afraid.

He submitted quietly to the binding of his hands with a leathern thong; other thongs were passed about his waist and ankles, and he was strapped securely to the stake. He saw David a long way off, struggling in the grip of two giant Comanches; his friend's broad hands were pinioned behind his back, and an agonised devotion filled his eyes as he looked at Shiloh. The secret alien faces of their foes were dark and immobile between them.

" Shiloh," called David across the intervening space, and Shiloh knew by his voice that he was very angry, " I couldn't do nothing to save you this time; you want to die, Shiloh, and I've known it all along; you wasn't really hankering to live, ever, and now you've got your god-damned crazy way and I hope to God you're satisfied at last! "

" David," said Shiloh, " perhaps you are right, you are often right. But please forgive me, David; even if it is true, you must forgive me."

David began to cry, noisily and without dignity; he was heedless of the scornful warriors at his shoulder, and Shiloh understood that he was beyond caring for a little thing like pride.

Shiloh stood with his back to the stake; he stood erect and noble in the sunlight, and now he was not conscious of his bonds. He thought of Prometheus, and of Laon's funeral pyre; in a sort of gentle philosophic trance he watched a trivial thread of smoke curl upward from the brushwood about his feet.

The thin translucent feather flew some signal to the assembled throng; in a moment an abominable clamour broke out among the Indians along the shore; a flight of arrows whistled bird-like about Shiloh's head, and the air was full of cries and violent wings.

He had preferred the silence; he was sorry that he was not to be allowed to die in quiet torment among the flames. Slowly he became aware that the smoke had thickened before his face, and that an arrow quivered in the stake above him. Even as he saw it, another arrow pierced his arm with a slender fiery sting; he regarded its plumed shaft with wonder.

There was a difference in the clamour along the shore; the cries were varied and increased by some new emotion. Shiloh was astounded to behold a score of moccasins trampling out the fire at his feet; as the smoke cleared he knew that his bonds were cut, and that the fallen arrows lay upon the ground like innocent dead birds whose wings are broken.

Now suddenly he felt the cruel ache of the wound over his temple; again he was conscious of the pains of mortality. He was visited by a horrid conviction that he was about to yield to a disgraceful faintness in full view of the Comanches; he believed that death were infinitely more desirable than this humiliation, and he was sincerely thankful for the stake firm behind his shoulderblades. For the second time that morning he put forth a preternatural effort and regained mastery of himself; he woke his spirit from its swoon; he stiffened all his sinews; he raised his head to stare around him.

5

A SLIM boy mounted upon a cream-coloured pony was watching him from the circle of braves; the lad appeared very proud and comely in a sleeveless tunic of soft white buckskin and long fringed leggings covered with an arabesque of beads. Across his forehead he wore a band of silver, and there were silver bracelets upon his arms and sea-shells in his ears.

"Good God, sir," said this young person coolly, reining in his pony with one slender hand, "you look precisely like the pictures of Saint Sebastian which the Spanish padre used to show me when I was a child; I protest that you are the veritable image of Saint Sebastian. If these silly fellows have made you suffer, depend upon it that they shall be punished as they deserve. Permit me to remove that arrow from your arm; it must be most uncomfortable."

Shiloh had no real prejudice against Saint Sebastian; that romantic martyr of the Christian mythology was not uncongenial to his secret mind. But the stranger's casual tone annoyed him, and he was further irritated by the debonair and somewhat dandified manner which winged the words with gaiety. He drew himself erect, and his eyes flashed rather fiercely as he replied.

"It's very kind of you, of course," said Shiloh, "but I think I can manage for myself, thank you. These friends of yours have displayed a senseless enmity towards me for which I am at a loss to account, but the folly and depravity of the human race have ever been my despair, and I suppose my misfortunes were inevitable in this savage land."

"Oh, but by no means, my dear young man; you are quite mistaken about that, I assure you. The Indians are uncommonly pleasant people for the most part, and you are certain to like them when you become better acquainted. I regret extremely that these hobbledehoys should have attempted to burn you, but they are little more than ignorant children, and I know you will bear them no malice for their inconsiderate outbreak."

"Really, I cannot agree with you upon that point," Shiloh answered. "I feel that I have very just cause to be offended by their conduct; they are adult, and entirely responsible for their uncivil behaviour. If you possess any authority over their nature, I trust that you will employ it to inculcate principles of wisdom and virtue more proper to their years."

"Well," replied the youth with a shrug of his graceful shoulders, "I dare say it is unavoidable that you should experience a passing resentment against these poor foolish Comanches; when you have had your breakfast you will be more forgiving. I don't

blame you the least for being cross at present; you look very
tired, and I perceive that someone has been striking you with a
tomahawk."

"You appear to regard that circumstance as a cause for mirth,"
said Shiloh with immense hauteur; he stared more closely at the
stranger's impudently smiling face, and observed that the boy
bore no resemblance to any Indian whom Shiloh had ever
encountered.

Shiloh saw that the young stranger had an innocently courageous nose, straight and blunt and childish, that his eyes were
brilliant hazel and set very wide apart, and that his short thick
hair was wavy and coloured like November beech-leaves. His
skin was tanned to a fine even bronze, but there was a rosiness of
blood beneath the sunburn which matched the small red lips. He
seemed to be about sixteen years old, slim and muscular and
moderately well grown for that tender age. His garments were
delicate and fresh in a barbaric fashion, and the silver bracelets
that he wore were scoured to a moonlight brightness.

"Whatever you are, you are not an Indian," Shiloh told him
sternly, "and I cannot admit your right to lecture me concerning
them. I have journeyed for a month among these violent people
without discovering anything but courtesy and kindness; my own
good intentions were everywhere the earnest of my safety. Now,
among the Comanches, I have found murder and malfeasance
beyond my dreams of hell; it is not fitting that you should laugh
in my face when you speak of it."

"Dear me, my good sir, you do take it all very seriously, don't
you?" said the boy with a flippant little grimace; Shiloh thought
him the most heartless person whom he had ever met.

"You see," the boy continued lightly, "it's purely a matter of
luck; my own experiences have taught me that. You were well
treated by the Pawnees, and now the Comanches have singed
your ankles and cut your head open for no reason at all except
that these activities amused them. I, on the other hand, was stolen
by the Pawnees and destined for a very dreadful fate; a band of
Cheyennes and Comanches rescued me from this, and I have,
naturally enough, become deeply attached to my preservers.
But let us talk of all this another time; I fear that my chatter is

wearying you, and you are quite palpably in need of food and slumber."

Shiloh disliked a certain condescension in the lad's cheerful voice; he would have preferred to refuse the offer, but his endurance was nearly at an end, and through a mist of exhaustion he heard David's voice in his ear.

" Come on now, Shiloh, quit arguing with the young lady and let her give you some nice hot breakfast."

Shiloh gazed at him in bewilderment; David's familiar features grew large and nebulous to his view, and he had scarcely the strength to whisper his surprise.

" What on earth do you mean, Davy? " he murmured dizzily. "There is no young lady here; what can you possibly mean? I see only a boy on a cream-coloured pony."

" Why, you crazy little fool," grinned David, " that there ain't a boy; that's a girl, and a mighty pretty one at that! "

David put out his arm, but not in time; the girl sprang from her pony with a soft and frightened cry. They were both too late; Shiloh had grown white as death upon the words, and fallen forward into the trampled snow, which showed a small red stain where his forehead touched it.

They knelt beside him, and down the face of each the tears were running; they tasted the cold salt tears upon their lips, and these tears tasted of winter and sorrow and the bitterness of love.

" Goldarn you, Miss! " cried David, " why did you have to go and tease and pester him like that, and him so tired? Couldn't you see he was wore to a frazzle with all these hellish goings-on? Seems like you was possessed of a devil or something, Miss, to mock him like you done, and him never able to stand women. That's what I've always declared; Shiloh can't stand women nohow; he's fond enough of 'em, I reckon, but if you'll excuse the liberty, Miss, they wears him out completely, and now you've been and killed him with your devilish mocking ways."

The girl knelt weeping in the snow; she lifted one of Shiloh's hands and kissed it, and the hand was cold and frightening against her lips.

" Oh, do you really believe that he is dead? Oh, do you really believe that he is dead, and that I have killed him by my cruelty? "

she asked David in a small and humble voice. "I am more savage than these ignorant Comanches; I am truly a devil, and I think that I am mad. I spoke to him scornfully because I loved him; I have never loved anyone, in all the years I can remember, and I loved him from the moment I saw him, loved him so that I was wounded by my love, so that it was like an arrow or a sword in my heart, so that I talked like a fool or a devil because my heart was broken by my love."

David was profoundly shocked; in all his life he had never listened to such wild and passionate words, and they were the more indecorous to his mind in that they were spoken childishly and in a small and tearful voice.

"Oh, my darling, my adorable, my beautiful!" cried the girl, addressing herself to Shiloh inanimate upon the snow, "please don't say that I have killed you; please be alive again and say that you forgive me for my devilish wickedness! You can't be so cold-hearted as to lie dead before my eyes and refuse to forgive me; if you will only listen while I tell you how I love you, you will never have the cruelty to die!"

She crouched in the snow; she raised Shiloh so that he lay upon his back with his head against her crossed knees. Her tears fell down upon his dishevelled hair and wetted his closed eyelids, and presently they had frozen into ice which sparkled crystalline against the dark hair and the shut secret eyelids.

A tall warrior approached the girl and laid his hand gently upon her shoulder; she started and looked up into his face with pitiful eyes. She said a few words in the Cheyenne language, and the warrior nodded briefly and withdrew to the river-bank.

"Let's get him into the fort," said David; he was sincerely shocked, but the girl's sorrow and wild regret had touched him with sympathy. He remembered that he had called to Shiloh upon the deck of the clipper ship, and that Shiloh had answered and returned from death; he knew some measure of the grief which shook this singular girl to madness.

"We'll get him into the fort," said David, "and we'll build a big fire and make some coffee; I've got brandy in my flask, and there's lots of blankets and buffalo robes in there where we left 'em this morning. There don't nobody need to touch him but you and me; I can't stomach these painted varmints laying a finger on him, and you're a strong girl; you lifted his head as easy as anything just now. Come on, Miss; we ain't got no time to lose a-crying if we wants to save him."

"You are right," said the girl at once; she dried her eyes and assumed an air of composure. "That will be best for the night; to-morrow, if he lives, I shall send for a litter and we can carry him to my father's lodge. Meanwhile I shall dispatch a messenger to bring us such comforts and remedies as our home provides; my father is the chief of the Cheyennes, and he will welcome this stranger with honour and affection for my sake."

"Well, Miss," replied David, "I can't rightly figger it out as yet how a white girl comes to have an Injun for a father, but if you say it's so I believes you, and there's plenty of time for explaining all that after we've got a drop of hot coffee into Shiloh. Now I'll take his shoulders and you take his feet and we'll have him into that there fort as slick as butter."

Several Indian braves rushed forward to relieve the girl of her burden as she stooped and prepared to raise Shiloh's feet from the ground, but she stopped them with an imperious movement of her head, and David knew that she was comforted by performing this humble service for his friend. He lifted Shiloh's thin body from the snow without difficulty; the girl did her part with a look of rapt devotion upon her face, and together they bore the unconscious figure between the silent watchful Comanches into the doorway of the fort. The silver winter sun glazed the white ice of the river with radiance, and David and the girl went slowly and in awe, because they loved Shiloh and feared to know that he was dead.

6

"WILL you forgive me for being rude to you, please?" asked the girl a little later; she knelt at the foot of Shiloh's couch of buffalo-skins, and suddenly she bent down and kissed the toes of his scorched moccasins.

David was boiling coffee over a driftwood fire; he wondered at the softness of the girl's voice and at her gentle and submissive manner. She was completely tamed; not a trace remained of her mockery or even of her passionate self-reproach. She moved about the rude interior of the fort with quiet peaceable steps, and her touch was exquisitely light and cool upon Shiloh's wound.

"Wonderful what love will do," mused David to himself as he added a dash of snow-water to the bubbling coffee. "She was a regular vixen, and now she's mild as a cream-syllabub."

"Will you please forgive me, out of the great goodness of your heart?" whispered the girl again, laying another airy and elusive kiss at Shiloh's feet.

"Of course; but you mustn't, you know," said Shiloh in a low voice; he still felt somewhat brittle and imponderable as he lay upon the couch, and he was not quite sure whether the girl and her kisses were real, or whether he and she and the shaggy buffalo-hides were all floating in a transcendental region of the soul.

"You see, I thought you were a boy, and rather an unfriendly boy at that," Shiloh explained patiently; it was a painful weariness to speak, but he saw that the girl's translucent hazel eyes were full of tears, and he had not the heart to disallow their sacred beseeching question.

"It was my horrid clothes; you couldn't know I was a girl in these ridiculous clothes," she assured him meekly.

"No; it was my own stupidity; I remember that my head ached, and then there was so much noise and confusion, and the smoke hurt my eyes and made me giddy," said Shiloh. "But I was an idiot not to know that you were a girl; you couldn't possibly be anything else, and I feel that I owe you an apology."

"No, no, no; the fault was entirely mine, and now I am going to get you a cup of coffee and to make you stop talking," the girl replied; she jumped to her feet and dried her eyes by rubbing them with her small brown knuckles. She moved with the grace and agility of a panther-kitten, and her golden skin rippled and shone over muscles smooth and quick as running water.

"'Course he'd 'a' rather had tea, but this coffee's more heartening-like on a cold day, as I reckon it, Miss," said David, giving her the tin cup. His prejudice against her was vanishing in the simplicity of his nature and her queer fantastic charm, even as the maple sugar was now melting in the amber warmth of Mocha.

"Lucky you was able to get back the mules and the baggage from them lousy — from them I should say cantankerous varmints, Miss," said David companionably, pouring hot coffee into the girl's cup and his own. "There was things there as Shiloh set great store by, specially some of them books and such-like trash and all."

"I am happy to have been privileged to be of service to him," the girl answered gravely.

7

"It cannot be good for you to hear so many solemn words before you sleep," said the girl that evening, shutting the book upon the *Misticay real Babilonia.* "The priests in Santa Fé compelled me to read these things when I was a mere child; my taste was vitiated by too much religion. If it were the *Galan fantasma,* now! that is amusing."

"As you will; we will read no more to-night, then," replied Shiloh, opening his eyes and smiling at her serious face. "Besides, it must be difficult to decipher the page by the lovely but wavering illumination of the flames. You had far better put the book away and tell me about yourself."

"It will tire you," said the girl, but it was plain to Shiloh that she longed to talk to him, and he was much too soft-hearted to disappoint her.

As a matter of fact he did not greatly care; he was comparatively comfortable now, and although he was weary he did not wish to sleep. He had been enchanted to discover that the girl read Spanish with fluency and a certain ingenuous music; it was a pity that she did not know Greek, as her voice was both harmonious and clear. Some natural elegance of diction was distinct in her speech, which seemed to hold the vague suggestion of an accent foreign and refined. Shiloh supposed, and rightly, that this was the result of her knowledge of three several tongues.

Shiloh had lately led an existence of such variety and adventure that his enforced idleness was a severe nervous trial to him, and if he had been permitted to choose he would have insisted upon an immediate departure for the Cheyenne camp. But David and the girl chimed in a maddening laughter at the thought, and told him that he would be exceedingly lucky if he were allowed to set forth upon the morrow.

"What, you crazy catawampus, do you reckon as you can get your head laid open afore breakfast and pay an elegant social call on your murderers the same goldarned day?" asked David, and the girl displayed a concurrent mirth as she evolved a remarkably nourishing soup out of venison and wild turkey.

Therefore Shiloh was a trifle bored, and ready enough to listen to her story. He had slept the winter afternoon away, soothed by some decoction of medicinal herbs, and now that he was wakeful he preferred to be amused. The ability to suffer a slight concussion at midnight and to enjoy the dramas of Calderón upon the evening of the same day is possessed by few mortals, but of this demi-Olympian company Shiloh was the shining superior star.

It was the girl and not he who had grown drowsy over the book; now her evident eagerness to confide in him appealed to every philanthropic instinct of his being. "Tell me about yourself," he repeated gently.

"My name is Anne, and I was born in New England," said the girl. "David pretends that he knew from the first that I must be a Yankee; perhaps he did, but that was very clever of him, since I was reared in Sante Fé and have spent the last three years of my life among the Indians."

"Knowed it all the same, Miss, the minute I clapped eyes on you," insisted David. "It's a sort of a look as is hard to explain if you ain't never seen it; up and coming, if I may say so, Miss."

"Well, never mind about that; if we both talk we shall tire him, and I have a great many interesting things to tell," said the girl, gazing fondly at Shiloh; she was ecstatically happy, but even in her happiness she remembered to speak in a mild submissive voice. She was not quite unselfish enough to keep perfectly silent, but at least she did not converse above a whisper, and she frowned most indignantly at David whenever his louder tones interrupted her narrative.

"Anne is a beautiful name," said Shiloh, who rarely forgot to be kind.

"I am glad you like it, as I know no other to tell you," the girl informed him with a radiant smile. "You are to understand that my father and mother both died when I was a child, and that I was adopted by the priest in Santa Fé and cared for out of the charity of his heart. That priest is also dead now; he was a nice old man, though rather too fat; for all that, he was a Spanish gentleman, and he made me study very hard. One eccentricity he had which annoyed me: he would never tell me my father's name."

At this point in the girl's story no scandalous suspicion leapt into Shiloh's mind; most innocently he waited for the truth, and in a moment he had it.

"You see," said the girl, "my poor father was a Protestant missionary; a Congregationalist, I think one calls it, if such a long word can possibly be right."

"That's right, Miss," David told her with an elder-brotherly air. "That's what my folks was; that's the proper thing for Yankees."

"For Yankees, perhaps; not for the inhabitants of Santa Fé," the girl explained. "And certainly my father was silly to attempt to come to Mexico and convert the people; I am afraid my poor father was a fool. The priest was quite charming to me about it, but of course he disapproved profoundly of the idea, and he believed that when my father and mother were killed by the Kiawas on the road to Santa Fé they only received the punishment which they richly deserved. The opinion is possibly extreme, but one cannot blame dear old Padre Francisco for holding it."

"I can," said Shiloh; "I think he was excessively intolerant and cruel."

"Oh, nonsense, although you are an angel to think so," Anne assured him. "You are too good for this world; the padre was an ordinary person, and that is the way people are. It is a pity, but you must get used to it."

"Never!" cried Shiloh, meaning it with all the fervour of his extraordinary soul.

"Now I hope you are not permitting the idea to worry you," the girl said tenderly. "You really must not let my simple story excite you; you will have a fever if you do, and it is all so unnecessary. I have led rather a quiet and uneventful life; a few adventures with the Indians, but that was to be expected."

"Please go on, please," Shiloh begged her; he knew that he would quite certainly have a fever if he listened to her, but the tale was too singular to leave unheard.

"Well, Padre Francisco obtained possession of me from the Kiawas; I was but seven years old at the time, and they had no earthly use for me," the girl went on. "Then he tore my father's and mother's names out of all their books and papers; most of the books he burned afterwards, but I think he kept them for a while out of natural curiosity, and I was fortunate enough to find several of them, and to steal them for my own purposes."

"It was not stealing," said Shiloh. "They were your parents' books to begin with, and the priest had stolen them from you."

"But that is absurd, my beautiful darling," Anne replied. "He was a grown person, and I was a disobedient child; of course I stole the books. You don't think I am ashamed of that, do you?"

"It is perhaps a matter of terminology, Anne," said Shiloh, which meant nothing to the girl beyond the pleasure of hearing his voice.

"I read the books; they were in English, but my father must have taught me to read, because I found I could read them quite easily," continued Anne. "I discovered from certain papers that my father had been a missionary, and I confessed my discovery to Padre Francisco; he was afraid I would feel the disgrace very keenly, but luckily I did not; it takes a great deal to shock me, you see."

"I see," said Shiloh, who could not help laughing. "And what were these terrible books, my child?"

"Oh, they were sermons by Mr. Cotton Mather and Mr. Jonathan Edwards, and hymn-books, and little books about witches," the girl answered airily. "Some of them were rather wicked, I admit, but no worse than the Indians when they are really out of temper. Merely details of damnation and that sort of thing; there's very little difference between that and some of the Comanches' more ingenious tortures."

"We are agreed upon that point," said Shiloh; if the girl had been observant she would have known that he had a fever already.

" Yes, but you are far more disapproving of it all than I," she said. " You cannot expect people to be soft-hearted, you see; it simply doesn't happen. Sometimes, yes, and for the few they truly love, as I love you, but not for all the world; not for enemy tribes. I am not soft-hearted myself about the Pawnees."

" I suppose not; the devils stole you, didn't they? " asked Shiloh anxiously.

" They did; they are not really devils, of course, although you are a darling to say so for my sake; still, I shall always consider them an unpleasant tribe, since they intended to roast me at a slow fire. A slow fire; think of it! "

" I can't! " Shiloh replied faintly.

" Well, I dare say that is because you were almost burned yourself this morning," said the girl indulgently, putting her cool hand upon Shiloh's brow; but in this supposition she was wrong. Shiloh was not thinking of himself; he was thinking of Anne, and he did not wish to think of a slow fire.

" Of course the poor Pawnees had a perfectly sensible purpose in stealing me," the girl said cheerfully. " That is, if you believe religion can ever be sensible; sometimes I am myself inclined to doubt it. Aren't you? "

" Often and often," Shiloh told her, with the light of something more than fever burning in his eyes.

" This was quite a simple idea; a little superstitious and silly, but then, what can you expect of ignorant savages? It appears that the Pawnees believe implicitly in sacrificing a young girl every spring; the theory is that this will propitiate the morning star or some such folderol, and that the morning star will send them plenty of corn and beans and pumpkins in consequence. Childish, isn't it? "

" Good God! " said Shiloh; he found it difficult to say even this.

" They treated me extremely well during the entire six months which I spent with them; I was stupid enough not to realise that they meant to kill me, and I had a charming time of it, to be perfectly honest. You see, Padre Francisco had just died, and I rather missed him, and then I was deadly tired of the Mexicans; such dull greasy people, much worse than the Pawnees! I never liked them; I was delighted when the Pawnees took me away. I was fourteen years old; that is two years ago now, of course, and I was still fond of juvenile games. I thought it great fun to play at being an Indian."

"Did you go with them of your own accord?" Shiloh asked her.

"To tell you the truth, I did, and it's very clever of you to have guessed it!" said the girl admiringly, kissing his hand. "But you must never give me away to the Cheyennes; I pretend to them that I always hated the Pawnees like poison. It flatters them, you see, and after all they did rescue me from a dreadful death, but to begin with I thought the Pawnees were delightful people. I went out for a walk one morning in the environs of the town, and met about a dozen of them on pretty little ponies; they looked so straight and tall compared to the dirty Mexicans that when they invited me to visit them I consented at once. They let me run home for my books and my Spanish shawl; in five hours we were miles and miles from Santa Fé, and they had given me a pony and taught me to say my prayers in the Pawnee language."

"Did you?" Shiloh inquired curiously.

"Sometimes; sometimes I said them in Latin like Padre Francisco, and sometimes I said a bit of Jonathan Edwards for a change. Do you think it really matters, my sweetest?"

"Not very much," said Shiloh, thinking that this was a child of nature's most fantastic marriage with a dream.

"And then," continued Anne in a vivacious whisper, "at last it was April, with little white clouds like swan's-down in the sky, and one showery morning I was taken to all the lodges in turn, and given silly pieces of painted wood, which I had to give back again to the warrior at my side, and that was so absurd that it made me cross. Not that I wanted the horrid scraps of wood, but it was such a senseless thing to do, you know. This mummery went on for two days, and then, if you please, I was varnished like a doll with vermilion and plumbago, so that I was half red and half black; fancy what a fool I must have looked! And that is not the worst, my love, if you will believe me; those hateful Pawnees actually intended to hang me on a gibbet and roast me alive over a slow fire; is not the idea in execrable taste? People are amazingly stupid and prejudiced when it comes to religion, or so it has always appeared to me. Later it seems I was to have been dispatched by means of tomahawks and arrows, but the slow fire is the most disagreeable part of it, isn't it? "

" It is," said Shiloh, to whom the thought was veritable hell-fire.

" I remember it all so clearly; it was an enchanting April day, coloured like my turquoise necklace; the streams were as blue as the skies, and along their edges the willows were turning silver and gold at the tips. Everything was gay and windy; it was such a dreadful waste of time to bother about burning me on a day like that. I was scared, I confess; I felt quite sick, and also very angry, because I did not want to die. That is all, I suppose, except that the Cheyennes came riding up in a cloudy powder of dust and rescued me just as the flames began to look like yellow flowers around my feet. I knew precisely how you felt this morning, my dearest; you see, the same thing had happened to me. Of course I didn't faint, but then no one had wounded me, and I was more frightened than hurt, as Padre Francisco used to say when I was a little girl."

8

SHILOH found it impossible to answer her; it is equally impossible to describe the horror which had sucked his words away.

" So then the Cheyenne chief took me home with him and treated me with the most distinguished kindness," Anne concluded. " His own daughter had recently perished in attempting to tame a wild horse, and as I was almost exactly the same age he soon grew very fond of me indeed. Finally he adopted me as his child; that is the reason that I always refer to him as my father. Probably he is much nicer than my real father was, and certainly he is much stronger and cleverer. He is the most powerful chief in this part of the country, which makes it pleasant for me; you may have noticed that those wretched Comanches were awed out of their wits this morning when I appeared; that is because they know I will stand no nonsense from anyone. That fellow who hurt you is a miserable sort of half-chief; it will be diverting to see what my father will do to him. My father is good enough to consider me fearless and original; I dare say a romantic person might say he doted upon me, but I am not romantic, except of course about you. In a word, the old man adores me; he is sorry that my hair is red and my skin the colour of cream, but that cannot be avoided, although it is a great pity."

She drew a long breath, and kissed the topmost feathery lock of Shiloh's hair.

"I don't think it a great pity to have a skin like lucent gold and hair like a magical bronze bell," said Shiloh; he had recovered his voice, and he employed it benevolently, but it must be confessed that he was very tired.

Anne perceived his state as soon as she stopped chattering; she controlled the passion of love and pity which convulsed her spirit, and went quite meekly to fetch him another bowl of soup. Shiloh lay still; his burning mind shone through his eyes in brightness.

"Aren't you hungry, my angel?" she inquired tenderly, putting a pinch of salt and a small peppercorn into the soup. "Please try to eat it for my sake; I will be so grateful to you if only you will eat a spoonful of my poor soup, which is longing to be eaten by an angel. Now you must not look as if you were going to die; you are frightening me and my little soup out of our lives, because we love you and live only for you. But I warned you that you would have a fever if you insisted upon hearing all that solemn twaddle about Babylon; it is worse even than Mr. Mather's witches. You are to think of the nice funny things I told you, and try to sleep."

"Don't you know as you've been a-harrowing of him with all that jabber about Injun wickedness?" asked David in an angry whisper. "Drat you, Miss, you surely are the queerest girl I ever seen in all my born days! 'Tain't the reading as done it; it's women; you ain't none of you got no sense, if you'll pardon the expression. Taking all that trouble to cook him up a pint of soup, and then spoiling his appetite with horrors; it's downright half-witted, that's what it is!"

"But those were not horrors; those were the everyday facts of my life, and my life upon the whole has been most amusing," said Anne in perfect simplicity and good faith.

Shiloh lay and watched her as she moved about the room as gently as a ripple of golden water; he wondered what mystery of soul her merry and casual talk concealed, and then, for no more than a passing instant, he wondered if indeed there were a soul obscured within the sunny glimmer of her body. This last conjecture faded before the visible adoration in the transparent hazel eyes which gazed into his own and were puzzled by their burning. Shiloh knew to whom Anne would say her prayers that night, although the only kiss she gave him was laid lightly and ridiculously at his feet.

" Good-night, my beautiful," she said; " I am going to leave you now, but David will take excellent care of you, and I shall see you at seven o'clock to-morrow morning. They've built a lodge for me before your door, a pretty little lodge all painted with deer and hawks and flying arrows; there's a cross old woman in it waiting to put me to bed, and I must kiss you good-night; I kiss the tips of your toes because I am your slave, your slave who loves you."

" Oh, surely not my slave; you must never be anyone's slave, my child," said Shiloh, but he was too tired to contest the point; she kissed the shaggy buffalo-skin in the place where she believed his narrow feet were hidden.

" A princess to the common people, but a slave to you, my sweet," she said as she vanished into the night, leaping softly through the door with the silent fluent grace of a panther-kitten.

" Good God, what a distressing idea! " thought poor Shiloh; he was shocked by Anne's unenlightened opinions and embarrassed by her humility; he was afraid that she was at once a sincere tyrant and a congenital slave. If such a creature could exist, it were no better than a lovely cockatrice; the fancy bothered him, for by this time he was very feverish.

He was feverish, he was weary, he was troubled by the bright and subtle fire of his own mind; it was like a too-bright lamp shining into his inward spiritual eyes, so that he could not sleep, or rest quietly upon his savage couch.

In a luminous splendour of delirium he saw the events of the preceding hours stream past his inward mind; the thing was like a radiant tapestry unrolled by an enchantment. The torches at midnight, the sparks against the glittering snow, the ripple of light like sunny water where Anne's own body moved, these several magics met and flowed into a single sheet of flame, and for a moment Shiloh believed that the heavens had opened in unnatural dawn.

Then he knew that it was only his memory playing monstrous tricks with his imagination, and he determined to be calm and to forget the Comanches' cruelty and Anne's hazel eyes.

"Might I have a drink of water, Davy?" he asked politely; his extreme politeness was more than David could endure.

"Aw, Shiloh, don't be so god-damned nice about it! If you was to swear at me or something, I'd know you wasn't going to die; I'd know that little hell-cat hadn't killed you with her jabbering. I'd 'a' liked to box her ears, princess or no princess; she's just a little red-headed Yankee like you'd see at any quilting-party and wouldn't bother to kiss, and her pretending to be someone grand's just to get you to take notice of her, I reckon. Aw, I know 'em, I know 'em all too well, and they're a bad lot when they're in love!"

It was impossible not to laugh; his amusement did Shiloh more good than the tin cup of snow-water, most of which David had spilled in conveying it from the calabash to the bed. All at once the world resumed the warm humane proportions of a mortal home; the nightmare was dispersed, and Shiloh was delighted to discover that he could sleep.

"Of course I am not going to die, Davy," he said. "There's nothing whatever the matter with me beyond a slight abrasion of the scalp, and you are aware of the amazing resiliency of my constitution. To-morrow we will go to the Cheyenne village; the change will be beneficial, and in three days I shall be perfectly well. There is nothing to worry about; you will see that I am always right."

"Reckon you are, you crazy critter," muttered David admiringly as he replaced the calabash upon its log and prepared to bank the embers of the fire.

Shiloh drew the miniature of Silver from his pocket; his fatigue rendered the act an effort, and his fingers refused to unfasten the clasp of the shagreen case. Nevertheless it was a comfort to hold the thing against his cheek and to dream the countenance which it concealed. Here was no violence or moving glitter of gold; here were colours silvery and pearly, and the shape of peace. The lips were cooler than snow-water, the eyes were softer than the end of sorrow, and Shiloh was asleep.

The Orphan Angel

IX

THE UNPASTURED DRAGON

SHILOH'S was a true prophecy: the morrow's journey performed a miracle of healing upon his light corporeal frame and revivified his mind with wonder. He did not really dislike the motion of the litter so long as he was permitted to gaze about him in silence; the girl walked by his side, but her mien was subdued into a docile melancholy when she perceived his desire for repose. She had dismissed her cream-coloured pony with a flick of her slim fingers, and now she went on foot, with bended head and downcast visionary eyes.

The litter was borne by four warriors of imposing aspect; it was quite evident that they stooped to the unaccustomed service only to humour a princess. They followed the meanderings of the river, and sometimes the way was rough, but fortunately they had but to traverse a distance of seven miles, and Shiloh supported the uneven pace with perfect equanimity. He was warm beneath a covering of splendid furs, and the circumstances of his progress were too romantic to be wholly displeasing to his taste.

Anne had awakened him at dawn with an armful of preposterously munificent gifts; he had tried hard to refuse the red and silver foxes, the velvet beaver, and the rich tawny marten which she carried, but finally her tears persuaded him against his will, and she had the satisfaction of flinging a king's ransom at his feet before she brewed him a cup of tea.

Now he was clad from top to toe in garments of pure white buckskin, exquisitely soft and supple save where their delicate surfaces grew stiff with an embroidery of turquoise beads and scarlet porcupine quills; his moccasins were two intricate patterns of colour. Shiloh was grateful for the cleanliness and comfort, but every ascetic nerve in his body revolted against this elaborate luxury, and he determined to be rid of his grandeur as soon as he was well enough to walk.

Nevertheless he derived a certain pleasure from the fact that he was clothed like a savage prince; he was ashamed of this feeling, but far too honest to deny it to his private mind.

"You are beautiful; so beautiful that you will draw my eyes from their sockets and my heart from my breast to hang at your belt like horrid trophies," breathed Anne in a low religious whisper. Shiloh laughed; he did not believe her in the least, but in truth he was very beautiful as he lay among the suave and heavy furs looking the slighter and the brighter by contrast with that rich and sombre fleece. In his hand he held one long feather of the golden eagle, which the girl had given him that morning; he liked it better than all her other gifts. He thought that he might perhaps wear it in his cap when he was strong again, and rushing over the prairie almost as swiftly as the shadow of a flying eagle.

Anne could not guess his thoughts; she gazed at him sidewise through her thick brown lashes and trembled with the intensity of her love. It was a great deprivation to her to be silent; only the authentic adoration of her soul for Shiloh could have kept her so for more than five minutes. Occasionally she would turn her haughty little head to frown resentfully at some unlucky brave who had disturbed the devotional stillness with a muffled shout; she felt extremely virtuous in spite of her disappointment, and the disapproving glances which she cast upon others consoled her in part for her own suffering.

The cavalcade passed slowly along the shimmering riverbank; the ice upon the river sparkled in the sun. Save for the braves who carried Shiloh, Anne and David alone of all the company went on foot; the Indian warriors reined in their ponies to a gentler pace, and David spoke to the mules in a mutter of remonstrance whenever they trotted near the litter whereon his friend lay stretched beneath a covering of sumptuous furs. It seemed half royal progress, half idolatrous procession; the circumstance that the cherished creature in its midst was a republican and an atheist adds a clear ironic lustre to its image in the eye of the mind.

At last they reached the outskirts of the Indian village; here the river widened to a curving basin, and the ice was strong and smooth as levelled stone. Upon this noble playground a number of Indian boys were engaged in contests of endurance and athletic skill; Shiloh saw to his amazement that they were stark naked. He stared enchanted at this spectacle of hardihood; his own detestation of the rigours of winter made the children's courage appear transcendent. In reality they were not in the least disturbed by the cold, having been accustomed since infancy to defy it; the armour of their copper skins was quite sufficient for their needs. To Shiloh, however, they seemed a brood of heroes; he thought of Sparta, and blushed among his comfortable furs. There was that in his nature which invariably desired to oppose the tyranny of danger and of pain; now his true inclination was to spring from the litter and dare the torturing elements to do their worst. Had he done so, he could scarcely have hoped to escape pneumonia; the mental blessing of a vindicated pride might possibly have compensated him for this annoyance. The sole reason that he delayed to put the matter to the test was that he knew very well what David and Anne would say, and how long and how loudly they would repeat it.

"What a bore it is," he reflected, "that there should always be someone to make a fuss about these things; I don't mean to be ungrateful, but I do wish that their affection did not interfere with my personal liberty."

"My dearest love," said Anne at this moment, "we are now coming to my father's lodge. Here is a headdress of eagles' feathers; it was taken from an Aricara chief who had come into our country, and who was very properly murdered by one of my most intimate friends. Let me bind it about your head, my beautiful; it will conceal that hateful bandage, and help convince my father that you are an important person."

"If you insist, my child," said Shiloh. "But I would far rather not wear it; it is stained with fear and anger. Besides, you know I am not really an important person."

"What nonsense," cried the girl indignantly. "Of course you are; the most important person in the world! And only look, there is hardly any blood upon the feathers; they are the feathers of the great gold war-eagle, and each one of them is worth the price of ten excellent horses."

Shiloh sighed as the plumes were bound about his brow; he wished that both the golden eagle and the Aricara chief were still alive and flying above the clouds, or across the cloudy shadows of the plain. The band about his brow made his head ache; Anne had bound it too straitly, but he had not the heart to tell her so. Her hazel eyes were bright with tears; the life-blood of the Aricara meant nothing to her, but the little drop of blood upon Shiloh's bandage drew the life from her own veins.

The Indian encampment numbered some three hundred lodges, and stretched for a considerable distance over the prairie; many dogs and horses roamed at large upon its borders, and the place was populous with dark-skinned squaws and children. Here were gathered the chiefs of the Comanches, the Arapahoes, the Cheyennes, and the Snakes, with a sprinkling of Kiawas among them; this village extended for a mile along the winter banks of the Arkansaw.

Shiloh was borne into the lodge of the Cheyenne chief; his litter was deposited upon the earthen floor, and he looked into the downward-gazing eyes of a tall and grizzled Indian of commanding appearance.

"This is my father," said Anne solemnly. "Father, this is the greatest chief of the eastern world, the King of England's eldest son."

Shiloh flushed with surprise and keen exasperation; the suggestion was too outrageous to be endured. He flung the silver foxes from about him and rose to his feet; impulsive fury tightened his muscles until it hardly needed his hand upon the tent-pole to steady him as he faced the Cheyenne chief. Their eyes were level as they met like flint and steel to make a fire.

"Really, Anne," said Shiloh, " you know perfectly well that your statement is slanderous and untrue. If you understood the moral and political infamy of the house of Hanover you would not presume to couple my name with any member of that house. Pray explain to your father that I am an honourable and virtuous person, or I must decline to trespass further upon your hospitality."

2

LARGE scintillating tears appeared within the aureate hazel of Anne's eyes; her voice was petulant as she answered.

"I only said that in order to make my father fonder of you," she said. "You are dreadfully silly, my sweetest, to be angry with me because of a little thing like that; for my own part I should much prefer to be a king's daughter; my father was a missionary, and yet I never trouble myself about the disgrace, or allow it to depress me. Now sit down like a sensible darling and let me fetch you something to eat."

"Good-day, sir; you are welcome to my house," said the Cheyenne to Shiloh in slow accurate English. " You must not permit this impertinent child of mine to weary you with her vagaries; she is a good child at heart, but excessively foolish. It will give me great pleasure to make you known to certain of our more distinguished chiefs to-night; you must be sick of the society of women and social inferiors."

"Thank you," Shiloh replied; his mind was whirling with bewilderment. " I should of course be glad to make the acquaintance of your friends; I cannot agree to your strictures upon the opposite sex, and I have never agreed to any theory whereby society is arbitrarily divided by certain rules inadmissible to an enlightened mind. At present I am grievously fatigued; may I depend upon your kindness to grant me a brief interval of rest? "

"Good heavens, my dear fellow, my entire household is at your service! " exclaimed the Cheyenne with obvious sincerity.

"Ask for anything your fancy dictates; a cloak of golden fox-skins lined with feathers, a milk-white Spanish horse broken to your rein, or a young virgin purer than the April moon; all these await you if you will take the trouble to accept them. Meanwhile, here are peltries from the Canadian mountains and seal-skins from California; I beg you to consider this couch as your exclusive property, unless you should prefer to share it with the fairest maiden of my tribe!"

"But, father, you have not arranged it in the least as I directed!" cried Anne with passionate scorn. "What are all these horrid moth-devoured furs doing here, when I told you there must be nothing but sable and beaver? By the body of Christ, I shall run away with the first horse-thief who importunes me rather than submit to this indignity! I have told you that I love this man, that I adore him with the ultimate fervour of my soul, and yet you dare to spread his resting-place with the mangy hides of nameless animals unknown to decent people! I declare to you, and by the holy cross I mean it with all my heart, that I will strip the skin from my own body and stretch it here for his comfort rather than permit my darling to sleep upon less than perfection, although the difference trembled in the splitting of a hair!"

"Anne, Anne!" Shiloh implored her, "I beg you to measure your words; this is the tongue of madness." He was repelled by her vehemence, and a look of strain and exhaustion drew his sensitive lips together and darkened the clear colour of his eyes.

"Gently, gently, my dear little girl; it is quite unnecessary to become so emphatic about a mere question of bedding; besides, you are embarrassing our guest," said the Cheyenne quietly. "I entreat you to excuse her, sir; her youth was subject to the most deplorable influences, and her education has been woefully neglected. I am endeavouring to correct its deficiencies, but sometimes I fear that the simplest principles of courtesy and self-control are beyond her powers of apprehension. Her physical courage is above reproach, but her mind is undisciplined and moonstruck in the extreme."

"Moonstruck? Of course I am moonstruck," cried Anne immediately. "Moonstruck, sunstruck, starstruck, and struck by the blue lightning of his glance; father, you have seen him, and you cannot be surprised."

" I am never surprised by any of your antics, my child," replied the Cheyenne. " But I will punish you severely if you persist in this frenzy; go to your room, and let us see no more of you until to-morrow. I shall send you seven grains of parched corn and a walnut-shell full of water for your supper; I trust that this enforced abstinence may medicine the temper of your brain."

" Oh, pray don't punish her because of me; I really can't bear that! " exclaimed Shiloh in horror. The joints of his knees became all at once unstable, and he sat down upon the couch and covered his eyes with his hands.

" But who will give my beautiful darling his supper, then? " Anne demanded tragically; she was far too deeply in love to have any appetite, but the thought of Shiloh deprived of her cherishing attentions gnawed at her soul like hunger.

" Why, anyone whom he pleases to select, of course," said the Cheyenne with cool serenity; if he had the least suspicion of his daughter's anguish his face did not betray him into pity. " I suppose he will choose an agreeable virgin for that office, or any other that his desires may relish."

" You won't, will you, my angel? " murmured Anne; she sank down beside Shiloh and laid her tawny head upon his knees.

" You won't; I know you won't," she whispered. " You could never have the heart to marry anyone else to-night, while I am shut up in my horrid stuffy room with seven grains of parched corn and twenty drops of water to console me. Remember me; remember how I love you; promise me that you will not let my father persuade you to marry an agreeable virgin while I am loving you all alone in a cruel locked room whose walls are painted with yellow rattlesnakes! "

" You decided upon that design yourself, Anne," the Cheyenne reminded her. " You said that it was cheerful, and that you liked it because it put you in mind of the garden of Eden. Now get up at once and go to your bed; I cannot have any more of this egregious folly."

" I promise, my child," said Shiloh at the same instant; the words were low, and strung upon a little laugh. " I shall certainly not marry anyone to-night; you may depend upon it that I will remember. I am sorry that you are to have no supper, but perhaps your father will relent when I tell him how very good you have been to a distressed traveller."

He patted the top of her tawny head, that was so like a magical bronze bell that he almost expected it to ring with music under his light touch.

" I don't care about my supper; I care about yours," said Anne in a tearful whisper. " You must be certain not to let them give you any of that horrible roasted dog; I wouldn't eat any dried pumpkins, either, if I were you, because they're rather indigestible. Father will make you smoke that ridiculous pipe; if you're not accustomed to strong tobacco you'll probably feel dizzy. Don't forget that you may have a fever again to-night; make the wretches get you everything you need and don't sit up too late talking to those silly old men; after all, you were severely wounded yesterday and you are entitled to some consideration. It's positively inhuman of father to send me away from you; I alone understand your angelic nature and the peculiar character of your injury, which requires to be kissed as well as treated with cold vinegar compresses; the kisses must not be cold, my beautiful, and in order that you may obtain their true benefit they should be administered every five minutes."

" Anne," said the Cheyenne sternly, " be silent, and go to your room. We have had enough of this disgusting balderdash."

" Oh, please don't speak to her like that! " cried Shiloh. " She is very impulsive, of course, but she has such an affectionate and feeling heart that it is diabolic to rebuff her."

" She is not a baby," said the Cheyenne. " She is nearly seventeen years old; she must be taught to manage her emotions as she manages a refractory horse. Girls who can manage neither the one nor the other come to grief; luckily she has good hands on a horse, but her emotions are unbroken to any curb."

Shiloh remembered with a sentiment of awe that the Indian's own daughter had been killed in taming a horse, and he marvelled at the chill indifference of the voice that spoke of grief.

" Good-night, my love," whispered Anne. She rose swiftly to

her feet, her pliant body springing upward like a flame; her hands were little darting flames about Shiloh's head. If she touched him even very lightly her caress was too fugitive to be realised; she gave him no kiss, but passed from the room like fire blown out by adverse breath.

"Do you think we have hurt the child?" asked Shiloh miserably.

"Not half so much as she has wearied us," was the Cheyenne's cool reply.

Shiloh was grateful for the tranquillity of the empty lodge after the Indian had left him; he stretched his long limbs upon the couch and prepared to question the universe in general and his own spirit in particular. A few minutes of this metaphysical exercise sufficed to wrap his mind in slumbers more profound than the deep peltries in which his bones were laid; he slept soundly, and awoke refreshed and soothed into contentment.

David was standing by the tent-pole and regarding him with a faintly quizzical expression upon his honest countenance. He looked clean and ruddy and restored to his best able-seaman temper.

"They're a-waiting for you in the big lodge next door," he told Shiloh with a broad grin. "Seems like they think I'm your valley-de-shawm or some such dunderheaded foolishness; I ain't invited to their lousy party, and the old codger's been and ordered me about like I was bound over to him for life. It's him as sent me in here to wake you; say the word and I'll tell him as you ain't a-going to come to his god-damned barbecue, for I reckon the food won't be much to your liking."

"I am afraid it would be discourteous to decline," said Shiloh regretfully, sitting up and rubbing his eyes, which were still large and vague with sleep.

"Oh, to hell with politeness if you're tired," David cried. "Only mebbe it might kinda cheer you up a bit if you was to go to their party, just to pass the time, like, and to see all them solemn old mummies setting round in their blankets same as a passel of grandmas in their Sunday shawls, and them handing a long painted pipe about in the silliest way I ever see in all my born days. Grunt like regular hogs, they do, and never crack a smile a-doing it. Guess you better go, Shiloh; you can take along a fistful of parched corn if you don't hanker after hound-dog fricassee."

"I fear that it is my duty to go," said Shiloh, rising from the couch. "I shall of course take you with me; it must be made clear to these people that you are my friend, and that the happiest equality has ever governed the relation of our hearts. I wish I might have a bath before I appear at this tiresome supper."

"You can, my lad," replied David. "There's hot water and oil and white sand a-laying ready for you in the next room, not to mention a new suit of yaller buckskin embroidered in purple, and about a peck of elegant silver jewelry."

"I much prefer these garments which Anne was kind enough to give me," said Shiloh. "The bath, however, I shall certainly take, and that was an excellent suggestion as to the parched corn."

An hour later Shiloh and David entered the enormous lodge where the chiefs were assembled; it needed but a word from Shiloh to the Cheyenne to make David welcome in that company. The word was gentle, but there was a glitter in Shiloh's eyes that convinced the Indian of its veracity.

The chiefs of the Cheyennes, the Comanches, the Arapahoes, and the Snakes were met together for a great feast; the festival was pacific, but it celebrated some bloodier anniversary of conquest. The calumet, passed from hand to hand with ceremonies of grave decorum, was indeed the emblem of peace; the smoke that wreathed the fraternal bosoms of the savages symbolised a more durable bond. Certain dark and ambiguous objects dangling from the rafters overhead failed to engage Shiloh's flying glances; David observed them, and knew them for what they were; he was glad that his friend's attention was deflected by the solemn ritual of the supper.

"If he knew them god-damned things was scalps," said David to himself, "there's no telling what he wouldn't say or do. Most likely there'd be ructions; mebbe our own hair would be kinda added to the collection afore the night was out. Well, they ain't said nothing about him sticking to parched corn and refusing roasted pup, and I reckon the old fools has the sense to like him; have to be a sight bigger fools than them fellers not to like Shiloh."

3

" My beautiful darling, I have brought you the finest present in the world! " cried Anne the next morning, entering the room with impetuous speed and turning a clever handspring in the centre of the floor.

She was in exuberant spirits, and the softest colours of flame danced in her lips and eyes and informed the texture of her hair. Nevertheless Shiloh's heart sank into his moccasins as he heard her; he was afraid that she had come to offer him her hand in marriage, and it was an invariable agony to his soul to be forced to refuse a favour to a woman.

Shiloh and David were seated quietly in front of a little fire; they were drinking tea and eating crisp johnny-cakes within the circle of its warmth. Anne was a disturbing element, although the element was clear and golden as the flames upon the hearth.

" What is that, my child? " inquired Shiloh; he was exquisitely gentle with her although she had overturned the tea-kettle in her leap to his side. " You know I have already told you, my dear little girl, that you must not give me any more presents; it is quite impossible that I should accept another, but please believe that I love your generosity and thank you from the depth of my soul."

" Oh, but this you must take, my sweet; it is far too splendid to decline! " cried Anne; her gaiety overflowed in a sunny stream of laughter, and she whirled into a fantastic waltz with her own shadow.

" What is this splendid gift, then? " asked Shiloh patiently.

" Why, the life of your enemy, to be sure, my angel! " said Anne with a pure chime of exaltation in her childish voice.

Shiloh set down his tea-cup with a hand that trembled very visibly; he leaned back against the wall of the lodge and regarded Anne with the wide bright eyes of fascination. If the girl had suddenly displayed a serpent's breast under the delicate fabric of her gown, if some loathsome blight had struck her into physical decay, his horror would have been as nothing compared to this repugnance of the heart.

"What can you mean, in the name of God?" asked Shiloh in a shuddering whisper.

"Merely precisely what I have said, my sweet; father has consented to have the man executed at once, and I came straight to tell you the delightful tidings. You see I lay awake all night and cried because I adored you so, and when my father saw how unhappy I was this morning he felt sorry for me and wished to comfort me; he gave me leave to choose whatever precious thing I desired, and of course I wanted revenge upon the enemy of my love. My father is a perfect darling, and I shall never say again that he is cross or unkind."

"Oh, Anne, Anne, do you know what you are saying?" Shiloh demanded with ashen lips.

"It's not so very surprising after all, my angel, although I confess that I feel proud and triumphant because I can give you this beautiful present," Anne continued; her felicity had not perceived that Shiloh was blanched and frozen by her words. "You remember that I explained that the dog was only a sort of half-chief; as a matter of fact he is the son-in-law of the true Comanche chief, and my father had little difficulty in getting him condemned to death. I don't think the old people like him very well; they have often spoken of his selfishness and bad temper. So the whole thing was quite easily arranged, and you need not be afraid that you have made the least trouble for anyone."

"Anne," asked Shiloh, sick with fear of the answer, "is the man dead?"

"You are a funny impatient angel, aren't you?" laughed Anne; her eyes were worshipful as she looked at him. "Do you know, I really believed that you might be vexed with me, and scold me for this? But no, the man isn't dead yet, my sweet; he soon will be, however, and then I shall have proved my love to you beyond a doubt."

"Anne," said Shiloh, "go, while there is yet time, and save this unhappy creature from the fate which your atrocious cruelty has prepared for him."

If every silvered lock of Shiloh's hair had been a rattlesnake venomed with the Gorgon magic, Anne could not have been stricken into a stiffer image of despair. Her light and flexible limbs appeared to turn to stone or bronze; her eyes stared round and empty into Shiloh's, and they were blinded like a statue's eyes. She was too warmly tinted by the sun to grow pale; only her lips ceased to be rosy. All pride and happiness were expunged from her little face, leaving it cold and vacant and forlorn as the ashes of a fire.

She stood upright in the precise centre of the lodge; her hands were clenched and laid against her narrow thighs, her small feet were set close together upon the floor. She swayed very slightly as she stood, not with the supple grace of a living girl, but like a meagre disastrous image broken from its pedestal.

"Anne," said Shiloh, "I am sorry that I spoke so harshly to you just now. You are ill; let David look to you while I go to save this wretched man from death."

Anne shook her head slowly from side to side; her face was quite expressionless and rather stupid. "No," she said to Shiloh, "I will go myself. Please let me go; please do not speak to me again, but let me go."

She turned and walked from the room with languid deliberate steps; her air was curiously apathetic, and she moved as though she were intolerably weary.

Presently she returned and sat down beside Shiloh; she kept her eyes averted from his countenance, and her thin rigid body seemed to shrink from him in pain and terror.

"I have done what you commanded," she said in a breathless tired voice. "I did not mean to offend you, my darling. I loved you; I wanted to be revenged upon your enemy. It was all quite simple; I suppose that I am very wicked, but I do not really understand. This much I know: that you have looked at me in horror and repulsion; it is enough; it is finished for ever."

"Anne, my child," said Shiloh, taking her cold hand in his, "what is finished? I do not know what you mean."

"Why, life, of course," Anne replied briefly; she smiled as she spoke, but her lips were colder than her little hands.

" Oh, no; truly it isn't," Shiloh told her; he put his arms around her and drew her to him with remorseful tenderness. "I was wrong, my child, to speak as I did; we were both of us in error, you to injure the Comanche and I to hurt you by the harshness of my words. Let us forgive each other and be friends; I cannot pretend that I was not rather shocked, but I think I am beginning to understand, and I am ashamed of myself for making you miserable."

His voice was so gentle that Anne tried in vain to stop her tears; as well might she have hoped to staunch a wound piercing into the very core of her heart. She began to cry, hiding her face against Shiloh's shoulder.

" Good-bye, my beautiful darling," she said presently. " My father has talked to me of your departure to-morrow; I am glad that you are to have the horses and the stick as a safe-conduct, since you will not accept an escort. He believes, poor old man, that you may return and marry me after you have settled your affairs in California; I know of course that this can never be, but the hope pleases him, because he has taken a great fancy to you, and he sees that I love you with my entire soul. I am not mad enough to dream of such happiness; I am better able to imagine hell than heaven; it is my Puritan inheritance, I suppose. Good-bye, my love, forever; do not forget that I love you. I am your bondwoman; I am your slave; perhaps in heaven I shall be permitted to serve you."

Shiloh had none of that pinched deformity of spirit which hates a love it cannot reciprocate in kind; his nature owned an innocent gratitude for all affection. Now he took the adoration of this singular child with a simplicity which comforted her tears and laid a delicate balsam of peace upon her heart.

He was too noble to hurt her by indifference and too sensitive to humiliate her by pity. " Good-bye, my dear child," he said. " I shall always remember you; I shall always love you, if you will believe it. Perhaps some day I may return; meanwhile there is a brotherly and sisterly pledge between us which shall never be broken."

" You are an angel," said Anne. " Good-bye, my darling."

She bent her head over his hands and kissed them; then quickly she stooped to lay a light elusive kiss upon the toes of his moccasins.

" That's my true way of kissing you, my love," she whispered as she went from him.

She went swiftly, like a flame blown out by the breath of doom; the flame was wild and fluttering and torn, but lovely again as a flower and brave as the fringed banner of a forlorn hope. It was a living girl who flew from the room on ragged wings of sorrow, and life was not really over, and the forlorn hope was a hope of heaven.

4

THE REMAINDER of the journey to Santa Fé was marked by many strange adventures, but these were fortunate and rapid in their course, and the two friends reached San Fernandez de Taos without serious mishap. It was obviously unwise of Shiloh to travel before the wound above his temple was completely healed; the fact remains that the hazard was unattended by unpleasant results.

When he removed the bandage for the last time it was evident that, although the scar was so neat as to be well-nigh invisible, a pale miraculous plume of pure silver had sprouted among the locks surrounding it; the circumstance cannot be said to have altered Shiloh's appearance for the worse. He looked an amazingly slim and comely creature astride the splendid horse which the Cheyenne chief had given him at parting.

These horses carried them over certain difficulties which might otherwise have soared into portentous dangers, and the painted stick with its eccentric characters of men and beasts was a sure passport from tribe to tribe of Indians. The Comanches accepted it as a friendly sign, and because the Pawnees had recently consummated a treaty with the Cheyennes, the Pawnees smiled when they beheld the Cheyenne figures carved upon the wood.

The mules were exceedingly useful as pack-animals; now that the snow lay deeper in the valleys and dry and shallow along the foothills of the mountains, it was pleasant to be mounted upon a pair of spirited horses, and Shiloh and David were very sensible of their good luck.

Some few experiences befell them which Shiloh in particular found distressing, but they themselves went unmolested and unscathed through snow-storms and a moiety of peril, and no great white grizzly crushed their bones for the vultures to pick. They found plenty of fresh game of several varieties, and the dried beans and maize wherewith Anne had stuffed their saddle-bags were frequently seasoned with venison and savoury wild geese.

It was disappointing to discover that the Republican Pawnees were not republican but savage in the extreme, and appalling to observe certain of their ceremonies; it is possible that Shiloh's silver feather of hair grew whiter after an evening spent among them. He met with nothing but kindness at their hands, but those hands were so deeply dyed in blood that he was loath to touch them. When he beheld them fling the scalps of their enemies upon the ground and stamp upon them with loud triumphant cries he turned from their lodge to sleep in the snow under the frozen azure arch of heaven. David made a strong shelter from a fallen tree, and their buffalo robes were numerous and warm, but even if he must have stiffened into winter ice Shiloh could not have remained in the lodge.

The Comanches were even worse; there was a nightmare festival into which Shiloh stumbled weary from a twenty-mile ride across the mountains; he could not believe the evidence of his outraged senses as he watched the scene.

A score of Comanche warriors were clad in the barbarous skins of bears and panthers; upon their dark bosoms were suspended necklaces made from the teeth and claws of these ravening beasts. They kneeled in a wide circle upon the floor, crawling upon their hands and knees and growling like the creatures whose rough or spotted pelts they wore. Between them they had laid the hearts of their enemies, cut into small pieces; they showed their hatred for these pitiful trophies of poor flesh by the bestial sounds which escaped their throats; their faces were fixed in a calm ecstasy of malevolence.

Shiloh fled from this revolting spectacle as though all the yelping packs of hell had been close behind him; later he wished to return and chastise the Comanches in a measured anger, but David caught his bridle and compelled him onward into the snowy passes of the hills.

Now did these hills continually rise higher into thin pellucid air, and the wind grew swifter and colder with each advancing hour. At last, upon a morning of fair weather flawless and chill as tempered steel, they crossed the Sangre de Cristo pass and gazed at the great plain beyond it; at their left hand and behind them the mountains ascended into heaven in purity and splendour. No word was said as the friends paused upon the summit of the path to survey this wonder; David blinked at the dazzle of majesty, but Shiloh was like a blue-eyed eagle as he stared into the sun. Some transmutation of glory was performed within his own mind, so that its actual convolutions came to hold the meaning of that crystal universe and to exalt it into a clear abstract perfection of language; there are those who would sell their souls into darkness for a knowledge of the syllables which flowed like a stream of snow-water through Shiloh's mind.

San Fernandez de Taos was a small town of white adobe houses; they approached it by the Spanish road as the Angelus was ringing, and beheld it like a holy city perched against the curtain of a steep blue hill. Once having gained its narrow streets, it was revealed to them as no more than a dusty village; they welcomed it as the end of the day's march and the meeting-place of their mortal kind. David might drink Taos lightning to his heart's content, and Shiloh might ask questions about politics in the fine literary periods he had learned from Calderón; it was good to rub shoulders with humanity again, and the world appeared warm and tractable in the light of a yellow moon to southward.

Contrary to their first expectations, they were not thrown into prison; the alcalde merely demanded the invoice of their goods, and later accepted a trifling gift in lieu of the non-existent document. When he realised that they had nothing to sell he was amazed but sympathetic; Shiloh's manners effected their usual enchantment upon the man, and by seven o'clock he had introduced them to the priest and invited them to a fandango at his own dwelling.

The occasion was cheerful, although somewhat shrill and odorous; Shiloh disliked the heat and clamour, but he confessed to a pleasure in the gay and childlike character of the assembly. He made a temperate supper of tortillas and milk; he did not greatly appreciate red peppers, and mescal appealed to him not at all. He attracted the favourable attention of at least twenty ladies, and for a while he talked to these in Spanish with that grave courtesy which gave the last refinement to his charm. Finally he grew tired of this exercise in patience; the last they saw of him that night was the flying fringe of his buckskins and the alarmed scintillation of his large blue eyes.

Shiloh and David slept in a neatly whitewashed room adorned with the image of a saint and a crucifix of brass nailed to a wooden cross. They agreed that they had been used with the utmost hospitality in Taos, and that it would be delightful to be gone along the road to Santa Fé.

"Davy, it is actually beginning to be warm in the sun at its meridian," cried Shiloh three days later, reining in his horse and flinging his coonskin cap to the moderated breeze.

"So it is, but I reckon you'll get too much of the goldarned sun afore you makes California," replied David rather sourly. He had drunk an excessive quantity of mescal overnight in the little hamlet of Elgidonis, and for once he envied Shiloh his devotion to China tea. The luminous glimmer of the distant snows was cool and sweet, but the heat of the sun upon his forehead was distinctly unpleasant.

"Pick up your cap, you crazy loon; it's a fine cap, and we can't afford to go chucking things away like that; a Mexican might give you a good gallon of mescal for that there cap."

"But I don't like mescal," said Shiloh; nevertheless he recovered the cap from the dusty ground, and he was enchanted to observe that the dust was warm beneath his moccasins.

"Well, I like mescal; reckon I like it too goldarned much," David admitted. "It tastes kinda like crab-apple cider we used to have in Maine."

It was perfectly true that the weather was changing with the winding downward road; the nights were still intensely cold, but the noons lay bright under a rain of arrows from the sun which pierced to the lively skeleton within Shiloh's skin and filled his very bones with rapture. He had always hated to be cold; now he was thawed and comforted like a golden snake in the spring-time.

Therefore he was inclined to be pleased with the city of Santa Fé de San Francisco; it wore an air sufficiently southern and out-landish to appear spiritually friendly to himself. The mountain towering to the east, veiled in perpetual whiteness, the cascading stream drawn from its glaciers, the houses pale or yellow against the extreme blue sky, the nameless colour of the aspens whose silver leaves were fallen into dust, these things were acceptable to him by reason of their austral form and atmosphere. To walk upon the flat roofs of the palacio in the cool of the evening was delightful; it was fortunate for Shiloh that the governor had re-ceived him as an honoured guest.

The large loud bells in all the churches began to ring for the Angelus; Shiloh was sorry that there was to be a feast and a fandango that evening, with a guitar and a violin, and a vast sup-per of beef and frijoles and chile, followed by wine from the Paso del Norte. He liked the chocolate, and hoped that he might be permitted to drink only that; the salads of green peppers were also innocuous to his taste. The Mexican ladies looked romantic from a distance, but when he spoke to them he was faintly troubled by the fact that a flavour of garlic still lingered upon lips marked by an epicene pencilling of moustache. He had a suspicion that they wanted to gobble him up with a clove of garlic.

"Davy, I wish we could run away to-night instead of to-morrow," he said to his friend with a plaintive sigh.

"Well, you gotta jabber a powerful lot of Spanish to-night to that old fool of a governor to make him give us a proper passport for California," replied David with his customary good sense. "Besides, by graminy, we need a bit of advice about Injuns, and crossing the desert, and that there canoe and everything; you'll be so took up with the old codger that none of them god-damned women can come a-pestering and a-plaguing of you, thank the Lord."

"I do," said Shiloh pensively, as he turned from the evening stars to the vociferous fandango.

" You see," explained Shiloh to the governor as soon as supper was over, " I have always been fond of boats; big boats and little boats, from the frailest cockleshell to the noblest galleon. Therefore your suggestion of proceeding down the Hila river by means of a canoe is particularly pleasing to my mind."

" My dear young friend," said the governor, thoughtfully lighting a cheroot, " I believe that the thing can be accomplished; the Indians have done it often, and if you are going to San Diego there is no manner of use in your taking the northerly Los Angeles trail. But the expedition will be both difficult and dangerous; I wish you would remain in Santa Fé."

" *Vive Dios!* " said Shiloh, who had heard these sentiments so often and from so many different people that he was beginning to weary of their sound. " But I really can't, you know; I never remain very long anywhere, to tell you the truth. I do not wish to appear discourteous, and of course your city is a charming spot, but I assure you that I must leave for California not later than to-morrow morning."

" Very well," replied the governor in a tone of resignation; " you know best about your own affairs, my boy; we shall be sorry to see you go, but I will give you excellent certificates and the most sagacious advice which it lies in my power to provide. Now, touching the matter of the canoe . . ."

In this fashion it came to pass that Shiloh and David set forth next morning under an unsullied sky, with every possible precaution against disaster neatly packed in their pockets and saddlebags. Their brains also were well stocked with admirable counsel, and their spirits rose in affinity with the fine ascension of the sun above their journey.

Shiloh indeed was so happy that he almost believed that his soul had left his body to fly beyond it along the western path; it might return to him at rapid intervals to circle about his head like a swallow, but it flew onward again each time. His happiness was far too swift to be held back by the galloping hooves of his horse; he knew that it had wings to leave the body, and he marvelled at its faithfulness in returning to its cage.

" I'll be switched if I see how you can stand this blazing hell-fire of a sun and never turn one of them crazy grey hairs," grumbled David long before they had reached the Hila river. The sun was not really hot; it was only glassy bright and shadowless at noon, and Shiloh's bones absorbed it to their marrow. He was beginning to forget that he had ever hated this season of the year. It was now the middle of February; the nights were still freezing, and winter prevailed upon the hills, but on the broad mesas about Albuquerque the thin dry air was delicately cold like wine.

They followed the course of the Rio del Norte southward, turning from it at last to find the young stream of the Hila among the sands. David swore that the land was no better than a barren waste; he would have fled to the water-brooks of the foot-hills with their groves of piñon and cedar if Shiloh had consented to come with him.

"Have you forgotten Silver?" Shiloh asked, and David shook his head and scowled at the horizon.

"There's something horrible a-laying for us over yonder," he said. "Can't rightly figger it out, whether it's a man or an animal or a ghost or just a kinda blurry wickedness, but it's there, and it's a-laying for us."

"Nonsense, Davy; I never listened to such nonsense in all my life." Shiloh laughed; he was in a continual effervescence of health and spirits, and he did not believe a word of David's melancholy predictions.

He loved the chances and changes of their roving life; the strange pale rainbow of the desert colours, the fantastic meals of aloes and beaver tails; he tasted the *miel de tuna* with approval because it was made from the juices of the prickly pear. The Indians of this country were mild and amicable; their festivals were not murderous, and although they looked fierce enough in their varnish of scarlet paint, Shiloh soon learned that this savage decoration was a sign of friendship.

"I think the practices of the Brothers of Light are far more barbarous," said Shiloh, turning pale with the recollection of the thing he had witnessed one midnight near Santa Fé.

Now that they had come to the Hila they remembered their intention of purchasing a canoe from the Indians; finally they succeeded in buying a small boat rudely hollowed from a tree-trunk. They had to pay several beaver-skins and a vast quantity of powder and ball for this, but when they had actually obtained it Shiloh's felicity was complete.

"Ah, this is something rather better than heaven," he said, lying supine in the bottom of the canoe and staring upward at the immaculate azure of the sky.

"Well," answered David, "you won't never make no progress a-laying on your back and looking at the sun with them saucer eyes of yours as ought to have been blinded afore this what with all them lousy books and all."

"What an adjective to apply to Æschylus!" said Shiloh, putting the unopened volume into his pocket and seizing the paddle with a pair of remarkably sunburnt hands.

It was difficult to compel Shiloh's spirited horse to learn the pace of a pack-animal, but by hook or by crook of fiery will the stubborn human creature charmed the beast into submission, and for ten enchanted days Shiloh floated down the surface of the river, living in magical reality the very progress of a dream.

"'Through death and birth to a diviner day,'" said Shiloh in the accents of beatitude.

A day came all too soon, mortal enough and sad, when he was forced to abandon the beloved boat and journey across the desert to the Red river, which the Spaniards call the Colorado. And even now he was happy; he was disembodied from his past and flying into a future which could only be beautiful and kind.

"Blamed if you wasn't patting the god-damned varmint on the head!" David declared when he discovered Shiloh gazing at a rattlesnake with innocent curiosity. Of course the statement was not strictly true, but it had enough of truth in it to make them both laugh uproariously. Nevertheless each slept with a hair riata wound around him, for it was senseless to perish on the threshold of adventure by the malice of a serpent's sting.

These were the days in which Shiloh made a number of little songs which he never took the trouble to transcribe; delightful little songs they were, dealing with snakes and coyotes and the queer burrowing owl which inhabits a hole in the ground. David liked them enormously, and they seemed an agreeable accompaniment to the fall of darkness over the opalescent shiver of light along the painted plain.

David had trapped a great many beavers on the Hila river, jerking their flesh in the pure dry sunshine, and they had plenty of parched corn and beans and coffee in their packs. By the time they reached the grassy prairies and the cottonwoods of the Colorado they had almost forgotten David's nightmare of prophecy.

The gigantic Yuma Indians of the Colorado wore loin-cloths given them by the Christians in the Spanish Settlements of California. This drew the hope of an ending to their journey warmly around the travellers' hearts. These Indians were dark-skinned and strong; they often went entirely naked, and the hair of the women fell to their narrow brown insteps.

David was appalled by their immodesty, but Shiloh thought it a very edifying state of nature, and wished he could have told Mr. and Mrs. Newton about it in Chester Square. He knew that this excellent couple would have shared his own horror at the Yumas' regrettable habit of dining upon the flesh of fatted dogs served without bread or salt.

These men carried bows of tough and elastic wood which the Spaniards call tarnio, fitted with reed arrows of an equal length. Their women wore snail-shells upon the ends of their long black tresses, and Shiloh thought that not even the Witch of Atlas had ever met with stranger creatures of the solitudes.

From these Indians David and Shiloh purchased another canoe; Shiloh was supremely glad of its possession, and as they floated downward towards the mouth of the Colorado, borne by a rapid current between banks of lofty cottonwood trees, it appeared indeed that they were nearing the glad conclusion of their toil. The new leaves of April flickered in the wind.

They floated pleasantly through warm and sunny airs; there was an abundance of beaver meat, and they saw numbers of wild geese and pelicans. So they floated for close upon a hundred miles; David himself was persuaded that their dangers were at an end, and Shiloh existed in a simple paradise of his own contriving which was fresh and innocent as April leaves.

He looked upon the face of Silver's miniature every evening before he slept; she seemed the titulary saint of this peacefulness, and her shadowy eyes held lovelier images than sleep or even death.

"'Of neither would I ask the boon . . .'" said Shiloh, as if he had been saying his prayers.

At last they met a great chief of the Yumas who told them by signs that he had been to the Spanish Settlements, giving a very tolerable imitation of the breaking of surf along the shore. This venerable man raised the expectations of the travellers to the point of tears; it seemed a wild and poignant thing to hear this echo of the sea in his voice. He was astonished at the whiteness of their skins, and gazed with awe and admiration at the flaxen gold of David's hair and the ocean colour of Shiloh's eyes.

They floated onward for three days, and then suddenly they knew that the current was against them, and that they were upon the eddies of a tidal river. The knowledge was bitterer than the brine mixed in the swirling waters under their bows.

"We cannot follow the river any longer," said Shiloh. "The governor's map may have been traced by guess-work, but it shows quite plainly that the river flows into a great gulf which is set on the wrong side of the peninsula. We must take the mules and horses and strike across country. It is a pity, but it cannot be helped."

"Away from the river?" asked David. "Aw, Shiloh, surely that's a god-damned crazy plan! It's getting terrible hot, and we can't never last long away from the river." His eyes ached with the fear of leaving the water and the young green of the cotton-wood trees.

"If you think there is danger from thirst," said Shiloh, "perhaps we had better set the pack-animals free; perhaps they will seek out a Yuma village, but I hope they may run wild over these plains for ever, defying man. It is a pleasant fancy in the midst of our considerable worries. If you wish, we may start out upon the horses; we can pack enough for a few days' travel on our saddle-bows, and then if the supply of water fails us we can free the horses also; I should be sorry to subject them to the tortures of thirst."

"But how about us ourselves?" inquired David. "Don't you give a rap about the tortures of thirst for us poor critters?"

"It's rather different, Davy," said Shiloh. "We are reasonable beings, and free to choose in this dilemma."

"Well, I ain't free to choose, not with you so goldarned stubborn as you are, unless I was to leave you to your fate, and that I'll never do, so help me God, even if it was deserved, which it ain't, you being the god-damn decentest man alive, if a bit lunatic, and I ain't forgotten that vow, and to hell with everything, I'm a-coming with you, old catawampus," replied David under his breath.

"The thing I can't exactly figger," he said presently, "is whether it's better to take the mules along and walk, and have more provisions, or take the hosses and ride, and so get along at a smarter rate of speed. Seems to me we'd better start with the whole shooting-match, and then see how things work out for us later."

"Very well; I will agree to that undertaking," said Shiloh. "Only we must send the poor things back to the river if we can find no water."

"And keep right on ourselves, no matter what happens?" asked David.

"Of course," said Shiloh. "That is what we came to do, isn't it? To go on until we had found Silver."

"I reckon so," said David. "Yes, I reckon as you're right, but well . . . for cris'sake!"

They filled every available canteen and flask with water, and started early in the clear and exquisite dawn, which turned to a brassy glare by midday. It was evident that they could never hope to carry enough water for the horses and mules; by noon Shiloh was so frantic with pity for their brute thirst that David with great difficulty prevented him from sharing his own portion of water with the animals. At the evening halt they turned the horses loose and watched them dash away in the direction of the river with a feeling of relief, which in David's mind was tinctured with a desperate envy.

"But anyways, we come pretty far to-day because of 'em, and I'm kinda thankful they're a-going to see them fresh green cottonwoods above the water again. Reckon the mules can hold out for another day; they're hardier, and mebbe we'll find water by to-morrow night."

But Shiloh could not wait for to-morrow night; he lay thinking how thirsty the mules must be, and he could not sleep, for he was rather thirsty himself, and his imagination credited the poor beasts with the endurance of torture. David was snoring peacefully, but he had piled all the water-bottles about his pillow, and Shiloh knew that he would wake the instant one of them was touched by the stealthiest hand. He rose, and stood looking at David; then he tiptoed very softly to the place where the mules were tethered and unloosed the ropes.

"*Adios, amigos,*" he whispered to them as they disappeared into the hot starry darkness. He had forgotten to remove the bell from about the neck of the little mare; it tinkled sweetly as she ran, and roused David from his slumbers.

"Might 'a' known you'd do it, drat me for a fool," was David's comment. "Well, I could see as you was half out of your wits all day, worrying about it; you was bound to take leave of your senses, I reckon, soon as you started figgering out how the poor dumb critters was a-feeling. Wish I'd 'a' told 'em to give my regards to them cottonwoods along the river, for I'd like goddamned well to get a sight of 'em to-night."

The morning revealed a singular landscape: for miles around them stretched a plain of harsh and salty sand; there was no tree, and no charitable sign of water. They took from the packs the little they were able to carry; already they were tired, for the heat was intense, and in their minds was a sorrowful assurance of ruin.

"I am afraid I rather sacrificed you to the mules, Davy, but I could not bear it another moment, and I hope you will forgive me," said Shiloh.

"You got to forgive yourself, too; it's as bad for you as it is for me," David told him sombrely. The words reminded Shiloh of Sir Philip Sidney, but there was not the pure customary delight in the recollection. The packs were heavy, and the water in the flasks could not last for ever.

"Good God almighty, is that a lake a-shining in the sun?"

cried David the next morning after they had walked for perhaps two hours under a blazing sky which turned continually from gold to cruel fire.

"It is; it must be," said Shiloh in a queer hoarse voice. He was very obstinate about not admitting that he was thirsty, but David guessed at his sensations from his own, and he was not surprised at the strange croaking sound of Shiloh's voice.

The water in the flasks had dwindled to a pitiful drop of mercy between themselves and hell, and now they were always thirsty and feverish, with a horrid crack-brained lightness in their heads. The sparkle of the lake in the sun was dizzy and sweet.

It was deliverance; they walked towards it slowly, because they were very tired, but at the last they ran and stumbled to its brink. They knelt down and tasted the water, and it was salter than the waters of the sea. Their eyes, which were withered with thirst like the rest of their bodies, refused them tears; nevertheless they felt their hearts as well as their brains crack within them with a crazy sound of drouth.

"Shiloh, are you thirsty?" asked David in the wide lunatic stare of the next noonday; he knew that he was trying to hurt Shiloh, and he had forgotten why he was doing it. His own torment was so acute that it had set a temporary madness upon his mind, and now for the first time in his life he tried to hurt his friend. There was no water left in the flasks; the drop upon their tongues last night had been hot and poisonous with despair.

"Are you thirsty?" he repeated, and wondered what he was saying.

"Not particularly," said Shiloh in a rustling whisper.

"You know you are, you know you are, and by God you got to admit it," persisted David; he moved and spoke like some dreadful automaton, and all his body was parched and burnt to the colour of dull red earth. Only his hair caught the brightness of the sun in brightness above the stupid agony of his forehead.

"No," said Shiloh, never moving his eyes from the far horizon.

Shiloh himself was shrivelled up into a scarecrow; he was so thin that the slight bones of his skeleton were plain to see, very elegantly formed and neatly articulated under the fragile tissue of his skin, that appeared no more substantial than a dead leaf in the wind.

His eyes were sunken in his head; the blue of the iris was incredibly brilliant in the hollows under the brow.

Last night after they had drunk the last feverish drop of water, they had scraped away the surface of the burning sand to find the cooler soil beneath; in these narrow graves they had lain down stark naked to endure the tortures of hell within their living flesh. David had slept for a few hours; Shiloh had never closed his eyes against the pointed fires of the stars. It was no wonder that his eyes were like consuming fires in their sockets.

Now he never moved his eyes from the far horizon, where a mountain of pure crystal glittered in the sunshine; Shiloh knew that the imponderable cloud of light was real, but it appeared silvery and dissolving as a single snowflake. It was far away, and very far away; it was not given to a mortal to attain such mountain-heights.

He was aware that he was traversing a little hill; he was so weary that it seemed a brutal labour to reach even the summit of a little hill. He climbed this mean eminence and paused because he could go no farther; his heart was knocking against his ribs, and all the veins of his body were filled with hellish flame. For a moment the clarity of his sight was darkened; when he looked at the earth again he perceived a small transparent stream of snow-water flowing softly under the hill. He could not believe his vision.

He touched David's arm and pointed to the water; he was beyond the power of speech, and a fear descended upon his heart lest he should die before he could reach the stream of snow-water.

He went forward lightly and quickly, moved by some obscure courage of the will; he fell down by the side of the water, and looking into it he saw quite plainly not his own face but that of another.

"Arethusa!" said Shiloh in no voice at all; of course he had meant to say Silver, but being very tired he called upon the glimmering image by the sweet name of Arethusa. Then he fainted quietly and lay with his face beneath the cool smooth surface of the stream; if David had not somehow found the strength to drag him backward, he must indubitably have been drowned.

The Orphan Angel

X

DOUBTLESS THERE IS A PLACE OF PEACE

WHEN the Indians carried Shiloh into the mission of Santa Caterina, the Dominicans all believed that he would die, but David knew better. After they had found the snow-stream there had never been any question of dying; suffering was another matter, and there had been plenty of that in the past fortnight, but Shiloh was alive, and David saw that he intended to remain so until he had come face to face with Silver.

Afterwards was still another question; David had a strange conviction that Shiloh might take it into his head to attempt to cross the Pacific on foot or to jump over a mountain-top or the moon, but for a time at least the silver cord remained unbroken which bound him to the earth, and ultimately it must lead him to San Diego.

For two weeks they had wandered like a pair of scorched revisitants from hell, over the high passes and along the valleys of the creeks bordered with palms and live-oaks, fainting and falling and rising to stumble onward, but always within touch and smell and blessed taste of water. The Indians had succoured them intermittently with roasted mescal and a thin gruel of maize, but their starvation was beyond hunger; it was the shadow of the trees and

618

the chill of the streams which they devoured like bread and wine. David soon regained the admirable power of his muscles, but his mind was shaken as by an assault of devils; Shiloh, who was worn away to a phantom, had never lost the piercing lightning of his intellect or the wildfire of his will. So they were enabled each to help the other during this period of their return to life, but when they entered the Dominican mission of Santa Caterina upon a clear evening of early May the shade of death was still visible over their countenances.

"But the poor boy cannot possibly recover; we must convert him to the faith, and then at least we shall have wrought a cure of the soul, but his body we cannot save," the good brothers told themselves concerning Shiloh. They little knew the gentleman who had come among them; it is difficult to say in which prophecy they were more lamentably at fault. In the matter of the conversion their disappointment was great; the fact that Shiloh did not die also affected them with a mild regret, because already he appeared to be a spirit divorced from the frail remnant of his flesh, and they loved him in a mood of elegy which was sadly wasted upon a living man.

"Told the goldarned idjits you was going to fool 'em yet, and you done it," said David triumphantly the morning they left the mission. His limited Spanish had not permitted him to speak his full mind to the Dominicans, but he had been annoyed by the manner in which they had prayed over Shiloh.

"Of course they were amazingly good to me," said Shiloh, who had been excruciatingly bored by the attentions which his body and soul had received.

They were travelling in a southwesterly direction, with letters for the neighbouring mission of San Sebastian. Their excellent certificates from the governor at Santa Fé had satisfied the military authorities, and they had been allowed to leave without an escort. Now they were approaching the sea-coast, and the surrounding vegetation was rich and paradisal with flowers.

Shiloh had made a truly surprising recovery; he sniffed the air flavoured with salt and honey and felt himself strong again. The skin-and-bone which was left of him composed a light effective engine for speed, and he was so deeply burned by the desert sun that he seemed to have absorbed a portion of its light, so that his fair complexion must hold colours of fire and gold for ever.

The scene was beautiful beyond imagination as they drew close to the shore, having traversed a range of lofty hills; the lower slopes of these were covered with a profusion of blue lupin and pale orange poppies, and as they descended into the green vineyards of the valley they moved in an atmosphere of honeysuckle and jasmine. The orange groves sheltered them at noon, but the wind was always cool from the Pacific, and along the King's Highway to San Sebastian there was no shadow more profound than the sweet shadow of the trees.

By this road, which the Spaniards call El Camino Real, they travelled from mission to mission, coming to San Diego in seven days, gathering wild honey from the blossoms of the mescal and supping on tortillas and fat mutton by candlelight. They reached the cliffs which overhang the sea, high pinnacles on which the waves are poured in tides, and beheld strange monsters, otters and seals and sharks and great whales spouting rainbows in the sunshine. The plains were spread with clover around the port of Todos Santos, where herds of horses and cattle roamed and pastured. This was the road which Junipero Serra had marked out by handfuls of mustard-seed flung along its sides, so that in spring he had walked between walls of yellow blossoms shoulder-high and loud with bees.

When at last they came to San Diego a soldier immediately arrested them, much to Shiloh's annoyance; he observed that the religious orders were more humane than the military. Their passports appeared to impress the corporal, and finally they were ushered into the general's presence. He looked at the certificates and smiled an amiable smile; they realised with relief that they would not be forced to spend the night in a cell among the legions of the Spanish fleas.

"Good," he said to Shiloh. "The governor at Santa Fé seems to have a high opinion of your characters; I trust that you will endeavour to deserve it. You are going to visit Don Narciso de Coronel upon important business; let me advise you to procure some more respectable clothes before doing so, lest he believe you to be persons of no importance whatever."

So it came about that at five o'clock on an afternoon of warm ambrosial May weather, Shiloh woke from a trance of hurry and fatigue to discover himself proceeding slowly along the gentle acclivity of a hill; he was aware that he was going to the *casa de campo* of Don Narciso de Coronel. He had a delightful sense of leisure and holiday; he had spent the entire morning in preparation for this event, and it had been a dull and wearisome affair to find lodgings where one was allowed to take a bath, and to buy the respectable apparel suitable for a visit to the country estate of a Californian gentleman. Now these details were happily arranged, and Shiloh felt extremely clean and civilised in his exotic new garments.

Exotic they certainly appeared to him; he had sought high and low for a suit with a reasonable English cut, but of course he had been forced to accept the Spanish mode at last. There was nothing else to be had in San Diego; Shiloh was the least self-conscious of men, but he had a light amused notion that he must look rather a fool in this black-and-silver raiment, which was nevertheless the plainest fashion to be purchased in town.

"Unless you dress like a peon," the general had advised him at parting. "And you must not present yourself before Don Narciso dressed like a peon."

Now the truth of the matter was that Shiloh bore not the remotest resemblance to a fool; he looked the most elegant and charming creature under heaven in his costume of a Spanish gentleman, and the fact that he was excessively thin and that his hair was silvered by fever and privation lent a subtle and distinguished grace to his aristocratic appearance.

It may be possible that a woman of sensibility could have beheld him at this moment and failed to fall in love with him; certainly no such extravagant miracle occurred that afternoon. Sylvie la Croix was sitting under a white rose-tree upon the confines of her cousin's garden; when she looked up from her needlework she perceived Shiloh approaching slowly along the road; he carried his broad-brimmed hat in his hand, and the wind was ruffling his hair into eccentric silver feathers. His sense of leisure and holiday had set a smile upon his lips; he was glad to be coming to this place at last, but his heart held no heaviness of awe or sorrow. The ecstasy of the instant was casual and delicious as the discovery of a wild strawberry or a white violet; here was no end to a long and hazardous quest, but the young untroubled beginning of happiness.

2

THE GARDEN was bounded by walls of cream-coloured stucco over which roses of all imaginable tints and fragrances made a tracery of summer, and there were hedges of cypress and beds of heliotrope. The house itself was almost hidden among trees, yellow acacia, and olive and dark evergreen; Shiloh could see its red Spanish tiles and the sun upon its whitewashed plaster. It looked cool and pleasant among the trees, as if it might be a house which peace had taken for a dwelling-place. It was the home of Sylvie la Croix, and Sylvie was sitting under a white rose-tree in the shadow of the cypress-hedge; even in the shadow he could see the silver-gold of her hair and the strange colour of her eyes.

Her eyes were of no known colour under the sun; under the moon, Shiloh believed it were better to say, for there was more of moonlight than of sunlight in their grey-and-golden depth, and more of dusk than of morning in their lashes. These eyes gazed at him from the shadow of the cypress-hedge, and even he, for whom all language was but the instrument of his art, could find no word to tell their colour.

"I believe," said Shiloh, whose manners were always enchanting, "that you must be Sylvie la Croix."

He said it with a smile; such a smile might have broken the heart of a stone to jocund spring-water. To his amazement Sylvie rose swiftly to her feet and ran across the garden into the doorway of the patio; he caught the frightened luminous glance she gave him as she passed.

If Shiloh had been in the habit of swearing he would have declared that he was damned; he whistled softly and unskilfully and walked towards the door of the house in silence. Five minutes later he had introduced himself to Don Narciso de Coronel, and had given him a letter from Monsieur Saint-Ange.

Don Narciso was a little man, very suave and gentle in his

speech; his tongue caressed the pure Castilian into music. His hair and pointed beard were inky against the pallor of his plump cheeks; his eyes were bright with urbanity and wisdom.

"But how kind of you to interest yourself in the poor child!" he cried with great cordiality after he had read the letter. "She is indeed fortunate to have the friendship of such an one as you, so obviously a man of the world and a person of impeccable breeding. Her own heredity is so deplorable, so tragic on her poor mother's side and so disgraceful on her father's, that I have despaired of settling her in life as I had once hoped to do. My wife dislikes her intensely, my daughters will have nothing to do with her, our friends are unaware of her existence. It is a thousand pities that I ever undertook to look after her; she is what the Orientals call a little white camel upon my hands."

"That is easily mended," said Shiloh rather stiffly. "I have promised Saint-Ange to bring her back to him if she will consent to come. I hope you will trust her in my keeping for the journey; I shall endeavour to acquit myself as a wise and tender guardian."

"I am sure you will, my dear sir," replied Don Narciso, laughing in a manner which affected Shiloh's mind most unpleasantly. "But why should you take all the trouble to carry her back to Saint-Ange? Why don't you keep her yourself? I should be overjoyed to have your superior presence among the somewhat dull society of this town, and I am sure that the climate of California would agree with you. You look rather delicate, you know, and as if the rigours of a northern winter might undo you; you had better settle down in California and take Sylvie off my hands for ever."

"Well," said Shiloh thoughtfully, "I have often considered the advisability of adopting an orphan, and naturally my sentiments towards Sylvie are the most affectionate and benevolent. But my affairs are greatly embarrassed at present, and I believe Saint-Ange were a more suitable guardian than myself for the child."

"I was not thinking of guardians," said Don Narciso in a soft and pensive voice. "After all, you are both young; you are patently a very charming person, and the girl has the merit of being pretty and docile in the extreme. I suggest that you find a small *casa de campo* with a shady garden, and permit yourself that rest and refreshment of the nerves of which you stand so obviously in need. It is evident to me that for this long while your life must have lacked the consolations which only a loving woman can bestow."

"But," said Shiloh, "I have to inform you that I am already married." He spoke haughtily, because he resented Don Narciso's comments upon his personal appearance and was profoundly shocked by the man's impertinence.

"So I supposed," replied Don Narciso. "No gentleman of your distinguished type ever escaped matrimony until his hair was grey; if you had escaped, my poor boy, those locks would not be whitened. I merely intended to propose an amicable arrangement whereby our little Sylvie may benefit by your chivalrous protection and you may find a cook and housekeeper who is also a loving friend. My own reward would lie in the assurance of your mutual happiness and my recovered domestic peace. My daughters are bitterly prejudiced against Sylvie, and my wife declares that it gives her an indigestion only to look at the child's pale putty-coloured hair and eyes like holes burned in a blanket."

"I should have said silver-gold and something else, possibly twilight," said Shiloh loyally. "But if I understand you rightly we are not talking of chivalry or of loving friends: you are plainly suggesting that this unfortunate girl should become my mistress."

He spoke with lofty indignation, and his eyes were cold and blue like Arctic ice. It cannot be denied that Shiloh had for a long time dreamed of Silver with a lover's mind; the thought of a mistress cherished and revered was not unnatural to his imagination or his life, and if another man had proposed the thing the event might have fallen with a different fortune. But Don Narciso was devoid of nobility and of that sensitive kindness which makes the rough world bearable; he was so wickedly eager to be rid of Sylvie and so cynically glad of Shiloh as her seducer that Shiloh shuddered in revolt against the base appeal. If the same suggestion had been made by Monsieur Saint-Ange it might have appeared innocuously romantic, gilded by that refined philosopher's gentle and ironic cast of soul; insinuated by Don Narciso de Coronel, the thing seemed foul and monstrous.

"Come, come," protested Don Narciso with a shrug, "this is very bald language indeed to apply to a poor orphan. Need we always call a fact by its ugliest name? I should prefer to think of my little cousin as the lady of your heart, or your true-love, or your valentine; there are twenty prettier words than the one you have employed."

If Don Narciso had shown Monsieur Saint-Ange's letter to Shiloh there is no telling what might have happened. This letter recommended Shiloh most highly to the Californian's hospitality; it also revealed a delicate suspicion that Shiloh's dearest hopes were set upon Sylvie la Croix. Monsieur Saint-Ange had written in that innocence of the spirit which the bitter cleverness of his brain could never quite destroy; he perceived no harm in the idyllic fancy of a union between these two children of his affection, and if Shiloh had read his exquisite dry phrases he would perhaps have been persuaded to the dream.

But now all was tarnished and polluted by the infamous pleasantries of Don Narciso de Coronel, and Shiloh turned away his countenance from the ruined vision thus unveiled. So by a singular chance a villain bound him to morality, where a virtuous man would have loosed him from its chains.

"I could never take such a cruel advantage of the child," said Shiloh firmly. "I marvel that you can calmly tender such a gift and look me in the face."

"These are very fine words, but they have no real meaning," replied Don Narciso with amusement. "My motives are perfectly disinterested, because you have already told me that you intend to convey Sylvie to St. Louis and return her to her former guardian; in any case I am rid of her, and that is all that matters. I am a soft-hearted fool, and I was sincerely desirous of seeing you comfortable and happy; if you choose to throw away your luck it is none of my business; I am sorry to have been officious."

Shiloh knew that he was speaking the truth; Don Narciso's character was certainly not elevated, but there was no mortal good in being angry with him. Like the rest of humanity, he lived according to his lights; these were not the stars, but no vehemence of righteous wrath could trim their wicks to splendour, and it were a waste of breath to blow them out entirely.

"But how, if I may ask," said Shiloh, because he wondered, "did you think that I could live in California, penniless as I am, and take proper care of Sylvie?"

"Because Saint-Ange writes that it is his intention to name you as his heir; for the present he means to make you a generous allowance in the contingency of your remaining in California. He wants you to return, of course, and yet he says that he is not too selfish to perceive that your own best happiness lies here; if you go back to St. Louis, where Sylvie was born, he could not honourably allow you to possess her; her mother was well known, and the higher circles of society are critical of such open sins. Here she has no position; my wife and daughters have never introduced her to their friends, nor allowed her to claim kinship with them. Her status is that of a governess or companion; it will cause no particular scandal if you seduce her."

"Good God," cried Shiloh, "have I taken leave of my senses?"

"I fancy," said Don Narciso suavely, "that the affecting farewell of which you speak occurred some time ago. Nevertheless you are the most engaging person whom I have ever met; the little fact that you dislike me is of no consequence in my estimate of your merit. Sylvie could not possibly have aspired to the hand of such a man; one sees at a glance that you are well born, well connected; your blood is gentle, perhaps noble, and I should not have been surprised to learn that you were a Spaniard."

"Thank you," said Shiloh crisply, "but I have no Latin blood; I am English." If he had ever been told that his ancestor was that Sir John Hawkwood whose wife was Donnina Visconti he had forgotten it long ago, and his opinion of baronets was not sufficiently high to tempt him to confirm Don Narciso's faith in his gentility.

"Well, I have always had an eye for a grandee; I confess that I am a bit of a snob, and your society would have been most acceptable to me in this neighbourhood," Don Narciso admitted with a sigh. "But you need not trouble to tell me how obstinate you are; you have fixed upon your course, and nothing can turn you aside. It is only such a pity, such a wild and foolish pity;

I wonder, my poor boy, do you realise all that you are rejecting when you turn away from California? Here is a country beautiful as heaven and far more amusing; here are women like pomegranates and men like Toledo blades; here are splendid horses to make the great land narrow to your impatience, and wine to strengthen you, and all manner of wholesome viands to steady you into health, and such wind and sunshine as might wake a dead man into impulsive ecstasies of living; can you turn from these things, you who are so tired, so desperately tired, and retrace your steps into the petty labyrinth and enigma of everyday? "

3

SHILOH did not answer him; of a sudden he was aware that he was indeed desperately tired. The face of Don Narciso de Coronel became bright with a wicked glittering brightness; his eyes were infernal diamonds for cutting the crystal of another's soul.

"Do you know, my poor boy," Don Narciso continued, " what it is you are losing when you turn away from Sylvie and give her to a desiccated old man to cherish in your stead? The old man will suck a little of her sweetness to prolong his dusty life; he will mean no harm, he will only make spiritual demands upon her, but her sweetness will be drained away; it will be a very horrid tragedy. Then the old man will die, having encumbered the earth too long, and Sylvie will never marry; she will wither into a poor little cobweb of grey sorrow, and all because she loves you, and has been waiting for you ever since she can remember. There she waits for you now, under the same cypress on the lawn; you may know her by the glimmer of the moonlight on her hair, for there is a crescent moon to-night, and Sylvie's hair is silver-gold like its curling gossamer."

Shiloh did not answer him: they stood and faced each other in the low white room among candle-flames kindled by magic on the moonlight-coloured walls. Shiloh stood very thin and erect as he faced Don Narciso, and it seemed to him that the infernal diamonds of the other's eyes were cutting into the quick of his soul as he stood there.

"Do you know, my poor boy," said Don Narciso, "what you have rejected in rejecting Sylvie? You have rejected yourself; you have rejected your desires, and your luminous dreaming mind; you have rejected your own soul. It is yourself that you reject in Sylvie, because you love her; you love this child, and when you turn from her you turn from all that is lovely, all that is innocent, all that is the peace of heaven."

"But that," said Shiloh suddenly, "is obviously absurd. You are turning it around, you are twisting it, you are blackening the moonlight and kindling an infernal planet in the nethermost pit to dizzy me. I cannot follow the whirl of this villainy; my mind is swift, but for once you go too fast for me; I know, however, that you are lying, and nothing can turn me widdershins against the power of my own will."

"Very well," replied Don Narciso with a whispering softness of music; "if that is the case, I shall say no more. You have beaten me, my fine lunatic grandee; you have held your own on ground that is mine by heredity and conquest, and perhaps I am not wholly sorry. Good-bye, and may God be with you if you care for His company."

"Who in heaven's name are you?" asked Shiloh with a shiver in his voice.

"You are perfectly well aware who I am," Don Narciso answered him. "Mine was an old name in heaven, and one that you have always admired."

"Good-bye," said Shiloh. "I suppose you are talking nonsense; I am too tired to follow you. I regret having been rude; I have not known what I was saying. Now I will bid you goodnight; to-morrow we must make some arrangement concerning Sylvie, in order to convey her to St. Louis; my friend David will wait upon you in the morning. I have the honour to wish you a very good-night."

"I shall not sleep a wink," said Don Narciso; "I shall be worrying about you, my poor demented child. Now let me send Sylvie to you with a refresco of lemons or a little wine and water. You appear quite exhausted; I am afraid our conversation has been too much for you."

"Not at all," said Shiloh. "You are completely mistaken.

Pray do not trouble Sylvie for anything of the kind; I am going immediately."

Shiloh turned and went from the room; as he passed into the moonlight he saw Sylvie waiting for him in the shadow of the porch. There was a small crescent moon in the sky which shed no more than the faintest glimmer upon her face, but he knew that she had been weeping.

"Sir," said Sylvie, speaking timidly in English, "is it true that you have brought me a letter from my guardian in St. Louis?"

Shiloh looked into her face; he saw that the nameless twilight of her eyes was intense and translucent with love for him. He saw the delicate pearly colours of her small face, the sweet heart-shape like a petal, the lips cooler than snow-water. He knew that the touch of her lips would be peace against the burning of his eyes.

He looked at her, not daring to speak, fearful lest his weariness should betray him by a word. He tried to send a subtle lightning of farewell from his mind to hers, he tried vainly to put the essence of his spirit into a look and teach her his heart for eternity. It was useless: Sylvie saw only a tall and haggard young man with hollow eyes like holes into the sky; she had fallen in love with this young man no later than five o'clock of that ambrosial afternoon, and it was sad that he was going to leave her without a word.

"Don't go," she said to him. "I wish you would wait for a little moment and tell me news of my home."

He shook his head, shaking his silvered locks into the air; she saw the stars of the sky through his hollow eyes, and he was gone upon the wind from the Pacific.

4

In the freshness of early morning Shiloh sat upon the summit of a hill and stared at the blue waters of the sea below him, where the waves were shattered into rainbows of cold spray against the coloured cliffs, which were deeply stained with ochre and orange and sunny rose. Dark ranks of cypresses were set between him and the east, and the sky's pure azure was unstained by any cloud.

He heard the bells ringing at the mission of Saint James of Alcala, and he wondered whether it might not be good to be a minor brother of an order dedicated to poverty like the Franciscans. He smiled to remember the day when he had walked with Peacock in the green English summer, and, coming to a vicarage with a corchorus in full flower along its garden wall, had all at once desired to enter the church and lead the quiet life of a scholar and a moralist. Peacock had been amazed into laughter; Shiloh had argued mildly that assent to the supernatural part of faith is merely technical, and Peacock had told him that he would find more restraint in the office than would suit his aspirations. Perhaps at that moment Peacock had been right, but now the sound of the Franciscan mission bell shed blessing like a fragrance upon the air.

"'Less oft is peace . . . less oft is peace . . .'" he repeated to himself, staring at the rainbows shattered along the cliffs.

Wrens and swallows were circling about his head, and the wind from the Pacific lifted the locks of his hair into wings. A Spanish brig was entering the harbour; the eagle clarity of his sight could distinguish the separate ropes of her rigging and the particoloured caps of the sailors upon her forward deck. Soon she would be departing for Valparaiso or China or other ends of the earth; there were great mountains in South America, and in China temples and lotus-flowers and the wisdom of a serpent mated with a dove.

He wondered idly whether David had reached the *casa de campo* of Don Narciso de Coronel, and whether his welcome would be worthy of David. For David was an honest boy, and kinder than bread to the hungry; Shiloh knew that David would die for him any plain working-day in the week.

"Aw, I'll go along to the old codger's and fix it with him about Silver," David had said the night before. "I was skeered to when you first asked me, but if you want me to, I'll go for you, and be damned to him for a Spanish galoot that ain't a-going to

awe me with no airs and graces. If you've got such a lousy headache as all that, I don't blame you for not hankering after another
walk to-morrow; I'll go up there instead of you, and you can lay
in the sun eating figs and grapes like it was the garden of Eden."

"Perhaps," said Shiloh, "if my head still aches in the morning,
I may be selfish enough to do precisely that." But there was no
"perhaps" in his mind as he said it; he meant very definitely to
send David to the Casa de Coronel to-morrow.

Now it was morning, and David had gone up the dust-
bloomed road in a rosy dawn, and Shiloh sat alone upon the summit of the cliffs and watched the past and the future, and the
present that was a succession of rainbows destroyed upon the
rocks below.

"Reckon I gotta tell her the truth about Jasper, Shiloh," David
had said with surprising finality before he departed. It seemed a
curious circumstance that David should dare such a decision, at
which even Shiloh might have boggled for an instant.

"I wonder, Davy; do you really believe that you must?" he
had inquired in some perturbation.

"I reckon it's my simple bounden duty to confess and ask her
to forgive me," replied David. "I'll just say to her sorta humble
and plain, 'Miss Silver, I was a-fighting with your brother, and I
fetched him a clip on the head that killed him, and as God is my
witness it wasn't never meant that way, and I'm sorry to the rock-
bottom of my soul, and I hope you'll excuse it and be friends.'"

"I see," said Shiloh. "I think you've put it very nicely, Davy;
but it may be rather a shock to her, you know."

"But don't I know it all too god-damned well, Shiloh, and
ain't that why I'm scared stiffer'n a new tarred rope when I think
about going up there alone?" cried David. "Aw, Shiloh, can't
you see your way to changing your mind and coming with me?
I can see as you feel like hell, but it don't seem natural in you,
somehow, to leave me go all alone when the hide's scared off me
at the idea."

Now Shiloh had his own motives for wishing David to go
alone; it was quite true that Don Narciso's conversation had given
him a splitting headache, but a headache could never have kept

Shiloh from performing what he conceived to be his duty, and his heart smote him as he told David a very noble lie.

"I would really rather not go to Casa Coronel again; I find myself exceedingly unwell, and I should only be a nuisance to you and a burden to myself. Go, Davy, and this once without me; after you have seen Silver you will not be frightened."

"Well, I reckon I'll just say to her that I'm in the place of her brother now, and that she's never to feel lonesome nor as if she hadn't nobody to protect her," declared David. "You don't figger it out that there's any real reason why her and me can't be friends, do you?"

"No real reason, Davy," said Shiloh.

"One other thing as I've been fixing to ask you, Shiloh," said David, "is whether or no — oh, I mean if — well, put it like this, sorta — was you — had you — that is to say, what was your intentions to Silver, in the way of loving?"

It was a relief to Shiloh to find that he could laugh, but nevertheless the phrase had a ridiculous poignancy that hurt him.

"'In the way of loving' my intentions are strictly honourable to Silver," he replied lightly. "I suppose there is no use in pretending that I don't know what you mean, Davy; you are asking me whether you have a clear field to win her for yourself if you can. You have; I should begin with the brotherly attitude if I were you, but there is no earthly obstacle . . ." He stopped, and David thought that he must have a very severe headache indeed.

"And I always had a notion that you was fond of her yourself, after you took to carrying her picture in your pocket," said David. "Funny, ain't it?"

"Very," said Shiloh. "I think I will go for a walk, Davy; wear your new clothes and don't forget that you must speak Spanish to Don Narciso. Tell him that you are prepared to take her back to St. Louis, and that you have sufficient money for her passage, and that you are a perfectly competent and reliable guardian for a regiment of orphans. Good luck to you, and don't use double negatives if you can avoid it."

Shiloh had hurried from their lodgings into the virginal dawn; it was very early, and a few stars swam like silver minnows in the violet pool of the sky. The sea was asleep; the waves were flattened and smooth as pearl, and a white mist softer than the breast of a gull rested upon the waters.

Shiloh had slept for perhaps three hours; he wrapped himself in his Spanish poncho and lay down on the dry grass at the summit of the cliff. He lay upon his back and stared at the stars, which presently swam into the invisible; then as the sun rose over the mountains he turned his head to watch it and took the flood of brightness into his eyes without blinking. It was as if a bitter golden balm had washed his eyes and brow; he was aware that his headache had quite disappeared, and that he was no longer unhappy.

He saw David come out of the yellow adobe house and walk quickly up the road which led to Casa Coronel; he would reach the place by nine o'clock. Shiloh had no doubt that by noon David and Sylvie would be friends; he wondered whether it would be one day or seven before they were innocent lovers.

"It is much the best way," he said aloud, and marvelled because he meant it.

5

THERE were many paths that he might take; they were spread fan-wise about him, like the spokes of a chariot wheel or the rays of the sun. Now that the bells were ringing in the mission of Saint James of Alcala he perceived that a little path led inland to the rose-red roofs and white adobe walls. The road to Casa Coronel lay broad and level in the sun; it climbed a hill, but the acclivity was never steep, and the fringe of the road was garlanded with honeysuckle. It would be an easy road to take; yesterday he had walked its entire length in a few hours. There was the road to Italy, which was very long and lay over his left shoulder as he faced the Pacific; to-night the sun would make another path for him along the sea, and pave it with a luminous moving pattern of ripples.

He did not remember that any path led back to Anne; his mind refused that dreadful way, which had burned in naked agony under the sun until death would have seemed a kindly shadow across it. Somewhere among his books, doubled back between the pages of Sophocles to mark a certain passage in the Antigone, he might one day find the feather of the great war-eagle that she had given him.

Last night he had been tired, but now he was not tired or troubled in any way; he sat under the pale blue sky in the centre of a circle of golden rays, and these were paths leading to the ends of the earth, or little paths leading to a church or a friend or a resting-place. The rainbows under the cliffs broke with a thunderous music among crystal flakes, and the music made words in his mind, but for the moment he was content to let them go free again like sea-birds and to sit above the waters all alone.

He knew that the miniature of Sylvie was in his pocket; he called her Silver to his own mind, and he could have made a song to her if he had chosen, but now she was no more to him than Arethusa rising from her couch of snows. Sylvie must be waking in Casa Coronel, and Shiloh hoped that she might wake in time to welcome David.

He would not take the trouble to draw the miniature of Sylvie from his pocket, but presently he would fumble with his slim brown fingers until he had found a pencil and a bit of paper, and he would catch the syllables that were filling his mind with music; they were wilder than sea-birds, but presently he would catch them quite easily in a little net of pencil-marks. It appeared a godlike prerogative, but for the moment he was content to wait.

His face was thin under the blowing wings of his hair, but its delicate bones were set in pure tranquillity. Only the incredible blue of his eyes, which were coloured like the sea, seemed variable with the sea's own brightness.

"'Less oft is peace . . . less oft is peace . . .'" said Shiloh, but smilingly, as if he loved the sound of the sad words.

Mr HODGE

& Mr HAZARD

"Why, let the stricken deer go weep,
  The hart ungallèd play;
  For some must watch while some must sleep:
  Thus runs the world away."

WITH A SPECIAL PREFACE BY
ISABEL PATERSON

FOR HELEN

Mr. Hodge and Mr. Hazard

PREFACE

THE LAST OF THE ROMANTICS

There is a word which has gone out of fashion, and the want of it caused difficulty and confusion in describing Elinor Wylie, for it defined the essence of both her person and her mind. She was reckoned a beauty, but that is not the word. She had many points of physical beauty: thick springing chestnut hair, expressive eyes of that mixed green-brown-grey miscalled hazel, the classic length of limb from hip to knee, and delicate wrists and ankles. Her neck especially was lovely as a marble column. She dressed with taste and care, in the newest mode; and made it her own. But it was her carriage, her air, that produced the total effect.

She had great elegance. It is a quality of universal range and strict meaning. Mathematicians say of a problem, a demonstration or a solution in their science, when it exhibits perfect lucidity and form, that it is elegant: the one remaining use of the term in its proper sense. In this austere region it reveals that the æsthetic prin-

*ciple is fundamental; intellect and emotion are ulti-
mately identical. And Elinor Wylie was all of a piece,
unlike many writers who compensate in literature what
nature failed to fulfil. Her work was her very self.*

*All her books, both prose and poetry, are interrelated
and continuous. This does not appear on the surface.
Not everyone recognized that* The Orphan Angel *and*
Mr. Hodge *and* Mr. Hazard *are supplementary, the
final chapters in the life of Shelley. The text to which
they are written may also be found in her last volume
of poetry, in the sonnet sequence of* Angels and Earthly
Creatures:

" *For I have moved companioned by a cloud,
     And lived indifferent to the blood's desire. . . .*

*A subtle spirit has my path attended,
In likeness not a lion but a pard. . . .*

*And happy I, who walked so well-defended,
With that translucid presence for a guard,
Under a sky reversed and evil-starred;
A woman by an archangel befriended.*"

*Shelley was the archangel, for whom she had cher-
ished a passion of the mind since her earliest years. In*
The Orphan Angel *she traced his influence after his
death; but for the convenience of the fable she had him*

saved physically from the sea, though the storm and shipwreck released him from his previous ties. Europe had cast him out; he turned his face to the New World, crossed the Atlantic, and travelled westward through America, an apparition of liberty. The narrative, for all its high-flown eighteenth-century style, has a singular ring of truth; one cannot but believe that Shelley would have been fantastically at home on the frontier, indifferent to its rude simplicities and happy in its natural freedom. He said of himself: "I always go on until I am stopped — and I never am stopped." Here he still went forward, as his spirit certainly did in his poems, which were scarcely read until after his death; their influence lives today.

But the whole story of Mr. Hodge and Mr. Hazard *is the absence of Shelley. This is England after it rejected Shelley; England revisited by a melancholy stranger in 1833. Mr. Hazard, described as returning from years of exile in the East, was variously identified as Byron or Trelawny; but he is rather a ghost, the Last of the Romantics. And he cut a very strange figure ten years after Byron expired at Missolonghi.*

He was thin and yellow with malaria; he had a touch of the sun; and his bronze hair was silvered under his brigandish black hat. The London fog bit into his bones, but he would not stoop to prosy means of keeping himself warm; he had a positive talent for discomfort. He talked of coffins and caught influenza, but did not die of it, perhaps for the reason hinted at in his own sombre question: " What makes you think I am alive? "

Of all his one-time friends and companions, Mr. Hartleigh alone was left. There is no harm in identifying Mr. Hartleigh as Leigh Hunt, for it would be impossible to invent a more suitable person to survive the Romantic movement. It is indeed difficult to account for Leigh Hunt ever having belonged to it, until one realizes that he was primarily a journalist and must have hovered on the edge of any contemporary movement whatever, fetched by his news sense. In his middle age Mr. Hartleigh had lapsed easily into a shabby domestic coziness. His offspring, born perhaps in the shadow of political prison or abroad, proved to be cheerful youngsters, attending homely evening parties with " a country cousin at the piano and custards for supper." They were the first of the Victorians.

Caroline Norton recognized Mr. Hazard; her handsome figure is significant, as marking the vanishment from the social scene of Lady Caroline Lamb. Poor Caro Lamb ended cracked and déclassée; and Caroline Norton was the last, presumably Platonic love of the ageing Lord Melbourne, once Caro Lamb's indulgent husband, William Lamb, who forgave her flagrant infidelity with Byron. But Caroline Norton, accused by a sullen husband, was vindicated in the courts of law from the Melbourne affair, and lived on in extreme respectability and a prosperous second marriage. She edited Books of Beauty and Keepsakes; and wrote little tinkling verses; she wrote Juanita, *that innocently meretricious echo of Byronism. She heaved a sigh for Mr. Hazard, but did not detain him. . . . Lord Melbourne was to become Victoria's first Prime Minister.*

Having cast a passing gloom on the fashionable London drawing-rooms, where he was no longer the fashion, Mr. Hazard went down into the country. There he met Lady Clara Hunting, whom it "would be a cruel wrong" to identify as the Lady Clara Vere de Vere, but scarcely unkind to call the Muse of Tennyson in such moments as he devoted to the aristocracy. Lady Clara's two daughters, Rosa and Allegra, were the choicest buds of Tennyson's rosebud garden of girls, not yet refrigerated into the icy nullity of Maud. They were early Tennyson. Mr. Hazard was smitten by their silver arrows. Lady Clara saw no harm in his darkling adoration. To her Mr. Hazard was neither mad, bad, nor dangerous to know. He was merely "an absurd creature" with "considerable talents" which could be appraised coolly. As the daughter of Lord Camphile, Lady Clara could patronize him. She could not recommend him to the prim Amelias and Edwinas of her acquaintance, whose bourgeois extraction necessitated greater circumspection.

Lady Clara had for tutor to her sons Mr. Hodge, who detested Mr. Hazard at sight.

And who is Mr. Hodge? Why, he is the schoolmaster

*of the Manchester school. Leaving out their virtues,
which need not be disputed, he is Dr. Arnold of Rugby,
and the father of John Stuart Mill, and Thomas Babing-
ton Macaulay, and the honest " plain business man." He
is, in short, the rising middle class at its worst. He de-
nounced Mr. Hazard to Lady Clara as " thoroughly un-
English," and suggested a strait jacket.*

*Metaphorically the strait jacket was applied. Tenny-
son wore it without complaint. Browning evaded it, by
an obscurity of phrase which frightened off readers.*

*Mr. Hodge was morosely in love with Lady Clara,
who laughed at him, secure in her position as a scion of
nobility. One foresees, with a shiver of horror, that ultimately he would get her; and that would be the end of
her. Mr. Hazard, of course, had not a chance against
Mr. Hodge, and knew it well enough. There was nothing for him to do but vanish finally, like a ghost at the
approach of daylight. Wherever he went, he would
nevermore revisit those glimpses of the moon in his
native land. Mr. Hodge is still in possession. Mr. Hazard's solitary footprints in the desert sands of the East
have been traced since by such exiles as Sir Richard Bur-
ton and Wilfrid Blunt and R. B. Cunninghame Gra-
ham, who followed the tradition of Childe Harold
without being able to say clearly what it was they fled
or what they sought.*

*It is curious to consider that Shelley and Byron had
no premonition of the nature of their temporal defeat.*

They raised the banner of revolt against an insolent aristocracy, or so they supposed; and they should have known, having been born into that aristocracy. They might have won posthumously, perhaps, had the conflict continued on the same front. They were beaten by an enemy who was scarcely in being during their lifetime — Mr. Hodge. Surely Shelley himself would have found Mr. Hodge ten times more intolerable than Castlereagh.

So this " symbolic romance of the mind " is the epilogue of that great drama of a lost cause, dedicated to the burning heart of Shelley and the perverse ego of Byron. There is a deal of erudition between the lines; Elinor Wylie had a fine aptitude for scholarship, and no one knew her chosen period more thoroughly or penetrated its significance more profoundly.

This also is her best prose. Here she chastened the abundance of her imagery and disciplined her luxuriant talent. Jennifer Lorn *is a dish of curds and cream flavoured with saffron.* The Venetian Glass Nephew *has the brittle exquisiteness of its title.* The Orphan Angel *is Shelley's own prose! In* Mr. Hodge and Mr. Hazard, *at moments perhaps Lady Clara's muslins billow about her too ethereally; she all but floats away in an Angelica Kauffman apotheosis. But the common little man, Mr. Hartleigh, and his petulant shallow vulgar Annamaria are clothed in sentences of the most austere distinction. The coarse-grained matter-of-fact Mr. Hodge is de-*

*picted in his most stultifying aspect without resort to
hyperbole or emphasis. He speaks, and he is there. This
is the very object of prose, to render the substance of
things so that the spirit is implicit. The prose of poets
usually tends to a " false gallop," as the verse of the born
prose-writer seldom quickens or lifts above a footpace.
Elinor Wylie had both gifts; and she never once let a
pedestrian line intrude into her verse, but at first her
prose occasionally escaped restraint. Here at the last she
compelled it to its true function.*

*If she had had five years longer, or even two or three
. . . But there is a special brightness in a flame which is
extinguished suddenly at its height; it is not seen diminishing and flickering down. Maybe her unwritten work
forms the fifth point of the star which illumines mysteriously the final paragraph of* Mr. Hodge and Mr. Hazard. *. . . " A fifth which set a crown upon the whole
. . . and remained a part of heaven."*

ISABEL PATERSON

Mr. Hodge and Mr. Hazard

CONTENTS

BOOK THREE: *MR. HODGE*

Advertisement

THE AUTHOR of the following little romance begs that the reader will accept it as a work of fiction pure and simple, nor seek to discover within its pages portraits of dead or living persons. The central character may indeed be regarded as a composite miniature of the whole generation of early nineteenth century romantics, but reduced to so small a scale and depicted in colours so subdued as to render the likeness invisible. No attempt has been made either to conceal or to emphasize the traits of the unlucky type to which Mr. Hazard belongs and whose imperfections he may serve to illustrate. He was evidently the victim of an excessive sensibility which the high order of his talents failed to stiffen into character. With gifts and natural abilities far above the common, he nevertheless lacked the power of self-discipline to a regrettable degree, and therefore fell an easy prey to morbid introspection and the disapproval of Mr. Hodge.

The author would be sorry to burden the illustrious shoulders of any genius with the hollow pack of Mr. Hazard's opinions; his eccentricities are his own, and if she has purloined a pistol ball or a black felt hat from his contemporary or hers she hopes to be forgiven. She has formed this little image of an idealist from various clays, and if, like the sculptor of a figurine, she has used an armature to uphold the practicable stuff, she believes the expedient justified. The novel of Mr. Hodge and Mr. Hazard is an everyday fable; its historical trappings are slight, and it must remain not a disguised biography but a brief symbolic romance of the mind.

Mr. Hodge and Mr. Hazard

BOOK I: MR. HAZARD

1

FUNERAL OF A MOUSE

WHEN Mr. Hazard was forty years old, he decided to revisit
England. Having been out of it for precisely fifteen years, he
had half forgotten its climate; his memory was incurably romantic, and through veils of far-away mist he saw the blackthorn more clearly than the mud. Also, it was true that he, who
so dearly loved the sun, had been rather too much in the sun of
late. Greece had been fever and chills by turns, and the cave of
the chief Odysseus a very rack for broken bones. Missolonghi had
been hot in the month of April 1824; a distinguished poet had perished there, and another, less distinguished, had merely had
malaria and miraculously neglected to die of it. The month of
May 1825 had been execrably hot, even in the grotto upon the
slopes of Mount Parnassus, in the captious opinion of a man mortally wounded. The temperature of such a man has a tropical
noon of its own.

If, like Mr. Hazard, you are mortally wounded and yet remain alive, you haven't been mortally wounded after all; you
have only the doubtful satisfaction of knowing that there is a
pistol ball somewhere behind your collar-bone. In the wet February of 1833 Mr. Hazard began to derive a perverse but gentle
pleasure from the conviction that if he continued to grow thin-

ner, he might soon be able to see the pistol ball as plainly as the collar-bone while he shaved by candlelight. He had never yet learned to button his night-shirt properly at the neck.

He had half forgotten the English climate when he landed at London Docks; the channel fogs had been clean as new milk compared to this tarnished verdigris smoke from which the face of his friend Hartleigh emerged with looming eyes like the spread wings of a soft dilapidated bat. The little man was shabby; his coat shared a certain worn furry look with his hair and thick eyelashes.

" My dear friend! " said Mr. Hazard; ten years ago, in Italy, he had cried " My dearest friend! " but now he lacked the requisite breath for the superlative syllable. The fog was heavy as seawater in his lungs, and a hundred times dirtier in its taste and smell.

" My dear fellow; my dear Hazard! " said Mr. Hartleigh; the beads of fog upon his thick shabby eyelashes grew more salty as he spoke. " And quite, quite unchanged since last we met; what happiness to see you still unchanged! "

" Hah! " said Mr. Hazard incredulously; it was his new way of laughing, which Mr. Hartleigh had never heard before. He supposed, accurately enough, that Hazard had picked it up in Greece; he concluded that modern Greek must be a harsh inhuman tongue.

" That was in '23, before we sailed for the Ionian Islands, I believe," said Mr. Hazard; " I should have thought, you know, that you'd notice a slight difference . . . however, you are yourself looking remarkably well." Which was so palpably untrue that he hastened to add: "And how is the excellent Annamaria? "

" Her health is good at the present moment; considering, you understand," said Mr. Hartleigh to Mr. Hazard, who perfectly understood. He had known Annamaria for a great many years.

" Those delightful winters in Spain and Arabia, with your wife and dear little Lionel," said Mr. Hartleigh, who was oppressed by the silence and by Mr. Hazard's large black hat, " how you must have enjoyed them! Of what inestimable benefit must they have been to your health! And Egypt, too; what did you think of the pyramids? I had hoped you would let me have a sonnet to the pyramids for the *Gossip*."

" Do you mind if I let down the window a bit? " asked Mr. Hazard. They were now in the hackney-coach; it was undoubtedly an extravagance, but since it was wordlessly agreed between them that the extravagance was Mr. Hazard's, nobody cared in the least about the money. Mr. Hazard was beginning to care rather painfully about the smell; the fancy visited him that the corpse of a mouse might be travelling to London with them in this extravagant hackney-coach.

Mr. Hartleigh glanced fearfully at Mr. Hazard, surprised again by the new and inhuman accent in his voice. " An unmelodious tongue, the modern Greek," thought Mr. Hartleigh in iambic pentameter. Having glanced once more at Mr. Hazard, he decided, not unreasonably, that his friend was about to faint. At the moment they were passing within the curdled nimbus of a street-lamp; Mr. Hartleigh perceived with warm-hearted concern that Mr. Hazard was precisely the colour of a vellum lectionary of the fifteenth century. A few ghostly freckles still lingered upon the thin bridge of his nose, but even these had changed from russet into dun. It was a truly shocking revelation; Mr. Hartleigh let down the window with a bang.

Mr. Hazard said: " Thank you; I prefer the fog to the mouse, don't you? " Mr. Hartleigh realized that Mr. Hazard had not the least intention of fainting; his words were clear and dry as scraps of mica.

Mr. Hartleigh, who had taken a small silver-plated flask from his pocket, put it back again with a thrifty sigh of relief.

" I thought you were ill, but happily it was but the unnatural hue of the fog," he said, his kindly eyes looming bat-like through the dusk.

" It is but the natural hue of my face, unhappily," said Mr. Hazard without apparent regret. " This is the celebrated Missolonghi tint, half-way between tallow and ship's buscuit. A really hot Arabian sun may toast the biscuit to a more agreeable brown, but this confounded voyage has turned it into toast-and-water. I assure you that I am quite well; I am only concerned lest Annamaria be annoyed with me for sacrificing my appearance to my principles."

"She is certain to admire you; you have the air of a distinguished foreigner," said Mr. Hartleigh, laughing. He was glad that his friend Hazard was not after all about to faint in a hackney-coach, and sincerely glad he had not wasted his brandy upon a fellow who did not care whether he drank cognac or cowslip wine.

Mr. Hazard said: "Hah!" which to Mr. Hartleigh's imagination had become modern Greek for a proper English chuckle; he pulled his large black hat over his large and rather alarming eyes and promptly fell asleep. Within the hackney-coach Mr. Hartleigh alone preserved his sharp and waking faculties; the corpse of the mouse and the slumbering form of Mr. Hazard travelled up to London in a darkling stillness equal and profound.

2

A COFFIN IN THE NEIGHBOURHOOD

AMONG Mr. Hazard's several sorts of genius, sombre and luminous by turns, the power of making himself uncomfortable lay shining and singular. Undoubtedly the gift of the most malicious of all his fairy godmothers, it remained a wicked talisman which invariably conducted him to the hardest arm-chair, the smokiest reading-lamp, and the coldest cup of tea. It was his lifelong habit to pour the tea out while it was still too weak, and this from natural impatience; an equally natural absence of mind prevented him from drinking it until he had read another chapter or written another stanza. Thus he never drank any but tepid tea, and the large ungenial cup which he lifted to his lips that evening at eleven o'clock was perhaps the chilliest in England.

It was as much Mr. Hartleigh's fault as Mr. Hazard's. Annamaria had given it to them boiling hot and almost black, but while the one gulped, choked, and proceeded with his pathetic narrative, the other sat, unmoving and apparently unmoved, until his friend had explained the failure of the *Gossip* down to its last distressing detail. Then he sipped his cold poison reflectively and spoke.

"But what did you expect, Hartleigh?" he asked in his new inhuman voice, which was chilly and bitter as the tea.

Mr. Hartleigh had expected anything but this cruel question; he had expected sympathy at the very least for the old venture, and possibly something more substantial for future trials of his perseverance as an editor.

"The difficulty of conducting a review . . ." began Mr. Hartleigh, and talked steadily for an hour by the stained ormolu clock. At the end of this period it struck seven and roused Annamaria from her nap. She sat up on the worn red velvet couch; one of Annamaria's cheeks was redder than the couch and impressed with the stamped pattern of its velvet.

"That means it's midnight," she said, with a polite yawn.

Mr. Hazard opened his eyes very wide and stared at the clock; the solitary hand pointed to twelve.

"So it's quite impossible to tell the hour, ever, I suppose," he murmured sadly.

"Not a bit of it," said Annamaria, "I know its tricks by heart. The children will be home any minute; they've gone to a little party. Quite simple; the country cousin at the pianoforte and custards for supper, but they enjoy it. They are cheerful young people; you'll make friends with them again in no time."

"I hope so," said Mr. Hazard. "They are too grown-up now to want me to pretend that I'm a savage creature; I needn't pretend that now, need I?"

"Of course not, Hazard; they're too old."

"I'm too old, Annamaria; it has become a work of supererogation," said Mr. Hazard.

"What does he mean, Hartleigh?" Annamaria inquired a trifle pettishly; she was dazed by sleep and possibly by something else.

"He means that he's already a savage creature, which is manifestly absurd; he is the tenderest-hearted man alive," said Hartleigh, loyal to the past, and hopeful for the future of the new review.

"What makes you think I am alive?" asked Mr. Hazard

alarmingly, twisting the locks above his brow into the same unicorn's horn which used to delight and frighten the Hartleigh
children out of their wits sixteen years before. Only it was not
quite the same unicorn's horn, after all, for now it was the colour
of silver instead of the colour of bronze.

"Have you found a coffin for me in the neighbourhood?"
asked Mr. Hazard. "You promised me faithfully in your last
letter that you'd find a bed for me in the neighbourhood. Savage
creatures hate being bothers to their friends, if they're lucky
enough to have any." He rose from the hardest of the arm-chairs
and stood looking at Hartleigh and Annamaria; you could see
from the expression in his eyes that he thought he was smiling.

"My dear fellow!" cried Hartleigh in genuine distress; his
thick furry eyelashes blinked back a tear.

"Hazard, I wish you would not talk so wildly; you terrify
me," said Annamaria rather unjustly, since Mr. Hazard had
spoken with the most frigid calm. "I think you must be ill; certainly you look shockingly ill. You are not yourself; it is quite
unlike you to terrify a woman."

"My dear Annamaria, you do not know me in my present
incarnation; I terrify every woman who beholds me, or even
hears my voice. You remember me as a herd-neglected deer;
now I am a wolf or a mad dog. An interesting example of
metempsychosis. But I am very sorry to have frightened you;
please forgive me."

"Ah, Hazard, it is nothing; I was only afraid that you were
ill," cried Annamaria warmly; her kindness, like the red velvet
couch, was worn but serviceable. "Sit down again and let me
give you a glass of port and a nice Bath Oliver before you go; I
remember well how fond you used to be of Bath Olivers. Yes,
we have found you quite a comfortable room, and only two
streets away from us. You must have a good sleep, and in the
morning you will have forgotten all that nonsense about wolves."

"Yes, yes," insisted Mr. Hartleigh. "In the morning you
must breakfast here; you will see all the children, and we shall
be a very cheerful little gathering. You need a good night's sleep
to cure you of these melancholy and erroneous ideas about yourself. In the morning you will be completely rested."

"How pleasant it would be," said Mr. Hazard, with averted eyes, which pretended to look at the clock while they really looked at the fire, "if what you so kindly say could come true; if in the morning I should have forgotten all this nonsense about wolves, and should find myself completely rested."

3

WARM WINE AND WATER

"You should have gone with him, Hartleigh," said Annamaria five minutes later. "He obviously isn't fit to go about alone. I think we shall both of us be struck dumb for the lies we told him; I was between laughing and crying when you swore to heaven that he was handsomer than ever. He never was, to my way of thinking, but now! Lord, I never saw such a dreadful alteration in my life! Why, the man looks half dead and wholly mad; you should have gone with him to his lodgings, if only for poor Mrs. Downing's sake. She will think him the devil, ringing her bell at midnight in that extraordinary hat."

Mr. Hartleigh poured out a second glass of port, the one which Mr. Hazard had not taken; Annamaria had the other decanter to herself, and that decanter's contents might easily have been sherry.

"I should have offended him, my love," he said meekly. "It was quite evident that he wished to go alone; he knows this part of Marylebone well, and I am not seriously alarmed for Mrs. Downing's peace of mind. I by no means agree with you about Hazard's ill-looks; he has endured great hardships in the past, as you know, and doubtless the fatigues of the journey and the agitations of his return to his native land have told upon him. But he has lost none of his elegance and distinction; he is thinner, of course, but the carving of the brow and cheek-bones is finer than ever; it is a beautiful head."

"Beautiful!" cried Annamaria rather shrilly; she was tired and cross, and beginning to be worried about the children. "If he is beautiful, then I am the Venus Anadyomene!"

"Not necessarily, Annamaria; the fancy is pleasing, but unfortunately it does not follow. It is a pity; it would be delightful if the thing were not *non sequitur,* for I assure you that Hazard is beautiful," said her husband, who in spite of his small vulgarities was a person of taste.

"Don't forget that I tried to model him in clay; he has not a regular feature," said Annamaria. "Put a few more coals upon the fire, will you? I think I hear the children coming; they will be wanting hot wine and water, I suppose, but we ought not to afford it."

"As well attempt to model Mercury in batter pudding, my dear; you might try quicksilver next time. Ah, forgive me if I've hurt your feelings; it's a great temptation to catch a flying likeness of him. His wife has tried it in her novels, over and over again."

"And failed," said Annamaria. "I don't want to be spiteful, but she does nag him, you know. You've said yourself that she'll never understand him; that she's too much like Baddeley to appreciate him."

"She's Baddeley's own daughter, to be sure; we must remember not to abuse the old villain now that Hazard's come home. He's so absurdly generous that he may still admire Baddeley." Mr. Hartleigh put the bits of coal upon the fire one by one, delicately, as if they had been lumps of sugar dropped into a fragile teacup.

"It wasn't the children after all; it must have been those rowdy young people next door," said Annamaria as disapprovingly as if her own children had never made a noise. "Hazard's come home; ah well, one can hardly call it that, poor fellow, can one?"

"I suppose not; Mrs. Downing's rooms are clean but cheerless, and he will never in this sad world demand a fire at midnight. The fog's worse than ever; I wish we need not have sent him forth from our cozy hearthside," murmured Mr. Hartleigh, relinquishing the poker and coaxing the frugal blaze with a folded newspaper.

The flames brightened under his fostering care; the lamp, turned thriftily low, diffused a softer light over the warm untidy room. Unlike Mrs. Downing's lodgings, the place was neither clean nor cheerless; it preserved a certain air of muddled comfort in the midst of shabbiness and confusion. The books had climbed up the walls to the very top to escape the litter of undarned stockings upon the couch, the pile of inky proof upon the table, the leaves of foolscap paper scattered underfoot. The stockings were white and gray and black, the couch was faded red, the armchairs were mustard colour, the curtains and the lamp-shade were a lively crimson, the table-cover combined these tints in a tapestry pattern. Mr. Hartleigh, who had presented it to Annamaria as a birthday gift, thought it rather like the table-cover in " The Eve of Saint Agnes." " A cloth of woven crimson, gold and jet "; yes, that was an exquisite description of the tapestry pattern, in Mr. Hartleigh's opinion.

" Cozy; very cozy; I wish with all my soul that he need not have fled away into the storm," sighed Mr. Hartleigh, with his mind still upon " The Eve of Saint Agnes."

" Storm, Hartleigh? There isn't a sign of a storm, though the fog's thicker than ever," said Annamaria, peering between the curtains. " It's too bad of those boys not to take better care of their sisters; I told them half past twelve at latest. Sometimes I think them quite irresponsible, I do indeed." She spoke as indignantly as if she had not been used all her life to irresponsible people.

" You see, my dear," she went on, taking up an irresponsible boy's sock and throwing it down again when she saw that both heel and toe were completely destroyed, " I didn't mean this sort of home for Hazard when I said you couldn't call it home for the poor fellow. If he leaves his wife and child in a castle in Spain, he can't expect this sort of home. I meant that with his family refusing to recognize him, and with Baddeley in a black fury, and his friends Piggott and Bird each absorbed in a mistress or a wife, England may be very cold comfort for him. And we can do so little, in these circumstances; it isn't like Hampstead, when he was a young and promising poet. If only your book on Lord Alonzo had been a success! "

" Annamaria, I asked you never to mention that detestable subject again; I hope I am as reasonable about reviews as most men, but the ferocity of those attacks . . . pray don't remind me of them. As to Hazard, of course all those Cambridge fellows admire and respect him deeply; you may depend upon it that they will seek him out at the earliest opportunity."

"If he depends upon it, he will be disappointed, my love. What is the Cambridge Union, to begin with?" asked Anna-maria sharply.

"Shall I explain it to you?" Mr. Hartleigh inquired with a harmless trace of irony.

"Certainly not; you know very well what I mean. What good can that ridiculous performance do him now? And then, he was beaten by seventy votes; a disgrace, I call it, to be publicly declared a lesser poet than that wretch Alonzo Raven. It is worse even than what happened to Shelley."

"*De mortuis,* Annamaria . . . please do not remind me of a painful subject. Poor Hazard! We must see what we can do for him. Perhaps Hallam . . ."

"It's quite hopeless, Hartleigh. A few years have probably turned several hot-headed Cambridge undergraduates into respectable fathers of families. There is a great prejudice against him still; what would happen if they introduced him to their wives?"

"The usual thing, my dear; their wives would fall in love with him," answered Mr. Hartleigh with a smile.

His wife was peering between the crimson curtains. She lifted the window a little, and a thin wave of fog slid into the room like a yellow wraith.

"There are the children at last," she cried. "They are just turning the corner. How very disobedient they are, to be sure! I suppose, since it is so late, I shall be teased into letting them have their wine and water."

4

AMBUSH AT A BREAKFAST-TABLE

MR. HAZARD's genius for making himself uncomfortable did not stop short of terrestrial immensities; its tempests were not confined to teacups, and its unkind enchantments were capable of plucking the waves up to heaven by their streaming hair and dissolving the skies, reversed within the Bay of Biscay. Earthquakes padded by his side like faithful heavy-footed beasts, and white unmoving glaciers shivered in his presence like tides beneath the moon. One of the lighter thunderstrokes of this tormenting magic was laid upon him when he chose to revisit London during an epidemic of influenza.

The fact that he had failed to go to Paris during the cholera epidemic of the previous year can only be explained by his deeprooted dislike of France and the bitter disillusionment he had suffered over the Revolution of 1830. Among the nomadic tribes of Arabia he had been regarded with veneration because of his apparent power of attracting and subduing sand-storms, and now that he had left his wife and little Lionel safe in San Sebastian, he felt confident that there would be fair weather and softly blowing winds along the Spanish coast during such time as he should spend in England. Many captains of East Indiamen had good cause to be grateful to Mr. Hazard during these months of lingering winter and of early island spring.

When he breakfasted with the Hartleighs upon the following morning, the influenza had already set its stigmata upon him. Annamaria marked the vivid flush upon his cheek-bones and the abnormal brilliance of his eyes and trembled for her children's health. There was small use in worrying over Hazard's health, because obviously he hadn't any, but the children were different; they were young and strong and their cheeks were suffused by a wholesome permanent pink and not by the uncertain colour of a flame. At the same moment she reflected that Hazard's eyes were unorthodox and rather appalling. Annamaria felt she could not call them fine; fine eyes were shaded velvet, like dear Hartleigh's. Hazard's eyes disconcerted her; they were too bright for a domestic breakfast-table. Annamaria knew that if she were to take the pretty Sheffield salt-cellar and fling its contents upon the fire, the variable flames would be tortured for a fleeting instant into the colour of Hazard's eyes.

The girls were chattering happily of the galop, and of the meringues which had so fortunately replaced the expected cus-

tards at the party. "And claret-cup," said the girls, "lovely, with
bits of pineapple in it!" The boys were occupied with their bacon
and eggs; they would none of them eat porridge any longer, now
that they were grown up.

"I must give them a dose of quinine all around," thought
Annamaria, and wondered if the younger ones would still expect
currant jelly afterwards.

Hartleigh was eating a small kipper; the little man blinked
his soft furry eyelashes and peered at Hazard, thinking that the
poor fellow looked wonderfully recovered. "He appears quite
his old self this morning," thought Hartleigh with innocent
satisfaction, dissecting his kipper.

Mr. Hazard noticed nothing whatever; he drank his tea
and did not like it, and forgot to eat the food with which Annamaria provided him. He thought that the night had been un-
seasonably hot for the time of year, and was vaguely aware that
he felt rather as if he had been climbing a very steep mountain.
He should, by sad experience, have learned a fever to match every
dead and living language that he knew, but he could not remember them so well as he remembered the languages, and
he had never expected the influenza to meet him in England.
The influenza was an Italian fever.

"Were you cold last night, Hazard?" Annamaria asked him
accusingly.

Mr. Hazard started violently, and dropped the copy of *Corn-
Law Rhymes* which he had just opened. "Yes," he said, "I found
it extremely cold at first, before the weather changed; do you
often have these extraordinary changes nowadays?"

"I knew it," cried Annamaria, between triumph and disgust.
"Hazard, you have the influenza; you'll have to go home and
go to bed at once."

"Nothing of the sort," protested Hartleigh. "He's looking
remarkably well, and, moreover, I wish to discuss the Reform
Bill with him. Pray don't interfere with us, my love; it is most
important that we discuss the Reform Bill without further loss
of time. Also, he's already promised to write a pamphlet advising the Government . . ."

"Stuff and nonsense," said Annamaria, "I tell you he has

the influenza. I wish we could find a bed for you here, Hazard, but there are the children to be considered. They mustn't catch it from you, you know, and unluckily it's highly infectious."

Mr. Hazard heard her words quite plainly, but at first they conveyed nothing to his truly remarkable intelligence save an impression that he was again in Greece and that someone had shot at him with an old-fashioned fowling-piece from behind a silver-plated tea-urn. But in Greece the ambush had been a clump of flowering laurel, and the report had been deadened by the long melody of waves breaking along a beach curved like an ivory crescent. The clump of flowering laurel had been far away, and only a stinging score of pellets had lodged in his shoulder and in the thin arm thrown so instinctively over the clear discerning eyes, which had seen the smoke like a tree of white blossoms rising above the rosy laurel. Now it was too late to cover his eyes against the ambushed shot. Stupid of him, not to have seen the white prophetic cloud above the tea-urn!

"You've startled him, Annamaria," said Mr. Hartleigh, "and he can't possibly have the influenza in Mrs. Downing's lodging-house."

"Of course I can," said Mr. Hazard, rising swiftly from the breakfast-table. The extreme quickness of his wits had unwound the delirious tangle of his nerves; his soul felt cold and sharp as an icicle within the skin and bone of his body, and behind his hot forehead his brain was frosty crystal.

"I'm sorry, Hazard," said Annamaria plaintively; the tears in her eyes made Mr. Hazard's unsubstantial figure waver and grow translucent like a ghost, "I hate to let you go; it's only for the children's sake. Hartleigh shall walk to Mrs. Downing's with you, and I'll send my doctor to you at once; one of the boys can take a message. I know you don't want any harm to come to the children because of you . . ."

"Good God!" said Mr. Hazard softly, and walked from the room in the implicit belief that he had taken leave of everyone according to the most rigid forms of etiquette in use among the Grecian chieftains.

"Don't come with me, Hartleigh; I beg of you not to come with me now," he said to Mr. Hartleigh in the narrow brown tunnel of the passage. "I assure you I shall be quite safe. They have most of them gone to Salona, and there is an enchanting moon tonight like the zone of a young virgin."

He gazed at Mr. Hartleigh coolly and haughtily; his eyes were clear as sea-water under his burning brows. If he did not speak precisely as the frosty crystal of his brain directed, it was because of the brightness of the crescent moon in his eyes. The innermost essence of his being, congealed into ice, longed coldly to be quit of Mr. Hartleigh.

5

DRIED PEAS AND RUSTY NEEDLES

LONG, long before Mr. Hazard was an atheist, or a Platonist, or a pantheist, he was declared regenerate, and grafted into the body of Christ's Church. The airy fine-spun feathers of an infant's hair were warily and discreetly wetted for the mystical washing away of sin; the infant's forehead, fragile as the shell wherefrom an eagle may be born, was duly signed with the cross of Christ's flock. Of the efficacy of this christening his impulsive youth could never be persuaded; the subtle convolutions of his later mind must ever be illumined by an intellectual beam peculiar to himself. In the opinion of the many that prayer had remained unanswered which desired for him power and strength to have victory, and to triumph, against the devil, the world, and the flesh. All things belonging to the spirit might live and grow in him, but they must grow alone, without the approval of the elect, or the help of his godfathers and godmothers in baptism.

Therefore it is improbable that Mr. Hazard had studied the second chapter of the Gospel according to Saint Matthew with special diligence for the past thirty-five years; it is a brilliant instance of his high powers of memory that all at once he seemed to have the thing by heart. He had been cruelly shaken by the brief struggle of wills between himself and the little man who had insisted upon taking his arm in the street; outwardly he had been glacially composed, but once or twice he had felt

the icicle of his inmost soul shiver and crack with the sick violence of despair. Nevertheless he had won; the little man had
turned and left him abruptly, with something like a blessing
uttered in the voice which most people reserve for oaths. Mr.
Hazard had watched him out of sight, coldly marvelling at the
broken droop of his shoulders and at the dinginess of the handkerchief with which he seemed to be mopping his soft shabby
eyes.

Mr. Hazard knew that his own eyes were hard; the strength
of his will had kept them hard as flint or the blue fabric of the
pole itself while they stared scornfully at the little man who
was talking of friendship and quinine and mustard foot-baths. But
now they were no longer flint; they were red-hot steel in the
hollows of his skull.

Mr. Hazard rejoiced to know that he had remained composed and haughty during his spiritual battle with the little man,
but he also knew what secret agonies and agitations had strained
his nerves and plucked his heart-strings to a hideous discord.
He looked at the house; the steps appeared giddily steep, and
at the end of their unnatural perspective the door was an ambiguous colour. He decided that he had far better walk to
Hampstead.

Suddenly he remembered everything with precise and delicate
clarity; he remembered the breakfast-table at the Hartleighs, and
the silver-plated tea-urn, stained rosy as an apple on the side
where the firelight touched it, and the breakfast china, which
was half willow-pattern crockery and half pink lustre ware, and
the kippers and the bacon, and the greengage jam which the
girls had wished were apricot. He remembered Annamaria's
purple stuff gown, and Hartleigh's worn brown jacket, and their
two faces, one so red and one so pasty. And he remembered the
grown-up children's smiling faces, florid or sallow as their parents'
types inclined them, and the solemn faces of the younger children
who had not yet been given their cups of tea. He remembered
the musty astringent taste of his own cup of tea, and he even
remembered the poached egg shrunk thin upon his plate,
wrinkled like a winter puddle. He had not seen it at the time,
but now he remembered its horrid chilliness, and his burning

mind shuddered at the memory. The whole was a *genre* picture, varnished brightly by the fever in his blood.

He remembered that he had the influenza, and that some of the plump and smiling children might even now nourish the seeds of it within their solid flesh. Annamaria had known quite well that he was the enemy of children; that he cast a blight upon them, that they withered in his presence like murdered flowers.

The Hartleigh children were not like flowers, yet Annamaria was right; it was not fair that they should die. And what of those other children who had died; were they not each one like a flower or a bird, and was it not his fault that they were dead? Or was it, perhaps, the fault of the Lord Chancellor?

The most exquisite images, the pure immortal music that the slight stops of human breath evolve from language, the extremest dizzying flight of thought into the void, were all imprisoned and confused within the agony of Mr. Hazard's mind. The exaltation, the mercurial elegance, the valour, and the strong vivacity were shrivelled up by fever until they rattled in his head like scorching peas and fled along his veins like rusty needles. He was in pain, but whether of the body or the soul his fever could not tell.

"Then Herod, when he saw that he was mocked of the wise men, was exceeding wroth, and sent forth, and slew all the children that were in Bethlehem, and in all the coasts thereof . . ." The harsh and breaking voice was Mr. Hazard's.

Mr. Hazard knew that he was not really Herod; he had been Herod for a little while in the thick fog, and he had pitied the king because the crown was heavy and brutal as it weighed upon his brow. They had tried to make Mr. Hazard King of Greece after Alonzo Raven had perished miserably of fever at Missolonghi. Now Mr. Hazard himself was perishing miserably of fever in Poland Street, Oxford Road. He was not in Hampstead after all; he was in Poland Street, standing before the house where he had lodged when he was first expelled from the university. He remembered, the pattern of trellises and green vine-leaves upon the walls, and how the fancy that the rooms were summer arbours had delighted his solitude.

He felt intelligent and sane and desperately tired. He refused to admit even to his own mind that he felt ill, but there can be no reasonable doubt that he felt very ill indeed. The fact that he walked slowly to Oxford Road and crawled into a cab must be conclusive proof of this, even without the additional evidence of his visit to a chemist's shop, where he purchased a small bottle of quinine pilules and rejected a quantity of excellent advice. His restored senses accomplished the journey to Mrs. Downing's front door, whose ambiguous colour had faded to a dirty buff.

Mrs. Downing met him upon the doorstep; the cabman was relieved, but Mr. Hazard was wearily fretted by her presence. He essayed to pass her with three syllables of apology.

"Mr. Hartleigh and the doctor's been and gone this half hour," she informed him sternly. "I think, sir, that the doctor was a bit put out. He says as you're to go to bed immejitly, and he's coming back at ten o'clock tomorrow morning."

"Thank you," said Mr. Hazard. He leaned against the iron railing of the steps and wished that she would let him pass.

"Will you be wanting any supper?" asked Mrs. Downing indignantly. "They said something about broth, but you'd have to have a soup-bone in for that, sir."

"No, thank you," said Mr. Hazard faintly, and fled to his room.

Here was no arbour of vine-leaves, but a travesty of roses traced in soot upon the walls. The counterpane's unclean design was like a nest of serpents. Mr. Hazard decided not to go to bed.

He sat upon the most uncomfortable chair, reading Mr. Tennyson's *Poems, Chiefly Lyrical* without any perceptible sensation of pleasure. His head ached abominably, and although he sat in his greatcoat, he was very cold.

Presently he could read no longer. While the chill shook his bones asunder, like breakable dice in a black dice-box, he lay staring out of the window into the impenetrable emptiness of the fog, wishing that the exaltation and valour of his mind had not been shrivelled up into scorched peas and rusty needles.

When at last he had survived the night and its delirium, he knew that the influenza could never kill him.

6

SPECIFIC FOR A FEVER

"What have you done with your hat, sir?" asked Mrs. Downing the next Sunday afternoon, as Mr. Hazard ascended her steps. It was all too true; his head was uncovered in the mild February twilight, which might so easily have been April had the trees been green instead of smoky lavender in the dusk. The church-bells were ringing in a circle around them, as cuckoos cry from every point of the compass, but with a solemn harmony of echo in their sound. It did not seem fitting to Mrs. Downing that Mr. Hazard should walk in the street with uncovered head while all the neighbouring church-bells rang to evensong. At the same time she hoped that his other hat, if he had one, would be smaller and paler than the satanic thing he had always worn pulled down over his eyes, as if he feared his eyes would frighten children.

"There is another hat exactly like it in the little corded box," said Mr. Hazard nonchalantly; he had not the faintest idea what he had done with the original hat. He believed that he might possibly have given it in lieu of sixpence to the cross-eyed fiddler who had been playing such melancholy music under a bow-window in Half-Moon Street. Certainly the fellow had held a black felt hat in his hand as Mr. Hazard strode away towards Piccadilly.

"The Half-Moon revisited," said Mr. Hazard to his own soul. "A fine Sunday afternoon spent among the sarcophagi of my dead selves. But at least I shall have missed the doctor." He spoke the last sentence aloud, and cheerfully.

"Yes, he's been and gone again, sir, and in a towering rage. He says he's finished with you, sir, and that you're bound to die, but Mr. Hartleigh made him leave a tranquillizing draught in hopes it would make you change your mind." Mrs. Downing spoke kindly; she liked Mr. Hazard much better now that he had taken her first floor sitting-room to hold the books which had been packed in the three larger corded boxes.

Mr. Hazard had managed his influenza very cleverly after all. Finding that the doctor affected his nerves to a wire-drawn extremity which had much in common with severe neuralgia he had avoided him by brilliant guess-work, and a series of long walks. The strangling bow-string of a sore throat, the obstinate helmet of pain clipping his temples, were evils slight and transitory compared to the dull aching lethargy to which the doctor's voice subdued him like a blow. Thus, in prolonged escapes, he had plenty of fresh air, and for the rest he contrived to exist upon tea and quinine and the peculiar tough and cindery toast which was the specialty of Mrs. Downing's kitchen.

The fatigues of this life of flights and evasions were numerous and at times excessive. Mr. Hazard frequently found it difficult to collect the strength to get up after a bad night, but as he took infinite pains and employed a variety of ingenious shifts and dodges, he was generally far upon his way by nine o'clock of the rainiest morning. Sunlight might waken his vitality half an hour earlier, but his own invention never failed to pull the scattered pieces of his faculties together in time to elude his foe.

No one ever knew where he went; he revisited every house wherein he had lodged during his vanished years in London, but even Mr. Hazard could not walk for ever in the rain with fever in his bones, and it is probable that he must occasionally have slept in the pews of churches, in the parlours of inns, and among the musty recesses of obscure book-shops. Wherever he went, he never went to the Hartleighs.

Once, to his intense and cold annoyance, he was brought home insensible in a costermonger's cart from Covent Garden Market, where he had wandered in an eccentric search for Roman hyacinths. Again, at stagnant midnight, he emerged from the emblazoned doors of a superb private carriage; he was pale and quivering with scorn, which, like a flame of the pit, consumed him to his hurt and wore him away to a proud skeleton. He thanked the owner of the carriage in words of exquisite politeness impregnate with vinegar and brimstone.

"I am afraid I have had the misfortune to offend him," said

the owner of the carriage, a slim and merry gentleman with auburn curls. "He fainted under my horses' hoofs; evidently he had preferred death to my poor assistance, but, being unconscious, he could not tell me so, and I made the excusable error of saving him. Pray tender him my compliments and apologies, and assure him of my willingness to drive a coach and four over him at his earliest convenience." And he gave Mrs. Downing a card engraved with a great name and a little coronet.

If Mr. Hazard suffered, in these adventures or in solitude, no one but himself was the wiser or the sorrier for that suffering. He avoided the Hartleighs as if they had been orpiment or aqua Tofana; the fear of infecting them with influenza had become an obsession with him, and he saw himself as poison to their domestic peace. Poor Hartleigh, who was sincerely attached to Mr. Hazard, visited Mrs. Downing's front door every day with touching futility; she was instructed never to admit him to the house. Now and then he had the good or evil luck to waylay Mr. Hazard in the street; he soon grew convinced of his friend's approaching dissolution and of the serious derangement of his exalted mind.

"Those incomparable powers," said Hartleigh to Annamaria, "quite, quite wasted. We must try to get him back to Spain and proper care. What a tragedy it is, to be sure!"

The incomparable powers of Mr. Hazard's mind were not really overthrown; in lucid and luminous intervals of evening light, in the divining crystal of the new morning, in the oracular silence of night, he perceived the universe and pierced it with the subtlest devices of the human soul. But not always; not at his worst moments, and hardly, even, at his middling moments.

This mild February afternoon, in which the church-bells cried like holy cuckoos from every point of the compass and from all the church towers between, was fair to middling, fair with an almost April fairness, and middling by the grace of a new moon. Nevertheless Mr. Hazard was very tired as he climbed the stair to his room; he wondered wearily why optimists like young Mr. Browning must hail unhappy poets by such titles as Suntreader and the false and flattering like.

7

CAMELOPARD AT A PARTY

Whether Mr. Hazard had influenza three times or only once must remain a mystery insoluble by the arts of medicine, the cabbalistic Tarots, or transcendental magic. No one, and least of all Mr. Hazard himself, was ever competent to decide whether the plague descended upon his head in three separate storms, or, waxing and waning like the inconstant moon, companioned his mortal loneliness from February until May.

This loneliness, although extreme, was of the spirit rather than the flesh, and by this time Mr. Hazard had far more spirit than flesh wherewith to be lonely. His nerves were constantly excoriated by fear of meeting the Hartleigh children in the street, for he believed that he might breathe destruction upon them as if he were Jehovah and they the elder sons of the Egyptians, but otherwise he was careless of others and himself alike, and he permitted both Piggott and Bird to call upon him whenever they were in London, which was seldom enough. He refused to visit them in turn in the country, because there were children in their houses, and at his worst moments, with his head aching atrociously, he still remembered King Herod, whose crown was sharp and heavy about his brow.

Several Cambridge graduates made a point of showing him every possible attention; his pride made the nature of such attentions narrow and difficult as climbing pinnacles of ice, and most of these gentlemen soon wearied in well-meaning. Young Mr. Browning was different; he could not be fobbed off, and his devotion was both tigerish and mulish in its intensity. Neither the forked lightning flash of Mr. Hazard's scorn nor the frozen profundity of his indifference could keep Mr. Browning from building fires and boiling kettles; Mr. Hazard might occasionally have found him a comfort if his boots had ever lost their abominable *parvenu* habit of creaking.

Mrs. Norton discovered him almost at once, by some hazel

wand of romantic intuition; she hoped that she had found the true Castalia among the stones of London. She was destined to be disappointed, but not before she had fallen in love with Mr. Hazard in a light Platonic way, fragile and sparkling as the Waterford wineglass brimming with champagne which she put into his thin hand. A few drops of champagne were spilled upon Mr. Hazard's black coat; he set down the glass and forgot to drink the wine, as he forgot to avail himself of the mirth and kindliness in Mrs. Norton's lovely eyes. Mr. Norton was from home; the little drawing-room in Storey's Gate was gay with flowers.

"It was charming of you to come to my party, Mr. Hazard," said Mrs. Norton. "People tell me that you are harder to catch than a camelopard."

It was at the giddy peak of Mr. Hazard's March influenza; the full moon of its fever cast its illumination upon his countenance, and everyone who had ever seen Mr. Hazard before declared that he was quite amazingly unchanged by fifteen years, that the silver in his hair was vastly becoming, and that he looked very young for his age. The colours of his youth were laid like a shining mask upon the worn contours of Mr. Hazard's face; nobody could deny his good looks.

"I could never have credited his eyes until I saw them," said Mrs. Norton. "But what fools they are who have called him gentle; he is the fiercest creature I ever beheld; he frightens me out of my wits, and without my wits I'm nothing."

She had her compliment, but not from Mr. Hazard. He knew that he was frightening Mrs. Norton, and therefore he refused to speak. He walked softly about, striving to subdue the brilliance of his eyes, striving to subdue the burning spirit within the slight fabric of his body, striving very patiently to contrive some veil, some fleece of lamb or delicate freckled deerskin, which might hide his soul.

He was glad that Mrs. Norton had called him a camelopard; it was a pleasanter form of metempsychosis than his own fancy concerning wolves.

"Do you know, Mr. Hazard," Mrs. Norton asked him in another vain and gallant attempt to make him talk, "that it was

your continual references to the Wandering Jew which first inspired me to write *The Undying One?* Does not the responsibility
weigh heavily upon your scrupulous conscience? "

Mr. Hazard, convinced that he was smiling, told her that
the burden was an honourable one. He refused to say more,
unaware that Mrs. Norton had a thousand times rather have
been frightened by his words than disappointed by his silences.
He listened while she told him of her enthusiastic intention of
writing a poem upon child labour; his sincere interest was
tinctured by delirium, and in the wild radiance of his eyes the
lady read the inspiration which his lips withheld.

Mrs. Norton wore white satin, with camellias in her shadowy
hair; she felt so truly the spiritual bride of Mr. Hazard that she
was startled when he left her. They sat together against a sombre
velvet curtain, under the downcast marble face of Clytie; the
fiery scintillation of their looks, their vital and uneven beauty,
the grace and the excellent violence of humanity, made them
appear more valuable by contrast with the Greek perfection of
the lifeless stone.

"Must you go? " asked Mrs. Norton, with more regret than
she considered it strictly decorous to express. She had not the
least suspicion that Mr. Hazard was feeling rather desperately
ill; his fever clothed the emaciation of his body with a garment
of light.

"I am sorry to hear that you have been unwell," said Mrs.
Norton. " You will, of course, take care of all that your friends
hold justly precious." Her lovely eyes declared her the most
affectionate of his friends.

"I will, of course," said Mr. Hazard; his voice was hoarse because he had the influenza, and ironical because he believed
that there was little left of him which the most partial of his
friends could regard as precious. Mrs. Norton found his odd
voice agreeable, because she was lightly and platonically in love
with him.

"Farewell, my dear friend," said Mrs. Norton when he left
her upon the stroke of midnight. She wished he would not go,
and yet the hour was a proper enchantment to win away a
spiritual bridegroom.

"Good-bye," said Mr. Hazard; twenty years ago he might have echoed her farewell as she desired. Now his exhaustion closed his lips upon the single word; he believed that he smiled, he knew that he touched her hand, and with that fainting effort he was gone.

Mrs. Norton gazed after him; she had a justified suspicion that she would never see him again. Her lovely eyes were full of laughter and a light and sparkling distillation of despair.

" What did he say? " asked everyone who had ever seen Mr. Hazard before or even heard of him; they crowded about Mrs. Norton, smiling with a voracious curiosity which she suddenly found abhorrent.

" Did he speak of her? " " Of his wife . . . ? " " No, I meant his first wife." " Does he expect his father to forgive him? " " What did he say of Alonzo Raven? He knew him well." " And the wards in Chancery; did both of them die? " " And had he not several other children? Are any of them living? " " But one was Raven's child, to be sure, Caroline." " I think him fascinating, though shockingly rude, my love."

" No, he scarcely spoke to me," said Mrs. Norton truthfully. " Perhaps he was composing an ode to my eyelashes, which I shall receive by the first post tomorrow, but I have a horrid notion that he was thinking of nothing nearer than Caucasus or Himalay. We agreed that it was ten thousand pities that Walter Scott was dead, and twenty thousand more that Doctor Arnold had ever been born. That is all, I vow upon my honour, except that I wonder why no one has ever told me how like a camelopard the creature is, a lithe and savage camelopard of the Libyan waste. No, I assure you, my sweet Henrietta, he said not a syllable about the entail."

8

SKELETON IN ARMOUR

In April, when he shaved by cloudy sunshine instead of candle-light, the vision of the pistol ball behind his collar-bone had become quite clear to Mr. Hazard. It needed far less effort upon the part of his imagination than the simple act of shaving required of his hand. His inventive mind, vivid in the midst of a pure silver pallor of dawn, played conjuring tricks with the pistol ball until it danced in air, flew skyward like a bird to pierce the risen day, or fell into his breast like a morning star.

The days began with showers, shot through and through with points of waking light. The colours were a rainbow's, but the shapes of cloud lacked the calm symmetry of a rainbow's arch; the wind and the wilder bursts of rain drove them hither and thither across the sky. Unquiet sparks of ecstasy, smaller than the sun's reflection in a drop of rain, lit the capricious twilight of Mr. Hazard's thoughts. The influenza had blown upon the mirror of his mind and misted it with a sorrowful fog: now the unquiet sparks of ecstasy moved over his mind and scoured it to brightness.

Years of the severest lessons of adversity had rendered Mr. Hazard's outward composure so nearly flawless that the sharp lancet of his self-contempt was blunted upon its surface. This superhuman armour was divided by no clumsy cracks and joinings; rather it resembled a coat of flexible mail, a cool marvel of contrived providence, a knitting up of nerves into invulnerable proof. Mr. Hazard's skill had woven it; he might have been proud of its difficult fabric. Yet he disliked the thing. It was a tough and stringent shield against the world, but after all it was only a makeshift. Even if his own skin had been but a beggarly tissue, he missed it sadly. He wished he might have patched and mended its tatters to last him into eternity.

Mr. Hazard cut himself inconsiderably upon his light and narrow jaw-bone; he hated the ravaged looks of the thin skull-face in the glass. The pliant coat of mail was cross-grained upon his limbs. The nights were never deep enough; they were like shallow straw pallets under his uneasy slumbers. There was no velvet profundity of oblivion to soothe him to repose. He reflected that ever since he had been flayed alive, he had remained a wretched sleeper.

Today he was to dine with the Hartleighs; his influenza had departed upon the wings of the last snow-storm, taking with it

King Herod's crown and half a stone of Mr. Hazard's body. The influenza had been unable to pick his bones to more purpose, since other fevers, called by the names of living tongues and the dead tongues of antiquity, had already tried their teeth upon him in the past. As it was, Mr. Hazard could ill spare those seven pounds of flesh.

People had been very kind, he supposed; to a herd-neglected deer even perfunctory attentions might have appeared a solace. But to a wolf or a mad dog such trifles were no more than a whistling of stones and a clattering of rusty tins at hunted heels. And now everyone was telling him that he must go back to Spain.

Mr. Hazard was not ready to go back to Spain; he could have tumbled his brown and gilded books, his black jackets, and his white shirts into the three boxes and corded them before another's slower pulses should have counted a hundred, but nevertheless he was not ready to go. He had been in England for nearly three months, and as yet he had done nothing. His plan when he landed at London Docks had been as plain as the map of a pirate's island drawn upon white vellum in the best India ink; now it was stained and ragged as though the cruel mutations of his fever had beaten upon it in cold rain and tropic heat. Yet he knew that he could still piece it together and decipher its characters if he tried.

He had followed a few of its arrows, drawn upon his memory in red or black, along those streets and squares where he had lodged in his youth. He had even, driven by a febrile impulse, walked swiftly across the bridge which spanned the little river in the park, and fled northward until exhaustion winged him neatly on Hampstead Heath and laid him asleep under an elm-tree. He had stood upon a terrace above the Thames, and watched its lights, like pearls dissolved in wine-coloured dusk, and wondered if it still flowed softly by the town of Gravelow and under the tall shadow of certain woods. And pursuing its course to the end of Cheyne Walk, he had beheld the great stream shrunk up into a straitened channel of green and silver, and the trees of Battersea lifted against the new moon into towers and battlements of April leaves. As the scene resumed its true proportions, he longed for the upper reaches of the river, which lay shallow as white ribbons among the grass.

Mr. Hazard regarded his thin face in the glass with an unjust dislike; his hair was thick, although its bronze was overlaid with silver; and his eyes were large and bright, although their sockets set their colour in the shade, as a cloud may darken the sea. For the rest, he might have sat for a romantic portrait of Yorick's skull, save that his nose was salient and pointed and his mouth too passionate and mobile for a mouth that has been stopped with dust.

He tied his black cravat with extreme care, and was glad that the fine linen of his shirt was starched so clearly and so delicately above the violent hammering of his heart. He believed that by these small vanities and disguises he might delude Annamaria into thinking him completely recovered; the fear of Annamaria's pity fretted his nerves as damp may fret the strings of a violin.

He brushed his satanic hat and stared defiantly at his own image in the mirror; he was silently challenging his face to betray him. His makeshift armour covered him adequately, but the mask upon his face was worn away to a brittle layer of pride. He did not trust it, in a glare of light, or under the bold scrutiny of Annamaria's pity.

Had Alonzo Raven been there in the flesh, he would undoubtedly have given his white eye-teeth to look precisely as his unfortunate friend Mr. Hazard looked at that moment. Mr. Hazard did not suspect this curious fantasy; had he been convinced of its truth he would not have cared a single steel button of the narrow waistcoat which was so obviously too wide for him. Nevertheless he looked a very elegant and lively ghost indeed as he turned from the ghostly image of himself in the mirror with a last defiant smile.

9

SEPULCHRAL MOTH

MR. HAZARD's liveliness had fled away in spectral laughter long before he had cracked a single walnut for the children or refused

a single glass of Mr. Hartleigh's port. Annamaria might have forgiven him for not drinking his soup, for then he was talking
rather wittily about "Yarrow Revisited," but it was impossible
to forgive him for not eating his dessert, for then he was silent
and listless while Hartleigh chattered about reform. Mr. Hazard
seemed to have lost his appetite for politics together with his appetite for almonds and raisins. His elegance remained to him,
but it was a graveyard elegance little to Annamaria's florid taste.
"A moth of which a coffin might have been the chrysalis";
someone had written that from Venice in a letter to Mr. Peacock.
Perhaps the writer had been thinking of gondolas, but to Annamaria's mind the words fitted Mr. Hazard like a long black
cloak.

"Bitter," said Annamaria to herself regretfully, "bitter as gall.
And I can remember him when he was the most affectionate,
open-hearted boy in the world, with such pretty manners too,
and so grateful for the little kindnesses we were able to show
him when we lived in the Vale of Health."

"Hazard," said Mr. Hartleigh to his friend, "I think you
ought to go back to Spain; the climate of England does not suit
you at all. It never did, my dear fellow."

Mr. Hazard glanced at Mr. Hartleigh with a quick suspicion
that he was being impertinent. An affectionate, open-hearted boy
would never have harboured this suspicion for an instant, but
perhaps while Mr. Hazard's hair had been changing from bronze
into silver, the virgin gold of his heart had been mixed with a
sad alloy. If a heart is open, iron may very easily enter it, to alter
the first purity of its metal.

But even the new Mr. Hazard, whose heart was sealed and
seared with fire, could not long suspect Mr. Hartleigh of impertinence. The looming eyes were shabby brown velvet like a
pair of bat's-wings. They were too soft for Mr. Hazard's irritable
taste; too kind by half, he called them to himself, yet not so kind
as Mr. Hartleigh. Mr. Hazard answered him politely, but his
voice was a plucked fiddlestring of impatience.

"I cannot go back to Spain," said Mr. Hazard, "until I have
seen certain people whom I hope to meet in England."

Both Annamaria and Mr. Hartleigh jumped to the comfortable conclusion that he meant his father and sisters, and even possibly his daughter. His other daughter was dead, of course; dead long since, in a vanished September, and the eldest boy, the one whom his father had taken, was dead of a decline these seven years. The second boy, he who had been so dear to Mr. Hazard, had lain quietly in his grave for so long that only Mr. Hazard remembered that he would have been seventeen years old had he lived. So, since his wife and Lionel were in San Sebastian, and since he had already seen Mr. Piggott and Mr. Bird, Annamaria and Hartleigh fell back on the soft cushioned thought that Mr. Hazard must mean his father, and thence were lulled to a dream of reconciliation and filial joy.

In spite of the sound but inexpensive port now warming their vitals, their hearts would have withered in their bosoms with pure horror had they suspected the truth. Mr. Hazard had no hope of meeting his father, or even the most broadminded of his sisters. It was precisely these same dead children whom Mr. Hazard so improbably hoped to meet before leaving England.

Not all the port and brandy in Annamaria's best cut-glass decanters could have removed the chill from their hearts could they have seen this hope within the secret mind of Mr. Hazard. But, even supposing that his mind had suddenly become transparent to their eyes, they would certainly have been so dazzled and amazed that this flying hope must have escaped them. Against the interwoven and concentric circles of his thought, against the colours of fire and crystal which informed its moons and stars, they would surely in their amazement have mistaken this hope for a darting bird or a dead leaf. It must have escaped them, even as it escaped them now in Mr. Hazard's few and casual words.

Deliberately he veiled his eyes against their wonder; he did not speak again for several long minutes. Annamaria was annoyed; she had taken a great deal of pains with the dinner, and had gone to the trouble of making the trifle herself. Mr. Hazard had eaten nothing to speak of, but that was no reason why he should not speak at all. He might have spoken about politics or literature, or the green April leaves waving like seaweed in the pool of the evening sky.

"Then you had better have a month in the country," said Mr. Hartleigh; he said it as he might have said: "Then you had better have some hot whisky and water," and indeed he thought of the country as a medicinal tonic rather than a spring of natural delight, for he was a true Cockney.

"I shall need a month, or even two months," said Mr. Hazard carelessly; he did not trouble to conceal his secret plan, for he knew that the influenza had done it for him. No one could possibly suspect Mr. Hazard of going to the country to chase wild geese or ghostly swans while he remained so excessively thin. To anyone with an ounce of common sense it must appear that Mr. Hazard was going to the country to eat butter and eggs, or new green peas and ducklings.

"The seaside, I suppose?" asked Annamaria, with kindly interest. "You wouldn't like Brighton?"

"No," said Mr. Hazard; the exquisite finality of the word was like a soundless charge of gunpowder to demolish the sea-front and lay the pavilion in ruins.

"The true pastoral country will be your best restorative," said Mr. Hartleigh. "The valleys and the verdant hills, the apple blossoms and the lilacs." Mr. Hartleigh saw no reason why a medicinal tonic should not be flavoured with honey and the extracted juice of flowers.

"Doubtless," said Mr. Hazard; courtesy drove him to a dissyllable, but he would have preferred a shorter word, or, better still, to be silent. It was too much trouble to unravel the spliced ends of the nerves which bound his body to his brain, but he was either very much bored or very much wearied by the Hartleighs' conversation. Already his laziness was cracking almonds instead of walnuts for the children, and now he began to make a neat and idle list of words of one syllable which might be employed in decent society. "Yes"; "no"; "quite"; "ah"; "oh"; "still" (this might be cleverly prolonged); "well" (the same rule applied); "thanks" (that was slightly vulgar); "so" (that was Germanic); "good" (excellent); "but" (French and affected; a shrug was implicit). Really, reflected Mr. Hazard above the litter of papery almond shells upon his plate, it was disgraceful, his native tongue's poverty in those polite monosyllables which may save the weariest breath to cool the bitterest porridge.

The room was a cube of hot bright air, moored fast among the thinner airs of twilight. It did not float, as the trees' branches floated and waved visibly in the green element above them, a sky like a lake reversed, grained and patterned like the surface of water, crossed by cool streams of radiance from the west. The room lay heavy and immovable like a drowned hulk at the bottom of this pool of ether; it did not hang suspended like the treetops, it was hopelessly weighed down by the soft imponderable air. It lay like a sunken ship, solid, painted with shining phosphorescence. The evening, so light over the tree-tops, was heavy enough to press upon the room, to crush its thick bright atmosphere closer and closer upon Mr. Hazard's mind. The flame of the lamp and the more gaseous flame of the fire, the dust spangling the bars of brightness with innumerable golden motes, these were emanations too difficult to breathe, too hot and dense for the delicate rhythm of breathing. Mr. Hazard thought how pleasant it would be if only he might be allowed to lift the black marble clock from the mantelpiece and hurl it through the shut window. The glittering splinters of glass would be neither so thin nor so sharp as the April air rushing in through the broken pane. Of course even to open the window in the old-fashioned way would be better than nothing, but Annamaria would be sure to shut it again. She would remind Mr. Hazard that he ought to be careful; she would pull the shawl about her shoulders and talk about toothache.

" I'll write to you, Hartleigh," said Mr. Hazard. " I'll send you an address when I write. Annamaria, I do not know how to thank you for your kindness. . . ."

10

'TIS TRUE 'TIS PITY

WHEN Mr. Hazard descended the narrow stairs of the Hartleighs' house in Marylebone upon the last night of April 1833 he stepped from a confined and breathless atmosphere into a fresh green twilight made chill and wholesome by increasing wind. The currents of air were electric with purpose, and the leaves snapped in the wind like little flags and crackled with cold fire overhead. It was an evening for love or the more severe resolves of ambition; as the breeze lifted the hair from Mr. Hazard's tense contracted forehead, it seemed to lift his heart also, though a moment before his heart had been heavier than a stone.

Now, if ever, was the moment for Mr. Hazard to declare himself a free spirit and a saviour of his kind. Such he had indeed set forth to be, and this with greater energy and impatience than remained in him tonight as he laid his hand upon Hartleigh's front door knob. A hundred fitful and intemperate schemes had flourished and died down within the past twenty years, whose fruits were to benefit the race of man from Niagara to the Straits of Propontis, so many exotics sprung from the fertile soil of Mr. Hazard's brain. His brain had yielded far too many of these harvests; nothing remained of them but chaff and worthless straw. Yet they had cost Mr. Hazard quite as dear as if they had been neatly stored in political granaries, safe from the teeth of rodents, locked away as accomplished laws. The four winds had taken his efforts and scattered them nobody knew where.

Tonight one wind was sufficient to blow an illusion of hope across his brain; it is sad to admit that this hope was concerned with nothing more important than his private happiness. Tonight his opportunity lay before him, had he possessed the strength to seize it, brighter and wider than the dingy street which filled his actual field of vision. Now he had the chance of stepping down four steps into the street, and with that descent entering the England of the time, and setting his thin shoulder to some useful revolution of a wheel in the machine. He did not choose to seize this chance; his fatigue and his indifference persuaded him that all such labours were in vain. He knew that his reputation, his character, his very name, were catchwords of conflict and failure; his physical exhaustion prevented him from knowing more, or desiring to know it.

Perhaps if someone had blown a charge upon a key-bugle or chromatic trumpet within Mr. Hazard's hearing at that moment, or had forced him to swallow one-twentieth part of a grain of strychnine or six-pennyworth of common brandy, his energies might have been so far recruited as to drive him into unselfish action. Things being as they were, and the street empty, and he tired and stifled by the Hartleighs' conversation, he had no mind except for his private affairs. Strangely and deplorably, these affairs seemed to him of the highest concern. He went down three steps into the street and paused; the influenza had left his body good for nothing more difficult than a night's sleep, but he might have set his mind to some firm and noble purpose. It is sad to record that he did nothing of the sort; he determined to do exactly as he pleased. He looked from side to side, pleased to be alone and to mature his selfish plans in solitude.

He paused, somewhat giddy from his quick descent of the stairs; he closed his eyes for one moment, but in that wink of darkness he had closed his eyes upon the whole world, upon the four remaining months of spring and summer, upon the turmoil of the public heart and the spirit of the time. He was going into the country to mind his own affairs; he was easily spared from the world and its destinies. The world would go round the sun as smoothly and as swiftly without the help of his affection; it could not be hastened or retarded by his pains. Therefore he was wise to leave it, and to live or die as he pleased.

Fortunately for the world, Mr. Hazard's contemporaries were more diligent than he; not one of them was to waste the long, sweet summer as he had determined to waste it. Southey and Lord Ashley were carrying on a correspondence about factory legislation; the first Reform Parliament had lately assembled, Buxton was taking up the work of Wilberforce, Althorpe was amending the poor-laws, and Roebuck bringing forward a vast new scheme of education. Lord John Russell was asking Thomas Moore to go to Ireland with him; "Your being a rebel may somewhat atone for my being a cabinet minister," said Lord John Russell, but Thomas Moore could not go to Ireland after all, because he, poor fellow, had promised to write lives of the literati for Dr. Lardner's *Cabinet Cyclopædia*. Wordsworth was worried about the realm, but delighted with his first grandchild; he was planning a walking tour in Scotland with Crabb Robinson as a holiday, but he would not stop composing Evening Voluntaries while he walked.

Mr. Macaulay was writing to his sister from the smoking-room of the House of Commons; in June he would be happy to inform her that in less than a fortnight he would dine with Lord Grey, Mr. Boddington, Mr. Price, Sir Robert Inglis, Lord Ripon, and Lord Morpeth. Everyone was busy and devoted. Young Mr. Whiteley was finishing his pamphlet " Three Months in Jamaica," and the Anti-Slavery Society was awaiting it with eagerness. Wilberforce was dying, and Haydon was painting the Reform Banquet and hearing plenty of excellent stories while he painted. Sometimes these tales were tragic; Sir Charles Bagot told him that Michelangelo's copy of Dante, with a wide margin and his own designs, fell into the hands of the Bishop of Derry and was lost on the passage to Marseilles. There were quantities of new books to offset such losses; Mr. Tennyson's exquisite lyrics, Mr. Browning's *Pauline,* Hartley Coleridge's poems.

Everyone was active for the future. Mr. Landor was preparing to plant thirteen hundred vines at Fiesole, and forty fruit-trees. Lord Nugent was upon the point of sailing for the Ionian Isles. The Oxford Movement was to be set in startling motion by Keble's sermon at Saint Mary's. Mr. Hallam was to die in Vienna, and Mr. Tennyson was to begin writing *In Memoriam*.

Everyone was very energetic. The Greek Islands were in revolt. Hussein Pasha had just left Constantinople for the front, and in the third week in May the ban of outlawry would be launched against Mehemet Ali. A few days later Ibrahim was to break down the gates of Gaza and storm the city of Acre. Upon the eighth of July, the eleventh anniversary of Mr. Shelley's death by drowning, a treaty was to be signed in the palace of Unkiar Skelessi. Meanwhile Mr. Gordon's *History of the Greek Revolution* would be published in London without a single reference to the unfortunate Mr. Hazard.

In France people were having their own adventures. Grisi had pleased the carping Parisian taste as Semiramide. George Sand had met Alfred de Musset at a dinner given by the *Revue des deux mondes;* already they were planning picnics at Fontaine-bleau; by September they would be *en route* for Venice. Amelia

Opie gave tea-parties in the Hôtel de la Paix, wearing a lawn cap with whimpers and crimped frills.

In England everyone was sedulous and earnest. Haydon, going to visit the graves of his children in Paddington New Churchyard, perceived that the name on Mrs. Siddons's headstone was almost obliterated; Malibran was playing at Drury Lane to the enchantment of thousands. After repeated applications the act was finally obtained permitting the extension of the Liverpool and Manchester Railway as far south as Birmingham. Mr. Cobbett had stopped riding about the country, but not before Mr. Trevor had been pelted out of Sunderland with rotten potatoes. Not everyone was lucky, but nearly everyone was industrious. Poor Mrs. Hemans had left her pretty " Dove's Nest " above Windermere and gone to live with her brother in Dublin; she had just sent Dora Wordsworth *The Remains of Lucretia David-son*. The Wordsworths missed her sadly, but were glad that even in idle Ireland she found time to work.

A few people were very unlucky, but nobody was lazy except Mr. Hazard. He had suffered a severe attack of influenza, but this was not sufficient reason for the complete prostration of his powers of will. If he felt incapable of returning to Greece, he might at least have gone to Limerick, to dissuade Gerald Griffin from joining the Society of Christian Brothers; he might have interested himself in the pathetic fate of John Clare. Mrs. Emmerson had given John Clare a cow, to be called by the charming name of Blossom or May; his cottage at Northborough was thatched, and covered with climbing roses. Nevertheless he was beginning to be haunted by evil spirits; Mr. Hazard, who was familiar with all spirits, might have helped him to exorcise these.

Even the women were working hard this summer; little Miss Landon was particularly hardworking, in her attic room at 22 Hans Place. Although the poor child lived circumspectly, as a boarder in the school establishment of the Misses Lance, she was pursued by cruel slanders; perhaps she was too young and too pretty to escape them save by an incautious dose of prussic acid. Mrs. Norton was busy with the *New Monthly,* and *Friendship's Offering,* and *The Keepsake,* and Mr. Norton was being detestable. Mrs. Shelley had made a sacrifice for Percy in leaving London and going to live at Harrow; she had begun *Lodore,* and undertaken a series of lives of the Italian literati for Dr. Lardner. Hogg's *Shelley Papers* had appeared in the *New Monthly Magazine;* Medwin had written a small volume of *Shelley Papers.* Mary was beginning to believe that she might attempt another edition of the poems, but she knew that Sir Timothy would never consent to a memoir. Leigh Hunt had published *The Masque of Anarchy,* with a preface.

Everyone was changing houses and opinions; Leigh Hunt had gone to Chelsea, and Trelawney had gone to America. When Lady Morgan went to France, her little black harp case was mistaken for a *petit mort* upon its last journey to Père Lachaise.

Coleridge was comfortable in the Gillmans' house at Highgate, but not everyone was so comfortable as Coleridge. Charles Lamb and his sister were living at Bay Cottage, Enfield, a mournful yellow house kept by a woman called Redford. It was believed that this atrocious person locked Miss Lamb in a dark cupboard as a punishment for cutting up a feather-bed and scattering the feathers out of window. Mr. Hazard was to be congratulated upon the superior patience of Mrs. Downing, for his conduct must often have been difficult for even the kindest landlady to understand. He never cut his mattress into pieces, but he frequently spent the night upon the hearth-rug when he did not spend it upon Hampstead Heath. If he had not paid his bills with such regularity, Mrs. Downing would have been glad to know that Mr. Hazard was going into the country to mind his own business and forget the progress of civilization.

11

ERE BABYLON WAS DUST

HE stood upon the pavement and drank the thin sharp air; it flowed about his head in a cool stream of felicity. He thought that if he followed it to its source, as if it were a true river, it might lead him wherever he desired to go. It seemed scarcely worth the pains of piecing the ragged map of his plan together if he followed this river of air to its source, which must be a spring of light among leaves far greener than these London leaves, on which a little soot already lay in flakes of black velvet.

If Mr. Hazard had eaten more mutton for dinner, or even a few of the macaroons in Annamaria's trifle, he might not so readily have believed that a river of air may be traced to its source, or that the source, once found, will reveal itself as a fountain of light. Out of the dark and odious pit of depression into which the powers of weariness had cast him his released soul sped like an arrow to a mark which his own mind had that instant traced upon the future. He had not the least doubt of the veracity of this vision. He did not know that his own mind, unreasonably swift and impetuous, had fled away in front of his wishes and struck the fountain of light from the blank rocky wall of the future. But he saw the light in the distance much more plainly than the dim brassy number above Mrs. Downing's door.

" I shall go there in the morning; early in the morning," said Mr. Hazard to himself as he climbed the stair. He pulled off his black jacket and his narrow black waistcoat with the steel buttons, and without waiting a moment beyond the flash of a tinder-box and the leap of a candle-flame, he began to throw his white shirts and his attenuated black trousers and his brown and gilded and vermilion books into the largest of his three boxes. He thought of nothing save the ecstasy of haste; he worked like a happy madman, like a slave driven by beatitude. When he caught a swift image of himself in the glass, he was far too profoundly enchanted by hurry to notice that he no longer wore a stretched and brittle mask of pride over a thin skull-face detestable in its own sight. He recognized the face, in rapid passing, as one he had known before, and casually accepted as a friend's. It was, thanks to the illumination of a baseless hope and the light of a single candle, almost precisely the same face, flushed, excited, bright-eyed, baffled, triumphant, intent upon a secret purpose, which he had been used to see glancing at him from behind the dark glass of a damp-spotted mirror some twenty years before.

The delicious useless violence of haste warmed more than Mr. Hazard's heart; his brow streamed with salty sweat, which ran into his eyes and twisted his hair into curlicues of silver. The clear green sky was darkened by a slanting tidal wave of rain; the rain beat wildly at the windows, and Mr. Hazard opened both the windows and let the rain drive in, along the dusty carpet, along the tops of the tables, with a prodigious sound of blown foolscap paper and the fluttering open leaves of books. The books and papers were spattered with rain as Mr. Hazard tumbled them helter-skelter into the boxes, and presently there was a bright pool of rain-water under the windows. The candle flared into a small pillar of fire and died in the wind, but there still remained enough pale and aqueous light within the room to permit Mr. Hazard to throw his books into the boxes, among a tangle of luminous white shirts and attenuated black trousers.

The white shirt that he wore was soaked with rain and sweat; he pulled it over his head and worked stripped to the waist in a cool whirlpool of wind and rain. He hitched his long trousers tighter about his waist, and the private wind of his own speed was added to the April wind from without. With a cutlass between his teeth and a handful of ingots among the gilded books he might have been a gentleman-pirate flinging Peru and India into triple sea-chests. His plan was patched together as he worked; he flew upon its quick previsions, lifted above all weariness and doubt, refreshed and medicined by certainty. He felt the cool sweat of his own body washed by the cooler stream of rain; after he had corded the boxes, he stood by the open window and let the storm sweep over him in waves of pure ravishment. He wondered why he had been so foolish as to have nightmares of late; it needed only a little haste and a few millions of clean raindrops to overcome such monstrous dreams for ever.

Mr. Hodge and Mr. Hazard

BOOK II: *THE YOUNG HUNTINGS*

1

REVERIE OVER AN APPLE-TART

THE NEXT morning, which happened to be the first of May, came up out of the east like an apple orchard in full bloom. Mr. Hazard was to travel westward; he knew that by nightfall he would be among true orchards of cherry and apple, and that the sun would go down in a golden forest of clouds. He was driven betimes to the inn from which the Gravelow coach set forth; he forgot to drink his tea, he confounded his boxes in a string of Greek oaths thicker than the actual cords which bound them, but at heart he was extremely happy. There was no longer a cracking icicle within his breast; the season's influence had melted it.

The day was fine, the weather was warm and sweet as new bread and honey, yet by eleven o'clock Mr. Hazard was wishing for his greatcoat. He knew he had rolled the clumsy thing into a wrinkled ball and tossed it into one of the boxes, but he was not sure whether it lay under Plato or on top of Lord Nugent's *Memorials of John Hampden*. The coach was stuffy and hot, and Mr. Hazard had pulled off his neckcloth and dropped his hat beneath a pair of muddy boots which did not belong to him. Nevertheless he wished he had been wise enough to wear his greatcoat.

Mr. Hazard's body did not match the breadth of his mind; he had always been tall, but he had never been wide. Therefore he was seldom afforded sufficient room in public and private conveyances; his memory in this matter was accurate to the brink of the cradle. As a child he had been nearly smothered by his mother's shawls and his sister's furbelows; his cousins, his tutors, and his friends had all taken an unfair half of any post-chaise. By forty he had been crushed and pummelled to the conclusion that in a fatted civilization he did well to wear a greatcoat.

The inclemency of winter wrought a natural cure of this injustice; Mr. Hazard was cold; he wore a greatcoat; his greatcoat was old-fashioned and voluminous, and he was falsely credited with the ability to fill its ample folds. In winter Mr. Hazard was frequently allowed breathing-space within a stage-coach. The capes of his greatcoat were deceptive, and very fat people preferred to sit beside timid old ladies in tippets, or poor little shivering boys going to school for the first time. But in summer the secret was out; the skeleton was uncovered. The minute his wife put his greatcoat away in camphor Mr. Hazard was at the mercy of the world.

There had been no stage-coaches upon the slopes of Mount Parnassus, and the peasants had often made way for him as he passed with his arm in a sling. In Arabia one could wear a burnous and appear capable of breaking a camel's back. In Spain and Italy the diligences carried a plague of priests, fat priests who battened upon garlic and strong red wine. The thin ones fixed their eyes upon their breviaries and let the populace squeeze them into corners; the fat ones sat down beside Mr. Hazard with complacent grunts. In England it was a secular scourge; the Gravelow coach was crammed with prosperous farmers and their wives and with shopkeepers who were undoubtedly successful. There was a crowd of pleasant young gentlemen on top who were not minded to make room for anyone whose age was over twenty-five and whose weight was under ten stone.

Within the coach Mr. Hazard was given as much indulgence as the least of the baskets and bandboxes. His neighbours regarded his long legs as a public nuisance, and he himself was unaware of the fate of his doubled-up knees amid the welter of top-boots, Bedford cord breeches, gaiters, black silk aprons, and merino petticoats which surrounded them. His smashed ribs, set by an eccentric Greek surgeon in the cave of the chief Odysseus, had never seemed so flimsy and unstable as they did now under the prodding elbows of the shopkeepers. He forgave the shopkeepers, but he was furiously angry with his broken ribs; he ground his teeth and longed to grind the ramshackle bones to graveyard dust.

Mr. Hazard's acute discomfort did not prevent him from being happy; the upper layer of his sensations was like a short and irritable piecrust over a deep and smiling apple-tart. He evolved this unpoetical simile as he ate his dinner in the parlour of the Holtspur at Beaconsfield; he finished his biscuit and cheese and fixed his eyes upon a blossoming enclosure whose tree-tops were tufted with the promise of a thousand apples.

Now his own mind bloomed with auguries; it was spring, the jocund freshness of a morning to which high summer will succeed as noon. The autumnal evening of such a time could not fail to be a harvest of contentment. Only good luck could grow in such a land and such a season. Some devil had sown tares in the garden he had sought to plant in this green valley, but his impatience had despaired too soon; he had let an army of wretched weeds drive him out of his inheritance. He had been infantile in his swift despair; he had never lacked courage, but he had lacked fidelity and that careless trust in his own powers which is worth more to a man than the affection of families and the approval of publics. He should have forgotten his gibbering peers; he should have ignored the brute commonalty. He should have let the world run softly by, as the Thames ran softly between water-meadows, until all his songs were ended.

In Italy, where pulses are reputed to beat quickly, a newly-wedded man will plant a hillside with silver olive saplings, and rest peacefully in the knowledge that not until his grandsons' day will any kin of his pluck profit from those trees. A slow harvest of yellow oil will ripen through the years to anoint the hands of future generations, but the man who planted them will go to his grave long before that treasure is pressed from the fruit of the olive-trees.

" A wise and instructive custom," mused Mr. Hazard, " flourishing in a soil made meagre by superstition and vice. I should have planted apple-trees in the Thames valley; my orcharding would have been in good heart by now."

Some river running softly through the shadowed valleys of his mind had washed them clear of bitterness and self-reproach; they were full of light, even as the low valley of the Thames overflowed with sunset. His mood, which should have been elegiac to suit the hour, preserved the plain simplicity of early morning. He had regained some lost innocence of the spirit; he spoke of planting orchards, but his hopes were as inviolate as though his first parents had never tasted apples.

He called for his bill in Arabic, and paid for his dinner in Spanish gold, but nobody minded these irregularities in the least, since the price of the dinner was three shillings in English currency, and Mr. Hazard did not ask for change.

At Gravelow the wide curving street brimmed with the flood of sunset above the brimming reaches of the Thames. By every rule of logic, by every impulse of sensibility, Mr. Hazard should have been drowned in sorrowful memories. His mood bore him like a strong swimmer across the double streams of light and water, and set him down quite safely in front of a little fire in the coffee-room of the Crown inn. He was not even out of breath; the waves of some mysterious power had laid him to rest in a comfortable arm-chair, and then receded, softly and more softly still, along the infinite conduits of the night.

2

SATAN FINDS SOME MISCHIEF STILL

Mr. Hazard knew that he must find lodgings, if only to have a mantelpiece upon which to range his seven Hebrew grammars. The next morning was gay with fickle sunshowers; it was a harlequin day, a strayed reveller from April, in glittering lozenges of blue and silver. Mr. Hazard and the erratic shadow of a cloud trod lightly down the High Street together, a grey shade and a black shade upon a pavement already dappled with raindrops and disks of brightness.

Mr. Hazard found lodgings without trouble because he refused to take any trouble; it was pure auspicious chance that the lodgings happened to possess plenty of clean window-panes to the east and south, through which the sun shone upon scrubbed paint and chintzes laundered into holes. He paid a week's rent in advance, believed that he would want no dinner, consented to the suggestion of an egg with his tea, and walked swiftly along West Street until he came to the little house where he had once lived. It was precisely as he had left it; he could have made a pencil sketch from memory before he turned the curve of the road. The larger house opposite, which had belonged to Mr. Bird, stood solid and unchanged.

He leaned against the red brick wall in front of this house and gazed at the green front door through which he had emerged so often into the mornings of a younger spring. He had a small precise picture of himself in his mind's eye, exact and critical, etched in sharp lines and bitten with the acid of irony. He laughed shortly under his breath and dismissed his own ghost to oblivion. The ghost of a living man must be a poor creature at best; a stuffless thing, projected into sunshine by a sick brain. But the ghosts of the dead are different; they are sustained and animated by spirits whole and entire, they possess their proper souls. Mr. Hazard watched the green door as though it had been the entrance to a forest glade and he a hunter awaiting with suspended pulses the delicate approach of a troop of wild deer.

The green door remained shut; the forest glade shimmered in the distance, caught in a criss-cross net of light and shade. No foot, however soft and fleeting, disturbed its feathery grass. Not even a solitary fawn fled down the forest glade with shy and subtle steps.

The hunter subdued his breathing and the beating of his heart and waited, his eyes upon the unopening door. Mr. Hazard knew it was in vain; he took the air into his lungs and the knowledge into his heart with a single sigh. This was not the morning for stalking wild deer; he must let them come of their own accord if they came at all.

He returned to his lodgings; he was so tired that he determined not to be idle. The influenza had given him a thirst for doing nothing which parched his mouth and turned his bones to powder, but he refused to slake his thirst in the cool depths of idleness. His luggage had been sent from the inn; he unpacked his boxes with speed and passion, leaving his garments in a heap in the middle of the floor while he arranged his books with extreme care upon the table, the chimney-piece, the chairs, and the shelves of the corner cupboard. The rows collapsed in clouds of dust, like castles builded of mighty cards, and he buttressed them at either end with piles of heavier volumes. Then he stood regarding them affectionately; his thin fingers were covered with London soot, and there was a streak of London soot across his forehead like a dark chrism. He had a wistful desire to read Lucian as a relaxation after his labours, and a passing regret that he had wasted so many guineas on Dyce's edition of Shirley's works. He had bought the books because of Shirley's melancholy end, and because he disliked Dryden.

Conquering these weaknesses, he turned to the seven Hebrew grammars and selected the heaviest with the inevitable instinct of the martyr. From the same shelf he took the King James version of the Holy Bible, the Septuagint, and the Old Testament in the original Hebrew characters. Hastily dropping a few notebooks and pencils into his pockets, he put the four thick volumes into a cracked leather knapsack and prepared to leave the room. The knapsack was slung over his shoulder, his foot was on the threshold, he had almost bumped his head against the lintel of the door, when he hesitated, wavered, and returned.

With a slightly guilty nonchalance he picked up his worn copy of *Paradise Lost* from the table and thrust it into his pocket among the pencils. Then he ran downstairs as if his cracked knapsack were a pair of wings.

"I must get on with it," thought Mr. Hazard, who was longing for the company of Satan and feeling abominably lazy about Job. He had always meant to write a poetic drama with Job for its hero; he felt that his own experiences had fitted him with acquired talents for the task. As a matter of fact, he had written the first act, with its magnificent lamenting strophe and anti-strophe, during the confusion of Lionel's Christmas holidays. Mr. Hazard was aware that the spiritual agony crying from his verse would have drawn blood from brutal adamant, but he was not quite content with the language.

It was noble; it was musical; it was tranced and ecstatic with sorrow. But was it better than the vulgar tongue of the prose version that certain anonymous gentlemen had dedicated to King James?

Mr. Hazard had decided to make his own translation. He did not trust the Greek, and so there was nothing for it but to turn the Hebrew straight into what the true lovers of his poetry were already beginning to call Hazardous English. This meant that Mr. Hazard must learn Hebrew, but the learning of Hebrew meant very little to Mr. Hazard, who had learnt Sanscrit and Chinese and the first thirteen letters of the Pali alphabet. He had begun his studies upon New Year's Eve, while Lionel was singing a Spanish carol, and at the end of four months he was proficient enough to answer Bildad and Zophar and Eliphaz and to argue eloquently with the Lord in his own language.

"I must get on with it," thought Mr. Hazard for the second time; he was so tired that he felt a fanatical horror of idleness. If he slipped into the cool depths of idleness, he might so easily forget about Job and fall asleep for ever.

"I shall walk to Medmenham Abbey," thought Mr. Hazard, "and I shall do the thirty-eighth chapter, with the Lord challenging Job from the whirlwind."

It is a singular instance of the folly of man's proposals that ten minutes later Mr. Hazard found himself in a light skiff with a pair of oars in his hands. The knapsack lay behind him unopened, but the copy of *Paradise Lost* was placed carefully upon the opposite seat, as if Mr. Hazard found Satan a more congenial vis-à-vis than Job. Twenty years of reading him had given Mr. Hazard Satan by heart; sometimes he regarded him as a beloved friend, but more often he identified the fallen angel with himself. It was the profoundest idleness to read Milton, for the words welled into his mind from his deeper memory; they were become a part of his mind, and to read them over was like murmuring a prayer learned in childhood, save that the words were not a prayer but a defiance.

The sound of the river, and its scent, and its cool colour, flowed past him in a dream; it was the distilled essence of idleness, the very element of peace. Upon its lifted banks the beech-trees were thin green flames that burned above the oaks.

"I shall row until I am tired," thought Mr. Hazard, who was already tired, "and then I shall find a quiet backwater where nothing can possibly come to bother me. Perhaps, after all, I deserve a little peace and quiet. 'Is my strength the strength of stones, or is my flesh of brass?' I shall go to sleep in a backwater and nothing shall worry me for the rest of the day."

3

SUNSHINE HOLY-DAY

"Excuse me, but would you very much mind waking up and giving me back my silver arrow? I can't shoot properly with any of the others."

The voice, which was sufficiently sweet, but high and chirping like a bird's, reached Mr. Hazard after a brief interval; it fell into the resounding cavern of his dream and waked him without a start. It did not fall suddenly; it drifted lightly down, it descended like a shuttlecock buoyed up by air, and touched him no more heavily than a feather or a leaf.

He did not move or even open his eyes; he lay supine in the hollow well of his dream. He was aware of no reason why he should answer the voice; if he had ever stolen silver arrows, that was in another life, upon another planet. He lay without speaking until someone spoke for him.

"It's rather ridiculous to ask the poor man to give you back your silver arrow, as if he were a thief and had taken it on purpose. Why don't you explain to him politely that you're a wretched shot and that it's sticking in his left shoulder instead of in the target?"

The other voice was a second shuttlecock, made of softer feathers; it was neither so merry nor so sharp as the first voice. Mr. Hazard wondered if it told the truth; without opening his eyes, he moved his hand until it brushed against a feathered shaft sprouting from his left shoulder. It was a curious circumstance; in his youth he might have called it miraculous. Even today, when he had meant to bother about nothing under heaven, he was tempted to look into this matter of the silver arrow.

He opened his eyes; he looked up, and at first he saw nothing but a dazzle of sunlight among translucent leaves like tongues of fire. Then, as the prismatic colours shifted and grew still, he saw the figures of two girls leaning from the bank above him. He saw them through the blindness of his dream, girls like trees dancing, like little birches turning the river-bank into a frieze.

"But would you mind giving it to me, whether I'm a bad shot or not?" said the chirping voice of one.

"He's asleep," said the other. "If you crawled along that branch and bent down, you might just manage to reach it, Allegra."

"But how silly to say he's asleep! His eyes are wide open."

Mr. Hazard's eyes were indeed wide open; he had not known that anyone was named Allegra nowadays. The music of the three familiar syllables was confused by echoes.

"That isn't really your name, is it?" asked Mr. Hazard with that slight impatient movement of the lips which he still believed to be a smile.

"Why shouldn't it be my name? Of course it is; I was named after a rich great-aunt. But give me my arrow, will you please? We're in a hurry." The voice of Allegra had a sweet scolding note in it, like a bird's.

"People are always surprised," said the softer voice. "It isn't really a great-aunt's name; we were named for poems, or something, because we weren't boys. I think it's rather a shame. I'm Rosa; Penserosa, you see."

"Is your mother fond of Milton?" asked Mr. Hazard, who had always wanted to meet a mother who was fond of Milton.

"No, of course not; she isn't in the least fond of him, and neither are we. It was a bet, I think; someone bet my father that we wouldn't be boys, and we weren't. The boys, you see, are always Tristram and Hilary. This detestable man thought it would be clever to invent the same sort of names for us; wasn't it horrid of him? "

Mr. Hazard sat up in the skiff and looked at the two girls; their heads were like preposterous and lovely flowers grafted upon the willow boughs. He thought them the prettiest children he had ever seen.

" The detestable man made rather a brilliant guess," he said. " How old were you when you were christened, and suppose he'd named you the other way round? "

" Yes, that's quite true," said Rosa. " But that makes it a little bit dull, having our names match our natures. The boys have come out wrong, which is much more amusing. Tristram's an agreeable rattle, and Hilary's as solemn as an owl."

" May I have my silver arrow, please? " asked Allegra for the fourth time, like an angry bird.

" Of course; I'm so sorry," said Mr. Hazard. He plucked the arrow from his shoulder; it had pierced his linen shirt without touching him. It was a queer plaything, with a silver varnished shaft and a blue feather.

Mr. Hazard stood up in the skiff and gave the arrow to Allegra. He thought her the most beautiful creature he had ever seen.

4

CLAIRVOYANT

PRECISELY why he thought this will never be known. Perhaps she slipped, like molten crystal, into some mould which his imagination had prepared since childhood; perhaps her changeling grace was sister to some necessity of his heart. Allegra was lovely, but Rosa was lovely as Allegra; Rosa was warmer, sweeter, and more pensive, softened by small compunctions and pities. They were twins in delicate flesh and bone, but barely kindred in their varying colours and in the light and darkness of their hair. Rosa was serious, and Mr. Hazard adored a contemplative brow banded with shadowy tresses; she was gentle, and Mr. Hazard was happiest in gentle presences. Nevertheless he chose the silver rather than the gold, the moon rather than the sun, the water rather than the fire, the sharp flower of the snow-flake rather than the tender flower of the earth.

Having chosen, he allowed his eyes the brief refreshment of another glance; his eyes, perpetually wearied by Hebrew grammars, were comforted by Allegra's cool regard. He was a beholder in whose eyes beauty dwelt at all times to enchant the visible world, but in this moment he was neither dazzled nor blinded; he saw the sprightly imperfections, the exquisite flaws in this being compact of grace and mockery, and he would not have altered her by the length of an eyelash or the smoothing of a hair.

"Thank you," said Allegra, taking the arrow with a smile, half of politeness and half of pleased amusement. Mr. Hazard looked so very odd in Allegra's cool blue eyes that she could not keep her pink mouth from turning up at the corners. Allegra was cheerfully practical; she wanted to laugh, and she also wanted to set Mr. Hazard among the strawberry beds to scare away the birds. In Allegra's merry and intolerant judgment Mr. Hazard would make an admirable scarecrow; as a man he was ridiculous.

Rosa's more charitable mind transmuted this opinion into a belief that Mr. Hazard might possibly be poor and that he must certainly be hungry. The ingenious goodness of her heart sought for some means of providing him with the wing of a chicken and a large slice of plum-cake. There was a red and green basket under the willow-trees, and several stone bottles of ginger-beer.

"Have you come far this afternoon?" asked Rosa. "Oh, I see; from Gravelow. And are you going back in time for dinner?"

"No," said Mr. Hazard, "I have my dinner with me." He picked up his coat and looked in all the pockets; he was sure he had put some bread and cheese into his pocket before he left his lodgings.

"So have we," said Rosa, "in that basket; it's nice eating one's dinner out of doors, isn't it?" She smiled, but she was very sorry for Mr. Hazard, because he couldn't find his bread and cheese.

"Do have some of ours," she said when she could bear it no longer; Mr. Hazard had found at least twenty pencils and a number of old letters, but not a single crumb of bread and cheese.

Allegra looked at Rosa, raising her arched eyebrows into light satiric wings above her amazement. Her small lips formed soundless words in the still air.

"Mama wouldn't let us," she breathed, inaudibly save to her sister's accustomed senses. "She wouldn't like his rowing up the backwater; I think she'd say he was a tramp."

Mr. Hazard was holding his coat upside-down and shaking it, and watching the pencils fall into the bottom of the skiff. His sensitive perceptions were distracted by his search; he failed to catch even the faintest whisper of Allegra's words. Had he heard them, nothing could have prevented him from racing back to Gravelow like a proud and somewhat ragged flash of lightning but he did not hear them, and he remained among the willows of the backwater, at the mercy of a sportive and capricious fate.

"That's absurd," said Rosa aloud. Mr. Hazard thought she meant his own behaviour; he accepted the comment with a laugh.

"It is, of course," he said, "I seem to have forgotten my dinner; sometimes I do. It doesn't matter in the least, as I don't happen to be hungry."

"You must be hungry; you've been rowing," said Rosa firmly; privately she thought he must have starved in an Irish famine, or been locked in an underground dungeon upon a diet of bread and water. Rosa was less practical than Allegra; she read romances and even occasionally poetry. But she was practical enough to open the basket and to give Mr. Hazard the wing of a chicken and three slices of brown bread and butter.

He sat in the skiff and the children sat upon the river-bank under the shadow of the willows. There were no apple blossoms to be seen, but the wind had lately blown over an orchard; it scattered invisible petals upon the surface of the water. The armour of a dragon-fly shone like a drift-wood flame.

Mr. Hazard was happy, happy as a hunter who watches a forest glade down which a troop of deer approach with shy and subtle steps. He looked at Allegra, and through the bright crystal of Allegra's face he perceived the vague and faintly tinted faces of other children, lovely, but no lovelier than Allegra, and perhaps, now that Allegra smiled at him, no dearer to his heart. He was content to have it so; to gaze into the clear, sharply faceted crystal of Allegra's face and to see therein the tragic past and the tired present and the austere future, melted into a single beam of light.

5

CAPTURE OF A BLACK SHEEP

LADY CLARA HUNTING was the youngest and by far the prettiest daughter of that Lord Camphile who had been Poynyard of the East India Company, and who had died the Earl of Camphile and Eden. It may be remembered by people who take an interest in such matters that Gerald Poynyard had the misfortune to lose his first wife; she perished in Persia under distressing circumstances, leaving Gerald a widower at the age of twenty-eight. Jennifer Poynyard had never been robust, either in body or soul; her strange Arcadian beauty perished with her, as she left no child, and little recollection of herself save in the grief of her parents and in Gerald's passing regret.

At the time he was Poynyard of India; he was far too deeply occupied by affairs of state to be melancholy except upon the rare occasions when he dined alone, and even then he found a good French novel a very fair substitute for a silent wife. He returned to England at the end of ten years, and remarried almost immediately, choosing a beautiful and well-bred girl from the outer branches of one of the great Whig houses. Augusta's beauty was not so pure and rarefied as Jennifer's, but her mind was strong and her stamina excellent. It would be untrue to say that she was never afraid of Gerald, but she hid her fear under her arrogant good looks and her composed and agreeable manner. She was witty; quite witty enough for Gerald, whose superior wit was contemptuous of gifts he could so easily outmatch. He was fond of her; he thought her handsome and healthy, if a little too self-assured. He was severely unaware of her talkative moods, and when her *jeux d'esprit* jarred upon his sensibilities, he philosophically thanked his stars that he had not after all married that minx Rosalba Berni, whom he had met at M. Voltaire's. Wit was a confounded nuisance with one's first cup of tea.

Augusta bore him three pretty little girls in rapid succession; Gerald was courteous, and often commented upon his daughters' comeliness, but although he appeared attached to Geraldine and tolerant of Sophia, he was distinctly annoyed by Clara's advent. His wife's friends were vastly relieved when her fourth child indulgently decided to be a boy.

Although named for his maternal grandfather, Charles Augustine was so precisely like Gerald that his mother found it impossible to make friends with him. If the thing had not been unthinkable, she might sometimes have thought that it was impossible to be fond of him. He was a brilliant and self-possessed child, and his father's features were so perfectly reproduced in miniature upon his small pale face that one might almost have believed that the Mexican savages had stolen Gerald's head and shrunk it up with red-hot sand into the minute proportions of a baby's skull.

Augustine was sent to school at the age of five; Gerald was even more Spartan with his children than with himself. In that same autumn Augusta took her girls to Paris, explaining politely that she disapproved of convents, and that if the poor children were to learn French properly, they must live in France. She had been extremely frivolous in a stately way of her own, yet she relinquished the prospect of London gaieties without a sigh, and her large grey eyes were luminous with relief as she gave her husband an affectionate farewell kiss.

Augusta and the three little girls grew calm and rosy during their first month in Paris; from being anæmic and nervous they bloomed into liveliness and dimples. From that time onward they were always pink and sweetly cheerful; their French was faultless, their complexions exquisite. It was no wonder that when Augusta brought them out in London, everyone fell in love with their ringlets and their laughter. It was their carefree laughter, even more than their irregular verbs, that their mother had sought to cultivate in the sunny seclusion of the faubourg Saint-Germain.

It had become a habit with them which Gerald had to accept whether he liked it or not. He liked it well enough when they laughed their way into three suitable matches, of which his favourite Geraldine's was inevitably the best. Lord Camphile's fortune was enormous, but he wanted it all for Augustine; his provision for his girls was comparatively modest, and he was rather proud of them for having contrived to marry themselves off so cleverly. Clara had not been so clever as the others, but he had never cared for Clara. Her mother adored her, a mere indulgence of self-love, for she was her mother over again in finer porcelain, turned on a lighter wheel and touched with brighter dyes. Her beauty was a flattering mirror to Augusta's face.

This was the lady whom Allegra called Mama, who now came down a narrow path among the willow-trees. Clara was three-and-thirty at this time, only seven years younger than Mr. Hazard, but no one seeing them together would have credited the calendar fact. Clara's fair hair, flaxen at twenty, was now pale chestnut quite unmarred by grey; her long-lashed eyes were dark and transparent as amethysts. Her skin, white as Allegra's, lacked the freckles which the sun had sprinkled like golden sequins on Allegra's little nose and smooth ingenuous brow. Clara was prettier than her daughters, more elegant and more composed. Her youthful laughter was now softened and diffused into a thousand slight enchanting smiles; the quality of her charm was evanescent, but although it appeared for ever fleeing, it filled the air about her like a perfume. Mr. Hazard watched her unhurried smooth approach with sentiments of pleasure; her gliding step, her gown of thin blue muslin, even the tinted cameo at her throat, seemed emblematical of peace. Mr. Hazard trusted such a lady to be kind as he would have trusted a cluster of white grapes to be sweet or a moss rose to be fragrant.

She looked at her daughters with a questioning smile which was nevertheless quick and insistent; her eyebrows elevated themselves into the waves of her hair and she waited, dubious and amused. Mr. Hazard, who had risen, made a long step to the riverbank, and Rosa spoke.

" We've forgotten to ask you your name . . ." said Rosa apologetically, blushing under her mother's scrutiny, which suspended
judgment and forebore to scold as yet.

"Hazard," said Mr. Hazard. Suddenly he despaired; reality
overwhelmed him like a muddy tide. He swallowed mud; he
breathed a suffocating darkness; he knew that the sound of his
name would break the tranquil surface of the scene, and drown
him in humiliation. He leaned against a tree, faint with the ap-
prehended stroke.

It did not fall. It hovered about his head, and slid into the
grasses at his feet as harmlessly as a deflected lightning flash. In
the vibrating balance of Clara's mind, curiosity weighed more
heavily than horror, and she smiled again.

" Then you're the Mr. Hazard who . . ." said Clara against
her well-bred will, and straightway poured a warm balsam of
words into the freezing pause that gaped between them like a
wound.

It was all true; Clara made it seem even truer. They had met
in Venice, soon after Mr. Hazard had returned from Greece with
his arm in a becoming black silk scarf. Everyone knew that the
chieftains had tried to make Mr. Hazard King of Greece, and
so several people in Venice had asked him to tea. Mr. Hazard
had refused all the invitations except one; his wife had wept
because he refused; and he had gone with her to a palace near
the Church of Saint John and Saint Paul, and sat for half an
hour in a hot room full of candlelight and tuberoses and the
tinkle of women's voices. Clara remembered his white face and
the dazed brilliance of his eyes, whose glances moved up and
down the long, crowded room seeking for a ladder of escape
above the roofs, for a stairway sunk into the bottom of the lagoons. While she ate a strawberry sherbet, she had decided that
he was a fool rather than a fiend.

He had changed a little in seven years; the silver of his hair
was startling against the parchment colour of his face. The dazed
brilliance of his glance moved up and down the river, seeking for
a channel of escape.

Clara felt inquisitive and sorry; she wondered very much
whether the wicked Mr. Hazard were not belied by his silvery

wolf's clothing. She knew how easily her evasive smiles could charm him even if he were a wolf. But of course he was only another black sheep; the thorns and briars of the reasonable world were tagged with locks of visionary wool from the fleece of such poor creatures.

6

THREE LADIES IN HALOES

THE MAKESHIFT armour contrived by Mr. Hazard's pride was doubled by a horrid lining; it might have been woven from nettles or horsehair and steeped in the blood of the dying centaur. It was, however, quite invisible; only its disastrous effect upon his nerves could be conjectured by Clara's bland judicious gaze. Her quick intelligence, undulled by excessive education, her perceptive sympathies, which rarely involved her heart, her experience, which swept lightly over humanity, bright and shallow as a summer rainfall, these qualities enabled her to look into the depths of Mr. Hazard's mind with a gracious ceremonial smile. If she had looked a thought further, she might have screamed; if she had beheld and comprehended all its pinnacles and caverns, she must certainly have swooned. The eccentric little that she saw affected her with a moderate pang of pity; her intuition was limited, but fair and lenient. It would be a cruel wrong to Clara to believe that rumour which at a later date identified her with the Lady Clara Vere de Vere of Mr. Tennyson's celebrated verses.

Mr. Hazard, on the other hand, saw a number of things which were not truly there, or perhaps it were juster to say that he perceived behind the shapes of actuality a multitude of informing spirits. The exact section of his mind into which Clara's neat pocket insight penetrated was the part wherewith he looked at Clara and the two girls and observed every charming detail of their forms and countenances, their lips and eyes and the ruffled locks of their hair making a magical spectrum of colour in the sun. Clara was pale chestnut and rose-ivory and amethystine-blue; Rosa was auburn and pink-coral and hazel-grey; Allegra was flax and snow and aquamarine. Mr. Hazard had never taken an interest in muslin frocks; the nymphs of his imagination were clothed in their own brightness, or in a cloud, or in the shadowy abundance of their tresses. The cashmeres and merinos, the grosgrain silks and Lyons velvet of his wife's wardrobe had made a sober rainbow of black and violet and crimson, but their rich fabric had evoked no mystery. Now he was bewitched by the fancy that the muslin frocks of Clara and her girls had been accurately matched to the several colours of their eyes. These greys and azures were at home among the willow-trees, between heaven and the curve of heaven reflected in the stream. The girls' thin skirts, which were so short as to leave their fragile ankles free, were spattered with river water; there was an engaging plumy disorder in their curls. Even Clara, the veritable looking-glass of grace and freshness, wore along the border of her blue gown a frosty pattern of dandelion feathers; a few of these winged seeds clung like snow-flakes to her soft brown hair.

From the swordblade edge of that sharp instant whereon his destiny had trembled, from the divided second of Clara's mercy or unkindness, Mr. Hazard's gratitude had sprung to meet her. His sick apprehension fell away from his heart; his pride was inviolate, she had not laid even the lightest finger-tip upon it. Yet she had known him, and known all about him; that lying all, that worse than nothing, that painstaking compilation of dead and rotting facts which his enemies would have called the truth. His pride scorned his enemies, and pitied them; it cared not a maggoty fig for their opinions. He cared for the opinions of very few; his friends need never be afraid of sitting down thirteen to table. Seven was a lucky number, and so, at the mouth of the pit, was three. Certainly he could count on three. But here, standing before him in a nimbus of sunset, were three more whom he desired as friends; by some incredible wizardry of fortune they did not turn away their faces from his wish.

Clara saw enough of his mind to be amused and flattered; had she seen even half of it, she would have fled from bother and responsibility like an elusive doe. She had a sensible faith in her own skill in dealing with black sheep of respectable family, and she knew there were no dove-cots to be fluttered within the confines of her garden. Her girls were darting swallows, who would chatter and laugh at wolves and poor black sheep alike.

In the far valleys and upon the mountain-tops of Mr. Hazard's mind walked shapes invisible to Clara. Each of the three figures standing before him in haloes of sunset had a brighter double upon the mountain-tops. These spirits stepped barefoot over the snows; they descended into the valleys to bathe in lucid streams. They were his sisters, and at the same time they were Clara and Rosa and Allegra. They were his children, and at the same time they were Rosa and Allegra.

It must be admitted that Lionel was not among this silver company. He was at San Sebastian with his adoring mother, quite safe, quite stout and healthy, quite satisfied with his worthy and important self. He was now nearly fourteen years old, and his firm little mind had already decided that he did not like his father. Lionel felt that this was a pity; he would never have expected to love Mr. Hazard, but he believed that with a few real efforts towards improvement upon his father's part it might have been possible to like him within reason. Mr. Hazard did not make these efforts. He seemed to consider it the whole duty of parents to be kind and devoted, to impart knowledge with brilliant patience, to listen indulgently to all one had to say, to take one for long lonely walks and to teach one to sail a fishing-smack. Mr. Hazard's theory of pleasures and accomplishments might have been evolved upon another planet than Lionel's. He never even tried to dress like other people's fathers, or to go to church, or to procure a pony or a tutor for Lionel. Lionel could not help disapproving of his father; he was far too virtuous to think this a correct filial sentiment, but he could not help it. Privately Lionel thought Mr. Hazard a thoroughly detrimental father.

Lionel's thoughts were not so private as his complacency supposed; Mr. Hazard was well aware of his son's sentiments. He was sincerely fond of Lionel, but he thought him a prig. Mr. Hazard felt that this was a pity. When Lionel regarded him with cold and ill-concealed disapprobation, Mr. Hazard forced himself to smile. When he was alone, he forced himself to laugh; nevertheless he suffered a profound mortification in the knowledge that Lionel did not like him. Lionel strongly resembled his dis-

tinguished grandfather Mr. Baddeley, and Mr. Baddeley detested
Mr. Hazard. Mr. Hazard had grown used to the situation; he
never worried his wife by referring to it. But he did not consider it necessary to allow Lionel to roam at will among the far
valleys and upon the mountain-tops of his secret mind. The lost
company of children was innocent of Lionel's presence; Lionel
would have disapproved of them all.

Clara watched Mr. Hazard; the cloud of these reflections
sent shadows of reverie across his face. Its lines were deepened
or erased as he contemplated a sorrow or an absurdity. He had not
spoken for at least three minutes.

" Ridiculous creature! " Clara thought tolerantly. " But I suppose he's had rather a hard time of it. He can't have found all
those odd dreary people particularly to his taste. He isn't vain or
bad-tempered, like Alonzo Raven; he's bewildered. ' Blank misgivings . . .' as someone says. It's not to be wondered at that he
finds us an agreeable change after *that* galley. I believe I shall ask
him to dinner one day; it's evident that he's never had enough to
eat since his family disowned him! "

7

DROWNED LYONNESSE

SIR JOHN HUNTING was in Persia; therefore he could not possibly
forbid his wife to ask Mr. Hazard to dinner one day. It is to be
presumed that he had his own reasons for going to Persia; certainly they were nobody else's reasons, for Sir John took nobody
into his confidence. It appeared to be his stubborn determination
to beat Colonel Passmore's detachment by at least six months;
since he went alone, the East India Company was contemptuously
silent. As Lord Camphile's son-in-law he had been a privileged
person; his vagaries were licensed during Gerald's lifetime. But
Gerald had been dead these three years, and now the directors
had received a letter from Lord William Bentinck begging them
not to allow Sir John to come to India again. The Governor-
General wrote pathetically of nervous dyspepsia and the strain

upon his good manners, and the board was happy to assure him that Sir John Hunting was by now exploring Susiana or Elymais, instructing a regiment of Azerbaijan infantry, or composing a memoir on the Atropatenian Ecbatana for the *Journal of the Royal Geographical Society*. As a matter of fact, he was attempting to decipher the cuneiform inscriptions on the rock tablets of Behistun; his discoveries antedated those of Major Rawlinson, but were not crowned with the same wreath of public honours.

Clara deplored his absence with dutiful regret, but she was too happily her mother's daughter to regard an erratic husband as a question of prime importance. Hers was a riddle rather than a question, but her desire to solve the riddle had languished into mild incurious content. She was interested in her children, who adored her. Clara was an enchanting mother; she teased and scolded them in dazzling turn. Her loving mockery was excellent discipline; she could be tender, and although she could be stern, she always forgave them by bedtime.

She felt a slight maternal interest in the unfortunate Mr. Hazard; she was younger than he, but she believed that she was infinitely wiser. She dispatched a pretty little note to his lodgings, inviting him to dine at Lyonnesse upon the following Friday evening.

"Lyonnesse? Can it really be called Lyonnesse?" thought Mr. Hazard as he read the note on a rainy afternoon, with the skies falling upon his smoking fire in sooty black drops. There was the name in gilt letters at the top of the cream-coloured note-paper, yet it seemed too good to be true. His memory of Clara and her girls was fading, as a rainbow fades among wet grey clouds. Allegra was the sea-blue fringe of a rainbow dissolving in the storm.

Mr. Hazard had returned several times to the green door through which he used to emerge into an earlier spring, but although he could see his former self quite plainly, a flushed and breathless stripling in a long brown coat with curling lamb's-wool collar and cuffs, he never caught, even from the corner of his eye, the briefest flicker of light from those younger ghosts whom he hunted along West Street. People emerged; senseless memories emerged at intervals, and then in the hush of waiting his heart would skip a beat, and he would be visited by a premonition of horror. So he would turn and stride back to his lodgings, and if he were not too brutally shaken by the blind encounter, he would apply himself with vehement diligence to the Book of Job, making of his verse a double bridle to bind leviathan.

At the end of five days his mind misgave him; he must be watching the wrong covert. He took various long walks, carrying *Paradise Lost* in one pocket and a hunch of bread and cheese in the other. The woods were freaked and pied with fresh transparent leaves and flowers; the sound of the birds fell with the sunlight, dizzily sweet from above. Nowhere between the forest-trees did he perceive his quarry. The conviction lay cold upon his spirit that only in the slender crystal facets of Allegra's face could he perceive it; perhaps he would never see Allegra again.

Therefore Clara's note came to him as a white dove out of the stormy afternoon; its olive-branch shone like a cluster of pearls. He had walked over to Windsor Great Park that morning; it was shrouded in unrevealing mist, and he had returned to Gravelow through a driving rain. Now he could not work, or even stop the fire from smoking. He was on the bleak point of deciding to go back to Spain when the lodging-house servant brought him Clara's note. It made pleasanter reading than young Mr. Bulwer's novel, *Eugene Aram,* which Annamaria had given him as a parting gift. It had been an error to suppose that *Eugene Aram* was light reading suitable to a rainy day; Clara had provided the only reading possible in such weather.

Friday was fine; the leaves glittered after the rain like the plumage of a million peacocks. Mr. Hazard was waked at four o'clock by a jagged rejoicing sound of cock-crow; his heart gave a leap and he was broad awake in an instant. He laughed to think that he had seized the earliest moments of this day because he desired it, because he could not lie submissively asleep after its bright edge had dipped itself in sunlight. The impatient hammering of his heart drummed him out of bed and into the garden; he walked up and down the garden in his dressing-gown, marvelling at the drops of dew as if each had been a special miracle.

When the clear amber of morning had turned into the cloudy

amber of afternoon, Mr. Hazard dressed himself with extreme care; his elegance was slightly formal and old-fashioned, but it became him the better for this singularity. It never occurred to him to hire a chaise from the inn; he considered the skiff, but in the end he set off on foot.

The rain had laid the dust; it was not unreasonable to go on foot through such an afternoon. A faint mist melted the morning's colours to opalescence, and blanched the sun to the moon's paler gold. Mr. Hazard climbed the winding paths of the Quarry Wood and went down into the valley. The hedgerows were like green waves whose crests of foam had been magically stayed at the moment of breaking. Mr. Hazard plucked the hawthorn and sniffed its bitter fragrance as he went.

Presently he saw a lane that ran between high walls, and at the corner of the lane a painted sign, with the word *Lyonnesse* written upon it. The lane was longer than he had supposed, and it had many turnings; now it ran under trees, and now between meadows where taller trees lifted their latticed branches against the cloudy hem of the west.

At last he saw the house clear at the end of a vista, and then it disappeared, and he saw it again under an archway of trees. It had been built less than forty years ago, of yellow brick and stone; he had seen it often, in sharp relief against the air and in wavering reflection in the stream, as he passed in his boat along the river. He remembered it very well now; it was a strange house, and he had always been charmed by its forward-thrusting shape above the water. It hung there like a castle or a crag; the severity of its outline was touched with Gothic fantasy.

From the river it was a promontory, but now its tawny fabric made it into a golden tower in the sun. Its lawns were striped and chequered with light, so that half lay like a field of gilt damask and half like a tapestry of blue and violet shade. There was a copper beech upon the lawn, and its thin new leaves were not metal, but flame.

Clara was waiting for Mr. Hazard upon the stone terrace; she did not appear in the least surprised to see him come on foot. She wore a frock of crisp white muslin, with wide diaphanous sleeves gathered into bands about her wrists like the sleeves of some pastoral bishop in a fairy-tale. There was a blue sash tied at her waist and a transparent blue kerchief knotted below her throat. She looked as fresh as if she had fallen from the rain-washed sky and were still wound in its tinted veils.

Mr. Hazard was somewhat tired, because he had been awake since four o'clock that morning; the sight of Clara was grateful to his senses as a glass of iced wine. He was aware that his shoes were dusty, and that Clara's hand was cool and fragile as she touched his hand.

"I am glad to see you," said Clara in her sweet voice, which held more intricate stops and modulations than most people's voices. "How nice that you could come to us today and what luck to have such perfect weather! Here are the girls coming up from the river; you will have to be properly introduced this time."

Mr. Hazard turned towards the river; he saw Rosa running up the path in a pink frock. Allegra followed three steps behind her, but Mr. Hazard could not see the colour of Allegra's frock. The delicate irregular radiance of Allegra's face was a clear crystal wherein Mr. Hazard beheld the pure and absolute image of beauty, clothed in its own brightness and borne along by the wind of its own speed. The crystal of Allegra's face was a clear chalice, filled with immaculate beauty to the brim.

8

UNLACING OF A BREASTPLATE

"SHALL we have tea in the saloon, or tell them to bring it out to the terrace?" asked Clara after dinner, certain that nobody but a blind man would choose the saloon with the prospect of sunset and moonrise before him. She knew that Mr. Hazard was not blind; his large disquieting eyes had rested longer upon her face than upon the laughing faces of her children, and already she had seen that Allegra's grace had tranced and enchanted his mind. He looked at Clara with his eyes and at Allegra with the inner vision of his mind. Clara was not disturbed by this trick of double perception upon the part of Mr. Hazard; she told herself that she was the only person present who was not a child or a bewildered dreamer more easily led than any child. She felt herself capable of leading Mr. Hazard away from his vision should occasion ever demand this measure, and she suspected that although he loved Allegra, the girl was no more to him than an alabaster shell filled with the light of his own spirit. If Mr. Hazard wished to find a friend among them, he must choose Clara.

Mr. Hazard had already chosen her; already she was invested in the splendour of his imagination. Whatever might have been one's opinion of Mr. Hazard in his twentieth year, at forty he looked invulnerable and coldly withdrawn. This frigid demeanour was a deliberately contrived effect; this was his armour. It was heavy and cross-grained upon his heart; he looked at Clara and he saw a friend, and little by little the joints of his armour were loosened. It fell away from his breast; it was as though the weight of a millstone had fallen. He laid aside the heaviness of years, and drew his breath lightly and without pain. His sharp sigh of relief drew kindness from the air; he was tired, and he wondered how he had ever borne that load of cruel steel over his heart.

"On the terrace, don't you think, in honour of the moon?" asked Clara with her most accomplished smile. Mr. Hazard thought with Clara, but if she had suggested the boot-hole he would have followed her choice contentedly. In showering Clara with the attributes of divinity Mr. Hazard denied her the power to do evil, even in lesser things. If she had bidden him drink the essential oil of bitter almonds instead of China tea, Mr. Hazard would have drained the venomous cup. He had not trusted a living soul for seven interminable years, and now it was a fire-new delight to trust Clara.

Mr. Hazard and Clara walked slowly up and down upon the terrace while the two girls ran races upon the lawn below. "Outrageous little hoydens," said Clara, knowing well that they were prettier than painted moths in the twilight. Presently she sat down in a great chair that was curved and silvered like a sea-shell. "They were made for the grotto, and then the grotto was too damp," said Clara, but Mr. Hazard felt that they had been made for Clara.

He sat upon the stone balustrade of the terrace; he would

have been more comfortable in one of the scalloped arm-chairs, but Mr. Hazard had never cared to be comfortable when he was happy. Perhaps the two states of being might not flourish together in his heart, and he had wearied of striving to reconcile them. He was very happy; he marvelled at his seven years of bitter and suspicious pride. He thought contemptuously of pride; it was not courage, it was after all a recreant and ignoble thing to go armed and armoured and panoplied in that precaution. He looked at Clara and Clara looked at him. The risen moon and the sun inclining towards the west mingled rose and silver-gold in the serene air; these beams were conformable to Clara's face, but not to Mr. Hazard's whose severely carven features shed their flattering dyes as a swimmer's forehead sheds the water.

"Amethystine," thought Mr. Hazard.

"Absurd creature," thought Clara, "I wish he did not look so ill, but perhaps it is only because he is wearing such a very odd cravat."

They talked of the children, and then because the children's antics wove a Grecian frieze upon Mr. Hazard's fancy, they talked of Athens, and from Athens their talk shifted by way of Sparta and Thermopylæ to Persian affairs, and soon they were talking of the East India Company and the late Lord Camphile, and Mr. Hazard was telling how he had once begged Mr. Bird to procure him employment at the court of an Indian prince, in some secret and political capacity. He had been sorry to learn that such employment was open only to regular servants of the Company.

"But I could not see why I should not be a regular servant," said Mr. Hazard with a slight smile, and Clara laughed and told him that he had not the air of a regular servant of anything so incorporated as a company.

"Of Prospero, perhaps," said Clara, being kind, and remembering the trapped and shining prisoner of the Venetian tea-party. Mr. Hazard's short laugh was merciless to himself; he thought of Caliban, but he did not care, because he was happy.

"'Have a new master, get a new man!'" thought Mr. Hazard.

9

PRIVATE VIEW OF THE INVISIBLE

Mr. Hazard walked home by moonlight; the dust seemed impalpable as air beneath his tread. He had forgotten all that austere and patient schooling with which he had sought to inform his mind during the last difficult years, or else his temerity was mocking its lessons in a mood of reckless elation. He had drunk several cups of green tea, but its pale infusion was not sufficient cause for the powerful impulse of joy which bore him onward along an airy path of moonlight. His everyday tastes would have bidden him listen for a nightingale under the flying arches of the wood, but tonight he did not bother about nightingales. The singing of the blood in his ears was set to a light vivacious measure, and he would have been sorry to have its sacred levity darkened by the voice of a bewailing nightingale.

"It will keep you awake, you know; you won't sleep a wink if you take another cup," Clara had told him maternally as she gave him the tea. She would have preferred to give him Turkish coffee, which she made in a pretty contrivance which her father had brought her from Constantinople. Clara loved to make the coffee; it was such a pleasant game that she was sure the sweet resulting syrup could keep nobody awake.

"Nothing ever keeps me awake," said Mr. Hazard mendaciously. He disliked Turkish coffee, because it resembled the muddy brew he had been reduced to drinking in the cave of the chief Odysseus. He had no wish to sleep or to dream while the true world contained Allegra and Clara.

Even as he left them and walked away from the Gothic tower of Lyonnesse, he was well content with the world and with his own share in its revolving fortunes. He compared his present condition to the worser states of the influenza and thought himself luckily recovered. All things were comparative; a boy of twenty hastening to his first assignation might believe this thin gentleman who walked so lightly upon dust to be broken and worn and middle-aged, but Mr. Hazard understood the liberal value of solitude, and he was glad to be alone and with his face turned from Lyonnesse. He had no more desire to steal its enchanting creatures for mortal employ than to fling a noose round the moon and pull it earthward to be cherished in his breast.

Nevertheless he was aware of his happy chance in having found a friend like Clara. She was the fine essence, the seventh distillation of his milder, more Platonic loves, those charming, melancholy loves which had been so much less exhausting than the passions. Yes, Clara was of that graceful number, but above them in her exquisite calm and distinction; she was as the evening-star to a wreath of bright tapers. She might never be willing to read Plutarch before breakfast or to play the guitar after tea, but she would be sure to turn such hours to uses of her own, to fill them with the casual poetry of her gestures and the musical concord of her voice. She was mistress of more influential harmonies than may be evoked from the strings of a guitar.

As to his few excessive passions, their memory pricked his nerves to a joyless agitation, and he did well to forget them if he was to endure the common stress of business with ease and self-command. Whether the business of his life was to be fomenting revolution or composing heroic verse, he did well to eschew the memory of those fevers. His Platonic loves were another matter; a cool, allaying recollection, temperate as Athenian marble.

It is not the province of this chronicle to pronounce a moral or intellectual judgment upon Mr. Hazard's virtues and defects. In the opinion of many persons of good sense and eminent faculties he had been a wiser and a more admirable man had he now proceeded to fall in love with his landlady's daughter or to take the barmaid of the Crown to his actual heart. Others would have advised him to make immediate haste to Portsmouth and to embark without delay upon a vessel bound for Spanish ports. Neither of these meritorious courses occurred to Mr. Hazard. He believed it a mistake to fall in love with one's inferiors; the ardent spirit of his youth had betrayed him into this error more than once, and the ensuing shocks had rendered him incapable of its repetition, and undesirous of the bad essay. The Spanish voyage was inevitable, but his conscience had set it for September, and it had not the barbarity to goad him to dutiful change of plan as he strode along the moonlit path to Gravelow. It would have been a harsh inflictive conscience that had harassed Mr. Hazard as he walked alone in the regenerated quiet of his soul.

For the first time in seven years he seemed to possess his soul in patience. Now for the moment he regretted nothing, he demanded nothing even of his own driven and conscripted powers. Beyond the light clear fabric of his thoughts, beyond the tranquillity of his thoughts unravelled from their horrid knots and smoothly braided into order, he perceived Allegra. Clara had untied the knots and soothed the tangles of his mind; she had accomplished this miracle without effort, by the subtle expedient of her smiles. But Allegra could do far more than this; the sharp irregular facets of her little face provided a glass for divination and subliminal wisdom. This emotion was not Platonic, or romantic, or animal; it was not love, but revelation.

To determine Mr. Hazard a madman and a fool would be precipitate and inept to the point of folly. It is enough to admit that he was mistaken. The emotion that he now experienced was love; Mr. Hazard was too proud, too scrupulous and too sensitive to recognize the recurrent spell. He had not been in love for five adventurous years, save for a brief passion of pity for a prostitute at Salonika, and he no longer believed himself to be a fit vessel for that holy element. He had never been vain, and certain private crosses had convinced him that he was too detached and bitter, too irritable, and, above all, too indifferent to inspire devotion in a fellow mortal. When he thought of Caliban, his thought was not ironical; Mr. Hazard would have made a preposterously refined monster, but his grotesque fancy was quite sincere. Moreover, he believed that he was so far insensible and disillusioned as to be sadly guarded against the assaults of love.

He was not, perhaps, unaware that in the past he had often filled a hollow alabaster shell with the light of his own spirit, but in the past his spirit had been volatile and brilliant, and evident as a burning planet within the trivial lantern where he had been pleased to kindle it. Now he did not recognize the darker star of his spirit within the image of Allegra, and if he had recognized it he would have been overcome by an impersonal anger against himself. He would have thought himself profoundly unfitted to feel a true and pitiful human love for Allegra; by force of scrupulous horror he would have murdered the sentiment in his own bosom. But Mr. Hazard did not suspect the pathetic fact; he was upheld by an implicit belief that the emotion which now possessed and pierced his heart was not love, but revelation.

He raised his eyes to the lineaments of heaven, and beheld the broad circle of stars dissolved in moonlight, drowning in the flood of thin radiance emanated from the moon. The eternal stars were small and perished flames in that vast, cold, pervasive flood of moonlight.

Mr. Hazard was happy, and so it never occurred to him to be afraid of the moon. He walked until the dawn came up with music from the east. The dawn, in Mr. Hazard's eyes as he turned homeward, seemed stained with the rose of predestined joy and plainly elected to a secret calendar of festivals. It is true that Mr. Hazard's odd theories concerning sunrise were untenable, but he had been awake for precisely twenty-four hours and had walked a mile for every hour of his waking.

10

BUTTER AND HONEY

Now, as the rainbow wave of spring arose and broke and flung a glittering spray of flowers into the air and then subsided into the long, smooth swell of summer, there began for Mr. Hazard a little silver age, so peaceable and hushed that it seemed secure against the hurry and violence of an ending. It was an age no longer golden, but it seemed the safer for that moderation; it was so small, so quiet, and so sweetly hedged about that it appeared exempt from envy and evil fortune. It was a paradise of children, but for Mr. Hazard, who was forty years old, it was no more than a middle land, a merciful limbo swept by tempered airs and calm with the lowered sun of twilight. After the ambiguous battles and the loud confusion of the past it was far better than happiness.

Clara was very kind to him. She soon learned him by heart, and

Clara's heart, though cool and thrifty, was quick to learn the symbols and curious traits which traced the outward character of Mr. Hazard. To her it was as simple as a nonsense alphabet, or a blind man's language to be deciphered by her clever finger-tips. Nevertheless, she liked Mr. Hazard; otherwise she would never have allowed him to come to Lyonnesse once or twice every week during May and June.

"He isn't a villain, and he isn't exactly a lunatic," she told her friends, who wondered how Clara could possibly put up with Mr. Hazard. "He is simply an absurd creature, an odd fish very much out of water among the Cockney illuminati, a black sheep unconsciously homesick for the fold. His talents are considerable, I assure you; you know that I have scant patience with poetry, but I believe his reputation is advancing by leaps and bounds and somersaults into places where even you may meet it. Him you will never meet; he wouldn't be a bit more tolerant of you than you are of him, dearest Edwina."

Edwina, or Matilda, or Amelia, as the case might be, would look delicately incredulous at this statement, but it was no stranger than the truth. The lady would no more hurriedly have let down her blonde lace veil and departed in her barouche than Mr. Hazard would have dropped his book, stooped to pick it up again, and fled to the point or the plantation. Clara had no trouble with cuts and *contretemps;* if the world regarded Mr. Hazard as defiling pitch, Mr. Hazard was at extreme pains to keep himself unspotted from the world. Clara was the best of good friends with both, for Clara belonged to the gay and self-sufficient world, and Mr. Hazard, in these hypnotic hours, belonged to Clara.

She liked him well enough to be carelessly flattered by his devotion; she thought his judgment sound in selecting her as a type of titulary saint, while he avoided the company of her acquaintances as though they had been so many elegant ghouls and succubi. It was a nice discriminating distinction, which stroked the pigeon feathers of Clara's gentle vanity until they shone like the outer skin of a pearl. The dreaming docility of Mr. Hazard's manner towards Clara was in piquant contrast to his wild runaway recoil from her country neighbours. In his more philosophic moods he would even submit to holding the Berlin wool for her embroidery, but if an inoffensive female in a fashionable bonnet approached with the tiniest rustle of silks, he turned chalky white and disappeared.

He was extraordinarily biddable, and his persistent innocence was a continual outrage to Clara's polished common sense. Nevertheless, it was a convenient quality; a dexterous touch might mould it, like clean wax, to any fabulous shape or pattern. It was a source of vexed amusement to Clara to observe how deeply her idlest word could impress the pure and malleable substance of Mr. Hazard's innocence.

" Let me see, how old will your Lionel be next November? " Clara would inquire sweetly. " Ah, fourteen; perhaps he's a trifle young for Allegra, but what fun if they should fancy each other! She's very much of a child at sixteen, isn't she? "

" Completely a child," Mr. Hazard would reply, his eyes upon Allegra's shining head as it dipped and skimmed in the distance. " It is a pity that she must ever grow up. But I should account myself the most fortunate of fathers to make such a water-nymph my daughter, if such dreams need not always go by contraries."

" He doesn't know I'm teasing him," thought Clara, suppressing both her mirth and her impatience. " He's impossible to snub, because he insists upon taking one's most frivolous remarks at their solemn face value. I meant to remind him that he's old enough to be Allegra's father, and to hint that it's ridiculous to adore her as he does, and instead I've only sent him into a happy reverie about settlements and silver-mounted corals."

Clara's verbal skill and Mr. Hazard's thin-skinned and fastidious taste were united in an effort to invalidate the fact of Mr. Hazard's tragic and unequal love. Between them they succeeded in an occult subversion of the truth which had the doubtful merit of deceiving them both. Clara began to remind herself that Lionel, in spite of his father's heterodox opinions, was the heir to solid advantages, and Mr. Hazard was so certain that his passion for Allegra was transcendentally paternal that any opposing arguments would have sickened him into memories of Saturn's reign.

" You must be kind to him, children; the poor creature loves you to distraction," Clara told her girls in discreet plural. It was evident to anyone with wide bright eyes in her head that Allegra was Mr. Hazard's favourite, yet Rosa was kinder to him than Allegra ever stopped to be. Rosa was just and compassionate; she never lost her temper with Mr. Hazard as Allegra occasionally did, and she even had the patience to lie in a punt and listen to the lesser choruses of *Job: A Lyrical Drama.*

"Appropriate!" said Allegra. "How can you possibly help laughing when he comes to the part about the island of the innocent and the pureness of hands? He *is* so fond of that bit! You are an angel, and I hope he's sufficiently grateful."

"I don't mind it very much," said Rosa charitably. "In fact, I'm not at all sure that I don't rather enjoy it, on a hot afternoon. '*Job: A Lyrical Lullaby*'; it's a nice sleepy sound, like far-away thunder."

Occasionally Mr. Hazard would write little verses upon the leaves of his note-book, and tear them out, and give them to Clara or Rosa. He never gave them to Allegra, because he knew that Allegra did not like verses. Perhaps Mr. Hazard had guessed this dislike, or perhaps Allegra had told him when she lost her temper. Neither Clara nor Rosa shared her prejudice; Mr. Hazard's verses were very short and very narrow, a light sprinkling of words down the middle of a torn page. "Lovely," Rosa would say with a smile, and Clara would say: "Charming," or "How pretty," and mean it.

Mr. Hazard was content with this middle state; he found it better than happiness. He moved in an elegiac atmosphere; he was secluded and absolved from all extremities of the heart, and his mind had forbidden himself to grieve or to provoke him by questions or commands. The populated waste of London, the withering storms and icy strictures of his fever, the quicksands and the broken bridges of the further past, these things receded and were whirled away from him, until they appeared no larger than a cone-shaped cloud, a pillar of sharp particles of dust. The present closed upon him like a hermit's cell, clear and symmetrical, and full of sunlight as a bee's cell is full of honey.

11

PLENTY OF CREAM WITH THE
STRAWBERRIES

THAT year's strawberry crop was uncommonly fine, which was fortunate, because Mr. Hazard was so very fond of strawberries that he had almost enough to eat so long as they were in season. Certainly they were an incomparable fruit for anyone who preferred not to lift his eyes from the pages of a book, even while he was dining. Cherries had stones, and gooseberries had hairy skins; an apple must be peeled and quartered, and that was an undertaking that stole his hands and eyes away from the Hebrew Testament. The dates of Arabia were both stony and sticky, and Seville oranges required one's entire mind. Peaches and grapes were almost worth the bother, but the bother was there, between him and the book; a melon was nearly as bad as a knock on the door. There was nothing in the world like a strawberry, cleanly moulded as a flower, and with its frilled stem providing a neat handle which even the most absent-minded person must appreciate. While there were strawberries to be had in the markets of Gravelow, there was no real danger that Mr. Hazard would starve.

For the sake of Job, and the virgin surface of his foolscap, Mr. Hazard ate his strawberries without sugar or cream when he dined alone in his lodgings. What else he ate is a matter for pure conjecture, not to be determined by an examination of Mr. Hazard's weekly bills. Fowls were bought; cutlets in immoderate quantities; ducks upon occasion, and profuse green peas and carrots. These were pleasant days for Mr. Hazard's landlady, but such is the rank ingratitude of human nature that by the end of June she resented Mr. Hazard's inroads upon his own brown loaf and Cheddar cheese, and stared indignantly at the empty dish when he was hungry enough to eat all his own strawberries.

Mr. Hazard had succeeded in reconciling Job and John Milton's Satan to a perfect concord; the other Satan, the Satan of the Hebrew Testament, was busy going to and fro in the earth, and walking up and down in it, while he devised elaborate torments for Job. This Satan was not a sympathetic character, yet sometimes Mr. Hazard liked him better than Job. He remained in the company of these from nine o'clock in the morning until the table was laid for dinner, but in the evening he escaped to John Milton's Satan. He wandered for miles up and down the valley of the Thames, sometimes in the skiff and sometimes on foot, and perhaps once a week Clara sent him a little gilt-edged note inviting him to Lyonnesse.

When he dined with Clara, he had plenty of cream with his strawberries; Clara saw to that, for she had a shrewd and amused suspicion that he lived upon watercress and monastic lentils when he was out of her sight. By intuitive enchantments untouched by vulgar curiosity Clara had discovered quite as much about the influenza and the broken ribs and the pistol ball as Mr. Hazard could remember, and possibly a little bit more. She was aware of Mr. Hazard's genius for making himself uncomfortable, and vaguely, carelessly aware of another and far different sort of genius, lighting its intermittent fires within the ravaged framework of his body. Partly in true charity of heart and partly in childlike vanity Clara took pains to make Mr. Hazard more comfortable than he had ever been since his family disowned him; she was very proud of the gentle wonders she accomplished without effort or particular thought. It was white magic, the more remarkable because she never exercised it above once or at most twice a week. It was pleasant to ameliorate the sad state of Mr. Hazard's nerves and to make the holes under his cheek-bones less conspicuous, but at the same time Clara felt that it would never do to spoil him. Once a week was enough; twice was a feast of indulgence.

It is an affecting commentary upon Mr. Hazard's way of life that such an amelioration should have been wrought in his comfort by Clara's casual kindness. He was quite capable of taking care of himself had he chosen to do so, but he did not choose; it never occurred to him to take care of himself. The project was too dull for his imagination; in a storm or a battle or a revolutionary plan he was eminently cool and courageous, but in lodgings in Gravelow he was not tempted to take thought to save his skin. In Mr. Hazard's sardonic opinion his skin was not worth saving. As to conserving his energies and guarding his powers, he had wasted and spent these things in a thousand vain endeavours, but at least he had flung them upon the hurricane, and scattered them upon the face of the sea. They were not worn away in fear and safety and avarice of the spirit.

Nevertheless his wild prodigality had been hard upon Mr. Hazard; the past ten years had exhausted him. Clara knew the limits of his strength better than he cared to know them; she saw that he had come to the thin frayed end of his tether, the strained and tightened thread. Softly and insensibly she drew him back through a labyrinth of weariness; he would never have retraced its arid paths alone. Her hand was light and fragile as it rested upon his, and with the utmost ease she drew him back to life.

She gave him plenty of cream with his strawberries, and she did not laugh when he looked at Allegra. Clara did not believe in spoiling Mr. Hazard, but perhaps she spoiled him a little, against her colder judgment. She felt very sorry for him when he looked at Allegra, and so she poured more cream upon his strawberries, and did not even smile.

"He works too hard at that ridiculous poem," thought Clara. "And of course he does not eat enough, or go to bed at a reasonable hour. It's entirely his own fault; I have no patience with such folly. But I wish he did not look so ill."

"We are going for a picnic next Wednesday afternoon," said Clara weakly. "Do come with us, if it would amuse you. When the boys come home for the holidays, we must have plenty of picnics."

12

SHEER O'ER THE CHRYSTAL
BATTLEMENTS

THE MONDAY before the picnic brought Mr. Hazard a long letter from Annamaria; he read it impatiently, crumpling its closely written sheets in irritable fingers. Her crossed and interlined pages closed upon his brain like a net upon a flying creature; the Hexateuch was less wearying to his eyes. By the time he had deciphered the letter he had a headache, and his conscience, which was even more sensitive than his optic nerve, was painfully affected.

"My dear Hazard," wrote Annamaria in vivid violet ink, "we are convinced that you are lonely. Coulson says he saw you in Maidenhead last week and that he could not in common honesty give us a good account of your looks. We are considering a little holiday in Dorset at Lulworth Cove or some such pretty spot and should be very happy for your company. The Carlyles have asked us to Craigenputtock, but naturally we cannot afford the journey. What would you say if we turned up at Gravelow one of these fine mornings and took lodgings next door to you? I am sure we should cheer you up amazingly in your 'retired leisure' and I would make it my particular care to tyrannize over you in the matter of flannel waistcoats and cod-liver oil."

Mr. Hazard leaned back against the broken springs of the sofa and closed his eyes; the letter fell to the floor, crushed into a crackling ball of paper. "Good God; cod-liver oil!" said Mr. Hazard in a whisper which rustled less audibly than the crushed pages of the letter.

He knew, of course, that he must ask the Hartleighs to visit him. His imagination conjured up a score of dutiful reasons, presented to his pity like so many waxwork groups wherein the Hartleighs' domestic misfortunes were modelled in crude emotional blood and tears. The forced and vulgar gaiety of Annamaria's letter was infinitely pathetic and infinitely repulsive to his mind. He would willingly have paid a thousand pounds by means of ruinous post-obits to be spared the necessity of writing the affectionate note which invited his friends to join him at Gravelow without delay.

"They are certain to come Wednesday," he told himself shortly; he had nothing but contempt for the cold inhospitable distaste at the core of his heart. But on Wednesday there was a letter by the first post explaining that someone had lent the Hartleighs a cottage at Hythe. "A rose-bowered cot," Anna-maria called it. "There will always be a bed for you, Hazard, and a welcome kept warm upon the hob."

"Excellent creature," said Mr. Hazard, with an acid smile for his happy deliverance; he had an honest scorn for his own squeamishness. He perceived quite plainly that Annamaria was possessed of sterling virtues which Clara's elegant mockery had thinned to gilded filigree; nevertheless he preferred Clara's cooler welcome, and the lighter clasp of her more delicate hand.

Clara's welcome was cool as the slim bottle of hock, sealed with mauve wax and necklaced with a princely coat of arms, which lay half hidden in green water under the willow-trees. The day was very hot; the sun absorbed the colour of the sky, which fainted through gradations of blue and crystal to transparency.

"I knew you would be tired," said Clara with a sidelong glance at Mr. Hazard; his boots and his black trousers were trimmed with a disreputable ermine of dust. "You look a little like one of those unlucky magic images which some enemy has melted away to nothingness in front of a raging fire. Why on earth didn't you come by the river on such a morning? We meant to make you row us to a more romantic solitude, but now we shall have to give you a very cold luncheon before you will be fit for it."

"I am not tired," said Mr. Hazard somewhat stiffly, "and I think this is a deplorably dull place for a picnic. I had far rather row you to Taplow or Bisham; it is too early for luncheon."

"Now you are cross," said Clara, laughing, "I knew that you were tired; you are never cross or rude except when you are tired. We are all of us starving, but I suppose we shall have to wait until you have rowed us up stream for ever before you will allow us a leaf of lettuce or a drop of ginger-beer; it is very tiresome of you."

To herself she murmured: "Absurd creature!" and "Preposterous vanity!" while her kind heart accorded him several excuses for petulance. It must be excessively fatiguing to walk five miles under a broiling sun, with one's pockets full of heavy books, and one's thin flesh fretted by mortifying thorns of weariness. It must be galling to know that one's hair was grey instead of silver-gold or russet; it must be vexing to wear a damp shirt and dusty black trousers while lovelier beings were immaculate in linen lawn. Clara forgave Mr. Hazard for his captious pride; she took the honey of compliment from it and neatly removed its sting. Mr. Hazard's gratitude and relief were extreme; her smile went over him like a small wave, washing the dust from his brow.

"We will compromise," said Clara in her teasing and caressing voice. "You shall row us as far as the weir, and we will make the greedy little girls eat drumsticks while you and I eat white meat, and we will drink a moderate quantity of Papa's Johannisberger out of brittle green glasses, and pour the rest into the river as a libation to Odin and a sacrifice to your principles. You will not appreciate it, but it will cure your headache. You may spare yourself the trouble of denying your headache, because at the end of half an hour it will be completely cured."

"How clever you are!" said Mr. Hazard as he fitted the oars into the rowlocks. "You make music without an instrument and compound medicines without a mortar and pestle. I never deny what you bid me believe; your advice is sibylline."

"You are very amiable to tell me so," said Clara, "and to give me pretty speeches in return for scolding you. Here are Rosa and Allegra longing to ask you whether you've remembered the songs; we hope you have the songs in your pocket and that you will read them to us before we've eaten the last strawberry. It will be delightful to have madrigals with our dessert."

"Yes," said Rosa, blushing with compassion, "we hope very

much you've brought the songs; it was so nice of you to write them specially for us."

"Yes," said Allegra, "it was nice of you bothering to write us songs."

Mr. Hazard was not deceived; he knew that the light creature of his love was indifferent to madrigals. The severe brilliance of his inner mind sent its beam beyond the sparkling translucence of Allegra's spirit; she was clear to him body and soul. She would not have given a hollow green rush or a bright new pin for all the songs he had ever made. Nevertheless she was courteous and not unkind; there was no shadow of cruelty to mar her pure impersonal laughter. Her nonchalance could neither inflict a hurt nor heal it; she was innocent of the desire to wound and innocent of pity.

For no better reason than that he loved her, Mr. Hazard was satisfied. He felt that Allegra would have been spoiled by the most trivial improvement; her flaws were more exquisite than perfections. He would never attempt to paint a snow-flake with the warmth and the rich odour of a rose.

"You think them pretty, don't you?" asked Clara with her gentlest mockery as she poured the yellow Rhine wine into the thin ice-coloured glasses. "No, I mean the little girls, not the engraved crystal."

After luncheon Mr. Hazard was tempted into reading his songs. The act was against his judgment and acquired wisdom, but Clara loosened the sinews of his will and he complied, aware of his own folly. He did not care; let him be ridiculous and have done with it, under the shade of the willows, to the Lethean murmur of the weir. The quiet, cool scent of the river, the music of Clara's voice, the wine like chilled sunlight in the thin glass, the wind silvering the willow leaves, had driven away his headache and tempered his pulses to the smooth flow of the stream. His nerves were released from pain; the water clasping his wrist like a miraculous bracelet drew the fever from his blood. The boat was moored in shadow; a radiance, strained and filtered through nets of blue and green, fell upon Allegra's hair. All shapes were softened, all colours were diffused and dimmed. Even the cushions in the boat had faded to the purple-red of *pot-*

pourri. Mr. Hazard had three of these cushions at his back; he drew his hand dripping from the river and found the songs in his pocket, as Clara bade him.

They were not really madrigals; they were small lyrics, in the simplest couplets and quatrains. Clara believed that Mr. Hazard had made the verses plain and simple to suit the understanding of children; she thought them charming and ingenuous.

"Mine is lovely," said Rosa, and Allegra said: "Mine is even nicer." They smiled, and wondered why Mr. Hazard's voice had grown hoarse upon the final syllables. He looked very tired, and more than ever like a scarecrow.

Mr. Hazard was tired, indeed, but singularly content. Clara had led him along a cool and level path of folly, and there was no punishment at the end of it, but only peace, and the children's thanks put into his hands like flowers. He regarded the wasted beauty of his songs as so many drops of honey wherewith to win the suffrages of butterflies.

"What fun we have had!" said Clara as he rowed them back to Lyonnesse on a river visibly dissolving in the rarer essence of evening light. "What a delicious afternoon! Next week the boys will be here; you must come again a week from today, and we will have another picnic, and you shall make friends with the boys and their tutor, Mr. Hodge. Good-bye, and don't forget to eat seven sensible dinners between now and next Wednesday."

The twilight was dissolving gold; Mr. Hazard was the one black mark upon the golden road to Gravelow. The day had drawn an unbroken circle of happiness round him, but now, as the day fell down for ever behind the curving edge of the earth, he shivered a little. He did not think of it as a prophetic shiver; there had been too many chills in the past, upon the slopes of Mount Parnassus and in the hollow vales of the Maremma, to put Mr. Hazard to the trouble of questioning the future about a little shiver along his spine.

BOOK THREE: *MR. HODGE*

1

A DEEP ROMANTIC CHASM

IF anyone ever takes the trouble nowadays to traverse the cloudy eminence of song which Mr. Hazard once builded upon the Book of Job, he may discover for himself that a certain peak of accomplishment outshines and ·overtops the rest. This is the third act; this is the lyric elevation which Mr. Hazard scaled during a week of June. This week contained the longest day of the year, that revolving chariot whose wheels are thirteen circles of moonlight. The longest day, and the brief shadow of darkness cast by it, sufficed for the last chorus, which glittered like snow upon the summit of the rest.

Mr. Hazard was well pleased with his work; he paused and surveyed the earthier kingdoms below him and preferred the isolated tower he had made. He was at once the architect and the explorer of this place; the flying buttresses which supported it were his own powers, and he had cut steps out of cold heaven as he climbed. Now he was satisfied with the height achieved, level with the lower planets and the superior vapours of the universe, and he looked forward quite happily to Wednesday afternoon. He recognized no absurdity in the proportion of his wishes; Lyonnesse was the inevitable valley which lay folded among these altitudes. It waited for him, drenched in light like honey from the broken clouds.

It was the only kingdom of the earth which appeared valuable to one who hovered upon wings of air, with an eagle's prerogative of choice in descending. The continents were spread before his eyes; Europe enamelled green, veined with the branching silver of rivers, embossed with a blue tracery of hills; Asia a mysterious colour like smoke, with fringes of brilliance and crystal spears of mountains; Africa wearing a bright disguise of lion skins clasped by a sapphire chain, and the breadth of America like roughened gold stretched between ribs of granite and enriched by the transparent blood of streams. He had travelled over the painted variations of this globe, whose curves sloped upward into a sky of reversed phantoms. Mirage had led him on and a pack of illusions had dogged his footsteps. Mr. Hazard was tired of distances; the small kingdom of Lyonnesse invited him. This valley kingdom, circumscribed and unperilous, gentle in its limitations, was a cure for his soul's vertigo. He surveyed it from the third act of his lyrical drama, and thought it a fit inheritance for his soul. He had no use for larger realms; if he should fall asleep in this valley, if he should fall asleep or die, Lyonnesse was a soft bed and a sweetly scented coffin. Say that from these heights it looked no wider than a grave spangled and plumed with summer grass, and you had said the sum of his desires.

He trusted Clara; even if he had been tempted to ask her for some rare and intricate indulgence he would have had faith in her charity. Knowing the ascetic measure of his appetites, he was doubly certain that she would not let him starve; crisp drops of spring water and spare and wholesome crusts could never be denied him. A long hour on the river once a week; a cup of tea on the terrace now and again when his head ached and Gravelow was a town beleaguered by evil; so much she was sure to give him, and he would ask for no more.

"Next summer you must bring your wife and Lionel," she had said to him; the light modulations of her voice had made music of the words and a sunny mirror for their sense. A delicately flattered picture had appeared, wherein Lionel and his mother smiled kindly upon Mr. Hazard, loving him, approving him, believing him. Mr. Hazard had agreed with Clara; a succession of Junes seemed to promise friendship and peace. Lionel and his mother could not fail to be happy here; Clara's voice made this assurance plain.

Now, as Mr. Hazard surveyed the hope of Wednesday afternoon from the calm summit of accomplishment, he was aware of a strict and exquisite proportion in his felicity. It was fairly divided into halves between the knowledge that he had carved a masterpiece out of the very air of heaven and the knowledge that in two days' time he might follow the level Thames to Lyonnesse. He did not smile or dream of smiling to compare such equal joys.

Gravelow was a beleaguered town tonight, but the hosts encamped upon the surrounding water-meadows were excellent spirits, armies of virtue and benevolence; their banners turned the sky into a field of lilies. These shapes of radiance filled the spaces of the wind blowing from the river; they entered the town and walked in light along its streets; they ascended the stairs of Mr. Hazard's lodgings and knocked invisibly upon his door.

"This," said Mr. Hazard to himself, "is your only secular trap for the soul. These spirits move among temporal matters in serenity and wisdom, but they are repelled by desperation. The violence of my longing drove them from me; they fled from the spectacle of my pain. Now that I am happy they come to me of their own accord; they are like angelic moths and may-flies, and he who would attract them must first kindle a taper. I have Clara and her children to thank for these admirable ghosts."

Tired by his conversation with himself and by certain metaphysical problems presented by those features of heaven perceptible from his window, Mr. Hazard fell asleep before the cocks began to crow. When he awoke, the spiritual hosts had disappeared from the water-meadows, but the scattered clouds revealed enough of gold and jacinth to attest their existence in other spheres.

2

WASPS IN THE JAM

THE WEEK rushed to its happy ending, swept onward by the triumphant speed of Mr. Hazard's third act. The morning of the seventh day was variable and pale; flashes of cool sunshine ran between the articulations of the rain like little fishes in a vast silvery net. It was impossible to foretell the weather, but all weathers are sanctified by such happiness as Mr. Hazard's, and he could not believe that the sky would not clear as soon as he had turned his face towards the east. He walked over the hollow plain and under dripping trees where the road curved up the hill and down again into the valley before his faith was vindicated. An oriel of blue opened overhead, permitting the suave light of afternoon to colour the falling raindrops. Mr. Hazard was wet to the skin by the time he reached Lyonnesse, but the oriel had widened to a great rose-window through which he beheld the sun above his left shoulder.

Mr. Hazard's sense of victory over a heaven of the mind and a more desirable earth lying at the turn of this narrow lane lent rapidity to his stride; it was unable to efface the lines of worry and fatigue from his brow or to stain his bleached and faded body with its original brightness. In the last month he had unlearnt every lesson of distrust wherein his pride had long and bitterly instructed him, but the marks of that distrustful pride were still visible upon his brow. He felt secure and strong and invulnerable; the third act of his drama was like a harnessed mountain moving under him. Nevertheless he did not look in the least like a man who has subdued a mountain by incomparable powers of will; he looked like a man who has forgotten to eat seven sensible dinners in seven days, and who has been wet to the skin on a chilly June evening. He looked ill and exhausted; his felicity was unapparent, but it was plain that one of his shoes wanted mending, and that there were several buttons missing from his coat.

To Mr. Hodge he seemed a horrid apparition. Mr. Hodge

was incapable of that flight of fancy which should liken him to a man hanged in chains or a blanched anatomy rejected by the sea, but the blurred shadows of these comparisons crossed his mind as Mr. Hazard approached. To Clara Mr. Hazard looked, as always, like a poor black sheep whose fleece is silvered by adversity; Rosa saw him charitably as the Prisoner of Chillon, and Allegra had grown accustomed to her scarecrow.

"An appalling person," said Mr. Hodge to Allegra, who was perched upon the balustrade beside him. She nodded absent-mindedly, knowing that Mr. Hazard could not frighten a single bird from a single cherry-tree.

"Ridiculous creature," said Clara to Rosa. "How very wet he is, poor darling! How has he contrived to be so very wet when we have had nothing but sunshowers?"

"You are late," said Clara to Mr. Hazard, with the slight comment of her smile, "but it doesn't matter; we have decided not to try the river today. Allegra has a new sash, or Rosa has curled her hair, or Mr. Hodge prefers to eat his lamb and green peas comfortably hot. I hope you are not too cruelly disappointed; of course you will have a far better dinner indoors, but I know you have a passion for picnics. And now I wonder what in the name of common sense I am to do with you."

"To do with me?" said Mr. Hazard, like a bewildered echo. "Must you do anything with me in the name of common sense?"

"To keep you from catching cold; don't you realize that you are in imminent danger of catching cold? You have swum the Thames in a fit of abstraction, and now you must ask Mr. Hodge to lend you some of his nice new clothes to wear while yours are drying."

"Of course," said Mr. Hodge without looking up. "Please; you must, of course." He tried to speak pleasantly. The attempt was a signal failure; Mr. Hodge was annoyed because Clara had called his clothes nice and new, and his antipathy to Mr. Hazard was dull and sullen, like a bruise upon his mind.

"Thank you," said Mr. Hazard, "you are very kind. But I beg you not to trouble about me; I am not really wet; the sun will dry me in a minute or two."

"I never catch cold," said Mr. Hazard to Clara, sitting down upon the stone balustrade of the terrace. He folded his arms tightly across his ribs and gritted his teeth; by a severe effort of the will he kept himself from shivering. His elbows pressed his clenched fists into his ribs, and the shudder passed from his bones obediently as his will directed.

"So I perceive," said Clara with a delicate flavour of malice in her voice. "It's not at all clever of you to refuse my good advice, but I see that you are past praying for. When you sneeze, I shan't even bother to say: 'God bless you.' But of course you won't sneeze; you're much too stubborn to sneeze."

"Mr. Hodge has a beautiful bottle-green coat," said Allegra, "with brass buttons; he's particularly proud of the brass buttons. You'd far better borrow it."

"But your shoes," said Rosa. "At least be reasonable about your shoes. . . ."

"It's quite hopeless, my dears," said Clara, "don't torment him; he must be allowed to catch his own colds in peace. It is almost dinner-time, and the boys have disappeared; will somebody please go hunt for them?"

"I will," said Mr. Hodge, jumping from his seat. His solid step went quickly down the path. He hunched his broad shoulders, shrugging a burden from his mind; he was relieved to be rid of Mr. Hazard's company, and he whistled as he went.

3

DRY BREAD AND RADISHES

MR. HAZARD had worn his shabbiest coat for the picnic, the same coat which had received such cruel usage at the hands of Omar Vrioni's troops during the fighting at Distomo in February 1827. It was a shocking coat; the celebrated bandit Polinario, meeting Mr. Hazard in the autumn of 1831 upon the solitary road between Madrilejos and Puerto Lapiche, had grinned compassionately at the rents in its lining and returned it to its owner with a courtly bow. Mr. Hazard had refused the robber's offer of a sheepskin jacket; he was fond of the coat, which had been made by an Athenian tailor in 1825. Tonight it was undoubtedly wet, but it had been wetter at Mauritius, in the hurricane of 1828; the *coup de vent* which had wrecked the East-Indiaman *George Canning* had blown away at least one of its buttons. It had seemed a suitable garment in which to study the condition of Mr. Telfair's slaves, but it was a curious blot upon the argent shield of Clara's dinner-table.

Clara intended to have the panelling tinted cream-colour as soon as she went north in August; she had never liked the cold pearly grey of its paint. This evening, however, she was well pleased with the look of the room; there was a glimmering play of rainbows upon the walls, and a faint reflected pattern of leaves and clouds touched with a counterfeited light. Her children's faces shone clear and fragile as four crescents set above the oval board. It was that lovely hour which preserves an equable balance between sunset and the radiance of the moon; the children's faces were rosy against the cold pearl-colored walls and the greenish glass of the window-panes. Their small faces, sharply carven, elfin and aquiline, shone rosy and freckled with gold in the light from the west.

"The translucid, or diaphane," said Mr. Hazard to Clara. "'The sun is its father, the moon is its mother.' The dogma of Hermes Trismegistus."

Clara nodded indulgently, hoping that he would drink his soup while it was hot and that the rain-water dripping from his clothes would not stain the delicate beasts and flowers of the Persian rug. She glanced at Mr. Hodge, aware of an acrid breath of intolerance in the crystalline air about her. Mr. Hodge appeared sedate and personable in his dark-blue coat; his nankeen trousers were neatly strapped under shapely and well-polished insteps. He was listening to Tristram's agreeable persiflage; only the corner of his lowered eye swerved suspiciously towards Mr. Hazard's last words.

"I wish the absurd creature would not choose this occasion upon which to talk transcendental folly," said Clara to herself. "He is doing it quite idly, to keep his teeth from chattering; he does not care tuppence for his athanors, elixers, and pantacles.

He is afraid he will have a chill if he admits he is human, and so he talks about Paracelsus and sidereal phantoms."

Perhaps Mr. Hazard was possessed of a nervous organism so sensitive that Clara's thought disturbed it like a command; perhaps he fell silent for some other reason. To Clara's relief he spoke no further word save in answer to the circumspect urbanity of her own conversation, which avoided hermetic pitfalls by a feminine magic peculiar to itself. Nobody else paid the slightest heed to Mr. Hazard; he sat eating bread and radishes, and staring at the children as if he had never seen them before. It was true that he had never seen the boys before, yet he looked oftener at Allegra. When he looked at Tristram and Hilary, he saw that Hilary was grave and regular as a golden coin, but that Tristram was harder to capture or apprehend by even the quickest senses. He was so volatile an essence that he escaped definition; Mr. Hazard admired his fiery and lively grace and the exquisite impudence of his bearing.

Either by accident or design, Mr. Hazard drank his soup while it was hot, and felt much recovered. He was now beyond the petty malice of a physical chill, and it had not yet occurred to him that the surrounding atmosphere contained a frigid element of antipathy. His quick susceptive wits were away upon an argosy of wool-gathering, or their burning course was benumbed by cold or stayed and averted by some alien spell. It was strange that the unfortunate Mr. Hazard should remain unmoved; it was stranger that the high-spirited Mr. Hazard should remain submissive; it was strangest that the proud and suspicious Mr. Hazard should remain unaware of an inimical humour. Nevertheless he so remained; Clara had mixed forgetfulness among her innumerable charms.

Presently Mr. Hodge's eyes swerved under lowered lids and rested for a second time upon Mr. Hazard; Mr. Hodge removed his eyes from Mr. Hazard's face as hastily as if they had been the horns of a snail brought into alarming contact with evil. He looked at Mr. Hazard's plate and looked away again in anger and contempt.

" He is eating salt with his bread like a fool, and buttering his radishes like a Frenchman," said Mr. Hodge to himself with energy. "A man who eats salt with his bread and butters his radishes is a loathsome phenomenon; I wonder that Lady Clara permits such a fellow at her table."

"I am afraid that Mr. Hodge is not liking poor Mr. Hazard," said Clara to herself. "It is a pity that there is so much prejudice in the world. I wonder whether I shall be able to reconcile their chemical differences; Lyonnesse is not the place for explosions. It was bound to happen sooner or later, I suppose, but I hope for poor Mr. Hazard's sake that I can postpone the inevitable."

"We will have tea on the terrace, children," said Clara in her clear unhurried voice, rising from the table in a rustle of India muslin.

4

UNSUBSTANTIAL PAGEANT FADED

Although Clara was cast in a porcelain mould, she was both liberal and humane. Her mind was temperate and well-bred; the sentimental and the intolerant were alike ludicrous in her sight. She was the calm sophisticated foe of cruelties and oppressions; if Kandler of the Albrechtsburg had ever elected to use the Samothracian Victory as a model for one of his life-size china ladies, his creation might have been Clara's double. She wore no cockades; her loyalties were not confessed by so much as a red or a white rose. She smiled, forgiving a rude variety of foibles; she sprinkled attar of bergamot upon factions and the tides of party strife. Of course she was heartily in favour of reform; her father had been known to be a Whig, her husband was said to be a rebel. Nevertheless if the Duke of Wellington or Sir Robert Peel sat next to her at dinner, she could not help feeling a gentle pity for the opposition, and she remembered that Lord Camphile had never approved of Mr. Macaulay.

Her father's firm opinions were still an article of faith for her, but her lighter and more flexible brain had altered them from a political decalogue into a set of pleasant sympathies. She was indifferent to Don Pedro and Don Miguel; she felt a moderate interest in the tea monopoly, and she was truly concerned that the Negroes must still submit to the cart-whip. She was a brilliant ornament of Lord Grey's routs, and the poor of the parish adored her.

Now it distressed her to witness the harsh disfavour with which Mr. Hodge so evidently regarded Mr. Hazard. Mr. Hodge was valuable to her in more ways than one; she could not ignore his prejudices. Her father had discovered Mr. Hodge; Lord Camphile had recognized the young man's eminent merits, and he had removed him from a desk in Leadenhall Street and exalted him into a private secretary. Mr. Hodge had been the comfort of Lord Camphile's closing years, which declined so fiercely into the grave that his family and friends were shrivelled into nonentities at his bedside. Mr. Hodge's bad manners and excellent abilities had sustained Lord Camphile through the cold fury of dying; no one else could be so admirably offensive to an importunate caller as Mr. Hodge.

Clara had inherited him; Lord Camphile would have preferred to leave him to Geraldine, but Mr. Hodge, who had a certain freedom of choice in the matter, had selected Clara from the beginning. Clara was the one Circe who had ever won him from his determined policy of rudeness; her long throat, her small and arrogant head with its coronet of gilded bronze, the lucent jewels of her eyes, formed a type of perfection for Mr. Hodge. Mr. Hodge had been a sceptic and a materialist ever since he was breeched; Clara was his first religion, and his devout novitiate was not yet ended.

He had not presumed to fall in love with her; she would never have permitted such an emotion to mar the deference of his attitude. He, whose habitual gesture towards the world was too discourteous to record, was on his knees to Clara. She was seven years his senior; in the grim secrecy of his soul he acknowledged her seven generations his better. He gloried in his subservience, and as he crushed the timid and the vain in his invincible progress towards success, he brought their limp bodies to Clara and laid them upon her altar like the spoils of war. She was often grieved by these pitiful trophies; this evening she was deeply grieved by his implied scorn for Mr. Hazard.

" He must not be allowed to hurt people's feelings," said Clara to Rosa. "Do you think Mr. Hazard has noticed a slight lack of cordiality, my love? It is very distressing to be present upon these occasions; there is a taint of the slaughter-house about the whole proceeding which is not to my taste. I must scold Hodge unmercifully as soon as Mr. Hazard goes home."

"I don't think Mr. Hazard has noticed anything as yet, Mama," said Rosa soothingly, "of course it's dreadfully evident to us, but Mr. Hazard is so very absent-minded, and he has been listening to Tristram and watching Allegra, and I really believe he is happy. He is always rather quiet, isn't he, when other people are talking? Perhaps he is tired, or has a headache, or has received bad news in a letter from Spain; perhaps he is only having trouble with Job. I truly don't think he has noticed anything amiss."

"I hope with all my heart that he has not," said Clara plaintively. "He is such a defenceless person, such a parcel of absurd sensibilities. But I don't want his feelings to be hurt; I wish he would go home. Is he looking more than usually ill, or is that simply a nervous imagination upon my part?"

"He always looks rather — well, you know the way he always looks, Mama," said Rosa. "Perhaps he does look a little less well than usual, but then he never looks very well."

"Heigh-ho," said Clara, "I suppose you are right, my dear. It's silly to worry about trifles; it spoils the complexion. But one does rather, about poor Mr. Hazard."

"One does," said Rosa, whose heart was soft for the unlucky.

The wind had fallen, with the subsiding rain, and now the evening was clear and warm; light strained through a thin fleece of clouds lay purified and distilled into dewdrops among the grass. Two great chairs curved and fluted like sea-shells stood upon the terrace; Clara sat in one, but the other was empty, since everyone else sat upon the balustrade. The empty chair, varnished in the several tints of nacre, was brim-full of green reflections. It was a chair for a naiad, and Mr. Hazard wished that Allegra might be persuaded to pause there for a moment. Yet to see her running down the path, as she was sure to do in the next moment, was as good or better; in the purified light she would fly like a swallow, swoop like a silver bat, be off into nothingness like the shadow of a cloud. Meanwhile the present interposed a globe of pearl between Mr. Hazard and his fate.

5

CRACK OF DOOM IN A TEACUP

MR. HAZARD had noticed so little that he was still happy. He had no desire to talk, but his silence was neither despondent nor afraid. He did as he pleased, sitting in a fair degree of comfort upon the balustrade, with his back against a marble urn. The marble urn was cold, and velvety with moss. He listened to Tristram, convinced that he smiled; he said: " Hah " in his brief new fashion of laughing, for the aerial performances of Tristram's wit were greatly to his mind. He watched Allegra, and had no quarrel with the universe which wheeled about her planet. His own sphere swung unguided in the hollow sky above them.

"How can he be so deaf, with that look of dismaying intelligence?" Clara asked herself resignedly. "Or so blind, with those preternatural eyes upon their faces? He is under a sleep-walking enchantment, but Hodge will wake him in a minute like the crack of doom."

Clara had wrapped her smooth shoulders in a violet scarf with bands of swan's-down along its edges; she felt a vague tremor of sorrow, which she mistook for the cool night wind, and she muffled her throat in the soft scarf and drew back into the depths of her chair. She had an irrelevant impulse to pray for Mr. Hazard's soul.

It was Rosa's courteous pity which shattered the crystal instant; she could not bear Mr. Hazard to suffer neglect, and to her glittering childish vision he appeared a tragic skeleton, a creature stripped of the bare necessities of joy. She cast about in the bright pool of her memory for consolation or praise.

"Have you finished your sonnet to Milton, Mr. Hazard?" asked Rosa; her voice was distinct and sweet as a bird's in the twilight.

Tristram stopped talking and looked at Mr. Hazard; he was surprised, but lenient and amused, as befitted his nature. Hilary was too polite and Allegra too careless even to glance in Mr. Hazard's direction; they turned the pages of a book of Flaxman drawings and laughed between themselves. Mr. Hodge stared straight at Mr. Hazard; his patience was at an end. He lowered his eyes as if he had stared at a nameless serpent, and spoke.

" Poor Milton," said Mr. Hodge in his heavy mysterious voice, which was yet plain enough for his meaning.

Mr. Hazard recognized the crack of doom; he could not believe his senses. He was startled as he had been startled at the Hartleighs' breakfast table upon the first morning of his influenza; the crystal instant was shattered, his nerves sustained the shock of an actual blow. By a violent exertion of his powers of self-command he reassumed his tranquillity; not his least eyelash or the smallest muscle of his face had betrayed him. Mr. Hodge was vexed by this apparent calm; he doubted whether Mr. Hazard had understood him, and he cursed the other for a blockhead and a fool.

Mr. Hodge did not suspect the truth. Mr. Hazard matched his will against the inimical will of Mr. Hodge, and at the cost of unmeasured spiritual energy he preserved the victory to himself. The truth, however, would have given the liveliest satisfaction to Mr. Hodge had he but known it. Behind the puny shield of his breastbone Mr. Hazard's heart paused in horror, knocked three times like a frantic prisoner, and went forward haltingly, as if its pulse were lamed. On the 13th of May, in Cold-bath Fields, a member of the Metropolitan police force had struck Mr. Hazard a smart blow with his stick; the blow had fallen with sickening impact upon Mr. Hazard's left temple, but it had caused him far less inconvenience than Mr. Hodge's words were now causing him. The strokes were similar, but Mr. Hodge's was the shrewder onslaught, and far more venomous in its effects.

Like execrable hebenon the poison entered Mr. Hazard's brain and was mixed into his blood and the marrow of his bones with immediate virulence. It was hatred, simple hatred, that rank poison fatal to Mr. Hazard's health, which now plagued his veins.

The constable had not hated Mr. Hazard, nor had his truncheon been doctored with contagion. Mr. Hazard was a bystander in Cold-bath Fields, a bystander as innocent as an embittered revolutionary can ever hope to be. The blow was a brisk reminder to move on, and so soon as his giddiness would permit, Mr. Hazard had moved on with the dispersing crowd. Nothing rankled within the cut on his forehead; a square of court-plaster covered it with oblivion. Mr. Hodge's words inflicted a severer wound; the three heavy syllables were pointed with hatred. Mr. Hazard knew hatred when he heard it, and the knowledge wrought no good in him.

There was that in Mr. Hazard's soul, tenable as strength or weakness, which considered the most ungenial theory with scrupulous faith. Above the anger and amazement which dissolved his joints his stricter intellect examined Mr. Hodge's words by its rational light. Was it possible that the sacred name of Milton was dishonoured in the sonnet which Mr. Hazard had written, or, more largely, was there anything in the obscurest corner of Mr. Hazard's spirit which rendered him unfit to celebrate this name in verse? Even as he sat wickedly entranced by hatred, even as his heart was stifled in his side, he considered very gravely whether or not he had done wrong.

The moment passed; only Mr. Hodge and Mr. Hazard were aware that such a moment had ticked suddenly upon the moonlight dial of the hour. Mr. Hodge was disappointed; Mr. Hazard was sensible of a profound fatigue. The moment's dull assault had shaken him, but now emotion and thought were gone from him and he cared not whether he fainted or fell asleep or died, if only he need not answer Mr. Hodge.

Mr. Hazard neither fainted nor fell asleep; a trivial hope had died within him, perishing between the limping pulses of his heart. He might possibly have chosen to die with it had he been given any choice in the matter, but the slight machinery of his flesh was not so simply stilled. It was too vital to be murdered outright by a diminished flow of happiness; it was accustomed to a more stringent diet than the honeyed fancies with which Clara had nurtured it for a while. Mr. Hazard realized for the thousandth time that it is difficult to die of that sharp and fugitive pang which is commonly miscalled a broken heart.

This pang may be inflicted by the most unimportant means; let it not be held a special folly upon the part of Mr. Hazard that he now experienced this pang. Mr. Hazard was conversant with many dead and living tongues, and it was his misfortune that among these none was more familiar to his ears than the forked vocabulary of hatred. He translated Mr. Hodge's two words with accurate skill; they informed him that he was an appalling person, unfit to associate with the innocent and the noble, that his appearance was odd, his principles outrageous, and his opinions contemptible. Their ten laconic letters told him that he was at all points detestable to Mr. Hodge. The lovely grave which was prepared for him in the valley of Lyonnesse was no longer his own; Mr. Hodge had filled it with the rotten body of the past.

Mr. Hazard's extreme fatigue followed upon this knowledge; the rigours of his late triumph over the mountains and the archangelic monsters of his brain had wearied him, but the last moment had tried his endurance by a harder proof. So short a space of clockwork time lay between Rosa's artless question and his answer that to the child the pause was unapparent.

"I have not finished the sonnet yet," said Mr. Hazard, "but I shall finish it tonight, and if I am to finish it tonight, I fear I must go home. Good-night, Lady Clara; I shall heed your excellent advice and go home. Good-night, little Rosa; Allegra, good-night."

Mr. Hazard, who was determined to finish the sonnet before he fell asleep, walked swiftly back to Gravelow along a narrow path cut from another world. He trod delicately, keeping his eyes upon the narrow path, stepping with infinite care over clustered shadows. On either side of him there bloomed a fresh profusion of weeds, festooned and knotted into walls which hid the sky and flourished wantonly with evil. Mr. Hazard looked neither to left nor to right, and as he walked, he strove to remember no words in the two worlds except the octave of his own sonnet to Milton.

6

PORTRAIT OF A NATURAL FORCE

"Obviously," said Mr. Hodge, "I cannot pretend to say what Sir John would think on the subject."

"Obviously you cannot," Clara told him with her most mischievous smile.

"But," continued Mr. Hodge, ignoring the snub, "I can tell you precisely what Lord Camphile would have thought. Your father would have considered this person a thoroughly undesirable acquaintance; such a person could never have crossed the threshold of your father's house."

"You are amazingly cool to lecture me, Hodge," said Clara. "And of course Papa was a horrid martinet in such matters. Poor Mr. Hazard is quite harmless, and you must admit that he is a gentleman. The children are really fond of him."

"I admit nothing of the sort," said Mr. Hodge. "On the contrary, I deny it flatly; Mr. Hazard does not fulfil my notion of a gentleman. But then, as you are aware, I am no judge."

"Don't be tiresome," said Clara. "I shall not give you the satisfaction of understanding you."

"Very well," said Mr. Hodge. "Now, as to the children, that is the most serious part of the business. I may appear cool when I lecture you, but, believe me, I am anything but cool; my blood boils to behold this man the companion of your children. You are a woman of the world, and as such protected against his influence; Rosa and Allegra are children, malleable as yet, innocent and unformed. He may impress their minds most dangerously."

"My dear Hodge," said Clara gaily, "have you seen them together? The girls patronize poor Mr. Hazard in the most outrageous manner; they laugh at his verse, his conversation, and the fashion of his cravats. It is very wrong, to be sure, but it relieves my mind of all anxiety concerning their malleable natures. They are a pair of minxes, and they regard poor Mr. Hazard as a cause for mirth. He will forgive them anything under heaven, but sometimes they drive him out of his wits with their teasing."

"Out of his wits!" cried Mr. Hodge. "That he is, and has always been; the man is mad. I could tell you a story or two of his school-days which you would not care to repeat to Tristram and Hilary. You know the disgraceful farce of his career at the University, but he was always a *mauvais sujet,* a pestilential player to the gallery. There is a sour hysteria in his make-up which is worse than positive crime. Not that he has always stopped short of crime, by certain credible reports; he has even advocated . . ."

"Never mind that juvenile nonsense," said Clara, "I dare say he was an uncommonly silly boy, but there is not an ounce of harm in the poor creature. I have tied him into a true-love knot round my little finger; if I took the trouble, I could quite easily turn him into a churchwarden and a justice of the peace."

"Your true-lover's knot is an asp," said Mr. Hodge. "He will but sting you for your pains."

"How poetic you are," said Clara, "and how illiberal! I thought you were a red-hot radical; Papa used always to laugh at your Jacobin rubbish, as he called it."

"I am a liberal," said Mr. Hodge sullenly, "but not a latitudinarian. I am a friend of liberty, but not a licenser of libertines. It was an ill day for freedom when Mr. Hazard sheltered his iniquities beneath her cloak; he is a born seducer, and he prostitutes the cause that he espouses."

"You talk like a nonconformist," said Clara, "but I believe you were, before you won your tripos and became a reformer. Please don't reform Mr. Hazard; your account of him is charmingly romantic. I wish he would fall in love with me, but I fear he has a humble admiration for that mocking Artemis, Allegra, who does nothing but flout him."

"You are very frivolous, Lady Clara," said Mr. Hodge, frowning heavily at a lunar moth. "I marvel that you can make a jest of this man's scandalous history. I suppose you are the fittest judge of your daughters' associates, and that I am impertinent in suggesting . . ."

"I am," said Clara with composure, "and you are excessively impertinent to advise me, my dear Hodge. Nevertheless I shall overlook it, because of my promise to Papa that no one but you should teach the boys mathematics. Though why the poor lambs must learn mathematics . . ."

"Mental discipline," said Mr. Hodge, "a control to which Mr. Hazard has never submitted his weakly rebellious brain. He is ignorant in the worst sense; misguided, ill-conditioned, ungovernable. He is a disastrous model for the boys."

"But he has most agreeable manners," said Clara. "Eccentric, perhaps, but agreeable, and delightfully self-effacing. I repeat, the poor creature is a gentleman. He has led a miserable life out of

his proper *milieu;* his folly has been punished by an inferno of
underbred bluestockings and shoddy philosophers. His pleasure
in our company is pathetic to witness. I have not the heart to
cast him off as his family did."

"Did you know that his scoundrelly old grandfather was
born in America?" asked Mr. Hodge. "It has become a parrot-
cry among his Cockney friends to say that the fellow's blood is
respectable if not distinguished, but his grandfather was an un-
scrupulous ruffian, a lucky adventurer. Your Mr. Hazard is
thoroughly un-English; he is the typical malcontent. You have
only to look at his hat . . ."

"To see that he has not a penny, Hodge," said Clara quickly.
"He has not inherited his grandfather's talents; he is a very unlucky adventurer. His conscience is an instrument of torture; he
cannot take a step without a scruple, and yet he is for ever taking
new steps. And of course he is fanatically honest; you see his
honesty in his eyes."

"I see nothing of the sort," said Mr. Hodge. "Forgive my
plain-speaking, which you may prefer to call rudeness, but I see
insanity in his eyes, and violence, and a base surrender to despair.
Do not talk to me of the look in his eyes, Lady Clara, or I shall
be thinking of strait jackets at once."

"Ah, you are too unkind," said Clara with a sigh, "you are
cruel, Hodge; why must you hate him so bitterly? He is ill; he
is broken by life. He would never forgive me for saying this, but
it must be clear to everyone who sees him. He is profoundly unhappy; have you not enough happiness of your own to be able
to spare him a crumb from my table?"

"No," said Mr. Hodge, looking square into Clara's blue
eyes, which were brilliant with tears, "no; frankly, no, since you
ask me. I have not a tithe of the happiness I desire; nor shall I
have it this side the grave. But I do not intend to share my crumbs
with Mr. Hazard."

Clara was not flattered by this profession; she thought it
indecorous and unbecoming upon the part of her sons' tutor.
At the same time she was perfectly capable of forgiving it; she
blinked her lovely eyes once, and considered it unsaid. Mr. Hodge
was a masterly teacher of mathematics, and far cleverer than any

agent in the management of her affairs. Her father had convinced her of his worth; his Cambridge honours and the esteem in which the Company had held him proved his practical ability. She blinked her eyes and was blind when he offended; she knew she could frighten him by lifting her eyebrows by the fraction of an inch. She was satisfied that he should adore her instead of one of her daughters; it might have been awkward if he had adored Rosa or Allegra. About Clara he could nurse no illusions, but if he loved Rosa or Allegra he might dare to reckon up his chances. Mr. Hodge was no bewildered dreamer, to be content with visions. He looked very discontented indeed as he sat with his eyes on the ground.

" 'Fallings from us, vanishings; blank misgivings of a creature moving about in worlds not realized . . .' " said Clara, thinking of poor Mr. Hazard.

"Does he teach you metaphysical poetry? " asked Mr. Hodge savagely. " I have the *Revue des deux mondes* in my pocket, with Musset's new play in it, but you won't care about Marianne's caprices now that you have taken to quoting Wordsworth."

Clara looked at Mr. Hodge; in the airy moonlight he appeared solid and well-proportioned, tall and muscular, and handsome in a heavy way of his own. His prosperity shone from his coat buttons and from the richer seals upon his watch chain. He scowled, but it was evident that he was a successful person.

"You mustn't be cruel, Hodge," said Clara firmly. "Good-night; you must read the thirteenth chapter of Corinthians and pray for charity. You will have to learn to share your crumbs with Mr. Hazard; I cannot let anyone starve upon my door-step. And he is hungrier than you, although he will never admit it. Remember, you must learn to share your crumbs."

"Must I? " asked Mr. Hodge, as she left him in the moonlight. "Must I indeed? I wonder." His voice was weighty with mysteries and projects. Presently he stopped scowling and strolled along the path by the river-bank, whistling between his strong white teeth.

" ' *Moi, pour un peu d'amour je donnerais mes jours,*
Et je les donnerais pour rien sans les amours,' "

whistled Mr. Hodge in the airy moonlight.

Mr. Hodge, also, was a dreamer after his own fashion; he was not content with visions, yet he too indulged a secret phantasmagoria of hope. Strange things had come to pass; a clerk in the East India Company had been made private secretary to Lord Camphile, and people had been known to die, even in Persia. There was no reason why Mr. Hodge should permit a stumbling-block to lie across his path. He kicked a pebble from his path, and it fell into the river, leaving a faint agitation of ripples to widen under the moon.

7

TIPTOE ON A TOMBSTONE

I⊤ was Susan's invariable rule to bring Mr. Hazard a cup of tea when she waked him at seven o'clock. Susan was a servant in the employ of Mr. Hazard's landlady; she was both virtuous and tender-hearted, and she had come to feel a loyal and benevolent affection for the eccentric lodger. Susan was nineteen years old, a tall fresh-coloured girl with an excessive quantity of reddish hair bundled under her mob-cap. The burning innocence of her eyes was shadowed by a starched ruffle, and the strength and litheness of her limbs were inconspicuous in pink and lavender prints. It was the rustle of these stiffened skirts which waked Mr. Hazard every morning; the curtain-rings played a jangling tune, the day drove a broad wedge of light into the room, and Susan set the little tea-tray down with a clatter within six inches of Mr. Hazard's head. By the time he had moved his head upon the pil- low she had disappeared beyond the brisk click of the door. The tea soothed Mr. Hazard more slowly than Susan had roused him; it revived him with leisurely warmth. The two slices of bread and butter looked no more edible than the fringed napkin under them, but the tea was welcome.

It was Susan's private conviction that Mr. Hazard was in grave danger of dying. In the first place, she believed him to be at least fifty, and in Susan's opinion fifty was not an unsuitable age at which to die. In the second place, she had seldom, if ever, seen anyone so thin as Mr. Hazard, and she observed with misgivings that the harder Mr. Hazard worked, the less he appeared to care for cutlets and potatoes. In the third place, and at this point Susan trembled as if her small felt slippers had advanced noiselessly into a churchyard, the sharp implacable morning, driving its rigid beam of light into the room, revealed Mr. Hazard laid asleep in such pallor and apathy as Susan had never beheld upon the pillow of a living man. It was her deep unspoken pride that each day she waked him, not from slumber, but from the stealthy approach of death. She let the curtain-rings jingle in merry discord; she set down the tea-tray with deliberate clatter of spoons and bent her childish face above Mr. Hazard for an instant, to make sure that he lived.

Each day she had succeeded in waking him; she was beginning to be confident that so long as she carried a cup of tea to him every morning at seven o'clock, he could not die. It was not difficult to wake him; Mr. Hazard was a light sleeper, and the window shone full upon his eyelids. In cold rainy reflections or in the richer colours of sun Susan bent her face above Mr. Hazard's pillow and, assured that he lived, shut the door joyfully upon her miracle.

Today she was not so certain; he did not move, although his eyes looked past her to the window, and past the window to the sky. Susan was all at once afraid; she went from the room without a backward glance, stepping as if she tiptoed across a grave. She closed the door softly, and then leaned against it, trembling until her starched apron rustled like leaves in the wind. In her crisp apron and pink print gown she trembled and shook like a tall young tree of laurel. She had not known, before she felt this sudden fear, how very fond she was of Mr. Hazard.

Mr. Hazard was alive, alive at first to a vague foreknowledge of evil, which broke in clear disaster over his mind, as the curtains were divided by the day, and left no smallest cloud upon his memory. He was unaware of Susan's presence; he closed his eyes again in a futile attempt to temper the unmerciful light to his mind. The light beat upon his pillow with a force like noise and sensible violence; he interposed the thin and insufficient tissue of his eyelids between his memory and the full radiance of morning, and it seemed to him that his eyelids cast no shadow upon his eyes or upon the memory behind them. He felt that the bones of his forehead were fragile and transparent under the light, and he wished that he lay asleep on the averted surface of the earth which was turned away from the sun and cool in the shadow of itself.

The feathers in Mr. Hazard's pillow were reassembled into wings; for a moment they bore him dizzily toward the sun. He had no power over their flight, which refused to turn westward into shadow or eastward into the valley of Lyonnesse. Their flight was straight toward the sun, and then that vast supremacy of fire melted the petty ligaments which bound the wings together, and they parted in mid-air and fell lightly back to the place from whence they came. Mr. Hazard fell heavily, head downward, without sense or power. It was a relief to him to find that he still lay upon his own bed in Gravelow; the feathers of his pillow were quiet within a linen pillow-case, and his mind was stunned into quiet within the transparent bones of his skull.

Mr. Hazard looked at the cup of tea which Susan had left by his bed; he wondered how it had been conveyed there, for he had no recollection of Susan's visit. Then he knew that the girl had come and gone, because there was the cup of tea upon the table, and the curtains flung wide to admit the sunlight. Mr. Hazard did not drink the tea, although he was somewhat thirsty; he pulled the curtains across the window and vainly imagined that he might sleep again. He could neither fly nor crawl into that cone of shadow cast by the earth, but he could make a little shadow of his own with three yards of faded cotton strung upon jingling rings.

Mr. Hazard did not sleep again that morning; in half an hour he arose and bathed and dressed. He pushed back the curtains impatiently and wished he could push back the walls of the house; he recognized the futility of evading the light. The sweet air entered with the light, not cruel, not sharp as a knife at his temple, but cool as spring water or dissolving snow. It was worse than useless to cower in an obscure cave of darkness while the air flowed with the suave freedom of the sea round the margins of sense and understanding. The pure air permeated the marrow of his bones, and his heart leaned upon its waves and was upheld in safety.

Mr. Hazard saw his tragedy in its true proportions; he realized the unimportance of his grief. Like every other mortal who remembers his childhood, he carried at the back of his brain a memory of soap-bubbles, of the clean pipe sticking to his lips, the pipe which was intended for a man, but whose fate it was to be broken between the hot fingers of a child, the taste of soap-suds in his mouth, and the vision of the hollow globes created out of childish breath and a basin of cloudy water, floating upward with the tints of a pigeon's wing upon their curves, melting in light against a sapphire sky. His grief had all the qualities of a soap-bubble, the impermanence and blown perfection of that flower of the atmosphere. Only, while its single leaf survived, it had appeared a type of universal happiness, and with its blossom fallen to less than smoke, to less than a drop of dew, it retained the shape of heaven.

Mr. Hazard sat by the open window; the sunlight moved a slanting finger across the pages of his book. "God will not withdraw his anger; the very helpers of the sea-dragon crouch under him." The book was the Book of Job, the Hebrew Hagiographa. Susan entered with the breakfast tray; she started as she saw Mr. Hazard surrounded by twenty volumes, their pages ruffled by the sunny wind. She looked at Mr. Hazard, and only the living mirrors of his eyes assured her that he had not died.

"But you have not drunk your tea, sir," said Susan. "You are alive, but you have not drunk your tea. You always drank your tea before today."

Mr. Hazard, to whom her language seemed reasonable enough, inclined his head in assent. Susan was horrified by her own words, but to Mr. Hazard they were clear as the Greek characters of the Septuagint. He noticed that her skin was like the lining of a conch-shell and that drops like sea-water lay along its rose.

"I'm sorry about your toast, sir," said Susan. Mr. Hazard looked at the toast, and perceived nothing wrong with it. He did not know that the sorrow in Susan's voice was for him. She was afraid; even the little living images of herself in Mr. Hazard's eyes failed to convince her that the clatter of a teaspoon had waked him at seven o'clock that morning.

8

THE OINTMENT OF THE APOTHECARY

IT was an unlucky circumstance for Mr. Hazard that he was not a fool. His mind was a constant traitor to his spirit in its quickness, its coldness, its unpitying and bitter mirth. To enchant this mind to lethargy, to drug it with spiced poppy and to bind its sinews with silk and the plaited strands of women's hair was no easy matter; Clara had accomplished it because she did not try, because she did not truly care whether or not she succeeded. Mr. Hazard had been grateful to her in proportion to the peace she had conferred upon his spirit. He was of his spirit's party, ever at odds with his own mind; his mind was a scorner, a tyrant, a torturer, and he delighted in any triumph over the enemy. With Clara's help he had kept the clever brute in prison for three months of pastoral holiday, and all the while the creature had slaved for him, performing barbarous labours which his spirit had transformed into this edifice of silver which was piled in foolscap pages under his hand.

Mr. Hodge had unlocked the prison and let loose the demoniacal mind, and now it sped, a lean and smiling monster, through the high chambers of the soul, splintering the crystal roofs, breaking the looking-glass walls with the vibrations of its laughter. His mind was no friend to Mr. Hazard; his mind was the sworn friend of Mr. Hodge. How swiftly, with what malicious pleasure in the deed, had his mind destroyed the brittle fabric of this dream! Now, retaining still the diminished form of heaven, the dream had escaped him for ever. This brutality his mind had wrought, with the aid and comfort of Mr. Hodge, upon his unsuspecting spirit. Clara, who had kept the key to the dungeon in her embroidered pocket, was miles away at Lyonnesse, sewing a fine seam in stitches like humming-bird's feathers, leaning back against a cushion of grass-green silk, sprinkling sugar in tiny snow-flakes over Mr. Hodge's strawberries.

The toast upon the breakfast tray was burnt, but Mr. Hazard had no appetite for toast and marmalade. He sat in the clean excellence of morning, in the full stream of light and scented air, a gentleman of forty, threadbare, reduced and worn to the structural integrity of the skeleton. The faults and misfortunes of earth and his own flesh, the temporal corrosion of the years, the inward-gnawing tooth of scruple, the stubborn and fanatic impulse of his pride, all these had stripped and bitten Mr. Hazard down to the ultimate framework of himself. He might serve to illustrate either an anatomy lesson or a text from Ecclesiastes. He was a simple pattern of mortality, drawn plain in intellectual black and white upon this summer day.

He sat with folded arms, regarding neither the breakfast tray nor the piles of books beyond it. Such things, set close together upon a table, were worthy to be burned; their level orderly rows annoyed him. Toast in a rack; curled shavings from a flitch of bacon; Fedor Glinka's metrical paraphrase of the Book of Job; a pat of butter embossed with clover leaves; a pair of boiled eggs, pale brown like biscuit porcelain; Eichorn's *Einleitung* and Holmes and Parson's new edition of the Septuagint; a napkin twisted into a cocked hat; a silver jug of milk; a little rose with cream-coloured petals; Kennicott and de Rossi's collation of the Hebrew manuscripts. Such things might have their uses, but for the life of him Mr. Hazard could not remember what he had to do with them. He was bothered by their presence; he thought of ringing for Susan and bidding her remove them from his table.

" I wish," said Mr. Hazard to his mind, " that you would have the common decency to stay where you belong, out of my sight and underground. Must I be for ever driven from pillar to post by your damnable mockery? "

" Out of sight, out of mind," said Mr. Hazard's mind rudely. " From the pillars of the temple to the whipping-post; yes, and back again. Mr. Hodge says you are out of your mind."

" My will subdued you," said Mr. Hazard, " I made you build a lyric tower out of all the tongues of Babel . . ."

"There sits the fellow who built your lyric tower, since you choose to call it by such a flowery name. There sits your immortal soul, Mr. Hazard, on the other side of your breakfast-table, and a precious fool he appears to be. He will make a charming incompetent second in your duel with Mr. Hodge," said Mr. Hazard's mind. "Now, if you would but leave the priming of the pistols to me . . ."

"Be quiet," said Mr. Hazard. "Will you have the goodness to be quiet, and to permit me to finish my breakfast in peace?"

"How can you finish what you haven't yet begun?" asked Mr. Hazard's mind with a hateful smile. "Shall I ring for fresh tea, or do you prefer to go straight on with the fourth act? You should take better care of your health if we are to make the fourth act a worthy successor to the third."

"Do as you please," said Mr. Hazard, "I shall hire a boat and spend the morning on the river. I hope you will not consider it necessary to inflict your company upon me; I am tired, and I wish to be alone."

"Have pity upon that poor fellow over there, and let him go with you," said Mr. Hazard's mind. "If you leave him with me, I shall torment him, and he looks quite unfit for such inhuman treatment. You, my friend, are accustomed to my rough manners, but that fellow with the feathered shoulder-blades is evidently afraid of me."

Mr. Hazard saw his mind distinctly, sitting in an attitude of negligent grace in the most comfortable chair the room afforded. The mind was attired in black; it wore an air elegant and satirical and seemed forever upon the point of taking snuff. There were no ruffles at its wrists, no sword at its side; it was clothed in a fluttering ambiguity of sable rags, and yet it contrived to suggest, by a turn of the head, a disdainful motion of the hand, the courtly cruel fashions of the past. Its stockings, like Prince Hamlet's, were ungartered, and there was that in the double disorder of its locks appropriate to both Pan and Lucifer. Mr. Hazard disliked the dark apparition in the arm-chair, and yet he could not deny his kinship to the thing. It was his mind; his spirit was another matter.

"Poor devil," said Mr. Hazard's mind, looking at his spirit.

Mr. Hazard realized that the words were wrong; his mind knew better than that. "Poor angel" was the proper name for the fellow with the feathered shoulder-blades.

Mr. Hazard wondered where this pitiful spirit had found the plumes which drooped in languor at its sides; they might be goose-feathers from the pillow-case or ravellings from the void of heaven. It was impossible to be sure, because the creature was invested in a faint and tarnished splendour which nevertheless clouded its exact lineaments from view. It crouched on the narrow window-seat, its chin on its clasped hands, its silly pinions strewing the drab carpet with flakes of pearl. It seemed caught up into a trance of pain and amazement, and the loosened strings of its hair hung over its large eyes and blinded them.

"Hah! hah!" said Mr. Hazard's mind. "I congratulate you upon your collaborator. He did very well for you in the original Hebrew; doubtless it is his native tongue. But Mr. Hodge can crush him like an hour's ephemeron. I advise you to keep away from Lyonnesse while you have that fellow upon your hands. Mr. Hodge's boot-heel has no bowels of compassion."

"Will you be silent, intolerable demon?" asked Mr. Hazard without hope. He felt a lively sympathy for the creature on the window-seat, which shrank within its wings and trembled at the discourteous accents of the mind.

"Good-bye," said Mr. Hazard's mind, with a gesture of farewell. "Spend the morning upon the river; you are sadly in need of sleep. I will refrain from comment upon your success as a reformer or a father; I will not demand your reasons for coming to England, or an account of your plans and escapades. You know that you have no voice in politics, no rank in letters, no honourable station in the world. A pretty mess you and your winged ephemeron have made of the business of life; even your pursuit of ghosts has been a failure. Moths and may-flies. 'Dead flies cause the ointment of the apothecary to send forth a stinking savour. . . . A wise man's heart is at his right hand, but a fool's heart at his left.' A little folly, Mr. Hazard. Need I remind you of Allegra?"

"Please don't," said Mr. Hazard.

9

CRUMBS FOR THE BIRDS

CLARA sat upon the terrace at Lyonnesse, bending her graceful head above twelve square inches of *petit point*. Her needle flashed in the sunlight and then stopped, quivering like a little arrow in the centre of a rose. The rose-coloured thread hung limp, not drawn into the mesh of the embroidery among the other stitches; Clara's hand remained poised in idleness. The star-sapphire which her father had given her shone like an evening planet against her hand.

She meditated; her eyes, which were bluer than the grey-blue jewel, searched the sky and returned to the *petit point*. She stabbed the rose to its heart and drew out the rose-coloured thread with deliberation.

"Here is a curious note from Mr. Hazard," she said to Mr. Hodge, who sat upon the balustrade. Mr. Hodge was pretending to correct Latin exercises, but under his heavy brows his eyes were never farther from Clara's face than the toe of her bronze slipper. "It was brought by hand from Gravelow; I suppose that means the absurd creature brought it himself, for he has nobody to run errands for him. It says . . . in substance . . . that he could not dine tonight. But it is so cryptic that I feel sure he is unwell."

"What is the matter with him?" asked Mr. Hodge, who knew without asking. "I thought he was never happy except at Lyonnesse. Is he beginning to tire of your hospitality?"

"From the tone of his note, I think he has rather languished for lack of it," said Clara, smiling. "His agitation is obvious. No, I won't show you the note, because you are certain to laugh at it. It is really a very odd note; it worries me."

"Then you had better let me see it, Lady Clara," said Mr. Hodge, looking chivalrous and solemn. "It is like the fellow's base ingratitude to worry you, who have been such a minister of grace to him. But it is of a piece with the rest of his impudence. You had far better let me see what he has written."

"Very well," said Clara, "but you are not to laugh at poor Mr. Hazard. He is not ungrateful, but I fear he is a little mad. There, you may see for yourself . . . only you mustn't look so scornful, Hodge, or I shall wish I had not let you see it."

Mr. Hodge took the note and read it slowly; in obedience to Clara's words he erased the sneer from his lips, but under his brows his eyes were hard and empty as a pair of grey shells. He had driven the contempt from his eyes at Clara's command; they were quite expressionless as he stared at Mr. Hazard's note.

"My dear friend," said the note, which was written in pencil, "I am sorry that I cannot dine with you tonight, but —

> 'Why, let the stricken deer go weep,
> The hart ungallèd play;
> For some must watch, while some must sleep:
> Thus runs the world away.'

Believe me ever most sensible of your kindness."

"But he has not even taken the trouble to sign it!" cried Mr. Hodge in spite of himself. "And in pencil; it is inexcusable that he should write to you in pencil. It is written upon — what? A page from a tradesman's book?"

"A leaf from a note-book," said Clara with inaudible mockery. "He always writes on the leaves of note-books. And it doesn't matter about his name; I know his handwriting very well, you see."

"My God, how long must I bear this?" said Mr. Hodge under his breath; he did not dare to say the words aloud. He tried to keep his voice calm and monotonous as he spoke.

"But what a letter!" said Mr. Hodge. "What a disgusting letter for a grown man to write! If a schoolboy were guilty of such repulsive self-pity, I should think it my duty to cane him. Ah, Hamlet, forsooth! It is Hamlet, is it not, that the fool is quoting? And his friend, Lady Clara, his dear friend. Do you see that he addresses you as his friend?"

"That is no more than the truth, Hodge," said Clara with composure, "I am his friend; I have given him the right to address me as a friend. Pray keep your temper; it is a pity I allowed you to see the note. As to Hamlet — do you think he is serious? He is out of spirits, of course; I dare say, like Hamlet, he is a little mad, but I am sure he is laughing at himself in this letter. He is not quite such a fool as you would have him."

"I would not have him at any price, mad or sane, wise or foolish," said Mr. Hodge with controlled fury. "Forgive me, Lady Clara, but the man sickens me; I am not myself when I consider him. I had as lief see you with a toad in your hand as with that revolting letter."

"We have had enough hard words," said Clara. "Let us try a few pearls and diamonds for a change. Now I am going to ask poor Mr. Hazard to dinner on Friday, and if you cannot promise to be kind and civil, then you must go and be rude elsewhere, for I will not tolerate it here. You might run up to London for the night to see the Water-Colour Exhibition or to improve your mind with the Elgin marbles. Or do you prefer to be good and stay at home?"

"I shall be good, as you are pleased to call it," said Mr. Hodge, "but you are mistaken; I shall merely be hypocritical. If I followed the dictates of my conscience in this matter, I should . . ."

"Horsewhip Mr. Hazard, I suppose," said Clara laughing. "Ah, my dear Hodge, I know your prejudices too well; you are as narrow as my little finger-nail. Nevertheless you have a sterling character; perhaps your virtue has earned its prejudices. But you must be kind to Mr. Hazard."

"I was not going to say anything about horsewhips; I am not a bully," said Mr. Hodge with dignity. "You may depend upon it that my manners on Friday will be no worse than usual."

"Then I must be content with moderate blessings," said Clara. "But listen; we will have turbot and a beautiful pair of ducks and the first of the raspberries; I may have a pineapple sent down from London. You shall choose the wines yourself, and drink them too, since the rest of us don't appreciate them. It will be a festival, a gala occasion; the girls shall put on their prettiest frocks and I will wear white satin and sapphires. We will build a triumphal arch for Mr. Hazard with 'Friendship's Garland' woven thereon in roses; we will have Roman candles and rockets and set pieces; we will persuade Paganini to sing for his supper on the violin, and Taglioni shall dance for us under the moon. It

will be a delightful party, and we shall all live happy ever
after."

"There will be no moon on Friday night," said Mr. Hodge
sombrely, "and please do not wear any more sapphires; you wear
far too many for my peace of mind."

Clara blinked her blue eyes and pretended not to hear. She
was relieved to know that Mr. Hodge's mood was softened by
her chatter, and she began to feel much less worried about Mr.
Hazard. After all, one could practise sorceries and glamours by
means of a few words of nonsense and a promise of early raspberries. If Mr. Hazard were ill, a slice of duckling and a glass
of white wine might be curative magic, and if he were melan-
choly-mad, it must inevitably medicine his spirits to see Rosa and
Allegra in their prettiest frocks.

<h1 style="text-align:center">10</h1>

THE SAGE IN MEDITATION

Mr. Hazard had set forth from Gravelow with every intention of
dining at Lyonnesse; it was only when its actual tower shadowed
the river at his right hand that his heart failed him. His fortitude went from him, and as the skiff left the sunlight and glided
into the darkened stretch of water, he relapsed into doubt and sad
self-questionings. A mist arose from the shaded water, and while
his lungs received it, he inhaled misgiving and suspired his final
breath of courage.

A small secretive beast slid from the bank of the river;
its shape of vole or weasel was indistinguishable in the dusk.
Whether the pursued or the pursuer, whether ravening or in
flight, the thing was to be envied. The ripples of its course were
soon dispersed; it was hidden in the glittering sunlit reach beyond. Mr. Hazard wished it well; for his own fate he could desire nothing better, unless indeed it were the lucky destiny of
a stone or a tree rooted in green shallows. He rowed past the
house, avoiding the high steps of the landing-place, and proceeding a little farther down the stream, he moored his boat in deep

obscurity. He bent his eyes close above the pages of his note-book, and there in the mist and luminous eclipse of day he wrote a letter to Clara. He laughed as he wrote it, beholding a stricken water-rat fleeing like a deer to the remoter bank. " Thus runs the world away! " said Mr. Hazard to himself, with noiseless laughter. Thus runs the world, thus flows the river, running softly, thus run and flow the pulses of the blood, running in the wrist, in the hollow temple, and under the ribs at the left hand of a fool.

When Mr. Hazard had written the note, he scrambled up the bank and looked about him. He was no great distance from the house, and he considered going to the front door and leaving the note in his proper person. He had proceeded half-way along the flagged path when he caught sight of Clara and Mr. Hodge upon the terrace. Clara's hair was powdered to pale silver-gold by the twilight; she threw back her head, regarding her embroidery at arm's length, and her profile and the faint colour of her hair were Allegra's. Even in the dusk Mr. Hazard could see the contours of her face, clear, aerial, aquiline, lifted upon invisible wings of pride, shining with an inner flame of mockery.

Mr. Hazard's bones were turned to water, and this water did not run softly and smoothly like the river Thames; it was rather a subterranean stream of cataracts and rapids. He stood hidden in the shadows, quiet as one of the leaden figures bordering the path, quiet as the moss-grown satyr in the hedge. He was absorbed into the darkness about him; he was conscious only of the bitter smell of yew and the sweet smell of jasmine, and of the little note fluttering between his fingers like a living thing, while his fingers did not tremble, but remained stiff and cold as stone or lead. How should he move his hands to still the fluttering of the note, or his feet to proceed along the path, when his bones were turned to water within the body of a leaden satyr?

Mr. Hazard was spared the trouble of delivering his note; a man emerged from the dusk carrying a flat basket of roses on his arm. He was evidently a gardener; he stared at Mr. Hazard for a moment, and then civilly demanded his business. Mr. Hazard gave him the letter with instructions to convey it to the house at once; he gave the gardener a piece of silver, and the man touched his cap and left him. The incident proved his own humanity to

Mr. Hazard; he perceived that he was alive, that he was after all a person capable of tipping servants and imposing his will on fellow mortals. He turned and walked with swift and resilient steps along the way he had come. He was no longer afraid of meeting Allegra; he knew that he would not meet her upon this retired path. When a white owl swooped from the shadows like a waning moon, Mr. Hazard was not halted in his light and even stride. Nevertheless he had been both lonely and afraid during that long moment while he stood like a leaden statue in the dusk, moveless except for the quick processes of his mind and the fluttering of the note between his fingers. He had felt remote from the comfortable bonds of flesh and blood, coldly and strangely severed from his kinship with mankind. The gardener had given him back the common stamp of humanity; he was glad of the assurance. Mr. Hazard thought he had purchased it cheaply with a single piece of silver, and he was sorry he had not given the man five shillings instead of half a crown.

He rowed slowly up the river to Gravelow; he rowed against the current and against the inner wishes of his heart, which were turned backward to Lyonnesse. Yet he knew that he could never have faced Clara and her children without some stupid blunder upon the part of his soul; he would have been stiff and cold as a statue, or, worse, he would have been a silly wild beast, struck in the side by a shaft of ridicule and dislike, ashamed of its wound, frantic for solitude. No, it was far wiser to go home; to go home to Gravelow.

"Hah," said Mr. Hazard, aware of his own weakness. "'Why, let the stricken deer go weep . . .' by all means, and in decent seclusion." He thought of Mr. Hodge's sleek dark head, bent over Latin exercises, while Clara regarded her bright embroidery at arm's length. "'The hart ungallèd play . . .'" He rowed faster, rowing until he was out of breath and almost out of the memory of Lyonnesse and the power of its spell. He rowed until he was blind and breathless, rowing away from Lyonnesse.

The next morning the spell had reassumed its power. About eleven o'clock Susan brought him a note, waiting by the door while he read it. "There's an answer," said Susan. "The man says there's an answer, sir, and you're please to send it back by him."

"Friday," said Mr. Hazard to himself, reading the note, "Day after tomorrow. I am to come without fail. Am I sure I am quite well? Isn't the weather delicious? The little girls have learned Hummel's duet sonata in E flat. Till Friday, she is mine most truly, Clara Hunting. Postcript. I am not to work too hard at what's-his-name."

"You needn't wait, Susan," said Mr. Hazard, "I'll bring the answer down myself when I've written it. Tell the man I shan't be five seconds."

It took him less than five seconds to make up his mind. Suddenly he knew the measure of his ingratitude and vanity. He laughed with joy to know himself mistaken, selfish, ill-conditioned; the knowledge relieved despair like a draught of sacrament. Knowing Clara right and himself wilfully wrong, the world swung round upon a noble axis, and the sun was once more within its proper quarter of the sky. The morning rose, expanding like a tree, towards the heights of noon; all sounds and odours grew clear and delicate, and the simple forms of earth were moulded with nicety and justice. The smallest leaf that hung against his window was scalloped and veined according to divine sanction.

Mr. Hazard wrote his answer to Clara in seven words, and ran downstairs to give it to the servant. Remembering that he had not rewarded the gardener as the man deserved, he put all his silver coins into this other servant's hands. It was extravagant, but not so extravagant as it might have been had Mr. Hazard ever carried many coins in his pocket, either of silver or gold.

11

A FINE PAIR OF SAPPHIRES

"Of course we will come, if Mama will let us," said Rosa. "Afternoon tea in Gravelow; it sounds lovely. Perhaps we might have the horses that afternoon, and come very grandly in the carriage; then we could wear our best clothes and be elegant young ladies, while the boys and Mr. Hodge go by way of the river. But wait; we must ask Mama."

"I had meant," said Mr. Hazard rather diffidently, "to ask your mother to do me the honour of coming with you next Wednesday. Perhaps it is too much to hope for, but it would be so very much happier a solution of the chaperon problem than a governess can ever be, and then . . . to have her with us . . . but I suppose it is impossible. In fact, I suppose the whole scheme is impossible; it is too charming to come true."

"Well," said Rosa, "we must ask her; she cannot be angry with you for asking. I am afraid she will say no, but then you won't be worse off than you are now, and she might just conceivably say yes, mightn't she?"

"Do you think she might?" asked Mr. Hazard; he looked at Clara, and her smile, and the meek fashion of her parted hair, and the sapphire dangling against her cheek, and the softer, more merciful jewels of her eyes, informed him of her kindness. He rose and crossed the terrace to her chair, and drew another chair close to it, and, choosing his words very carefully, he asked her to drink tea with him next Wednesday afternoon.

Mr. Hodge, who sat upon the balustrade between Tristram and Allegra, could not hear Mr. Hazard's carefully chosen words, but he could hear the absurd vibration of Mr. Hazard's nerves made audible in his voice. Mr. Hazard was nervous; he had set his heart upon persuading Clara to say yes instead of no, and now his heart was in his mouth and evident in the uneven sound of his voice. Mr. Hodge wondered what the fool was saying with such unnecessary fervour; it might have been a declaration of love or an appeal against a capital sentence.

It was both; Mr. Hazard felt his destiny dependent upon Clara's nod, which would let her sapphire ear-rings fall forward in line with her eyelashes, or the shake of her head, which would fling them sparkling from side to side. He watched her face, his thin hands gripping the carven bosses of the chair.

"You see," explained Mr. Hazard, "it shouldn't be such an unfair division of pleasures. You have given, and given again and again, and I have taken your charity and brought nothing in return."

"Hospitality," said Clara, "and of the simplest sort. Please don't call it charity, Mr. Hazard; you make me feel as if I had been giving you soup and flannels."

She laughed, and Mr. Hazard laughed with her, but Mr. Hodge could have sworn that there was no conviction in the fellow's lunatic mirth.

"You have," said Mr. Hazard, "food and raiment, and these for a starving man. It is charity, and sheer munificence; I have nothing to give you in exchange. But if you would allow me to have a tea-party for the children; a tea-party seems the only possible thing for summer. If it were winter, I suppose there would still be pantomimes. But by next winter I shall be in Spain."

It was the forlorn echoes in the last sentence which decided Clara, and the inevitable ring of parting in the last word. Spain was distant enough, in reality, and Mr. Hazard's voice made it sound more distant than the moon. Clara, who had once glanced into *The Conquest of Granada,* had a picture of Mr. Hazard sitting lonely as Boabdil in a small Moorish palace, while happier people went to pantomimes. Also, she remembered that by September Mr. Hazard would be on his way to Spain; she would be sorry to see the poor creature go, and yet she knew that his going would lift a little burden from her mind and cut the trivial knot of perplexities tangled about his presence.

"Very well," she said sweetly; her ear-rings swung forward as she bowed her head in consent. Her smile was teasing and lenient; her sidelong glance at Mr. Hazard observed that his fingers had relaxed upon the arms of his chair. His sigh of relief touched her lightly with amusement and pity. He looked at Allegra, and Clara looked away.

When Mr. Hazard had gone home that evening, Mr. Hodge was afraid to ask Clara any questions. He wondered very much what cause Mr. Hazard had been pleading as he leaned towards Clara, his knuckles white against the arms of his chair, his voice tense and uneven. Mr. Hodge found it difficult to believe the ridiculous truth when he heard it, and yet the truth displeased him.

"Is that the vastly important project he was discussing?" asked Mr. Hodge. "I thought it was a life-and-death matter, that he had got his precious neck in jeopardy or was planning an elopement to the Cyclades. A tea-party! How infantile! At the same time, Lady Clara, I doubt your wisdom in having yielded to his wishes. You are too tender-hearted; he imposes upon you at every turn."

Clara could not help laughing, though Mr. Hodge's vehemence annoyed her. "Thank you," she said, "I do not like insults to my common sense, my dear Hodge, even as the price of compliments to my kind heart. If Mr. Hazard is capable of imposing upon me, I must be amazingly simple-minded. I assure you that if the poor darling had a little pane of glass set in that speculative brow of his, his thoughts could be no plainer to me than they are."

"I am glad to hear it," said Mr. Hodge, "I am glad to know that you cannot by any chance be deceived in his character."

"But he is such an innocent creature, Hodge!" said Clara. "He is clever enough at writing verse, I suppose, but he knows nothing of the world. It is stupid of you to talk as if he were a sort of Lovelace. Am I a silly Clarissa, a simpleton of fifteen? I tell you I can wind him round my little finger like this poor bit of black silk."

"But he is wound about Allegra's little finger," said Mr. Hodge solemnly. "It is Allegra whom he loves, Lady Clara; that has been ludicrously clear from the beginning."

Clara looked at Mr. Hodge, and in the thin summer darkness her amethystine eyes were inscrutable. Slowly she unwound the strand of black silk from about her little finger and allowed it to drift to the grass at her feet. She lifted her hand, and the sapphire rings upon her fingers caught the starlight and held it.

"Ah, Hodge, why need you have said that?" she asked softly. "I am sorry you said it in so many words. It is cruel to define these things too plainly; we must pretend they aren't true, if they are sad enough, and there is no help for them. I have not said it so plainly even to myself, and I am sure Mr. Hazard has never dreamed of saying it."

"Then so much the worse for Mr. Hazard," said Mr. Hodge. "He has no moral honesty; he refuses to face the bare facts of

existence. His passion is laughable, but it is none the less dangerous for being undignified."

"It is not laughable," said Clara gravely. "It is a pitiable passion, if passion it is. We may smile at these things while they
remain unsaid, but you have broken our poor conspiracy of
silence. Yes, yes, of course he is in love with Allegra; I, too, have
known it from the beginning, but it is so deplorable that I have
tried to pretend it isn't true. I have played a harmless comedy to
save his pride."

"Surely it would have been kinder . . ." began Mr. Hodge,
but Clara interrupted him impatiently. She was angry with him
for making her cry; she dabbed at her eyes with a fine lace
handkerchief, reflecting that her handkerchiefs were not accustomed to tears. Tears were a rare indulgence with Clara; she
thought them more expensive than the amber essence with which
her handkerchief was scented.

"It would not have been kinder," she said with spirit. "It
would have been the most malicious cruelty I could have contrived to hurt him. He does not like to be pitied, you know; nobody likes to be pitied. Do not insist upon turning my comedy
into a tragedy by making me pity Mr. Hazard."

"As you please," said Mr. Hodge. "Your policy of blissful
ignorance has much to recommend it to the moral coward. But
for myself I prefer to face the issue at all costs. You pay a doubtful
compliment to your Mr. Hazard in obscuring the truth."

"But I thought he was Allegra's Mr. Hazard," said Clara.
"Thank you for making me laugh again, Hodge; tears have always bored me to distraction. It is an heroic portrait you draw of
yourself; Haydon would be glad of it for his next historical piece.
Let us stop quarrelling and be friends; there are no issues to be
faced between friends. Only, you must not dot your i's and cross
your t's in this tiresome manner, for it turns all life into a moral
lesson."

"Good-night, Hodge," said Clara with recovered gaiety.
"You must come to poor Mr. Hazard's tea-party with me next
Wednesday. But, remember, never cross your t's until you come
to them."

"How frivolous she is!" thought Mr. Hodge, staring at the

sapphire heavens, whose infinite mocking brilliance was after all no more inscrutable than Clara's dark blue eyes.

12

LESS THAN ARCHANGEL RUINED

In Gravelow at this time there lived a woman who kept a small bakery in West Street. This woman was half Saxon peasant and half gipsy; she was neither young nor old, neither handsome nor notably plain. She was the sort of woman who keeps her shop-window in good order, but may possibly drink a little gin in secret.

Mr. Hazard was easily touched to pity or disgust; he was the sort of man who saves a commonplace woman from a burning house at the casual cost of his own life, but is spiritually exhausted by a quarter of an hour's conversation with her. Had he met her in a ditch, he would have shared his last crust with her, but he might have refused to employ her as kitchen-maid because she had ugly hands.

He was a connoisseur of obsidian and sardonyx; at a glance he could tell the Etruscan from the Island gems, and smile at one of Pichler's eighteenth-century Psyches. But he could not tell a stale rock-cake from a fresh one, or yesterday's buns from today's. The woman was an excellent pastry-cook, but she had rarely been able to resist the temptation to turn a dishonest halfpenny. She was therefore precisely the woman to sell yesterday's cream buns, and Mr. Hazard was precisely the man to buy them.

"A dozen buns, if you please," said Mr. Hazard, not asking for any particular kind of bun, or even inquiring the price. He looked very tall, and although his eyes were preternaturally bright, they gazed through the ceiling of the shop and ignored the cakes upon the counter.

The woman felt well-disposed towards Mr. Hazard; nevertheless she sold him a dozen of her most undesirable buns, wrapping them in a trim brown-paper parcel. "Thank you, sir," she said civilly, as she put his money into the till.

Mr. Hazard walked home to his lodgings; it was three o'clock of as exquisite an afternoon as even his fastidious taste could have chosen. If some power had permitted him selection among all the days of that July, if he had been allowed to turn them over beneath his hand like a heap of roses varying from warm to white, his preference must have fallen upon this afternoon. With honey at its core, and powdered grains of gold like fine Arabian spices dusting its inner leaves, the flower of this afternoon was cool and cloud-coloured; its blowing fringes were silver in the wind. It would not rain, and the wind blowing from the west could be trusted to blow the petals of light towards Gravelow. Mr. Hazard was content with his afternoon.

The true flowers in the green glass vases perished in the confined space of his sitting-room; as soon as he entered the room, he perceived that the flowers were dying. He had cut them himself in the small garden, and putting them into the watery glass, he had forgotten to pour actual water upon their stems. Now they were drooping and dying in the tall green vases. He rang for Susan, who brought a jug of water to refresh them; her face was grave and doubtful as she looked at the flowers.

Mr. Hazard was not used to gathering flowers; in other years ladies had gathered flowers for him, but he preferred to leave a rose upon its stalk. He hoped that the cold water would revive the stems of these flowers.

"I tidied up a bit, as you told me to, sir," said Susan. "I'm afraid some of your books and papers may be hard to find in those pigeon-holes, but they're all safe, and the place looks beautiful. Did you remember the seed-cake, sir?"

"No," said Mr. Hazard, "I forgot it. Did you tell me to buy a seed-cake, Susan?"

"Yes, sir," said Susan, "but it doesn't matter. Everything will be very nice; we've got some lovely raspberries for you. Here's a letter, sir, come by the last post."

Mr. Hazard took the letter, believing that it came from Clara. The habitual pallor of his complexion was increased until he was as white as the thin sheaves of paper thrust into the pigeon-holes of the desk. He sat down on the edge of the desk and forced himself to look at the letter. The London postmark saved him from the tiresome necessity of fainting.

Susan was appalled. She had seen Mr. Hazard painfully affected by trifles, but she had never seen him overthrown as now. "Are you quite well, sir?" asked Susan, being very sure that he was ill.

"Quite," said Mr. Hazard rather crossly. "Please don't bother me, Susan; go downstairs and wait until I ring for you."

The letter was from Annamaria. The Hartleighs had not gone to Hythe after all; they were still in Marylebone. Also, they were in trouble. Annamaria hated to worry her dear Hazard while he was engaged upon his lyric drama, but as a matter of fact poor Hartleigh had the influenza. The boys were with a friend in Cornwall; the younger children had been sent to the Isle of Wight. These summer influenzas were particularly distressing. Hartleigh was miserable, and they were in serious financial difficulties.

At this moment Mr. Hazard heard the carriage coming along West Street; it drew up before his door with a clatter of hoofs and a smart jingle of harness. The coachman cracked his whip for no reason, and Tristram's laughter sounded, cold and bright as sleigh-bells in the summer air. Mr. Hazard crammed the letter into his pocket and rang furiously for Susan. He stood waiting, his face turned towards the door; his veins were filled with a fever of impatience, and all the while the letter uncurled itself in his pocket with a crackling noise like fire.

Mr. Hodge came into the room, followed by Tristram and Hilary; the passage was empty behind them and there were no more footsteps on the stairs.

"Where . . . ?" said Mr. Hazard, and felt the question stick in his throat like a sharp fishbone. All words were knives and splinters in his throat, and he was silent.

"Lady Clara decided not to come this afternoon," said Mr. Hodge; his manner was courteous and even gentle. "She feared that it might rain. Also her brother is arriving from Camphile Eden tonight, and she has various arrangements to make for his comfort. But she has sent us in her stead; we are the bearers of many apologies and regrets."

"The girls sent you their special love, Mr. Hazard," said Hilary. "They think it's very bad luck that they're not allowed to come with us."

"I've a note for you from my mother," said Tristram; the exquisite arrogance of his bearing was tempered by a cool and friendly smile. He turned out his pockets one by one, and found several notes, but not the note for Mr. Hazard.

"I'm frightfully sorry," said Tristram, "I must have lost it, or else she forgot to give it to me. I'm frightfully sorry, Mr. Hazard. Perhaps she gave it to you, Hodge."

"Never mind," said Mr. Hazard, who felt their blue eyes like so many knives at his throat. He knew that they had told him all that the note could say, and yet he wished that Tristram had not lost that scrap of Clara's handwriting.

Susan came in with the tea; she had cut the bread and butter delicately thin and piled the raspberries into a pyramid of damask. The cream buns were stale, but Susan hoped that Mr. Hazard would not eat any cream buns.

Mr. Hazard ate nothing at all. He knew that Susan had spread a large tea upon his writing-table; he wished that she had not filled the quiet of his room with tea-kettles and plates and spoons. He was sincerely grateful to Mr. Hodge for pouring out the tea.

13

A MOONSTONE INTAGLIO

THE BOYS made an excellent tea; the cream buns disappointed them, but the perfection of the raspberries more than atoned for this. Mr. Hodge ate a slice of bread and butter, and looked at Mr. Hazard. Mr. Hazard seemed quite unaware of his duty as a host.

"You had better have a cup of tea," said Mr. Hodge in a kindly voice, his hand upon the tea-pot. Mr. Hodge did not like pouring out tea, but he realized that Mr. Hazard was, for the moment, incapable of the effort. There was no use in their all going hungry because Mr. Hazard had been born a pitiful fool.

" No, thank you," said Mr. Hazard, who was not hungry. He watched the faces of the boys, their slight aquiline features, the freckles gold against the bright colour on their cheek-bones. He listened to their animated tones and to the running chorus of Tristram's laughter. He was glad that they were making such an excellent tea, but he longed for Clara's note that Tristram had forgotten.

Mr. Hodge was speaking to him in a low portentous voice, which was tuned to darker secrets than the children's voices. Mr. Hazard turned to him, hearing the end of the world in the heavy reverberations of that voice.

" She thought it wiser not to come, and more considerate of your feelings," said Mr. Hodge. " I assured her that you would understand; you would not wish to cause a moment's disquietude to Allegra's mother. You do understand, don't you? "

" Of course," said Mr. Hazard. It was true; Mr. Hazard understood, and the thing that Mr. Hazard understood grew clearer than the air and more exactly carven than the moon's shell within the glass of an astronomer.

It was not the end of the world; it was the strange countenance of the moon, brought close, and staring with calm-lidded eyes at Mr. Hazard. Mr. Hazard's own eyes were supernaturally turned into a pair of star-gazing crystals, and his perceptions were increased to angelic power. He knew rather more than he wanted to know, but the thing that he knew was familiar, now that he saw it clearly in the glass.

He understood that Mr. Hodge believed him to be in love with Allegra. This was inevitable and to be forgiven; he had believed it himself until the last instant, although he had never confessed it to his mind. He had loved Allegra in the first moment of beholding her; nay, he had adored her with the burning remnant of his flesh and the insensate passions of his spirit. He had starved and thirsted for lack of her; he had accepted dry crumbs and dew-drop morsels in place of food, and been satisfied with deprivation. Moved by this true radical force of love, he had harnessed mountains and broken them to his rein and cut a path from the cold extreme of heaven. He had made his love an Archimedean lever whereby the world was tilted one degree nearer to the universal good. These things he had accomplished, knowing that she would not care a silver pin for such wonders, and she had not cared.

She had not cared, and his accomplishment had wearied him, and his love for Allegra had fallen into a decline, and died of languor and exhaustion. Dry crumbs and dew-drops are thin fare to support the vitality of the heart, and while his starved and baffled love lay dying, Clara had come to Mr. Hazard and stood at his left hand, a little apart, not smiling, not pitying him or seeming to divine his pain. He had loved her for this and he loved her still; it was possible that he would always love her. He was sure that she was aware of this, and that, upon the whole, she considered it a compliment.

What else she knew could only be conjectured; certainly he would never ask her, but if he were to ask her a hundred times, he would get no more than the least fraction of a smile for answer. Perhaps her graceful and neglectful air, the bright eyes turned the other way, the light mind absent upon more amusing errands, had been delicate acts of mercy; perhaps they had been simple laziness. She had watched the entire course of his ridiculous and tragic love without a sign; she had blinked her dark blue eyes and played tricks with the musical stops of her voice, and by means of these innocent diversions she had won him from despair. She had seen him look to her from Allegra, and still she had given no sign, and by means of pretence she had kept his pride inviolate and saved his face. He hated his face, and yet while its precarious mask was fitted round his mind, it assured him a little privacy. He loved Clara for saving his face, even if she had done it to save trouble for herself.

Mr. Hazard remembered Clara, and a pang of intense desire cut his heart in two. He longed for the woman in ten thousand idle ways which, being added together and summed up, became a crying hunger, an instinctive need, an immediate infantile wailing within the spirit. What difference, earthly or divine, did it make to Mr. Hazard whether Clara were invested in supernal wisdom or in the careless and enchanting attributes of flesh and blood? She had been his friend and saviour, and now he loved the narrow ground she walked upon, although she might be a mere piece of that fair ground, a lady of clay. Perhaps she was a goddess and had contrived it all from above, but he suspected her strongly of being a woman, and he loved her better for the fault. He longed for the bit of paper whereon her hand had inscribed a set of gentle and untrue excuses for failing him today.

Mr. Hazard saw that Mr. Hodge and the boys were going; he rose and said good-bye to them with fluency and ease. The engaging manners of his youth returned for a moment, like a ghostly reflection, to flicker in his lips and eyes. For this brief moment he was as polite as Hilary, as witty as Tristram, and several inches taller than Mr. Hodge.

He stood with his hands in his trousers' pockets, regarding the others with a faintly metaphysical smile. His fingers touched Annamaria's letter, and he drew it forth. He had forgotten it, and yet it was precisely what he had been needing for the past three minutes.

"I have had a letter from London," he said to Mr. Hodge, "which calls me away at once upon important business. The business will be long and complicated, and although it may only take me to Marylebone, it may quite conceivably take me to Abyssinia. As I leave Gravelow tomorrow, I am afraid I shall not see Lady Clara again before next summer."

The breath was knocked from Mr. Hodge's magnificent chest by these amazing words; he was incredulous of his facile triumph. The boys' young voices were lifted in a babble of surprise, but Mr. Hodge was unable to speak. He was a sceptic, and yet he thanked the author of this blessing in a mood of religious awe. Doubtless, thought Mr. Hodge, its true author was the beautiful Clara Hunting, that gold and ivory image of his idolatry. Yet he spared an approving glance for Tristram, for Tristram had lost his mother's note to Mr. Hazard. It is impossible for a poor mortal to foretell with any degree of certainty the oracular message that a gold and ivory image may compress into a small three-cornered note.

"If you are leaving tomorrow, you will want to pack," said Mr. Hodge rather unsteadily. He looked at the books, at the accumulated rows of Greek poets and Hebrew prophets and kings. He looked at Mr. Hazard; an actual sensation of pity caught him unprepared. Mr. Hazard was teetering back and forth on his heels and toes and smiling a secret philosophical smile, but to Mr. Hodge's eyes he looked more than ever a contemptible anatomy. He was as thin as a storm-bitten scarecrow and as pale as a rain-washed rag.

"Don't you want me to help you pack those books?" asked Mr. Hodge, stirred by an humane impulse. "There are a tremendous lot of them, you know; you'll find it rather a job to finish by yourself."

Mr. Hazard looked at Mr. Hodge; he saw plainly that Mr. Hodge was moved by a laudable impulse, but he also saw that such an impulse would never have moved Mr. Hodge had Mr. Hazard not been going to London tomorrow.

Mr. Hazard had scared away a multitude of crows by his blacker pride; he opened his smiling lips to emit a politely scornful negative, and then thought better of it. After all, he felt wretchedly tired and ill; there were far too many dying flowers in the room, and the windows had never been wide enough. Why should he hesitate to employ Mr. Hodge's excess and prodigality of muscle to perform those gross gymnastics which must wear the body to its death and leave the soul unstrengthened? For years he had worn away the precious metal of his body by such trumpery pains.

"It would be pure good nature upon your part to help me," said Mr. Hazard with his smallest and most subliminal smile. He raised his fine ironic eyebrows, and began to sort his books into neat and rational piles. He was very careful to lay his own fragile sallow hands upon none save the slenderer volumes; he left all the heavier and duller books to Mr. Hodge. He put the *Symposium* and *Paradise Lost* into his two coat-pockets, and dropped Miss Barrett's *Prometheus Bound* into the waste-paper-basket. His white vellum set of the Greek dramatists went next to Shelley and Coleridge in the pigskin box.

So soon as the exertion of packing had wearied Mr. Hazard, which happened within five minutes of his first effort, he sank into the most comfortable arm-chair that the room afforded and observed Mr. Hodge with sympathetic interest. Mr. Hodge was very hot; his sleek dark hair had fallen into his eyes, and his broadcloth coat would have fared better upon the back of a chair than stretched across Mr. Hodge's splendid shoulders. Mr. Hazard examined the cluster of seals upon his watch-chain, and, choosing the most curious, detached it from the rest.

" Tristram," he said in his light dry voice, " may I impose upon your memory in so far as to ask you to give this little intaglio to your mother? It is a pretty antique; a Greek scarabæoid of the happiest period. Beg her to accept it as a token of my gratitude and an earnest of my friendship, and bid her good-bye until next summer, or perhaps until a later day."

Tristram looked critically at the seal which Mr. Hazard had given him; it appeared to be a blond and frosted moonstone, bearing upon its surface the figures of a lion and a stag. The lion's teeth were sunk in the stag's flying shoulder; the gem itself was clipped by a worn silver band.

" I will show it to my mother," said Tristram rather haughtily, " but I don't believe she will wish to take it, Mr. Hazard. It is too valuable to be given away."

" Do you think so, Tristram? " asked Mr. Hazard with his imperceptible smile.

He sat in the small room, among the dying constellations of the flowers, among the teacups glimmering like sea-shells on the table, with the three restless presences fixed opposite him in the disorder of the place. Hilary whistled the march from *Faniska* and drummed with his fingers upon the straitened window frames; Tristram frowned over the intaglio seal; Mr. Hodge sweated at his labours. Mr. Hazard leaned his head against the comfortable cushions of his chair; the intellectual colour of his eyes was full of laughter.

He knew that tomorrow, in the London coach, he would feel faint and suffocated among its odours of mortality, and crossed in love and fortune, but for the moment he was happy. There were five points to a star; these three uneasy presences were in the room, and himself, making four, and a fifth which set a crown upon the whole and was superior to the others and remained a part of heaven.

FUGITIVE PROSE

WITH A SPECIAL PREFACE BY
WILLIAM ROSE BENÉT

Fugitive Prose

PREFACE

Besides her four distinguished novels, Elinor Wylie wrote a few short stories and a few essays, both short and long, which appeared in various periodicals. The most sustained work of the latter kind was done by her for the literary supplement, Books, *of the* New York Herald Tribune, *during the month of February in 1927, when Irita Van Doren, editor of that section of the newspaper, invited her to contribute four articles in successive issues on writers to be chosen by herself. As for Elinor's short stories, they were never her principal interest. As many as three appeared in popular magazines, two of them admittedly light, and one of which Emily Clark speaks in her chapter on Elinor in her volume of reminiscences, "Innocence Abroad." These are not included here. The story to which Miss Clark refers was called "King's Pity," and dealt with the romance of Mary Tudor. She says of it:*

"It appeared in [wrong magazine given] and [Elinor]

had, naturally, been well paid for it. But she told me, looking almost ill, that its composition had been an ordeal to which she could never again subject herself.”

Of the stories she wrote con amore, *the first that I have chosen for this section of Elinor Wylie's fugitive prose, appeared before our marriage in 1923, in* Playboy, *edited and published by Egmont Arens, Volume 2, Number 1. It dates from a decade ago, and I fear to touch it clumsily. I think it was the first brief imaginative prose of Elinor Wylie's to be published in a magazine.*

The second story, “ Gideon's Revenge,” appeared in the then extant Century Magazine *during the period when Carl Van Doren was its literary editor. Shortly after, in 1925, he printed serially Elinor Wylie's “ The Venetian Glass Nephew,” the only novel of hers ever to appear in this fashion. While “ Gideon's Revenge” is not written in her most characteristic satirical spirit, it is deeply ironic and, in my opinion, most subtly philosophical. Upon the composition of this section of the book I consulted one of Elinor's oldest literary friends and most astute admirers, Carl Van Vechten. Concerning “ Gideon's Revenge ” we amiably disagreed. The next inclusion, however, he regards as probably the best of her fugitive pieces. It is “ The Life Story of Lydia Greensmith,” and appeared in* The New Republic, *November 24, 1926. At that time Elinor was a contributing editor of this weekly, and its masthead bore her name among others for a considerable period, during which both prose and poetry by her appeared in its pages. Several years prior to this a page of her first published poems had been printed in the same periodical by Ridgely Torrence.*

The next story, which was accepted for Harper's Bazaar *by Charles Hanson Towne, and appeared in the issue of that magazine for September, 1927, I have placed just before the papers concerning Shelley, as it develops a delightful speculation concerning Shelley. It is interesting to note, in connection with it, that Somes' Sound is actually adjacent to the town of Somesville, in Maine, where Elinor Wylie first began to write poetry again after having laid aside that practice almost since the days of the publication of her first very rare anonymous little book, "Incidental Numbers." An early sonnet of hers, "Atavism," in "Nets to Catch the Wind," recalls the same locality. Maine, I think, remained Elinor's favorite among the New England States, as many of the summers of her childhood and young girlhood were identified with it.*

The story of which I have just spoken is properly followed by perhaps the best of Elinor's contributions to Books, *an essay-review which contains, among other matter, interesting comment upon a dear friend of hers, the editor of the Julian Edition of Shelley. And I can identify the man she speaks of as encountering "along Sixth Avenue under the spiteful thunder of the 'L,'" as Philip Moeller, who has directed the best productions of the Theatre Guild. I chanced to be present at this first real meeting of two Shelley enthusiasts.*

" Mr. Shelley Speaking " was published in The Bookman, *to explain, if not to justify — since to those truly familiar with Shelley's language in his letters and reported conversations it needed no justification — his manner of speech in " The Orphan Angel." The paper was printed soon after the book had gained wide notice.*

" The Sage in Meditation " appeared in The Saturday Review of Literature *for January 19, 1929; that is, posthumously. It was set down in England, when Elinor was perfecting her finest volume of poems, " Angels and Earthly Creatures." I have already written of this period:*

" During the Autumn of 1928 she lived quietly in The Old Cottage in the town of Henley-on-Thames, taking long daily walks alone through the surrounding countryside, and ' strictly meditating the Muse,' to her never ' Thankless.' "

The essay, as I then said, was " a by-product of many months given over, despite the dangerous accident that intervened, to the writing of poetry." It is an essay distinctly for poets. It is a defense of the well-nigh frantic industry of poets against those who will ever regard them as mere idlers. And it is the truest exposition of the industry of a great poet that I have ever read.

The review-essay on the " Autobiographies " of William Butler Yeats, that follows, was printed in Books *during the month to which I have referred above. It is a sensitive tribute from a great American poet to one who remains the greatest living poet in the English language.*

The three slighter papers whose inclusion completes this section, appeared: "The Pearl Diver" in the then Literary Review *of* The New York Evening Post *for September 30, 1922; "Jewelled Bindings," in* The New Republic *for December 5, 1923; and "Symbols in Literature" in* The English Journal *for June, 1928. All three papers contain valuable hints as to Elinor Wylie's attitude toward her art. She touches with lightness upon methods of research (the indefatigable and inspired precision of her own research being something at which to marvel), makes a graceful and adroit defense of strict discipline in the poetic art, and explains why novels are sometimes written in a manner "to avoid the bitterness of being understood."*

In closing, I have before me several unfinished fragments of the author's prose manuscripts. Here is the beginning of a story, the first section of which is succinctly entitled "Album," presenting, as on old cartes de visite, portraits of the forebears of those who were, apparently, to move through a novel concerned with modernity. The two families represented were to be the Damons and the Angells: there were a Mr. and Mrs. John Damon and a Mr. and Mrs. Archer Angell. As to the forebears, "you may further learn that the sand beneath Mrs.

Damon's ridiculous slipper, the tree-top above Mr. An-
gell's equally preposterous but much larger hat, were
respectively indigenous to a seaside resort upon the coast
of Rhode Island and a celebrated Spa among the moun-
tains of New York."

In section two, " Romantic Encounter," we are intro-
duced to the Linda Damon of 1910:

" On the whole she remained, for at least half a block,
no more than a charming gently-nurtured girl, pink-
cheeked and pretty in a new black frock. Then, with
sudden and amazing sharpness, as one who steps from
the discreet shadow of trees into a frenzy of outrageous
noon, the girl stepped across a certain invisible dividing
line; upon her descended a shining loveliness like a gar-
ment of light. Although her path was still shaded, she
was now completely surrounded by radiance; she
walked in beauty. The beauty was in the eye of the
beholder."

There is a brief " short story synopsis," outlining the
love story of an Eighteenth Century English Civil Serv-
ant, " of the Bengal military establishment," one Cap-
tain Mordaunt, who is " cursing his own folly for being
such a blockhead as to quit the Paradise of Hindustan to
visit England." At " Mrs. Weston's famous receptacle
in Berkeley Row," he " drinks a few glasses of wine
with the girls." "They next proceed to Mrs. Kelly's
similar establishment in Arlington Street," and there he
meets Mrs. Kelly's entirely innocent young daughter of

sixteen. For his aloofness in dissipation, Captain Mor-
daunt is nicknamed " Surly Nabob," which was also to
be the title of the story. His romantic rescue of Miss
Kelly — and the misunderstanding thereof — was to
supply the chief matter of the narrative.

But more seriously contemplated was the beginning
of another novel, typed on yellow copy-paper under the
title of " A Tenpenny Ash Plant." It concerns the for-
tunes of Elfrida Follett, " the daughter of the organist
of Autrelieu Abbey," pronounced, naturally, Otterlee.
Unbeknown to all and sundry, she has for seven years
been the mistress, because she deeply loved him, of Tris-
tram Ashleigh — being also his daughters' governess.
Of course, Elfrida's present employer, Mrs. Tredin-
nick,

" would never have allowed Olwen and Ettarre to be
educated by anyone's mistress, not even the mistress of
so remarkable a man as Mr. Ashleigh of Bayneleis Brook.

" ' You're in love with someone at home, of course,'
Mrs. Tredinnick had said casually at the end of the fifth
year, after Elfrida had repulsed both the honourable pro-
posals of Mr. Tredinnick's architect and the dishonour-
able proposals of Mr. Tredinnick. ' I hope it's that nice
young pianist, but I'm afraid it's not.' "

Again, Elfrida, feeling " most unhappy," supposes
" that she must, in some subtle way, be ruining the
characters of two innocent girls, only she was such a
good governess, and had such a superior touch upon the

piano, thanks to her father's training, and such reserves of patience, thanks to Mr. Ashleigh's, that she knew no one else would suit Mrs. Tredinnick so well. Besides, she realized that Mrs. Tredinnick would not object to having a mistress as a friend, however quickly she might have dismissed such a person from the position of governess. There were many such among the acquaintances of anyone so well-connected as Mrs. Tredinnick."

The humour of this hardly needs laboring. The affair of the quite adorable Elfrida with Mr. Ashleigh begins upon entirely idyllic terms, and he is charmingly described. But the manuscript runs to but seventeen pages, and hence the romance of Bayneleis Brook is lost to the world. It is natural that Elfrida's father should make several references to Mr. Rochester, in the course of the narrative, governesses being such favorite heroines with at least one of the Brontës. But Elinor Wylie's variant of the " governess novel " would have been sure to possess her own inimitable compound of great romantic beauty and needlepoint satire.

A number of literary people still recall her projected novel on the general subject of the Salem witches, a book in the thought of which she expressed delight and for which she collected many reference volumes. She was not to live to write it. This completes a brief survey of the most important fragmentary prose she had near her when she died.

Peculiarly rare fragrance arises from these aloof par-

*terres, these dew-bright landscapes. The author seemed
while she yet lived the embodiment of all that hyaline
ecstasy and quicksilver intelligence she so adored; the
exemplification of her own intricate patterns of frost —
of all delicate, nimble, fragile, translucent, and nobly
quickened emotion and thought. The cloak of her imagination was a broidered black damask wherethrough the
rapier of her wit caught essential moonlight upon its
blade. But the other face of her masked, ironic spirit was
the face of a crisp-frocked curly-headed child, surprised
in mischievous laughter among the wild flowers of some
fabulous upland pasture, where the wounds of Life are
not and the winds of Time blow not. Her spiritual home
lay west of the moon.*

WILLIAM ROSE BENÉT

MAY, 1933,
NEW YORK CITY.

Fugitive Prose

CONTENTS

Fugitive Prose

THE HOUND

THE COLD white dish of *antipasto* blossomed like a flower garden into lovely colours, but he was very pale. His hair stood up in a ruffled crest. The carven angels ever eager-eyed, with hair blown back. . . .

" What's the matter, old man? "

The radishes were as pretty as rosebuds in a valentine. The wine cast a prismed gleam of crimson upon the table, such a gleam as might have stained the sunlight falling through the windows of the Sainte Chapelle. It was not even Chianti; it was California claret. Curious colour. Curious. . . .

" No — but what? Something bad? "

" The Hound — the Hound of Heaven. "

" Again? " Impossible not to be a bit sardonic with a knife like a candle flame in your heart. Dissolving it in — something. Fire or water.

> " *As I was going round,*
> *I saw a hound*
> *Lying on the ground*
> *Dying of a wound.*"

In such a pool as that the fallen sunlight lies, staining the floor of the Sainte Chapelle. The radishes were like waxen rosebuds.

789

The hound had lain there ever since you were a child. The voice of the Ulster woman who had been your nurse rhymed the words in a sepulchral groan. The hound lay at the foot of the Tower of London, not the real Tower, but the imagined one of infancy, cold and white and obstinate above this mortal agony. The hound lay in a puddle of blood. The pavement was white where it was not red.

"An illustrated edition. It came into the office this afternoon. I was — looking at it."

An illustrated edition. You could picture the slim-waisted Dulacish dog to which some artist had striven to impart a Christ-like expression of countenance. Or wouldn't they dare? Would it just be twirly lines and mist? If they did, it would be a greyhound of course, and it would be white. Towers topped by soap bubbles would be white in the background. Heart-shaped lattices would bloom from the pencil in rosebuds. There would be clouds. You had the book, so, in a swift image. Suppose you were to read the Sermons of John Donne, or even Holy Living and Dying, in an edition illustrated by Arthur Rackham? But then you wouldn't, your mind was too salty. Peppery and salty. Besides, the words of those books would crunch such phantasmagoria to pieces and spit them out in disgust. The poem had italics. What a pity! It left a loop-hole, somehow, for the illustrations to creep in. It was dastardly, in that beauty. Their angel plucked them from me by the hair. Poor child, his hair was standing straight up in the wild air. . . .

"I hate you to be unhappy! Why don't you go and be one? There's a place — just a door — on the south side of the square. In French and Italian — and of course English. But they wouldn't listen to you until you were one. They'd be polite and kind, but completely detached. They never reach out for you — visibly. They seem rather bored. When you are, really and truly, it must be different. Why don't you try?"

"Can't, I never could. That's the trouble. It's a sort of nostalgia. But to swallow all that . . ."

"The only other way is mine, a perfect conviction of a death-bed repentance. I don't plan it. I'm quite ashamed, but I know myself, and that makes it simpler. You don't."

"Know you? O . . ."

"No, darling; know yourself."

"It must be wonderful to be a fanatic."

"Yes . . . but that's not what you're looking for tonight. Incense, rather, and then that almost intolerable tinkle of the bell. The Salvation Army would do for the other thing; their faces are eaten away by exaltations. Only . . . it's ugly; a desert where a fastidious hermit would search his robe continually for fleas. That's not for you, my lamb."

The Lamb of God, and other lambs, some not so white. The shepherd and the sheep. There were sheep-dogs more beautiful by far than greyhounds; such were clothed in gold and silver fur and bore ruffs and frills upon their proud breasts. They loved the lambs. Very seldom did a sheep-dog go mad and devour the flocks of his master.

"The fried potatoes will make you a little fatter, I hope. No, take the rest of the wine, I don't want it. I'd rather have spinach. Please."

"Tonight you're the Renaissance page."

"To run at your stirrup."

Your bronze hair like a rococo bell, your doublet black and grey. Those Chinese dragons might be heraldic beasts, if you wanted them to be. He would, tonight. Another time, perhaps, he might prefer them to swim palely in the Emperor's lotus-pond. A fanatic was by no means the same thing as an ascetic. Simply because the bridge of his nose curved like the ivory paper-cutter at home he could not call himself an ascetic. The Hapsburg lip despised underdone beef, but was quite fond of mushrooms.

"I'm puzzled; always puzzled. Life's so queer. Puzzled."

"I'm not, a bit."

You said it instinctively, for fear they would think you afraid. It was not strictly true; perhaps it was true in spirit. If you groped your way down a damp basaltic corridor you were puzzled. If you marched straight ahead and pretended you didn't give a damn about daggers between your ribs, you weren't. You really didn't care, and so you didn't wonder. Torchlight running scarlet along swords.

" My father was a gallant man,
He laughed at death and dangers;
He stormed the very gates of hell
With a company of the rangers."

" Ha, the personal application! No, that sounds cross; I'm sorry. Only, women always do."

" I'm sorry."

" No, I'm sorry."

You smiled brilliantly, biting into a stalk of celery that was ringletted like a flaxen child fresh from the curling-stick. You were the only person on earth who remembered curling-sticks. How many curls there used to be in the world, sleeked and burnished around curling-sticks until they resembled the silken twists of French candy which were only meant for parties! Candies pale green and tender pink, to match the flowers in the cut glass bowl that you could never lift. Standing in the middle of a mirror; floating there, yet heavy, and sharper than a pineapple to touch.

" Funny, funny the way your tears jump off your cheeks and fly into the air! Why? I never saw anything so funny as your tears; jumping, jumping, and so bright. What makes them? "

" I know . . . always like that. So are Mollie's. I remember in church, the Easter after Father died. The hymns, you see, and both of us at once. Carl laughed. . . . O, but nicely, I mean! It must have been funny; two girls, so tall and slim, and in those days quite fantastically pretty. The bright tears flying straight out into air full of lilies; glass birds flying and falling. Funny."

" Not so very, after all; don't be sad. The hard green pear for you; the nice pink apple for me; that's right. And now about that other thing. . . . I'm not sad, either. It's merely a recurrent madness; a tremendous pull, but I can't quite go it. Hairsplitting . . . all the minutiæ. Saying you believed them. I couldn't."

Chrysoprase grapes that they never touched; cheese veined like marble. Unaccountable idea of his; that he was the only one. But then, he was. Unaccountable, always. Surely, everybody; everybody was pulled by that. How could you help it? It was your ancestors; silly not to see that.

Pulled back and back, until you were in a fishing-boat on a tilted sea that appeared miraculously solid in a flash of lightning, under steps that came steadily across its undulations. How could you forget? How could he expect to forget? You must sit still and wait; in life, march straight ahead; in this, which was above life, and perhaps beyond it, sit still and wait.

Tawny nets, all spangled with new drops of the sea that were green and clear, and old drops that were dried and crystalline.

A long white beach; parrot-coloured shells that sang like nightingales. You could lie down like a tired child; he could lie down like a tired child. He looked very young and very pale.

You could both lie down like tired children on the beach at Naples. Poor, poor Shelley. Another; not so different from this dearer child. Tall and thin, hair standing up in a crest of darkness, blue eyes instead of brown. An eagle's feather . . . an eagle's feather from the Caucasus. Shelley thought he would be satisfied by that content surpassing wealth the sage in meditation found. Only, he knew he hadn't found it, on the beach at Naples.

For me that cup hath been dealt in another measure! You see; you always return to it. The accent of those words was unmistakable. Even Shelley, and in spite of Plato. That was why you liked Socrates so much better; the hemlock, yes, the hemlock.

Truly the chicory in the coffee made its blackness as bitter as gall. He, who so loved coffee, was making a grimace and laughing. Brave to laugh, when the coffee was so bitter and he was so tired.

> " *As I was going round*
> *I saw a hound*
> *Lying on the ground*
> *Dying of a wound.*"

The tall white Tower of London did not care. From a great distance the Woolworth Building looked as if it did care; the sun painted it with gold; it was a thin gold pencil pointing at something wonderful among the clouds. But when you came to it, it was cold and white. It would not care even if you jumped out of it and were a red splash on the clean pavement.

You must lie very quietly upon the long white beach until at last the net fell over you, first soft as the breast of a mother, then stringent as her defending arms.

His eyes were the colour of the coffee; it was not really black; gold floated somewhere in its darkness. He was still smiling.

" Ah, I hate you to be unhappy! "

" I'm not. Tired; a little tired."

" I know, my lamb; I know."

If your heart really burst the whole room would at once be filled with golden light, beautiful and inhuman. Raying, streaming, like broad swords or narrow pennons, from the little crack in the heart, the heart so inadequate to hold such splendour; no bigger, hardly brighter, than the smallest red apple in the dish. All this reminded you of something sorrowful, and the lamb reminded you of the same thing.

" Poor lamb! "

The hungry lambs look up and are not fed; that wasn't quite right. Grim wolf with privy paw! Funny to think of it like that. Well, people had their prejudices; Milton, and Torquemada, for instance. Wolves . . . but wolves might always be of Gubbio. But that was sentimental; that was your mind at seventeen or so; that was an illustrated edition, in fact, of the Little Flowers. Not Dulac or Rackham; Boutet de Monvel, precisely. Thin flat colours, pale grey and fawn, kind, a little wild, but far more shy than wild. Stiff and innocent, like wood carving of the middle ages seen through blue and violet fog.

Now the fierce ones seemed better, somehow.

That was long ago; going with Nannie Morse instead of Mama and Mollie. To hear someone . . . someone Nannie liked to hear.

Uglier inside, certainly, than even queer Saint John's. That proved that Beauvais and Chartres hadn't started the pulling. They wouldn't take the trouble; beside, they had so much else to give, such wreaths of stone and glass, such flowers, such faces lovely and malign, such flying arches. You might be the wickedest person in the world, or the most scornful and mocking, and they would still show you those things with noble pride, before turning their backs on you. The ugly ones were different; there was something there for you or there wasn't; it could never be other than that one thing.

You could sit down and wait for it. For it, surely, or so nearly it that you would never know the distinction. You made fun of Francie, but really because she was so blonde. The façade of a Presbyterian church fell down on her without hurting her at all, but that made no sense, because of course she used to be an Episcopalian before she did it. She was funny; rather amateurish. That's what you always felt; if you waited until you were dying the very real ones couldn't laugh at you. Or probably not . . . much.

The pulling began long ago, but for you there was nothing for it but to sit down and wait. You could do that if you tried.

The beloved creature across the table, leaning his head on his hand, couldn't. He ran back and forth; he was tired. Heartbreakingly tired. But now, if you breathed softly and slowly, there was little fear that the room would ever fill with golden light from a red apple broken in two and bleeding.

> " As I was going round
> I saw a hound
> Lying on the ground
> Dying of a wound."

This time you said it aloud, by mistake. The sound of the words made the tessellated pavement and the tall white tower; the body of the dog was mirrored in a pool of red.

" That's cheerful, I must say. I thought we were going to have a cheerful evening."

" I'm sorry; it's nothing, just a rhyme. Scary, I used to think; it has a sort of scary beauty. Not ' macabre '; quite clear and primitive. Giotto in a nightmare."

" I don't know what you mean."

" I'm sorry; truly I'm sorry. I know I'm stupid."

He was annoyed; he was looking away; his profile was remotely proud. The nose more like the ivory paper-cutter than before; the chin trying to be haughtier than it ever could be. A very fine effect, even if you hadn't loved him; only his throat wasn't long enough. That was better than the bridge of a nose for pride; round marble columns lifted over Olympus. You would always go to those people for a certain kind of counsel; they weren't real, but they were there first, above the grey headland and among the olives.

" Be friends! "

" Of course, angel rabbit! "

It would be nice to be one, in some celestial fairy-story that was told over and over again into starred eternity. It would be far easier than being a Renaissance page in a black and silver doublet, with bronze hair clustering hot and thick around your brow as you ran breathless at his stirrup. The horse was black; the hound was white and gold; all three served the knight who wore cuirass and greaves of cold blue steel; the plume in his helmet was rippling like cold blue sea-water.

What if you were the hound instead of the page; was not the hound the humbler of the two? Not the Hound of Heaven, of course; an earthly hound, dusty and panting; whose heart was bursting in a golden flame of love for his master. The wolf of Gubbio turned Christian and a slave. The weary hound looks up at the knight and wishes he were an angel rabbit, and that the knight were really God, instead of only Don John of Austria.

What if you loved God as much as you loved this boy? Try to imagine that. O easier to imagine the thinnest ether and the uttermost stars than that! You must sit still and wait! A prismed stain of crimson upon the tablecloth is like the pool of tinted sunlight upon the floor of the Sainte Chapelle. In the pool a white hound lies forever dying.

" Hello, honey."

You are walking quickly through the lighted square; snow lies sparingly upon stone and grass alike. Your hand is under his arm; he pulls you close. You smile and say " Hello, old kid." He has passed the door without noticing it; he has never known it was there, the mysterious door on the south side of the square; the door which was, somehow, a confessional.

The pattern of lamps in the square makes a great golden net; the snow is softly dusted with gold.

" Wonderful air; wonderful night. I'd like to fly; I'd like to take a ferry-boat as we did last spring. Wonderful; wasn't it wonderful?"

"Might be a bit chilly tonight. Your overcoat . . ."

Your casual tone is as elaborate as the stiff lace-paper frill around a valentine with pink rosebuds at its four corners; its careful quiet is more loving than a million silver kisses. Funny, funny boy; not to know that ferry-boats are as useless as aeroplanes! He runs back and forth; he is dreadfully tired. You sit still and wait, until the tawny nets enfold you.

"I'll write a poem instead; I have a wonderful idea. . . ."

You step in rhythm; long legs, slim ankles, narrow feet hurry in unison. He is happy. A poem; instead of what? Instead of the ferry-boat, of course; he never saw the door. He wanted to be a fanatic, but he read an illustrated edition. It sounds like an epitaph. You have a salty peppery mind, my girl; sometimes you read the Mural Quadrant instead of the Oil Cruet, but you prefer such words as these. . . . "The ashes of an oak in a chimney are no epitaph of that oak. . . . The dust of great persons' graves is speechless to. .. ." The sky is powdered with points of an almost intolerable beauty; the tinkle of the bell is more intolerable than the stars. Sit still and wait for the golden net, dragged dripping from a sky that is a sea of infinite amazement to the humble.

"A wonderful idea . . ."

He is happy. You thank God, but you would rather thank him; you would like to kiss his hand because he is happy. And yet, you have a salty mind; listen to your own laughter.

"A wonder came to light
Which showed the rogues they lied . . ."

"But why? Why 'The dog it was that died'? "

"Dear lamb!"

Listen to your own laughter. He is happy. He will write a poem; it will be the border of a missal book or gilded chronicle magnified into painted clouds along the horizon. It will be the apotheosis of his paper-cutter nose in the air. You will sit on the floor at his feet and lay your cheek in the palm of his hand. You must not cry; he is very tired and your tears would fly around his head like bright glass birds; you must not even let them sleep in his hand tonight; he is very tired. All birds and fishes, however silver and gold, however wild, may sleep at last, lying down together like the lion and the lamb, folded in the tawny meshes of the net; dragged dripping, dripping from the deep sea and the deeper sky.

The tall white tower is the Tower of London, but the pool of blood has fallen like rain through the coloured windows of the Sainte Chapelle. Within the pool, mirrored by its smoothness, a white hound lies forever dying.

> " *As I was going round*
> *I saw a hound*
> *Lying on the ground*
> *Dying of a wound."*

You dreamt the groaning words; you must not cry. Breathe softly; he is very tired. Breathe softly; you must neither of you wake, for he is very tired, and your heart is breaking in your breast like a small red apple which at the sound of tears or voices must burst into swords and banners, filling the room with the beauty of golden light and the intolerable tinkling of bells.

1923

Fugitive Prose

GIDEON'S REVENGE

GIDEON extinguished the flame wherewith he had lit his pipe; he dropped the match tidily behind the wallflowers, and looked about him with quiet, but incredulous, joy. Standing at the door of the cottage, his head was stooped a little beneath the lintel, partly from actual necessity and partly in a courteous gesture of apology to this exquisite scene in which only children or delicately formed and tinted women might appear appropriate and untarnished. Above him the freshness of the honey-colored thatch contrasted pleasantly with the rose-purple of ancient brick; the watery sheen of the upper windows reflected a few hanging strands of straw, like gilded seaweed observed in the profundity of a wave. Inclosed by its clipped hedge, the garden lay like a small square pool of flowers drawn together in concentrated brightness, as if many larger and grosser gardens had been melted into one and poured into this narrow space. Across the green a dew pond reversed the sky to another pool, and permitted Gideon's vision to plumb without fatigue the utmost depth of the empyrean.

Gideon was a tall old man; his age was perhaps seventy. His face had more of the falcon than the eagle in its lines; the beaked nose, the bony setting of the large, bright eyes, the hollowed cheek and temple, were all carved and polished to a pattern sufficiently bold, but light and restless and uneasy. His eyes were gray; his hair, which had once been reddish, had now the faintly yellowed whiteness of flax; it rose steeply to a crest above his brow. The garments which he wore hung somewhat awkwardly upon his emaciation — an emaciation suggesting austerity rather than weakness. The correct and shabby tweeds were excellent in themselves, molded to fit with easy perfection the scene and circumstance, but although they clothed with tolerable grace the mortal form of Gideon, they did not fit his soul. You saw him preferably in rusty black, with a hat remotely Spanish, and a cloak; decidedly the soul of Gideon wore a black cloak. And indeed at this very moment, within the cottage, Caroline was brushing just such a cloak preparatory to putting it away forever with beautiful cakes of gum camphor crumbling like soft and fragrant ice among its mysterious folds.

Gideon turned and entered the cottage; the rooms appeared deliciously chilled and shadowed by the green orchard to the east. Avoiding the larger chamber, where Caroline whisked fantastic garments into the bland, golden obscurity of a tulip-wood chest of drawers, he turned into the kitchen and surveyed its cool and ordered colors with minute approval. It was a room decorous and subtly bright, a place for the concoction of junkets and cherry-pies. Gideon sighed with pleasure; it was a miracle that he, a lawless, bitter man, should have imagined this room and made it. Of course there had been the skeleton ready to his hand — the stone floor, the beams, the fireplace — but he had breathed upon cold ashes, and they had flowered like a domestic rose.

Caroline had climbed the steep little stairs to the attic; he could hear portmanteaus bumping about overhead, like huge frolicsome beasts; he had a sudden picture of the trim, pink-faced servant surrounded by portmanteaus and kit-bags, labeled in dusty, barbaric scarlet, enormous in the gloom. He reflected with satisfaction that all his papers were already neatly pigeonholed in his grandfather's desk and his mother's boule cabinet; Caroline was merely rummaging among ponchos and sombreros.

Slowly, with a fastidious, yet sensual, savoring of his delights, Gideon entered the other room and strolled down its entire length, stopping here and there to touch the lovely surface of wood per-

versely satin-skinned, or velvet worn and rosy as immemorial
lichen. Here again was something more than human in the happy
confluence of various times and manners; he had seen these objects scattered in obscure exile among the Victorian ineptitudes
of his mother's vast drawing-rooms, or lately huddled ignomini-
ously in storage warehouses; he had purchased some of them carelessly at the ragged ends of the earth, and now they were gathered
together under the green and glazing twilight of the apple-trees
to make a miraculous whole. He had bought a cottage, knocked
down a partition or two, and engaged a certain number of pan-
technicon vans; he had expected the place to be comfortable and
rather absurd, and by some curious necromancy of chance it
was grave and exquisite. It was as if it had always been so,
and his. Between open windows, his desk was flooded by calm
radiance.

As he fingered the firmly packed bundles of letters, bound with
pink legal tape, or more sentimentally confined by blue ribbons,
he considered the future with approval. It was eminently fitting;
it was, indeed, inevitable. How, save under conditions of the most
shining peace, could he hope to relax into that judicial clarity of
mind so necessary to his great project? The hardships, the astringent horrors of his past career, had precisely steeled his hand to
execution; it now remained for a poor, but honest, gentleman to
judge the culprits before killing them, and Gideon was acutely
aware of the propriety of being equitable to begin with, if only to
augment the pleasure of being savage in the final sentence, the
final act of revenge.

He stared retrospectively down the lurid vista of the last
twenty-five years, his mind's eye blinking, for all its falcon look,
in the full chemical glare of recollection. There had been, quite
literally, singularly little sunlight in the vista, and that little had
quivered to a tropical intensity removed by several continents from
this subaqueous glimmer stained by apple-trees. But mostly, he
remembered, things had happened at night; that was, perhaps,
the reason he had achieved so flattering and profitable a reputation
as special correspondent.

Special! Oh, very special indeed! For who but Gideon would
have been clever enough to be forever on the spot, the often bloody

and unhealthy spot, where things were happening at night? What other nocturnal vigilance had so well observed, what vitriolic pen recorded, alike the curious minutiæ and the vast apocalypse of life? From the beginning to the end of that bewildering vista he had contrived to see the event strangely, and to make the strangeness vivid by his words. Also, he had advanced in wisdom and cunning; he recalled with contempt how crudely he had daubed hell-fire and sanguine upon his earlier efforts. In ninety-eight, when he had seen the *Maine* intemperately uncurl a million fronds of brilliance against the plushy dark, he could not, telling the dreadful thing beheld, curdle the reader's veins as now his lightest, coolest whisper curdled them. The latest of all his writings, the wry, amused account of Lenine stretched upon his crimson upholstery under the great glass bell like some horrible wax flower, blooming through unnatural, and electric, days, that was excellent, that was art.

2

AND now, the quarter-century past, he was quit of restraints, of delicacies and decencies; now he was free of galling secret vows and public scruples. The very last of the Pennimans had died twenty years ago in the person of old Joseph; Gideon had kept his promise to Millicent, and Millicent herself had been dead for twenty-five years.

He was free to turn that intricate and fiery engine, his mind, upon the people he had hated and had, for a measured space of time, striven to forget. At first, after his wife's death, he had acidly regretted his promise to her — the promise given to the expiring appeal of her large blue eyes, but never ratified by their wedded spirits in this world or the vaguer one into whose ambiguities she had at once departed. He had kept the promise because it was a promise; he had been totally untrammeled by sympathy for its purpose or its beneficiaries. He had spared the Pennimans for a score of years; he had not written a book, no, not so much as an epitaph upon any of them until two decades had yellowed the latest of their tombs. It had been a hellish bore, but now he was glad he had refrained. The long and lenten abstinence from revenge had but given edge to his appetite and sharpened his powers to austere perfection.

Gideon drew a dozen slim and pointed pencils from a drawer of the desk; upon its dark-amber surface he placed a formidable pile of copy-paper. The book loomed before his happy contemplation, tremendous, Protean, monstrous, yet alluring. A book, but not alone a book; a mighty chase, a dexterous unmasking, a trial, and an execution. And Gideon, at once Justice incarnate and the instrument of Justice, Gideon must be both judge and executioner. The book was to be a headsman's ax, savage, medieval, elegant, and efficient. Then, picturing a row of Penniman faces upon the spikes of Temple Bar, Gideon smiled a slight abstemious smile.

Apart from fancies, however charming, the facts were these; he reviewed them swiftly, leaning back luxuriously in a chair whose polished curves were as velvet to his neuralgic bones. The book was a debt to his own soul, long overdue, heavy with accretion of interest. He had waited, for Millicent's darling and ridiculous sake, until all kith and kin of hers were moldered into complete indifference. She had desired to shield them from anger and annoyance, for surely their fatted, gelded souls were incapable of pain; she had interposed her threadbare little body between their torpor and his vengeance. Very well; it had been so, but now he would remember it all, and set it down, and verily the page should shrivel beneath the fire of his revelation. Though they skulked in their sepulchers, shrouded in this their last cowardice, he would burn them out of oblivion; the flame of their destruction should ascend forever, purified and fervent, sweet in the nostrils of the brave. He would tell the tale; he would release that holy indignation which for so long had made his heart a fever.

Milly — that foolish nickname wherein her family, with characteristic impertinence, had clothed the golden pallor of her girlhood! If Gideon pronounced her name, he enriched the vowels with a foreign inflection which made it more Melisande than Millicent. That was her proper appellation, that long soft veil of sound, fitting her sallow-flaxen beauty with an enduring garment.

She, who had lain so long asleep in his heart, should be brought forth once more into the wide, bright chamber of his mind; he would look at her in the unpitying glare of that illumination. She would stand, willowy and disarming, lovely and ineffectual, beside the solid, stolid forms of her murderers, the Pennimans. Gideon would look at them all; the Pennimans would tremble and grow pale, they would even grow thin perhaps; Millicent would smile. It would not be the smile of her later days, painted narrow and colorless by despair; it would be the smile of the beginning, of hope and casual courage and unconsidered joy. Gideon ground his teeth, thinking how the Pennimans had destroyed her gaiety and trust. She had loved her father and mother; she had even loved the unspeakable Ambrose, with his long nose and liquid, languid eyes; by love she had been broken and undone.

Of course they had opposed the match; they were obstructive by instinct and conviction, and Gideon, who had refused to be a barrister in order to write for the lesser journals, was sufficiently above them in family and below them in fortune to irritate their every prejudice. His wit inflamed their mental tissues like cayenne pepper; his tongue was gall and vinegar. They resented his height and were half afraid of his hair, which was never properly brushed; he seemed an enigma designed to insult them; his doing could not be other than wrong, but his mere being was the radical error. Gideon knew that, and the reflection soothed him; it meant that he had always, even without trying, done his best to please them: his best must always fail with the Pennimans, and he was glad he had not tried too hard. Millicent had tried too hard, and, in foredoomed endeavor, been destroyed.

He had been a strange son-in-law for the Pennimans; he had fluttered that dove-cote with a vengeance. Fat pigeons they were, and Ambrose with the melting gaze of a turtle above his little waistcoat's curve. And Millicent among them, white and fluttering, with her perpetual olive branch: she was truly a dove!

Without the Pennimans, pecking and obese, how far might they not have flown together, Gideon and Millicent, the falcon and the dove! God knew she had always wanted to be free; God had known it all along, in fact, and that was Gideon's quarrel with God, second only to his quarrel with the Pennimans. For the Deity, frequently invoked by that pious family, had apparently been moved by their flatteries rather than by Gideon's dignified silence; God had not saved Millicent even at the last minute: he had, by allowing her to die, given her back to the Pennimans. Gideon, who had never believed in God, found this impossible to forgive; in his indignation he realized that he was a Christian.

The Pennimans, outrageous to the last, had always blamed him for his wife's death; they had pecked her into shreds while he was cynically examining the Spanish-American War. They had not even taken the trouble to cable news of her illness; he had returned to find her *in extremis*. Gideon was frantic; the Pennimans were sorrowful and mildly complacent. They expressed surprise at his reappearance, and disgust at what they were pleased to term his neglect. Millicent had, apparently, been killed by the absence of a husband whose presence had always, according to the Pennimans, constituted a criminal menace to her health and sanity. The bronze door of the Penniman vault shut firmly upon her mortal remains; the family, in solemn conclave, decided that Gideon was sailing for South Africa with Milly's blood upon his hands. Gideon knew that their own hands were dabbled in her innocence.

Gideon found the South African War a personal convenience, but against the Pennimans he was very bitter, and his amazing despatches, colored and brilliant with hate, were only a partial relief to his feelings. He found it impossible to dislike the Boers with the authentic fervor so desirable in a special correspondent; quite deliberately he dipped his pen into his private gall before writing, and his passionate loathing for a respectable family at Wimbledon fired half England to a pure flame of patriotism. But it was all very unsatisfactory and rather troublesome, this inner pretense that Cronje and Wessels were in reality Mrs. Penniman and Ambrose. His despatches were devoured raw by the popular appetite, but he himself went hungry; he starved for his revenge. Gideon, remembering those days, laughed heartily. How fierce he had been, and how frustrate!

The sunlight fell across his dusky golden desk, and still he remembered, and did not write. That was twenty-five years ago, and this was England, and he was old, but neither frustrate nor starving. The Gideon of the Transvaal had been a widowed Gideon of forty-odd, bereaved and raging — a Gideon who had but just observed the wife of his romantic youth go down to the grave shrunken to premature decay, quenched in body and soul, the clear flame withered, the bright stem trodden underfoot. For a long and parching term of years he had beheld her obliquely in the flawed mirror of her dying face; later he had shut his eyes while she slept in his heart. Now he looked at her again, in the cool and blessed light of these windows, in the peace of this quiet room; she was a girl again, and beautiful. But Millicent had always been beautiful.

It was the other Pennimans who had been ugly; how ugly he shuddered to recall. He drew a packet of papers toward him. These were photographs of the criminals, letters from Milly, letters from Ambrose, his own wild scrawls. Gideon adjusted his spectacles.

3

At seven o'clock Caroline lit the lamp; it was a pale unluminous yellow against the western window-panes, where rose color was fading. Half an hour later she placed a small tray at Gideon's elbow; the noiseless hand was also skilful, for the cutlet was done to a turn, the coffee superlative. Gideon ate and drank, thanking the stars now set in chrysoprase above the apple-trees. At nine he put down the last of the letters and, lifting one of the photographs, examined it intently. A curious trembling seized him; he appeared a prey to obscure emotions, and his face was visibly convulsed.

The picture, a highly glazed *carte-de-visite* of the eighties, showed a family group augmented by one stranger: it showed, clearly enough, the four Pennimans and Gideon. There, seated side by side, were old Joseph and his wife; at their feet was Ambrose; behind them, poised as if for flight, the less substantial forms of Gideon and Millicent wavered against a painted frieze of foliage. The faces were remarkably distinct — distinct as the golden syllables of Harrogate bitten into grayish cardboard below them.

The photograph completed at a single shattering blow the annihilation of Gideon's hard-won calm. The tears poured from his eyes upon the glassy countenance of Ambrose, while Gideon laughed and laughed.

Here, presented upon a little slip of grimy cardboard, was the whole stupendous farce; the farce was here reduced to such miniature proportions that the human eye could grasp it and the human understanding contain it without effort. During the last three hours, while letter after letter passed into the relentless illumination of his mind, Gideon had gradually perceived the outlines of this farce; they were at first too huge for his comprehension. But now, under the complacent glow of the lamp, the picture made them very plain, very clear and definite.

The Pennimans were funny, and he was a fool. They had always been funny, and he had always been a blazing fool not to see it. They were harmless and absurd; any one with eyes in his head could see that now. Joseph was funny and innately charming; a perfect Cruikshank portrait of a blustering, heavy father born fifty years too late. Mrs. Penniman was funny and pathetic and rather a dear; yes, she was entirely a dear, with her cotton-wool hair and her face like a frightened baby's. And Ambrose was funny, and — well, Ambrose was enormously funny; Gideon left it at that. As for Millicent and Gideon, they were funniest of all; they were, he realized, tremendous.

There was Milly — and oh, how right the Pennimans had been to call her Milly! — there she was, in her famous green silk frock from Liberty's, looking like a Du Maurier drawing executed not in ink, but in China tea, the sweet little ghost of a Du Maurier drawing. How sweet she looked, and how extraordinarily silly! Yes, of course, that was the word; that was precisely it — silly Milly, adorably silly Milly, clinging to the arm of her devoted young husband. To the stalwart arm? Perhaps not quite to the stalwart arm, but at least to the protecting arm of a fiercely possessive Gideon in the first of all the black cloaks, with the biggest and blackest of all the sombreros pulled down over smoldering eyes, whose expression was accurately compounded of love for his bride and haughty malevolence for the rest of the world. Which meant, mostly, the Pennimans. No wonder poor Ambrose lifted his own eyes in alarm to the face of his tall brother-in-law.

Was it possible that he had ever believed himself a suitable husband for that delightful little idiot in green silk and Italian corals who was so obviously made of pink sugar candy? Both sun and rain must inevitably melt the pretty creature; the chills and ardors of common life must reduce her to crumbs of sugary dust. Brittle and soft and sweet, Milly was always sweet. Oh, he had loved her right enough, and she had loved him; but Milly had loved every one, and Gideon had loved no one but Milly.

Was it possible that he had ever expected the Pennimans to understand his plans, his ambitions, for Milly and himself? He laughed again to remember the mixture of frigid courtesy and contempt with which he had invariably met their suggestions and advice. He might as well have worn a black mask in addition to the outrageous sombrero for all he had ever let them see of his thoughts or intensities of feeling. Not that it mattered; he was such piercing vinegar to their emollient oil. It was nobody's fault: they were all of them good and kind; Milly was an angel, a sugar angel; and the young, thin, eager Gideon no more than an impulsive and infatuated fool. What a fool he had been to burden himself with such confectionary! What a fool she had been to intrust herself to his hot and sticky grasp! It was a miracle that they had survived so long in each other's strange company.

Gideon again bent his falcon gaze upon the photograph, and his laughter was quenched in pity. The people in the picture were all so ridiculous and serious and profoundly innocent, and now he might laugh at them as much as he liked. He could never laugh with them, and it was nobody's fault.

And the book? Gone, like a gorgeous thunder-cloud, tiger-streaked, into profound oblivion. Dead, like the Pennimans, who, in its death, were prodigally revenged.

Gideon stooped, and set a match to the fire. It flew upward like a sanguine flower, and the room was roseate instead of amber-yellow in the lamp-light. Its colors glowed from new planes and facets; its shapes were subtly altered and enhanced. Caroline came in quietly with the whisky and soda.

Presently Gideon rose, and lit his pipe. A tall and solitary figure, he stood gazing into the lambent mystery of the fire; he sighed gently.

"I suppose I shall have to learn to dislike my neighbors," he told himself in a low voice. " One might write a grim realistic novel about those squat dark people at Skatt's Farm."

But at the back of his mind was a sick conviction that they were probably quite pleasant, harmless people, and after a little while he took his candlestick from the hall table and went upstairs to bed.

He jumped very quickly between the cool sheets, and fell asleep trying hard to hate the squat dark people at Skatt's Farm. But the dreadful part of it was that Gideon could not hate them.

1924

Fugitive Prose

THE LIFE STORY OF LYDIA
GREENSMITH

THEY could not have had a more delicious day for the Grand
Prix if they had ordered it beforehand, leaving time for at least
three fittings, from Patou or Poiret. Therefore I had made fairly
certain of not meeting an American at the Musée Carnavalet; the
sudden vision of Miss Lydia Greensmith was a miraculous shock
to my nerves. These were already slightly shaken, because the
cabman had cursed so very heartily when he discovered that I
was not, after all and in spite of my new ashen-rose-colored raiment, for Longchamps and the races. I stood staring at the glass
case with its little dusty dead rats and their goblin printing-press
and thinking that art is long, perhaps, but excessively thin. I was
alone save for the sinister plaster presences in the next room and
the scarcely more vivacious creature selling postcards to nobody
at the door. Then Lydia Greensmith entered from the garden
and I was amazed into a voice.

"Oh," I said, "*Oh!*" She was so charming and so absurd,
from the enameled pansy at her throat to her small elastic-sided
boots, and she was obviously too soft to be plaster and too warm
to be wax.

"Bonjour, mademoiselle," she said politely and I trust quite sincerely. It is true that my great-grandmother was a Huguenot, and one does not expect to meet an American at the Carnavalet on the day of the Grand Prix. The moment she spoke I perceived that she came from Connecticut.

"Do let me help you with that heavy bag," I cried at once, seizing it by its worn handle. "And your box; goodness gracious, you haven't been dragging a great leather box across the court-yard, have you? Isn't there a porter somewhere about?"

"At the races," said Miss Greensmith sadly. "You see, I tipped them all last night; the chambermaid, too. It's always a mistake; one gets no service the next day. A taxi, perhaps."

"The animal at the door might find one," I suggested, but she shook her head.

"Really they're all cross with me for leaving," she murmured. "I know it's flattering, but so awkward about the bags. And you, my dear . . . no, really, you mustn't spoil your pretty gloves. But if you could see whether there is a taxi in the street . . ."

"There is," I said, "mine; it's waiting for me. May I take you anywhere?"

"I thought I would go first to the brasserie on the corner, for a 'fine,'" Miss Greensmith replied timidly. "It's melancholy, this parting. . . . Goujon's darling lions . . . ah me, how I shall miss it all! I've been very happy; I've loved it so, you see; perhaps I'm making a mistake." And she began to cry.

"A 'fine' is indicated," I thought. Aloud I said, "I'll tell the taxi man to keep an eye on your luggage."

"Please," she whispered. "But are you quite sure, my dear, that the man's reliable? I have one or two little trifles . . ."

"Not from the Carnavalet?" I asked; I couldn't help it. The bag had seemed mysteriously heavy. We turned into the rue des Francs-Bourgeois.

"Only from the cellars, child, and gifts, all of them; gifts from the government. Defective pieces; broken fans and bits of porce-lain. It's a matter of sentiment, entirely, but so kind of the dear Ministers to understand."

"But do you mean," I cried, when we were seated at the small green table with a "fine" between us, "that you were actually living there?"

" Yes," said Miss Greensmith simply.

" No," I said to the waiter, " I prefer an infusion. Camomile. Better for the nerves."

" They permitted it out of pure kindness, and because my uncle had been Governor of Connecticut. Yes, the fact that I am a gentlewoman undoubtedly had something to do with it, but that doesn't alter the circumstances of their amazing kindness."

" You're very pretty, you know," I said somewhat impertinently. It was true; she had enormous lavender-gray eyes in a fragile three-cornered face. I guessed that her curls had once been dark, but now they were silvery and shining with a moonlight fairness.

" That has nothing to do with it," she answered with an air of pride and soft reproof. " It was pure altruistic kindness on the part of the Ministers, I assure you. I asked the government if I might, mentioning my uncle and a few distinguished ancestors, and I was allowed to live in three small rooms in the attic. No modern conveniences, of course, but an exquisite view. It is not generally known; I hope you will not speak of it, my dear, particularly as I am leaving."

" Ah, such a lovely, lovely place to live! How have you the heart to leave it? " I demanded. " Remember the quiet courtyard and the sunlight on the frosty stone, and the rooms as clear and elegant as the inner shapes of flowers! Remember the little coach and horses carved from mother of pearl and gold, and you might look at it every single hour! Ah, but you were lucky, and I think you are rather an idiot to go home! "

" I liked the earrings made in the form of a guillotine even better," said Miss Greensmith wistfully. " Only, my dear, I'm not going home to America, you see. I've had quite enough of the Grand Central Station, thank you.

" Yes, I was born in Connecticut; you are entirely right about that," she continued shyly. " Near Fairfield; pleasant country, especially in the spring. Lilacs and apple-blossoms; there was a hedge of white lilacs before the door. But I was always afraid to go out of the door; I never was properly adventurous until I grew up. I rarely left the house until I was past thirty, and then only in the cool of the evening, in a blonde lace veil. Ours was a huge old house; the roofs were as broad and green as other people's front lawns, and one hot summer I had actually a little garden of lilies of the valley in the shade of the north chimney. The peaks and gables used to rise above me like green hills; they were covered with moss, and the treetops made other hills beyond them."

"But why did you go away?" I asked. "And what about the Grand Central Station? Another 'fine'?"

"Please," said Miss Greensmith. "À l'eau. Well, my child, my dear parents died for one thing, and my brother married a film star. I did not care for the curtains she selected for the drawing-room, and I thought I might be happier in New York."

"And were you?" I inquired, pouring out another cup of camomile tea.

"I never saw New York," said Miss Greensmith, "except from the Grand Central Station. I never dared to venture into the street. I lived in the Grand Central Station for fifteen years.

"I arrived before it was really finished," she went on, "and at first it was somewhat uncomfortable, but I soon grew accustomed to it, and then for a time I was very happy. It was beautiful, you know, in a queer way; that great floor glittering like golden ice, and all the strange long corridors and lighted galleries. And then the shops; I did enjoy the shops, I must confess."

"But where did you sleep?" I asked rather nervously, sipping my infusion.

"Oh, at the Biltmore, sometimes, and sometimes at the Commodore, and then towards the end I tried the Roosevelt for a change," said Miss Greensmith with a pensive smile.

"Didn't you ever have the curiosity to go to the Belmont?"

"I considered it, but I couldn't bring myself to cross Forty-second Street, my dear," Miss Greensmith admitted, sighing. "But what did it matter, with my whole world under one vast zodiacal roof? I had everything I needed for that fifteen years."

"Then you must know that little shop where I used to have tea with William, and the buttermilk place, and the place where they sell Irish dulse, and the secret entrance from the Yale Club!"

"But naturally," said Miss Greensmith, "I know it all; nobody else knows it as I do. But of course I prefer the Carnavalet."

"I can quite comprehend that," I answered sympathetically.

"And now you are leaving it forever. Why? In the name of all adorable gimcracks, why?"

"I am going to Rome," said Miss Greensmith. "Not over, you know; I am an Episcopalian. Just to Rome."

"'Which is the sepulchre . . .'" I said. "'Go thou to Rome, at once the Paradise . . .'"

"Precisely," Miss Greensmith replied. "That is precisely what I mean."

"Oh, is it, really and truly?" I cried, trembling a little in spite of the camomile tea. "But do you mean what I mean, I wonder? Is that the reason you are going to Rome?"

"Yes," said Miss Greensmith, "the Protestant cemetery." And she began to cry.

"Don't," I begged her, which was unfair, because I also had begun to cry.

"The authorities have given me permission," she whispered finally, touching her wet lashes with a cobweb handkerchief. "I shall sit there all day long, every day for the rest of my life. 'From the world's bitter wind, seek shelter in the shadow . . .' I love the adorable gimcracks of the Carnavalet, but I believe I've outgrown them, just as I outgrew Connecticut and the Grand Central Station. I don't care for anything now, except — except the Protestant cemetery. And in the evening I shall drink Asti Spumante and read . . ."

"Of course," I said, "you're quite right. I think, if you don't mind, I shall go to Rome with you. But first, you must come with me to the Ritz Bar to have a champagne cocktail."

"Yes," said Miss Lydia Greensmith, "I'd like to do that, my dear. Only don't forget that we've left my luggage at the Carnavalet."

Then, as I went to fetch it, she took a volume of Shelley out of her reticule and laid it upon the little green table. The book fell open in the middle, where the blue silk marker divided its enchanted leaves.

"Another 'fine,' if you please," I heard her murmur to the waiter in her French of Fairfield in Connecticut.

1926

Fugitive Prose

A BIRTHDAY CAKE FOR LIONEL

" ' For this purpose,' said Shelley, ' I wish to find two young persons of not more than four or five years of age; and should prefer females, as they are usually more precocious than males. I would undertake to make a provision for the parents; and would bind myself to watch over the children as if I were their own father. If you can assist me in this scheme, I will withdraw from the world with my charge, and in some sequestered spot direct their education. They shall know nothing of men or manners until their minds shall have been sufficiently matured to enable me to ascertain when brought into play, what the impressions of the world are upon the mind when it has been veiled from human prejudice.' " — *A Newspaper Editor's Reminiscences in Fraser's Magazine for June, 1841.*

It was the fourth of August in the year 1832, and upon the round piny islet which lies at the head of Somes' Sound two little girls were engaged in icing a birthday cake. The suave and windless air of afternoon hung warm between the spruce and hemlock boughs, and above the children's candid foreheads their damp hair clung in glittering whorls and rings of red and brown. The face of Artemis was pallid with the excessive heat, but Jezebel's cheeks kept the delicate brightness of snow-apples as she bent over the yellow bowl of caramel and honey. The syrup creamed under her silver spoon; she licked the spoon with the tip of her pink tongue and laughed.

"It's good, thank goodness, but it's damned hot," she announced to her companion. "I'm glad, all the same, that we boiled it; the beaten white-of-egg sort of thing would never have survived in such weather as this, Missie, and you know he does like the icing better than the cake. It's very important that the icing should be perfect, particularly for his birthday."

"I don't think Lionel quite likes you to swear, Jess; of course he's never precisely spoken of it, but he always looks rather shocked by profanity. Last night when you said, 'God blast my eternal soul to hell if I don't prefer the purple calico,' he turned quite pale; I know it made him nervous. You should be more considerate now that you're grown-up."

"Yes, Miss, and you're an excellent person to lecture me upon that score; who was it that forgot to tell Loren about the tea yesterday, and who was it that dropped bayberry candle-wax on Plato? I'll swear as much as ever I please; if you truly think Christian swearing upsets him I'll say *nom d'un chien* or *Zeus soter.*"

"That would be much nicer and politer, dear, and I'm sure Lionel would appreciate it. He never scolds us, and so we're apt to get a bit careless, but his own manners are so beautiful that I think we should strive to emulate them."

"Ah, the angel, the angel, angel love! As if we ever could be like him; that's quite utterly hopeless, Missie. Nevertheless, you're right; we must try to please him and to make him happy. If only my birch-bark book-marker were a little more worthy of him I shouldn't mind so much; I should never have attempted to copy that steel engraving of the Coliseum on such a small piece of birch-bark."

"My pincushion is rather pretty, only he rarely uses pins," said Artemis with a mournful shake of her flame-colored curls. "Next year I believe I shall make him a balsam pillow."

"Needles and pins . . ." sang Jezebel laughing; then for no

apparent reason she blushed until her cheeks were rosier even than snow-apples. "Next year we shall be in the world, I suppose. What a horrid bore it sounds, doesn't it?"

"Terrifying, to me; I can't think darling Lionel will ever be so hard-hearted as to take us there, among the wicked rich and the oppressors and the tyrants. If I ever see a Lord Chancellor I shall perish of fear upon the spot."

"The critics are the worst, but if I meet one I shall kill him for killing John Keats," cried Jezebel with spirit, tossing her pale bronze ringlets in the quiet air and allowing the golden lightnings of her eyes to flash defiantly at some invisible foe.

"Bloodshed is invariably wrong, save as an act of courage to protect the weak," Artemis declared gravely. "Yours would be revenge; I don't think Lionel would like that."

"Can't help it; I'm always sorry to worry the precious, but of course I expect to kill plenty of people when we go into the world. I shall simply have to kill Godwin, and the wretched beast on the Quarterly, and that lawyer fellow Whitton; I shouldn't be surprised to find that I must kill Sir Timothy too, one of these days. When I think of Lionel actually hounded by bailiffs in the waste of London I could cry!" said Jezebel, and forthwith proved the truth of her words by a shower of glittering tears.

The clear gray eyes of Artemis had each of them a crystal drop upon their lashes, but she replied with admirable composure as she smoothed the icing over the surface of the birthday cake.

"To be consistent, you would have to kill the bailiffs also, and then you would most certainly be hanged, and that would make Lionel frightfully nervous, as you know very well indeed. Jess, if we are really going into the world, I must learn to be brave and you must learn to be calm; otherwise Lionel will find us a great nuisance."

"I know, I know, Missie; poor angel, we're quite enough bother to him as it is, and he is so ridiculously good to us, far kinder than we deserve. We're spoilt, I'm afraid; he has been such a darling that he's been imposed upon by the pair of us. Fancy his letting me choose such a hideous name as Jezebel merely because I was obstinate and had always felt sorry for her because she was eaten by dogs! What a stubborn little brute I must have been in those days!"

"Well, dear, you were only five years old at the time, and Lionel wanted us to be perfectly free to choose our own names; I don't think he blamed you in the least for choosing Jezebel. He told me once that for one so young you had displayed a touching sympathy for the unfortunate; he doesn't care very much for Jehu, or for Elijah the Tishbite."

"I know he understands; it is so pitiful that nothing was left of her but her feet and the palms of her poor little hands! Only when I go into the world it may be better to call myself Jessica; I shall be fifteen then and Jezebel sounds silly for a girl of fifteen, though it's all very well for a child."

"I wish we might be children forever, for my part," said Artemis with a sigh, leaning her cheek upon her slender hand; the transparent pallor of her skin was luminous like a sea-shell in the green shadow of the pine-trees. Her hair was brighter than the gilded pine cones; it was bright as the little fire that danced in the stone oven over sweet-scented fuel. A shining tin kettle jigged above the flame; there was a willow-pattern teapot and a silver spoon conveniently near the cup and saucer.

"Loren has remembered the milk to-day, at all events," said Jezebel happily, smiling at the birthday cake. "I wrote down everything, milk and candles and gingernuts and Gibraltars and raisins and angelica and a jar of Mrs. Fernald's wild-strawberry jam. What a splendid supper, and how delighted Lionel will be that we have arranged it all as a surprise! He loves surprises."

"Fancy needing forty candles for the darling; it doesn't seem possible that he should be so old," Artemis murmured pensively. "Forty really is rather old, Jess, if you come to think of it quite seriously; I dare say we shall be grandmothers when we are forty, and wear caps, and perhaps suffer from rheumatism. Lionel isn't a bit like that, of course; he's divinely beautiful, for one thing, and then somehow he's so extraordinarily swift and light and dashing. Even his gray hair isn't a bit like other people's gray hair; it's more like quicksilver."

"Gray!" Jezebel shone and sparkled with scorn; it was as if some one had suddenly kindled a light behind the soft colors of her pink-and-white face and her hazel eyes. "Do you call that gray? It's like the moon; it's like the sun burning away the fog; it's like the crests of the waves breaking under the stars! You ought to be ashamed of yourself; how dare you tell me that Lionel's hair is gray?"

"But I said it wasn't; I said it was like quicksilver," Artemis protested plaintively. "Don't be cross, Jessie; he'll be here any minute, and he mustn't find us quarreling. You know how it upsets him, and we mustn't spoil his birthday supper with nonsensical arguments and squabbles. Besides, I love him as much as you do; I'm not so clever at putting it into words, but you know how much I love him."

"I know, Missie dear; you're a good girl, and I'm a plumb fool, as Loren says." Jezebel was laughing again; she leaned across a bar of sunlight and kissed her sister's downcast cheek. "Don't be sad, my poppet; you look like a little drowned pearl; you mustn't cry. We both love him with all our hearts; we love him equally and he belongs to us both and to nobody else. He's ours, and we're his; nobody can ever, ever take him away from us, for all our lives forever."

"Suppose he should die!" Artemis shivered; she was so pale that her gray eyes were black.

"Missie! What infernal folderol! Lionel isn't going to die," cried Jezebel triumphantly; she leaped to her feet and sang the joyful words like an incantation. "He's going to live, to live for years and marvelous years to come; so long as we love him he cannot die!"

"Suppose he should get married," said Artemis faintly. "Suppose, Missie, that Lionel should get married."

"Married! But you know quite well that he's married already; that he has a tiresome wife somewhere who doesn't like him very much any more. Imagine what an idiot the woman must be; imagine how ludicrous it would be not to love Lionel!"

"Didn't you ever think he might be rather fond of that lady in black who used to live at Prettymarsh? The one whose husband was drowned at sea on his way home from South America; the one who had the white Persian shawl and the seed-pearl earrings. Lionel used often to lend her books; they used to take walks together on Sundays while the other people were in church."

"Oh, but that lady's gone to Boston, Missie, and besides, she must be more than thirty; her hair has little white feathers in it over her forehead. She isn't a bit the sort of person whom Lionel would marry. Would love, I mean; of course he doesn't approve of marriage."

"What sort of person would he marry, or love, if you prefer the expression?" asked Artemis in a low voice; she stared at Jezebel with dark dilated eyes, and her small breasts rose and fell quickly under her sprigged calico frock.

"Why, some one . . . some one pretty . . . and young . . . some one like us, I suppose," said Jezebel cheerfully, skipping beneath the hemlock arch which leaned toward the sea. "But let's not bother about it any more; let's have a nice little swim before supper instead. There's plenty of time, because there's the catboat now, putting off from Captain Pray's slip. I'm hot as the seven hinges of hell — excuse me, Missie — and the water will be colder than the melted emerald of icebergs; it's flowed straight from the frozen Pole itself. 'A sunny pleasure dome with caves of ice.' One for the money, two for the show, three to make ready, and four . . . to . . . go! "

She pulled her faded pink calico frock over her curly head and flung it to the unmoving air; she dived from a pinnacle of rock into the sea. Her slim body flashed upward into sunlight like Excalibur's naked blade emerging from the stream; she clove the water like a straight gold sword, and then suddenly she was supple and tenuous as a trail of bright seaweed. Artemis followed her slowly, dropping her sprigged blue calico upon the pine-needles and picking her way delicately across the slippery rocks. She slid into the waves with a peaceful shiver of contentment, and her milky skin was turned to moon-color in their tinted depths.

Between the tall violet hills the Sound was a channel of fallen sky, profoundly azure, but under the shadow of the island's pines and hemlocks the pool lay clear and green as well water. The children disported themselves happily for five minutes; then they scrambled up the steep rocks, shaking the moisture from their curls and chattering like a pair of birds. The warm August air soon dried their curls, at the same time painting them with the earliest fresh hues of sunset.

They stood together under the dark hemlock arch and waved their hands to the approaching boat; their fingers made the fringes of two flowers, one white and the other golden. A man at the tiller of the boat waved back at them, and they blew him kisses across the windless air; their laughter carried their kisses to him upon a private breeze. He laughed at them although they could not hear him, and blew them a single kiss apiece.

"Let us wear our muslin frocks to-night, Missie; it is a most suitable occasion for our muslin frocks," said Jezebel as they strolled toward the log hut.

"He will call them outrageously fine feathers, but he will admire them all the same," replied Artemis, "especially if we wear the blue sashes and the amber beads; it was kind of the lady from Prettymarsh to send us the amber beads."

It took them precisely seven minutes to dress; they tied each other's sashes, and sleeked each other's curls with a tortoise-shell comb. There was no mirror in the log hut, but there was a superb set of the Greek dramatists, a rich row of Elizabethans, a splendid Plato, and the English poets from Chaucer to Keats adequately clothed in red morocco. The eastern wall was a fine mosaic of the French and Italian classics; the Spaniards and the Germans were ranged to westward. Between the children's cots were neatly disposed *The Last of the Mohicans, The Spy, The Pilot,* and *The Prairie,* together with Washington Irving's *Sketch Book* and a few volumes of *The Token,* containing some of Nathaniel Hawthorne's earlier pieces. A Latin grammar or two and a Beginner's Greek Book were flung invidiously upon the puncheon floor.

In addition to these comforts and extravagances, the hut contained furniture of the simplest and most durable description; several bandboxes from Boston were piled upon the rustic shelves, to which a sylvan tissue of birch-bark still adhered.

The sisters attired themselves in transparent book-muslin frocks, one butter-colored and the other ivory-white; they encircled their slender throats with necklaces of amber. The blue silk sashes rustled gaily as they whisked them through the door and down the path to the landing-place.

A tall gentleman leaped from the catboat to the slip with a pantherish bound which made you believe him twenty until you saw his hair, and knew that it had taken twice as many years to refine its frosty silver and carve the delicate lines upon the brow beneath. Such noble and eccentric tracery was lightly etched at the corners of the mouth and about the eyelids; its faint hieroglyphics were beautiful in themselves, and doubly beautiful because they spelt gentleness and courage and a subtle sensitive grief, which turned to laughter on the lips and in the amazing brilliance of the eyes. The eyes were blue, like the sea between the channel of the mountains; their color was deeper even than the farthest sea. The gentleman was sunburnt; he was very thin, but sinewy and strong as a wild creature of the forest. At the same time he looked excessively fastidious and civilized; he wore rough clothes of country homespun, but his linen was exquisite and admirably laundered. There was a faint suggestion of the savage in his swift and haughty bearing, but you had only to look at his hands and feet to perceive that he was quite preposterously well-bred.

He disengaged himself carefully and kindly from the children's vehement embraces, and kissed them each upon the brow.

" Are you good, are you happy, are you hungry, have you studied your Greek, and what are we to have for supper? " he asked them with a charming smile.

" Birthday cake, angel cake, birthday cake for an angel! " they cried in chorus, jumping up and down in an innocent frenzy of excitement. " You thought we'd forgotten, darling idiot, didn't you, didn't you? Or had you forgotten it yourself, you angel, angel, funny funny angel? We haven't studied our Greek, and we've had a swim, and we've made you a book-mark and a pincushion, and we've Gibraltars for you, and angelica, and gingernuts, and strawberry jam, and the kettle's boiling, and there's fresh loaf sugar and new milk and a caddy of China tea from Boston! And we love you, love you, love and adore you, and we demand to be allowed to kiss you forty times for good luck! "

Mr. Lionel Anon, for so he was known in the little village of

Somesville where he had lived for the last ten years, sank upon a rustic seat and warded away the two sisters with nervous but effectual haste. His slender hands were both gentle and elusive; nevertheless Jezebel succeeded in capturing one of them for an instant; she had covered it with kisses before it had time to evade her, quick as were its gestures of protest and control.

"Easy, easy there; draw it mild, my dears," he said pacifically, with a humorous lift of his rather serious dark eyebrows; the words were careless and colloquial, but the diction was clear and elegant in the extreme. One saw now where the girls had acquired their pretty manner of speech; their soft voices cut each word crisply and deliberately, and their laughter was pleasant and decorous even as they danced like infant mænads in the falling sunlight.

"Listen, listen, Lionel, when are we sailing south, and must we really and truly go into the horrid old world, and will you ever marry any one else except ourselves so long as you live?" cried Jezebel in one jocund breath, sinking like a yellow blossom upon the shining pine-needles and clasping Lionel's thin knees with both her arms. "We are so very curious about your plans for the winter; we don't care about Chesapeake Bay again; we had far rather go to Florida and live on a river among the oranges and the alligators. We want most frightfully to go to Florida, but we are afraid that you intend to marry that pale lady from Prettymarsh and take us all to Boston to be educated properly and to visit the poor. Promise us that we need not go to Boston, and that you will never on any account marry any one except ourselves."

"You know, darling, you really should decide at once if you are going to have the catboat completely overhauled this autumn," Artemis suggested tenderly, bending her lovely translucent cheek above Lionel's cracked and salty sea-boots. "You mustn't stay on the island until November this year, or you will be catching pneumonia again and driving us out of our poor little heads with terror. I protest that you owe it to yourself to go to Florida, or at least to that harbor on the coast of South Carolina of which Captain Pray has so often spoken; the climate of Maryland didn't really suit you at all, and the catboat is brave enough to go wherever you choose to steer her. Do please, please swear to us that you will do as we ask you this once, and not be a stubborn angel any longer; you know we are grown-up now, and we only ask to be allowed to take care of you and to adore you always."

Lionel, for so we must continue to name him, stared at the two bright heads with pained and puzzled eyes; he ran his thin brown fingers through his frosty hair, and his hand so trembled with agitation that the locks above his brow were sprayed into the air like silver foam.

"Really, my dear little girls, I hardly know how to answer so many questions all at once," he said slowly in a somewhat shaken voice; he patted their curls with a gesture of absent-minded affection, but his large blue eyes searched the distance as if eager for an avenue of escape.

The polished tin kettle still jigged above the pine-knot fire; he heard its song, he saw its comfortable shininess, and his worried gaze grew brilliant with relief.

"I'm rather tired, you know," he said gently. "I shouldn't very much mind having a bite to eat. If you would be so extraordinarily kind as to give me a cup of tea and a slice of birthday cake I should be uncommonly obliged to you, my dears."

A chorus confused and musical arose in unison from the throats of the two sisters; together they made a soft hysteria of concerted sound, which grew articulate upon such phrases as "Beasts that we are!" "Poor darling! Poor angel! Out beyond Little Cranberry since six o'clock this morning!" and "I dare say that silly old fool gave you nothing but salt pork for luncheon!"

Jezebel tugged distractedly at the salty sea-boots; Artemis ran to fetch a homespun coat unwetted by the spray of the deep seas beyond Little Cranberry. One girl filled a tin basin with hot water and the other produced a pickle jar full of strong brown soap; the huckaback towel smelled sweetly of juniper. An air of childish domesticity possessed them; the island was their doll's house and Lionel was undoubtedly their favorite doll.

He accepted their attentions with detached and indolent amiability; he was as quiet and very nearly as limp as if he had actually been stuffed with sawdust, but one knew that this composure was a defensive measure; as a man of flesh and blood he must needs adopt it in order to avoid being torn limb from living limb by the children's love. He smiled; he murmured a courteous gratitude, but he looked upon the exhausted point of being killed by kindness.

"Tired as the devil, aren't you, my archangel?" Jezebel asked him; he shook his head and laughed, then ducked gracefully as she flew to kiss him. He rose lazily and sauntered to the woodpile, his hands in his breeches' pockets. The axe stood upright in a cleft tree-stump; he swung its steel blade skyward until it flashed like a streak of moonlight in the sun.

"Ah," he said, "I perceive that Loren has left you plenty of kindling; so much the better for a starving man. Forgive me if I fail to assist you in setting the table; you know I always drop the teacups and mislay the sugar-tongs."

"Don't be ridiculous, darling; you're not to do a stroke of work upon your birthday. Loren has chopped the wood and brought crystal gallons of water from the spring; we've cooked you the most delightful supper short of heaven. Now sit down and don't interrupt us upon any account until we call you." The gray eyes of Artemis melted into tenderness as she spoke. Lionel sat down upon the pine-needles and leaned his back against the comfortable girth of an ancient tree; he drew a book from his pocket with a thanksgiving sigh, and bent his eyes above its fair broad pages.

"Little goat bleat, little table appear!" cried Artemis ecstatically, while Jezebel danced about with the willow-pattern teapot in one hand and a wreath of smooth and verdant leaves in the other. "I'm Ganymede; I'm Ganymede," she was saying. "We haven't any laurel for a crown, nor violets, but we've mixed a little parsley in with the wintergreen and it really looks rather well. Now I must pour out a cup of tea, because I'm Ganymede."

The table bloomed like a miracle of shining damask and silver spoons; it grew up among the pine-trees like some exquisite mushroom. The girls seized long wax tapers and lit the diadem of forty snow-white candles which crowned the birthday cake. There was a bunch of pink dahlias in the center of the table, which matched the stripes upon the Gibraltars; the angelica was the color of icicles. There was a fairy-tale prettiness about it all which touched Lionel to the heart, but he wished very much for a small mutton-chop or even a boiled egg. He had been fishing the deep waters beyond Little Cranberry since six o'clock that morning.

Lionel placed the wreath of wintergreen upon his head without a trace of embarrassment; he seated himself at the table and helped himself to a spoonful of strawberry jam and a gingernut.

" I have never in all my life seen anything one half so beautiful as my birthday cake," he said; his manner was impeccably courtly and grave; his smile was charming without mockery. " It is an enchanting combination of the Alpine Mountains and the Milky Way, a fabulous mingling of frost and fire. You are the cleverest little girls in the world to have made it, and the kindest little girls in the world to have made it for me."

" Oh, but we loved doing it, and we are so glad you like it, and we adore you, and would slave our hands to the bone for you if only you would let us! " they cried in a long unanimous breath. " You have always worked so hard to take care of us, and to teach us Greek, and good manners, and kindness to animals, and the principles of democratic government, and the noblest poetry of ancient and modern times, and you are such an incredible darling, and we do wish so dreadfully that we might be your wives. We would make such very devoted wives; only try us, dear, dear, dearest Lionel, and you will see what excellent wives we shall make if only you will give us the chance! "

If some portions of this speech were pronounced in Jezebel's clear soprano accents and others in the lower more poignant tones of Artemis, its complicated murmur reached Lionel as a single cry of passionate entreaty. Under his sunburn he turned distinctly pale; his eyes showed a wild rim of white around their dark blue irises; his head jerked backward in a gesture of alarm. Of a sudden he assumed the air of a blooded horse who is preparing to bolt, maddened by the near approach of some remembered scourge.

" Wives! " he exclaimed in a voice vibrant with nervousness. " My dears, have you by any unlucky chance gone mad? What earthly need have I for any more wives . . . for any wives . . .

for any wife, in fact? You know all about Mary . . . at least, you have questioned me relentlessly concerning her for the past ten years, and you have learned quite as much as is good for you. You should have the common sense to understand that Mary is my wife, and that therefore I cannot possibly be married again."

"Ah, but my precious angel, who has said a word about marriage?" inquired Jezebel, smoothing his coat sleeve with pacifying fingers. "You really must not be so absurdly excitable, darling; your nerves are in a shocking state. Stop trembling; stop spilling your tea; now attend to what I am saying, Lionel. We have not asked you to marry us; we have only told you that we would like to be your wives. Surely the ceremony itself is of slight importance compared to our love for you; it is a mere remnant of superstition; as the legal tie is an outworn chain. We have often heard you say so, my sweet, when something in the newspapers has annoyed you."

"I was not saying it to you, Jessie; I may have murmured it aloud in a reverie; how can I tell? Certainly I never intended my words to be taken seriously by two little girls of fourteen."

"Juliet!" answered Artemis, quick as a wink of lightning, while Jezebel cried shrilly as a bird, "But darling, do we not take all your words seriously and to our hearts? Have you not taught us everything we know, and did you not intend to teach us to love you?"

"As a father; of course I wish you to love me as a father . . ." said Lionel weakly.

"Lionel, what nonsense! You are not in the least like any father we have ever seen. We remember our own father quite well; he was short and plump, and he wore a red beard. We have seen plenty of fathers in the village when we looked through the telescope, and they are all very much like him and not in the least like you. Don't be an angel idiot; you cannot honestly expect us to love you as a father," Jezebel protested with lively scorn.

"As a brother then; you can love me quite suitably as a brother, I assure you," Lionel began; both girls interrupted him before the words were out of his startled mouth.

"You know you're not our brother, you're too old to be our

brother, and too wise, and far too beautiful, and besides, you simply aren't, and that's all there is to it," said Artemis tearfully, hiding her wet lashes against his homespun coat.

"You're no more like a brother than you are like a father; we've seen all the brothers of Somesville through the spy-glass, for don't they spend every Sunday afternoon trying to get a glimpse of us from Captain Pray's slip, and do you suppose we haven't noticed their pink faces and their yellow hair and their funny shy smiles? They're nice; I can't help rather liking them, but if those are brothers — and you've always said they were the brothers of those pretty girls in gingham frocks — then you are something entirely different," said Jezebel; a star had risen in each of her eyes.

"You might just conceivably be a cousin," she went on, thinking of Laon and Cythna. "You might be a god, and often I believe you are; sometimes when you are worried you might be the poor maniac in your own poem. But mostly, judging from your books, and from Shakespeare and Keats and so forth, I should think you must be either a lover or a very superior sort of husband."

"Good God, what in heaven's name have I done to you, my children?" cried Lionel. He buried his face in his hands and his silver hair fell forward in a shower of light; he was laughing, yet several tears trickled between his thin brown fingers as he laughed.

"That's hysterics; that's what Mrs. Fernald had when her little boy was drowned in the pond," Jezebel warned him solemnly. "Loren told me about it; she laughed and cried exactly as you are doing now. You must pull yourself together and be sensible, or we shall have to throw cold water in your face and make you smell burnt goose feathers, and you won't like that, you know. You mustn't spoil the birthday party; we're sorry if we've upset you, darling, but you truly must be calm and eat your cake."

"And have it too?" asked Lionel rather wildly, "must I have it too, Jessie, even if I don't want it?" He lifted his head and smiled at her, and shook the hair back from his forehead.

"If it's the word *wives* to which you object, dear Lionel," said

Artemis suddenly, in a small meek voice, "we can call ourselves anything else you like — we can call ourselves your — what is it — thingumabobs — those ladies in novels who aren't married to their husbands."

"No, Artemis; a thousand times no; you must call yourselves nothing in the least like those ladies. They are usually charming females, I admit, but they are inappropriate models for children of your tender age. You must be content to remain my wards, my beloved little sisters. You must be good, and patient for the present; if you will only do as I ask you I will take you to Boston this winter, and our kind friend Marianna shall buy you bonnets trimmed with ostrich feathers, and you shall learn the *galop,* and be introduced to the young poet Longfellow, who occasionally honors the town with a visit, and who has written a very creditable ode for the graduating class at Bowdoin. You shall have all the sherbets and chocolate eclairs that your hearts may desire, and even if you should wish to go to church I should not seriously oppose the idea, as I think young people are entitled to a certain amount of innocent dissipation, and Marianna informs me that the organ recitals are frequently very fine," said Lionel, speaking extremely fast and trembling more than ever as his charges stared at him with large dilated eyes.

"Don't be silly, darling Lionel; we don't want Marianna or ostrich plumes or chocolate eclairs; we want you," Jezebel replied firmly, clasping his arm with both her strong and slender hands. "Marianna is all very well for Prettymarsh; her Persian shawl is nicer than anything the Somesville ladies wear, and we are grateful for our amber necklaces, but we don't wish to bother with Marianna this winter. She is your friend, at a pinch she serves as some one worthy to amuse you during the summer, since you will not allow us to leave the island. But our plans for the winter are quite definite; they have nothing to do with poor dear Marianna. We don't care about the *galop* or Longfellow; we are determined to go to Florida, and to eat wild oranges, and to have a baby alligator as a pet, and to be your devoted wives, and to love you and take care of you forever."

"Both of you?" Lionel asked her in a shaken voice. "Do both of you together intend to be my wives?" He was so pale that Jezebel feared that he might faint; accordingly she put her arms about him and crooned to him in a peculiar music of lullaby while Artemis answered for her.

"Of course," said Artemis, "why should we quarrel over a ridiculous little point like that? Have you not always taught us to go share and share alike? Have you not instructed us to be generous, and never to permit the petty vice of jealousy to poison our sisterly affection? How can you expect us to quarrel about you, when all your dear advice has taught us love and tolerance and charity to each other?"

"My God, my God!" said Lionel. "Is it possible that I have erred in this respect also, having intended so supremely well toward these innocents?" And he laughed more wildly than ever, running his fingers through his hair until it flew as fiercely as a meteor's above his worried brow.

"I am a fool," said Lionel aloud, but to himself, "I always was, I ever will be a fool. But it is a pity that I contrive to involve others in my particular madness. Marianna warned me before she went to Boston, but I did not, I could not, believe her. I thought that her own — ah, flattering preference for me had given her illusory notions about the little girls. She was right, and I was blindly, doltishly, ludicrously wrong. I am a fool, a damnable insensate fool."

"Lionel, Lionel, you are not! How dare you call yourself such hideous names, when you know quite well that you are a darling and a saint?" cried Artemis in a soft storm of indignation; she fluttered like a dove defending its violated nest. "How dare you, Lionel, how dare you to our faces, while we adore you as we do?"

Jezebel was trembling with rage and loyalty; she pounded Lionel with her hard little fists and at the same moment essayed to kiss him. "Angel, my precious angel, will you take back those wicked words this instant, or do you wish to break our hearts?" she demanded in a breathless whisper.

"Decidedly not," replied Lionel. "That's the whole trouble, my dears; I don't wish to break any one's heart. I have never wished it, but apparently I have always accomplished it with sinister ease. You are fourteen, but so, as you have said, was Juliet. I am forty; I am far too thin for symmetry, my hair is gray;

I rarely meet with a looking-glass, but it is highly improbable that my countenance, which has been engraven with lines of care since I was twenty-five, has grown more comely with the years. No, Jezebel, it's no good calling me an archangel; I am a very mortal man, sufficiently intelligent, but neither strong nor beautiful nor wise. If you must fall in love, let it be with some one of your own age; I will take you to Boston as soon as I can possibly manage it, and Marianna shall give a dance for you at Christmas-time, and you shall have favors and ices and all the things that you have always wanted."

"But Lionel dear, those things are frivolous and unimportant; you have taught us to care for lovelier things than those," said Artemis gently. "Would it not be far better to go sailing down a river in Florida, between green banks where the birds are bright as flowers and the wild oranges brighter than stars? The three of us together; could anything be sweeter or more peaceful than that? And the Boston climate will be very bad for your chest, remember; you will quite likely go into a consumption. Be a lamb and decide upon Florida for all our sakes."

"It would not be peaceful, my dear," said Lionel sadly. "I do most earnestly assure you that such a plan would not be peaceful, now that you have both of you determined to fall in love with me."

"Ah, Lionel, don't be so unsympathetic; it is not a question of determination; we have fallen in love with you because we cannot help ourselves," cried Jezebel. "You are obviously the most marvelous person in the world, or out of it, for that matter. You are our darling, our treasure, our own; we can divide you quite happily between our hearts. Why, you have said it all, over and over again, in your poetry, in the tales you have told us. 'True love in this differs from gold and clay, that to divide is not to take away . . .' Can anything be plainer than that, darling?"

"Really and truly, Lionel, Jessie is right; you mustn't be selfish, you mustn't forget 'If you divide suffering and dross, you may diminish till it is consumed away; if you divide pleasure and love and thought, each part exceeds the whole. . . .' Now there you have it in a nutshell, and you wrote it yourself."

"I," said Jezebel radiantly, "could be 'the comrade of your wanderings over heaven'; I'd like that best, and Missie could always be soothing and quiet like the lady in the 'Sensitive Plant.' It would be an ideal arrangement, in my opinion." She kissed his hand, and gazed at him with golden reverential eyes.

"'Ideal,'" Lionel repeated wearily. "Quite so, my child; it would be an ideal arrangement, but not a practical one. It grieves me beyond words to disappoint two dear little girls, but the plan is visionary and fantastic past all reason."

"Reason be damned," cried Jezebel with a grandiloquent gesture of contempt. "Excuse me, sweetest, I mean to hell with reason. It is you who are fantastic; you are denying all your principles, and talking in the most prejudiced and narrow-minded manner. 'This truth is that deep well, whence sages draw the unenvied light of hope.' If that teaches anything at all, Lionel, you are being uncommonly silly."

"Well," said Lionel a little drily, "some one has certainly been silly, but who that person was, or at what precise time his silliness was perpetrated I am not prepared to admit. Leave it at this; you are too young to understand 'Epipsychidion.'"

"Then why did you read it aloud to us when we were seven?" Artemis asked him reproachfully. "You know we had learned most of your poetry by heart before we were grown-up, and you never told us that it wasn't suitable and true."

"And don't forget, while you are being so superior," Jezebel added, "that Harriet was only sixteen when you married her, and Mary only sixteen when you ran away with her to France. We should be delighted to go to France, although we prefer Florida because of the alligators."

"That was different," said Lionel, but without fire or conviction. He looked profoundly depressed and rather ill; every tiring minute of his forty years was traced in the lines upon his brow.

"But why, but why?" "We will wait another twelvemonth if we must, but you have often said that our minds were remarkably mature." "Darling, you have no notion how happy we can make you if you will allow us to try," and, "ah, my angel, don't be sad; I can't bear you to be sad"; these ascending cries and several others echoed in Lionel's ears and circled about his head like sea-birds. He was aware of a severe neuralgic pain in his temples and a strong impulse to escape from the island immediately and at all costs.

"But why is it different, why on earth is it different?" reiterated the children's musical voices. Suppressing a nervous desire to scream, Lionel answered gently, "I suppose it is I that am different; I suppose, as a matter of fact, that I am too old. I am far too tired to run away with you, my dears; I will take you to Boston, but I will never run away with any one again so long as I live, and that I must warn you will not be long unless you will consent to keep quiet for at least a moment."

They were awed by his words; a sudden silence fell like balsam from the air. Lionel relaxed to a peace which was so nearly pure weariness that he lacked the energy to pour himself another cup of tea; the first stood cold and untasted beside the birthday cake upon the shining supper table.

The forty candles were coals of fire to his imagination; he felt almost intolerably sorry for the children in beholding the frosting upon the cake, the pink dahlias, the glittering silver spoons. But he was even more tired than he was sorry; the travail of pity was beyond his strength, and he closed his eyes so that he should not see the veil of tears over the face of Artemis and the amazed and innocent anguish of Jezebel's regard.

It must be remembered that Lionel had been fishing the deep waters past Little Cranberry since six o'clock that morning, and that he had eaten an insufficient lunch and no supper at all. If the children had been blessed with the common sense to provide their idol with two boiled eggs or a mutton-chop he might possibly have come to another decision regarding them; the question must remain forever unanswered upon the scroll of time. His sentiments toward them were benevolent rather than romantic, but he was an excessively soft-hearted person and for the delicate dividing of a second their fate may have trembled in the balance of his mind.

It was his wretched headache which upset that balance; that, and the recollection of the striped Gibraltars. Lionel loved to scour the sapphire waters of the Western Way, but he was an indifferent sailor and the dead flat calm of the afternoon had been most unpleasantly lifted upon the long rollers of the Atlantic. At this moment he was feeling far from well, and even the terrified silence of the children failed to persuade him to unclose his eyes and promise to take them to Florida. He was aware of their entreaty in every sensitive nerve of his body, but, as the neuralgia drove a horrid tenpenny nail of pain into his forehead, he grew more and more determined upon Boston and the assistance of Marianna Bland in the matter of female education.

Ah, yes, Marianna had been right all along; she had warned him tenderly and repeatedly of this danger, and he had been deaf as an adder and blind as a bat. " My dear friend," she had told him upon the occasion of their last Sunday night supper together, " the responsibility of those two charming but impulsive children is too much for you; you are beginning to look sadly worn and worried." And she had put another spoonful of chicken salad upon his plate, and filled his glass with the very light white wine which agreed so well with his taste and digestion. She made an enchanting picture in her soft black frock and creamy cashmere shawl; her hair and eyes were quiet and shadowy as the twilight beyond the open window. A faint perfume of syringa entered with the air; the lilacs had been dead since June, but a long succession of flowers flourished in these northern latitudes, and nowhere better than in Marianna's summer garden. It was a pleasant evening on which to walk among roses and heliotrope and mignonette and tall white hollyhocks like clustered moons.

It was a pity, perhaps, said Lionel to himself as he sat with closed eyes before the glimmering birthday cake, that Marianna's husband had been of so fiery and jealous a disposition; the terms of the will were a bit hard upon Marianna. If she married again she forfeited all her comfortable life; the house at Prettymarsh, the smaller house in Boston. Sea-captains are notoriously tyrannical; Captain Bland had desired to possess his lovely wife even beyond the grave. But Marianna had always declared that she didn't care in the least; that she was sick of marriage; that she adored her freedom and her mitigated solitude. And Marianna read Plato; she was capable of friendship.

An enchanting creature, Marianna; so cool, so kind, so undemanding and so intelligent. "If a star from heaven falls into my apple orchard, do you suppose I am such a fool as to make it into an apple turnover? " she had asked him once with delicious reassuring laughter. Lionel felt that he could trust Marianna; she was as safe as the white church on the hill, as silent as a pretty ivy-covered tomb, as exquisite as a gossamer web spun upon the grass at dawn. She would never offend his sensibilities, she would never ask questions, and by some peculiar magic of sympathy untouched by inconvenient violence, she would always do exactly as he pleased. She could love him, and then again, by a transcendent act of devotion, she could quite easily not love him if he didn't wish to be loved. She could not fail to be a remarkable influence for good upon the girls' impetuous natures.

What was it that she had said to him before she left? Something about a simple fête *champêtre* or picnic which she proposed to arrange for the children's pleasure when she returned in September. "Poor little darlings, they've never known any one of their own age, Lionel; how tragic, when you come to think of it! Of course they have had every possible advantage of education; association with your brilliant mind is the highest privilege upon earth, as I have long realized to my delight, and your spirit is so noble, your manners so flawless, that the girls have learned much from the perfections they observed. But — forgive me, my dear friend, you need not be assured that I adore you — you are possibly — but are you not, dear Lionel — a thought eccentric, a thin hair's breadth beyond the boundaries of common wisdom of the world? My friend, do not mistake me; it is your charm, the rarest of your spiritual graces — but nevertheless, you must confess you are eccentric. I think perhaps we should afford Jessie and Missie the opportunity to meet some few companions of their age even before we take them to town. These village people are decent souls; nay, they are more than that. They have not the advantages of wealth and wide culture, but they come from excellent stock; their characters, and indeed their breeding, are above reproach. I shall not hesitate to ask the Somes lads and the sons of Mr. Fernald and Captain Pray to my picnic."

Lionel remembered Marianna's words quite plainly as he sat with closed eyes before the birthday supper-table; they came to his senses as softly as the notes of a wood pigeon. He could recall her tranquilizing murmur like the music of a dream; his headache receded in long waves of diminished pain as he listened to the memory of her words.

At this particular hour of dusk, he knew that the Somes lads and the sons of Captain Pray and Mr. Fernald would be lounging upon the porch of the village store or strolling toward the wharf where the schooner from Bangor swung to and fro under yellow riding lights. Doubtless these lusty fair-haired fellows would already have supped heartily upon salt pork and beans or corned beef and cabbage, but he had no reason to suppose, with his mind's eye perceiving their ingenuous visages, that they would accept with reluctance a dessert of gingernuts, angelica, and birthday cake.

" Dear children," said Lionel, opening his wild blue eyes and smiling sweetly at Artemis and Jezebel, " please don't be frightened; stop crying, my dear little girls, and hear what I have to say. I am not angry; I have no intention of scolding you any more. My idiotic head has been aching rather badly, but that's of no consequence, except that for a moment it made me slightly cross. Never mind; it's better, and you must forgive my rudeness. Only, it seems a thousand pities to waste all this magnificent supper; the three of us cannot possibly eat it all. What would you think if I were to take the dinghy over to the village, and bring back a few of those agreeable yellow-haired brothers? A party on Saturday night never comes amiss. They are all of them good boys, and very fond of frosting, I assure you. No, Jessie, the exertion will not do me any harm; on the contrary, it is precisely what I need. You may kiss me good-by, but be quick about it; I shall be back in half an hour."

He was gone, so swiftly that the wind of his speed ruffled their curls even as their hearts were stirred by amazement. He ran rapidly down the path to the landing-place and leaped into the dinghy; he had fitted the oars to the row-locks and was flying across the smooth harbor before they had recovered their quickened breath. The moon rose over the eastern mountain, and presently the dinghy was lost among the shadows of the willow trees which lined the farther shore.

" Well," said Jezebel in a faint and solemn whisper, " so that's the end of that. I suppose you know he's given us the slip forever. He'll always be kind and charming, but we shall never have him to ourselves again. There's no use crying over spilt nectar; we must let him go gracefully and make the best of a damned bad business."

" Oh, Jessie, Jessie, how shall we ever bear it? " cried Artemis, lifting her little white face to the moon. " And now of course Marianna will get him. I knew it all the time; I never really liked her, in spite of the amber necklaces."

" No more did I; but what can we do? We mustn't bother Lionel any longer; we may make him unhappy, we may even make him ill, but we cannot make him change his mind. We had better go to Boston and forget our sorrow in a whirl of frivolity. Stop being a woman wailing for her demon lover, Missie dear, and set your thoughts upon the *galop* and young Mr. Longfellow! " Jezebel's eyes were preternaturally bright; it was impossible to say whether it was moonlight or tears which shone within their depth.

" I dare say you're right, Jess; my heart is broken, but perhaps time may heal the wound; I'm sure I sincerely hope so. Now what about these wretched louts who are coming to devour Lionel's birthday cake; do you suppose it will be necessary to be civil to them? "

" We shall have to be civil; Lionel will never forgive us if we are rude to our social inferiors. He says we have none, but that's sheer nonsense; these silly boys are obviously our inferiors in every respect. Nevertheless, let us be polite to them; it will please Lionel, and serve to distract our minds from our misfortune."

The sisters rose simultaneously in a crisp rustle of book muslin; by the illumination of the summer moon they smoothed each other's crumpled frocks and straightened each other's sashes. If their faces were stained with tears, such marks were no more than a dust of dew upon two unfolding flowers. Even in the cold and silvery moonlight their bright curls were pale gold and flame color above their candid brows.

" I wish we might have a mirror," said Artemis with a plaintive sigh. The sound of oars was audible in the stillness; Lionel's laughter chimed far away, and was answered by a loud guffaw.

"Perhaps when we go to Boston, Marianna will give us a mirror; I rather believe she will," said Jezebel, rumpling her pretty curls above her childish forehead and her large excited eyes.

1927

Fugitive Prose

"EXCESS OF CHARITY"

EVER since I have known Roger Ingpen, I have wished that
Shelley might have had him for a friend; it would have been
so great a happiness to each to know the other. But, as
things have fallen out in this middling world, Shelley's loss is
the greater, since in all ways of the heart and mind Roger Ingpen
does, of course, know Shelley very well, whereas Shelley himself
had to be content with such persons as the shadowy Dr. Lind,
of Windsor, and that most execrable of mentors, William Godwin. Nevertheless, even Shelley is fortunate in this friendship,
sundered as it is by a hundred years from the look into the living
eyes and the clasp of the actual hand; he is lucky to have Mr.
Ingpen for his editor, the executor as it were of his spiritual
effects and the rich estate of his immortal soul.

It is not necessary to believe in a future life in order to call
Shelley's soul immortal. He lives continuously and increasingly
in the intellects and the affections of those who love him. While
I would desire a true eternity for Shelley, a stretch of time made
smooth enough and golden enough to foster his capacity for joy,
it is evident that even without heaven his essence survives in the
quickened blood of a child who reads for the first time the "Ode
to the West Wind" and runs across an autumn field shouting its

words to the air; it is evident that it survives in steady brightness in the brain of a scholar such as Mr. Ingpen. Francis Thompson has certain unforgivable words to say of the cold and bitter quality of an immortality such as this; he is indeed fortunate if he has found a better paradise for himself. It is possible to-day, after the long lapse of a century dimmed by the smoke of soft coal and the fumes of petroleum, to find more friends of Shelley's among your casual acquaintances than remained by his breathing side during the course of his brief existence.

It is possible to walk along Sixth Avenue under the spiteful thunder of the " L " and, meeting a man whom you have known only slightly, to have that man within half an hour put into your hands a letter from Shelley to Peacock. It is possible to discover in talking with this man that he feels precisely as you do about the character of Shelley and is as indifferent as you to the danger of being considered a lunatic. " I live over again the days of my infancy and youth . . ."; so runs the beginning of this letter, written in Bath upon some September day, and as this man and I read it together, the days of Shelley's infancy and youth are relived for a third time in our minds. It is possible to be sitting one morning above the petty clatter of a typewriter and to have a messenger give you a note from a friend which miraculously incloses a check upon Messrs. Brookes and Company, of Chancery Lane, and this check is drawn in favor of W. Godwin, Esq., and signed Percy Bysshe Shelley; this particular excess of charity is for the sum of forty pounds, and the cold old bloodsucker received it from the boy upon a January day in the year 1818. So again it becomes a symbol of generosity, this time for my more grateful benefit. It is possible to sit among beloved companions a few winter evenings later, and setting this frail slip of paper too suddenly before the eyes of a high lyrical poet, to see those green eyes fill with tears as at the evocation of a spirit. These things are possible by the chances of every day; if they were miracles they would not be half so kind. It is possible to meet a woman with a singularly musical name who has driven her little car across the downs to dine at a great house in Wiltshire and to have her say to you before two hours have passed, " If you and I had been alive we might have done something." You may look at her by the pale rose-colored light of a late June sunset and shake your head and reply, "I doubt it; I very much doubt it," thinking how powerless you would have been in the adamantine face of the Lord Chancellor and the "Quarterly Review"; yet even this lovely nonsense seems a sort of immortality.

It is even possible, by a sort of divine good luck, to sit for long delighted hours in a house in Bedford Park, listening to the editor of the Julian Edition of Shelley, and occasionally interrupting him to cap a quotation from a letter, and smiling with him at a hundred beloved recollections of some one we have never seen. I have wondered what other fraternity of interest may constitute so strong a bond or so infallible a test of liking, and I have thought that fishermen must come next, with your true veteran golfers a poor third. For this is "shop" of the most intoxicating kind; "a bright fire, a clean hearth, and the rigor of the game," might be its motto, although those charming words were written about whist players. It is pleasant to drink champagne cocktails in Paris while you talk about the shoes of the Princess de Lamballe, but it is far, far pleasanter to drink tea in Bedford Park while you talk about the youthful "printing freaks" of Mr. Shelley or the beautiful silk pantaloons he wore when he came home for the holidays. The laughter of the unskilful and the grieved sighs of the judicious cannot persuade me that I have ever been happier than upon certain evenings in that house, with a cup of tea in my hand at the proper early-nineteenth-century hour, and in my lap and laid on either side of me a shining treasure of scrap-books and manuscripts and pictures. And this volatile inebriation has illuminated the chill white tunnels leading underground to Charing Cross; it has sung among the wheels of the last tired train to London.

It is possible to lie upon heaven-scented pine-needles under the smooth blue crystal of Monadnock and to read that surprising book, "Shelley and the Unromantics" with sentiments of admiration and wonder not unmixed with shame. This book was written by a woman, Olwen Ward Campbell, and it is a curious fusion of elements, a subtle and sensitive vision of Shelley set strangely beside a rather cruel and intolerant view of all his friends. I can hate Godwin as a Catholic hates Judas, and I cannot love Godwin's daughter, Mary, but Mrs. Campbell will not even forgive Hogg his passing treachery or Peacock his constitutional coldness. I wish I might be so fastidious, but Hogg and Peacock will always win me to themselves, however imperfect they may have proved as friends of Mr. Shelley's. Nevertheless, this book is revealing and beautiful, and its discovery was pleasant and profitable to my mind. I do most passionately agree with its conclusions as to Shelley; of those who never knew him in life, only Browning and Swinburne have spoken with an equal understanding, and since their words are after all more magnificent than Mrs. Campbell's, perhaps their comprehension is a little less. Her book is further precious in that its author is patently a very good person; too few of those who love him have done him sufficient honor in this respect. The beauty of this bad thought must be that Shelley would not have been likely to be hard upon our faults. I cannot pardon Francis Thompson for his damnable patronage, or Canon Kingsley for his brute stupidity, or Matthew Arnold for his blindness; Mrs. Campbell cannot pardon those "people of obvious instability of temperament and unsuitability to life" who have loved Shelley as such men failed to love him. But the happy chances are that Shelley would have forgiven the lot of us and the tangle of our loves and dislikes; this is his "excess of charity."

To me the most valuable tributes to Shelley must come from fine and virtuous persons like Mr. Ingpen and Mrs. Campbell; this is the praise best worth his taking, though not the only praise which might have pleased him. It weighs more heavily in the scales against detraction than a dozen romantic essays or half a hundred sonnets. So among the various magics of Mr. Yeats's "Autobiographies" it was a joyful shock to come upon such high eulogy of "Prometheus," as it was a dull distress to learn the long-suspected secret that Dowden's smaller spirit could not lift itself into a true approval of the marvelous creature whose life he has recorded with mild uncritical tact.

If you really love Shelley you are not uncritical; you do not need to be. "For" — to paraphrase Swinburne's words about his Queen of Scots — "surely he was something better than innocent." Is it then necessary to pretend that he was never mistaken, never reckless, never forgetful of others as he was so often forgetful of himself? When Shelley was nineteen he was actually in many ways a ridiculous though lovable and brilliant child; he had already a mind like his own solar microscope, yet his wild imagination and impulsive nature, together with what he would himself have called "the delicacy of his constitution," led him into absurdities and cruelties such as the Hitchener affair. By the time he was twenty-nine he had grown so wise, so patient and so kind that to any superstitious person his drowning must appear inevitable. If any ten years of the world have ever witnessed a more amazing development and flowering of nobility from imperfection, I should be glad to celebrate that decade in letters of pure silver.

The theory that Shelley was completely unaware of his own defects seems to me especially preposterous. By the circumstances of his life he was caught up into a situation where any loud bewailing of the past, any open self-reproaches or laments would have cut a living woman to the heart and left a dead one none the better for her revenge. Both Hunt and Peacock knew something of the lively and voracious wolf which the boy carried under his cloak until he died; to admit to Mary a remorse for Harriet's suicide would have been a form of self-indulgence more distasteful to Shelley than all the bottles of claret which Byron swallowed in his shaken presence in that fantastic house in Pisa.

It is an ironical comment on the impossibility of pleasing every one, or indeed any one, that while Shelley is often criticized for his hardness of heart and lack of warm humanity, and this apparently upon the strength of the undoubted truth that he continued to live and to write divine poetry and brilliant letters even after he had made some grave and tragic errors of judgment, he is also often criticized for being over-sensitive and over-sad, and this upon the strength, which is called weakness, of his mood in such poems as "Stanzas Written in Dejection" and "Lines Written Among the Euganean Hills." As a matter of fact he was extraordinarily courageous about his sufferings both physical and mental, but the poems rather than the letters represent the personal essence of his soul. He could always be depended upon to write Peacock a masterly description of the Coliseum or Mary a tender admonition to be a good girl and get along with her novel, but he could not depend upon his own spirit never to fail him in secret, he could not always be so charitable to himself as he invariably was to his friends. It is hard to realize, now that the least of his lyrics seems written in starry gold upon the mind, that in those moments when his hand of flesh and blood scribbled them upon paper, his own mind never dreamt of such a consummation; he believed that very few people would ever read these words and fewer still would cherish them.

Now if in turn you cannot believe this moving wonder, you have only to look at his own letters to have it proved to your entire satisfaction or despairing pity, according to your temperament and habit of thought. He truly believed that few would read his verses, and he hid them from Mary for fear of wounding her, as she herself will tell you in her " Note for the Poems Written in 1818." It is comforting to read the end of this; " but with one or two that he loved, he gave way to wild and joyous spirits, or in more serious conversation expounded his opinions with vivacity and eloquence."

Somewhere, and I am almost glad that I have not the time to turn to the actual letter, Shelley writes of himself that there are a dozen persons at most who regard him with anything but hatred and contempt. This is a strange and melancholy thing to set beside Hunt's description of Shelley; the words are not Hunt's but Lord Bacon's, and for aught I know Hunt may misquote them. " Excess of charity, and it is not possible that man or angel should come in danger by it."

Perhaps not ultimate danger. Certainly there is no danger to-day that Shelley may not be beloved. But this " excess of charity " made his life more vulnerable than most, and it is pleasant to consider his reward in the opinion of the future. His future is already our own past. Some of us have loved him for longer years than composed the span of his whole life. Roger Ingpen told me that he bought his first book of Shelley's poems when he was fourteen years old, or was it twelve? At least he said to me generously: " You see you beat me." I did. I first read " The

Cloud" and "The Skylark" in my Third Reader, and I think I was seven years old. This was the same winter when my innocent young mother read "Christabel" aloud to me. My admiration for it was so nearly pure horror that "The Skylark" was a great consolation after dark. "If we were things born not to shed a tear"; even a child can understand those words. Then when I was eleven we were no longer in that Victorian high-ceiled house in Philadelphia, where "The Skylark" first sang to me. It was September in Washington and the air was warm and sweet as if all the grapes and peaches of Maryland and Virginia had flavored it to my taste. I stood before the smallest book-case in the library, and from its shelves I drew Trelawny's "Recollections." The window was wide open; there was plenty of light and soft autumnal wind in the room. I did not move except to turn the pages. Even the black leather chair was too far away from the scene within the covers of the book. I stood quite still and turned the pages, and the curtains blew in at the window and a few golden leaves blew in between them.

So I read for the first time of Shelley's death and burial. I can remember what I felt in that moment of past time, but never what I thought. It is therefore impossible to tell of it except to draw the picture of the room full of light and softer air and of the child standing in the center of the room and turning the pages of the book, afraid to move, afraid to cry for fear the scene within the pages of the book might be hidden from her eyes, wondering and wondering why the bright creature who had lived within that scene should have died and fallen into dust no stronger than the golden leaves blowing in at the window.

1927

The Complete Works of Percy Bysshe Shelley: Julian Edition. *Edited by Roger Ingpen and Walter E. Peck.*

Fugitive Prose

MR. SHELLEY SPEAKING

" I prithee deliver thyself like a man of this world."

We are informed by Aristotle that in order to acquire the probabilities of opinion, which are the premises of dialectical syllogism, the process is induction as in science, but dialectical induction by interrogation from the opinions of the answerers until the universal is conceded, whereupon the dialectical syllogism deduces consequent opinions in the conclusion. It is my intention in this little paper to invoke the opinion of several answerers; I entertain small hope that the universal will be conceded, but I am very certain that my premises are not fallacious.

So much for Aristotle; after I have quoted Hazlitt I shall be my age and get down to cases. Hazlitt wrote of Shelley in these scornful yet glittering words: " The author of ' Prometheus Unbound ' has a fire in his eye, a fever in his blood, a hectic flutter in his speech, a maggot in his brain, which mark out the philosophical fanatic. . . . The shock of accident, the weight of authority, make no impression on his opinions, which retire like a feather, or rise from the encounter unhurt through their own buoyancy." But then Shelley was a Platonist and Hazlitt was frequently wrong; he was wrong when he wrote of the same young gentleman: " There is no *caput mortuum* of wornout threadbare

846

experience to serve as ballast to his mind; it is all volatile, intellectual salt-of-tartar, that refuses to combine its evanescent, inflammable essence with anything solid or anything lasting." Poor Shelley had more than one death's head at his intellectual feast before he was five and twenty; his mind contained the salt of sorrow and pity. Meeting Hazlitt at dinner in London upon the eve of his own departure for Italy, he probably talked very good sense in an excitable and nervous manner; he may easily have talked a little nonsense at the same time, for he was ill and the fever in his blood was actual. I would forgive Hazlitt all his sneers for this one crystalline beam of insight; it was written after Shelley's death, of course, but there is no use in being bitter about that. " Mr. Shelley was a remarkable man. His person was a type and shadow of his genius. His complexion, fair, golden, freckled, seemed transparent with an inward light, and his spirit within him —

> ' So divinely wrought,
> That you might almost say his body thought.' "

" His body thought "; yes, and indeed how divinely; the poetry is part of that divinity. But also his body spoke, and sometimes it spoke in concealment of his simpler meanings. " The pure and eloquent blood " often clothed itself in language which can only be called elevated; the words are like the robes of an Augustan orator upon the limbs of a Grecian athlete. As such, they have for me a delicate and incongruous charm, a stately absurdity, a fantastic innocence which wins my heart and provokes my laughter. It is thus that I have attempted, in " The Orphan Angel," to reproduce the essential quality of Shelley's speech; to balance my patent adoration I have faintly caricatured his dear and ridiculous mannerisms. Perhaps I have been too painstaking; my " ingeniously woven wreath," as Miss Newman names it, may be too intricately woven for your taste. But my Aristotelian answers gave me the materials for this wreath, and I am going to turn a few leaves of it to prove that it isn't artificial.

First, because I like him best, there is Thomas Jefferson Hogg. His Life of Shelley remains for me by far the most brilliant, moving, and sympathetic account of " my incomparable friend." That it is mocking no less than loving is the secret of half its charm; it is full of recollections of Shelley's youthful talk from the lively memory of his most intimate companion.

Here is Shelley, speaking of a small boy whom the two encountered upon one of their walks near Oxford:

"That little ragged fellow knows as much as the wisest philosopher," he presently cried, clapping the wings of his soul and crowing aloud with shrill triumph at this felicitous union of the true with the ridiculous, — "but he will not communicate any portion of his knowledge; it is not from churlishness, however, for of that his nature is plainly incapable; but the sophisticated urchin will persist in thinking that he has forgotten all that he knows so well. I was about to ask him myself to communicate some of the doctrines Plato unfolds in his 'Dialogues': but I felt that it would do no good: the rogue would have laughed at me, and so would his little sister."

And so would Mr. Hogg, and so would I, for the matter of that, at the same time believing him the most enchanting creature under heaven. Now listen to his own reply to our amusement:

He looked grave, and said mournfully, "You laugh at everything: I am convinced there can be no entire regeneration of mankind until laughter is put down!"

Now here is Scythrop, out of "Nightmare Abbey," and he is employing that same elevated language which you may have found so irritating in Shiloh. "Very true, sir," he says, "but liberty of action, between individuals, consists in their being differently influenced, or modified, by the same universal necessity; so that the results are unconsentaneous, and their respective necessitated volitions clash and fly off in a tangent. . . ." "Unconsentaneous!" Is not that a fine word for Shiloh, or the Duke of Noodlesoup? No wonder Marionetta then quoted, with a very arch look, "'I prithee deliver thyself like a man of this world.'"

Scythrop is a caricature, but Peacock drew this caricature with affection and considerable understanding. Shelley was himself charmed by the fantastic portrait, and provided Peacock with the motto which prefaces the book, from Ben Jonson's "Every Man in His Humour." "Have you a stool there to be melancholy upon?" is its apposite conclusion.

To turn from Peacock's caricature to Peacock's serious Memoir of Shelley is to find various conversations reasonably reported by a person of clear and piercing common sense. The measured eighteenth century cadences of these speeches is evident to the most undiscerning ear; as literature they are as inferior to Shelley's poetry as Shelley's prose is always, save for a few exquisite and noble lines, inferior to his poetry, but they are beyond all doubt the words of the same young man who spoke so grandiloquently to Hogg in the water meadows of Oxford. Imagine, for instance, the solemn comedy of the scene, demurely recounted by Peacock, when Shelley takes a sudden fancy to enter the Church of England and his friend warns him gently of the difficulties inherent in such a plan!

"It is an admirable institution," says Shelley with stubborn meekness, "that admits the possibility of diffusing such men over the surface of the land. And am I to deprive myself of the advantages of this admirable institution because there are certain technicalities to which I cannot give my adhesion, but which I need not bring prominently forward?"

The most valid charge which can be brought against the idiom of Scythrop and of Shiloh is the undisputed fact that the Shelley of Trelawny's Recollections uses more full stops and fewer semicolons. But allowing for Trelawny's peculiar staccato style, which is always vivid and characteristic, it may credibly be assumed that he occasionally clipped and weeded Shelley's flowers of rhetoric after the habit of his own mind. It is possible, of course, that Shelley actually became more concise in speech during the Italian exile, but his letters give no hint of this change, which is so slight as to be very nearly expunged by the substitution of a few semicolons for the full stops upon the printed page.

"Why," asks Trelawny, "do you call yourself an atheist? It annihilates you in this world." Trelawny himself is, after all, not precisely monosyllabic.

"It is a word of abuse to stop discussion," Shelley replies. "A painted devil to frighten the foolish, a threat to intimidate the wise and good. I used it to express my horror of superstition;

I took up the word, as a knight took up a gauntlet, in defiance of injustice. The delusions of Christianity are fatal to genius and originality: they limit thought."

There is other eloquence of the same magnificent sort; it is more convincing in Trelawny's nervous English than in M. Maurois's elegant and witty French. "The Pythian priestesses uttered their oracles from below — now they are uttered from above. Listen to the mournful music in the pine-tops — don't you hear the mournful murmurings of the sea? Sometimes they rave and roar, shriek and howl, like a rabble of priests; in a tempest, when a ship sinks, they catch the despairing groans of drowning mariners. Their chorus is the eternal wailing of wretched men." It is Mr. Shelley speaking, the same Mr. Shelley who wrote " The Witch of Atlas," who would nevertheless never say " sailor " while sufficient breath remained in his body to permit him to pronounce the word " mariner."

It was part of Shelley's essential nature to express himself in long words. As a child he delighted in the romances of the Gothic school, those same ludicrous romances of which Miss Austen makes such delicious fun in " Northanger Abbey." Instead of laughing at Horace Walpole and Mrs. Radcliffe, Shelley imitated them in the poetico-pompous periods of St. Irvyne and Zastrozzi. Later he swallowed the eighteenth century philosophers whole and without a single grain of salt, and he was passionately addicted to the sentimental novels of the American, Browne. His devotion to Godwin's "Political Justice" is notorious; it must also be remembered that he talked frequently with Godwin and incessantly with Godwin's daughter Mary, whose own prose style, even in the intimacy of her journal, is both windy and stilted. If the notes which Mary wrote for Shelley's poems be compared with those written by Shelley himself it will be seen that the idiom, though inferior, is strikingly similar; it is in fact the language of the eighteenth century, faintly inflated and warmed by the breath of the romantic revival.

After all, Shelley had his earliest schooling in the England of the eighteenth century, not only in the spirit but in the flesh. He was eight years old when the new century began, and it is quite certain that his preceptors did not immediately alter their manner of speech in order to welcome it. Both Mr. Timothy and Mr. Godwin were products of the old century; so were Dr. Lind and Madame de Boinville and Mrs. Gisborne. When any of these ladies and gentlemen was informing or misinforming Mr. Shelley, she or he was assuredly doing so in a language which might well sound strangely stately to modern ears. Even when Shelley was learning Greek or Italian, his teacher was turning those lovely tongues into the idiom of the eighteenth century.

Keats was taught English literature by Cowden Clarke, and he stepped straight out of Cockney London into the country of Spenser and the brave Elizabethans. His own speech, if one may be permitted to judge by his letters, was probably a fine mixture of these two lively elements. Byron talked and wrote like a Regency wit and rake who was also a genius; he was a law unto himself, yet even he was far more influenced by Mr. Pope and Mr. Dryden than by his own contemporaries. Shelley read with hunger and passion; he read most of the high masterpieces of his own island and of Greece; he read much Latin and Italian, and toward the end of his life he read Spanish; French and German he knew as a matter of course. One can detect many threads in the shining fabric of his mind; Milton occasionally cries from " Prometheus," and certainly " The Cenci " is uncommonly good Webster. But in the main I think he wrote English prose rather as the elders of his childhood had written it, and talked it, too, a little in their graver manner, with his own wild spirit sometimes lighting the words to flame.

It was a queer, and to me infinitely lovable, quirk in Shelley's nature which constrained him to say to Godwin, "I have experienced a decisive pulmonary attack," when he meant that his lungs were slightly touched, and to write thus to Mary in the midst of his agony at the moment of Harriet's discovered suicide: " It is through you that I can entertain without despair the recollection of the horrors of unutterable villainy which led to this dark, dreadful death. . . . There is but one voice in condemnation of the detestable Westbrooks."

It was typical of Shelley that when he was depressed or ill he could write to his nearest and dearest, to Claire and to Mary, " I can do you no other good than in keeping up the unnatural con-

nection between this feeble mass of diseases and infirmities and
the vapid and weary spirit doomed to drag it through the world,"
or, " Imagine my despair of good! Imagine how it is possible that
one of so weak and sensitive a nature as mine can run further
the gauntlet through this hellish society of men! " At the same
time he was quite capable of walking thirty miles with Peacock
or twenty with Trelawny, laughing and cracking bad jokes in
Greek. Many persons might have been annoyed by the puns;
perhaps Claire was annoyed by her letter, which bears this significant note: " Here some words are blotted out by Miss Clair-
mont." The other quotation I put into the mouth of Shiloh during one of his less cheerful moods; and a critic subsequently took
me to task for insulting Shelley and suggesting that he was a
misanthrope. He was anything but a misanthrope; it was said of
him by Leigh Hunt, ". . . we never met, in short, with a being
who came nearer, perhaps so near, to that height of humanity
mentioned in the conclusion of an essay of Lord Bacon's, where
he speaks of excess of Charity, and of its not being in the power
of 'man or angel to come in danger by it.' " But it may be admitted that Shelley had his ups and downs; I think that possibly
he possessed what is known as the artistic temperament.

Shelley could write the " Ode to the West Wind " and write
no single word that is less than divine in all the swelling music of
its flight. He could, on the other hand, append this note to it:
" This poem was conceived and chiefly written in a wood that
skirts the Arno, near Florence, and on a day when that tempestuous wind, whose temperature is at once mild and animating, was
collecting the vapours which pour down the autumnal rains."
Which is monstrous fine, as Dr. Johnson would say, but hardly
the voice of Ariel.

Yet it is the voice of Shelley, the very living voice, and this to
me must make it ever valuable and beloved. I reserve the right
to laugh at it if I please; I can never grow tired of it, whether it
sings or whether it becomes forensic; it is delightful in its more
childish moments, and its tones can be at once touching and
sublime. By far the best way to hear it is to read the poems from
beginning to end, including the notes by Mary and by Shelley
himself, and Thomas Jefferson Hogg's Life, and Peacock's Mem-

oir, and Trelawny's Recollections, and the Letters as edited by
Mr. Ingpen, and the innumerable books about the poet of which
the best, to my mind, is Mrs. Campbell's "Shelley and the Unromantics." When you've done this, and particularly if you've
been doing it since you were seven years old, you are certain to
adore Mr. Shelley; his voice will be ringing in your ears, and
you may even go so far as to write a book about him. I, for one,
will never blame you.

1927

Fugitive Prose

THE SAGE IN MEDITATION

DURING the latter half of the second decade of the nineteenth century, when Mr. Shelley was sitting atop of the Baths of Caracalla composing the choruses of "Prometheus Unbound," there were plenty of busy people in Rome. Busy minds and busy-bodies among the ladies and gentlemen of the English Colony, and many industrious brown pairs of hands among the poor Italians themselves, who have always been rather good at manual labor, whether this was a question of hewn stone, water drawn bodily over stone arches, or paint splashed upon the ceiling of the Sistine Chapel. The eyes, brown or gold or impudent hazel, which matched these pairs of hands, probably regarded Mr. Shelley with indulgence or downright approval; he must, in the year 1819, have been a medicinal sight to any eyes which had not grown horny with stupidity or prejudice. The eyes of the busybodies, bent over the pages of the *Fortnightly,* or carefully measuring Suchong in a silver spoon, were thick and dull indeed; they had been purged neither with euphrasy nor rue. They had seen too many "disgraceful spectacles" and "disgusting exhibitions" in their time to burn with a kindlier light than hatred at the spectacle of Mr. Shelley and the Baths of Caracalla.

"Clambering about among those ruins all day long, when his

wife is going to have a baby!" they muttered morosely to the leaves of the *Fortnightly* and of the Suchong, and if they met him at the Bank or the Reading Room they cut him with extreme acerbity or with gusto attempted to knock him down, according to their temperament and sex. "If she calls herself his wife!" said the cutters, but the knockers-down cried, "And he dares to call himself an Englishman!" Lord Byron was wasting his substance in riotous living, but Mr. Shelley was wasting his time atop of the Baths of Caracalla, and his offence was the worser in the nostrils of the English Colony.

This theory, which may be called a conviction of the essential laziness of poets, undoubtedly prevailed in Rome in the year 1819; in the year 1929 it prevails over the entire *ci-devant* civilized world. It is a fine, finicky, useless sort of business at best, this writing of verse, with a deal of idleness about it, and a general air of sitting on a cushion and sewing a seam of feather-stitches. Which is, of course, pernicious nonsense. It is a bore to wash dishes and an expense to feed the swine, but it is damned hard labor to write a passable sonnet. If they be regarded as luxuries rather than necessities, though if they are something more than passable they may slip into the necessity class along with the white hyacinths, this does not in the least lessen the difficulty of their manufacture; people are always worrying about the hardships of artificial flower makers and rollers of scented cigarettes, and a really hard-worked sonneteer may be a shocking sight when he is sweating over the sestet. The seam is fine, or as fine as he can contrive to make it, but if there is a cushion at all it is probably that bit of carpet covering the seat of a third class railway carriage, or that nettle-bed plush in a "day-coach" coming down from Albany, or that exiguous place in the subway which the stoutish gentleman from Bucharest has lately miraculously occupied. The sonneteer falls into the place and catches the sestet as he relinquishes the strap, but can he manage to write it down on the manila envelope? His salary — and let us hope it is not less than twenty-five dollars — is in the manila envelope if it has the good luck to be Friday, and perhaps he will dine sumptuously on macaroni and red wine, or perhaps he will prefer a tin of baked beans by the comfort of his own gas-ring. But the really important thing is to make the little pencil marks into a recognizable Italian sestet more recognizable as a sestet than the red wine will be recognizable as wine. Ah, the thing is done, and the platform of Astor Place glides gracefully into view, not very like a whale, but far more like a whale than an antelope. It is work, of sorts, this trapping of sestets in the subway, and if the sonneteer fails to turn it to its proper use, it may all count as good training in short-hand and prestidigitation. At least this work (of sorts) can be done without a kit of tools or special training of any kind, though pencil and paper and a fair degree of quiet are useful things to have about you. You may get very dirty doing it; you may deserve a rubber collar and paper cuffs and the respect of your fellow-man. But, if you are thinking of setting up as a sonneteer, you mustn't make the mistake of believing that you'll have it. Your hands will be black, but the fact that the blackness is ink instead of motor oil robs it of the lustre of honest toil; your back as well as your head will ache like blazes, but you cannot pretend that this pain was acquired in a machine shop, and a typewriter lacks the nobility of labor unless it belongs to a large herd of typewriters in the offices of an important wholesale business. My poor sonneteer, you will find there is a prejudice against you; if I were you I should either become a mustard broker or accept the inevitable and continue to write sonnets, which is more amusing than mustard broking and far less lucrative.

Milton could put it better than I; he knew the uncessant care and the strict meditation that are necessary in his trade. Whose was the error, in the beginning? Did some merchant of the seaports, passing inland under Thessalian olive trees, envy the homely slighted shepherd and his pipes, or was the fair and ruddy countenance of David the first offence to the Philistine? It is impossible to say; the sonneteer will never know. It now becomes convenient for this creature to change his sex, like Tiresias; he must be a woman in the next sentence, and myself. I only know that this highly respectable trade, which was Milton's, and at which I labor as a humble artisan, fills the average neighbor of the average sonneteer with clucking suspicions and prejudices. She has cooked her father's dinners for twenty years; very right and proper, too, but what of it, and how?

If my neighbor's father wanted watercress in his salad, and there was none at the greengrocer's, and she had to bicycle eleven miles to get it, since the watercress beds are eleven miles from town, she would think herself both virtuous and energetic, and she would be right in so thinking. But because I have walked ten miles to fetch an abstract idea from the top of a hill, she thinks me both lazy and eccentric, and she is wrong in so thinking. I have cooked many dinners, and good dinners at that, but she has not written even a passable sonnet. I know and recognize the decency and dignity of her work, but in me, or any other poet, she sees only a wild look of having been scrambling over brambles or among the ruins of the Baths of Caracalla.

There is not the slightest doubt that in that incredible Uranian year which saw the birth of Prometheus and the nobler odes, all the English inhabitants of Rome regarded Mr. Shelley as a very idle as well as a very wicked young man. Whatever cruel things were rumored of the real or reputed children of his loins, these fair and vigorous children of his brain were ignored or forgotten. He was a blot upon the face of nature, a slap in the face of society; a scapegrace, a seducer, and an infidel. Therefore it went without saying that he never worked, save as a dangerous yeast to disturb the established orders; he was incapable of honest toil. The phenomenon of his swift ascent of the Coliseum was no better than the agility of a goat; these creatures nibbled grass and Mr. Shelley nibbled pencils, and the morals of all were notorious. A young male goat might be occasionally persuaded to draw a cart, but Mr. Shelley drew no carts, but only little pictures of trees among the fluttering pages of his note-book. Also he scribbled among these pages, when he was not scrambling among the stones of the Coliseum. The idea that Mr. Shelley was an industrious person never entered the frequently-shaken heads of the English Colony.

The poor Italians perceived that he was industrious, because they saw that he was never idle. If they did not always know what was the precise work that he did, they saw clearly that he worked hard at some matter of importance. It would not have surprised them to learn that like Leonardo he invented flying machines or flew among the higher mathematics, but the chances were that he wrote poetry, though he might very likely paint pictures at the same time. The workmen of the arts were versatile and patient; any market gardener knew that, and how the ink of Dante and the pigments of Michael Angelo had been dredged up from hell and pulled down from heaven. An artist was an honest artisan, who worked in the sweat of the brow and made the sinews of his body serve his mind.

Mr. Shelley employed his sinews in a great deal of scrambling, and yet the more intelligent of the market-gardeners knew that it was the incessant scribbling that counted. Here, in the light scrape of the lead upon the paper, so much lighter and slighter than the scrape of catgut upon catgut even, lay the long labor and the uncounted pains, "Alas, what boots it with uncessant care . . . to strictly meditate the thankless Muse?" Almost any Italian market-gardener knows the answer. These, who flourished with their white grapes and lettuces in the year 1819, knew beyond the disputes of a thousand tea-parties, how very hard Mr. Shelley was working.

When he reached the top of the Coliseum, his thin freckled face, so strangely illuminated by the heaven-color of the eyes, would be, perhaps, beaded with sweat and bright with exertion of the swift ascent, but this was nothing; the dark-eyed children and the frolicking goats knew the same lively beating of the heart. But when he rose, a little stiffly, from the flower-encumbered grass, and put his note-book in his pocket, and walked home to Mary, the market-gardeners and the farmers from the Campagna recognized his look and respected it, and, being poor Italians, wondered not at all that an honest artist should be tired to the extreme marrow of his bones by the exertion of scribbling. Their blood remembered the Renascence and their brains retained the teachings of a handful of Grecian slaves. They were not astonished to observe that the cheek-bones may grow salient and the eyes hollow from the slight exertion of composing the lesser choruses of "Prometheus Unbound." The tying-up of vines and the pitching of hay may achieve this alchemy, but they had Dante, at the tired back of the brain, to remind them that both heaven and hell may be as hard as shovelled earth when such an one as Mr. Shelley is set to work among their illimitable fields and vineyards.

No such interpreter was invited to the tea-parties of the English Colony; Mr. Shelley remained an idler and an infidel. And yet, day by day and hour by hour, as he lay among the rustling blades of the flower-encumbered grass, the whole of "Prometheus Unbound" was unwinding itself from the convolutions of his mind, until the dazzling fabric was erected into words, and dispatched to Ollier to be printed. There is no other art like this, that without instrument or material substance creates itself in beauty. The memory alone would serve, upon a desert island or in a prison cell, to prolong this beauty for an eternity of time; neither wood nor marble nor the pigments of clay are necessary for this divinest art of all. Who, therefore, unless in 1819 he was a determined reader of the Tory reviews, can reasonably doubt the effort and the mortal pains required of the mind in manufacturing these wonders? The mind's own stuff, the essential matter of the brain, is literally spun away and twisted into the making of such works of art and pure inspired nature.

An agreeable madman or a fine inconsequent lady may believe, may persuade his or her exquisite perversity that genius or the humbler talent is a bird or butterfly hovering to alight when it pleases, kissing the averted cheek of the artist with a feathery wing, descending from heaven like a secular holy ghost for a brief moment of ecstasy or fulfillment. The laborer is unworthy of his hire who credits such heresies. Good work is accomplished in the sweat of the brow and the draining away of the heart's blood; there is no other means or method to produce it.

Mr. Shelley knew this truth as he walked home to Mary, a little stiffly, through the long shadows of the fine Italian landscape. He did not waste much thought upon the evident fact; he was tired, though he would inevitably lack the sense to go to bed; he was hungry, though he would inevitably lack the practical appetite to eat his supper. His thoughts were all concerned, and wisely for the purpose of his art, with Prometheus and the spirits. "Light of life, thy limbs are burning through the veil which seems to hide them." If such fiery songs are to escape into the full clarity of the mind there are always a brace of eggs to remain uneaten and a duster to be avoided, and these evasions require a high degree of ingenuity and skill. Mr. Shelley lacked neither energy nor intelligence in the ordinary business of life; he went to the Bank, he provided his household with gold pieces; he hunted villas in post-chaises and took no harm from the upsetting of the same; he said a great many kind words to Mary and wrote a great many kind letters to Claire; he lent money to the Gisbornes and gave it to the Leigh Hunts; he was even thinking of building a boat, when he should have sufficient leisure to afford such luxuries. Meanwhile, he worked so hard that there was nothing left of him but bright skin and lively bone, and that increasing pile of scribbling which he would send to Ollier to be printed, when, in the sweat of his brow, he had finished his scribbling. He would be tired when he had finished it; he might reasonably liken himself to an orange which the Muses have squeezed for their own purposes, save that his empty skin would be fair and freckled like an English apple rather than the fruit of a classic soil. The Roman farmers, bearing their white grapes from the vineyards, observed to themselves that the tall Englishman was tired; they did not interrogate the stoop in his shoulders as to its exact origin among the sinews of the body and of the immortal soul.

If the common thoughts of the brain are bent to consider Milton or Shakespeare instead of Mr. Shelley, they will falter to realize the industry required of these. Milton, laboring in darkness and the sacred light of his own spirit, was bound to a harder daily task than Samson Agonistes; no galley-slave, no convict breaking stones upon the road, has accomplished, even under the lash or the punishment of starvation, one-half the work which Shakespeare did for stubborn desperate love of the work itself. It is not only profane but stupid to doubt these truths; you need only put "Paradise Lost" or a dozen plays of Shakespeare into the scales of any honest greengrocer to prove the actual weight of ink and paper of which their mighty substance is composed.

Even the London Telephone Directory was not compiled by a single intelligence; the most grudging greengrocer must admit that there is a pound of flesh and Christian blood in Shakespeare.

If anyone believes that, because Byron drank excessive quantities of claret and French brandy and cohabited with the wives of Venetian gondoliers, he did not at the same time work like a navvy and nigger rolled into one disreputable Apollo, that person should make some little effort to rewrite " Don Juan," or even copy the original version on his Corona. He will have his work cut out for him by a sharp pair of shears. If he likes the exercise, he may then try his hand at transcribing " Prometheus Unbound," and end by dashing off a few fair copies of " Adonais," with, one hopes, his own improvements and emendations.

When, and of course if, this interesting person has completed his experiments, he will no longer be surprised to learn that when Mr. Shelley had remembered to eat his supper, having sung for it to such good purpose, he tumbled into sleep, if not precisely like a felled ox, at least like a very thoroughly stricken deer. He was quite as tired as the anonymous experimenter would be the morning after the big party for the buyer from Kansas City. Let us refresh the tired experimenter by presenting him with two tickets for Mr. Ziegfeld's latest production, and let us permit Mr. Shelley his interval of sleep upon the hearth-rug. He has, as he might himself have put it in a letter to Peacock, earned this brief repose. So let us leave him in peace, nor wake him when a few sparks fly into his hair from the fire; to-day he has climbed to the top of the Baths of Caracalla, and to-morrow he may finish " Prometheus Unbound."

1928

Fugitive Prose

PATH OF THE CHAMELEON

THESE chapters of a single symmetrical book compose one of the great poetic romances of the world. I had meant to say, one of the great romantic novels, but as my dazzled eyes withdrew themselves from the final page I knew that the word was too frivolous and too unspiritual. Nevertheless, for all its dignity and verisimilitude, the book has the luminous visionary inner strangeness of the higher legends and fabulous tales of antiquity, and this together with the fine simplicity of truth. These far-off things are not older than the short half of a century nor these battles longer ago than the other day, but they have become one with some imperishable fabric of mythology by virtue of their own beauty and the beauty of the language which clothes them in light.

Do not read this book until you may be alone with it and free to think of it when you have done. It will weary you; not with any weariness of the mind, for it is as exciting as wine or the air of high altitudes, but because you will feel when you have finished it that you have climbed a cloud and that the breath has gone out of your body on the steep ascent. I wish it might be my privilege to retire for a week into a good monastery or a cavern in the side of a hill, there to sleep and wake to a small supper of locusts and wild honey before I should emerge to write this testament. For me this cannot be, but at least you may benefit by my experience; by no means read this book until you have a space of clear leisure about you. Only, as you value your mortal happiness, do not delay too long in scooping that clear cave of leisure out of the surrounding hours, for you must not deny yourself the joy of this book by one unnecessary moment.

I have heard it said by a wise man that this book and "Ulysses" are the two true masterpieces of modern Irish literature. But I have also heard it said by a woman sufficiently wise — if indeed women can ever be wise — that "Ulysses" can be understood only by Dubliners, and by them but imperfectly at times. This gives me a baffled feeling, because I know only too well that I was born in a certain Somerset County not far from New York and that my father's people came from another Somerset County in England, which makes me a Saxo-American as ever was. So I have always taken it for granted that I could never understand "Ulysses," and I believe precisely the same sad thing of all the poor young men who have dyed themselves so deeply in the imperial stain of this rare foreign murex. They can imitate Mr. Joyce a little, they can industriously dab themselves with the queer color of his prose, as if the blue murex were woad and they were ancient Britons instead of modern Americans. But, or so I am told, they don't really know what Mr. Joyce has fished up out of the depths of his mind.

Now, here is another sort of book entirely, and the beauty of it is that nobody on earth can imitate it and every one worth his salt can understand it. Homer might have written such a book in the wisdom of his blindness, or Shelley if he had lived to be sixty and ceased to be persecuted, even by his own soul. The one would have been in Greek and the other in an English grown tall enough to stand beside Prometheus, but neither would have belonged to any narrow land or time or people. We should all have shared them together like a consecrated bread, just as a hungry German may eat the substance of Shakespeare and be strengthened by it for all the jeers of Shakespeare's loyal countrymen. This is the sort of book to write, if one has the God-given power; this book is a free gift to all minds worthy of it. Even if

Mr. Yeats would not choose it to be so, he could not withhold the beauty of this book from a single person who possessed a certain spiritual grace and the power to buy, borrow, or steal, a copy of it.

So far as imitating goes, the thing is quite impossible, for which heaven be praised. Heaven, although I named it idly, is the proper place to praise for giving Mr. Yeats a manner of writing which will not easily encourage imitators. He has a manner, and that manner is, in the good sense, grand; he has few mannerisms, those alluring baby murexes which tempt the fishers of great men. The exquisite simplicity of his prose is solemn and pure; " the fascination of what's difficult " may lure us to lag along behind him; few of us will catch up with him. If I may be permitted one of those paradoxes which Englishmen call bulls and believe to be mistakes, most of the people who could catch up with him have gone before, " to sup with Landor and with Donne."

This art is no miracle, after all; a sentence like this, from " The Trembling of the Veil," is charmingly significant: " When in my twenty-second year I had finished ' The Wanderings of Usheen,' my style seemed too ornamental, too elaborate, and I thought for some weeks of sleeping upon a board." Here is a young person who is taking his work very seriously. I hope it is not a serious fault in myself that I must smile at this; I do not smile in mockery but in delighted memory of kindred impulses of my youth. The book is full of such things; it is a beautiful intensification and heightening of the mental ecstasies and despairs of every artist. In it any one of us who has lived even half as long as Mr. Yeats may read his own spiritual autobiography, enriched and ennobled by a stranger scene and a higher talent, which here springs up into genius.

Only one other autobiographical book, setting aside the published letters of a few poets, has moved me and exalted me as this book has done. That other book was marvelously removed from this, as indeed it seemed to me removed from all life but its Arcadian own. That book, which stands like a solitary golden tree in my recollection, was W. H. Hudson's " Far Away and Long Ago." I read it first when I had recovered from what was all but actual death; I was coward enough to distrust my love for it a little, to half believe that it was my own unnaturally sensitive perceptions which made it live so clearly in my mind and heart. I know now that I was wrong, but it was animating to feel again, as I read the "Reveries" of Mr. Yeats's childhood. Here is the same unreality which is so much more real than reality, the same vision of a new heaven and a new earth which is nevertheless half familiar, which " scarce seemed a vision " when we knew it first. It is the sense of finding some lovely thing forgotten since you were a child; "fallings from us, vanishings." Impossible things to put into words, unless a genius is doing it. These two books are as different in all outward ways as is the Argentine from Ireland; Hudson's book is golden and calm as the Garden of Eden, Yeats's book is sad as a weeping April twilight. Hudson is like a child lying in a trance in the sun and watching small living creatures, birds and snakes, moving in a haze of warmth. Yeats, in his " Reveries," is like a child lying in the moonlight and crying mysteriously, yet each is full of enchantment, and each confers a peculiar peace by reason of its beauty. It seems strange that the happy child should have died at last in a poor lodging house and the unhappy child should now be a senator.

It is impossible within the limits of this paper to convey the palest impression of the amazing richness and variety of the later chapters of the book. Never was such a story set down in such a manner; it is too good to be true long after you have finished, and yet you know it is true. When Keats heard that a gold ring of Anne Hathaway's had been found in a field at Stratford-on-Avon, he wrote to a friend, "I shall go mad! " I have felt this precise incredulous ecstasy at moments when I beheld some word or thing which seemed too wonderful to be true; there are stories in this book which so affect my spirits. Like Keats, I imagine for an instant that I shall go mad. This I feel when I see, through language transparent as a sheet of crystal, the proud and touching figure of Lionel Johnson proceed to his doom. I have always loved this lonely and incredibly distinguished creature, not only for his delicate and bitter verse, but for his virtues and defects as I knew them from slight, inadequate accounts. Now I have him before me as clearly as if Mr. Yeats's Christian

Cabbala had been potent to summon him from his grave. The picture of the rooms in Charlotte Street, with the gray corduroy curtains and the innumerable bookshelves and the elegant, scornful, fanatical little Lionel reading all night because he could not sleep; this is as I had imagined it, and now that I truly see it it is like something foreknown in a dream. "Talking there by candlelight it never seemed very difficult to murmur Villiers de l'Isle Adam's proud words, 'As for living — our servants will do that for us.' Yet I can now see that Johnson himself in some half-conscious part of him desired the world he had renounced." Small wonder; it must have been sad to live alone with a dark angel.

The tale of the Rhymers Club is so tragic that only its vast excitement makes it bearable. Dowson and Davidson and Lionel Johnson himself all came to cruel ends; it is to be presumed that the gods loved them, especially the two younger. I am glad to know one delightful story of the scholarly Lionel; I think I like it even better than "Morfydd." He said once to Yeats: "One should use a colon where other people use a semicolon, and a semicolon where other people use a comma." He would of course always say precisely that, and how I love him for it!

The account of Oscar Wilde and the tragedy of his ruin is extraordinary. Here for the first time I have been able to see a dignity behind the horror; Mr. Yeats has unsealed my eyes and made me more generous and more just. "'Wilde will never lift his head again,' said the art critic, Gleeson White, 'for he has against him all men of infamous life.' When the verdict was announced the harlots in the street outside danced upon the pavement."

Aubrey Beardsley, dragged down by Wilde's destruction through no fault of his own, save that he was unpopular and it was "the moment for getting rid of unpopular people"; Henley, like a wounded lion after the death of his little girl; John Synge — these names make it indeed "The Tragic Generation"! Of Synge Mr. Yeats has a wise and profound saying, which I will quote for the pleasure it gives me:

"No mind can engender till divided into two, but that of a Keats or a Shelley falls into an intellectual part that follows and a hidden emotional flying image, whereas in a mind like that of

Synge the emotional part is dreaded and stagnant, while the intellectual part is a clear mirror-like technical achievement."

This book is as much for painters as poets; the stories of the Pre-Raphaelites of Bedford Park, of Morris and the eccentric Nettleship are all of an extreme fascination. The figure of Maude Gonne seems itself like a painting by a true Pre-Raphaelite; it has the early innocence of art. I suppose it is most of all like a statue of gold and ivory made by the elder, which is to say the younger, Greeks. This is a noble creature; my heart does not warm to her as it does to the red-haired girl of good family who was so poor that she lived on a pennyworth of bread and cocoa shells a day and yet hired a woman to go with her to the art school, because she did not think that a lady should walk in the street alone. But it is all the fabric of romance; there is not a page which fails to shine with some peculiar light.

I suppose I must find a flaw or two — no emerald is real without them. I might say, and truly, that sometimes I do not very much like Mr. Yeats himself; he seems very solemn and very selfish at times. But then this makes it all so much truer, and gives me the excuse that I want, to say that as I read I have often seen myself in this far greater artist, and that I believe every one who reads the book will in some measure see the image of himself in its crystal.

1927

Autobiographies: Reveries Over Childhood and Youth — and The Trembling of the Veil.—*By W. B. Yeats.*

Fugitive Prose

THE PEARL DIVER

THE GREAT ship, moved at her anchorage by a motion supremely
indolent and gracile, has sunk into blue water a swaying shaft of
greenish darkness wherein float bubbles of light among conjectured fins and scales; vainly the hot-eyed sun has striven to
penetrate this inverted tower of shade, tilted so dexterously in
accord with the most languid tremor of the vessel. The time is
the incredibly high noon of the East; the place is that richly
sinister Port of Aden, on whose quays romance forever awaits
the traveller, her lovely visage veiled in rags of a detestable filthi-
ness. Some valued friend of yours, who encircled the globe
during the early '90s, has long since familiarized you with the
setting and taught you to observe the details. There stand the
ladies, their filmy raiment foaming over the rail like flower boxes
upon a house boat; behind them tall, bronzed men in blond
cavalry mustaches and pith helmets shine with a blinding radiance of new white ducks and flannels. *Chota hazri* has been devoured like the first dews of morning; tiffin will presently be
served; the voyagers are eager to taste the more ambiguous
flavors of the town. Meanwhile, to vary the monotony of the
hour, a myriad lithe, brown creatures sport like dolphins in
the subaqueous gloom and upon the sunlit surface of the water;

between voracious shadows, pluck pearls and florins from the sea's pavement with casual facility and pleasure.

I venture to perceive an analogy between the rebellious pearl diver and myself, in my slight experience with public libraries. If you stigmatize the analogy as far-fetched, I am quite prepared to agree with you. The exiguous coping of the Pierian spring confines the depths in which I must now and again submerge my mind in a search for the florin of information and the pearl of authentic knowledge. In profundity this narrow well compares not unfavorably with the Indian Ocean; if it cannot boast a solitary shark, it contains a profusion of leeches and poisonous tadpoles. The advanced state of civilization under which I am privileged to exist offers me sundry diving suits in the form of stately edifices housing large collections of books; my native sloth and stubbornness assure me that I shall be swifter and nimbler in an unclothed ingenuity of my own contriving.

I am but too bitterly aware of my barbarism; the charges of ingratitude and light-mindedness are verified by my conscience. And yet, how much more delightful, how much more stimulating, to abandon the paraphernalia of card indexes and mahogany desks and slip unhampered into cool water; to snatch in the middle of a bursting breath the adventurous jewel or antique coin upon which one's fingers chance to fall! In solitude, and in solitude alone, the mind may achieve the noble nakedness of the classic bronze, the muscular adroitness of the savage.

I own to an affectionate memory of many libraries; I am fond of saying I have read in the British Museum, though in truth patrician or official influence to permit one to enjoy its shabby books in the decent privacy of the hovel. The Public Library of our fair City of New York is the spiritual home of many gifted poets and distinguished critics of my acquaintance; editors — aye, and publishers themselves — have here polished the richness of their learning with paper and printer's ink, even as the jewellers of the Middle Ages polished their enamels with stretched goat skin and pulverized pottery. I sit at the feet of these lofty ones much as they sit at the feet of Clio or Melpomene, but deeply as I venerate true knowledge, I admit that for my own purposes I would rather obtain undisputed possession of an empty room, a clear but tempered light, a comfortable chair, and a stray volume of Mr. Thomas Carlyle or Mr. John Webster than be made free of a whole Bayeux tapestry of his-books may be breathlessly sought, preferably upon sliding ladders or along perilous strange galleries where the librarian never ventures, libraries are among the most beneficent of human inventions. As places wherein to ponder, under the shadow of a great rock, upon the sacred pattern of words scrolling a mighty page, they are but prison houses. Refused the inestimable boon of lying prone before rose-red embers, or supine upon cushions with the feet at an elevation commensurate with that occupied by the head, the reader of sensitive and high-strung nature becomes distressingly torpid and morose. He knows only too well that he cannot proceed with his researches into the history of ceramics while he dawdles listlessly over the " Memoirs of a French Diplomat in Cochin China During the Seventeenth Century " or the " Life of the Empress Dowager." He realizes, if he is wicked and sagacious like myself, how much better he would have done to stop quietly at home and read Mr. Austin Dobson's " Proverbs in Porcelain," a book fully as apposite to his subject as either of his other discoveries and which he happens to possess in the seclusion of his own well-stocked library shelves.

Forgive the levity and irrelevance of the foregoing confession; no doubt if I were to study the question at the Public Library I would alter my shocking opinions. Meanwhile, I must prepare for another unaided dive; perhaps you will throw me a small coin from your own mental purse that so clinks with gold and silver; perhaps I shall find a pearl for myself at the bottom of this narrow well which is nevertheless so very deep.

1922

Fugitive Prose

JEWELLED BINDINGS

I HAVE purloined my title, as I am fond of doing, from the literary imagination of another, to whom my thanks are hereby offered. John Webster furnished me with Nets to Catch the Wind; I took Black Armour from Lionel Johnson; to the anonymous author of an announcement of a sale at the Anderson galleries I am indebted for this present caption. The phrase, as it originally stood upon the pages of a fairly prominent review, was Superb Jewelled Bindings, but I am forced to let the sumptuous qualification go the way of all too many brave things, and thus sink into oblivion. The bindings of which I propose to write are hardly superb; they are elaborate, neat, enamelled, elegant, perhaps exquisite, but they lack the vast suavity of the truly superb in art. They are the bindings, the spiritual bonds, the sharp and delicately turned shapes and forms which so decoratively constrict the essence of contemporary lyric verse.

Permit me to quote from the picturesque bit of prose whence my title was stolen. " Surrounding this is a large wreath of laurel, tied with a mauve ribbon, and studded with fifty-eight pearls set in gold. Disposed around the cover are two hundred and twenty-three garnets and four opals. The design of the back cover is equally brilliant and contains forty-eight garnets, eight opals, eight moonstones, twenty-eight turquoises, twelve blue chalcedonies, two hundred and fifty-four amethysts, and nine topazes. There are scores of similar bindings, elaborate in design and lavish in the use of precious stones."

Surrounding what? you may well ask. At the Anderson Galleries all this intricacy surrounds Some Poems by John Keats, but in the curious museum of our own time some, nay many, poems by eminent young lyricists appear, if not similarly tied with mauve ribbon, at least painstakingly inlaid with seven moonstones and twelve blue chalcedonies. The large laurel wreath, though it has not yet been permanently awarded, has been bespoke by several, and he is poor indeed who cannot afford a few garnets and amethysts, or a mild freshwater pearl.

So I figure us to myself, dwindled to the jewel brightness of the picture in a camera obscura, hunched over our filing and fitting, careful lapidaries, clever goldsmiths, excellent workmen for the most part, but a thought too intent upon the binding. Of course there are obvious exceptions; your personal predilections will supply their names. If I hesitate to say that I am one of the chief offenders, it is only because a writer's claim to distinction, even in crime, annoys the intelligent reader. So — bowing always in the direction of the obvious exceptions — let me refer to us as a group, enchanted by a midas-touch or a colder silver madness into workers in metal and glass, in substances hard and brittle, in crisp and sharp-edged forms. From this company I exclude all persons whose poetry the Dial will publish, whether their lines rhyme or no. I include only the lyric poets, more or less young, entirely modern, who are, among a hundred and something million Americans, leaving little verse unto that enormous clan.

When I say little, I mean literally diminutive; short lines, clear small stanzas, brilliant and compact. I don't mean inferior or contemptible or negligible. Neither do I mean great.

One of the most enchanting conceits of the eighteenth century was the enamelled snuff-box, which opened to reveal not brown tobacco dust but a bright and singing bird. And although some few of our modern boxes have nothing but powdery dryness under their neat painted lids, most of them are music-boxes, whose gilded birds repeat a fine variety of tunes, melodious, bitter, passionate, or intellectual, as the case may be. And for this sort of singing a small jewelled receptacle of two or three well-polished stanzas is no bad thing; it is comfortable and fitting. Did I suspect for a moment, as in my own case I have not dared to suspect, that my bird was a live one, I should let him out.

I should let him out into freedom, but not necessarily into free verse. I should try to remember that he was born in a snuff-box, and be prepared to build him another house, a stone dovecote or a wicker cage, according to his nature. I should let him perch in the groves of Academe if he liked, or upon a bramble bush of ballads. If he were a real bird he would know his own mind, and his own music.

But the question remains unanswered, in my opinion at least, as to whether we have shut up any eagles or nightingales in our snuff-boxes. And I believe we are good workmen, dexterous and clean in our handling of gold and silver and precious — or even semi-precious — stones. I believe we are careful and conscientious, but not so much so as our detractors declare. I think rather that we have found a manner which very justly encloses our matter, a letter which very nicely defines our spirit. As to the decoration, the setting of words transparent or opaque in a pattern upon our jewelled bindings, I am by no means ready to discard it. It is a deliberate art, perhaps, but as such it is a discipline and a struggle not to be too impetuously scorned. If our spirit is greater than the thing that holds it, it will go free of its own accord; our work is notoriously brittle, and I have no fear that its forms will ever imprison an authentic genius. And, in the remote possibility that some of us are not geniuses, but only adroit and talented young people with a passion for writing verse, it may be an excellent thing after all that we have cultivated a small clean technique. A number of minor poets are far better employed in being brittle and bright and metallic than in being soft and opulently luscious. It keeps the workshop tidier, and leaves a little elbow-room in which the very great may move their hammers and chisels in serenity.

1923

Fugitive Prose

SYMBOLS IN LITERATURE

THERE was once an apocryphal German professor who proposed an amended version of certain lines from *As You Like It.* Shakespeare, he suggested, had drunk rather too much canary or Rhenish when he wrote, "Sermons in stones, books in the running brooks." It should obviously, said the Herr Professor, be reversed; sermons belonged in books and stones were frequently found in brooks. And this is true enough, as any mere clergyman or geologist can affirm, and yet it is not half so true as the thing Shakespeare said.

In another book, even greater than *As You Like It,* there is a prolonged and consistent use of parables. When, in the 80th Psalm, the history of Israel is compared to the growth of a vine, the device of metaphor is magnificently successful. If you dislike a rich man, and find it hard to believe that he will ever go to heaven, you will think of the eye of a needle even quicker than you will think of Dives. The Unwise Virgin is so present an image in every one's mind that it is possible to-day to call a play *Behold the Bridegroom* and make your meaning plain to the population of Broadway.

Therefore I do not, in this paper, intend to apologize for allegories. I believe that no single person who reads my words has not accepted allegories as the very essence of truth, and grown so familiar with that truth that he has forgotten that they were allegories. It is simply that in the older stories, the ones which have become part not only of our literature but of our lives, the symbol has become a name for the thing itself, the mask is immediately recognized. Perhaps it is not accurate nowadays to say that every one will immediately recognize Punch and Judy as a wife-beater and a shrew, but certainly every one will recognize Charlie Chaplin as a tragic clown and Mary Pickford as a good little girl. If the most literal-minded person among us wishes to describe a man whose generosity passes the bounds of worldly wisdom, he will not cast his mind's eye up and down Main Street for a comparison; he will say that the man is quixotic, and all his literal and realistic friends will accept the word as descriptive. In every circus traveling over the dusty length and breadth of the American summer, the dwarfs will be called Lilliputians, and all the little children will understand quite well that they are not giants. It is too much to expect of the average person to remember that these words came from the bitter and brilliant allegories of Cervantes and Swift, but I ask the readers of this paper to remember it, and to marvel at the lasting power of the symbolical in art.

I wish to avoid the word "fantasy"; it reminds too many people of Dr. Freud of Vienna, and it reminds me of those blithe patterns upon printed silks which the French call *fantaisie*. It is not a word of sufficient dignity and worth to describe *The Faerie Queene,* or *Pilgrim's Progress,* or *Gulliver's Travels.* I myself should hesitate to apply it to *Lady into Fox;* certainly it is not a noble enough name for *Mr. Weston's Good Wine.* These things are all allegories, of less or greater merit and grandeur; some are slight, and some are heroic, but they are all too good to be called fantasies.

Now the literal-minded may ask — or so I am credibly informed — why Mr. Bunyan did not tell the realistic story of a persecuted dissenter, and why Mr. Powys did not tell the naturalistic tale of an English village. But for some unknown reason he will ask this question more indignantly in the case of Mr. Powys than in the case of Mr. Bunyan, for to many people it seems forgivable to be allegorical in the seventeenth century and excessively foolish to be allegorical in the twentieth. I think, although it is impossible to be sure about anything so mysterious as this theory, that the explanation is quite simple; to the literal-minded, Mr. Bunyan's real history is very nearly as fantastic as the story of Christian's pilgrimage, and the steel helmet of the Parliamentary soldier as strange as Christian's staff and scrip. Whereas Mr. Powys lives to-day, and recognizes the existence of Fords and the Woolworth Stores, and these things should disinfect a man's imagination against all danger of visions. Only, thank God, they don't, and if you stop to think of it, Mr. Bunyan's flintlock probably seemed as prosaic and modern to him as Mr. Powys's umbrella undoubtedly seems to Mr. Powys. In the same way, Mr. Literal-Minded really sees very little difference between the court of Queen Anne and the court of Brobdignag, and he thinks the Rev. Dean Swift quite justified in being savage and insanely fanciful about politics and morals. He wishes, however — or so I am credibly informed — that modern writers would be sensibly modern, and stick to their Gopher Prairies and their American Tragedies.

Now as a matter of cold fact, both Mr. Lewis's books and the even more amazing books of Mr. Dreiser are full of allegorical figures. Over the books of Mr. Dreiser there broods a terrific figure of blind and tragic Chance, blinder by far than Mr. Hardy's Chance, who did after all in the final analysis belong to the Church of England. Mr. Dreiser's Chance is a sort of Cyclops with his eye put out; he frightens Mr. Dreiser more than the Cyclops ever frightened Ulysses. As for Mr. Lewis, his Babbitt is one of the lesser gods of the American mythology; he is a mere metaphor. He is really no more realistic than Gargantua, though he is not nearly so lovable.

I admit, however, that these gentlemen are not meaning to write allegories. They are doing it in spite of themselves, and against all their principles and convictions. Among those who are speaking in parables and violating no principles in so doing, the most distinguished examples are Mr. T. F. Powys, Mr. David Garnett, and Miss Sylvia Townsend Warner. In the books of these three English writers, the events of the story are sometimes supernatural; the forces of the universe of good and evil, the common

courses of nature are changed and twisted into miracles and portents. The same thing happens in any fairy story; it happens in
Cinderella and in Little Red Riding Hood. But this is no reason
for laughing at these books, or for stupidly wondering; the same
thing happens in Homer's *Odyssey* and in *Hamlet*. There is even
an element of the supernatural in the Bible, and the best critics
do not hold that the power and majesty of that book is lessened
thereby.

Another and less clearly defined form of allegory is that in
which the story is possible, but frankly improbable and strange.
In this class belong many books of adventure; whether the writer
knew it or not, I believe that a writer has seldom assumed a toga
or a periwig save as a mask or disguise for his deeper meaning.
I am not, of course, speaking of the ruck of historical novels, but
I think I see Mr. Thackeray's blacker moods dressed up as Es-
mond, and Stevenson happily escaping with Jim Hawkins. Into
this class I put my own books, with the single exception of the
Venetian Glass Nephew, which contains a light hint of the supernatural, perfectly susceptible of being explained away by the sober-
minded.

Now why should anyone wish to wear a pair of wings or a
periwig, and pretend to be an angel or a *chevalier d'industrie?*
The answer is somewhat complicated, but nowhere has it been
more happily expressed than in a short essay by Mr. Christopher
Morley, dealing with a brief allegorical novel of several years ago
which Mr. Morley was kind enough to admire. I will quote his
opening paragraph,

There are always excellent reasons for silence. One worthy reason is
that you have nothing to say. Another is that what you are thinking is
too important to be said, or would become untrue if uttered. The recourse of those who feel that they have something to say, but desire
to avoid the bitterness of being understood, has been (ever since Aesop)
the fable of fantasy. The importance of any fable can be gauged by
the area of silence it covers. Abraham Lincoln, a very Aesopian person,
could conceal the whole blackness of Civil War in an anecdote.

That is excellent and exact. " To avoid the bitterness of being
understood " — that holds good for the mighty Swift, although it

was written about one of the least of the allegorists of this genera-tion. And to avoid the bitterness of understanding; sometimes it is that. And to be able to put a red beard or a lion's skin on your worst enemy, or to seize a rapier or an old-fashioned squirrel rifle, and have at them without explanation or apology. If Swift had written about the king's mistresses he would have been impris-oned, but by calling them cushions he could be as bitter as he pleased, or very nearly, for nobody was ever so bitter as the Dean pleased. If you call a spade a diamond some people will think you are frivolous and affected, but other people will understand how much blacker things may be said about spades by the simple trick of pretending that they are diamonds.

1928

THIS BOOK IS SET IN GRANJON,
a type named in compliment to Robert Granjon, type-
cutter and printer — Antwerp, Lyons, Rome, Paris —
active from 1523 to 1590. The face was designed by
George W. Jones, who based his drawings upon a type
used by Claude Garamond (1510–1561).

       This book was composed, printed, and
bound by The Plimpton Press, Norwood, Massachusetts. The typographical scheme is by W. A. Dwiggins.
The paper was made by the Ticonderoga Pulp and
Paper Co., Ticonderoga, N. Y.